WOLF STREAK BETA: AWARENESS

by

M.G. Brown

DORRANCE PUBLISHING CO
EST. 1920
PITTSBURGH, PENNSYLVANIA 15238

Dorrance Publishing Co
585 Alpha Drive
Pittsburgh, PA 15238
Visit our website at www.dorrancebookstore.com

ISBN: 978-1-6366-1542-4
eISBN: 978-1-6366-1555-4

Wolf Streak Beta: Awareness is a tale of science fiction. All characters, all sci-technology, all places, and all names and term for such, and all situations are merely from author's imagination. No actual person nor place nor event is intended. Any resemblance to the past or present reality is totally coincidental.

PROLOGUE:
SWYLLO AT STEPPINGSTONE STATION QUINTO

Cheers of spectators faded in background as Swyllo stomped frustrated along the tunnel from Pulseball dome. However, cheers of victory were not for her team now. No, now toxx foxes had prevailed in tournament. Her wolves had failed to win all important final competition. Now immediate mission of Wolf Streak was in limbo until choices were finalized. Vulching nasty, she thought silently. She had played for victory now to claim alpha role tomorrow.

"Nasty vulching lucky! They were just lucky!" Swyllo whined in her high-pitched voice as she stomped into locker room and thumped the padded head of her Zapstik against chairs aligned near player lockers.

From behind her came a low, almost growling voice of her crewmate Domyn, saying, "Somewhat lucky, yes, but foxes played very good game, just as we did, Swyllo. Double overtime! I don't remember ever hearing of a final championship game going double overtime. We just played in a classic Pulseball match. Audience back in Zerosolis System should have witnessed greatest game ever. We will have left our finest image with population there. People of Zerosolis System so critically need some hope and positive entertainment…"

People of the faraway solar system of Homeworld should witness action of recent Pulseball competition. Relayed from Steppingstone to Steppingstone, sanbeam transmission of event would travel back through many light years of space from Steppingstone Quinto to Homeworld in Zerosolis System. Populations there needed such entertaining distraction very critically as they continued to struggle to repair and renew planet. Swyllo knew her efforts here on Quinto would be part of history of all people so far away. She felt a mixture of pride of her role within Blue Jay and also some shame for being on team, which lost deciding competition. Yet she would continue regardless of her disappointment of Wolf Streak, perhaps losing prime scout for this mission. At very worst, Wolf Streak would be second spacecraft to leave Steppingstone Quinto on long journey to the next likely solar system for Blue Jay Project. Hopefully her crew would win glory of final success.

"Vulch, if Jamyk could have stopped last pulse shot by Bhiros," interrupted baritone voice of a very tall boy entering locker room behind Domyn. "If only I could have latched onto vulching crazy ricochet, we could have had another chance score winner. If only…"

"Awright, Milyr, you know 'if only' never really counts," large young man Domyn sighed. "We live with what happens, not with 'what if.' Awe knows we played in a historic Pulseball match just now. We must be satisfied with such reality now. We have done our contribution to total project. We will continue to do our share of ambition of Blue Jay."

"Vulch, at least it's cherp! Maybe we'll be legends now," Milyr laughed as he ripped off helmet, exposing his elongated, bald, and very sweaty head.

"Awright, perhaps, but I believe the crew who finds colonials first in Sexto System will be real legends of Blue Jay," Domyn declared, also lifting off his helmet and unpeeling the top most portion of blue McAnderwike uniform, before continuing, "Maybe foxes will get glory now after their victory today. They deserve honor. Bhiros had his foxes primed for their best."

Competition between Wolf Streak and Fox Flash had been very spirited over past years since their departure from the Zerosolis System. Spirited but not nasty, their friendly battles mostly during Pulseball tournaments on several Steppingstones had provided some needed recreation from their intense training and operations of spacecraft over light years of distance between Homeworld and Steppingstone Quinto, furthest settlement of human expansion into galaxy. Well, Swyllo reminded herself in her mind, not really furthest human travel from Zerosolis since the very colonials who Blue Jay sought had launched huge colony ships many hundreds of years past in exodus from Homeworld. Somewhere beyond Steppingstone Quinto was a solar system or three giant colony ships with descendants of those desperate and bold people of original colonial exodus. Wolf Streak and Fox Flash and Lynx Blaze were spacecrafts of the sixth phase of the long duration of Blue Jay Project. Their ambition was to locate and contact present descendants of past brave colonials. Swyllo had hoped her crew would win honor of discovery.

Sputtering with frustration and whipping her blue helmet into cubicle of locker, Swyllo retorted, "But it was still vulching lucky toxx foxes won the game. Why do they get to be first to go into Sexto System? We could easily have been champions. We've could have been alpha Jayer crew. We were just so vulching close. I'm goaded nasty knowing billions of fans back in Zerosolis System will remember us wolves as losers. I'm no loser! None of us wolves is losers!"

"Vulching foxes will be gloating like arrogant toxx now," Milyr exclaimed, slamming padded head of his Zapstik into his open-gloved palm, "I just hope they dare say something goading to us. I'll show them who is really a Jayer legend. Oh, I hope fool Chitir says his glory!"

"Let it go, Milyr. Flash Fox will only be about nineteen days ahead of us when we get to Sexto System, if Cap Bhiros chooses alpha position. After almost revol of journey through LaOgres, nineteen days is not much of a head start as space travel goes. You know so!" Domyn reminded his crewmate in strong firm tome, which Swyllo and everyone else respected. "Awe knows if Cap Bhiros will even select alpha position."

Muttering low enough not to project her grumbling, Swyllo considered possible repercussions of the loss to foxes. Neer Domyn's previous words reminded her of mission for Blue Jay Project, which had engulfed crew of wolves on Wolf Streak for so many years. Ultimate goal was finding and hopefully reunion with descendants of colonists who had departed Zerosolis System many centuries in past. In far past, Homeworld had nearly fallen to over-population and then consequent wars for scant remaining resources of the planet. Not even few terra-formed colonies on outer planets and moons had relieved nasty ruin of environment for human life on Homeworld. So some of the ancestors had fled likely devastation and sought new world somewhere else far away in the galaxy.

Since exodus human species of Zerosolis had been separated by vast galactic distance and many hundreds of years of time. After centuries following era of Despoliation of Homeworld, human civilization in Zerosolis System had struggled back to space-faring technology. Blue Jay Project was enormous undertaking spanning at least six generations while humans, who stayed in Zerosolis System, attempted to reunite with descendants who had left for some far distant new world of better environment to allow humans to survive and populate into the future.

Now as result of competition via spectator-viewed tournament of Pulseball games, Fox Flash had choice to lead or to be back-up in the next phase of the journey. Swyllo groaned in low voice in chagrin.

Only slight moment of satisfaction tweaked her despair as she realized at least she was not one of the cats of Lynx Blaze, which over years of training and competitions had fallen to third position of order of three spacecraft and crews. Cats would not care which crew won the tournament since Lynx Blaze could not gain precedence over either Wolf Streak or Fox Flash now. Cats had lost their position at Steppingstone Tercero when their prime pilot Kiblin had been killed by deranged steppers who had some unreasonable hatred for astronauts of Blue Jay. By being one position short then, Lynx Blaze did not retain confidence of MisCom to continue as contender for prime spacecraft. But cats had loyally continued with spirit as redundant back-up just in case of failure of either of the two prime spacecraft. MisCom needed every option for present sixth phase of project after spending so much time over five generations at minimum to get Blue Jay to current point in mission.

Standing in front of her personal cubicle, Swyllo leaned her Zapstik against the locker and agreed, "Yeah, Bhiros is vulching unpredictable. He may desire to stay here on Quinto and rec some more. And Chitir might convince him to linger here at Quinto just to ogle kittens of Lynx Blaze when they get here tomorrow. But other foxes will be gloating! They'll convince him to take alpha position. They will wish to be heroes of Blue Jay who finally find elusive colonials. Especially Chitir will think going into Sexto System first will get him far ahead of me, maybe to meet some new bodacious girls. No, not ever can he get away so easily!"

Laughing in his hoarse baritone, Milyr chortled while he stooped to pull down his sweat-soaked pants and reveal his long slender legs below the low hanging shirt, "Ha, first you claim he's ogling kittens and then you worry he'll sneak peeks at colonial fems in Sexto System. Vulch, tiny fem, you are uncherply goaded by your clutch for his skinny toxx. I don't think he wants to get away. Manly peener as he thinks he is, Chitir wants your toxx for himself. He won't seek out any colonial fems."

"Yeah, maybe not, but I don't plan on letting big oaf get chance," a small girl stated emphatically as she peeled down wet pants of her McAnderwike uniform. "Especially if there might be cherp girls out there in Sexto System already. My Chitir is very easily swayed by bodacious fems."

Beside her a large-bodied young man Domyn with a very deep voice tossed his wide pants into his locker while he said, "So, Swyllo, you have feelings for

Chitir? Are you sure? You know Doc has told us repeatedly our awakening sexuality will be inhibited for years yet because of chemical…ant…um…damn, can never remember name. But you know toxx drug in our food nutrient. I do not believe you can lust for him at your present stage in maturity."

"Vulch, Domyn, our drive is inhibited, not actually stopped, or so Prof says," exclaimed rather tall Milyr as he crumpled the hem of the shirt up his torso into a bundle of fabric encircling his lanky chest, and by such action, revealed his naked figure and then he chuckled as he said, "And girls do mature faster than us men. Maybe our little fem here has clutch for Chitir now already?"

With an exasperated glare at her male companions, especially bare toxx of Milyr showing he had not worn JMO shorts under his McAnderwike again as seemed his habit for adornment in competition, Swyllo snorted and slammed her palms onto her waist, and a tiny girl of nearly nineteen years snapped brusquely, "I said feelings for him, not clutch! We have been cherp friends always, Chitir and me. Just because he's in a different crew doesn't mean we lose our friendship. And besides, vulch, I don't want to lose what control over him I now have, big Sasquatch would be lost without me. Vulch, he needs my very mature and wise guidance."

"And you don't trust vixens on Fox Flash to keep their paws from him, do you? Swyllo, you're so openly jealous. You can't wait for a mission to be finished, can you? Then you can tame Chitir way you really want him," Milyr snorted with leer and then casually inquired while still bent at his waist with the shirt rumpled around his upper torso, "So, my fine fem, will you pull sticky shirt over my shoulders and head now for me. You know I'm always getting my muscular body stuck in vulcher garment…"

"Vulch, Milyr, you can squirm and wriggle your scrawny self out of the shirt on your own. You don't know anything. You just talk. You just dream about sex and pretend you're more manly mature than everyone else. Even though we're all about the same age and same maturity, you think you're just a big handsome peener," Swyllo retorted glaring at him and then folding her own shirt up over her breasts and shoulders to show him how a real athlete undresses from piece of McAnderwike uniform, taking it past her own perspiring bald head and whipping it into her locker all in one smooth motion.

Milyr had been tallest of crew since the very first days of their meeting as crew of Wolf Streak on Steppingstone Primero. In past time nearly five years ago, he had been easy to look upon for her. His slender boyish body had seemed beautiful to her childish eyes. However, whenever he opened his mouth in his goading speech,

Milyr had nearly always goaded her sensitivity with his obnoxious manners and opinions mostly of himself. Aging over the years had not improved his nature as he related to Swyllo. His skill as pilot and communications primary for Wolf Streak had kept him tolerable to her as cherp crewmate, but her childish dreaming of his body had faded many years ago. Chitir had walked into such maturing role with handsome and charming ease. Swyllo smiled at her dreamy thought.

Sitting in chair beside her, Domyn declared with warning in his voice, "Awright, let's be civil wolves here together. We need to stay as one crew and one team. Do not act like youngling pups!"

However, a lanky boy with long narrow face ignored or did not hear Domyn's caution and instead continued to tease loudly yet slightly muffled as he worked in mild awkwardness with his head inside crumpled folds of shirt while he tried to shake and wriggle out of binding shirt, "Tiny fem, Swyllo, I am big handsome peener. Just ask any fems who flock around Pulseball games at each Steppingstone when we play. Vulch, they are most likely waiting outside for my bigness..."

"Just you, Milyr! One big vulching peener!" she snarled, plopping into her chair and smoothing undergarment of yellow color which covered her torso from just over her breasts down to just past her hips with both hands. "You toxx, you are so charmed by yourself and so clutched by yourself! And you can't even learn how to undress your vulching self!"

Leaning forward in bent posture and finally shaking the blue shirt from his long arms, Milyr sneered, "Only telling honesty, tiny fem. We are not all as inhibited as Chitir. Don't get so vulching jealous just because I can resist effects of antemgebemarzex better than your toxx friend."

Feeling her pulse rate increase and her face grow hotter, Swyllo glared at the grinning elongated sweating face and knew he had gotten to her. With his usual waspish manner, Milyr had intruded into her tiny private sense of comfort and forced her into feelings of confusion and discomfort. Why did she let him goad her so? Why did she get so frantic when he ridiculed her maturing sensual feelings? Cursing herself for her weakness, Swyllo sulked in the chair and let her bald scalp nod into her sweating palms. Milyr was such vulching toxx, she thought silently.

If she could arrange to trade between two lead spacecrafts and get Chitir here and send toxx Milyr away, Swyllo would beg Cap Nyba for such a splendid gift. But crews were fixed so many years ago at Steppingstone Primero when selection had been finalized to create best balances for three spacecrafts on present phase of Blue Jay project. She was stuck with the obnoxious presence of Milyr until culmination in Sexto System, where hopefully colonial population would be rediscovered. Once the mission was finished, then she could snare Chitir into her future. Once their phase of Blue Jay was ended in Sexto System, she and Chitir and all others would be free to return to life outside Blue Jay and stay at future Steppingstone Sexto, or with colonials if invited, or return to any of the five Steppingstones back toward Zerosolis System, or of course dwell in Homeworld or any of planetary terra-formed bases in the solar system. Wherever they finished their lives, Swyllo planned to snare Chitir with her. Boy had no choice in her mind, she mused vehemently.

"Awright, enough! Toxx damn, it's, enough!" the deep voice of Neer Domyn growled sternly.

Quiet silences fell over the trio in the locker room. Intensity of big young man's exasperation reached into consciousness of others. Swyllo felt emotion from his annoyance as a wave of warning strong enough to subdue any idea of pursuing slinging of insults. Perhaps they should act like true Blue Jayers, she mused, and not like snipping pups. Since his appointment as Neer of Wolf Streak at Steppingstone Secundo, Domyn had earned the respect of all in Blue Jay. His firmness of discipline had squashed many puppy actions of crew before events had become nasty and captain or counselors had been required to demand punishment. Domyn ruled Wolf Streak surely!

Sheepishly Swyllo peered toward Milyr and caught his gaze. Usually a piercing glare of an almost nineteen revol old boy had been abashed into glimpse of embarrassment. They shared common nod. Swyllo continued disrobing from their blue Pulseball uniform in silence. Upon her bared skin, new sweat added to perspiration of the game on Swyllo. Milyr pivoted his tall, naked figure toward his cubicle to place sweat-stained shirt inside. His sweating face gazed into the cubicle. Swyllo sensed his chagrin. She also hoped he would pluck out his JMO shorts and put them on his nude and distracting body.

Not many moments later, a sudden boisterous cry came from the doorway into quiet, "Did you wolves know Jamyk passed out again? Just as we were coming out of the arena, he just passed out. He just fell over onto the floor."

Standing abruptly and staring at the newcomer, Swyllo asked in worry, "Passed out? Is he okay?"

Striding purposely into locker room, a girl with a sweaty bald head and rounded face glistening with perspiration exclaimed vociferously, "Yes, boy passed out. Doc and Prof are with him in Med. Prof helped me carry him to Med. Jamyk collapsed not long after you left the arena. He just fell to floor. I was almost inside the tunnel then. But heard noise from foxes who were around him!"

Also, on his feet, Milyr murmured with an unusual sober seriousness to his tone, "But, Whyvvi, is little peener okay? Was he hurt in flurry of strikes and saves at end of overtime? Is little onad okay? He seemed cherp while he was grinning with Chitir and Bhiros when they were interviewed by reporters. And what was his interviewing about if he was on a losing team?"

Young woman Whyvvi peeled the helmet from her bald and perspiring head and replied with a smug tone, "If you had stayed for the tournament awards, you toxx, you would know Jamyk was named player of the game for his goalkeeping. Such award is not always earned by one of a winning team. Goalies have gotten the award often since first games at Steppingstone Primero."

"Vulch, I know that, but Bhiros gets it many times also," Milyr protested tersely and then asked again, "But is onad really okay now? Should we go to check and support him?"

"Since we haven't heard any alarm from Doc yet, we can probably assume he is fine," Domyn said calmly, though his voice was not as strong as Swyllo normally heard from a big young man and caused her some momentary panic.

Stopping at cubicle next to Milyr and setting her Zapstik blue pad onto the floor and white tip against the locker, a round-faced girl called Whyvvi replied, "Well, yes, he is okay. At least so is what Doc told me. She thinks it is usual dehydration and low level of nutrient, which seems to always affect Jamyk in contests. Little peener never prepares his body for exertion of playing Pulseball. He always waits for the last moment to take in fluids. Then when he remembers finally, he never drinks enough."

"No broken bones? No torn muscles? Is our little peener okay physically?" Milyr inquired while stroking his fingers up and down his long torso before taking purple JMO shorts from the cubicle and bending to pull the garment up his long legs to around his waist.

Domyn stated very matter-of-factly, "His suit is titan-flexed armor strengthened. All our McAnderwike uniforms for Pulseball competition have protection. Trait should have protected him from any serious physical strike or fall occurring in the arena."

Reaching into the cubicle to hang her blue helmet, Whyvvi declared with assurance, "Yes, he is healthy. He sustained no broken or torn anything. He is just tired out and depleted of fluids, according to Doc. Cap Nyba is there with others in Med, probably scolding Jamyk for his carelessness. She should be here soon. She had to meet also with official rep and Cap Bhiros to certify game results. Then of course ritual ceremony with pressers for sanbeam message back to other Steppingstones and eventually Zerosolis System. You know! All typical stuff!"

"But he's okay, right? Little peener is okay?" Swyllo asked in a concerned tone, which surprised herself with her unusual worry for the younger boy, who was so often her annoying social nemesis and irritating toxx pup almost as annoying as Milyr at times.

Whyvvi spat miffed by inquiry apparently, "Yes…yes…he is just cherp. If you do not believe me, then just go ask Doc Kymil. Doc says Jamyk will be ready for our journey to Sexto System. Now since we have lost a pivotal game, we will be Beta crew. We should have longer wait on Steppingstone Quinto. Fox Flash will get prime Alpha position. Jamyk will have plenty of time to recover."

Slightly winded by his attempt to extricate his large muscular arms and shoulders from tight-fitting McAnderwike shirt, Domyn gasped in his deep voice, "Whyvvi, you are assuming Cap Bhiros will choose to be Alpha crew. Win by foxes does not necessarily mean they will accept Alpha mission. Cap Bhiros may elect to let his crew take more rec time here at Steppingstone Quinto. He knows glory will find both of our spacecraft regardless when we arrive in Sexto System."

Swyllo nodded with understanding as she stripped from her full-body JMO suit, and as she tossed a wet sweaty garment to the floor of her cubicle, she said, "Oh, yes…so much cooler on my skin now! But Domyn, Bhiros is very audacious. He'll want to be first into Sexto. Foxes will want glory! They are very competitive. And you know he'll let Chitir and Khebol convince him to go for glory!"

While she enjoyed the cooling sensation on her perspiring skin in relief from clinging adherence of JMO to her torso and waist, Swyllo watched Whyvvi reach upwards to the back of the struggling huge form of Domyn to help the young man escape confining garment and heard the other girl agree, "Damn, right! Cap Bhiros is a daredevil and risk-taker! Being Alpha on our mission is just his desire. After their win now, foxes have shown to MisCom they are worthier than us. They did win overall series. Bhiros should choose Alpha lead. We should get useful time to prep for our last journey."

After McAnderwike garment fell to the floor, Domyn stepped from the tangle of pants and shirt around his large feet, as he then wore only his favorite tan JMO running shorts and said, "Thank you, Whyvvi. I believe you are most likely correct

Cap Bhiros will choose Alpha role. But let's wait for official designation. Let's not make any long-term rec plans just yet."

Snapping the waist band of his purple shorts against his taut lower belly, Milyr chortled with leer, "I've got vulching great desire for much reccing to do now. I hope vulching foxes do go for Alpha. All my fem fans here on Quinto will appreciate my extended presence."

As Whyvvi stepped by him, she laughed when she tugged sharply at the back of his shorts, dropping them slightly down his buttocks, and she declared, "Milyr, you are so skinny. I do not know what keeps your JMOs from sliding right down your bony frame once you unmeld front. What about your body could attract eyes of any womanly fems on Quinto?"

 Milyr smiled as he left drooping shorts down his buttocks and then he spread his long arms and then posed his tall six-foot, six-inch figure and boasted, "Yeah, nothing but the most perfect masculine body in galaxy. Muscles could lift up planets, never mind a mere piece of clothing. Muscles are bulging energy, purely full of power! Yeah, what my fems all want is my bulging powerful muscle!"

Giggling in spite of her attempt to be less caustic to her normally irritating crewmate for sake of Domyn, Swyllo could not help but retort, "Vulching strange now I don't see any bulging on your scrawny body, you hunk of skin and bone."

As she plucked her yellow JMO body suit from her cubicle, Swyllo observed his grin slip from his long face and his arms pause in posing to slap his taut belly, and Milyr leered, "Yeah, tiny fem, no bulging for you. But plenty power in the body. Body to be cleaned up for all my fem fans waiting outside. They will adore my great and handsome self."

"Washing up, now a very cherp notion," Domyn intruded on exchange while he pulled a cleaner pair of tan shorts up over his hips and waist, but only amusement tainted his deep voice as he added, "We have some private time in the sauna pool, just us and our friends from Fox Flash. No stone techs, no instructs, no MisCom, no pressers, and no toxx fans, just we will be there now. Let's go now, men, women, and Milyr. Let's relax for a while!"

Kicking her McAnderwike from around her feet, Whyvvi smoothed the wrinkles of her pink one piece, full-torso JMO running suit over her figure and scowled as she complained, "Well, Neer Domyn, you do not mean to just leave our gear here all over the floor. We always pick up and secure our gear before leaving any locker room. One of your standard routines…"

"We can take little time to get our McAnderwikes picked up," Swyllo agreed. "It will only take a few minutes. We can keep Cap Nyba happy by doing so."

Frowning with his hands on his hips clothed in tan JMO shorts, Domyn declared sternly with a serious tone yet mirth in his voice, "Now is time for just doing. Now is time for enjoying. Not time for picking up. I will talk to Cap later. We will go to the pool...now! Before Milyr gets even more obnoxious or impatient to see his adoring fans, we go now!"

Shocked by the intensity of his command, Swyllo followed the six-foot tall muscular young man toward shower entry. As she plucked at edges of her yellow JMO running suit to hoist top above her still only slightly developed breasts, Swyllo heard a gasped shriek from Whyvvi. Her friend had to strip from her sweaty JMOs and hastily change to clean suit for requirement of pool of Steppingstone Quinto. Then tentative footsteps of other two young people slapped on the floor behind Swyllo. Whyvvi mumbled sourly in low hushed voice. Her typical favor for Domyn seemed lost in her sour mumbling then.

Soon standing aside Domyn under showers, Swyllo felt a gentle and misty spray strike her body and bald head. She stretched her arms above her shoulders and let water wash over her entire torso. Soaking JMO suit against her torso and hips, steamy, warm water soothed her fatigue and soreness from prior vigorous exertion of Pulseball game. Warm spray felt really cherp on her body. She had not been so aware of bumps and bruises on her body. Apparently titan-flex armoring trait of McAnderwike could not totally protect the athlete from all injuries in competition of a game, just most severe. In the moment, spray of heated showers soothed soreness. She felt cleansed of grime, sweat, and defeat.

Yes, defeat at play of foxes, Swyllo thought sourly. Such sadness she felt for her mood just before the final phase of a long journey over many years, hopping from Steppingstone to Steppingstone across a vast distance of light years. Each hop had averaged about one standard revol of her life and then a relatively short visit to Steppingstone for replenishment of supply for spacecraft and crew. Also, time was allocated for the Pulseball tournament at each Steppingstone. Such athletic extravaganza was necessary show for people of Homeworld in Zerosolis System and all prior Steppingstones in back-trail of Blue Jay Project. Some annual viewing of progress of present Blue Jay mission had been necessary to bolster hopes and spirits of those billions of people. Since no real discovery of colonials, other than minor trails of residue of propulsion or comm transmissions, had been found thus far, MisCom appeased masses behind with games of Pulseball intermixed with reports of scientific discoveries and sights of new solar systems. People living still on Homeworld in the far distant Zerosolis system and intervening Steppingstones behind present phase of Blue Jay needed much encouragement and hope for a successful Blue Jay ending. Swyllo could not argue the benefit of such use of her playing time in games.

When she moved from showering sprays, Swyllo saw moisture-drenched form of Domyn waiting by closed door leading from shower chamber, and he admitted with a wide grin, "Felt really cherp, awspir cherp, didn't it, Swyllo? Obviously we get so used to titan-flex armor of McAnderwikes protecting us, we don't realize how many mostly insignificant bumps we attain in game. But an awspir shower of heated water sure feels amazingly cherp!"

Momentarily stunned by strange similarity of his comment with her prior thought, she looked up into his wide-set eyes and stammered, "Ahh...yeah...it was...luxurious! You are a surprising man, Neer Domyn, and wise leader. I believe sauna pool will be better still."

From steamy spray, she heard Milyr's croaking voice suddenly squeal, "Vulch, don't do to my toxx, Whyvvi. Don't poke me like so! Vulch poking me like makes me puddy!"

High-pitched laugh exploded from mist and then Whyvvi's voice sang, "But I thought you were planning to see your fem fans. I just wanted to give you prod. You need helping poke, just for your fem fans, do you not, oh, great and handsome Milyr?"

"Vulch, fem, I have to go out there with our friends first," groaned Milyr, "Guy like me can't walk out to pool with my bigness projecting how great I am. Surely would not look proper to friends. They expect some charm and maturity from me often."

"You should not need to worry, Milyr. It is cherp for you water pastes your JMOs to your skin. You would not want scant projection of your greatness hurting your vulching reputation, now would you, oh, great Milyr?" Whyvvi laughed.

"Awe, help me! You damn pups will goad me yet," Domyn muttered in a low voice just loud enough for Swyllo to overhear.

Watching watery figures of her two crewmates appear from showery mists, she giggled to Domyn, "Yeah, just pups, but our pups, aren't they, Domyn? Damn, Milyr, you appear less appealing in wet than you do normally."

Scowling at Whyvvi and then Swyllo, Milyr grumbled as he fluttered and straightened wet JMO shorts around his waist and hips, "Vulch, guy can't get respect from you fems! In spite of a handsome, gorgeous profile, you still give me vulching nastiness. Not even wow...or...cherp what manly body! Just nasty vulching toxxness!"

Stepping past him to stand beside Swyllo, Whyvvi stated, "Profile belonging to great manhood, yep! But only when you look at him from behind! Do you not agree, Swyllo?"

Stalking to them, Milyr towered his six-foot, six-inch figure over the girls, glared down at them, and then grinned as he said, "Indeed, centuries ago, according to Prof Lyndyn, women of great wisdom often judged potential of man by his toxx. Now if you are sincere, Whyvvi, I guess you think I'm a very manly guy! I'm a manly guy! I'm a manly guy!"

"Oh, awe save us!" groaned Domyn, and Swyllo almost laughed at him as a big man tried to keep a smirk from his face as he punched the panel to open a door to pool area, "Let's get to the pool. Maybe water will be cold enough to dowse some of our overwhelming nasty silliness. Maybe we can behave reasonably mature in front of our fellow Blue Jayers from Fox Flash. Do you think we could now, my wolf mates?"

Just before pivoting to go into the pool area, Swyllo snorted and inquired skeptically, "And, Milyr, since when do you ever pay attention to Prof Lyndyn's ramblings?"

"Vulch, I listen always. I just don't use his wisdom very often," Milyr admitted with a smirk, and then pushing past her through the doorway, he cried in direction of the pool, "Hey...hello, fine fems of Fox Flash. How did you luscious vixens like my form in game today? My wolf fems say I was absolutely manly cherp today."

As her eyes adjusted to increased sunlight filtering through a huge globe over the pool, Swyllo observed a trio of girls in their JMO suits splashing and treading water along the curve of the closest side of a large pool, which was shaped like a figure eight, and she called gaily, "Yeah, cherp game today. You foxes were cherp Jayers today! But beware of vulching tall, walking puddy. He thinks he's gorgeous manly today. Toxx is more obnoxious than usual..."

"Don't mind her, beautiful vixens! She's just jealous because I won't give her any attention," Milyr shouted over his shoulder at Swyllo as he approached a cluster of laughing girls in a sparkling pool. "How's the water today? Not too cold, I hope. I don't want any shrinking of my cherp body. I like cherp warm water now, just right for a little cuddling! Perhaps, fine fems?"

Carhel splashed water at him when he squatted down at the edge of the pool, and another girl, Emkhat, shouted with a laugh, "Milyr, you big toxx, stay away from us. We don't trust you now!"

With her bald head bobbing just above water, a third girl, Radhin, chirped with a high shrill voice, "You toxx, you might be nasty to us after losing game. We don't trust you."

Then they all laughed and giggled again, singing, "We don't trust you, you walking puddy! We don't trust you, you walking puddy!"

Peering at Swyllo, Milyr complained half-heartedly, "Vulch, tiny fem, see what you started! You fine fems are going to be the death of me yet. But then… what splendid death it could be! Now, vulch, maybe not death! Too far to go for fem! What do you think, Domyn? Us manly guys should not need to die for our fems, should we?"

"For my own future possibilities with bodacious young lasses, Milyr, I believe I will not answer a question. You are on your own for now. Awe knows what kind of trouble a guy can get into if responding to questions like so," a big young man in light brown JMO shorts chuckled just before he dove in a shallow arc into the pool and capturing gaze of Swyllo.

Witnessing lithe but wide form glide through clear water, Swyllo decided to follow his example. Without waiting to listen to Milyr's next ridiculous remark, she leaped her body into her dive. Her arms, then her bald head, and finally her torso plunged into cooling water. Flow of water along her body was exhilarating. She felt the flow caress along her smooth scalp, her slender torso, her narrow waist, and lastly her thin legs. She sensed moment of relief and peace while she glided through refreshing water.

Then her hands touched the wall of the pool. She surfaced with rapid exhalation of her breath. As she inhaled the next breath, Swyllo regretted shortness of glide and necessity of renewing breath at expense of such an invigorating moment. Yet such was life, she mused, cherp events were almost always temporary.

Her dive and glide had taken her about half an arc of circular pool from commotion between Milyr and young women from Fox Flash. Very tall boy was trying still to impress them with himself, his wit, and his charm. However, three noisy and giggling girls were rejecting his shenanigans with what Swyllo thought were false motives while they joyously laughed in group not far from the edge of the pool where Milyr stooped still. Such silly pups, Swyllo snickered to herself, yet then Milyr had such effect on fems.

Movement attracted her sight. Behind Milyr, a thin tall figure of Khebol was sneaking toward commotion. She knew her friend Khebol to be a prankster of highest order. She suspected he was about to perform one of his mischievous deeds on Milyr. Cherping nasty, she thought to herself. Why not give him assisting help? Perhaps she could provide diversion, she mused.

Smoothly breast-stroking across the surface of the water, Swyllo called heartily, "Are you still trying to clutch with my friends? Milyr, don't you get it? We don't clutch with skinny puddies."

Dodging more splashed water, though he was wet already, Milyr exclaimed to girls, "Hey, I'm cuddly guy. Just ask all fem fans on Steppingstone Quinto. I just want to be friends with cherpest young and bodacious vixens in Quinto System. You, fine fems, and my pretty young vixens. You're most bodacious vixens for any man to gaze upon."

Swimming to a trio of girls treading water about two yards now from the edge of the pool, Swyllo sputtered through watery breath, "Vulcher, boy, you've got puddy idea of yourself! Girls, let's go teach him some reality."

With challenge Swyllo led other girls closer toward pool edge, all time watching Khebol closing behind Milyr. Tall young man had a wide grin on his narrow face. There was no question, Swyllo thought. Milyr was soon to be in the pool. Unless nasty toxx realized Khebol was behind him, she suddenly worried.

Radhin shrieked loudly, "Yeah, girls, let's teach him reality. He's such pompous toxx!"

"Hey, yeah, come teach me, young vixens…" Milyr started to say, beginning to rise from his hunched crouch and waving his long arms in welcoming gesture.

However, Swyllo observed as Khebol rushed silently from behind and pushed the tall boy toward the pool and cried out with glee, "Wet time for big puddies!"

As Milyr soared over heads of girls and splashed with his long arms and legs splayed out around his lanky torso onto his side into the water, Swyllo laughed with a high-pitched tone of elation and cried out, "Cherping great! So cherp entry into pool for puddy guy! Cherping was the best way for him to get wet!"

"Vulching great! Really cefacious!" exclaimed gravelly a voice of moderately tall and rather thin Khebol. "Cherp timing, Swyllo, we make a good team. I'm slightly abashed though for such whipping for our favorite arrogant toxx Milyr!"

"Vulch, yeah, it was cherply cefacious! Especially since our obnoxious toxx took dowse was cherp," Swyllo declared with a watery smile as she watched other girls from Fox Flash swim over a sunken form of Milyr to continue dunking and harassment.

From the other half of an hour-glass-shaped pool, Whyvvi shouted suddenly with an aggrieved tone to her voice, "Khebol you toxx, where have you been? Get your nasty toxx over here. You will most likely be leaving soon for Sexto System. I will not see you for almost revol! Get your toxx over here now!"

While a loud roar from Milyr rose from noisy ruckus in middle of the pool and screams of three girls gaily chorused his displeasure, Swyllo noticed a grin on Khebol's face contort to a frown, and the tall boy protested, "Argh! Vulch, she can't let me alone for a bit even. You'd think we were already mated. And we know our mating is not likely for years yet."

Blinking her wet eyelids at him and smiling, Swyllo giggled, "I don't believe you feel as sourly as you complain, Khebol. You're a lot like your friend Chitir. He pretends not to desire me, yet his face and body language tell me differently. You guys are such easy toxx for us young women."

His eyes rolled beneath his squinting eyelids before a tall boy in tan JMO shorts muttered, "And you're a lot like rest of Jayer girls. If you get your hands on any of us men now, then you seem to believe you've got us forever. Vulch, you girls do mature faster, even with inhibition of antemgebemarzex. It's not fair, just not vulching fair!"

"But, Khebol, eventually you guys like it, I'm sure," Swyllo grinned and then hastily scowled as another worry crossed her mind, and she groaned tersely, "Where is toxx oaf Chitir? Khebol, where is the vulching young lad? He should be here with you by now."

Before he could answer her, another demanding shout came from Whyvvi in the other portion of the pool, "Khebol! I am getting whipped! Get your skinny toxx over here right now!"

"Argh!" he grunted, starting to turn away, and then before leaving, said, "I believe he's with Jamyk. As soon as he heard about Jamyk passing out, he left the locker room to check in Med. He should be here soon if Jamyk is alright!"

Growling just barely audibly, Swyllo said with mixed emotions, "Thanks, Khebol. We have heard Jamyk is okay. But toxx Chitir had better get his body here soon, or big oaf will be in vulching nasty trouble. I'm goaded waiting here while he plays around with fool Jamyk!"

"Such a big threat from such a small young woman," Khebol called back over his shoulder as he slowly walked away along the edge of the pool. "Still I'd not want to be Chitir, if you ever get really whipped. Would be a nasty time for him then, hey, Swyllo?"

Whipped? She was getting whipped? Over the big oaf of toxx boy, she was getting agitated? What was wrong with her, she wondered. Emotional sensations had never before troubled her at previous Steppingstones, at least emotions about Chitir. But then she had never been nearly nineteen before either. At Steppingstone Cuatro, she had been about one revol younger, and so had he. Their relationship had been one of close friendship, except when they were competing on opposing teams in Pulseball tournament. But now, one revol older, she felt different about him. More possessive, more…jealous…she asked herself abruptly. Was it possible, could she be jealous now of Chitir spending time with his other friend Jamyk? What were such new feelings in her heart and mind? Was antemgebemarzex inhibition failing now? Was she feeling some of the natural hormones then?

Aggravated with her own thoughts, she inhaled a deep breath, submerged beneath the surface of the water, and pushed off with a powerful thrust of her short legs from the wall of the pool. Soothing torment within her mind at same time as relieving strains of her bruised body, coolness flowed along her slender body as she glided through clear water. Her light-yellow JMO suit stuck to her torso like second skin. What a cherping great feeling, she mused silently beneath water. Though, she thought silently, tightness of JMO seemed more binding around her torso, especially her upper torso now than at Steppingstone Cuatro. Was she getting fat now? Would change in her body be attractive to Chitir? Or would he see her as toxx chubby now?

She swam course beneath and around thrashing legs of four people frolicking in center of the pool surface. From the pool bottom squirted several streams of bubbling water heated and oxygenized to provide pulsating sauna effect. As her peripheral vision noticed similar bubbling streams flowing from the pool walls, her main focus was on a large body whose powerful breaststroke and thrusting kick paced her spear-like glide easily. With her lungs filling with carbon dioxide and beginning to ache mildly for exhalation, Swyllo curved her form upwards and stroked toward the surface. Beside her Domyn copied her route. His effort seemed so easy compared to the strain she felt in her swimming.

When her bald head popped from water into sunlight streaming through the globe above, Swyllo gasped out a lungful of air and watery spray and then hastily inhaled new breath of warm air. From the center of the pool, she heard laughs, giggles, and often curses of three Fox Flash vixens and their nemesis Milyr. Only moment after her surfacing, the wide bald head of Domyn erupted from churning waster. She listened to the blow of his exhalation as she treaded water near the pool edge.

From a wide-lipped smile under skein of clear dripping water, he gasped taking a deep breath, "Awspir!... Sure…helps our tired muscles, eh, Swyllo? Even effort to swim seems to relax soreness of an intensely played Pulseball game. I feel relaxing only starting in my body!"

Sputtering watery breathes and grinning simultaneously, Swyllo replied, "Pooling is one of my favorite rewards after playing Pulseball games. I'm so very thankful Steppingstones allow us their recycled water for pools. Water feels so cherp to jump into after games. We are truly vulching lucky to be Blue Jayers on Steppingstones, aren't we, Domyn?"

"Awright, we are lucky for sure. One of the rewards we Blue Jayers get for putting our lives at risk on our many years of travel to Sexto System. We do give up normal life to be Blue Jayers, Swyllo. People back in Zerosolis System and on all of Steppingstones live relatively normal lives, but they do lack flare of adventure we experience on Blue Jay mission," Domyn said, and then after a few seconds as they both rested, he continued with some confused mirth in his tone, "We do deserve reward of a pool. However, after playing such strenuous games in such intense competition with Fox Flash and home teams of Steppingstones, every time we seem to have so much energy left in our exhausted bodies to play and frolic with foxes in pools. Maybe next time we wolves will need to expend more effort in game to beat foxes of Cap Bhiros. Yet his players also seem to have plenty of energy to contend with our Milyr."

"Maybe, Domyn, but we did play very well today. I must admit even rascal Jamyk seemed on focus today. Only last lucky shot by Bhiros was only let down, I noticed, by Jamyk," she exclaimed with mild annoyance and slight slap of water to emphasize her chagrin.

"Shot wasn't lucky. Shot was plain skill by one of most skilled guys to ever play game, Swyllo," boasted a familiar deep voice from above and outside the curved edge of the pool.

Peering upwards through water droplets running down her smooth-skinned forehead and eyelids, Swyllo noticed approaching silhouettes of two people against the backdrop of a bright dome above pool. Without doubt she recognized stout figures as Captains Bhiros and Nyba. Neither leader was much over, five feet six inches in height. However, their natural stance and presence declared them to be people of authority to Swyllo at least.

Cap Bhiros was well-muscled at his shoulders, arms, and chest. His torso tapered to a relatively narrow waist now covered by his favorite orange JMO shorts. His hips and thighs widened out again beneath shorts with muscles and faint hint of wide-boned frame he would most likely grow into at adulthood not many years into future. If she had not been captivated by Chitir, Swyllo might have felt clutch for Bhiros. Now why was she thinking so then? Man was captain and had responsibilities as leader. Bhiros would not be interested in her, would he?

Embarrassed by her own thoughts, Swyllo hastily averted her glance to Nyba, her captain of Wolf Streak. Cap Nyba showed already some of her adult wide-boned figure from slightly flattened peak of her bald head to broad hips and torso to muscled, firm stance of her presently bare feet. As usual her big arms were crooked at elbows in her most common posture with hands on hips clad in her blue JMO suit. Swyllo had no question in her mind Cap Nyba's expression was one of serious authority as she stood there observing her crew playing in the pool. Very intense young woman, Swyllo thought, but one who exuded respect and confidence to her fellow Blue Jayers.

From beside her in waving water, Swyllo heard Domyn declare quickly, "Cap Bhiros, it was a very acrobatic move you made to get rebound and get off least shot. But if I had been two inches taller, then I could have knocked you from your course when you leaped from the pedestal. Then you would not have had a chance at play. Awe knows what would have happened then. Maybe we'd be playing still!"

"And if Jamyk had been in better position after his last save, then maybe he could have prevented your shot from hitting target," Swyllo groaned hastily, "Little toxx got himself out of position and did not give himself any chance to move back in front of target. What was he thinking then?"

Waving his hands and arms in a negative crossing gesture in front of his torso, Bhiros laughed, "No, no, no, don't blame Jamyk. My super leaping twist to snare rebounding pulse and then my amazing spin to shoot pulse were my best moves ever. Was just skill, my great cherping skill!"

"Awe, yes, quite amazing moves they were. So were Jamyk's saves entire game! Everybody played a very awspir game today," Domyn said diplomatically while he treaded water not far from Swyllo, "All of your foxes played their best today, Bhiros."

Without changing her stance and in her mellow but very controlled voice, Cap Nyba announced, "Yes, everyone in game today played exceptionally cherp, especially rascal Jamyk, and all foxes. According to the official observer, Jamyk made fifty-three saves today. Most likely a tourney record! Foxes managed sixty-one shots, another tournament record. Their quickness and pedestal leaping during game will provide experts and fans much to talk about back in Zerosolis System and all Steppingstones between there and here. Many of observers here at Quinto are saying already foxes have set strategy model of future for game of Pulseball today."

"Jamyk's performance will astound them all once fans of Zerosolis view the game," Bhiros stated with true honesty in his throaty voice. "Wolf Streak is lucky to have him as crewmate."

About to retort something about the younger boy's mischievous tendencies, Swyllo then felt approach of other swimmers around her, so held her tongue when Milyr's baritone voice asked with real concern, "How is our little peener, Cap? Is he okay? Was he just dehydrated and depleted of nutrition?"

"Rascal is fine now. Doc Kymil put him into a nutria-bath after Prof Lyndyn carried him to Med. Just like typical Jamyk to not eat enough before a game, but now he's okay. He should be out soon. Doc Kymil said she would order him to get some sunlight today, even if he did not wish to go pooling. Prof Lyndyn agreed with her and told lad so in rather long lecture. However, you know Jamyk, little toxx doesn't listen very often. Although I do not believe he will turn down any chance to jump into the pool," Nyba explained in her mothering voice rather than her forceful authoritative voice Swyllo knew so well.

Chuckling in a water spraying gasp, Milyr chortled, "Vulching right, he's not a listener. But cherp to hear little onad is okay now, right Swyllo?"

As he exclaimed last remark, his long-fingered hand pressed down on her shoulder. Caught by surprise, Swyllo swallowed water as her small body was pushed beneath the surface. Choking water and partial breath of air from her throat and mouth, she spun her lithe body from under pressure of Milyr's one hand, and with her arm, pushed the offending hand away from her shoulder. In a few seconds while she was underwater, Swyllo observed kicking the legs of several people and pulsating bubbles streaming from the wall of the pool. However, her awareness noticed little of such as she kicked frantically back to surface.

When her smooth-skinned head burst into the warmth of sunshine again, she heard several people laughing, and she gasped with fury, "Toxx vulcher, I hope you can't get puddy until you're older than Prof and Doc combined. You're such a vulching toxx, Milyr!"

From above bobbing heads in pool, Cap Nyba scolded in her voice of irate annoyance, "Wolves, let's not act like pups now. Try to behave while we're with foxes."

"Vulch, Cap, but we are just pups," shouted Milyr. "We're all just young pups enjoying a playful swim in great cherping sunshine. Not very often do we get to do so with our friends of Fox Flash while we are both on our journey through space for Blue Jay. Vulching for sure, we all know not any real sunshine in LaOgres space for next revol or so, don't we?"

"Now you are righter than you may realize, Milyr. We won't be able to rec for much longer," announced Cap Bhiros. "Official departure for the last leg of our mission for Blue Jay is now determined. We will be leaving very soon."

"But, Cap, we don't have to go real soon, do we?" whined Emkhat, not far away from Swyllo.

"Vulch, Bhiros, can't we stay here longer?" complained Khebol. "Our journey will be so long to Sexto System. We'll be in LaOgres space for almost one revol. We'll miss our friends here…"

Clutching the pool edge next to Khebol, Whyvvi pleaded, "Do not make him go so soon, Cap. Let Khebol and your crew get more rest here. We can all rest here on Steppingstone Quinto together. We should be able to postpone next phase of Blue Jay slightly. We have done so much already."

Then Swyllo heard and sensed firmness in Domyn's tone when he declared loudly, "Awright, enough! Don't act like whining pups. We are Blue Jayers, and we have a mission to finish. We must not complain about commands of our captains."

Abruptly quiet spread amongst swimmers along the edge of the pool, so Cap Bhiros said to Domyn, "Thank you, Neer. We have been with present mission Blue Jay for most of our lives. Now we have a chance to see finish finally. Whyvvi, if you really desire to mate Khebol, then you should be happy to see finish of mission into Sexto System. Then you two people can go back to Zerosolis System…or… wherever you wish to sneak away for the rest of your lives."

"Vulch, Bhiros, don't encourage her!" wailed Khebol.

While Whyvvi gave a bony shoulder next to her one quick sharp rap with her knuckles, Cap Nyba stated with firm soberness, "We have been to sanbeam communication with MisCom. Blue Jay to Sexto is go. Decisions have been made now. Alpha and Beta designations have been authorized. Our rest here at Quinto is almost over. We resume our journey very soon."

Several gasps and moans could be heard around her. Swyllo was surprised at internal excitement and nervousness churning in her stomach. Never before had she believed a moment would affect her so. For most of their lives, as Bhiros had just said, they had trained for and been educated to journey Blue Jay mission to Sexto System. Now suddenly time was upon them. It was a bit scary, she realized, and a bit exhilarating. They were to travel many light years further into the galaxy in search of descendants of legendary colonials who had departed Zerosolis System over 500 years ago. Now time was theirs to become legends themselves if they were successful. Swyllo inhaled a very deep breath, held it, and then exhaled to calm herself. She was surprised to feel such anxious exhilaration.

Standing in partial silhouette with sunshine behind him, Bhiros said sternly, "Yes, we start for our last part of the journey. Need is great for us to successfully find colonials and whatever new world they have discovered or created with terra-forming science, which was aboard three colony ships when they left Homeworld and Zerosolis System many centuries in our past."

Nyba continued as if they had planned such spiel, "We all remember, I'm sure, planets of Zerosolis System are at best only models of terra-formed nature. They are best humanity could manage in response to failing of those of our ancestors who churned our world into terrible Despoliation Era. Billions of people living in scattered domes of terra-formed recovery have only fleeting hope colonists found planet or planets of replacement to lost nature of our Homeworld. Our mission is to find colonists and their marvelous new planet and methods…"

"Yes, and once we do so in Sexto System, all of our people, both of Zerosolis now and who in Sexto live as we hope, should live in environment proper for humanity. We will correct horrors of ancestors on Homeworld who created Despoliation," Bhiros declared in unusual soberness.

With formality of ceremony, Cap Nyba stretched her arms toward Bhiros and solemnly announced to young swimmers in the pool, "As agreed prior to our travel from Steppingstone Cuatro, champion of Pulseball tournament between the final two most qualified crews of project Blue Jay would choose either Alpha or Beta role. As captain of Fox Flash and winner of tournament here on Steppingstone Quinto, Cap Bhiros has been allowed by MisCom to select a role of his choice. I now have honor to introduce us all to captain of Fox Flash Alpha, Cap Bhiros. May journey to Sexto System be without mishap and with glory!"

In silence of announcement of moment, Cap Bhiros stretched his arms toward Nyba, and as they hugged, he replied in an unusually serious tone for him, "May your journey to Sexto System be without mishap and with glory. May crew of Wolf Streak Beta enjoy their days of recreation!"

"Damn...vulching nastiness!" muttered Khebol in a barely audible voice not far from Swyllo, but then she witnessed grimace on his face realign to sober respectfulness when he asked in a normal voice, "When do we leave, Cap?"

Peering down at Khebol's bobbing bald head and then to all other young swimmers, Cap Bhiros answered, "Neer Khebol, Fox Flash Alpha departs from Steppingstone Quinto in five days. We will go over mission protocols tomorrow with full crew. Today we will relax. Today we will enjoy our time with our friends and fellow Blue Jayers of Wolf Streak Beta. We may yet share moments with Hlankam's crew of Lynx Blaze before we depart."

"Vulch, toxx cats don't deserve our time," Milyr griped loudly and harshly.

Neer Khebol swatted the bare shoulder of Milyr and then scolded, "You are toxx, Milyr. Cats are as valuable as we of our two craft. Only one terrible killing altered their chance of being one of two lead scout craft of Blue Jay. And slaying was not by their hands of crew but another!"

"Yes, and you should not say any nasty words to them once they arrive here," Whyvvi demanded tartly treading water almost on top of Khebol.

"Wolves, Wolf Streak Beta will leave in about nineteen days later according to Blue Jay scheduling," Cap Nyba stated and then added more cheerfully, "But as Bhiros just said, let's play now present day. Let's enjoy the presence of our friends. It will be soon enough we will all be plunging into LaOgres to journey toward an unexplored region of space. We, all of us Blue Jayers, will be the first humans of our time to scout and explore Sexto System."

"We will have chance to be Blue Jayers to finally make contact with descendants of our ancestral colonists who left Zerosolis System over 500 years ago. We could be most famous Jayers of all time. None of the previous five missions were able to find super colony ships. We will have a chance now," Bhiros proclaimed and then suddenly cried out with cracking in his voice as he leaped into air, "But now...let's play! Jayers in thevpool!"

While she watched him somersault over her head into the pool, Swyllo was even more surprised to hear stoic Cap Nyba shout with a trilling melodious laugh, "Cannonball!"

Then while Cap Nyba leaped her squat form over swimmers and tucked her body into what resembled ball, Swyllo grabbed for handrail along the pool edge against sudden splashing waves from two falling bodies. Although captains of Blue Jay spacecraft, Nyba and Bhiros were still merely nineteen years in age, as Swyllo reminded herself while her face felt a splatter of huge splashes.

Whyvvi wailed in midst of churning water, "Five days! You leave in only five days. Khebol, we will not have much time."

"Less than you say, Whyvvi. I'll be spending many hours over the next three days calibrating and checking maintenance performed on Fox Flash by Quinto engineers," griped Khebol in a gravelly cracking voice, even as his hand stroked the bare shoulder of Whyvvi aside him in the pool.

"Nasty luck for you two cuddlers," Milyr smirked before he grinned at the other girls around him and suggested, "Yeah, vixens, only five days to catch me before you travel to Sexto. It is your last chance to be with my cuddly, very adult, and manly person."

As she listened to the three young women shriek in unison and hastily swim away from the long arms of Milyr, Swyllo snorted sourly, "Argh! How vulching disgusting toxx can be sometimes!"

"Yeah, Swyllo…are you…jealous?" Milyr retorted, spitting water from his mouth with his narrow face partially submerged beneath the choppy water. "I'll make time for you, cherp fem. But then we will see each other everyday while coasting through LaOgres. I thought I'd give foxy vixens a chance first while they're still here. Seems to be a fair thing to do!"

"Argh! No way, you vulching toxx! And I hate coasting LaOgres. But not enough to vulching cuddle with you, Milyr," she snarled at him before turning to swim rapidly along the arc of the curved pool edge.

After about eleven yards of freestyle swimming, she paused to check to learn if Milyr had followed her. Instead a long figure was swimming slowly toward giggling and splashing girls on the far side of the pool. Vulch him, she cursed silently to herself, he was just so vulching arrogant. Such puddy, toxx personality in such a handsome male body, she mused. No, she was not jealous, she could not be! But he had followed them and not her. He had given them his attention and not her.

Vulch, she scolded herself more harshly, she was not jealous. She could not be. Jealously was an emotion requiring some form of physical sexual attraction, didn't it, she wondered. Yet could not be the case because all hormonal drives, which could lead to sexual desire, were inhibited during the journey in space for duration of the Blue Jay mission. She could not be attracted to him. Antemgebemarzex would inhibit any such loving emotions. And he was obnoxious Milyr. She could not be jealous over him with other girls.

Then why did his taunts bother her so much? She felt something, she realized. And then what about Chitir, what about her feelings toward the big oaf? She felt for him in different but similar sensation as she did for Milyr. She would have to ask Doc Kymil. Being almost nineteen now, almost a Blue Jayer woman, was more confusing than being about a revol younger back on Steppingstone Cuatro.

Would a bewildering feeling be any less when she was older in Sexto System after coasting through LaOgres? Vulch, LaOgres space, she swore to herself. Seems like aging happens too quickly in LaOgres travel, she reminded herself, thinking back to the trip from Steppingstone Cuatro to Steppingstone Quinto. Vulching, LaOgres travel, too much sleeping, not enough awakenings, she grumbled, too fast to be aware of one's aging consciousness, too fast for proper maturation. Vulching LaOgres, she cursed silently. Her body and mind seemed to age faster than she was aware.

A flurry of water movement beneath her forewarned her. Then a wide-browed head surfaced beside her. Water flowed from his smooth, hairless face while his bigger than average eyes peered at her. With no sign of effort, Domyn tread water near her. His mouth smiled in kindness.

Then smile changed to a mild frown, and Domyn asked in concern, "What is your worry, Swyllo? Your face looks like serious nastiness, to use one of your slang terms. Is it teasing of our often rambunctious Milyr? If he's obnoxious to you, I'll simmer his intentions fast!"

While she clung to the handrail and her legs kicked slowly in a relaxing sauna burst from the pool wall, Swyllo was forced to grin at her companion and say, "Nastiness… Neer, you almost never use my slang. It sounds funny from you. Don't worry about me now. I can handle Milyr, big foolish toxx! He's just such a vulching toxx. Handsome to gaze upon, but till he opens his mouth to say his mind, what little is there!"

A smile on a big face continued as Domyn said, "I believe you can. However, your face did express some turmoil. What really bothers you, Swyllo? Your distress concerns me as Neer and as your friend. I would be poor Neer if I did not help you with any problem."

Embarrassed by her befuddlement over her possible relationships with boys, which she did not wish to discuss with Domyn, Swyllo replied instead, "Coasting LaOgres makes me worry, Neer. Even though we've done it several times already since leaving Zerosolis System, I still don't like it. Odd, very strange, and scary space gives me vulching nerves!"

"If you're sure Milyr is not a problem," Domyn said, staring at her for a moment as if reading her expressions like Prof Lyndyn often did, then continued,

"Seems as if you know you can handle coasting LaOgres as well. We'll be in it only little less than year! And asleep in stasis much of travel!"

With an abrupt slap at water with one hand, she whined, "But I still hate it. Every time we plunge, I feel like we'll never get back to real space, see real stars again. I don't like the feeling. It makes me too nervous. I don't feel cherp."

"Yet I know you understand LaOgres is real space, Swyllo. It is just a different aspect with different macro forces than those humans had observed originally, then measured and unraveled. You learned all science basics years ago in school before we were finally selected for Blue Jay," his calming voice explained while his muscular arms stroked gently back and forth, keeping him afloat in water.

Feeling a flush of heat in her cheeks as blush of uncontrollable embarrassment crept up her neck to compete with warmth of sunshine on her bald head, Swyllo swallowed in a gulp and muttered, "I know... I know... Domyn but... I still don't trust LaOgres. I feel helpless there, out of control, coasting on forces we really don't control."

"I probably should not admit now in moment, but we don't really control gravity and quantals in what you call real space. In Debordo space, we use natural forces such as gravity, but we do not control them. We leave such to universal deity, if you believe in such. We are mere humans. We use natural physics we can understand but don't control such forces completely," his deep voice said while his large eyes held hers with compassion.

She was about to retort her misgivings when suddenly two hands pushed against her legs and thrust her upwards from the water. Shrieking with her startled surprise, Swyllo inhaled hastily a lungful of warm air before plunging back down into clear water. Under water she twisted her body toward the pool wall. Through pulsating bubbles of sauna streams, she saw two sets of legs and thighs. One was clad in tan JMO shorts, obviously Domyn by the very thick legs.

Other wore orange JMO shorts. Man was obviously Bhiros with his shorter and slightly slender, though muscular legs beneath a narrow waist. She was angry enough to hit him in the crotch where he would hurt to extreme. However, her sense of hierarchical decorum and common knowledge of boyish impulses of young man stopped her. She suspected he was playing only.

Once she surfaced again, instead of responding with physical retaliation, she yelled shrilly with a spitting watery gasp, "Vulch...you...toxx... Bhiros! You scared vapors out of me, you vulcher."

His square-jawed visage revealed his wide-mouthed boyish grin beneath mischievous sparkling eyes, and Bhiros laughed, "Vulcher? Are you calling me vulcher? What kind of mouth is so? You used to tell me I was a big and tasty treat of manly boy."

"Not you, too, Bhiros?" she wailed, reaching the handrail on the pool edge. "Vulching guys all think they're clutches for girls. Vulching guys!"

"Damn, Swyllo, I didn't mean anything nasty," the young man sputtered with his face twisting in confused anxiety before he continued, "I just was trying to bring some play into what seemed too serious a conversation between you and Domyn. We're in day for fun, not serious!"

Treading water beside her, Domyn explained hastily, "Cap Bhiros, she has just had a moment of trouble with Milyr not long ago. He was being himself too over-enthusiastically. Also, she is having a little nervousness about coasting LaOgres."

"I'm sorry, Swyllo. I didn't intend anything uncherp. You know me! My timing is always wrong! I seem to joke and play at most inappropriate moments," Bhiros apologized but could not extinguish his big boyish smile across his face. "I'm just your old big and tasty treat!"

"Argh! Guys!" she growled and then with slight giggle retorted, "But you were never big and tasty, Bhiros. You were only big. Chitir was big and tasty, not you. Where is the big oaf anyway? Didn't you let him pool today? Is he hiding away with fool boy Jamyk?"

With a pout replacing a grin from his lips, Bhiros groaned, somewhat falsely she thought, "Not big and tasty? I'm only big? Maybe I won't let him come to the pool today, if I can't be big and tasty."

"Whoa, what's up, guy? I thought I was big and tasty," squealed a cracking gravelly voice as Khebol swam toward them with his awkward breaststroke.

Not far behind him, Whyvvi complained sourly and slightly angry as she also approached, "What is big and tasty? Khebol, what is your reference? Why do I not know about it? I should know about some big and tasty phrase, if about you!"

While Domyn choked on water as he laughed beside her, Swyllo splashed water at Khebol's bald head and chuckled, "No, no, guys, get it right. Bhiros was big. Chitir was big and tasty. Khebol was tasty. And Whyvvi, it doesn't mean anything important. It's just cherp fun from many years ago before Steppingstone Secundo if I remember right. Not any reality anyway, anyhow! Long ago! Years now!"

"Way back?" Whyvvi paused, and then after thinking briefly, continued, "You say before Secundo? Why do I not know about…joke, Khebol? I was around during pup years! You never told me? Khebol?"

Before she lost her thought of recent threat by Bhiros, Swyllo suddenly interrupted, "Cap Bhiros, don't you dare prevent Chitir from getting into the pool today. Not with you leaving in five days and plunging LaOgres soon after, you'd better make him get in here soon!"

"Khebol, what is the 'tasty' reference?" Whyvvi persisted swimming to the thin boy and gripping his shoulders, "Tell me now! Before you spend time hiding in Fox Flash in prep soon!"

Wincing, Khebol stammered, "Whoa, girl, it was long ago. It was nothing important, just pup toxx fun. Don't get all whipped over it!"

"Bhiros, where is Chitir?" Swyllo griped, swimming aggressively towards him. "Why isn't he here yet? You'll be plunging soon. Your Fox Flash will be off to Sexto."

As his big eyes glimmered amusement, Bhiros pleaded, backing away from her thrashing arms, "Hey, Swyllo cherp! He's with Jamyk. He'll be here soon. We don't plunge for days yet."

Whyvvi continued her tirade at Khebol, yelling, "Long ago? Swyllo just mentioned it. Joke is still vulching alive. How is it I do not know about it? Khebol, why have you never mentioned it before? Khebol, what is meaning for 'tasty?' Tell me now or feel my anger!"

"Jamyk? Why is he still with Jamyk? He'll be in LaOgres in five days. I need him here with me. I need to see him before plunging. And then we'll be apart for almost a whole revol before Sexto. I need to be with him again first," Swyllo squealed with intense chagrin.

"Before LaOgres, Khebol? Were you going to tell me before you left for your plunging into LaOgres? Were you going to tell me about your manly joke before you left, Khebol?" Whyvvi shrieked.

"LaOgres, I hate LaOgres. No Chitir in LaOgres! I may lose him in LaOgres. I don't trust LaOgres. I may never see him again after LaOgres," Swyllo cried out as a sense of terror swelled in her awareness and tears began to weep from her eyes.

Through unexpected turmoil in her mind and dripping water off her brow and salty tears, Swyllo saw Domyn glide in front of her, grip her flailing hands, and say firmly, "Awright, enough, Swyllo, calm down. Khebol, come over here. She needs to hear you and me tell LaOgres is safe. Whyvvi, let him go now. Go abuse Milyr for a while. I need Khebol here now."

"Is she suffering her fear reaction to LaOgres space again?" Bhiros asked with worry while Swyllo felt rather than heard a shrug from Domyn, and then Bhiros continued, "Whyvvi, let's go irritate Milyr. He's always cherp for some goading fun. Let Neers take care of Swyllo."

While she floated in a pulsating warmth of sauna streams, strong clasps of big hands of Neer Domyn began to steady her panic. She was very irritated at herself for giving in to her fears. They were right. She had travelled through LaOgres space many times before. Great spacecraft had plunged successfully each time before. She had always seen Chitir and all other companions after each pop out back into Debordo space. She realized her fears were irrational, yet they were still powerful enough to conquer her emotional stability. She needed Chitir. Still she felt annoyed at herself for need...to be reliant on big oaf.

From not far away, she heard Khebol with a tremor in his cracking voice ask, "Is she okay? Do you really need me, Domyn? I'm not a cherp counselor or doctor. I'm an engineer like you. I'm not very cherp with lofty psych stuff. Where's Lyndyn or Hethep when we need them?"

"Take her hand and help me reassure her," Domyn interrupted in his deep soothing voice as one hand released her right hand from his grasp. "It's awright, Swyllo. Khebol will take your hand as well."

Then a long, bony hand clutched her right hand, and Khebol murmured softly, "Swyllo, don't be afraid. Coasting LaOgres is a normal function of space travel now. Been no mishaps, no disasters since Blue Jay missions began. Been so many travels before us. Tech is well-tested now. We'll be very secure on our journey. Don't worry so you fear our operations!"

Comforted slightly by nearness and touch of her two male friends, she gasped with her mouth just above the waving water, "I know! I'm so whipped about myself now. Let myself be so scared! Doesn't make sense. I know LaOgres is just...another...part of space."

"Whoa, just right, Swyllo, another part of space," Khebol reaffirmed. "It's just an aspect inside or between curved nature of original Debordo space. We are familiar with Debordo space as original emptiness around our birth world in Zerosolis System. As you remember, LaOgres is just like an opposite of our normal space. All anti-gravity based!"

To her left, Domyn added gently, "Yes, you must recall an old basic inflating balloon concept of original Debordo space. We all learned of ancient concept of expanding universe theories while we were in academy back before and at Steppingstone Primero many years ago…"

"I remember, I remember," she insisted impatiently, and then not to seem toxx in front of her intelligent friends, she continued stubbornly, "and space was theorized to be curved as inside of a balloon. I remember! I'm not totally cefacious, you guys!"

Gripping her hand more tightly, Khebol declared with some excitement, "Yes, whoa, cefacious, Swyllo! Elasticity of balloon represented a force of gravity pulling all bodies of mass toward each other along with ancient term strong force."

"And ever expanding balloon was viewed as expanding universe," Domyn said in his deep voice. "At a time many centuries ago, humans could comprehend only an inside layer of balloon as total universe. Nothing outside, nothing inside, only plastic of a curved balloon was known to them then…"

"Vulch, were they wrong!" chortled Khebol.

Now feeling part of discussion rather than timid recipient of their lecture, Swyllo grinned and said, "Yeah, until people explored by robotic devices and then in person space outside Zerosolis System. Then they discovered laws of universe as observed and theorized by ancients were not correct. Since past ancient laws had been based upon observations and measurements within gravity well of the Zerosolis System, they did not allow for concepts such as anti-gravity and null-gravity."

"Yeah, very cefacious now, Swyllo! You're so much more cherp now, aren't you? In fact some of telemetry sent back to the Zerosolis System from departing super colony ships helped guide ancient theorists in new directions," Khebol exclaimed, and then he added, "I wonder if colonials figured out about LaOgres and Weznuski space themselves. I wonder if they discovered Kil-Kols."

In spite of the warmth of the sun on her head, she shivered when she offered, "Yeah, LaOgres, unknown space inside the balloon, I wonder if they discovered yet. I wonder if they know about a new aspect of universal space with its different and opposite laws of gravitational physics."

"Awright, I believe you are with us again, Swyllo. Yes, different laws of gravity and an opposite strong force of repulsion are both traits of LaOgres space. Yet these are traits which humans could theorize, study, and create technology to travel and explore," Domyn interjected hastily.

"Yes, the very basis of Blue Jay missions, it's what developed from a more modern understanding of the universe," Khebol declared with obvious glee.

"I'm feeling much more cherp now, Neer," Swyllo confided, smiling at her friends. "Having cherp friends makes me feel more in control. I won't let vulching anti-dimension of LaOgres zap my spirit again. Cherp, guys! Maybe we swim and frolic now?"

With twinkle in his squinting eyes, Khebol grinned and said, "You'll be in control of space, Swyllo. You'll be taming vulching monster as we coast through LaOgres. We all know you're one of best harvesters in Blue Jay history. As a harvester, you'll be the boss of LaOgres energy!"

"Yeah, guy, don't put a kind of vulching stress on me! We all know artigences handle LaOgres flight while we sleep most of the journey," she cried, trying to playfully kick his legs under the surface but failing as her kick was deflected by fluid resistance of water.

Either ignoring or not sensing her foot movement, Khebol smiled, "Still you'll control monster, Swyllo. You're too cherp harvester to let powers of light, gravity, anti-gravity, or whatever defeat your control. Why, you're one of best. You're a true Blue Jayer!"

"I just collect and harness physical forces. Pilots do flying and controlling. No, not even control, just use them, right, Domyn?" she said, glancing to the wide face on her left.

However, his sight was directed over her head, and Domyn chuckled, "Speaking of pilots, here is a rather strange pair from showers."

Wrenching her hands from the holds of two boys, Swyllo splashed and kicked her body around in water. There he was walking toward the pool. His slightly rounded cheeks puffed with exertion as he carried over his left shoulder small figure of another boy whose sporadic cursing reached pool. Her heart rhythm beat faster. Chitir was coming.

As six feet tall and lanky, but athletic boy clad in his light green JMO shorts approached the water edge of the pool, Swyllo glared at him as she gripped the handrail tighter than she needed and shouted, "About vulching time! Where have you been, you big sasquatch? I've been waiting for you."

When he came within one yard of the pool, Chitir halted and laughed at his cargo, "Stop wiggling, you little squirm. Prof Lyndyn ordered me to bring you out here and make sure you join the crowd. So, you toxx squirm, join the crowd. You stink still anyway even after the shower!"

"Nope," rasped a hoarse voice from above Chitir's head.

Swyllo stared at Chitir while he lifted a small body, also clothed by green

JMO shorts, and then heaved the squirming boy into the air over the pool and then she demanded tersely, "Now get in here, you big sasquatch. You'll be leaving in five days. I want some of your time with me."

Flailing legs and arms in what appeared uncontrolled motions, Jamyk fell with an explosive splash into water as Chitir's dimpled face smiled at her, he said, "Get me in the pool, hey? Why do you want me in the pool, lovely Swyllo? Some devious intention for my luscious body maybe?"

"Just get your oaf toxx into water," she scolded him but then more meekly murmured, "I need you, Chitir. Come chase away my fear."

"She just suffered a brief panic attack, guy. Treat her cherp," declared Khebol as he began to swim away, and then added with a mischievous grin, "After all you are big and tasty!"

Instant bewildered frown chased away his smiling dimples, and Chitir stammered, "Huh...what big and tasty? Guy, what are you jabbering about?"

"Something happened years ago at academy on Steppingstone Primero when you little pups used to den together, I believe is what he is referring about, but who remembers from back then," called Domyn swimming away towards the narrow nexus between two circles of the pool.

"Steppingstone Primero, what's about? I can't remember far back then either," sputtered Chitir in an almost whispered, mellow voice. "How can I remember pup vulch from long ago? I have trouble remembering last week. Swyllo, what's about big and tasty?"

"Don't pretend not to remember. And where the vulch have you been?" Swyllo growled, spattering him with water and rejoicing in his brief trembling at a sudden chill onto his probably heated skin.

Kneeling down and reaching for her hand on the pool edge, Chitir answered, "I've been with Jamyk in Med after he collapsed. Didn't someone tell you?"

Swyllo desired to grip his long-fingered hand, jump from water, and hug him, but instead for some obscure reason, her mouth snarled, "With Jamyk? You would rather be with him than with me? What could you have done for him Doc Kymil couldn't? I needed you!"

"But I didn't know!" Chitir squawked as his eyes widened in distress, and then he continued, "Jamyk seemed to need me, I thought at the moment. You seemed to be bonding with your teammates as you left arena. I've learned not to intrude into another team's bonding right after an emotional game, even if they are my friends."

While his hand paused just before touching her hand, Swyllo desired to lift hers up to him, but her irate emotions still overwhelmed her intention and her speech, and she snapped peevishly, "But you should have known I needed you. And you went to see little onad peener. And you stayed there for so long while I needed you. I was vulching whipped!"

Leaning back on his haunches and pulling his hand away, Chitir stated with a mild grin, "Whoa, Swyllo, it was little peener who caused me to come out here when I did. Really...it was weird! He was in a nutria-bath and was half conscious. Doc Kymil was monitoring his fluid and nutrient levels. Then suddenly he started muttering your name and woke up alertly. He began to get out of the bath. Doc tried to keep him there, but he was insistent! Rather powerful lil' boy when he gets riled!"

"Vulch damn pup, he's always just so uncherp! Never does as he's ordered," Swyllo interrupted sharply. "But why did you need to stay there? Jamyk just probably wanted to cause more mischief. You didn't have to stay with him. He's always being toxx fool!"

"Really, I did. Next Doc Kymil decided Jamyk was healthy enough to be released from Med since he was giving her trouble anyway. Prof Lyndyn told me to make sure Jamyk got through your locker room and shower without hurting himself or short-cutting sanitation protocols. Pup was very hyper about you for some reason. Worried me, Swyllo, and goaded me vulching huge!"

"But you still took time to shower with him. You still stayed with him longer. I needed you here," she accused him with her voice shaking, her vision blurring his face in her fury.

"Hey, whoa, Swyllo, ease up! I came out as..." Chitir began to say.

Interrupting him with a splash of water in his direction, she felt a heat of her emotion spite her words as she spat, "You don't care about me. Only little peener Jamyk! Not me at all! I needed you. But you were with him. Don't you care about me at all?"

For a few moments, his face frowned in obvious hurt and puzzlement, and then his eyes squinted into slits, and Chitir declared in a low serious tone, "I was in Med with a sick friend. Lot more important, I believe, than rushing to play with the whipped girl in a jealous mood."

"Whipped? Jealous? Jealous of whom? Over you?" she shrieked in a high-pitched voice and then immediately regretted her outburst and feeling of intensely rising body temp in her face and neck.

His face slackened to taut smoothness devoid of his normal dimpled smile, and he responded coldly and sadly, "What's wrong with you, Swyllo? You're being an uncherp toxx. Over-reaction to me staying with Jamyk just now! What's really the problem?"

"Hey, you do seem to like little onad peener better than me. You did stay with him today all way through showering to the pool here," she accused him tartly.

However, she silently cursed herself, wondering what was she doing? She needed his closeness, his support, his friendship, and his love. Why was she snapping at him like so? Was she jealous? Was she afraid of coming separation? Too many uncertainties, she admitted to herself, too much confusion. What was she really doing now to Chitir?

To her right, a long figure pulled itself from the water, stood rigidly in front of Chitir, and snarled, "Are you toxx vulching with my little fem here? Is vulcher fox goading you nasty, Swyllo? I can take care of very nasty right now. Like kicking foxy toxx!"

Peering upwards she saw two tall boys glaring at each other. Milyr was a good six inches taller than Chitir. Yet Chitir was just as leanly muscular and just as determined under threat. However, boys fighting for her in the moment was not what she wanted now. How had previous conversation gotten so out of control? Why was she irate with Chitir for his loyalty to pal Jamyk? Not her normal reaction!

Hesitantly she stammered, "It...it's...okay... Milyr... Just leave us alone now."

"I should kick his vulching toxx anyway," snorted Milyr, and then added with a sneer, "Never did trust foxy peener chasing after you. He's not a good cuddle for you. He's not cherp for you, fine fem."

While she observed, Chitir step back with one foot and crouch slightly at the knees in a defensive fighting stance, Swyllo pleaded sincerely, "Guys, no! Milyr, go back to your other girl vixens. Chitir, please come in the pool with me. I don't want sourness on our last days together on Quinto. Please, guys..."

From the other circle of the hour-glass-shaped pool came a shrill cry from Nyba above a noisy merriment of other swimmers, "Aiyee, vulch, I wish he wouldn't do toxx stunt again!"

When she witnessed two adversaries avert their glares toward a sudden shriek, Swyllo looked in same direction and groaned, "What now? What's happening over there?"

Nyba bellowed again, "I hate when little toxx does his silly dares! Every time I hate it. Damn vulching rascal! Domyn, please watch him carefully. We need him healthy for our mission."

Chitir asked loudly across pool, "What's he doing now?"

"Just staying on the bottom of the pool and holding his breath," Bhiros replied calmly, treading water.

Domyn growled in complaint, "Foolish imp, he does so at each Steppingstone with pool. He never tells us why he must try to break his previous time of holding breath. But he does it still again!"

Through fluctuating waves of the pool, Swyllo thought she could see a tiny form in green shorts somewhere near the nexus of the two pools. Jamyk was motionless to her sight, but he must be waving his arms to keep himself from floating to the surface again with lungs full of air. Or maybe he found some drain or other pool assembly to latch onto and hold himself down there. Whatever he did, his small form just seemed to sit quietly at the bottom of the pool, seemingly motionless to her view in angle through the water.

As other boys and girls paused in their antics to watch the thin form in green JMO shorts sitting on the bottom of the pool, Milyr chuckled sourly, "He does have a way of suddenly getting attention, little peener!"

"Yes, and not with my favor," Nyba protested sourly.

Domyn grumbled with distaste, "He is annoying at best, Cap. Do you want me to go down to get him before he gets himself into nastiness?"

"Let him try to break his prior time, Nyba," Emkhat pleaded in enthusiasm.

"He'll kill himself with his foolish challenges to his stamina," Nyba griped, walking to the edge above where Jamyk sat, "Such lil' nasty toxx he is to my nerves!"

Chitir trotted promptly away from Milyr and her toward the edge near Jamyk and exclaimed in obvious excitement, "He's trying to beat five minutes, I think. He came close to the time at Steppingstone Cuarto. My tiny friend will do it today, I know."

In spite of her usual antagonism toward Jamyk, Swyllo felt a then common bond of exuberance she shared with Chitir as she observed him bounce on his feet while staring into the pool. His enthusiasm warmed Swyllo's spirit, in spite of his attention on Jamyk now. His boyish joy for sudden excitement soothed her prior despair. One trait, which was what she loved about him. Almost irresponsible boyishness still appealed to her. If Jamyk could bring the trait out of Chitir now, then she would thank the annoying rascal boy with big hug. But probably not kiss the scamp, she snorted silently in her mind.

Khebol called out in wonderment and then more shrilly, "Vulch, how can his tiny lungs carry so much breath? And all after he played such an energized game today?"

From a central narrow point of the pool, Bhiros shouted enthusiastically as he treaded water on surface, "Vulch, I wish I had stamina and such lungs."

Rapidly gulping an inhaled breath, she heard Chitir shout, "Did almost five at Steppingstone Cuarto. Come on, Jamyk! You can make it."

"He can't vulching hear you, you toxx," laughed Milyr, standing above her still on the poolside patio. "He's just a young pup toxx trying to show off for you, you big fool. But he's our toxx, our pal who is cherper than any of cats who hate to be in water…"

"Argh, toxx boy Ylustun seems fish in pools when he finally gets here," Swyllo retorted.

"Vulcher tomcat, Lusty is more skin than fish in water. I hope Hlankam makes him wear JMOs next time. His pathetic peener is still not worth showing to fems…" Milyr chortled, laughing.

"Humph, you toxx, yours isn't grand either," Nyba scoffed from a side of the pool, and then with a frown, as if embarrassed, continued sheepishly, "Not I stare at you in showers, you ugly piece of toxx manhood!"

"Ho, ha, you do know me cherper than I thought. But your eyes might need testing soon," Milyr exclaimed and then chuckled loudly as he stalked poolside watching Jamyk but moving toward Nyba.

"Oh, vulching damn!" groaned Nyba, and Swyllo wondered if her dismay was for remark of Milyr or reckless performance of Jamyk, even as her eyes seemed to follow approach of Milyr along the poolside.

"You're Jayer, Jamyk!" yelled Khebol, and Chitir almost simultaneously from their different positions on patio, and Khebol announced then, "Just passed five minutes and still going!"

"Vulching little onad did it!" grinned Milyr, and obvious admiration in his voice surprised Swyllo, and then he continued with more pride, "He's our little peener pilot, Swyllo."

Soon, maybe thirty seconds more, a small form in green JMOs rose from a place on the bottom of the pool. Suddenly air burst from the surface, and a few seconds later, a small bald head popped into the air from the water. Close set eyes blinked away the streaming water, and a thin-lipped mouth gaped wide as Jamyk gasped for breath. Then while everyone around pooled, cheered, and sang his name, Jamyk floated face-up, exhaling and inhaling in deep rhythmic breathes. His thin legs kicked weakly below his green JMO shorts. His thin arms paddled tiredly around his body. He appeared to disregard cheering friends around the pool.

While Swyllo stroked freestyle across the pool surface toward him, she witnessed both Milyr and Chitir leap into the water. By the time she swam to the narrow nexus, they had reached Jamyk, grabbed his arms, and slowly floated him toward the side of the pool. Each tall boy had one of the arms and shoulders of Jamyk in their grasp. Spitting out breathes of watery spray and stroking with one arm, two boys cradled Jamyk between them with their other arm. Feuding of minute earlier was washed away by common silent consent.

"Almost seven minutes, I think! Holding his breath for long, impossible!" exclaimed Khebol as Swyllo approached the trio in the water by the edge of the pool.

"No, it's Jayer!" murmured Carhel, treading water between grinning figures of Emkhat and Radhin in pool. "It's truly a Blue Jayer triumph!"

"Damn lil' rascal will give me an ulcer," muttered Nyba, standing over gathering a throng of swimmers around Jamyk. "Don't do again now as long as we are here at Steppingstone Quinto. It's an order, boy!"

His eyes glanced up hastily and briefly at Nyba, and Jamyk, in a weary lethargy in the hands of two young men, rasped just barely above a croaked whisper, "Tired."

Seeing sparkle in Chitir's eyes, Swyllo felt contagion of his spirit when he exclaimed, "Really, cherp Jamyk! More than last time, you're Jayer today for sure. You are full Blue Jayer."

Stifling an automatic envious response, Swyllo smiled at the small boy and instead praised, "Yeah, you really did it. Cherping great performance, you little peener!"

His eyes twitched side to side first at Milyr and then at Chitir, and Jamyk grinned at her when he croaked, "Yup!"

"Are you okay, you little peener?" Milyr asked with a smile and released his supporting hold from Jamyk's arm and added with almost an embarrassed lowering of his voice, "I've got other people to see…vixens to cuddle…fems waiting…"

"Here you go again," interrupted Whyvvi sarcastically.

"Cherp!" Jamyk yelled in a squeaky rasp, and then shaking off the clutching hand of Chitir, he murmured, "Thanks! Go Swyllo!"

Taking opportunity Swyllo swam toward Chitir, brushed against his arm still treading water, and said solemnly, almost humbly, "I understand, Chitir. We are all friends first. I'm actually proud of you for helping Jamyk, both now and earlier. I'm also proud of him for doing so cherp today, both now and in Pulseball earlier today when we almost won!"

Deep voice of Domyn declared, "Right! Awe wills, we are all Blue Jayers here today. Whether we wear blue and white or brown and orange in the arena, we are all Jayers. Whether we travel on Fox Flash Alpha or Wolf Streak Beta, we are all Blue Jayers. We are only Blue Jayers now on Quinto and will soon be going to Sexto System. Let's relish our friends and enjoy our recreation today."

"Don't forget, Docs and Profs," reminded Whyvvi.

Khebol moved closer to a young woman in pink JMO suit and declared, "Don't forget our Blue Jay mates on Lynx Blaze. Because they're always last to arrive isn't reason to ignore them!"

"Of course not, but our older crewmates, Docs and Profs, don't seem to get to pooling very often. Did you ever notice that?" Bhiros inquired with a chuckle.

"Yeah, of course, Cap," Radhin chortled. "I mean Docs and Profs don't join us in pooling. Our other Jayers from Lynx Blaze are still travelling from Steppingstone Cuatro. Who knows what crew of weird kittens does together? Cap Hlankam isn't a most sensible leader!"

"Probably reccing with each other! Cats are weirder than us. Maybe why they are backups to Blue Jay mission," Milyr smirked, and then as if he rethought his remark, hastily added, "They have no sexual hormones in their kitten bodies. At least they act so little, we see them at each Steppingstone. However, Docs and Profs were our age once on their previous missions built and populated Steppingstone Quinto. Now they are space elders. I wonder if antemgebemarzex still works on them…"

"Awright, enough! You're almost being too insulting of our fellow Blue Jayers!" warned Domyn with deep growl, and then he continued in much more mellow voice, "Before you say something inappropriate, Milyr, be silent. Our comrades in Lynx Blaze are Blue Jayers, too! And our Doc Kymil and Prof Lyndyn, and Doc Thebon and Prof Hethep of Fox Flash, they are all Blue Jayers also. They were Blue Jayers before we were born. Without their guidance, we would be just an ordinary spacer…"

Snuggling against Chitir, Swyllo tuned out Domyn's voice and whispered, "Let's sneak away, Chitir, my guy. Jamyk seems healthy now. I need to talk while we can. You'll be departing for Sexto System soon. We'll be so many, many light years apart then."

"My young lass, not really many, many light years…" Chitir started to reply.

However, abruptly Jamyk shoved against Chitir and demanded in whispered voice, "Go!"

As small form pushed off the wall to float out to the center of the pool, Nyba requested firmly, "Keep an eye on him please, Neer Domyn."

Surprised Jamyk had heard and acted upon her urging of Chitir, Swyllo peered into the wide eyes of her dimpled rogue and suggested, "Let's get a bit of space for ourselves. I need to talk with you. Yeah, journey is not really nasty long, but it still seems too long to be away from you."

His eyes sparkled with some water dripping from his eyelids, and his mouth widened to form his dimples in his cheeks, and then Chitir said in a hushed voice for her only, "You are right. Even numerous awakenings can seem too long without your smiling and pleasant presence."

"Are you teasing me now? Don't be toxx now!" she scolded.

"How can your big and tasty ever be toxx?" Chitir grinned.

Then with smirk of her own, Swyllo asked, "Shall we dive to the bottom and retrace part of Jamyk's feat? You can do for me, can't you, my bold oaf of a man?"

With a sudden dismay spoiling mirth on his face, Chitir sputtered, "Uh… argh… I don't really like underwater. Swimming up here is about my limit in water. And I'm not cherp with so, even now!"

"I believe you can do anything, you big oaf! You jumped in when you wished to help Jamyk," Swyllo reminded him while stroking his shoulder and upper arm. "Just follow me."

Without waiting for him to argue, Swyllo inhaled a deep breath and ducked under the pool surface. Pushing off the pool wall with her short strong legs, she headed toward bottom. In moments she reached seventeen feet in depth and spun to peer upwards.

Surprisingly and joyously to her present perspective, lanky, long form was descending behind her. His gangly and awkward attempt to coordinate his frog kicks with his breaststrokes almost made her laugh. However, she was thrilled he had followed her. Was not his typical activity under water!

When he arrived before her, Swyllo reached out, hugged her short arms around him, and pushed off from the pool bottom. With her head against his chest, she could hear his beating heart. As they rose towards the surface, she thought, what a nice sound, so strong, so vibrant, and so comforting.

After her head popped from the warm water into the air, Swyllo exhaled and inhaled hastily. Before he could finish, a grin spreading over his water dripping face, she kissed him.

As their lips parted, she watched his face of confusion gradually widen into dimpled smile so intrigued her, and Chitir asked, "What is your kissing now about?"

"I love you," Swyllo whispered, almost afraid of her own words. "I'm sorry I can be so nasty at times. But I do love you, you big toxx oaf! Even in hold of our anti-sex feeling drug, I love you!"

Then, before he could reply, she reached a hand to the back of his bald head and pulled him toward her. Swyllo kissed him again. As their torsos made contact, she thought she felt an increase in their heartbeats and warming of their bodies, even against slight cooling from the pool waters. Her fingers flushed warm at contact on back of his bald head. Tiny depressions and bumps of his skull seemed to mesh perfectly with spread of her fingers. Chitir was so perfect for her, she mused.

"Can we feel love now? Is it possible?" he asked softly after the kiss had ended, and then with a gasp of breath, he continued looking into her face, "At our young age and with inhibition of antemgebemarzex, can we feel any real physical love yet? But... I... I did just feel something now. I did feel clutched when we kissed. It was cherp! Didn't know could feel so!"

Kneading the back of his head with her fingers of one hand and gripping a gently warm and wet shoulder with other, she chuckled, "Of course it's possible, you oaf! Not all love is hormonal. At least it is what Prof Lyndyn often repeats in his ramblings. I can love your personality and your spirit. And besides biochemical inhibition of our hormones isn't perfectly effective."

"Whoa, so right! Milyr is always boasting about his adventures with fems of Steppingstones. I did feel a strong tingle when you kissed me. Maybe being almost nineteen and learning about sex during group discussions on long journeys in LaOgres allows us to feel partial hormone sensations," Chitir grinned with renewed hope on his boyish face and in his mellow voice.

"Don't be so analytical! Why don't we experiment about your theory over a few days before you go?" she suggested with an impish grin just above splashing water as her hand stroked his bald, warm head gently with steady rhythmic contact to the nape of the neck and back up his scalp.

"Huh...er...how do we do that?" he asked, gulping as a wave of water splashed up onto his grinning face, and soon his smile ceased briefly in a mild frown at a slight entry of water.

"You big toxx, I think you can create some investigative propositions to allow us to test whether we are still inhibited by antemgebemarzex. I have cherp confidence in potency of your brain," Swyllo said with leer and then another kiss on his wet dimpled face.

When she released his mouth from her aggressive advance, Chitir smiled again and whispered in a low husky voice, "Kiss was somewhat stimulating again, Swyllo. I did really feel my body heat up. Maybe you are right about our hormones not paying attention to alleged effects of antemgebemarzex. I suppose we could do some testing of our new theory."

"Oh, you big toxx, just let's not waste any of our precious time with planning," Swyllo teased as her hand on his head stroked down his warming neck. "Let's just begin testing."

"Er, does feel right to me now," Chitir agreed, and his hands were caressing her shoulders now. "We do need to get to know each other so much better before our long separation."

"Yeah, we do," Swyllo replied with smile, but then with a half-hearted warning, declared, "But just one notion now, my Chitir, before we begin, if we stimulate any response now, then you'll behave yourself in Sexto System just in case you should come across any bodacious ladies amongst colonials. Bargain me so, my cherp Chitir! I'll trust you to keep your promise!"

"You are my only bodacious lass," he sighed, staring wide-eyed into her squinting eyes.

Swyllo leered, "And you are my only big and tasty guy."

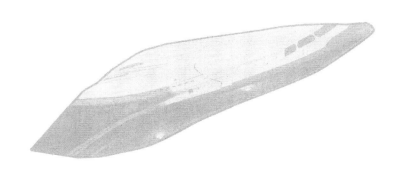

SPEC ONE: DOMYN THROUGH LAOGRES
CHAPTER 1

Awe and comfort embrace.

His head rests upon warm, moist sand of the shore. Slightly cooler but very comfortable water line rises and falls subtly along his neck. His shoulders, torso, arms, and legs float on the surface of a nearly calm pond. Like numerous fingers, knuckles, and palms, gentle movements of water caress his skin, knead his muscles, and stroke his flesh.

Awe and serenity encompass.

From across the pond, soft, pleasant patter of a small waterfall comingles with music of tiny waves just beneath his ears. Multitude of chirping insects, peeping frogs, hooting owls, and yipping coyotes fill the night with song. Flutter of leaves and creaking of branches whispers in the breeze through trees around the pond.

Awe and tranquility entwine.

From branches silhouetted against the moonlighted night sky above, fragrance of sweet blossoms delights his nostrils. Strong scent of wild mint competes with a natural bouquet of flowers. With his breath sweetness seeps into his mouth, across his tongue, and down his throat, a taste of honey, hint of wine, tease of mother's milk. Through air aroma of pleasant pine needles, spruce trees, and evergreen boughs tickles his nose.

Awe and enchantment enthrall.

Far above in the night sky, countless stars shimmer through soft mists hovering over the pond and waterfall. His blinking eyes follow the sway of branches above and also coasting form an owl passing silently over the shoreline. Not far to the

1

side, he observes a leaping form of nervous frog jump into water.

Awe and awareness engage.

"Awaken, Neer Domyn."

Warm water flows away from the shore and begins to recede from his prone figure. Massaging hands drift away with the water. Sounds of night fade into darkness. Scents of forest evaporate into starless sky. Consciousness beckons!

Awe and comfort dissipate.

"Awaken, Neer Domyn."

An awareness of awakening stirred his consciousness. Frantically his mind tried to retain tranquility of dream. When he rolled to his side, sensation of warm, soft sand and soothing water was replaced by annoying chill and confining scratch of cloth against his body. Pleasant fragrances of nature were replaced by musky, stale stench. Joyous raptures of sleep eluded his tenacious attempt to avoid awakening.

"Awaken, Neer Domyn," a female voice repeated.

When his bladder pained him for release, however, he knew for certain he was awake. His Saphyndenlairoum was soon to disconnect. His nineteen days of ultra-slow metabolic sleep within protection of Saphyndenlairoum had come to a sudden end. His bodily functions would be his responsibility once again. Saphyndenlairoum would pamper his body no longer. He released his bladder into the Saphyndenlairoum diaper.

"Neer Domyn," repeated a female voice nearly inside his ears. "Accepting your urine sample."

Stubbornly still trying to recapture sleep and comforting dream, he squirmed onto his back and then over to his other side, but the sleeping garment entangled his legs and arms. Saphyndenlairoum garment was no longer as supportive as second skin but now irritation to his body movement. Saphyndenlairoum bed was no longer soft and cozy warm. He should stop pretending sleep, Domyn thought to himself. He was not so lazy as his male companions... usually!

"Neer Domyn," said a female voice of Bodacia from the garment around his head and ears. "You are awake. Your vital signs confirm reality. You must prepare for disconnect."

With sleep-atrophied tongue and micro-tubules still in his mouth, Domyn mumbled, "Aw...dam...bo...as...a...be...zee."

"Neer Domyn, your command is gibberish," announced artigence Bodacia in a matter-of-fact manner. "Disconnect is beginning."

"Aw…damn…bo…asha…," he garbled as the garment, against his will, twisted and stretched his form onto his back, arms to his sides, legs straight in line from his hips and torso on top of the bed.

Then tingling, sometimes prickling sensations spread over his flesh as hundreds of micro-electrodes and micro-tubules were retracted from his body back into the Saphyndenlairoum garment. From his legs, arms, and torso, electrodes responsible for periodic muscle stimulation during his long sleep now oozed away from his flesh. From his groin and buttocks, a suction diaper now pulled away from his flesh with irritating abrasiveness. From his stomach micro-tubules for nutrient feeding now slid from his flesh with pinching and pulling annoyance. Slowly, meticulously, after nineteen days of sustaining his body, former protrusions into his flesh retracted back into Saphyndenlairoum garment. His lazy days were over for certain now, Domyn grumbled in low mumble to himself.

After micro-tubules in his mouth and nose had exited, he swore hoarsely, still addled-tongued, "Damn…Bo…da…sha…go…eee…zee."

"Do not be childish, Neer Domyn," a female voice chided from the garment fabric near his ears. "You are almost a man adult, Neer Domyn. You have experienced awakening for five years. Accept so!"

"An… Bo…da…sha…you…still…got…no…tuh," he stammered, trying to chuckle and grin with his still uncoordinated facial muscles inside the Saphyndenlairoum garment.

Ignoring his comment, Bodacia said into his ears, "Prepare for uncovering."

"Yea…mum…ope…roo…wam…tis…ime," Domyn mumbled

"Begin uncovering," Bodacia said with terse warning.

Then the garment split open on top of his face and began falling around his temples and ears. A sudden rush of cooler air bathed his abruptly exposed face. Along the upper side of the shoulders, arms, torso, and legs, he felt the Saphyndenlairoum garment split open. As fabric slid down his skin along the length of his body, air-conditioned atmosphere of room chilled a thin layer of sweat and analgesic gel over his naked body. All around him, he felt garment morphing into the bed support of Saphyndenlairoum. Sudden chill sent goosebumps over his naked skin but feeling helped to awaken him more fully. Domyn smiled. At least he was alive again after a long sleep.

Then suddenly a different, gentler woman's voice asked from not far away, "How do you feel, Domyn? Do you know where you are?"

As his face attempted to form a smile around his mouth, Domyn recognized a low, melodious voice of Doc Kymil. She was the first person he encountered upon each awakening from slow metabolic sleep while they travelled LaOgres space. Though only in her upper forties and not of his bio-blood, she was often appreciated by him and many of others in the crew of Wolf Streak Beta as matriarch of crew.

Knowing his brain was functioning well enough to remember the name of the spacecraft and their current situation in LaOgres space, he was pleased with himself and rasped with dry throat and numb tongue, "Fee...ing...azy... Doc... Not like...when young. Am in Med...on Wolf...in La...gres..."

"Not too bad, but was that 'hazy' that you said or 'crazy?' I can never quite tell from you elderly teenagers," Doc Kymil's voice sang with obvious mirth and slight laughter.

"Nah, Doc...el...azy... Awe help...my tung. Least...know...where...am. We are on... Wolf...reek," he struggled with his words and then added bit whimsically, "Awe...back...to...sleep?"

Even-toned voice of Bodacia said with very slight hint of tartness, "No, sleep, Neer Domyn. This artigence is finished as your nursemaid for at least the next twenty-three hours. You are awake. You should behave as such."

From a few feet to the side of Saphyndenlairoum, Doc Kymil chuckled and then said, "Your age may be making you feel lazy and sluggish, Domyn. Your mind seems relatively attuned. I believe your body is rebelling. When males reach around your age of nineteen years, their bodies are almost fully grown, but heart is slower to develop and mature in muscle. It must work more strenuously now to feed blood to your recently grown body. You have grown in the past nineteen days while you slept."

"Awe...damn, Bodacia, how much...weight...taller?" Domyn queried artigence while beginning to control his vocalizations.

"Neer Domyn, you have added 6.79 pounds. You have grown taller by .53 inches since your past awakening," Bodacia responded.

"Don't tell me that I'm getting fat, Bodacia," he griped to bio-med artigence, even though his brain told him that response was merely measured statistics and had been requested by him.

However, Bodacia could not read his thoughts, and said matter-of-factly, "No, Neer Domyn, you have not added percentage of fat to indicate you are fatter. Your primary addition is of 41 percent muscle, 11 percent..."

4

"Bodacia," Doc Kymil interrupted abruptly, "please begin prep of Jamyk for awakening."

"Yes, Doc Kymil," Bodacia acknowledged and then was silent.

"Bodacia does take every comment almost literally, doesn't she?" Domyn remarked, happy to be able to vocalize entire sentences now instead of previous mumbling, and then asked, "Okay if I start working my arms and legs now?"

"Good idea! Just start with usual simple arm curls and reaches. I'll need you to keep your head still while I take off your eye parches. Remember, don't open your eyes suddenly. Even though Med lights are at low setting, you have a history of being light sensitive after awakening," she reminded him as her voice moved closer and her faint scent, comforting, entered his nostrils with his next breath.

"Vulch, nasty awakening! Awe, maybe someday I'll acclimate better in Saphyndenlairoum. Maybe Bodacia can help me. She is so motherly to me while I'm swaddled in Saphyndenlairoum. Maybe, Bodacia, you can make my eyes less sensitive to light and more sensitive to your beauty," he exclaimed into the air-conditioned atmosphere and waved his flexing arms to emphasize his remark.

"No, Neer Domyn, such is impossible. I am not programmed to perform surgical operations. Neer Domyn, I do not have an attribute that can correlate with your term 'beauty.' I am sure you know so already. Are you using your human form of comedy now?"

"Sorry, Bodacia, just state of confusion on my part! Please ignore my idiocy," Domyn tried to say without laughing.

"Neer Domyn, are you suffering brain ailment? No such reading now occurs on scans of my sensors regarding your internal health," Bodacia said, and Domyn thought he heard the hint of bewilderment in the voice of artigence.

As her hands dabbed and dried sweat and gel from his face, Doc Kymil commanded, "Bodacia, Domyn is fine medically. Please focus your sensors upon Jamyk. I'll handle the comic patient."

While slowly curling his hands to his shoulders by bending at elbows in repetitive motions and feeling sleep fatigue gradually leave his arms, Domyn whispered, "Bodacia really does take every comment as if it were absolute seriousness, doesn't she? Even jokes and teases, she doesn't understand those forms of human speech. She is serious about everything, isn't she?"

"Yes, Bodacia being artigence does react to each word that we say as if it were simple data. Domyn, you must remember, as human and feminine as her voice may sound, Bodacia is artificial intelligence exclusively aligned and programmed to interface with Wolf Streak Beta and crew, especially Prof Lyndyn and me as medical personnel," Doc Kymil reminded him as she gently worked at the eye covering over his left eye.

Continuing his arm exercise, Domyn chuckled and whispered, "Awright then, even though I've caught her in few instances of almost snide human remarks, I'll constantly remind myself that she is artigence with little human perspective."

Almost imperceptibly from theh air around him, he heard a hushed voice retort, "Not human, yes, but at least I cannot get fat like some boyish man who thinks so high of himself."

Domyn caught his breath with a slight gasp, and noticed hands peeling a patch from his eye, pause abruptly as Doc Kymil asked with obvious surprise in her voice, "Bodacia, did you just try to say joke?"

For several heartbeats and held breaths, room was quiet, but then an even-toned female voice said, "Sorry, Doc Kymil, just state of confusion on my part. No doubt, comments, of present company have affected my perceptions. Please pardon any idiocy on my part. I should attend to Jamyk now."

"Oh my, don't worry, Bodacia. Yes, please focus on prepping Jamyk for awakening," Doc Kymil instructed and then asked, "Domyn, do you know where you are now? Does light from the room bother your eyes now in awakening?"

While room light filtering through his closed eyelids created orange-red glare before his eyes, Domyn, knowing from past experience, Doc Kymil's question was an attempt to check alertness then of his awareness, answered, "We are in Med on Wolf Streak Beta, just as we have been at each awakening since leaving Steppingstone Station Primero some five years ago."

"What is Wolf Streak Beta? Where is it now?" she asked now, patting gently but thoroughly onto his forehead and face with moisture absorbing mitten.

"Awright, Doc, easy one! Wolf Streak is the finest spacecraft on Blue Jay mission," Domyn replied with pride while staring still at the reddish glow through his closed eyelids. "We are travelling in LaOgres space on our way to Sexto System and our fated meeting with long missing colonials. Now is my second awakening since plunging into LaOgres since leaving Quinto. Hope am aware of self!"

"Oh well, Domyn, you do seem to be optimistic about our success and aware of situation. Then, Bodacia, I do certify Neer Domyn has awakened from Saphyndenlairoum sleep mentally and physically able to perform his duties, as always," Doc Kymil stated more loudly, so artigence Bodacia could record certification into official log archives for day cycle.

"Awspir!" he sang enthusiastically and then more morosely complained, "But if I could only get my lazy toxx off the bed. I want to check Flandecams soon during present awakening."

"Now, Neer, don't rush procedure. We'll have you ready soon. Besides Vivacio is always monitoring Wolf Streak Beta's systems. He'll alert you if there is anything close to a problem," Doc Kymil promised in her smooth voice as it moved around his prone position on the bed of Saphyndenlairoum and then continued, "I'll rub off gel now, Domyn. You continue with arm exercise. I'll start with your legs just as I have so many awakenings before."

"Awright, my most favorite part of awakening process!" Domyn laughed heartily.

Though his eyelids were closed still, when he felt stroking on his right foot, his memory saw large puffy mittens on her hands begin their work. Out of prior experience, he lifted his right leg slightly off bed to allow her easier access. Especially designed to absorb mixture of sweat and analgesic gel used to coat his body for contact within Saphyndenlairoum garment, mittens cleaned his skin with each swipe. Doc Kymil's meticulously thorough yet tender, striking touches over his damp skin had been one of joys of awakening during usually year-long voyages through LaOgres space between Steppingstones. How many times had she cared for him thus far, he wondered. He had lost count!

As her hands in mittens caressed along his calf, around his knee, and over his thigh, she commented, "With each awakening, you have more skin surface to clean. Domyn, your thighs are remarkably thick now. Bodacia was correct before. You are now an adult man, physically grown man. We'll expect more of you from now on, Neer Domyn."

"I've thought always I behaved as a man since Steppingstone Station Tercero. Didn't I, Doc? Although I was only about seventeen then, I could do a job as well as any Blue Jayer. Did my duty well, didn't I, Doc?" he pleaded with a slight hint of doubt in his voice, which caused him to feel foolish and unmanly for his tentative avowal of his own progress in maturity.

Combination of snort and giggle in her voice told him she had detected voice tremor as well, and while her mittens began a slow, tickling stroke over his left foot, Doc Kymil said with mirth in her tone, "Oh my, yes, Domyn, you have performed your engineering and other professional duties quite proficiently since beginning our Blue Jay mission well before Steppingstone Tercero. As all Blue Jayers, you have been ahead of normal educational and technological pace of average young people. We have no complaints, Prof and I, or our Cap Nyba, as she has alluded to me."

"But…" he qualified her statement for her, and after a brief pause while he blinked his eyelids hesitantly against light of Med, he continued, "Our bodies do not mature as fast as normal adolescent, correct? Or so Prof Lyndyn and you have so often reminded us."

As her mittens swathed across and around his left thigh to his hip, she agreed, "Oh, yes, because of antemgebemarzex inhibition, your sexual maturity has been postponed and thus delayed some developmental aspects of physical growth and also consequently social growth. Nothing to be alarmed about, Domyn. You'll mature rather quickly henceforth now!"

"Not if you listen to Milyr!" he protested, however, to himself, he wondered if perhaps he should have had some reaction when Doc Kymil swathed his genitalia, but not wishing to mention so to her just then, he continued, "But sometimes I believe he's just yelping through his toxx. All that bragging and claims about fems in every Steppingstone! Don't really believe his tales!"

Apparently she read his dismay and doubt in his voice for Doc Kymil replied with genuine concern, "Oh my, don't worry, Domyn. You and all Blue Jayers are special people with a special destiny. You do not need to base your maturity comparisons on pattern of average human adolescent development. Don't let Milyr's fantasies and desires, as artificial as they are, cause you to doubt or belittle your own development. Trust me, Domyn! I have medical expertise to tell you are truly a physically mature man. I'll say so as your doctor, as well as friend."

After a sequence of eyelid blinking as he forced his eyelids to open, Domyn looked through watery haze to see finally her face with its small nose, close set eyes, and pert mouth fully intent and focused on her nursing function. White shirt, adorning upper part of her torso, flexed at narrow shoulders when she leaned into the stroking of his abdomen. Silvery-colored mittens appeared moisture-laden on ends of her short thin arms. Yet with each stroke, his skin became dryer and felt less oily. Skin-tight white headpiece covered her entire head. Except for lack of usual visor over her face, Doc Kymil now wore her standard dionboda uniform for working inside the Med of scoutcraft Wolf Streak Beta.

Observing her exposed face as she slid mittens over his right shoulder, along his arm, and down to his hand, Domyn witnessed her eyes scan over his body length, and prior experience of many awakenings prompted him to ask, "How's my PEQA, Doc? Has it changed any now I'm manly?"

8

After releasing his right hand and then while walking around Saphyndenlairoum to his left side, a smile creased cheeks around her pert mouth, and she replied, "No, looks same as always to me. After all I can see but a general glow of person's PEQA, not quantal level precision of PEQA scanner."

"Awright, well, I was hoping maybe there would be difference in my PEQA you could see to substantiate physical changes in my body to more maturity," he sighed in disappointment and then with sudden confidence continued, "However, my PEQA does change, Doc, right? It's why we have to recalibrate on Dionjossad for our dionjocus at each awakening. Right, Doc, isn't it?"

After letting go of his left hand, she instructed with professional firmness, "Turn over now, Domyn. I need to do your backside. You know procedure."

With considerable soreness and weakness, he forced his large body to roll onto his stomach without falling off Saphyndenlairoum. Task was much more effort than his normally fit body required, he mused with worry, just to turn over. Lazy nineteen, he muttered to himself! At least Physio Electromag Quantal Aura of his body had not changed to her sight and was reliably fit. Some cherp info, he thought! After all PEQA of a person was so very specific, such aura of electromagnetic energies on quantum level was basis of all interfaces with artificial intelligences, which controlled spacecraft in conjunction with human personnel. Domyn was very pleased to know his Physio Electromag Quantal Aura was just where it should be in Doc Kymil's special vision.

"You are correct about changes though, Domyn. Dionjossad scanner can measure minute differences in an individual's PEQA as body grows and cells and molecules change. But my rare ability can just barely discern a PEQA of a person. With experience I have learned to observe whether PEQA is healthy or unhealthy but not any greater detail. In fact everyone's PEQA seems to look identical to my limited vision. Yet I know with scientific sureness each person's PEQA is as unique, or perhaps more unique than fingerprint and retinal pattern. Just limitation in my sight prevents me from seeing individual uniqueness," Doc Kymil stated swiping her mittens over his buttocks.

"At least you can see PEQA. Almost nobody else can see them. You're very special, Doc," he told her with sincerity, and then with a moan of pleasure, added, "Awright, and you give great backrubs also. You're a woman of many talents, Doc."

Her melodious laugh struck his ears at the same time as a mitten slapped abruptly onto his toxx, and she quipped. "Only less than one tenth of one percent of people can see PEQA with their own eyesight. And I have to look at your big toxx for my reward? Not much reward for being so special. Now speaking of special sight, I've also spotted one consistently rebellious growth of hair just above your ugly toxx, Domyn. Lay still while I remove it. It's more pronounced now, probably sign of inevitable maturing manliness has tried to take hold of your body."

"Awright, Doc, but please don't rub it out again! It's my only sign of being manly," he groaned and then thought with chagrin of how much like Milyr he had just sounded.

"Oh my, Domyn, you know we can't have any external hair anywhere on our bodies. Such hair would interfere with PEQA field interface with artigences of Wolf Streak Beta, especially Dionjossad interface," she stated seriously, and then as afterthought, added, "Also external hair might be a health hazard here on the spacecraft where we Jayers need to be careful over long journeys."

"I know!" he pouted at rebuke to his scientific knowledge. "But I still have emotional need to be manly. I guess it's another symptom of being nineteen. Seems like all Blue Jay males about the same age who I know suffer from such condition."

Sudden chill of medication hit his skin between the base of his spine and his left buttock, and Doc Kymil said with a trace of exasperation in her voice, "Oh my, not only nineteen-year-olds! I know one aging man of forty-seven years who seems to suffer the same problem on occasion. There, Domyn, you are a handsome young man of hairless perfection once again. No difference to your perfect PEQA either! Just like your mature body, you have perfectly glowing PEQA."

"Awright, enough, Doc, don't tease me so," he laughed while a chill on his backside warmed, and then he sighed half-heartedly, "Awe help me keep my manliness. I need to face Milyr and Lyndyn as manly peers. Especially Milyr, who is boastful always of his manliness!"

After snort of derision, she chuckled, "Oh my, don't worry about them, Domyn. You are a man in such group of peers. Throw in Bhiros, Khebol, Chitir, and Thebon as well! Ask Nyba or Whyvvi! They will agree about which male seems most adult or manly of current Blue Jayers. Don't worry at all, Domyn. Trust me to say you are manliest of our pack of wolves and foxes and throw in lynxes also."

"Doctor Kymil," announced Bodacia, "Jamyk will be ready for your attention in eleven minutes."

After a few seconds of silence following sudden interruption of Bodacia's broadcast, Domyn squirmed from off his stomach, sat upright on the

Saphyndenlairoum bed, and admitted sheepishly, "Awe, damn, Doc, I've taken too long to awaken. Not very manly of me, do you think?"

"Don't ponder it, Domyn. As I've said, much of your sluggishness is your age and sudden growth. Not something you can control while you are sleeping for nineteen days. You are much quicker to awaken than Milyr. And not as annoying as elder wolf Lyndyn, as much as I care about him," she stated, stepping in front of him and placing her small hands on his wrists.

"It's time to walk around, right, Doc?" he asked rhetorically, realizing intent of her maneuver. "Awe praise Saphyndenlairoum for its thorough care of my body. And of course, thank you, Bodacia, for monitoring such care."

"Neer Domyn, I acknowledge your gratitude. Now prepare your fat, manly body for ejection," Bodacia said in a less than even-toned voice with hint of mirth hidden within.

Then instantly Saphyndenlairoum began tilting from its normal horizontal position to vertical position. With irritating resistance, his buttocks gripped the bed surface briefly and then slid down incline of repositioned Saphyndenlairoum. As his feet hit the floor, Doc Kymil stabilized his slide with her hands. Silently Domyn thanked fates Bodacia, in her present oddly humorous mood, had not inclined the bed in opposite direction for his form to slide onto head instead.

Hastily he laughed at himself for fantasizing such action by artigence, yet still exclaimed, just in case, "Thank you, Bodacia. I will try to be easier next awakening."

Bodacia said, "Acknowledged, Neer Domyn. You are not as difficult a patient to monitor as young one Jamyk. You are annoying sometimes but not...difficult."

Surprised Domyn stared at Doc Kymil, who also appeared stunned by apparent hesitation and near stammer in voice of artigence, and then he said, "Bodacia, you are sounding more like us each awakening. Please don't change. I like you as you are. You're very comfortable to rely upon."

"Acknowledged, Neer Domyn," artigence responded tersely, and then after pause, said, "I must attend to boy...difficult... Jamyk...in present awakening!"

While Doc Kymil held his wrists to steady his standing position and stared with amazement at him, Med remained quiet for several seconds, and then Doc Kymil whispered, "Not like Bodacia to comment about one patient to another, nor to even suggest humorous reaction nor to appear confused. Some variance is with her and Jamyk today!"

"Perhaps with us as examples for almost five years, she has begun to evolve in whatever way artigence does," Domyn whispered in turn. "She'll be interesting to study on LaOgres trip. We have several more awakenings yet to go."

"I'll be certain to monitor Bodacia carefully. We all depend on her intelligent and impartial supervision of Saphyndenlairoum functions. It's critical! Development of possible humor and confusion is sign of some emotional response. Not in her programming! I'll talk to Prof Lyndyn about it. As you say, there may be some natural evolving occurring within her artificial intelligence. But for now, let's get you walking about and putting your big leg muscles into action," Kymil commanded, backing away and leading him forward with her support.

Domyn suggested then as he stepped slowly forward, "We can instruct Vivacio to check her operational condition. May tell us something useful!"

"Wise precaution," Doc Kymil agreed, walking backwards slowly and carefully still.

"Do you know of previous artigence, which has evolved emotions, Doc? Even during all sci-tech instruction we received in our training at Steppingstone Primero, I don't recall learning of such odd occurrence," Domyn admitted while stepping stiff-legged for a few strides and grateful for her assistance with his current awkward and much too clumsy balance for his opinion.

"Any feeling of cramps or unusual pain?" Doc Kymil asked as she watched his legs and hips perform a walking maneuver. "I have no memory myself of emotional evolution of any artigence. You might ask Nyba. Her hobby interest of past history may have some information. Or of course Prof Lyndyn may know of some socio-psych studies in artificial intelligence field. Let's get you off to your cardio-exercise. Cap Nyba has a busy schedule planned as always."

"Maybe I'll check with Nyba. She doesn't ramble as much as Prof Lyndyn," he suggested, and then feeling coordination and strength of his legs improving rapidly, added, "I feel ready to go now, Doc. Awe praise creator of Saphyndenlairoum and Bodacia for keeping me fit while letting me sleep for nineteen days. Nineteen-year-old male's dream existence."

"Then you're on your own," she announced, letting go of his wrists. "You know routine. Walk around Med a few times and prove to me you are capable of more intense cardio exercise. You have been quick to recover at all prior awakenings. Bodacia would have given warning if your vital stats were inappropriate. Get your big toxx moving, Neer!"

Swinging his arms vigorously enough to gently twist his torso side to side, Domyn strode from her support and increased his pace. He watched her shorter figure in white medical garb turn from him to approach green Saphyndenlairoum slowly rising from the floor.

On the bed thrashed a figure clad within a green garment connected to the bed. Jamyk! He realized it was Jamyk within the green Saphyndenlairoum garment. Short, slim form was unbelievably twisted and entangled. Only Jamyk could force the Saphyndenlairoum garment, which was part of and connected to the bed, into such a knotted shape. Boy was as much rascal imp in sleep stasis as when awake perhaps!

"Awe, incredible, he looks like a pretzel every awakening," Domyn exclaimed amazed. "How can Saphyndenlairoum contort so? Bodacia, is Jamyk healthy inside the blanket covering thing?"

"Neer Domyn, Jamyk is physically correct based on his normal vital stats. But he is…difficult…in present awakening," Bodacia answered in less than her usual even tone of conviction.

Observing Doc Kymil hesitate in her approach towards green Saphyndenlairoum, Domyn asked abruptly, "Doc, is there something wrong? Bodacia seems uncertain!"

Her face showed puzzlement, then wonder, and she whispered with doubt in her voice, "I'm not sure, Domyn. Was it his PEQA that I just glimpsed? No, it couldn't be! I don't see PEQAs while sleepers are inside the Saphyndenlairoum garment, too much interference. But I thought I could now just briefly. Bodacia, what stage of sleep is he in now?"

"Doctor Kymil, Jamyk is just beyond REM sleep but not yet at post REM," Bodacia responded and then added, "Data is beyond my programming parameters to be any more precise. Jamyk is…difficult…awakening now."

"What is beyond REM?" Domyn queried, striding around the green Saphyndenlairoum with greater nervous energy. "I never heard of such before."

"We don't have a delineation term of stage between REM and post REM," Kymil stated with both excitement and worry intermixing in her tone, and then she flipped visor from atop her white cap down in front of her right eye and asked, "I'll check her data reads in my visor… Bodacia, is current data common with Jamyk? Have you recorded condition before present awakening? I don't recall getting any notes about such data. But you wouldn't delete a data report, I'm sure!"

While small figure inside the Saphyndenlairoum writhed into uncomfortable appearing positions, Domyn wondered to himself if he looked like so in his sleep, and then heard Bodacia answer, "Behavior is beyond my parameters, Doc Kymil. If I had witnessed such behavior prior, I am not programmed to define or analyze such behavior. I have recorded patient Jamyk is…difficult…when in sleep stasis."

"How often has Jamyk been difficult, Bodacia?" Domyn asked curious and worried.

"Neer Domyn, Jamyk is difficult many times in the Saphyndenlairoum sleep," Bodacia reported.

"Bodacia, does difficult status threaten his vital signs or overall health?" Doc Kymil asked, now standing beside the green Saphyndenlairoum with her hands raised as if to reach out and assist the boy, yet not sure how. "I don't see any such problem on my visor scan. His vital signs seem within his norm."

"Neer Domyn, my records indicate seventeen such states have occurred present sleep cycle," Bodacia responded and then hastily added, "Doctor Kymil, according to life vitals for Jamyk, no emergency was detected during present sleep cycle. Patient Jamyk has been…difficult…in sleep cycle."

Suddenly Kymil gasped loudly, and then in a more hushed voice, muttered, "Oh my…no…could…not be! No, not Szczygiel Shine, no, impossible!"

"Difficult? Awright, he looks vulching uncomfortable in there. Bodacia, are you sure his vitals are okay? Looks really nasty to me," Domyn groaned, and then his awareness tried to comprehend what Kymil had just whispered, and he asked, "What was it you just said, Doc? What was about some kind of shine? Did you say 'seagull shine?' I've never heard about anything like so!"

"Neer Domyn, life vitals for Jamyk are within parameters for him. But… difficult…status has postponed his awakening for at least twenty-three minutes," Bodacia informed him; and then abruptly as Jamyk lay still suddenly, Bodacia said abruptly, "Jamyk is now in post REM sleep."

Doc Kymil asked firmly as if her surprise of moments before had vanished, "And his vital stats, are they within his normal parameters still, Bodacia?"

"Doctor Kymil, vital stats for Jamyk are within parameters for him in post REM sleep," Bodacia replied in her even-toned voice.

"Is Jamyk difficult now, Bodacia?" Domyn asked. "Was it shine Doc mentioned?"

"Neer Domyn, such designation is not in my programming for human patient," Bodacia replied and then added, "Doc Kymil, Jamyk will now awaken in less than seventeen minutes."

Observing a bewildered and strained expression of Doc Kymil, Domyn whispered as he walked toward her from around the Saphyndenlairoum bed, "Do you know what just happened? Is he okay? What did you say about some kind of shine?"

Her left eye stared at him from the perspiration covered face as she answered, "I don't really know. But Bodacia reads healthy vital signs, and he has passed into post REM sleep. He seems calmer now, Domyn. Jamyk has always been restless sleeper at least in the Saphyndenlairoum. I believe he is okay."

"Can we be sure? You thought you saw his PEQA through cover. And then some kind of shine? Very strange! And Bodacia's behavior has been weird. Are you certain he's okay?" Domyn pressed her with his intense stare, quite concerned for his small friend in the Saphyndenlairoum.

As her hand went to his chest and wiped gleaming sweat from his skin, Kymil said firmly and in a motherly tone, "Oh my now, Domyn, I can see you are ready and warmed up enough to do your cardio exercise. Don't worry, I trust Bodacia's programming. I trust the program for her responsibility to us as her patients. Now you, young man, must get to running the corridor soon."

Turning and peering down at his small younger crewmate and friend hidden within the rumpled Saphyndenlairoum garment, Domyn admitted in a sympathetic, sad tone, "I do worry, Doc. As frustrating pup as he is, I still care for him. I worry. You know how anxious I can get when our sci-tech doesn't work as it should. Are we sure now, Bodacia, or Saphyndenlairoum, or your dionboda are functioning properly? Should we have Vivacio check them all now before I go?"

Beside him Kymil murmured, "I do know your feeling, Neer Domyn. I feel same anxiety when one of my people, my organic machines as we could be called, becomes injured or sick. Remember you still can have Vivacio do a diagnostic check while you do your exercise. Vivacio can do so at any time you or we command. Don't worry! It's not all your responsibility."

"And now do you truly believe the situation is okay? What about the strange shine you thought you had viewed? You did sound very anxious then, Doc? Almost in panic!" Domyn argued.

"Oh my, it is not a likely occurrence, Domyn. My mind was surely playing tricks on my eyes. Shine I imagined is nothing but postulated possibility, not real phenomenon. I'm satisfied with the current status in Med now," Doc Kymil said in her mothering tone, which he knew would not allow any further argument. "Here, Domyn, so go do your exercise and catch up with Cap Nyba.

She has been waiting for you over nearly an hour now. She will be whipped at you if you don't show on time!"

When he turned to face her, she handed him a light brown pair of Clarinkev running shoes and his usual tan JMO shorts. From where she had procured such garb so suddenly, he had no notion. Calm, peaceful expression on her face prevented him any retort. He could never argue with such a look, now never could. Instead he slipped on JMO shorts over his muscular legs and then put on Clarinkev shoes. It was time to get on with the awake day. Awareness of self and his responsibilities commanded him!

Yet as he sauntered toward the exit, Domyn overheard Doc Kymil murmur to herself in uncertainty, "Could have been Szczygiel Shine? Is it possible? No one ever showed so to my eyes!"

"Awe protect little rascal," Domyn whispered as he heard the hatch close behind him.

Then he went on toward his duty in exercise and meeting with Cap Nyba.

Hopefully he was not tardy in her opinion already!

SPEC ONE: DOMYN THROUGH LAOGRES
CHAPTER 2

In midst of sparkling reflections of sunlight, clustered little group of mallards swam in swampy pond to his left, muskrat glided rippling through water between tufts of marsh grass and decaying pieces of branches sticking from the dark surface near the bank. Walking along a well-trodden path, Domyn lost sight of a muskrat briefly when a stand of cattails with brown heads blocked his view.

Not really a dirt path, he reminded himself. Actually he was strolling along an exercise corridor in Wolf Streak Beta. In fact a dirt path was brownish colored floor with firm but slightly springy consistency, allowing safe walking and running conditions for the crew. This was as close as he could get now in space to cross country running.

Upon each wakening from Saphyndenlairoum, Doc Kymil ordered an aerobic exercise session for each crew member. With long walking strides, Domyn felt tightness of sleep withdraw slowly from thick muscles in his naked legs. As he circled his bare arms briskly with each step, his heart rate increased gradually. He felt good on this third wakening since departing from Steppingstone Quinto.

In warmth and brightness of summer sun overhead, Domyn's mild exertion produced slight sweat over his naked shoulders, torso, and legs. Wearing only his light brown JMO running shorts around his waist and hips and his brown Clarinkevs on his large feet, Domyn felt the warmth of the sun seep into his flesh. Very pleasant feeling, he mused grinning!

However, he realized the blue sky and bright sun above his head were in reality portions of an artificial scene portrayed on the corridor ceiling. Apparent sensation of summer heat was provided by low level ultra-violet and infra-red lighting to settings designed to safely expos crew to appropriate doses of these waves required for physical and psychological development of humans. Awe be praised for Blue Jay sci-tech, which provided this scenario, Domyn thought. After nineteen days of Saphyndenlairoum sleep, heat felt soothing on his large body.

As the path turned gently left round the edge of the pond, two box turtles scurried from the muddy bank into dark water. To his right, two chattering squirrels raced between green bushes of mountain laurel and then scampered noisily up trunk of white birch tree. Their loud and hasty climb startled a small flock of mourning doves that flew off with a sudden whistling wail into the forest of tall oaks, firs, pines, and more birches.

While persistent screech of red-tailed hawk pierced the artificial sky above, path swerved to the right way from the pond scene. Wiping sweat from the smooth skin of his brow and eyelids, Domyn increased his pace to fast walk. His eyes observed many creatures and plants of scenario round him. He wondered how many of such life forms now actually existed back on Homeworld in Zerosolis System. Perhaps Nyba would know information. She was living archive of most info from history…usually.

Momentarily his joy dissipated with sad thought of mass extinctions of creatures of old world. Yet his mind was not attuned to dwell on ancient trauma. Domyn was more enthused by present technology, which did bring creatures and plants back into his life now for his exercise routine. At least memory of their past existence could be honored, he mused happily.

As he reminded himself to ask Nyba about ancient history of age of extinctions, Domyn quickened his pace. He knew from many trips round course, which his present direction along corridor would have longer bends to left than to right as it followed circular shape of horizontal center plane of Wolf Streak Beta. However, overall, 200-yard circular route was designed to be subtle zigzag to reduce boredom and to allow runners to lean in both directions on alternate turns. For some unknown reason, all crew tended to choose the overall left leaning direction. Probably some ancient, instinctive drive, Domyn thought. He would ask Prof Lyndyn later. Surely Prof would know the reason for the psychological need to run left more often than lean right.

As he strolled at fast pace and swayed his arms in vigorous circles, loosening his shoulders, Domyn heard a gurgle and splatter of narrow stream flow from briar and grapevine-laden forest floor beneath leaning poplars and scrubby sumac trees.

After flowing from the hillside to his right, the stream disappeared from sight when it met the path or corridor floor and then reappeared suddenly from the floor into scene on his left.

In spite of consistency of scene integrity from one wall to other, passage under the floor had yet to be programmed into effect. Sight reminded him always the environment, which he now passed through, was still only very sophisticated compilation of three-dimensional images. Yes, he mused, sci-tech of his Blue Jay was quite marvelous yet did have some flaws.

Perhaps Khebol could program the bridge, he thought, or perhaps a little trickle across the floor for runners to leap over in their run. Awright, he admitted to himself, technology had its limits, and existing show was well worth little discrepancies, which his astute eyes uncovered. After all, and fortunately, no scampering rabbit had ever vanished from his sight attempting to cross over the path. Startle might have been too annoying and disconcerting after long sleep in the Saphyndenlairoum. His brain needed refreshing and pleasant stimulation after approximately nineteen days in sleep stasis just as much as his muscles.

While he followed the path along the curve back to the left, Domyn twisted his gradually warming and sweating torso side to side in cadence with his fast, long strides. Muscles and tendons in his naked legs were still mildly tight on his third wakening during current voyage through LaOgres space. Yet he realized soon he would begin running pace and could feel his body almost demanding such exertion already.

However, his heart rate and lung expansion were still a bit sluggish to increase to running pace just then. Despite artificial muscle stimulation of the Saphyndenlairoum, nineteen days of sleep left his very human body lethargic. His heart and breathing needed gradual increase in rhythm. He needed to be ready for fast running pace when Nyba came around the curve of the path shortly.

As she had so many times before in all previous awakenings, Nyba would be coming up behind him soon after having completed number of 200-yard laps. It was her routine. Cap Nyba woke before him. Her role as captain of Wolf Streak Beta required her to be active and in conference with three artigences of spacecraft before organizing the crew. She was like the spacecraft's mother-figure for the crew, more so than even Doc Kymil, who was in reality the eldest woman onboard.

Although only nineteen-years-old herself, Cap Nyba had important duty and responsibility. Domyn had never complained about her preference for current environ program, through which he now walked rapidly. Nyba deserved opportunity to choose the northern latitude forest environ. He realized she had affinity to honor the memory of so many of the extinct creatures depicted in program. Actually he felt more wake after his runs through the northern forest environ than any of the others, especially tropical jungle, which tended to be darker and more sleep evoking to him. He liked routine. He liked Cap Nyba's choices.

The forest to his right opened into a small meadow of assorted short grasses and wildflowers, milkweeds, reddish-purple briars, and cawing crows and gobbling turkeys. Then suddenly over noises of holovistic wild fowl, he heard familiar humming and vibration of Flandecams not too far down the corridor ahead. Domyn experienced again his sensation of routine, cherp security of routine. Awesome sensation, he praised to himself, power, steadiness, majesty of his favorite tech, Flandecams. Even discontinuity of service ladders and access ports infringing on the environ scene did not dampen his glee, his almost ecstatic happiness now. Such pleasure had motivated him through past education to become Neer of scoutcraft.

When he paused in his quick trot within the humming warmth of two Flandecams, one above and one below the corridor, a wide grin spread across his large face presently dripping with perspiration. Instantly his memory reminded him he was nearing number two and number six of eight Flandecams positioned around the outer structure of the great spacecraft Wolf Streak Beta. Four were in upper portion of spacecraft above crew quarters and ConCen. Four were in lower portion under living section.

Domyn laughed with gaiety and waved his arms at three fat woodchucks eating grass merely twenty-three feet behind one service ladder and access. Holographic woodchucks ignored him. Thank awspir Blue Jay tech for sensation, he mused to himself smiling broadly. Raucous blue jays flew over sun-lighted meadow cawing and chirping at fat woodchucks, but Domyn's attention was upon his Flandecams.

Flandecams were primary propulsion generators for spacecraft. In Domyn's mind, they were a greatest advancement in human technology over the past 200 years. They were the main reason LaOgres space travel was now possible. Flandecam created each of the three aspects of gravity known to humans, posi-grav, an-grav, and null-grav. Spacecraft from the Debordo aspect, posi-grav, which humans had originated in the Zerosolis System, could safely pass through LaOgres space aspect where anti-grav was aspect. In addition to propulsion, Flandecam provided protection and insulation of null-grav field around the spacecraft to keep the tiny bubble of Debordo space intact in vastness of LaOgres space. Flandecams were awspir, Domyn wanted to shout to fat woodchucks and noisy flighty blue jays.

"About time you got in here for your running," Domyn heard her panting voice call before he noticed her treading footsteps and was embarrassed to realize his daydreaming had prevented him from hearing Nyba's approaching heavy steps.

Suddenly feeling his cheeks flush with heat, Domyn quipped defensively, dripping sweat from his bald head down his temples and neck, "Nineteen-year men are slower to get started. Or so Doc says! Give me a chance, Nyba! I'm trying to wake up!"

With sheen of perspiration on her wide, bald forehead and scalp, Nyba retorted with smile, "So would be...normal older boys! But Domyn...not wolves! Wolves are...not norm. We are cherp!"

As she approached at a jog, Domyn noticed new muscle in her bare arms and shoulders above light, sweat-stained, blue JMO full-torso running suit. He wondered silently, when had she gained such muscle?

"Awright, we're wolves truly, but one is still bit lazy," he chuckled honestly to her.

With her short arms pumping in rhythm with each jogging stride, sweat-drenched JMO flexed side-to-side over her squat torso. For the first time, he noticed her rounded breasts pushing garment out from her chest. Damn, he swore silently to himself, when had she developed those? Between second and third awakenings, or had he not noticed before? Had his attention been so lax?

When she jogged past him, Nyba slapped his bare belly with her soft sweaty hand and commanded with a gasping laugh, "Don't stand there with a big mouth open. Let's go! Let's go! Start your running! Get your fat legs moving! See if you can keep up. Get your manly, nineteen-year-old body moving. We've got lots to organize today before others arise from stasis..."

While the after-sting of her playful slap dissipated from his belly, Domyn spun around and began loping to catch her. Steady noisy clap, clap, clap of her heavy tread emphasized powerful stockiness of her build. Pasted tight to her backside and hips, the JMO outfit revealed wideness and muscularity of her toxx and her thighs. Nyba's hips had rounded out more than her waist since last wakening. His knowledge of physiology and biology told Domyn such roundness was a sign of womanhood as much as development of her breasts. When had his childhood friend become woman? Why had he not noticed before now?

Sprinting to catch Nyba, his peripheral awareness saw leaves of the trees on each side of the path were then yellows, oranges, reds, browns, and purples. Sun was lower in the artificial sky and behind his back. Heat of his running exertion had replaced simulated summer heat. Autumn was portrayed on corridor walls. Cooler temperature did not lessen dripping sweat from his body nor sweat stains on Nyba's flexing JMO garment. But the slight chill in the air in exercise course felt rather nice to him then.

While the line of trotting black and gray wild turkeys paced them on the right side of the path, Domyn grinned through his panting breathing at sight and at Nyba's racing figure only a few yards head. Momentary enticing vision of Nyba, by which he should be biologically stimulated, he abruptly realized intellectually. Yet why was he not feeling any hormonal excitement? Why was he analyzing rather than reacting to her womanly form? Was it the anti-sex drug in nutrient supply? Was it his prior social friendship blocking sexual interest? He could not remember what Prof Lyndyn had said about the topic, even though middle-aged man had lectured about such stage of human growth many times by then on far way Steppingstones. Then as he reached her side and began pacing with her stride, Domyn did remember vaguely something about biochemical with a strange name…anti…what was it? Ant...something…sex?

However, while a parade of trotting turkeys veered up the artificial hillside and through green tangle of grapevines draping oak and cedar trees, his thought faded way when Cap Nyba announced with a panting breath, "Now you have caught me, we can discuss mission arrangements for awakening, Neer Domyn."

As last of turkeys disappeared up false forest slope, Domyn heard command authority in her voice and knew her usage of his rank title ended play and began scoutcraft business, so he responded, "Awe wills it, Cap! What would you like of me today?"

While they continued to lope long side-by-side at a good but comfortable pace, Cap Nyba said, "I'll launch Buffalardi today with Milyr, Whyvvi, and Doc Kymil."

Feeling the vibration of another pair of Flandecams and observing a briefly service ladder and access port, Domyn exclaimed gleefully as they ran through the artificial forest, "Awspir, then I can inspect Flandecams personally. Been two awakenings since last check to three through five!"

"You should sit in on Prof's session with Swyllo and Jamyk," Nyba declared pointedly firm.

"Is it really necessary?" Domyn asked, saddened by unexpected prospect.

"Prof requested your presence," Cap Nyba announced with a gasp and then added emphatically, "Vivacio reports today all Flandecams are at maximum operating efficiency."

"I like to confirm the status of Flandecams on my own," Domyn explained while they ran by brown and purple leaves on trees displayed along holovistic walls on each flank of path.

"Neer Domyn, Prof Lyndyn asked for you to be there. He would not want you if it weren't important," she stated and then repeated with greater emphasis, "Vivacio reports maximum efficiency."

Awe damn artigence, Domyn growled quietly. Vivacio was the artificial intelligence computer of spacecraft. Specialized artigence was responsible for interfacing with the crew in conjunction with internal technical maintenance of spacecraft. Vivacio would have reported to Cap Nyba earlier in awakening about status of all Flandecams amongst many other spec details for scoutcraft.

Damn, Domyn cursed gain silently, he did not wish to sit through another bout of bickering. He liked other crew members, but they could be damn annoying at times. Listening to Swyllo and Jamyk yakking at each other was not how he wanted to pass current awakening.

As a high-pierced shriek of a red-tailed hawk sounded overhead and was instantly answered by another not far away in scene on the wall, Domyn muttered sourly, "They've been squabbling gain, hey, Cap?"

"Obviously, or Prof would not deem the session important," Nyba declared with huffiness to her panting breath, and then with slight worry, asked, "Did you notice any sign of disturbance with Jamyk in Saphyndenlairoum earlier? I received report from Doc last awakening informing me there has been some difficulty with his sleep cycles during our present trip."

Domyn replied, gasping from his wide chest, "Bodacia…did not…complain as much today as last awakening. I did not notice anything myself. Doc Kymil seemed to wish me gone much quicker than normal from Med to exercise routine. Maybe toxx problem has been resolved?"

"Now would be cherp to hear! We need rascal alert and Bodacia not distracted," Cap Nyba declared and then suddenly chortled with gasp and pointed toward the fast-flying, elongated, and darting creatures on the left side of the path, "Look, Domyn! Are those…dragonflies?"

His eyes spotted insects as creatures flew behind a service ladder of another Flandecam junction, and he responded, "Awright, they do look like what I recall as dragonflies. Must be one of Khebol's new additions to our corridor program. I wonder where he finds long-lost creatures to populate the program. Our buddy, Neer Khebol, is a wizard I'm beginning to believe."

Running beside him stride for stride, Nyba laughed through heavy breaths, "Yes, cherp! I never know what he is adding to holovision programs. I'm surprised myself when he can discover an animal from ancient files which I did not remember myself. So cherp!"

Still a bit unnerved at a possible counseling session with Swyllo and Jamyk, and already missing hum and strong vibes of Flandecams not far behind to the corridor, Domyn grumbled, "Awe be wise, hope Khebol doesn't program anything really annoying or scary. He's known to have a weird sense of humor. Yet, just as you, I'm stunned myself how he manages to get real action habits from ancient archives of extinct animals. Ancient files must be very precise."

Over repetition of footfalls thudding on the path, Nyba said, "Maybe the surprises Khebol gives us will help ease some of our worries. I like seeing animals and birds active once again if only in our artificial program. Hopefully our own wild creatures, Jamyk and Swyllo, will enjoy surprises as well?"

"Yeah, awright, best description for them! Rash minds, rash deeds, but really smart, two pups are truly!" Domyn agreed and then continued feeling obligation to speak some praise about them, "Jamyk has become a good repairman with Flandecams. Maybe I can use him in my inspections today..."

"Neer Domyn," Nyba interrupted chuckling, "You are a stubborn one! You would have been true ancient in the Zerosolis System. Your interest is purely sci-tech and machines. Like vulching ancients, you might not worry about the loss of other species to human technology and unwise energy programs..."

Trying to prevent her from going into one of her long tirades about foolish mistakes of ancients of over 500 years ago, Domyn interrupted her hastily, "Awe be true, Cap. You're probably right! However, now I'm just trying to help. Just like our mission so many years from the Zerosolis System tries to help our people on humanity's home planet deal with slow reclamation of planet. Do you believe our exploration and our Pulseball tournament comms, which we send back via Steppingstones, really give people back in Zerosolis hope and inspiration in their renovation of Homeworld? I've lots of doubt!"

"Now I do like to believe we give them hope," Nyba huffed as they ran still. "We must always believe in our mission toward the Sexto System."

"And do you believe still of likelihood of finding colonials there and discovering a new lush and green world which they have inhabited?" Domyn asked, keeping stride with her.

She glimpsed to him just briefly, and her eyes glistened with what he thought to be enthusiasm as she replied, "I do wish so is reality there in Sexto. Our home world is renewing much too slowly for my liking. I dream of finding colonials in paradise of bounty for human population. Then we can comm Blue Jay MisCom with the so important discovery! They can begin migration to better life in the Sexto System."

"We can merely hope awesomeness of the universe does hear your pleas and heed your dreams, Cap," he sighed through his panting breath and then in a chuckle continued, "So much like potential of me helping Prof with the curing of Swyllo and Jamyk in their puppy behaviors."

"Your notion is cherp. Now then help Prof by being to his session, Neer Domyn," Cap Nyba declared with authoritative emphasis to her breathless voice.

Peering down for an instant at his striding light brown Clarinkevs covering his long feet, Domyn recognized the familiar power of her decision-making, her stubborn determination to be right, and was glad she had seemingly dropped her momentary focus on ancient neglect of climate and life on Homeworld in the Zerosolis System, so he agreed hastily, "Sure, Cap, I'll be there. I'll help with rascals."

As a large flock of grackles and red-wing blackbirds whirled in unison on the right side of the path, Nyba waved at them with her right hand and then said, "I know you will. Yet remind Prof Lyndyn everyone should be on ConCen for communication with Fox Flash Alpha. I want all of us wolves there today. We were lacking in our respective regard during our last cycle of awakening."

"Yeah, Cap, would be cherp for Swyllo and Jamyk to see others, especially Chitir," Domyn agreed, just barely sensing the passing junction of Flandecams in midst of colorful leaves falling from trees in scenes flowing alongside them as their footfalls pounded on the pathway through the artificial terrain.

Slightly twisting her torso towards him as they ran, Nyba looked into his face and suddenly stated, "After communication with Fox Flash Alpha, I want to have full crew rehearsal for popping to Weznuski. We skipped so last awakening. Not exactly simple procedure to do when we must! You know so!"

Within the sweat-drenched JMO outfit flexing of her upper body highlighted her breasts, and he realized that her command ability was just as mature then as her physical maturity, but his focus in moment required him to reply, "Yes, Cap, even though we will not pop for several more awakenings, we should be prepared for procedure. You're very wise as well for thinking about popping back into the Debordo space should help Swyllo with her fear of LaOgres space."

"Just what I had in mind. I wish to get their attention on mission operations and eventually rejoining our friends on Fox Flash Alpha," Cap Nyba said, and after few running steps, added, "And, Neer, we'll need to foresee successful finish to our mission into Sexto System."

"Awe will it, Cap!" Domyn huffed as he loped aside her.

"Vulch, Domyn, are you still believing in some universal deity nonsense? Isn't it so silly for someone like you with your incredible scientific mind?" she snorted in amusement but then returned to her prior train-of-thought and declared, "But never mind so now! We only need to feel how cherp it will be to see and hear from our friends on Fox Flash Alpha again."

Slightly dismayed by her ridicule of his speculative philosophical belief, Domyn decided not to argue with her in moment and replied instead, "Yes, hearing from our comrades on Fox Flash will be especially cherp for Jamyk and Swyllo. They have very close bonds with Chitir."

"Maybe why they quarrel so much and get on each other's nerves?" Nyba suggested with a motherly tone to her mellow voice. "Perhaps they share a bit of jealousy concerning Chitir."

"Uh, yes, worth mentioning to Prof," Domyn said, and then when another thought came to him, he added, "How many awakenings yet before we pop into the Sexto System?"

"Do you want to know how long you have to end the bickering?" Nyba laughed.

"No, I want to know how long Prof Lyndyn has to fix quarrelling," he laughed as they ran along weaving path for...how many laps now?

While he chided himself silently for having lost count awhile ago, Domyn listened to Nyba chuckle between her own panting breaths, "I believe we have more than half of the awakenings to go yet. Most likely about seven, I believe, but will not be long to wait. We will be sleeping for most of the time duration. We'll be in Sexto with Fox Flash Alpha before we know."

"For pups like Jamyk and Swyllo, seven awakenings are long time. Especially if they're under stress," Domyn suggested solemnly in serious thought then.

"We're not much older than them," Nyba said over honking of several geese flying overhead in some v-shaped general formation across false skyline on the ceiling and continued, "Actually Swyllo is our age, Domyn, within a few months if I recall! Although she doesn't act it very often, does she?"

Again his eyes observed flexing of her wet blue JMO garment over tautness of her figure, and he thought to himself, not really older than Swyllo, yet Nyba was so much more mature, and then he said loud, "No, I feel older today...than other past awakenings...since we were Jamyk's age on Steppingstone Tercero, I believe. Boy is two years younger than us, isn't he?"

"Now I think you're right! I don't pay much attention to his personal issues, like age. Yet we were pups ourselves...between Steppingstones Tercero and Cuarto," Nyba confirmed with a slight glance toward him when they rounded the bend to the right in the path in the moment.

"Awe remembers, Cap! We were once just pups," he agreed with grin as he looked to her running form beside him, then he added with admiration in his voice, "And, I must admit, how we have changed since then. Both of us in body and in way we think, I guess also!"

For a few moments they were silent while they ran through then leafless trees on walls of the corridor and observed reddish-tan white-tail deer drinking from the false stream, but then Nyba continued, "Yes, Domyn, we have changed, but not so long ago we, too, were merely young pups...pups with command authority...command responsibility...surely! But just pups in on our Blue Jay spacecraft."

When deer suddenly bolted into the forest with its white tail straight erect as if frightened by their presence, Domyn asked with curiosity, "Was creature acting like a natural in interactive surprise from us now? Did Khebol include such? I don't recall seeing creatures flee from us as if we were threat to them."

"Maybe it's new to me! Many new additions to north program since we left Steppingstone Cuatro. Khebol has been at our Vivacio often with his updates and pranks," Nyba chuckled glibly.

"Yes, he has given us so many new surprises during our years of being pups. Yet we were and still are pups with dreams of glory...of being Jayer heroes. All of us Blue Jayers dream of being ones to finally find colonials. Should be our glory!"

With giggle and then a sudden groan, Cap Nyba gasped with serious anxiety, "Now we're mature! At least we're supposed to be mature to lead our crew to their destiny. I hope we're mature for our Blue Jay mission. Perhaps even Khebol...should he be mature by now? I hope...and Cap Bhiros...and Chitir...and all foxes! They'll have first chance to find colonials. They'll be first to get into the Sexto System. I hope they're ready for the challenge. And I'm slightly envious of them, too!"

"Awright, they do have advantage now," Domyn agreed, and then after several strides, giggled in spite of his own displeasure with gigglers, "But you claim we're mature. Are we sure? Do adult bodies make us mature enough to perform challenges of our mission? I hope so! But have doubts, too!"

As she partially turned her head toward him, Domyn saw a puzzled expression on her face and then heard her bewildered voice ask, "Adult bodies? Is so why I feel…different? Is so why you look so…umm…so…different to me today's awakening?"

Frowning with his own befuddlement, Domyn inquired with a slight squeak to his normally deep voice, "I look different? Vulch, am I fatter? Do I need to run more?"

Smiling at his evident discomfort, Nyba answered, "No, I don't think you are fatter than last awakening, Domyn. You're just…bigger…more muscles…more bulges on your body. You look so much manlier to me now. Only way I can describe what I see now!"

"More bulges? More manly? What does it really mean, Nyba? I want to believe you. But I don't feel so about myself yet," he grumbled with some embarrassment and then admitted somewhat hesitantly, "Awe knows I'd like to keep up with your rapid growth to maturity, Nyba. You are so much more womanly now today in present awakening…"

Regaining her expression of bewilderment, Nyba stared at him for few strides and then asked suspiciously, "Womanly? What do you mean? Doc Kymil said same thing in Med just earlier! What do you two mean to imply by term 'womanly?' Am I looking older finally? Losing my youth?"

"Argh! Well, perhaps Doc meant to say you have developed into a mature and…well…beautiful young woman," Domyn stammered, not knowing how to vocalize his observations of recent. "You look more cherp now, Nyba. You have more…more bulges…more mature muscles!"

Then with both amusement and consternation battling in her voice, Nyba chortled, "Cherp? More bulges? Sounds like how I described you, you toxx! Some leaders we are! We can't even tell each other what we really see or how we regard each other. Mature? Us? It was easier when we were just pups…on Steppingstone Tercero. Doing what Prof and Doc suggested to us! No rule or responsibilities!"

"Awright, I guess you are right! We are just pups still with dreams of glory," Domyn grinned.

"Perhaps, my friend, now we're mature…and with bulges," she laughed nervously.

"Yes, with bulges and dreams of glory! Do you believe that we're ready for our challenge in the Sexto System?" Domyn asked, huffing in panting breath as he loped beside her perspiring figure.

"Yes, my friend, and soon we must act very mature to grab our glory," Nyba panted as she quickened the pace. "We must not just dream of glory. We must seek it out and grab ahold tightly."

"Yeah, we must seek glory not only for ourselves but also the multitude of people relying on us back in the Zerosolis System and five Steppingstones between there and here," Domyn declared with exuberance.

"Now are you, Domyn, the same boy who I have travelled alongside for so many years? Do you show new trait of maturity?" Nyba inquire somewhat facetiously perhaps and with huffing snicker.

While he matched her pace, Domyn glanced to her and said breathlessly, "Awright, maybe meaning of being mature, don't you think, Cap Nyba? Even a boy like me can grow into a man."

Nyba declared, "You are a wise man now, my friend, and Neer."

They loped long the path with purpose for Wolf Streak Beta and crew.

29

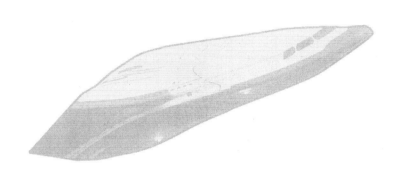

SPEC ONE: DOMYN THROUGH LAOGRES
CHAPTER 3

During the fifth awakening since plunging into LaOgres space, Domyn watched with amusement his two friends running and shouting around the gym recreation chamber.

Jamyk twisted aside and laughed.

As her Zapstik descended, just missing along the length of his blue figure, Swyllo cried out with a snarl, "Argh! Tiny peener toxx, stand still! Maybe your onad sways too much for you to be still!"

Instead Jamyk poked her backside with his padded Zapstik and then leaped quickly just ahead of her attempt to undercut his legs with a floor sweep of her own blue Zapstik.

"Vulching, tiny peener!" Swyllo shrieked in obvious agitation and ire.

Still wearing only his brown JMO shorts, Clarinkevs on his feet, and a rank layer of sweat from his recent running exercise, Domyn watched as two blue figures battled around chamber, and he chuckled to Prof Lyndyn standing beside him, "Toxx rascal seems to anticipate her strikes. I don't believe she has hit him yet since they began the session."

"Indeed," Lyndyn agreed in his slightly nasal voice. "Typical of their sessions, Domyn. Swyllo selects Zapstik combat believing she is slightly more muscular and more adept at offensive maneuvers than Jamyk, as he is most often goal tender in gaming. However, she loses her skill advantage as she gets emotionally upset almost as soon as combat begins. I believe she enters sessions with emotional turmoil. But then, after all, purpose of sessions is to use and release emotions and frustrations held within. No doubt Swyllo does release significant quantity of emotion in their dual sessions, especially in combat with Jamyk. She will…"

"Yes, Prof," Domyn interrupted, smiling to himself at man's tendency to ramble his conversation, and then he continued, "But I wonder how he does his anticipation. It seems to be same as he does in real Pulseball games. Jamyk knows or guesses a move of the shooter. How does he do so? He is so effortless and also so careless. How can he do it with precision?"

Laughing hysterically Jamyk stumbled to the floor. Swyllo pummeled his small form with several harsh strikes of her Zapstik. Still giggling, in spite of the attack, the boy rolled side to side on the floor trying to avoid the attack. Not letting her adversary escape, Swyllo continued her assault grunting her favorite expletives in process. No doubt she was very intent in aim to strike his smaller body.

Not concerned by the situation or seemingly brutal smashes to the boy, Domyn knew vicious attacks were absorbed by the McAnderwike suit covering Jamyk. Just as in a competitive game of Pulseball, half-inch thick, titan-flex construction of McAnderwike protected wearer against blunt force hit another human was capable of generating. Both participants wore the same blue McAnderwikes they had used on Steppingstone Quinto in the historic final match versus Fox Flash Alpha. They were quite safe from blows of each other. And so they hit with fury often in their emotional conflict.

In an apparently wild, reflexive attempt at self-defense, Jamyk swung his Zapstik at Swyllo. Caught in an unbalanced stance, Swyllo took blow and fell to the floor. Well, Domyn thought to himself, McAnderwike would not prevent the body from being knocked over.

"Argh! Damn little vulcher!" Swyllo's curse filled the room to be followed by another bout of raspy laughter from Jamyk.

"Exceedingly well, indeed therapy is going exceedingly well," Prof Lyndyn announced, and then turning to Domyn, continued, "When he is concentrating and not playing, as he is now, Jamyk has no doubt honed his reflexes over numerous experiences of goal tending. I believe he was original goal tender of Wolf Streak at such a young age as he was then when you first entered Pulseball tournament some five years ago now on Steppingstone Primero. Yes, indeed all those games since then and countless practices you and Nyba have put the crew through have no doubt sharpened Jamyk's anticipation and reflexes. He is indeed…"

"But, Prof, he was just as sharp before Steppingstone Primero as he has been recently," Domyn argued persistently with the shorter man wearing a gray dionboda uniform, which covered his entire form, except for his slightly pudgy face, "My guess is he owns some innate gift to think ahead?"

From behind the visor over his left eye, Prof Lyndyn's wide face frowned briefly before he replied, "More than five years ago now. No doubt your memory is tricking you, Domyn. As time passes, we tend to embellish some memories of our earlier and more youthful days, especially athletic or professional attributes. Indeed to our memories, we were always much better at whatever we did than we most likely were in truth. We often reminisce of how good we were then. How much better and tougher we were than current athletes of today! We are always..."

"Prof," Domyn interrupted rambling diatribe, "it may be five years for you and Doc, but the rest of us slept most of the time. Our memories probably don't add up to more than year total, including stays at Steppingstones. I'm sure I can remember quite accurately only year of awareness."

With his visor-covered eye apparently attentive to two figures writhing on the floor, Prof Lyndyn responded never-the-less, "Domyn, you of all people with your vast sci-tech knowledge must remember conscious awareness is not only memory we create in our lives. Even asleep the brain continues to process stimuli from around us and includes such stimuli into our memories, usually subconscious I admit, but memory. Also, our physical body, independent of our conscious awareness, can make memory. So not to belabor issue, I'll just say your brain has accumulated more memories than you may think..."

"My vast sci-tech knowledge isn't very strong on human bio-med info," Domyn admitted sheepishly. "In fact reminds me, Prof, I wanted to ask you something. What is See... Seegla? Awe help me... Seagull Shine? Don't know if I say it right!"

As an eye beneath the visor turned toward him, Domyn witnessed sudden sharpness to the older man's face, which had not been there before. When man remained silent for several seconds, Domyn thought Lyndyn perhaps was viewing some image on the monitor in the visor, some display of medical or psychological importance involving two combatants, then running around the room again. Perhaps Prof Lyndyn would ask Bodacia for some more detailed precision visor of dionboda interface provided. Lyndyn stood quietly.

However, instead Prof Lyndyn asked tersely, bluntly, "Where did you hear of Szczygiel Shine, Neer Domyn? And under what circumstances?"

Taken aback by the man's much more pointed and sharp tone, Domyn stammered, "Well…urgh…in Med…we were doing normal awakening procedure. Doc Kymil thought she saw something involving Jamyk while he was still in Saphyndenlairoum…"

"What did she say she saw?" interrupted Lyndyn, not at all like his normal tolerant personality.

"Awright, well, Doc asked Bodacia if she had recorded See… Shine. Bodacia said her programming was not prepared to record shine because no human had ever been observed as displaying shine. But Bodacia was acting strange during awakening. Doc wasn't sure if she had seen something in her visor or perhaps PEQA with her special vision. I didn't know what was going on," Domyn said, staring at the unusually focused man before him.

As a blue form lightly brushed past his large body, Domyn listened when Lyndyn nodded and agreed with mellow nasal twang, "Indeed, Bodacia is correct. No human has ever displayed Szczygiel Shine by self-natural means, either instinctively or by intent. You say Bodacia was acting strangely? How do you mean?"

"Well, yes, she seemed confused. She referred to Jamyk as being difficult. Bodacia could not define his situation more precisely. Her programming had no parameters for his behavior. Something about being in some unusual sleep stage," Domyn tried to explain but then asked impatiently, "What is shine, Prof? I don't recall learning about it. Doc was very mysterious about it…"

Interrupting again Lyndyn stated, "No doubt, Domyn, you had Vivacio check Bodacia. Did he find any malfunction? No, if there had been malfunction, I would have been informed. Doc Kymil did say she thought Bodacia was telling jokes but is just the case of artigence mimicking our speech. Bodacia has performed as expected for two sleep cycles and two awakenings since then, is it not correct, Neer Domyn? You have not had any warning from Vivacio since then, have you?"

"No, Prof, Bodacia has been fine since then, although she still grumbles about Jamyk being difficult once in while. Vivacio confirms her positive status. I've checked her programming and circuit myself. She's not a problem, Prof. Now what's such shine? What's vulching secret?" Domyn asked more abruptly and more forcefully than he would normally talk to a mid-aged man whom he respected.

"Bodacia," Lyndyn called loudly, "is auditory dampening currently active in McAnderwikes of Swyllo and Jamyk?"

"Yes, Professor Lyndyn," Bodacia replied curtly from some speaker comm in the chamber then.

"Vivacio, is evidence of malfunction in the current status of Bodacia?" Lyndyn asked again a bit louder than normal and shuffling his feet in Clarinkevs more restlessly than his typical low-keyed habit.

"Professor Lyndyn, Bodacia is currently operating within parameters at maximum efficiency," said Vivacio's resonant male voice also into the air of the chamber from perhaps the same speaker as Bodacia prior.

Now his attention was so focused upon his debate with Prof Lyndyn, Domyn had lost his visual awareness of two combatants. Yet their noises and actions as they danced and pounded and shout at each other still entered his peripheral sight. He did notice effusive laughter, which before had engulfed Jamyk was now absent. Younger boy was active still but vocally silent. Swyllo was making all the noise now. Her shrill voice dominated the chamber when artigences became silent again.

Wondering why Prof was avoiding the topic of Shine, Domyn pressed his question firmly and asked with a low growl, "Awright, Prof, Shine, what is it? Doc thought it was important. What is it?"

Hesitating for several seconds, Prof Lyndyn seemed perturbed to Domyn but then said, "No doubt she did! Woman can see more than the rest of us. Doc Kymil has the ability to see PEQA…"

"Yes, yes, Prof, I know," Domyn interrupted with a tone of frustration creeping into his voice. "Shine, Prof, what is it? Why so evasive now?"

"Indeed, Shine," Lyndyn began slowly, as if it pained him to reveal the subject to anyone, and then finally continued, "Szczygiel Shine is theoretical phenomenon, Domyn. One has never been recorded by any device from person in natural state without artificial stimulation. Stimulation was performed during very carefully designed experimental research during mappings of the brain. I don't understand how Kymil could have seen one, even in her display monitor through enhancements of Bodacia, and even with her special vision for PEQA viewing. We don't know if Szczygiel Shine and PEQA are connected…"

Then more irritated by the man's reluctant stalling, Domyn growled with frustration, "Awright, Prof, what is it though? What vulcher is toxx Shine?"

With a trace of dismay in his nasal voice, Lyndyn answered hesitantly, "As I was starting to say, Szczygiel Shine is artificial creation only. When micro-electrode stimulates psychic nerve center…or what recent research over the last century has discovered to be nerve formation in the brain may be psychic…"

35

"Zachymatis!" Domyn blurted impatiently and wondered where he had found info in his own memory, usually loaded by mech tech specs and designs but less with psych and med data.

"So you do know some of med-info after all, Domyn," Prof Lyndyn declared with a nasal chuckle and then continued, "Yes, indeed zachymatis, when stimulated at a certain level, will send out a pulse or shine through much of brain. Special pulse can be recorded by quantal tech monitoring systems we have in Blue Jay project, including our own Bodacia and Wolf Streak Beta. We refer to such pulse of neural activity as Szczygiel Shine. Now remember, Domyn, shining pulse is not a phenomenon anyone or any device has recorded from any human subject under naturally occurring situations. We've witnessed pulse only by chance and only when artificially created when first studying zachymatis and its function involving psychic activity. Doc Kymil should know!"

When Lyndyn paused for breath, Domyn said in a hushed voice, "Yet our Doc Kymil suspected she had glimpsed one of special shines in her monitor. And from our own rascal Jamyk!"

Except for panting breaths of the two young people, then laying prone on the floor not far from each other, the room was very quiet contrasted to just moments before, so Lyndyn's almost whispered words sounded loud when he said, "Domyn, don't exaggerate the importance of your belief. After all Doc Kymil only thought she saw something. Szczygiel Shine has never been reported or recorded by normal occurrence. Bodacia can't confirm anything of strange possibility. It's most likely a lot of confusion and imagination, almost like your obsession with your universal awareness speculations."

"My thoughts of universal awareness have little to do with what Doc said, Prof. But maybe Jamyk has some limited psychic ability helping with his anticipation," Domyn suggested hopefully, and leaning toward Lyndyn as if to keep speculation secret from exhausted combatants, he whispered, "So might explain some of his ability and timely moves. He must have some talent to be able to move so rapidly when dodging Swyllo's blows or stopping shots in Pulseball game. He does seem to do so much more effectively than anyone else I've seen."

"Indeed perhaps! I can tell you since you probably know already, most of the Blue Jay members have higher psychic scores than average population. We now strongly suspect zachymatis is a portion of the human brain directly connected to psychic ability in humans. Our Blue Jay crews do have higher than average intelligence and memory retention. Some Blue Jay researchers have postulated our higher than average psychic scores, especially when zachymatis is tested, provide further evidence intelligence and memory may have a psychic component as well. Yet has not been thoroughly studied as of now. However, what was once just an idea of magic or fictional fantasy, topic of psychic talents has been given some scientific credence in the last 200 years. Though don't get overly encouraged with your speculations, Domyn! We do not have enough knowledge about such yet to seriously measure and research with any precision. We are at a beginning of psychic science only, Neer Domyn. Anything is possible, but most of our speculations are probably not quantifiable and thus not convenient to be proven. Odds are more than, let's say, a billion to one anyone we know will be abnormal psychic phenomenon, one to leap science ahead."

As he witnessed Jamyk staring at him through mist and a sweat splattered face-shield, Domyn interrupted Lyndyn's lecture and murmured, "But it would be awspir if it were real, Prof. If we have one in a billion pup right here on Wolf Streak Beta, wouldn't it be awspir?"

"No doubt, would be almost as unusual as having our best sci-tech engineer educated in complex technology of Blue Jay project who insists on believing in metaphy spirits," Lyndyn chuckled at Domyn and at same the time pointed at Jamyk and asked the boy, "Now, young man, are you bored yet?"

Jamyk replied in his tired, raspy voice, "Yup!"

"Vulch...he's just...whipped! I beat his toxx...nasty!" Swyllo chirped through panting breath.

"Indeed, Swyllo, perhaps, you've worn him out. We still have time in the session before you people need to go to your next duty. What would you select to do, my young pups?" Lyndyn asked in his occasionally comic fatherly persona. "We can sit around and discuss many psychotherapeutic educational techniques. Would you likethis topic, Jamyk, Swyllo?"

Together they respond immediately and loudly, "No!"

Only sense of obligation to his role as assistant for Prof Lyndyn in the current particular session prevented Domyn from joining in with their dissent, and then he asked, just barely controlling laughter in his voice, "Well, what will you try next, more combat with Zapstiks? Wrestling? Pulseball keep away? Time still, I guess, for two impish rogues to terrorize Prof and me yet!"

Right away Lyndyn gripped, almost squealing, "No for me to be involved, young rascals!"

37

"Vulch, no!" Swyllo groaned almost simultaneously. "I'm not going to wrestle slimy little peener! Stinks too much like rotten toxx! And always slick with his slippery sweat!"

As he took off his McAnderwike helmet, a wide grin spread across his narrow face, and Jamyk proclaimed in a hearty and somewhat demanding recommendation, "Splat...bulbs!"

"Awe no!" Domyn heard his own deep voice comingle with Swyllo's shrill moan immediately.

"No doubt Jamyk had such planned when he allowed Swyllo to select first contest. Did you not, my young lad?" Prof Lyndyn grinned while shaking his bald head at the boy.

Only response from the boy still sprawled on the floor as he then began to sit up was a shrug of his slim shoulders and slight raise of his hands out from his sides, palm up as if to indicate in mime, who, me?

With a sigh and mild chuckle, Domyn said, "Awe knows I guess I must have had psychic sense not to have showered after my exercise running and decided to wear my JMOs to session. It seems their splatter bulb affairs tend to get observers as well as contestants."

"Whatever do you mean?" Swyllo smiled with a strange quick nod to Jamyk. "Neer Domyn, we would never involve you in one of our battles. After all you don't seriously believe little onad and me would ever join forces against you, do you? Seems so very vulching unlikely, doesn't it? He's such little peener toxx. And I never favor him or his idiot ideas ever...now...do I, Domyn?"

"Nope," Jamyk rasped with grin, a rather mischievous grin to Domyn's perspective, and then the boy added, still grinning, "Never!"

"I believe I'll let you supervise next bout, Domyn. I hear Doc Kymil calling for my assistance in some consultation," Prof Lyndyn chuckled, turning toward the hatch quickly and with a surprising quick gait.

"Awright, now, Prof, enough of your joking," Domyn grinned toward the slightly older man. "Session is your responsibility. I'm just socially ignorant sci-tech specialist. Field of counseling is yours. Don't you dare desert me now against young rascals."

"No doubt you are more than a tech genius, young man, or should I say young Neer? Anyone with belief, no, more like scientific theory of supreme awareness overseeing vast universe must be more than a simple tech specialist," Prof Lyndyn suggested with a hint of humor in his nasal voice. "Indeed if you are correct in theory, then you won't be alone here in the chamber with two mischievous wolf pups. You'll have your supreme awareness to guide guard you."

Off to the side where two blue figures sat on the floor, Swyllo chirped with sudden enthusiasm, "Is it to be splatter bulbs then, puny onad? Do you have nad for type of dirty competition? I will vulching love to paint your skinny toxx with splatter bulbs."

As he heard Jamyk laugh in a short snort, Domyn replied with a laugh, "Prof, I've never claimed to believe in actual one specific entity. My speculation has not advanced to degree yet. So you should really stay here and aid me from terror of two wild pups. In sense you are my true supreme elder wolf primary of Wolf streak Beta. Prof, you are my entity of protection in today's awakening."

While he spoke, his eyes watched Jamyk arise from the floor, walk toward the wall where he punched a spot with a blue glove on his fist. After the window slid open about three feet up from the floor, the boy reached into opening. Within moments Jamyk pulled the container from the opening.

When his grinning face turned toward Swyllo, Jamyk displayed the contents of the container by tipping it slightly downward, so she could see into the top, and then he asked, "Enough?"

Swyllo yelled with a squeaking wail as she giggled, "Vulcher enough for the entire crew, you toxx! Why don't you get a smaller bag? We'll never get our McAnderwikes clean if we use many bulbs."

Jamyk looked down at his blue uniform and frowned, "Clean?"

"Yeah, you little peener, we will need to clean the suits after we're finished here. You do wash your clothes when they get dirty, don't you?" Swyllo shouted with a scolding tone.

"Nope," Jamyk rasped and then let his mouth flash into a wide smile at her. "Maybe!"

"Erhh! Boys, don't you guys ever think about things like that?" Swyllo griped as she rolled onto her haunches and seemed prepared to rise to stand soon.

"Indeed are too many bulbs," Prof Lyndyn groaned. "Are you sure you really want to play with many for just the two of you, Jamyk?"

"Two?" Jamyk asked with a smile, and then after he pointed at four people in the chamber, he chuckled, "Four!"

"Awright, you are definitely not leaving me alone with devious two rascals, Prof," Domyn declared with a hearty laugh. "My universal awareness is but speculation of existence, not a specific single protecting guardian. No, my friend and mentor, you are here with me. You asked for my help in session. Now I am here for you, but it is still your session, Prof. Your obligation per Cap Nyba's mind!"

"Vulch, no, Jamyk," Swyllo cried out while she arose from the floor to stand on her legs. "Vulching too many to try to wash off my McAnderwike before I use it again. Let's use…"

"Nope!" Jamyk interrupted her before she could finish her remark and then the boy rasped with a broad and widening grin, "No suits!"

"Vulch, yes, just JMOs, hey, little peener?" Swyllo inquired with a tone of approval in her voice. "Yes, why not, just our JMOs. Will make it fairer for our observers, if by some chance they were to become involved in contest. Yes, onad, JMOs will be most cherp!"

"Awright, now, you two rascals, don't get nasty silly now," Domyn pleaded with mock concern.

"Nope!" Jamyk laughed as he punched a spot on his chest, opening his McAnderwike to begin unmelding process, and then while he peeled the top layer from the inner layer, he giggled, "Naked!"

"Awe help me!" Domyn sighed with sudden embarrassed anxiety, "I guess we are fortunate a private session is not broadcast back to humanity on Steppingstones and in Zerosolis."

"Indeed I distinctly hear Doc Kymil, and now I believe also Cap Nyba calls for my services now," Prof Lyndyn moaned, slowly sneaking toward the hatchway from chamber.

"No, no, Prof," Swyllo giggled as she disrobed from her McAnderwike. "As Neer Domyn has just said, you are supervisor of sessions. You can't run off now. And by your own rules, we must play contest by vulching odd rules Jamyk chooses because it is his turn to select a contest. Even if little peener is being nasty toxx, we should play by the rules."

"No doubt, Domyn, your metaphy will protect me also, if I ask politely," Prof Lyndyn said with some resigned pessimism. "Even though I'm not much of philosophical believer in silliness, I hope your universal awareness will grant me some slack now. Indeed we are lucky not to be in a broadcast scenario in moment. My old body would scare the life from poor viewers in the Zerosolis System."

"No, Prof, you don't hear me. I said we have no guardian here. My speculation only suggests we, or our iotas of awareness, are but each part of universal awareness existing in universe as we are but not to oversee us or our activities.

My thought has been so far universal awareness is psychic aspect of universe compliments physical aspect. Universal awareness experiences universe through infinite iotas of its awareness from energize life-forms throughout time. We are on our own here now in the gym with two young...um...maybe...demons?"

"Vulch, Domyn, now is not time for silly toxx theory," Swyllo chirped almost out of her blue McAnderwike. "Time for having some vulching nasty fun!"

"Yup!" rasped Jamyk as he wriggled McAnderwike down his skinny figure.

"Perhaps then we can convince our young friend to relent in his choice of attire, or lack of it, for competitive session," Prof Lyndyn suggested with a slight hint of hopeful pleading in his voice. "After all, if you are correct, each of us is part of a universal thing. Now, my young friend, Jamyk, you would not splatter universal thing with wet slushy paint, would you?"

"Nope!" Jamyk grinned as he stepped out of the crumpled McAnderwike at his feet, and then pointing at Swyllo and then Domyn, the boy declared, "Friends!"

"Indeed I can live with that," Lyndyn said, stepping backward into a corner away from the disrobing players. "They're all yours, Domyn. I'll satisfy my responsibility by being observer."

"Oh, Prof, you're a big help!" Domyn chuckled, watching the older man move into a corner of the gym chamber, but at least he had stopped trying to make for exit. "Awright, may my universal awareness enjoy foray into wet and wild messiness. I suppose any experience has some universal value. Awright, my friends, shall we keep our JMOs on to at least pretend we are mature enough to be in the presence of universal awareness of some maybe modest perspective?"

"Vulch, Domyn, if you are right about awareness, then it has seen us naked before. No big deal to me, especially little peener over there!" Swyllo laughed, looking at Jamyk.

"Ha, ha!" Jamyk chuckled, setting the container of splatter bulbs in the center of the gym and then stepping back with one colorful bulb in each hand, he rasped with glee, "Naked!"

"Awe help me!" Domyn prayed as he watched Swyllo walk to the container to retrieve her first supply of splatter bulbs. "You wouldn't make an exception for your good friend and Neer, would you, Jamyk and Swyllo?"

"Nope!" they said in unison with smiles while they peeled out of their JMOs.

"No doubt, matter of principle for young people, Domyn," Prof Lyndyn said from his corner away from likely contest. "They do enjoy making rules now, don't they? Very good for release of their tensions and stress, don't you agree?"

"Awright, easy for you to ramble on about while you're over there where you believe you are safe," Domyn said to Lyndyn, and then with another thought in mind, he continued, "However, I do not think your position will guard you from some collateral damage there, Prof. I suspect bulbs will find their way around most of chamber. You might as well join in the contest aggressively. You may have some desire to relieve some of your own stress and tension today."

"Vulch, yeah, Prof," Swyllo retorted, "Come on, join the contest. Relieve some of your own stress. You must have some after trying to take care of us toxx pups for many times."

"Yup!" Jamyk rasped with a smile at Lyndyn. "Relieve!"

"No doubt you young pups would love to get me into your battle now," Lyndyn laughed. "Perhaps you are correct. I must think about participating very carefully now. Give me some time to consider ramifications of joining you in competitive playful nonsense."

"Vulch, Prof, I thought it was a serious session for relief of psycho-stress," Swyllo declared. "Were you goading us before? Are you trying to trick us now?"

"No, no, my young friends, session of great importance for you," Lyndyn said with his nasal voice revealing signs of concern, and Domyn realized the man was suddenly worried he had spoken poorly for sake of purpose of session and future sessions of similar nature.

Trying to help Prof Lyndyn from a possible cleverly designed trap by Swyllo, Domyn said with a laugh, "Sure, Prof, every session is serious, right, even those totally embarrassing to us. Come along now, elder wolf, show us just how seriously puppy you can be now. We all need to be foolishly puppy at times, no matter our age or our status in society. Don't you agree, Prof?"

"Yup," Jamyk rasped, "pups!"

"Indeed you are very astute, young Neer," Lyndyn conceded as he hesitantly stepped forward. "If you will allow me some adult dignity and let me wear my professional uniform, I will feel less awkward and less intrusive to your contest. I should try to retain my professionalism at least."

"Vulch, Prof, Bodacia is here somewhere to do duty now," Swyllo protested. "And besides, like I tried to say before, Domyn's great and grand universal whatever has already seen all of us naked before. Natural way we came into life, isn't it? Or perhaps were you born with a dionboda attached?"

"Naked!" Jamyk rasped with smile. "Natural!"

"Indeed you do know how to argue against me with some logic, you two young wolves. No doubt, Whyvvi has had some affect upon your reasoning habits. I suppose you are correct. I really have no excuse not to join your contest and follow your rules, Jamyk," Lyndyn sighed with some dismay.

"Yup!" Jamyk declared with laugh. "Everyone!"

"Vulch, will be nasty cherp! I'll still paint your skinny toxx with most of my splatters, you little toxx," Swyllo said as she shook her two bulbs already in her hands at Jamyk.

"Awright, then we'll all be involved now. However, do we really need to get naked?" Domyn protested with some chagrin, surprising him after having lived and showered with a crew for most of his life on board an enclosed spacecraft. "I don't suppose your friend Chitir would want us to play in nude like you have requested? Would he want his best friends getting naked and splashing each other with messy paint? And would he wish his girl Swyllo naked and messy with paint…"

Briefly Swyllo and Jamyk peered at one another and then they declared together, "Yup!"

However, Domyn, even though he realized probably so not so long ago, was now of belief Chitir would be feeling same reservations he was feeling now they were both upon the threshold of true adulthood and not pups anymore, so he continued his argument half-heartedly, "Are you certain, Swyllo? Do you really believe Chitir would want you naked before other young men now? I did notice how you two were cuddling on Steppingstone Quinto before mission to the Sexto System left. Are you sure he would approve now if he were here?"

"Chitir," Jamyk rasped in moderately sober tone. "Man…now!"

"Yeah, maybe, he might have some reservation about me getting naked now. Vulch, little onad, your friend is quite protective of me recently. I'm not sure if Chitir would like me doing pup acts anymore. I am growing into a woman now. I am growing out of my pup days," Swyllo said almost in disappointment, and then she suggested, "Perhaps we keep on our JMOs, Jamyk, for Chitir's sake."

"Chitir," Jamyk said almost in a whisper, and his face lost the boyish grin for a moment and instead appeared almost vacantly stoic while he tossed splatter bulbs gently in his hands, and then he looked at Domyn and said in an apparent change of mind, "JMOs!"

"Awe much better!" Domyn smiled, thanking Chitir in his mind, and then he glanced over at Prof Lyndyn in the corner and suggested, "Awright, old wolf, you have no excuse now not to participate in fun. Come join us. I have feeling I will need someone to provide alternate target for my young friends…"

"Yup!" Jamyk chortled, now showing the childish glee again as he glanced at Prof Lyndyn. "Prof!"

"No doubt, Domyn, your universal awareness entity will find experience interesting and indeed amusing," Prof Lyndyn groaned with mild sarcasm as he peeled off his dionboda cap. "Yet I am manly enough to help my young wards in their attempt to release their stress. Bodacia, I am going off monitor for the next period of time. You will need to monitor the rest of session. You do not need to forward session to Doc Kymil until I have chance to edit the recording. Do you understand the request?"

Bodacia said in her even-toned female voice, "Professor Lyndyn, I will record your session. I will monitor vitals of all participants. I will not forward recording to Doctor Kymil until you have approved."

"Correct, Bodacia," Prof Lyndyn replied as he let the gray dionboda garment fall to the floor and then stepped from the pile of clothing, wearing his gray JMO running shorts.

Swyllo grinned as she adorned her yellow JMOs and asked, "Little onad, do you think we should double-team him for changing your naked rule?"

"Yup!" Jamyk laughed, stepping back into his green JMO shorts and then waved a hand towards Domyn and laughed heartily with evident gusto, "Cheat!"

"Awe help me!" Domyn laughed loudly, knowing he would probably not reach the container in the center of the gym before receiving first a wet and messy attack. "You owe me, Prof!"

"Domyn," Jamyk rasped with a devious grin and pointed toward the container in the center of the gym. "Go!"

Then Domyn ran toward the container. His speculation had been correct. He never reached the container before bulbs splashed onto his large body.

Universal awareness must be enjoying play of foolish human creatures now, he thought silently while he laughed.

Spec One: Domyn Through LaOgres
Chapter 4

"Cinsilono," Jamyk rasped, "Twenty...three."

Viewing malfunctioning coil in Flandecam through a visor eye-piece over his left eye, Domyn observed the same sight as his younger crewmate and agreed, "Awright, yes, that's a problem. We'll need to replace faulty Cinsilono. I'm confident that you can do that now, Jamyk."

When the thin boy above him in working shaft looked down at him, Domyn lost view from micro-cam in Jamyk's dionjocu helmet and instead his left eye saw himself peering up the shaft. His own wide shoulders just barely squeezed into the narrowing work shaft. His tan dionjocu helmet with its one eye-piece over his left eye adorned his large head not more than two feet below green Clarinkevs on Jamyk's small feet. Damn, Domyn thought to himself, his days of doing repairs alone were over now for sure. His big body would not fit into the work shaft anymore.

"Do you remember how to disconnect bad Cinsilono?" Domyn asked the almost seventeen-year-old boy clad in his light green dionjocu uniform, which already revealed sweat stains under the armpits.

Grimace convulsed over the young face showing from the green dionjocu helmet, which covered the entire head of Jamyk, except for face, and Jamyk snorted with annoyance, "Yup."

Slightly ashamed with himself for asking a question in the first place, Domyn announced hastily, "Of course you can, Jamyk. I'm sorry vulching toxx. You're as good with your hands as any Blue Jayer that I've ever known. You'll need..."

"Goodaure," Jamyk interrupted with a sharp hasty reply, "Thomaselli."

In his visor eyepiece, Domyn witnessed himself smile when he laughed, "Awright, you did learn very well, Jamyk. Did you hear that, Prof?"

From beneath him in the corridor below the access work shaft, a mellow, slightly nasal voice of Prof Lyndyn responded, "Indeed I did, Domyn. Rascal lad continues to surprise us all the time. His educational scores just barely kept him qualified for Blue Jay project. Yet when he needs to apply himself to piloting or mechanics, little rascal comes through…"

"Prof, please get pieces of equipment that he asks for," Domyn interrupted the older man, "we need to get this Flandecam back in acceptable condition."

"Yes, indeed we must fix this machine. I'll get pieces from mechbot that's been chasing me along this corridor. Damn, mechbot keeps bumping my legs. It won't let me alone down here. One would believe that it is afraid to be alone. But I am getting off my focus now. Yes, I must get the Thomaselli morpher to remove faulty Cinsilono, and of course the Goodaure torch to begin that process…" a nasal voice conversed with itself amidst sounds of feet shuffling and mechbot humming down below in corridor.

"Krispher," Jamyk yelled hoarsely with agitation down the work shaft, "girst."

As he wriggled his large body down the shaft to point where he could bend his torso to reach downward with his hand and arm, Domyn chuckled to himself about the situation with the boy of almost no words above and the man of constant flow of words below. They were both very good at their primary responsibilities. Now they did need to repair the Flandecam soon. Very strange trio of personnel had responsibility here now. They must work well as a unit. Domyn realized that Vivacio would not have brought them out of Saphyndenlairoum sleep midway through the cycle if there was not an emergency situation anticipated by artigence. They were currently between scheduled awakenings seven and eight. Yet they were here and they would do task, Domyn expected with confidence.

"Hurry!" Jamyk growled hoarsely and surprised Domyn by his potent demand.

Yes, Domyn pondered silently to himself, there was not any doubt that Jamyk was much testier present awakening than normal for the young lad. Was unusual irritability due to having been forcefully awakened midway through the regular Saphyndenlairoum sleep cycle? Would it somehow adversely affect the natural rhythm of Jamyk's zachymatis? Was that why the boy was agitated ntcurre awakening?

Domyn felt some personal discomfort and lack of focus himself. Were their bodies and minds adversely affected by not finishing the sleep which they were accustomed? Would so affect quality of their performance? Was it possible that they would make some unwitting mistake in repair of Flandecam? For a brief moment, Domyn experienced sense of panic.

Then Jamyk whispered with weariness, "Please... Friend."

While he waited for Prof Lyndyn below, Domyn heard what sounded almost like subdued repentance from the boy above. In the visor over his left eye, Domyn witnessed a brief smile escape from beneath the dionjocu visor over the sweating face of Jamyk. Smile eased panic and worry of Domyn. He felt little optimism flow into his awareness.

Yes, most likely Jamyk was exhausted and perhaps surly due to weariness. Yet Domyn sensed that his young comrade would find focus and determination to perform task efficiently and properly. That was a typical trait of Jamyk when under stress, Domyn mused. The lad seemed to tap into internal energy and focus when he became overwhelmed or challenged. Was this part of a mysterious anticipation that Domyn had often recently ascribed to enhanced zachymatis within the brain of Jamyk? Was this a realistic thought or just some wishful imagination? Domyn was not sure.

"Of course, of course I should send up Krispher gloves first. How could I forget this? Yet know it only makes sense to my feeble brain. And then the Neytier shield should be put in place before any torching," the man of forty-seven years of age muttered to himself in the corridor below, and then his round face within the gray dionboda cap with a one-eyed visor appeared at the bottom of the access shaft as Lyndyn continued his conversation, "Here, Domyn, can you reach these Krispher gloves? I'll climb up to you if you can't. I'm not so elderly yet that I can't do that kind of activity. No, indeed not yet am I that elderly..."

"That's fine, Prof. I can get them now," Domyn said hastily and then reached downwards past his tan Clarinkevs to grab the Krispher gloves from the rising hand of Prof Lyndyn. "I can take Neytier now also. My big hand is useful for something at least. I can't fit up there into the work port, but I can grip those tools without any problem. Here, Prof, give me the tools."

Below him Domyn watched the older man in the gray dionboda twist slightly to raise the other hand with the Neytier shield upwards toward his own sweating hands. With Prof Lyndyn now reaching up with both tools, his face showed to Domyn slight film of perspiration, even down there in the corridor. Flandecam did generate very substantial amount of heat through this access port. Domyn hoped that his sweaty grip could hold the extra weight of the Neytier shield, along with the Krispher gloves. His hand strength should be more than sufficient to compensate for any slippage due to sweat. He gripped the tools, twisted his body back to upright, and reached upward toward the green Clarinkevs on the feet of Jamyk.

"Krispher," rasped the boy, already having contorted his body at his narrow waist to enable him to reach down to Domyn.

Rivulets of sweat streaked down short thin legs inside the green dionjocu suit and pooled in the Clarinkevs to saturate the fabric. Droplets of perspiration fell from Jamyk's short thin fingers as he reached for and grasped pair of Krispher gloves from Domyn's much larger hand. Domyn observed the glistening sheen covering the face and neck of the boy.

While he watched Jamyk put on the gloves, still in contorted position, Domyn asked with genuine concern, "How are you doing with heat? Are you feeling okay?"

From beneath dionjocu the helmet and visor eye-piece over his right eye, the younger boy rolled his left eye, snarled to bare his teeth, and snorted in annoyance, "Yup... Neytier."

"I'm not disrespecting you, Jamyk. I'm just concerned. This heat is nasty enough to take energy right out of anyone," Domyn said, hastily sensing discomfort of the lad with any older person showing worry for him.

Small hand waved its fingers at Domyn, and Jamyk demanded brusquely, "Neytier."

As he handed up the Neytier shield to the hand gloved in the Krispher glove, Domyn's hand brushed against the wet feet inside the green Clarinkevs of Jamyk. He could feel heat radiate out of the small feet and hands of the boy. He could smell heat-stressed odor from Jamyk's appendages. The young lad was overheating now, Domyn worried. Yet should they stop this repair?

From the corridor below, Prof Lyndyn announced, "His temp is high but within specs for him. He seems in past to be able to handle more physical torment than the rest of us. That has amazed me during these many years how he can push his body to his limits and beyond when necessary. He should be okay for awhile, at least hopefully long enough to finish repair of the Flandecam. Don't worry, Neer Domyn. I'm watching his bio-specs. Bodacia is as well. The young lad is surprisingly resilient despite of his frail appearance. However, he should have some water though..."

"Yes, you're right, Prof. We do have to get this Cinsilono fixed soon to get this Flandecam back to perfect performance. Vivacio won't let us go back to sleep until the generator is repaired," said Domyn, and then after a moment of pause to take a deep breath in the heated air, he added, "Prof, get the Goodaure torch ready. If you can give that to me now, then we'll have that ready for him when he needs it shortly. Anything that we can do to help make this operation go quicker will aid our repairman up there. Then we can get him down into cooler air and some cherp cool shower."

Watching Jamyk with his exposed left eye, Domyn saw the younger boy straighten upward toward the open panel along the large Flandecam generator. With his right eye, Domyn observed the same sight as Jamyk currently viewed. The small, thin hands inside the gloves meticulously positioned Neytier shield around the Cinsilono coil to be replaced. Neytier shield would protect all surrounding coils and related parts of the Flandecam from the heat of the Goodaure torch.

With some personal pride in his own ability to teach this young rascal some of the techniques now being used in this repair, Domyn realized just how expertly Jamyk, though only seventeen years of age now, was performing this chore. In spite of his past lackadaisical attitude during hundreds of lessons during five years of this journey from the Zerosolis system toward the Sexto System, Jamyk had somehow managed to learn these mechanical skills. Yet Domyn had known for many years now that was who this rascal really was, a surprisingly unpredictable package in human form.

However, his thoughts were disturbed by reality suddenly as he reminded himself that one of his Flandecams was malfunctioning. Domyn felt an almost personal affront because the Flandecam was not operating at maximum efficiency. Well, he mused, at least it was not totally dysfunctional. Only one of the Cinsilono coils was faulty. However, as primary engineer of Wolf Streak Beta, Domyn felt an obligation to keep all of the mechanisms of Wolf Streak Beta functioning at maximum performance.

While the spacecraft traveled LaOgres space, maximum performance of the Flandecams was more than a worthy goal for personal pride. It was life necessity for each of his crewmates on the spacecraft. Domyn never let himself forget just how dangerous a predicament could be if the null-grav field around the spacecraft dissipated while in LaOgres space. The particles of the spacecraft and all humans onboard would most likely lose their cohesion of normal space and instead repulse apart as is norm in LaOgres space. That would not be very cherp for crew of Wolf Streak Beta, he mused. Now that critical reality required concentration and skills of the young rascal above.

The view in his visor eye-piece on the dionjocu helmet showed Domyn that the Neytier shield was in place, and then abrupt dizziness from sudden movement by Jamyk, the causing camera in the boy's helmet to blur a view teased Domyn's sight, and then he heard a croaking voice from above request with some authority, "Goodaure."

"The Neytier looks perfectly placed, Jamyk. You are doing cherp work," Domyn complimented and then reminded his younger mate, "be careful with the burn. You know how important this Flandecam is for the safety shield around this spacecraft."

"Yup," rasped the boy with obvious testiness, "now!"

Yes, Domyn pondered to himself, this Flandecam was very important to safety and propulsion of spacecraft. Actually all eight of the Flandecams were equally important. These generators worked in precise patterns to both drive the spacecraft through either LaOgres space or Debordo space and to also provide a null-space shield barrier around the Wolf Streak Beta while travelling through LaOgres space. Domyn hoped that Jamyk not only knew intricacies of a repair that the boy now attempted but also understood critical importance of correctly manipulating new Cinsilono when that was installed. However, that was several steps yet to be done, Domyn reminded himself. He must allow the boy time to perform the task with patience.

"You are doing very good work now, Jamyk. Just be cautious," Domyn said again, trying to let Jamyk know that his effort was appreciated, and then Domyn remembered that he should next tool for the boy so-called down the access shaft, "Prof, hand me that Goodaure torch. Jamyk is ready to morph off old Cinsilono. Do you have the Goodaure now?"

While Domyn twisted his large bulk in confines of the access shaft again to reach downward, he listened to Prof Lyndyn reply with slight huffiness in his nasal voice, "Indeed, of course I do. I've had it for some time now since you demanded of me to get it ready. Here, Domyn, I'll climb up a few steps on the access ladder to get this to you quicker. Are you feeling alright yourself? Is excessive heat up there beginning to bother you? Your big body may not react as well to that heat as Jamyk's thin body. You do have history of not adapting to very high temps as well…"

"Awright, Prof, I'm fine. Just get that Goodaure into my hand now," Domyn grumbled with agitation at the man's insinuation about his stamina, and yet he wondered to himself if he had been adversely affected by the intense heat already.

From above Jamyk called with his hoarse voice cracking with impatience, "Goodaure!"

When he finally could look downward toward Prof Lyndyn, Domyn saw the Goodaure torch waving in the tight opening of the access shaft and hastily grabbed at a tool with one hand, and then said with less terseness, "Thanks you, Prof, your foresight has made this chore go more efficiently for all of us. And perhaps I am feeling bit ornery now due to this heat. We all know how important this correction to the Flandecam is for safety of this spacecraft. There now, I've got it. My hand is sweaty, but I can grip this one tool well enough to bring it up to Jamyk."

Yes, Domyn thought, this was critically important chore. Without null-grav field surrounding this spacecraft, physical laws of LaOgres space would tear any normal molecules and matter in general into smallest bits of matter possible. That would definitely not be very cherp, Domyn reminded himself. He needed to keep his mind on task and on well-being of his crew here with him now trying to do this chore. He could not let himself be hindered by his own bout with the heat of this situation.

With his body slipping inside his dionjocu suit with all the sweat wetting his skin, Domyn carefully twisted his figure back upright and held the Goodaure torch up for Jamyk, and he said, trying not to let his own weariness enter into his voice, "Here, Jamyk, take this tool. Handle it carefully. Don't let your sweat allow it to slip from your hand. You may find that your gloves are beginning to loosen around your skin now because of sweat. Take that into account when you grasp this Goodaure. I know you know this already, but I do need to remind you for my own sake."

Jamyk's one exposed eye stared down at Domyn, and the boy said calmly, "Yup."

Then while Domyn watched this scene from both his own exposed eye and also from the perspective of the camera in Jamyk's helmet from his other eye, he experienced a strangeness of this dual opposing view, and his eyes blurred momentarily. Yet he did manage to see the boy grip the tool securely in a small hand and begin to contort himself back upright to continue the task on Cinsilono. Within seconds with changed view of Jamyk and his helmet, Domyn shook off the confusing dizziness.

Was this also an affect of the heat, he wondered, or just unnatural double view? He was not certain. He would be very happy when this chore was finished. His mind was taking too many side trips into his imagination than he would really like. He had briefly wondered if the boy could survive this odd and heated situation because of his possible connection to some mystical psychic realm tied to his very unusual zachymatis. Was Jamyk sustaining himself now with some unnatural strength?

Yet this was not a very useful consideration now during this critical repair, Domyn scolded himself. Yes, Flandecam was malfunctioning and it was giving off tremendous amount of heat. Most of this heat was shunted throughout the ship to provide heat for survival of human crew. But much was still here in this confined working shaft. Awright, Domyn insisted to himself, this heat was affecting his rather large body and sweat flowed freely in heat of this work shaft so close to the Flandecam. This was undoubtedly a reason for his discomfort now and his loss of focus. He needed to regain that focus for the sake of Jamyk, who was doing most of the task up there in the worst of the heat.

Now suddenly worried about the boy again so close to the heated proximity to the generator itself, Domyn asked while he wiped salty sweat from his face and eyes under the dionjocu helmet, "Prof, how are we doing concerning our health? Are there any signs of over-stressing our bodies yet? Is Jamyk still okay up there?"

"Both of you are pushing your upper limits on your bio-specs. Jamyk is just at his upper edge. He should be okay a short time more based upon his past history with stress. But he does need to take in water. We really need a portable air-conditioner as well, but we didn't think to supply mechbot with one. We were probably overly concerned with the emergency status, which triggered Vivacio to cause Bodacia to awaken you. But still this Flandecam does seem to be functioning, although apparently Vivacio read some fault within mechanism…"

"Awright, Prof, that's enough! That was more than I needed," sighed Domyn while watching Goodaure torch melt substance of older Cinsilono coil, and then he suggested, "Prof, get replacement coil. Jamyk will be ready for that piece soon."

"Indeed, right, yes, no doubt that is sensible notion. I'll get a new Cinsilono could from mechbot. We can save him some time from being in heat up there if we are ready with the next coil. I will be right back. Now if that mechbot hasn't moved off somewhere…" a voice of a man trailed away as Prof Lyndyn returned down into the corridor below and his gray dionboda cap disappeared from the bottom of the shaft.

With his left eye observing the scene in the visor eye-piece of his tan dionjocu helmet, Domyn was satisfied that Jamyk was doing unmorphing with torch according to standard procedure. The old Cinsilono coil would be out soon. The protective null-grav shield should be safely at full maximum strength. The an-grav currents and repellent forces of LaOgres space should be merely interesting phenomenon of universe through, which Wolf Streak Beta must travel to reach its destination in the Sexto System.

Just how many more sleeps before reaching the Sexto System? Domyn tried to calculate quickly in his head, but this heat was making his awareness sluggish for this mental activity. Was there eleven more, or maybe less? His mind could not focus. Domyn was moderately angered at his lack of mental awareness at that moment. His large body seemed to react poorly to intense heat. Again he worried that he might make a critical mistake during this repair operation. Perhaps destiny had selected the younger boy to be there just then to perform more mechanically challenging portions of process, Domyn thought abruptly.

His concentration of this long of thought dissipated when he witnessed Jamyk's gloved hand slowly pull the old Cinsilono coil from inside of the compartment of Flandecam. Jamyk's head was extremely steady in spite of his exhaustion and discomfort of heat. Jamyk was as usual very good when he needed to be and when he was forced by circumstance to focus on one specific activity.

"Old...ready," the sweating boy reported as he bent through the narrow work access shaft with coil in his hand, and then as Domyn reached up to take the old coil, Jamyk halted his downward reach suddenly and scolded harshly, "Stop!... Hot!"

Abruptly Domyn noticed his own bare hand not inches from the recently unmorphed coil, which would be very hot still after the Goodaure torch had heated composite, and with considerable embarrassment by his own careless forgetfulness, Domyn swore, "Awe damn my foolishness! How foolish can I be? Prof, get my pair of Krispher gloves. And you should put on yours as well. How foolish! This part will be very hot now."

By the time he contorted his wide torso downward, Domyn observed that Prof Lyndyn held up the light brown gloves, and the older man smiled knowingly, "I had already thought of that myself. Belatedly I must admit, but still it occurred to me just before Jamyk shouted. Here's your gloves, Domyn, and here's the replacement coil. The delay might do both of you some good anyway. Jamyk can probably use slight rest. In fact, Jamyk, you should drink some water now. You are most likely very dehydrated by now up in that concentrated heat. I can get water very soon, if you have patience..."

"Nope!" the tired boy gasped as he finally handed the old Cinsilono coil to Domyn, who now had his gloves in place, and then before pulling his small hand upward, Jamyk wiggled his fingers hastily and demanded, "Give."

Hastily Domyn gripped the old coil in one hand, and while he bent back downward toward Prof Lyndyn, exclaimed with renewed confidence and authority, "Awright, yes, Prof, hand me that replacement Cinsilono. I've learned over the years to let Jamyk go when he wants to do something important. This repair is almost finished and is still important. You're doing cherp, Jamyk. Take your time, be steady, and align the coil exactly in place. I'm sure that you know all that. But I feel as if I should help you in some way since I'm too fat now to fit up there myself."

"Not...fat," Jamyk rasped with a very slight chuckle, "giganormous!"

While he made this speech of encouragement to his younger friend and then listened to Jamyk's own words of friendship, Domyn twisted back upward with the new coil, and then with his wet hand within the Krispher glove, passed the new Cinsilono coil up to the gloved hand of sweating boy, saw the firm grip of a small hand around the coil, and then called down to Prof Lyndyn, "Prof, get Thomaselli morpher next. We're almost finished now. Let's hurry this process along. I'm not getting any cooler up here with my very large giganormous body."

"No doubt that is an appropriate term for you, Neer Domyn. However, I must still assert that Jamyk must get some water and at least short rest," stated Lyndyn from below and then continued with a sigh of resignation, "However, I also respected that you two stubborn young lads would disagree, so I also have this Thomaselli, which no doubt you need about now."

As he watched the older man hoist the other hand into view in the opening at the base of the access shaft, Domyn was somewhat surprised to see him holding the Thomaselli morpher, and Domyn chuckled with a hoarse voice, "Awright, that was cherp thinking, Prof. You seem to be more intuitive than me this awakening. Perhaps you have a bit of espersense yourself, Prof."

"Or no doubt, I am so much more acclimated to being awake during this middle part of the normal sleep cycle, my young Neer," Prof Lyndyn suggested with his own nasal chuckle. "Yet we must all have open mind to new possibilities. I would not mind having that type of talent. Indeed with such talent perhaps I could more readily psychoanalyze you two stubborn and often rebellious young lads. Then I would feel more cherp about helping you through your difficult years now..."

"Yup," interrupted Jamyk with a rasping and giggling sigh, "cherp!"

Squeezing his large arm and hand with the Thomaselli morpher alongside his body dressed in the wet and sweaty tan dionjocu, Domyn exclaimed with renewed optimistic enthusiasm, "Awright, we make cherp team, don't we? Even when one of us makes mistake or forgets some detail of our process, we back each other up for good of the task. We are truly a united pack of wolves."

Skinny fingers in the green Krispher glove meticulously gripped the Thomaselli morpher from Domyn's hand. The youngster was obviously exhausted, Domyn realized. The boy's arm rose slowly alongside his sweating torso in a very wet appearing green dionjocu suit. The Thomaselli seemed to be a heavy weight to the lanky arm. Domyn wished that he could go up the shaft and do the task for Jamyk. But he could not. He must hope that Jamyk had learned lessons well over five or more years of education and practice for this Blue Jay mission. He had to rely on the youngster to finish the repair and get the Flandecam back to maximum efficiency. Maybe Jamyk could tap into his odd espersense strength. That is if he really had such ability. Awe only knows, Domyn mused.

With apprehension and confidence dueling in his thoughts, Domyn watched in his visor eye-piece the young hands work the Thomaselli morpher on the replacement Cinsilono coil, and he praised with conviction in his tone, "That looks quite good, Jamyk. You are doing the job right. Just be steady and careful."

"Yup," Jamyk rasped with little emotion in his voice, "working."

From below Prof Lyndyn asked in his nasal voice, "No doubt you young lads have everything under control up there now, don't you? I've handed up all appropriate tools for you now, haven't I? I don't want to hold up the process by forgetting anything that you might need…"

Interrupting the older man, Domyn replied tiredly, "We're almost finished with the replacement, Prof. You can prepare the mechbot for the return to its bay soon. This appears to be the last step in the process, other than sending down tools and of course our little monkey up there."

"Monkey?" Jamyk laughed and yet his camera and hands held very steady as he continued the morphing task on the new Cinsilono. "Me?"

"Awright, yes, you are so like monkey at times, my friend," Domyn chuckled, trying to keep the boy positive and relaxed with some humor. "Your uncanny skills at climbing and twisting and going into places that rest of us can't or don't dare, all these traits are special to you, and I'm a bit envious that I can't do those things. Yes, my little friend, at times you remind me of ancient tapes of creatures called monkeys. And, awe knows, that is a very cherp compliment and not insult."

"Indeed, young lad, I must agree with this big gorilla of a young man," Prof Lyndyn joined in metaphorical humor, and then continued, "Your skills of acrobatics and leaping and contorting your body are astounding to me. Indeed, you do have the best attributes of a monkey, my young lad."

After few seconds and with a laugh, Jamyk ceased work with the Thomaselli morpher and gasped, "Finish... Check... Vivacio."

"Hold, Vivacio," Domyn ordered loudly and firmly. "Jamyk, come down from there. I don't want you that close to Flandecam at first check at full power. I believe that you have done the job correctly. Come down now. We don't need you to risk yourself up there now."

From the bottom of the access shaft, Prof Lyndyn stated with authority, "Vivacio, be prepared to perform preliminary check of the Flandecam six Cinsilono coil twenty-three. Partial power only, and wait for direct command by Neer Domyn."

"Nope," Jamyk refused with stubbornness in spite of his obvious exhaustion. "Not...back...up."

Neer Domyn swore to himself. He hated to make these types of decisions. Jamyk was probably correct in that once down from the working platform by the Flandecam, the boy could not climb back up in his present fatigue. If the boy stayed up there during the test, then his health could be harmed maybe. If he comes down and the test fails, how to proceed with repair, Domyn wondered. Should he wake Swyllo, who could fit up there as well? Or maybe Milyr, who might be thin enough for this access port? But that would mean a longer delay in repair. What should he do now? Domyn swore to himself again. He really did hate to make these decisions.

"Awright, enough!" he chastised himself tersely, and then with anguish in his voice, declared, "Awe guide my commands. Jamyk, come down now. You've done your part. Come down, my young friend. Hand me your tools first. You can't carry them and climb down the ladder at same time."

"Nope," Jamyk protested still as he cautiously pulled the Neytier shield from around the coils and then said adamantly, "stay... Test."

In a very firm and much more commanding voice than normal from the older man, Prof Lyndyn declared, "Obey Neer Domyn, Jamyk. Your bio-med reading is well beyond your upper stamina limit now. Even for you, Jamyk, any more heat, stress, and strenuous activity would be hazardous. Come down from the Flandecam now, my lad."

Domyn observed the boy hesitate for several more seconds, the Neytier shield dangling from one hand, the Thomaselli morpher from other, and then he croaked, "Tired."

"Now, Jamyk, before you fall, give me the shield and morpher," Domyn ordered sternly. "No, just drop the shield. It's of no use now. Come on, my friend. Drop the shield. You've done your duty up there. Come down now."

Swaying on trembling legs on the scant platform above, Jamyk peered down at Domyn. His narrow face dripped with sweat beneath the dionjocu visor and helmet. His visible left eye was flickering open and shut against the sting of salty perspiration. Finally he released the Neytier shield to the gravity of the shaft. It fell toward Domyn's large hand.

Batting useless light-weight shield off to the side, Domyn commanded, "That's good, now hang on tight and hand down the Thomaselli morpher, Jamyk. Vivacio must test the Flandecam soon. You must get down now. Let me have the morpher."

"Down," gasped a croaking voice, and Jamyk leaned downward through the narrow working shaft, morpher in his hand.

As Domyn felt the morpher hit his extended palm, he heard Jamyk mutter with calm clarity, "Fall."

Suddenly the small boy slid down the access shaft. His thin legs scuffed the ladder by Domyn's uplifted arm with the morpher in hand. Hastily grasping theladder rung with his other hand, Domyn cradled the falling boy between his own chest and ladder. His arm with the morpher swung reflexively around the lanky body. In this position, he made temporary nest for the boy.

"I'm dropping the Thomaselli now, Prof," Domyn shouted, releasing the morpher from his hand, not caring now whether it shattered on the corridor below.

"Just hang onto Jamyk, Domyn, and to that ladder," yelled Lyndyn. "I've got the tool. You take care of yourselves. I'm ready to catch you if you lose your handhold. I can climb up and help support Jamyk's weight."

"That's not necessary, Prof. We can manage ourselves," Domyn breathed heavily while nestling the thin body between him and the ladder, and then after a moment to catch his breath again, he asked, "Awright, Jamyk, are you okay to get down now? I can feel your squirming and panting. Are you ready to hang on to my neck with your arms? Then I can slowly get us both down this ladder."

Feeling Jamyk's head slide up against his chest, Domyn listened to the boy mutter, "Yup."

Then two thin arms snaked up his chest, over his shoulders, and then locked hands behind his thick neck. Carefully and gradually, Domyn climbed down the ladder with Jamyk hanging limp along his wide torso. Awe help me, Domyn thought. The dangling legs of Jamyk made his steps difficult but not impossible. Domyn's large strong hands easily clung to and released from the rungs of the ladder in cautious and sure rhythm until he felt his feet touch the corridor floor.

"I can take him now, Domyn," Prof Lyndyn offered.

Swinging one arm and hand under Jamyk's legs and the other behind the thin bony back, Domyn picked up the boy like a very small child and said through gasping breath, "No, that's okay, Prof. I've got my friend. Let's get him to a cool shower and then Med. I'm sure that Doc Kymil must have been awakened for this emergency as well as us."

The small face against his chest whispered, "Vivacio."

"Awright, Jamyk. Can you believe this, Prof?" Domyn laughed and then he called loudly, "Vivacio, run check at full power on Flandecam six Cinsilono twenty-three now. We might as well go for a win now, friends. Win or fail now, don't you think?"

A monotone male voice responded from corridor walls, "Neer Domyn, testing Flandecam six Cinsilono coil twenty-three at full power. I am beginning test now."

While they waited exhausted in the corridor for artigence Vivacio to grade their effort at repair, Domyn felt a cooler temp chill sweat on his back right through the damp dionjocu suit, and he sighed, "Damn, we do need a cool shower, Jamyk. Awe grant us cherp the Flandecam now."

"Indeed, my young lads, you could certainly improve your health situation with a good soapy, deodorizing shower," Prof Lyndyn grinned under a twitching nose as he gently pulled off their dionjocu helmets from their heated heads. "Indeed, lads, long session in the shower will do both of you some good. Let's hope that Vivacio has good data to relate for us now. He must have decided by now how the repair has functioned, shouldn't he?"

"Awe, damn test," Domyn grunted, surprising himself at his own careless disregard, and yet he felt irresponsibly nonchalant about results suddenly and continued, "To the showers now, shall we, friends?"

"No doubt, Neer Domyn, if that's what you wish now. But as long as you are both unharmed, other than some overheating and some dehydration, should we not confirm results of your efforts," chided Prof Lyndyn with a knowing grin.

"Vivacio, what is happening with the test on Flandecam six?" Domyn inquired with exasperation as he repositioned Jamyk's bony body in his arms.

Male artificial voice replied, "Neer Domyn, test of Flandecam six Cinsilono coil twenty-three results are positive at 99.6 percent of normal efficiency. Estimated longevity of this capacity is 137 days."

"Awright, Vivacio, why didn't you report this sooner?" Domyn complained wearily.

"Neer Domyn, you did not specify a time frame for my report," said artigence.

"Indeed well done, lads, well done," praised Prof Lyndyn as he stored the two dionjocu helmets on the mechbot.

"Damn, artigences, they're too literal with my commands," Domyn muttered in a hushed whisper, and then much louder, called, "Thank you, Vivacio."

"Neer Domyn, you are welcome, this is my function," Vivacio acknowledged.

Feeling satisfaction of a successful repair, Domyn chuckled, "Yes, we all did cherp work this awakening, especially you, Jamyk, you little Jayer. You'll be taking my position someday."

Hoisting the lanky small boy tighter and higher against his chest, Domyn felt a breath of Jamyk's words flutter against wet dionjocu over his chest as the boy mumbled, "Domyn...taught."

"Yeah, I suppose that I did try to teach you some of my engineering knowledge. At least we have cherp possibility to continue our mission toward the Sexto System. We may yet discover whereabouts of descendents of those daring and adventurous colonials of so many hundreds of years ago. You are a cherp student of my wayward teaching, Jamyk," Domyn exclaimed.

"Indeed he is, my lad. And you are fine teacher," praised Prof Lyndyn. "And now off to those cleansing showers."

Without protest Domyn carried Jamyk after the older man through the corridor.

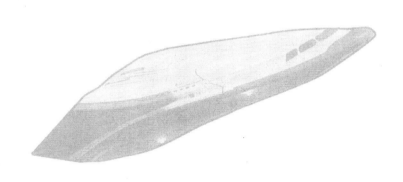

Spec One: Domyn Through LaOgres
Chapter 5

"Vulching fine mams on Whyvvi now, hey, little peener," blurted Milyr. "You toxx vulchers did notice her new womanhood, didn't you?"

Domyn chuckled and then said, "I'm just surprised that you haven't made any remarks about this until we are in the eleventh awakening in LaOgres, Milyr. I was sure that you would start this topic at the very start of this stage of our journey to Sexto System. Are you not paying attention to our girls anymore with all your fem fans on all five Steppingstones?"

"Vulch, Domyn, you know that's not the case. I'm always watching our own wolf bitches for eventual maturing into fine young ladies. But they just seem to be so slow to show their mams compared to females on Steppingstones. However, finally our Whyvvi is starting to show her mams now. With that slender figure, those mams really stand out and attract my eyes. She's not flat. I sure could not avoid seeing mams this awakening."

Catching a glowing pulse on the receiving end of his Zapstik, Domyn smiled at his taller teammate and agreed, "Yes, definitely, she is a young woman now. I noticed Nyba earlier this voyage since leaving Steppingstone Quinto. Our girls of Wolf Streak Beta are starting to reveal their maturing bods..."

"Ha...yeah, like she was the last voyage between Cuatro and Quinto. Not flatty anymore! She certainly does not look like Jamyk here anymore," Milyr joked while patting his lanky chest with one hand and holding his Zapstik in the other.

"Mams!" Jamyk giggled as he grinned and pretended to cup his nipples on his very thin chest with his hands while also holding his Zapstik. "Muscles?"

As he pressed the trigger on his own Zapstik to release pulse and toss it toward Jamyk, Domyn laughed at their antics and called to Jamyk, "Little man, you don't have much of either yet. Awright, be ready, here it comes."

While saying this, Domyn watched the thin boy in green JMO shorts swiftly swing his Zapstik away from his chest and deftly catch pulse on end. There the pulse glowed briefly a fluorescent orange. Jamyk grunted loudly with smile perhaps in agreement. Then with a slight twist of his scrawny torso, threw the pulse to Milyr.

"The pup may not have much up there yet, but he's almost more than Swyllo. That little wolf bitch Swyllo is still vulching flatty. Isn't she nineteen like us, Domyn? You have noticed how slow she is to get the round mams, haven't you, Domyn? I'm sure Jamyk has noticed this," Milyr quipped as he snagged the glowing orange pulse on the end of his Zapstik and then continued with sudden sarcasm to his tone, "Vulch, maybe that's why Chitir gets clutch for her. Maybe he likes flatties. Hey, that big vulcher, maybe he doesn't like girls!"

"Nope," Jamyk retorted in defense of his friend, "Loves...girl."

Spinning dramatically to emphasize his remark and then tossing the pulse back to Jamyk, Milyr sneered, "Vulching for sure, Chitir likes flatties, like you and Swyllo, little peener. The big toxx gets vulching clutches for flatties. He doesn't know about love!"

"Love!" repeated the small boy as he plucked a rapid moving pulse from the air, spun in pirouette, and released the orange pulse back to Milyr, "Love!"

Easily catching the pulse on the end of his Zapstik, Milyr leered with grin, "Love, not vulching likely, Chitir just wants pure vulching sex, if he can get his sorry manhood to work right. That's what he really wants, pure sex. But I'm not even sure that big toxx likes girls at all."

While he observed Milyr reposition his tall, lanky figure to pass the pulse toward him, Domyn said in his deep calm voice, "Don't believe Chitir likes Swyllo for looks or sex alone, Milyr. That relationship is beyond hormonal. Of course with sex inhibiter in our nutrient, that's probably a cherp situation for them. I believe that they have been close friends for our entire Blue Jay journey since we met back in outer stations of the Zerosolis System. They are friends who have found connection beyond hormones and biology."

"Maybe, Domyn, but vulching antemgebemarzex is only an inhibiter for postponement. It doesn't totally stop our maturation or our desires. I vulching know that for certain. Look at me, I'm rutting primo to fems throughout the Steppingstone chain," chirped the six-and-a-half-foot tall nineteen-year-old boy dressed in only his lavender JMO shorts and Clarinkev running shoes as he tossed the pulse to Domyn.

"Hah!" laughed Jamyk loudly and sharply with mocking disdain and disbelief in his voice, "Nope!"

Apparently an abrupt bark from Jamyk caused Milyr to lose concentration for his toss of pulse was aimed at Domyn's tan Clarinkev covered feet, well off normal accuracy of young athlete. Twirling his Zapstik swiftly, Domyn caught the glowing pulse just above his feet. A glance downward revealed slight coating of sweat on his bare legs. The tan JMOs were clinging to his hips with moist sweat. Glancing upwards again, he noticed gleaming perspiration on lanky form of Milyr. Then with a turn of his head, he saw a similar sheen on skin of a shorter form of Jamyk.

"Awright, I can see that we're warmed up enough to do some shooting on goal. Let's do some two on ones with three of us here now," Domyn declared, and then with smirk at Milyr, added, "Awe help your accuracy, super stud. We do want to get a few shots in against Jamyk this awakening."

"Vulch, Domyn, I'm sorry about that! But it was an accident," whined Milyr, and then with more confidence, boasted, "I'll get many vulching goals this awakening against this little one nad peener."

"Nope!" declared Jamyk in his raspy hoarse voice and laugh, "None!"

"Vulching yeah, I will, you little peener. I'm ready and warmed up now. Talking about wolf bitches and fine mams gets me hot. When I'm hot, I can score vulching lot of goals. Be ready, little one nad," warned Milyr with a grin and challenging wave of his Zapstik at Jamyk.

"Ready," stated Jamyk with an answering grin and tone of confidence in his short reply. "Try."

As he sauntered to a small recessed alcove in the wall, Domyn suggested, "I'm thirsty. Anyone else thirsty? Jamyk, Doc Kymil says to make sure that you stay hydrated. Milyr, you wouldn't want to cramp up in the middle of your best move, would you?"

"Yup," Jamyk agreed, following him to the wall. "Thirsty."

Milyr paused and complained, "I'm always thirsty. But, vulch, I hate drinking that nasty nutrient with vulching antemgebemarzex in it. Knowing as long as I drink toxx nastiness, it'll slow my sexual maturation. That's vulching nasty, especially for a primo guy like me!"

At the alcove in the wall, Domyn pulled out a cup of liquid nutrient composed mostly of water with appropriate sustenance within that was required for the human crew of Wolf Streak Beta, handed it to Jamyk, and then chuckled, "Yet, super stud, you're claiming to be always immune to its affects and always was ahead of the rest of us males in maturity. Your tales about all fems at five Steppingstones…"

"Vulch, don't believe everything I say," Milyr protested, but then after a few seconds of silence, added vigorously in his own rebuttal, "But they are all true, of course. Trust me, guys, they are all vulching true. Would I make up tales like that just to impress you?"

"Yup!" Jamyk snorted with a hint of disbelief in his voice, and then after drinking a liquid nutrient, he rasped with laugh, "Toxx!"

"Don't laugh, little one nad peener! You're at least two years behind the rest of us. I never heard Doc talking about any hair removal from your body," Milyr sneered with a mix of compassionate joking and some malicious mocking in his voice as Domyn interpreted tone, and then Milyr added with grin, "It could be vulching years before you mature into manly adulthood."

"Nope!" Jamyk smiled, glanced down into his JMO shorts now pulled open with one hand, and then rasped with a laugh, "Huge!"

"Awright, enough of this silliness!" Domyn laughed, and then trying to regain sense of mature composure, continued, "We're all maturing, slow as it seems, according to Doc. Well, just look at our girls, as womanly as they are getting, even with sex inhibiter. Doc says my hair tuft gets more vigorous with each awakening. Drink up, Milyr. A nutrient won't make you lose your manhood."

"Nope!" Jamyk agreed, still peering down into his green JMO shorts. "Manly!"

Dropping his Zapstik to floor, Milyr strolled to Jamyk, gently cuffed the smaller boy in the shoulder, and chortled, "You can't lose something you never had, pup."

While drinking down his own cup of nutrient, Domyn heard Jamyk quip with almost comic resignation, "Never."

"Drink that vulching antemgebemarzex, pup, and you may never," Milyr teased while shaking the boy's neck lightly from the back and then continued, "But, vulch, you're right, Domyn, about the hair. Doc Kymil did tell me the same thing. My hairy streak seems to grow back thicker with each sleep cycle. My natural manliness is just too vulching powerful for even anti-hair protocol through genetics and bio-chemicals designed for us by Blue Jay. I'm just too vulching manly to be stopped!"

"Awe enlightens! There you see, Milyr, drinking this nutrient doesn't stop your growth to eventual manhood. Here, have a drink. It'll help your athletic effort," Domyn stated in as an encouraging tone as he could muster while grinning and handing a cup of nutrient to his taller companion.

While his long fingers traced a path from his navel down his lanky lower abdomen to the top of his light violet JMOs, Milyr said with speculative anticipation, "Perhaps I can convince Doc not to remove my hairy streak when we get to Sexto. It will be such a convenient conversation starter with fems. They could follow it down to our mutual delight…"

"Hah!" blurted Jamyk, glancing up at his taller friend, "Talk?"

"Well, Milyr, I don't believe that you really have an interest in conversation with girls, do you?" Domyn chuckled, still holding the drink out to the other young man.

As long fingers continued to absently stroke a patch of currently bare skin between his JMOs and his navel, Milyr took a drink with his other hand and admitted with a throaty laugh, "Vulch, now, Domyn. I guess talk is not on my mind when I plan for fems. Talk is only the starter, then to more cherp clutches perhaps when I'm lucky. My manliness will amaze colonial girls in Sexto."

Witnessing Milyr gulp down the nutrient, Domyn commanded, "Awright, enough of this fantasy talk. Let's get back to our practice before we cool down again. Jamyk, are you ready?"

Just finishing the second cup of nutrient, Jamyk tossed the empty cup into hollow in the base of the alcove in the wall and replied in his raspy voice, "Yup."

As they retrieved their respective Zapstiks, Milyr muttered with a leering tone to his baritone voice, "But I wasn't talking fantasy. I really do have ambitions of clutching fine fems, especially fine colonial fems with big mams. But first let's score many goals on this one nad little peener."

Running to the wall where the goal circle was attached eleven feet above the floor, Jamyk challenged loudly and defiantly, "Try!"

Then the five-foot tall boy leaped up and reached with an extended arm to the center of the one-yard wide goal. When the end of the Zapstik touched the center dot, an electrified orange pulse in shape of a sphere about seven inches in diameter suddenly appeared to jump from the dot onto Jamyk's Zapstik. Domyn realized from many years of experience that Jamyk had initiated a pulse with a pull of the trigger on the rod of the Zapstik. Before the boy's feet landed back to the floor, Jamyk twisted his narrow torso and threw the pulse from end of his Zapstik toward Milyr.

As the electrified pulse ball flew straight at Milyr's crotch, Jamyk yelled with a laugh, "Nads!"

"Vulch!" Milyr shrieked while hastily spinning his Zapstik to intercept the pulse.

"Hah!" Jamyk laughed with gleeful gaiety, "Manly!"

Laughing at Milyr's sudden terror, Domyn reminded himself from personal experience of a jolt of discomfort that the pulse could give to flesh unprotected by a McAnderwike uniform, but he still called out in support, "Here, quick, before Jamyk is ready."

"Vulch, little peener!" Milyr shouted with trembling irritation to his voice, and then he spun as if to pass to Domyn but instead continued momentum of his long arms into a shot at the goal above Jamyk's head and yelled at same time with a gasp, "Are you trying to make me like you? Only one nad now?"

Although the pulse moved toward the goal very rapidly at a sharp angle, Jamyk jumped and reached with his Zapstik to catch the orange pulse before it contacted the circle, and the boy panted after the catch, "Manly...nads."

Startled by the seemingly graceful ease with which Jamyk stopped the unexpected shot, Domyn wondered if the boy's feet had ever touched the floor from his earlier leap? Had the boy leaped before Milyr had made the shot? For a second, his speculations caused Domyn to hesitate. Was he seeking to discover too much in anticipation of Jamyk? Was he letting his imagination intrude on his athletic attention? Awright, enough, he chastised himself, this was not time for this.

"Vulching lucky little peener!" Milyr cursed.

However, Domyn rejected his temptation to trace his memory of the previous minute to check what he remembered of Jamyk's actions. Instead his focus keyed on the younger boy as Jamyk released the pulse in an arc high over Domyn's head. Jumping from a standstill, Domyn lifted his Zapstik as high as his muscular arm could stretch to just barely snare the pulse before it flew over his head to the far end of the court. If the pulse had gotten past his reach to the end of the gym, it probably would have faded into nonexistence if no Zapstik renewed energy within seven seconds.

As he descended with a captured pulse, Domyn tried to catch Jamyk out of position and unprepared. He swung his arm and the Zapstik downward and released the pulse in an underhanded shot near the floor with intention of rising sharply upward toward the exposed goal. However, just as Domyn released the pulse, Jamyk stepped forward two strides, leaped into the rising pulse, and caught it on the end of his Zapstik. As the end of the boy's Zapstik glowed fluorescent orange not yards from his face, Domyn wondered, how had the boy anticipated that unusual underhand shot?

Without his permission, his mind wandered into his usual imaginative foray. Domyn asked himself, would Bodacia have recorded Szczygiel Shine in the brain of Jamyk just then? Would artigence have found an unusually high intensity of zachymatis activity? Then as Jamyk threw the pulse hastily between his two opponents, Domyn scolded himself silently, no, no, you big toxx, don't focus on fantasy now, pay attention to what you are doing. Pay attention to this practice.

"I got it, Domyn," Milyr shouted, and then with his long legs, ran rapidly to the other end of the court where the pulse had bounced off the far wall.

Shaking his head at his own befuddlement, Domyn prepared to get back into the mental aspect of this exercise. His eyes watched his tall companion snag the fading pulse on the end of the Zapstik. His mind tried to focus on scoring goals against their very talented and apparently lucky adversary, Jamyk. Then as Milyr raced him toward Jamyk, Domyn felt ready to challenge the boy.

But no matter what type of shot they tried, Jamyk blocked, caught, and deflected everything that they tossed at his goal. When they feigned shots and then tried tip-ins, which were tricky to perform due to the time delay between absorbing the pulse and then triggering release for the shot, Jamyk stopped them. Although a much quicker release, shooting on the fly where the Zapstik did not absorb the pulse but merely deflected it, were no more successful. Not even constant swearing and threatening taunts from Milyr could disturb the younger boy from preventing any goals.

After almost eleven minutes of various offensive strategies and two on goalie shooting sequences, Domyn and Milyr were frustrated thoroughly by their lack of success. Breathing heavily and sweating profusely after their various and vigorous attempt to breach Jamyk's goal, two companions eyed each other at the other end of the gymnasium after chasing down the pulse batted away from their possession by Jamyk. With hands on knees, Domyn wondered against his own better judgment if Jamyk had used something more than his own physical skills and normal senses to throttle their attempts. Awe only knows, Domyn mused quietly to himself.

As Milyr bounced the pulse off the wall in obvious annoyance and then recaptured it on the end of his Zapstik, he muttered through a panting breath, "Vulch, what's wrong with us, Domyn? Is little one nad peener just that vulching good, or do we just lick toxx?"

"More!" called their rival from the far end of the gymnasium as Jamyk skipped lightly on floor beneath goal circle. "Come!"

Turning his head to glance at the small boy, Domyn admitted, "Awe knows, it does seem like he is so much better at focusing now while we are in LaOgres travel than when we play competitions at Steppingstones. But then during those contests, there are so many more interfering factors to his concentration. Here he must only watch two of us."

"Vulch, he's kicking our toxx nasty!" Milyr griped, bouncing the pulse off the floor with his Zapstik repeatedly and nervously. "I would vulching like to get at least one score off him this awakening."

"Come!" shouted Jamyk hoarsely while waving his Zapstik at them and then at the goal circle, "Try!"

Still bent over at his waist and drawing in deep breaths of air, Domyn suggested in a low hushed voice, "Let's charge him with cycling give-and-go about half court. After you get the pulse back from me there, give me a second or two to set the screen for you."

"Vulch, yeah, let's see if one nad can stop what he can't see. Vulching cherp notion, Domyn," agreed Milyr with a conspiratorial whisper and smile, and then loudly he shouted, "Here we come, you little peener!"

As Milyr trotted toward half court, Domyn circled around behind him. When he passed his companion again, Domyn caught the orange pulse from Milyr and then veered toward the center about seven yards in front of Jamyk. There he feigned the shot while Milyr circled around his position. Then when Milyr ran by him, Domyn passed the pulse back to Milyr. Then he ran directly in front of Jamyk no more than two yards away. He could hear Milyr's heavy footfalls moving around him and behind him. Jamyk had not shifted his position during the entire sequence of this maneuver.

Knowing that Milyr was now positioning behind him for quick release shot over his head, Domyn stepped closer to Jamyk to further block the smaller boy's sight with his large body. Before Domyn set his last step though, he witnessed Jamyk jump up and block pulse just as it buzzed just over his own head. Domyn could feel the electric tingle of the pulse on his bald scalp; it was so close just before Jamyk batted it away.

When pulse bounced freely to side wall, Milyr swore loudly from behind Domyn, "Vulching no! That's not possible!"

"Hah!" rasped Jamyk in a gleeful voice as he twisted his form in mid-air in direction of the bouncing pulse and then called, "Chase!"

"Vulch!" Milyr cursed again from the side of the court away from the pulse where his running momentum had moved him after his shot. "You'll have to get it, Domyn, hurry!"

However, as he turned to go after the pulse, Domyn witnessed Jamyk land on one foot and begin running stride with the other the moment his second foot touched the floor. Laughing the younger boy in green JMO shorts raced to free the pulse and snatched it on the end of his Zapstik. With continued laughter as his Zapstik glowed fluorescent orange at the lifted end, Jamyk dashed to the far end of the gymnasium.

"You toxx little peener pup!" Milyr cried out with frustration in his cracking baritone voice while he chased the shorter boy, "Give me that vulching pulse, you little one nad peener!"

"Nope!" Jamyk shouted back at Milyr through laughter and panting breaths, "Come!"

Trotting to the center of the court with the intention of cutting off the return lane alongside of the court on which Jamyk seemed to be heading, Domyn chuckled as he watched the boy running from the taller young man in lavender JMO shorts. Both of their slender bodies glistened with wet sweat. Their JMOs stuck to their hips and waists as if glued. In a few seconds of viewing this action, Domyn thought to himself, guess they had a cherp workout so far, cherp enough for Doc Kymil's requirement for cardio exercise.

But then his mind reminded him that they had been at this high level of activity for less than nineteen minutes or maybe as much twenty-three minutes, he could not be certain. When he made his attempt to corral Jamyk alongside the wall, Domyn was less than enthusiastic actually since he did not mind if this running and chasing went on for several more minutes. With a rapid scamper and a sudden dart-like rabbit, Jamyk eluded his half-hearted try at stealing the pulse from the boy's Zapstik.

Barely avoiding collision with Domyn, Milyr's lanky figure dashed by in sweaty pursuit and cursed breathlessly, "Vulch...hah...yah...little...peener... hah...I'll...kick...hah...your toxx... Maybe... I'll chop off your one nad, hah!"

For more than a few minutes, this new game of keep away continued with Jamyk panting and giggling. With many curses gasped into the warm air, Milyr tried to follow and intercept the younger boy. As Jamyk scurried around the court, he held his Zapstik high above his head. At the upper most tip of the Zapstik, the prize of fluorescent orange glowed brightly. Each time Milyr seemed about to close on the smaller boy and steal the pulse Zapstik-on-Zapstik, Jamyk ducked, dodged, or darted in a sudden direction, the taller boy could not manage as rapidly or as deftly.

"Vulch this!" Milyr yelled suddenly as he threw his Zapstik to the floor, and then shortly after few loping strides he tackled Jamyk contrary to etiquette of sport. "I'm not letting this little peener make fool out of me this long. I've got your toxx now!"

As two bodies fell to the floor, Jamyk tried to swing his Zapstik with the electrified pulse toward Milyr. However, Domyn was close enough to reach out with his own Zapstik and steal the pulse from the Zapstik of Jamyk. While his eyes viewed two rolling and squirming forms on the floor, Domyn pulled the trigger to release the pulse into the farthest corner where it would fade to nothing within seven seconds.

"Awright... I guess...it is cherp time...for break," Domyn panted while confirming with his eyes that the pulse faded out harmlessly in the corner.

"Nope!" giggled Jamyk, starting to rise from the floor, "More!"

However, Milyr reached out with his long arm, grabbed the thin leg just above the ankle, and snorted, "Oh, no, you're not getting away yet, you little peener!"

"Vulch!" Jamyk swore, trying to kick and twist away. "More!"

"Vulching no way, get back here," Milyr demanded as his left hand snagged onto the waist band of the green JMO shorts around the hips of Jamyk, then while swinging the struggling boy off balance to the floor again, he snorted, "Yeah, you're not going to get away from me now."

"No!" Jamyk whined, squirming still to stand up again, "Milyr!"

"Vulch no, little one nad, you're not even going to be able to run right out of your shorts now. I've got you for sure now," Milyr yelled wearily as he rolled his almost seven-foot tall figure on top of the five-foot tall form of Jamyk, and then as his lanky torso settled perpendicular across Jamyk's chest, he ordered firmly, "Vulching rest now, you toxx pup! Stop squirming and take time to rest. Give me some peace!"

Observing the thin form of Jamyk writhe briefly beneath Milyr and then concede to entrapment, Domyn agreed with Milyr, "Awright, yes, let's rest a short time. Maybe we can take some more nutrient drink. Then we can go back to more practice."

Slowly turning his bald perspiring head to peer at Domyn, Jamyk asked with a sudden calm seriousness to his voice, "Why?"

Taken aback by the unusually thoughtful tone of query and steadiness of gaze of the narrow face of Jamyk, Domyn was silent for several seconds while only panting breaths sounded in gymnasium, but then finally he replied, "Well, we want to be ready to defeat Fox Flash Alpha next time we play them in real competition."

"Next?" Jamyk asked, still holding Domyn's eyes with a calm steady gaze, "Next?"

"Awright, well, yes, next game against Fox Flash Alpha," Domyn repeated with bewilderment about what exactly Jamyk was concerned.

After another moment of quiet, Milyr inquired in solemn, unusually serious tone for him as well, "Domyn, will there be a next game? Will there ever be another tournament for us Jayers? We have been wondering, what will we really be doing from now on when we get to Sexto System? Even our very sensible and logical Whyvvi has mentioned her doubt about this. When we reach Sexto, will there be more Pulseball games against Fox Flash or Lynx Blaze or anyone?"

"Again?" Jamyk asked hoarsely, "Sexto?"

Their sober tone and their unmistakable worry about not playing anymore games stunned Domyn. He did not know how to answer this confusion. He had never really thought about this situation as a problem. This going to the Sexto System and facing the unknown there had been in the future for his entire life so far. What could he say to his friends now to relieve their concern? How could he get them to return their attention to their play and practice? Or was that important anymore, he wondered silently to himself.

Yet his natural spirit and jovial outlook brought possibilities from his memory, and Domyn replied with enthusiasm, "Awright, of course we will play Pulseball again. The tournament has followed the Blue Jay mission faithfully all the way through hundreds of years of history of this Blue Jay mission from home world in Zerosolis System to each of Steppingstones as they were created and populated. Steppingstone Sexto won't be any different."

"Maybe," Jamyk declared, "Different."

"Vulch, Domyn, there is no Steppingstone Sexto there," Milyr protested, peering up from his prone sprawled position on top of Jamyk. "We may be only humans when we get to Sexto System, maybe foxes will be there, too. Suppose we don't find missing colonials? Vulch, what if we are ordered to return to Quinto? Domyn, you must have thought about what happens when our part of Blue Jay is over. What vulch happens to us then? Will we be remembered by billions of people and all my fans back in the Zerosolis System?"

As two familiar faces of his constant companions of most of his lifetime stared at him with puzzled and worried expressions, Domyn suddenly realized that he had not really considered this aspect of their Blue Jay journey. What happens when they fulfill their mission? Since joining Blue Jay, his concerns had been a pursuit of project, learning science, and maintaining sci-tech. Yet had he ever thought about completion of mission, and then what would occur afterwards? Domyn was not sure at that moment. However, he reminded himself that Blue Jay was ongoing always. There was a plan, he mused, wasn't there?

Yes, a plan, Domyn thought to himself and took enough encouragement from believing in a possible plan to answer his companions while dropping to his knees so as not look down at them, and he replied, "Awright, we all know that the Blue Jay Corp of Engineers is already prepping spacecraft with construction materials for Stepping Stone Sexto. Once we scout the Sexto System, whether we find colonials or not, we will sanbeam comm by way of Buffalardi beacons back to Steppingstone Quinto. Then Blue Jay MisCom can decide what construction parameters are most appropriate. They should launch most likely within a month of our comm. Corp of Engineers should arrive in less than year to Sexto System just as we will after we get through LaOgres. There will be Steppingstone Sexto. And, if our predictions are correct, then there will be colonials there to greet us and show us their wondrous achievements."

"Us?" Jamyk squeaked, "Wolf?"

"What about us, Domyn? Our part ends at the Sexto System. Once we report to the Blue Jay MisCom, Wolf Streak Beta's mission ends at Sexto. And really so does duty of Fox Flash Alpha! What if we don't find colonials there in Sexto? Do you really want to go back to Zerosolis and live a normal life just like all billions there? Vulch no, Domyn, we're Jayers!" Milyr exclaimed, slapping the floor with both of his hands for emphasis.

When a young man did so, apparently the full weight of his upper torso settled onto the chest of the smaller thin boy, for Jamyk suddenly wailed in torment, "Ah!... Hurt!"

"Awright, let him up, Milyr," Domyn demanded hastily though the long figure was already rolling off the trapped boy.

"Sorry, peener pup! I get nasty careless sometimes. Are you okay?" Milyr asked with genuine sincerity to his voice as he arose into a sitting position not far from Jamyk, and then with a sudden laugh, Milyr added, "Vulch, wolf pups are nasty tough anyway. Jamyk, you're tough toxx!"

Still laying face up on the floor, Jamyk glanced at Milyr and gasped with a mild grin, "Toxx!"

"Yeah, vulching toxx, all of us Jayers, aren't we? But we're tough toxx! Let's hope we find colonials. I wager fems are tired of men there. They will be looking for some new primo young lads like us, hey, Jamyk?" Milyr exclaimed while he leaned back on his long arms with hands splayed slightly behind his back for support, but then he peered to Domyn and asked again with soberness, "But, Domyn, what will happen to us in Sexto? Will Jayers there be forgotten? And what will be the fate of vulchers on Lynx Blaze? What will they do next, just go home to Zerosolis? Will they just sit their collective toxx on Quinto if they get that far?"

"Awright, Milyr, why do you have so many serious thoughts now? This is totally not like you," Domyn laughed, trying to get the other boy to get back to his normal irresponsible self, and then he continued with mirth in his voice, "Vulch, you two pups should be having fun now at your age on this historic journey. We are famous Jayers who will be legends to go into the Sexto System. Nearly everyone in Zerosolis will be blue with envy. Anyone of them would wish to be one of you pups!"

"Pups?" Jamyk asked with his bare forehead wrinkled in a comic scowl, "Nope...wolves!"

"Vulch, yeah, little peener, by the time we pop into Sexto and then find those lost colonial fems, you will be a vulching wolf. Oh, you'll not be as wolfy as my primo self but more wolf than that toxx Chitir," Milyr laughed, and then after a moment of hilarity, added, snickering, "Vulch, yeah, even with only one nad, you'll be more wolf than vulching Chitir."

"More than," Jamyk rasped in a panting breath, "...toxx lynx!"

"Vulcher for sure, you'll be more man than any of those tomcats of lynxes, especially toxx Lusty who is their bare toxx runner for their kittens to chase..." Milyr scoffed with glee.

Now listening to the banter of his companions, Domyn was pleased to have their attention on more trivial issues again. This was the way he liked to have them relax when they were here in the gym. This was not the place for overly serious considerations, he thought.

While their laughter continued, Domyn abruptly discovered himself to be daydreaming about what possible sci-tech advances colonials had made in over 500 years since their ancestors departed from Zerosolis. This was an odd daydreamm he mused, but let his mind wander into such questions as how had colonials adapted their sci-tech during years of isolation from other civilizations of humans? Whatever colonials had managed to achieve, there should be some very intriguing sci-tech to discover in Sexto System, Domyn thought optimistically. Yes, he told himself silently, he did have something to look forward to in the near future in Sexto System.

Maybe life after Blue Jay would not require honing his skills at Pulseball after all, he mused, and then asked aloud with some relief, "Awright, wolves, you won't mind if we halt this Pulseball practice and instead finish Doc's required exercise session in running the corridor, would you?"

"Vulch," they both yelled in unison, "No!"

"Awright, then let's go to do some running. Put away our gear here. Get another drink of nutrient, enough to energize you for about three fast-paced miles," Domyn commanded, and then as he stood up, asked, "What program do you want to input for this exercise session?"

"Rain forest jungle," Milyr replied hastily.

"Night," Jamyk added before Domyn could ask for starting time, and then the boy added, "Moonlight."

"Awright then we'll run at night in full moon in the jungle forest," Domyn declared, and then as he watched others arise from the floor, "You lads won't be afraid of running in darkness with all those wild animal and bird noises all around you, will you?"

"Vulch no! Wolves run best at night. We own vulching night!" Milyr boasted as he playfully swung his long arm at Jamyk. "You're not afraid of the dark are you, little man?"

"Nope," Jamyk rasped.

"Even with some devious and surprising interactive creatures sometimes appearing in programs of Khebol, you will not be afraid, will you?" Domyn laughed, striding to the alcove with the nutrient dispenser.

While picking up three Zapstiks and heading to the equipment cubicle, Milyr bragged, "Wolves can outrun and outwit any surprise created by that toxx Khebol. Vulch his foxy toxx, Khebol creates only ghost creatures, right, Jamyk?"

"Yup," Jamyk replied as he joined Domyn at the nutrient alcove and then asked, "Drink?"

"Of course, little man, here," Domyn replied and then reached into the alcove for a cup of nutrient for his younger comrade. "You should drink some also, Milyr."

While Milyr responded with his usual pessimistic opinion of value of nutrient and his future sex life, Domyn smiled to himself. Should he be alert for a ritual ambush somewhere along the running path? Would two lads scheme to dash ahead in the moonlight and set a trap for him again this time? He smiled again at the thought, most likely. They needed to have that type of sneaky camaraderie against him on occasion. They usually deserved opportunity.

Domyn laughed again. Only universe could really know what was in the minds of those two young men now. Their thoughts were most likely much more than either spoke into conversation. And this was presuming much in the mind of Milyr, who spoke often in habit. Yet Jamyk kept his words to such a minimum that no one truly knew his inner thoughts or feelings most of the time. Between them these young men were the unlikeliest comrades to play in this universe.

Awe knows, probably the universe could use a cherp laugh now anyway.

SPEC ONE: DOMYN THROUGH LAOGRES
CHAPTER 6

On the thirteenth awakening while journeying in LaOgres space, Neer Domyn sat comfortably in a brown chair on the ConCen of Wolf Streak Beta.

"There is Kil-Kol ahead along our current course, Neer Domyn," reported Whyvvi, seated in the red chair three positions to left of Domyn along the semi-circular arc of the formation of the colored chairs in ConCen of spacecraft.

After flexing his ring finger of his left hand inside his tan dionjocu glove, Domyn viewed in the visor over his right eye the same long-range sensor scene as Whyvvi. In the scene, a cloud-like patch of diffuse twinkling light glimmered in the dim gray light of LaOgres space. Domyn recognized this immediately as Kilczek-Kolrain. This phenomenon was region of Debordo space, where normal gravity or posi-grav became balanced or zero between solar systems and other spatial bodies and systems. What he now viewed was the inverse side of Kil-Kol that presented into LaOgres space. Usually every solar system in the Debordo space had at least one Kil-Kol zone. Of course there was the inverse portion in LaOgres space as well. These two opposing aspects of same phenomenon joined together by passing through the Weznuski space barrier of the null-grav. Domyn remembered this in a fraction of a second.

Since he viewed the visor with only one eye, he did not have the benefit of binocular vision as did Whyvvi, whose dionjocu helm required both eyes, so Domyn asked, "Do you scan any sign of recent braiding, Whyvvi?"

With his naked left eye, Domyn observed a pink figure in a red chair swivel toward him as she replied, "No, Domyn, Kil-Kol is too far away still. We should be close enough soon. Do you suspect that Fox Flash Alpha deployed their Buffalardi through this particular Kil-Kol?"

"Most likely, I believe. Remember, Fox Flash Alpha would have been on a similar course and nineteen-day sleep cycle as we are. Their awake cycles would occur in about the same position of space as ours. We traverse approximately the same expanse of LaOgres space, unless the an-grav currents have been disturbed and severely distorted since their passage about nineteen days ago. Although space is in flux constantly, even the entire year might not dramatically change texture of this space. To our short-term perspective, this would all be about the same as when Fox Flash Alpha passed here," Domyn explained with assurance in his deep voice, and then as slight doubt entered his mind, he hastily continued, "Awe alone knows odds of travelling past two totally different Kil-Kols when on similar route with same cycles of awakening."

Pouting beneath the visor over her eyes, the nineteen-year-old girl sighed, "Yes, you are correct, Neer Domyn. I should have remembered that basic physical fact. This Kil-Kol must be the same used by the Fox Flash Alpha. I should be able to discern the braiding signature of Khebol soon. Cap Bhiros assigns Khebol to oversee their launches of Buffalardi every time. And I certainly know Khebol's handiwork."

From across the semi-circle of chairs, a tall lanky figure in lavender attire laughed from the violet chair, "Vulching for sure, Whyvvi! You wish you could get Khebol's hand...he...work!"

"Well, performance of Neer Khebol at most Blue Jay functions is much more reliable and proficient than some...boys...that I know," retorted Whyvvi, spinning her red chair toward the tall young man slouching in the violet chair.

"Perhaps, Milyr, you should concentrate on getting Wolf Streak Beta closer to that Kil-Kol. My Chitir would have found the best currents of an-grav to get us there by now," bragged a small girl in a yellow dionjocu seated immediately to Milyr's left.

With his long arms swaying and bending in intricate patterns while he flew the spacecraft with his dionjocu gloves, Milyr sneered and laughed even louder than before, "Hah, vulch Chitir and his flying. I repeat, Khebol's hand...he...work, his very special hand...he...work for our Whyvvi is rarer than Kil-Kols with full strength of sun in LaOgres space. And we all know how rare those are..."

Yes, very rare, Domyn thought to himself, that is Kilczek-Kolrain with a light intensity of normal sun in Debordo space. Actually Domyn corrected his own thoughts, the reflected light and not original sunlight came from Kil-Kol on

LaOgres side of Weznuski barrier of null-grav space. With no suns in LaOgres space, only light was that which had passed through from Debordo space and was now reflected by zillions of zillions of spergits trapped in nether region along the boundary between LaOgres space and Weznuski space.

According to the most recent sub-atomic particle theories known to Domyn, spergits or spinning energy bits were the tiniest sub-quark composition of matter. Here in LaOgres space, instead of attracting together to form quarks, protons, neutrons, atoms, molecules, and then increasingly larger pieces of matter as occurs in Debordo space, these spergits are repulsed apart in conjunction with nature of antigravity of LaOgres space. The spergits cannot form together in this space, so are dispersed as far apart as possible into the very edges of this aspect of space.

However, intrusion of Kil-Kol into the outer fabric of this LaOgres space does provide minimum of posi-grav that exudes from Debordo space through connection in Weznuski space. This minimum posi-grav attracts many of freely roaming spergits into clustered, yet non-coalescing mass or cloud. Even though still separate spergits, an incalculable number of these spergits in such relatively close proximity could reflect free light almost to intensity of the moons of the home world in Zerosolis System.

Domyn was impressed by sight in visor. However, he realized that almost never did these clusters of spergits captured by Kil-Kols simulate brightness of true sun of Debordo space. This particular Kil-Kol did seem to be about as bright as he had ever witnessed himself over many years of his voyages through LaOgres space.

"Vulching nasty, don't I know that," swore Swyllo, sitting two chairs to the right of Domyn, and her shrill voice snapped him from his foray into old lessons of former physics instructors, and then her voice said sarcastically with some chagrin, "These toxx Kil-Kols are best sources of light energy in this vulching LaOgres space and there are hardly any as powerful as the sun. Those really cherp Kil-Kols are as scarce as reliable man, right, Whyvvi?"

"That is for toxx certain, Swyllo. Especially on this crew!" agreed Whyvvi tersely with a snide chuckle but then added hastily after glancing at Domyn, "Except for our Neer, of course!"

Spinning in a violet chair to Swyllo's right, Milyr chortled with merriment, "Swyllo, Whyvvi, I'm here. I'm as reliably primo as men come. I'm here. Anytime you want me, I'm here for you."

While Whyvvi grunted in disgust, Swyllo groaned, leaning away from her taller crewmate, "Argh! All I desire from you, you toxx, is to get Wolf Streak Beta closer to that Kil-Kol. I need to harvest more energy to replenish the power supply. You use up too much stored energy with your ridiculous haphazard flying. Just get us straight to Kil-Kol. And that's all you vulching toxx!"

Domyn witnessed a leering grin flash white teeth beneath the full visor covering the young man's eyes just before Milyr chuckled, "I can get straight to the target for you, tiny fem. Vulch, I'm here for you anytime. I can get straight... and with much power...for you, Swyllo, whenever you want me."

"Argh! Keep your vulching hands away from me," Swyllo protested, turning her yellow chair away from the swinging and gesticulating long arms and hands clothed by pastel purple dionjocu gloves. "Swivel yourself away from me, Milyr. You're nasty into my zone now. Turn your nastiness toward the wall, you stunted toxx pud!"

As he controlled the flight of Wolf Streak Beta with movements of his hands and fingers within his dionjocu gloves now in interface with Joculatus, Milyr retorted in his smooth baritone voice, "I'm just flying this spacecraft, tiny fem. Don't believe I'm trying to cuddle with you, do you? You do want me to get... straight...to Kil-Kol, don't you?"

"Swivel away! You're such a vulching arrogant toxx puddy!" Swyllo snarled with both anger and yet a hint of mirth in her high soprano voice, and then with what seemed like a more serious insult, she complained, "An-grav currents out there can't be as zigzag as your flying. I'm not sure if you can fly straight, you crooked toxx!"

"Awright, that's enough!" Domyn scolded with his deep voice growling with sternness more firmly than normal. "Let's not act like foolish pups, people. We've got job to perform. Cap is expecting Buffalardi launch on schedule. Milyr, pilot us toward a close favorable point near that Kil-Kol. Swyllo, harvest as much new energy from the reflecting spergits as you can, Whyvvi, coordinate with Joculatus for the most efficient timing for braid of the probe. Now, people, let's focus on our functions."

Instantly silence hushed ConCen. The silence so quiet that Domyn could hear a subtle flutter and swish of three pairs of moving arms, hands, and fingers, and he smiled to himself. These young people were very verbose much too often, yet they did know their duties quite well. The dionjocu uniform with a cap and special visor gave each crewmember interactive view and supplemental information pertinent to the respective function. These dionjocu garments connected PEQA of each crewmember with artigence controlling all outside operational activities of spacecraft. This artigence was called Joculatus.

Now as he listened to the noises of the dionjocu garments, Domyn felt uncomfortable in silence that he had created with his scolding. As he scanned the gradually approaching Kil-Kol in the visor over his right eye, he reminded himself just how much he hated the disciplinary part of leadership. He realized that in spite of their previous annoying banter, young pups had been performing their functions. Yet Cap Nyba expected him to push and guide the crew of Wolf Streak Beta. That was part of his duty as Neer. All of these people were nineteen years of age or very close to that age now. Only Jamyk was younger. Cap Nyba and he were officers and were supposed to lead and so sometimes such meant discipline and guidance, at least from what Prof Lyndyn often lectured him in private.

From her yellow chair, Swyllo broke short the quiet in ConCen when she reported with a casually sober tone, "This Kil-Kol is exceptionally bright. It seems so much brighter than most Kil-Kols. I should be able to bring our power supply back up by several levels. That will be one cherp happening in this awful LaOgres. At least this scrawny toxx on my right is piloting us close to this cherp Kil-Kol."

Surprisingly Milyr did not make a remark after her reference to his talent, so with some relief in his awareness that his scolding had not dampened spirit of his people, Domyn said with encouragement, "That's good, Swyllo. Take advantage of this powerful Kil-Kol. I have confidence in your skills as a cherp harvester of whatever light is out there for us to capture. Milyr, be cautious of any unusually strong currents in grav flows as we get closer. Sometimes different gravities that can occur near Kil-Kol can intermix and form whirlpools or other vortex eddies very like our artificial braids."

Joculatus announced in a monotone male voice in Domyn's earpiece, "Neer Domyn, fifty-three minutes to scheduled launch of Buffalardi probe."

Milyr said with some indignation in his baritone voice, "That I already knew, Domyn. There are some unusual swirls in periphery of this Kil-Kol. And also strong central whirlpool that likes almost like a black hole in Debordo space. This is something that you might want to check on pilot view."

Hearing this hastily Domyn flexed his little finger inside the right dionjocu glove to switch the view in his visor to that of the pilot, and he commanded before he observed the new view, "Keep us away from any conflicting currents or suctions, Milyr. We don't need to lose any voyage time by unexpectedly popping back into Debordo space. That has happened to the other Blue Jay spacecraft, even without activation of their braid. If we don't control our popping through Weznuski, we don't know where we will return in Debordo space. We might need days to plot the course to Sexto System and then plunge back into LaOgres space to resume the timely journey."

"Well, that would not be very cherp," Whyvvi stated from her red chair on the other side of the ConCen from Milyr and Swyllo. "If we ever need to travel to Sexto System in Debordo space, then we would be very old spacers by the time we reached our destination. Our voyage is so much faster when we use space-time of LaOgres space."

"Vulch, I'd almost rather grow to be a very old woman and travel through real Debordo space than go through this toxx LaOgres," Swyllo griped sourly in a lowered voice.

"Don't worry, tiny fems. Don't worry, Neer Domyn. I am the vulching best pilot in Blue Jay. I can fly through or around any nasty," Milyr boasted loudly, but then after a few seconds, his voice became more defensive and almost surly to Domyn's perspective when Milyr remarked, "Don't you have any confidence in me, Domyn? Don't I ever get any credit for being able to see these problems and adjust my flying to avoid them?"

As his right eye observed the fluctuating green, yellow, orange, and red colors representing ever-changing currents and intensities of gravity fields of LaOgres space between Wolf Streak Beta and Kil-Kol, Domyn forced himself now to comment on his crewmate's slightly insolent mood. This was typically Milyr trait, Domyn thought to himself. His friend often heard affront when none was intended. Milyr could be just as emotionally fluctuating as gravity eddies in space were physically changeable. Milyr could often transform from egotistical braggart to insecure pouter in seconds. Yet, Domyn told himself, that was Prof Lyndyn's challenge.

At the moment, more concerned with the swirling red representing a very strong and strange gravitational vortex at the center of Kil-Kol, Domyn said aloud with some puzzlement, "That looks like the braid never closed. What do you believe, Milyr? And, Whyvvi, you should scan this with your sensors as soon as you can free away from Joculatus and calculations for launch."

The lanky figure in the light purple dionjocu uniform kept his back to Domyn and others on ConCen, and after a few moments, responded, "I don't see any sign of posi-grav flow, Neer Domyn. But there is definitely residual twining of an-grav and null-grav. It's too far away yet to be sure. That could have been a full three-pronged braid recently."

"A really strong and long running braid might account for this unusually dense gathering of spergits," Swyllo said in a cheery high voice and then continued, "a really cherp density of light reflecting spergits is very cherp for me to harvest light energy. But why is it not closed if it is from the braid? That is not so cherp, I think."

Whyvvi declared with consternation in her voice, "Why just an-grav and null-grav in the twining? The braid is not supposed to be like that. Khebol would have done the proper braid with all three gravs. His braid would have closed correctly. This does not appear to be the Khebol creation."

"Vulch, where is posi-grav strand? Why is this not closed?" Swyllo complained shrilly.

"If vulchers on Fox Flash Alpha hadn't missed comm last awakening, maybe we would know," griped Milyr, gesticulating with his hands and arms as he piloted the spacecraft.

"But why did they not comm us last time?" Whyvvi asked puzzled.

With no ready answer to Whyvvi's question coming in mind, Domyn instead responded to Swyllo's train-of-thought, "Awright, yes, repulsive nature of LaOgres space would push spergits into the braid rift like air leaking from a punctured balloon. But the if braid reached through to the Debordo space, then the null-grav nature of Weznuski space would not have influenced spergits to cluster so densely. Something is very unusual here."

From her red chair, Whyvvi exclaimed loudly, "Well, we are postulating that the braid did not reach through to the Debordo space. And yet it did not close on this side of Weznuski. That the braid should have closed. If Khebol made that braid, then it should have closed."

"I guess that toxx is not as good as you would like to think, hey, Whyvvi?" chortled Milyr with amusement in his baritone voice.

Just then Joculatus said in Domyn's earpiece, "Neer Domyn, forty-seven minutes to the scheduled launch of Buffalardi probe."

However, Domyn needed to prevent any squabbling amongst his crew at that moment, so he growled in warning hastily, "Not now, people! Stay focused on your functions and not on any silly bickering. We've got to launch our Buffalardi soon. This twining vortex is problem. Will it affect our launch? Does anyone have any input on that topic? Our time is now limited for this required launch."

Memory of viewing the model schematic of Buffalardi probe the braiding through the Weznuski space into Debordo space and then deploying two communication beacons abruptly flashed into consciousness of Neer Domyn. The memory from the training session many years ago on the now distant Steppingstone reminded him of importance of deploying Buffalardis during voyage from

Steppingstone Quinto to Sexto System where hopefully the next Steppingstone station was to be established. The Buffalardi chain of relay beacons served as communication stretching through almost eighty-nine light year distance between last Steppingstone and now active Blue Jay spacecraft. Buffalardi beacons were essential for Blue Jay communication over such long distances in Debordo space. Domyn reminded himself again that each awakening required launch of Buffalardi back through the Weznuski barrier into the Debordo space to keep comm chain intact and operationally efficient.

While these memories flashed through his mind, Domyn listened to Milyr say, "I don't see any sign of the full braid through to Debordo space. I see on my pilot view no signs of gravities intermixing other than this twining. Why not use this twining as portal entry for our braid? Maybe that will save us some time and energy for our launch."

"Actually, this toxx might have cherp notion for once," retorted Swyllo. "His suggestion might use less energy for probe launch. If the energy of twining enhances momentum of Buffalardi probe, then we might be able to conserve energy in the launch and maybe during full braid. We could let that twining throw probe through Weznuski into Debordo."

"Is our energy conservation important now?" Domyn asked, immediately knowing the answer and then berating himself silently for inane question that he had put forth just to stall on making decision.

Swyllo replied, "Not really, Neer. Energy supply is positive and increasing. This very bright Kil-Kol on this side of Weznuski barrier is very cherp with light energy to harvest now."

"But why did the braid not close at this end? Braids always close behind the passage of Buffalardis or spacecraft. Why not this time?" Whyvvi asked empathically. "And why does no posi-grav strand show in what is left of this apparent braid. Can we chance launching through thesame part of Kil-Kol where error anomaly seems to have occurred? Neer, we must be careful here. I wish that Fox Flash Alpha had reported to us last awakening. I wonder why they did not."

Vulch, Domyn swore to himself, where was Cap Nyba? Should he summon her to ConCen? Would there be time for the rest of the crew to calibrate their dionjocus with Joculatus in order to function on the ConCen? Could he oversee this problem, or should he pass on the responsibility to Cap Nyba? After all she was the captain of Wolf Streak Beta. She had proven her ability to lead over their many years of schooling, space flight training, and mastering of Blue Jay sci-tech and Wolf Streak Beta mission. Vulch, could he handle this without Cap Nyba?

In his earpiece, Joculatus said, "Neer Domyn, forty-three minutes to the scheduled launch of the probe."

"I don't really know if anyone has ever vulching launched through such a mysterious twining of gravities," admitted Milyr while waving his arms and hands in meticulous patterns, and then slowly turning his violet chair toward Domyn, continued, "Vulch, this twining is wider, that braid should be for the Buffalardi passage. And I'm getting what might be the opposite flow around the outer edges of this vulching thing. Toxx never saw such vulching gravity action in any aspect of space!"

"If this is the leftover braid, then where is other end? Where is posi-grav strand? This doesn't make logical sense," Swyllo cried in a high, slightly stressed voice. "I vulching hate LaOgres!"

"If this is the braid from Fox Flash Alpha, then it must at least nineteen-days-old now," exclaimed Whyvvi from her red chair. "Can braids last that long? I do not believe that Khebol could make such mistake. None of us Jayers could make such mistake with simple Buffalardi launch. There must be something very different about this."

With his naked left eye, Domyn peered at the pink clothed girl sitting three chairs to his left and inquired firmly, "Do you scan anything unexpected to confirm your opinion? Have you used your sensors at the highest setting? Give me something, Whyvvi. Our Buffalardi launch must take place soon."

"I am scanning on my highest zeta ray frequency, Neer. Yet I do not read any clear sign of the complete braid there. I read nothing but very dense spergits. Even that reading is confused with interference of twining gravities, which are somehow affecting electromagnetic spectrum," Whyvvi replied, struggling to keep a steady voice, and this tremor worried Domyn for Whyvvi was last to become emotionally distraught of the crew.

To appear to have the situation in control and to take any guilt from the focus of his crew, Domyn called out loudly, "Vivacio, is there any error or malfunction in sensor scans of Joculatus?"

Within seconds a male voice of artigence Vivacio said, "Neer Domyn, all systems of Joculatus are functioning within programmed parameters."

Then flicking thering finger of his tan dionjocu glove on his right hand, Domyn viewed the colors of the pulsing gravities change to a scene of silver, gold, and white luminescence depicting intensities of light energy as seen now by Swyllo, and he asked, "Is a core of grayish silver typical of a center of such a vibrant Kil-Kol, Swyllo? This seems to be near scanning limit of this twining vortex."

"Neer Domyn, such dense cluster of spergits usually shows much brighter in my visor view as they reflect light that I can see. This reflection almost reminds me of...vulch... I don't know...maybe...moonlight from the ancient pictures of moon of home world in Zerosolis," Swyllo stammered as she obviously tried to relate to some memory. "It's almost like a shadowy...cloud cover in the center here now at this Kil-Kol. I don't know what else to call it, Domyn."

In the earpiece of his dionjocu cap, Domyn heard a monotone voice of Joculatus say, "Neer Domyn, low intensity sanbeam is trying to communicate with this spacecraft."

"Whyvvi, switch to neutrino scan immediately," Domyn commanded hastily as his mind tried to work on the image that Swyllo had tried to convey, and then he announced to ConCen, "We are receiving sanbeam transmission. Joculatus, from where is this sanbeam originating?"

The artigence replied, "Neer Domyn, sanbeam is travelling from the center of the vortex as defined by pilot Milyr."

Suddenly,Whyvvi shrieked excitedly, "It is Khebol. I know his voice. It is Khebol. But this is a very poor reception, but I am certain it is Khebol."

"Awright, Whyvvi!" Domyn demanded in his deep authoritative voice. "Try to be calm. What is the message? Is it real time or delayed?"

His left eye witnessed her face scowl in annoyance at him or perhaps in concentration on her sensor scan now that she received signal, he was not sure, which as she paused momentarily and then reported, "Again I have poor reception, Neer Domyn. I believe it is repeating the message. It should be clearer but seems to be the same message over and over. It is most likely an automated recording, probably delayed and programmed into Buffalardi beacon that Fox Flash Alpha launched here. Khebol would have wished for us to know something important and specific, or he would have announced himself and kept open-ended conversation possible."

"If that was possible," Milyr grumbled sarcastically from his purple chair.

Flexing his ring finger inside his left dionjocu glove, Domyn then observed the visor image before his right eye change to a very fuzzy video picture and static charged audio transmission in his ear-piece, yet he heard a voice repeat, "Target... Beta...launch...before...center...target... Beta...launch..."

While he listened to this repeating message, he heard Whyvvi ask with confusion, "Where is he transmitting from? We never get comm from Fox Flash Alpha before our own launches. The system needs our beacons to be deployed before we can get reception from them. This is not logical. Khebol should not be able to reach us yet without our beacon in operation."

Joculatus said, "Neer Domyn, thirty-seven minutes until the scheduled launch of Buffalardi probe."

From the end of the semi-circular arrangement of chairs, Milyr declared with strain in his cracking baritone voice, "Neer Domyn, these currents are getting more robust. There seems to be vulching counter flow as we get closer to the edge of the Kil-Kol extension into LaOgres space. This vortex of the twining gravs sticks out from Kil-Kol much farther than normal currents by Kil-Kol. I am nasty tough time trying to fly any closer. Sometimes this Wolf Streak feels like the twining is pulling at us with a tremendous force and then abruptly seems to be pushing at us with just as much force. This is not vulching normal!"

"Just keep us steady enough and along our intended course for Buffalardi launch," Domyn ordered while he continued to listen to repeating message in his ear-piece from Fox Flash Alpha and mused confidently to himself, at least there was now comm from their partner craft.

"I'm doing the best I can. There seems to be duplicity about this vortex I've not seen before. It almost acts like a passage of craft after the braid, except with no posi-grav strand this time. As we continue to get closer, I believe that I can feel, if not see another outer twining flowing back at LaOgres space from the center of Kil-Kol. This other outer twining appears to surround inner twining at considerable distance. Both vulchers are going in opposite directions. That just doesn't make any vulching sense to me," whined Milyr as his arms tried to flail with movements of his piloting.

Hearing frustration and mild worry in the young man's tone, Domyn said with assurance while he tried to concentrate upon the message sent by Khebol over his own visor, "Just keep us steady on our planned course, Milyr. Use your superb skills and knowledge to guide Wolf Streak Beta. Let us deal with this anomaly. You focus on piloting."

"Yeah, Domyn," a tall figure in a lavender dionjocu replied with mild sarcasm.

He heard pessimism in the voice of Milyr but did not respond or put any attention into that bit of emotional frustration. Instead Domyn thought to himself as he watched the blurred face of Khebol continue with a short repeating message, this situation did not make any sense. Milyr was right about that. Braids go one way from one spatial aspect through Weznuski space, then into opposite aspect. If this was the braid initiated by Fox Flash Alpha, why was it incomplete into

Debordo space? Why was it still open in LaOgres space? And now if Milyr was correct, why was it folding back over itself? Could he really deal with this situation? Should he call emergency and summon full crew to ConCen? Damn, maintaining his spacecraft and its sci-tech was so much simpler than leading ConCen, Domyn groaned to himself.

"Neer Domyn, if we received transmission from Khebol, they must have launched successful Buffalardi," Whyvvi stated with surety in her tone.

"Vulch, of course," Swyllo agreed. "That's cherp obvious!"

Awe of course, Domyn agreed silently, why hadn't he realized that sooner? Too many ongoing pieces of information shuffling in his consciousness, he surmised. His own preference to be involved in every technical puzzle and activity would not allow him to focus on any one factor. Awe help me against my own stubborn arrogance, Domyn mused to himself.

Then with some reluctance, he tapped his right heel onto theemergency pedal on the lower portion of his chair. After a two second pause, he tapped it again. Vivacio, internal artigence for Wolf Streak Beta would now notify all other members of the crew to report to the bridge as soon as possible. At least then there would be more brains to unravel this predicament, he mused.

"I've just summoned the rest of the crew and decided this qualifies as an emergency situation," Domyn announced in a calm firm voice. "I do not mean be belittle your ability to solve this situation. I believe that we can use all brainpower available to Wolf Streak Beta. Now, Whyvvi, normally Khebol launches the Buffalardi probe through the center of Kil-Kol, doesn't he?"

"Well, every time that we follow on the voyage, then he always has used the center. I do not know what he does when we lead..." Whyvvi began to reply from her red chair.

Interrupting her hastily, Domyn asked while trying to force himself to focus on this and not get involved in the piloting challenge of Milyr just then, "Whyvvi, his message repeats...before center... Is that how you hear it? Could Khebol be telling us to launch away from the center before we get there?"

From the right side of the chairs, Milyr complained tiredly, "The gravitational pulsations are getting much more erratic. This spacecraft is handling like a toxx drunken wolf now. These grav currents outside are nothing like navigational scans that we observed near any other Kil-Kol."

Ignoring the young man for a moment, Domyn continued with Whyvvi, "If Fox Flash Alpha launched their Buffalardi successfully, then that braid would have closed behind the probe after it passed through Weznuski. Do you believe that Khebol would have launched before targeting the center of that Kil-Kol?"

In this earpiece, Domyn listened to Joculatus as artigence updated the launch to be scheduled in about twenty-nine minutes, and at the same time, heard Whyvvi reply, "No, Domyn. Khebol would behave consistently. I believe that he wishes for us to launch before reaching the center-oriented trajectory. Khebol repeats... Beta and launch...each repetition prior to words...before and center. He most likely would know that he had launched for center trajectory and had not been successful. The foxes must have launched the second Buffalardi probe beyond center before travelling out of range of this Kil-Kol. That is very unusual for Khebol. He is not one to do unusual, unless there is major problem."

"Or vulcher is playing some prank on someone!" Milyr scoffed wearily from his purple chair.

"Not now, please, Milyr!" Domyn sighed and then asked, "Whyvvi, is our Buffalardi ready for launch?"

"Yes, standard launch mode is ready and coordinated with Joculatus," Whyvvi replied, but then asked with concern, "But that would target our original center intent. Is this what we want to do now? I am not confident that with these abnormal grav currents that we can pinpoint as precise a target direction as usual. Do we really wish to launch toward the center of that Kil-Kol?"

"Vulching unlikely, Domyn! These pulsations pulling and pushing at us are getting much worse. Even normal braiding may be difficult," warned Milyr from within his light lavender dionjocu, now showing darker stains of sweat in spite of the cooling function of the garment.

Awe help, Domyn thought, he could use some inspiration now. He could not wait for Cap Nyba to get to ConCen. Joculatus counted down to nineteen minutes to the original launch position. Was Whyvvi correct? Was Milyr right to voice concern? Domyn realized that he must make a decision soon. But, damn, he did not want to accept this responsibility to take action beyond tje norm. Awe inspiration, he prayed silently. Would he help or hinder mission with any choice that was out of the ordinary now? This was so much more difficult than repairing machinery, he groaned quietly.

Then with a deep breath and renewed prayer for supreme universal aid, Domyn commanded in a firm voice, "Joculatus, coordinate with Whyvvi for new launch trajectory toward the farthest backward edge of Kil-Kol based upon our current course perspective. Make new launch time minus five minutes from the original schedule. Use hurry mode, both of you!"

"Neer Domyn, requested hurry mode with such time constraint may over-exert some of my programming parameters," said a monotone male voice of artigence Joculatus.

"That may be so, but I do have strong confidence in you Joculatus and in your partner Whyvvi," Domyn stated, and then as he turned his glance toward Whyvvi, continued loudly, "Vivacio, monitor and be prepared to support or repair any difficulty that Joculatus may experience. And you, my friend Whyvvi, quickness and concentration are now critical to this change of plan, especially if you are correct about possible actions and intentions of Khebol. Don't let us down now. Use that superior wit and logic of yours to prep us into our new launch window."

"Yes, Neer Domyn," Vivacio responded into the air of ConCen.

As Whyvvi did not remark and instead immediately busied herself with task with Joculatus, Domyn listened to Milyr complain, "It is much worse, Domyn, very toxx...difficult to...keep us...on course for any launch before our original plan. And, Domyn, opposing pulsations seem to be increasing our velocity and drawing us closer to Kil-Kol than is normal for standard Kil-Kol flyby. I don't think we have as much time as you'd like. And worse yet, Domyn, I don't like the looks of that central vortex between two pulsations. It reads so much like the pocket of pure null-grav that it vulching scares me. I don't know if I will be able to generate any posi grav or an-grav fields if we get sucked into that pocket. Anything I can't do while piloting scares toxx off me!"

Flicking his visor back to the scene as read by Milyr on pilot view, Domyn briefly observed multi-colored streams and eddies of various gravities near Kil-Kol and saw a darker, more vague core of vortex just as Milyr had indicated, yet before he could focus his intellect upon this sight, Swyllo cried shrilly with agitation, "Vulch, my light sensor is now getting very abnormally low intensity from that area you pointed out before. That nasty central spot just doesn't give me any reflected light to harvest. I should be collecting prime reflection from that spot as I was just minutes ago but not any longer. There is something nasty vulching toxx about that spot now!"

What now, Domyn winced internally in his mind, and then he ordered, "Swyllo, take maximum recordings of all data. Also, tap into sensor scans for both Milyr and Whyvvi and record these also onto your system. They have too much to do now. You will have all the recording function and authority now. We should try to gather as much data as we can about that anomaly. But the rest of us need to focus on duties involving launch and piloting. Did you hear that, Joculatus and Vivacio? You are both to coordinate your recording functions into Swyllo's system now."

Two male voices responded simultaneously, "Yes, Neer Domyn."

"I recommend that you extend Wilchrison prior to launch. The extra early braiding may help pull Buffalardi away from the suction of the vortex and toward your intended target zone," Milyr suggested through gasping breath, and Domyn noticed a muscular strain in lanky arms and large wet stains in lavender dionjocu. "Vulch, this vortex is just so nasty toxx. I never thought that I would be frightened of any spatial gravitational phenomenon. But this vulcher scares me!"

With the countdown passing thirteen minutes, Domyn wondered if artigence had updated this count to a new revised launch request. But only for the moment, for his real attention was now upon fear displayed by normally fearless and often obnoxiously a brazen young man. Yet in spite of his fear, Milyr had mentioned extending Wilchrison early. That was not a normal step in routine, but would this notion help situation? Would this new process improve chance of success?

Domyn knew that Wilchrison was a device that when extended above the outer surface of Buffalardi or a spacecraft, and then activated performed the braiding of three gravity fields generated by the Flandecams. Wilchrison created the braid effect of three differing gravity fields to allow an-grav and posi-grav to coincide briefly alongside each other with a buffer of strand of null-grav. This braid was only wide enough to allow probe, or craft, channel through which to traverse the narrow barrier of Weznuski space. The extended Wilchrison was not a common feature of normal launch of Buffalardi probe but should not adversely affect the launch nor impede course programmed by Joculatus and Whyvvi. Awe willing, Domyn sighed, it should work now.

"Do you have any problem with extending Wilchrison early, Whyvvi?" Domyn inquired, and then while the girl frowned in thought for a few seconds, he continued, "We will need to get that probe as far toward edge of this Kil-Kol as we can and as rapidly as we can. Joculatus, do you have any problems with this maneuver?"

Whyvvi replied, "That should add only about a minute to reprogramming. By making this change in procedure, we should be able to shorten the overall duration of full launching."

Unusually slow to respond, finally Joculatus said, "That is an unprecedented departure from my programming, Neer Domyn. I do not foresee any negative results with this change in procedure. My program does not have any historical information available to form a complete analysis."

"Awspir! Let's do it then before we get much closer to that gravity vortex," Domyn commanded and then added with a bit of humor to help relieve building tension of his crew on ConCen, "Piloting in this situation is making Milyr sweat like a rutting horse. You know how he hates work."

"Vulch, I'm not only sweating like a rutting horse in the middle of summer," gasped Milyr with panting breaths as his arms moved, still piloting spacecraft, "but even I can smell that I stink like one, too. And I'm not even getting enjoyment of rutting. Vulch, such nasty notion this is!"

With her back to the violet chair, Swyllo wrinkled her nose and puckered her lips beneath her yellow dionjocu cap and visor as she agreed sourly, "Nasty vulch is right! You others don't have to sit next to him. Even some of his drops of sweat fly over at me when he flails his arms. That's nasty!"

"Hah, Swyllo fem, you only dream that you could be rained upon by some of my fluids," laughed Milyr between grunts of effort.

"Awright, are we ready to launch yet?" Domyn inquired now, not worrying about the banter as his crew released some of their nervousness, and probably good that they did, or so Prof Lyndyn would have thought.

Gasping with her exertion, Whyvvi gasped, "Thirty seconds... Neer Domyn... Then we can launch Buffalardi toward the outer rim of Kil-Kol."

"Hold Wolf Streak Beta steady on course now, Milyr. Until we launch at the correct inclination to Kil-Kol edge, you will need to keep us directly on course," commanded Domyn, glancing over at the sweating young man in the wet lavender dionjocu. "You're doing cherp, Milyr."

"I always do my best, Domyn. I just hope that we can get out of this turbulent pattern soon. I just hope that one launch will solve the problem. Then we can get vulch away from that nasty vortex that shrivels my nads just looking at it," Milyr retorted breathlessly.

"The Buffalardi is ready. Wilchrison is extended on probe," stated Whyvvi.

"Joculatus, launch in one minute at a time that Wolf Streak Beta is at the most precise inclination toward target zone," ordered Domyn, relinquishing the rest of the procedure to artigence.

Except for grunts and gasps of Milyr as he tried to keep alignment of the large spacecraft to best possible inclination for launch, ConCen fell silent. Domyn found himself holding his breath. His palms inside his tan dionjocu gloves were slick with sweat. His right eye watched the scene as Milyr saw it. The view was a confusion of red and orange with a sprinkling of yellow, like the ancient kaleidoscopic vision of some now unknown video artist. There was a vortex of red pulsing not far from the path of Wolf Streak Beta. Was this what worried Milyr, Domyn wondered?

In quietness of ConCen, footsteps of others scuffed softly across the carpeted floor. Domyn realized without looking around that Cap Nyba and the rest of the crew were now in ConCen. To his right, the blue chair swung around. Then a feminine figure in blue settled in this chair just as quick, a very short jolt of launch swept subtly through structure of spacecraft.

Joculatus said through ConCen, "Neer Domyn, launch has been completed."

"Thank you, Joculatus. As protocol requires, keep precise recording of the Buffalardi course and the braiding into Kil-Kol. Whyvvi, let's check on zeta ray scans into that vortex. Make sure we have record. Milyr, you can fly as you must now to avoid vortex and those nasty gravitational pulsations. I'm sure that will make you so much happier," Domyn sighed as he made eye contact with Nyba and then asked tiredly, "Are you ready to assume command now, Cap?"

However, before she could respond, Milyr groaned loudly and swore, "Damn, vulch, it's too late. We're trapped in vortex current. And it's pulling us right into null gravity between twinings. We're vulched for sure now. We're vulching trapped!"

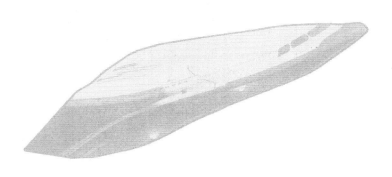

Spec One: Domyn Through LaOgres
Chapter 7

"Trapped?" Nyba inquired with anxiety, "How are we trapped?"

With frustration and some fear in his baritone voice, Milyr groaned, "Vulch, Cap, I really tried to stay clear, but Wolf Streak Beta is caught in a zone of null-grav between two opposing grav twinings. I can't get us to move. The vulching null-grav zone keeps negating any posi-grav or an-grav field that I try to create with the Flandecams. Wolf Streak Beta is nasty stuck here. I couldn't help it, Nyba!"

"That is not typical of a Kil-Kol flyby. Neer Domyn, this situation has been confirmed, hasn't it?" Cap Nyba asked in tone of a slight disbelief as she turned her blue chair toward him.

Hearing doubt in her voice, Domyn replied hastily and with whatever resolve that he could muster against her strong personal presence, "Cap, this is not typical Kil-Kol. There seemed to be remnant of the braid that was possibly begun by the Fox Flash Alpha nineteen days ago. This braid is still open at this side of Weznuski and after nineteen days! That should not happen..."

"Vulch, yes, that does sound very abnormal. Are you sure of data coming from sensors?" Nyba inquired tersely, and Domyn could hear that she was obviously still very doubtful about this information.

"Awe yes, Cap, we had Vivacio check all systems involved," Domyn replied, feeling guilty of some forgotten step during his control of ConCen, but then he continued with more conviction as his eye viewed the massive red splotch that appeared centrally in display in his visor, "I am certain that what Milyr now claims is true, Cap. The remnant of the original braid from the Fox Flash Alpha seems to be doubling back on the outside of itself, creating this zone of null-grav. This is causing Weznuski to intrude into this portion of LaOgres where there is connection with Kil-Kol. Apparently Wolf Streak Beta is caught in this null-grav zone between the original inner braid and outer twining."

With the visor raised still above her blue cap covering her scalp and forehead, Nyba glared at him and then asked sourly, "Did we launch Buffalardi at least? Did we perform that operation successfully? I should hope that we could do that without failure."

Even though he realized that she was seeking to vent her agitation and also get information and meaning from current situation, the sarcastic tone of her voice hurt his professional pride, so Domyn struggled with his own inclination to snap back at her and instead reported, "Yes, Cap, Buffalardi was launched. However, we received a sanbeam recording from Fox Flash requesting that we not aim through the center of Kil-Kol. I judged that we should aim instead for periphery, which we have done."

"Then Buffalardi wasn't trapped in this null-space?" Nyba inquired, and then turning her blue chair toward Whyvvi, continued, "Whyvvi, how is Buffalardi tracking? How soon should it deploy its beacons into Debordo space?"

Dressed in a pink dionjocu uniform and seated two chairs to Nyba's left, Whyvvi spun her red chair to face Nyba and reported, "Buffalardi probe is now at the LaOgres rim of Kil-Kol. Since we launched, it has had no disorientation from course and no unusual gravitational pull from abnormal twinings. It has made braid for itself and should be into the Weznuski space in less than a minute. Under normal conditions, it should reach Debordo space in less than thirteen minutes."

"Are these normal conditions?" snarled Cap Nyba with irritation and then added, "Keep read on that Buffalardi, Whyvvi."

"Toxx vulching can't get any grav field to stay coherent long enough to push or pull us," Milyr sputtered to himself just loud enough to reach the ears of Domyn from three seats to his right, and then the young man muttered again, "Toxx vulch, just can't get a grip!"

Nyba asked into the air of ConCen, "Joculatus, can you confirm Whyvvi's predictions for deployment of beacons into the Debordo space?"

While viewing in his visor screen over his right eye, the pulsating red-purple representations of twinings creating pocket of null-space around spaceship, Domyn listened to Joculatus reply, "Cap Nyba, Buffalardi probe should deploy beacons in Debordo space in eleven minutes."

"Swyllo, what is our energy supply?" Domyn asked in a hushed voice so as not to disturb Nyba's conversation.

Swyllo replied with a tremor of nervousness in her high voice, "Energy looks…okay…for now… But I wish I could get more light intensity from that center. Now there is nothing but vulching dimness from that center. All around this Kil-Kol is a very cherp brightness, but not from that vulching center anymore where it should be strongest."

From his left, Cap Nyba demanded abruptly, "Milyr, stop generating grav pulses for moment. Rest a little and keep an eye on the automatic cycling of null-grav shield generation. We may be inside null-space now, but we don't want to be surprised to be suddenly into the an-grav space."

"Vulch, Cap, we don't want that for sure. The an-grav space could rip us apart very rapidly. But, Cap, we really don't want to get trapped here forever like ancient astronauts Kolrain and Kilczek did," Milyr complained nervously. "I should really try to keep Wolf Streak Beta rocking gently just in case. Maybe the null-grav zone will have an intermittent opening. It really is not that wide."

"Neer, is that wise?" Cap Nyba asked, turning toward Domyn, and then from his ear-piece on audio frequency designed to allow Cap Nyba to limit audio feed to specific members of crew, she asked in whisper, "Doc, how is Milyr's health and stamina at this moment?"

Trying to stall on a direct response while Doc Kymil diagnosed Milyr's current condition through her dionboda, Domyn replied, "Well, Cap, I don't see any breaks in consistency of twinings on either side of null-grav pocket. Unless energy powering these opposing twinings is disrupted or ceases on its own, twining walls of this anomaly would have no intermittent gaps. However, we don't know if two opposing twinings are directly connected. We don't know what is powering them. This is a new anomaly to our knowledge and experience."

"Yeah, it is new, vulching unheard of by any Jayer," Milyr whined, still trying to direct movement of the spacecraft with some flailing of his lavender dionjocu gloves. "I'm afraid to just stop trying. Remember vulching nasty that stranded Kilczek and Kolrain? We heard about that many times when we were very young pups before Steppingstone Primero."

In his earpiece, Domyn listened to Doc Kymil say, "Milyr is physically tired. His vital signs are outside active level parameters for him. He should rest, at least briefly. He needs some water and nutrient sustenance now also. Bodacia, do you concur?"

On restricted audio feed only, Bodacia said, "Doctor Kymil, I concur with your diagnosis on the current health of pilot Milyr."

Aloud across the ConCen, Cap Nyba explained with a steady, almost tutorial manner, "Remember, Milyr, ancient astronauts Kilczek and Kolrain did not have the same sci-tech that we have now. Their flight occurred in an era before humans knew of Kil-Kols or three aspects of space..."

"Our vulching sci-tech isn't doing us much cherp good now," Milyr protested, "its vulching useless! We will become toxx legends of our time, new Kilczek and Kolrain corpses lost in space."

To Domyn's perspective, Nyba seemed surprisingly patient with Milyr as she continued with her lesson, "I'm sure that we all remember that astronauts Kilczek and Kolrain were pioneers and explorers looking to study dark matter beyond gravity well of Zerosolis System. Unfortunately for them, they happened upon and into the grip of Kil-Kol just outside the region of Zerosolis. They were stranded within the null-grav aspect of then unknown Kil-Kol and Weznuski space, which eventually entrapped their ancient spaceship. The limited knowledge and design of their ancient ship did not give them sci-tech to generate any gravity fields with which to form the braid to travel the null-space region."

"Awright, yes, Milyr, they had no braiding technology then. I have confidence in our sci-tech now. We will find a way to propel ourselves out of this situation," Domyn said with assurance, trying to aid Nyba as she tried to calm and encourage the crew.

On restricted audio frequency, Prof Lyndyn announced in a hushed voice, "Cap Nyba, his stress is not critical but a higher than preferred level for him. I agree with Kymil, brief rest will benefit Milyr. We do have another pilot on the ConCen now. We may need both healthy to get out of this situation."

When Domyn heard a muttered groan of annoyance from Cap Nyba on the ear-piece audio, probably as she considered assigning Jamyk to pilot function, he also listened to Milyr grumble, "Yeah, vulch, look what happened to them. They were stranded and died before the rescue mission could reach them. only memorial they earned was naming of spatial anomaly that killed them. Vulch, I don't want this anomaly with my name on it a hundred years from now."

"Hey, Milyr's Hole!" laughed Swyllo with hilarity.

"No, but maybe Nothingness of Milyr," suggested Whyvvi with a nervous laugh.

"Argh, now is no time for comic silliness!" Nyba groaned sourly at either quips of young women or thought of placing Jamyk into pilot function, Domyn was not certain, but then he heard her command, "Jamyk, prep to assume pilot function immediately. I don't want any stalling and no shenanigans! Milyr, halt all attempts at movement of Wolf Streak Beta until we understand this situation better. Do you agree, Neer Domyn?"

"Vulch, I can pilot now, Cap. I'm alright," whined Milyr as he waved his long arms tiredly and his lavender dionjocu dripped moisture from several spots due to concentration of his sweat.

"Awright, enough, Milyr!" Domyn growled sternly, and then with more moderation in his tone, continued, "Milyr, you've worked very strenuously more this entire difficult experience. You do need rest. Follow Cap's order. We'll need you ready when we finally fly away from this place. Go take rest. Get a drink of nutrient and just plain water. That agrees with your recommendation, right, Doc?"

"Oh my, that would certainly be my instruction," the melodious voice of Doc Kymil said from her white chair next to Domyn on his right.

"Buffalardi had deployed beacons into the Debordo space," announced Whyvvi, and then added with a hint of doubt, "At least I believe that it has. The zeta ray sensors are not as precise as normal with this strange vortex near this Kil-Kol. It should have deployed by now is what I should say."

. "Vulch, nutrient and that nasty antemgebemarzex again, you're trying to shove that nasty drink down my throat all time, Doc," Milyr protested with frustrated resignation in his baritone voice as his arms gradually stopped their movements and his fingers flicked less often inside his dionjocu gloves than before when he was flying a craft without Jamyk. "However, I guess I won't need my manliness anyway. We may get stranded here until we die."

While watching Jamyk clip his pilot visor to the light green cap on his head, Domyn said firmly to the other pilot, "Awright, Milyr, stop acting like toxx pup now. Enough of your griping! We'll find way to get out of this vortex. We're Jayers after all!"

Beside him to his left, Domyn felt a swish of Cap Nyba's chair and heard her voice ask, "Joculatus, do you confirm deployment of beacons in Debordo space?"

"Cap Nyba, Buffalardi beacons have deployed in Debordo space," replied artigence Joculatus, and then almost immediately after this, he announced, "A sanbeam comm is arriving from Fox Flash Alpha now."

"Khebol!" blurted Whyvvi excitedly.

Domyn witnessed Cap Nyba flick the ring finger in the blue dionjocu glove on her left hand at the same time as he performed the exact movement in his tan glove. Then the image of the fluctuating red and purple and orange colors of gravity currents and twinings on his visor changed to slightly blurred video transmission of a large-headed, bald young man. A smile momentarily expressed the greeting of cheer on the face of Cap Bhiros.

However, very shortly Domyn saw the very hasty transformation to expression of concern and seriousness, and then Cap Bhiros said with soberness in his deep voice, "Wolf Streak, this is Fox Flash. We have anticipated a possible problem or confusion that you may have come upon. This transmission originated eleven minutes before we estimated your deployment of your Buffalardi occurred. Neer Khebol determined eleven minutes would be most likely the time delay between our positions. We hope that recorded message left with our Buffalardi of your present Kil-Kol reached you and was of aid…"

"Vulching it is about time we heard from Fox Flash Alpha," muttered Swyllo. "They didn't even transmit the last awakening."

Deep voice of Cap Bhiros continued in Domyn's ear-piece, "…imbedded on tier two within this comm are recording we made of our sensor reads during our passage by your present Kil-Kol. We pray our recordings can be value to your situation. Respond by normal sanbeam comm. If you received Khebol's automated recording, we suggest that you aim your sanbeam into the center of Kil-Kol. Khebol believes our original Buffalardi is functioning still somewhere central to Kil-Kol. We don't understand how this can occur…"

"What vulch! That's a lot of help!" moaned Milyr sarcastically.

Domyn listened to Cap Bhiros say, "…believes this strongly. If you did not get Khebol's recording, and this is first comm to you at your current position, then aim your sanbeam at your recently deployed Buffalardi…"

"Don't they know what vulch they did?" Swyllo cried stressfully. "How can they help if they're vulching guessing? Toxx, this is not cherp!"

"Quiet, Swyllo. He is talking about Khebol," scolded Whyvvi.

"…Khebol will be the most knowledgeable and useful member of Fox Flash to aid you while we are in range of our recently deployed beacons. I've asked Khebol to comm with you at next sequence. He calculates we may have four or five exchanges before we are out of range. Give us precise information as you can about your situation. We hope that your only problem is one of confusion, but Khebol suspects that you may be in a serious nasty toxx now. I pray he is wrong for once. Fox Flash awaits your comm. Be briefer than I have been to speed up exchanges. Time delay is about eleven minutes. Fox Flash ended," and then the face and voice of Cap Bhiros vanished from the visor in front of the right eye of Domyn.

Slightly overwhelmed and perturbed by speculation in the message by Cap Bhiros, Domyn welcomed Nyba's rapid decisiveness when she commanded, "Whyvvi, put together as complete record of our recent sensor reads. Joculatus, include pilot view screen recordings of flight passage reads three minutes prior to Buffalardi launch through to current time. Whyvvi, Joculatus, you've got three minutes to compile and then send whatever is ready by then. Domyn, you've got those three minutes to comment to Fox Flash Alpha. Then I need your ready to analyze recordings that they have sent to us. Our entire comm must be ended in no more than seven minutes. Let's be very efficient with our comm to get as many exchanges with Fox Flash Alpha while they are in range. Let's go, boys and girls!"

"Vulching time delay!" muttered Milyr as he peeled off his lavender dionjocu cap and visor from his bald head. "How can we be effective while communications are so scattered and one-way?"

"Okay, you boys and girls, we can't change time delay. Let's do our functions. Let's think our way out of this. Clock is ticking, boys and girls! It is truly Jayer time now!" Nyba called, strongly filling ConCen with her confidence, and then is his ear-piece, Domyn heard her say to him only, "Neer, use restricted Tier Three to talk with Fox Flash Alpha. Keep our crew off your comm unless you specifically need someone for expert or pertinent comment. I'm counting on you to focus on getting us away. You don't need chatter of our crew distracting you now. I'll listen in on Tier Three and try not to interfere. You're down to two minutes and thirteen seconds, Neer."

Two minutes? Awe help me, Domyn groaned silently. What should he report to Fox Flash? What should he ask them or Khebol? Two minutes? Why had Nyba put this burden on him? Could he think of way to get Wolf Streak out of this nasty mess? Two minutes to comm with Fox Flash, he moaned, awe help me!

Kicking the pedal on the base of his brown chair with his right heel, Domyn activated the comm system and ordered, "Joculatus, this is Neer Domyn. Establish Tier Three comm at my control and send to Fox Flash by sanbeam at the time appointed by Cap Nyba. Target the general area of center of Kil-Kol. Expect sub tracts from Whyvvi and yourself as ordered by Cap Nyba."

"Neer Domyn, sanbeam is enroute," Joculatus said in Domyn's earpiece. "You have one minute, forty-three seconds per Cap Nyba's instructions."

Awe damn, now artigence is pressuring him, Domyn sighed bitterly to himself, and then said aloud, "Fox Flash, this is Wolf Streak. Khebol, we have received your prior message, which suggests that your Buffalardi and one or more of beacons is in center of Kil-Kol. Was this first the for you? Did you perform second launch?"

This was impossibly difficult, Domyn whined to himself and wondered if he was asking pertinent and useful questions, but he continued still, "We are trapped in an anomaly of null-grav between two undefined twinings of an-grav and null-grav.The inner twining seems to be narrow enough to be remnant of your braid of central launch. This is still open, which suggests that braid did not reach the other side of Weznuski space. The outer twining is flowing in opposite direction away from Kil-Kol at a slight angle outward. Likely that your Buffalardi must have some connection with these unusual twinings. Nyba has limited my talking time to speed up our exchanges. We will compare your sensor read with ours as soon as I end this comm. We are sending some of our own recordings on Tier Two of this sanbeam. I'm on Tier Three with Nyba. Awe help us, if you can't! Wolf Streak ended."

In spite of the air-condition cooling off his tan dionjocu uniform, Domyn felt wet sweat covering his body. Vulch, that was worse than exercising with Milyr and Jamyk. He had no inspirational or invigorating sensation as usually followed an active physical workout with friends. Just cold, damp sweat and tired, befuddled mind stunned him as he kicked off the comm pedal with his right heel. Domyn wondered, had he accomplished anything? Had he given Khebol anything to consider, anything to stimulate that creative brain given to Khebol at birth?

"Neer Domyn," Nyba said loudly beside him. "Our sanbeam has been sent to Fox Flash Alpha. We have eleven minutes to come up with our next exchange, or, of course, how we're going to get out of this vortex. What do you need from us?"

As her strident voice shook his lethargy, Domyn replied with trepidation, "Kil-Kol reads sent by Fox Flash should be put on ConCen holovision for best resolution and analytical viewing."

"Do you have a theory, Neer?" Cap Nyba asked.

"Vulch, I have theory that we're all vulched here forever," Milyr whined from his slouched position in his purple chair.

"Now that is not very helpful, you toxx!" yelled Whyvvi from across ConCen.

Ignoring comments by others, Domyn sighed wearily while nervously rocking his chair side-to-side in short slow movements and said, "Not really, Cap, just seemingly unrelated data swirling about in my mind. I need something specific, something truly correct as basis for my speculation to create a useful theory."

While he spoke to Nyba and swayed his chair back and forth, Domyn noticed a figure in white arise from a white chair and step to the lanky form in the purple chair. They talked in low whispers and then both departed the ConCen. Well, now that was cherp to observe, he thought to himself. At least Milyr would get some rest and attention from Doc Kymil.

Between the now empty chairs on his side of the ConCen, Swyllo sat in her yellow chair. She had been on the ConCen as long as he had since beginning the Buffalardi launch assignment. How long ago this awakening had that been, Domyn wondered briefly. But that was not what he should be focusing upon now, he scolded himself silently. If Swyllo could stay focused upon her task, so could he.

Nyba was saying to his left, "…know that we are not moving, that is solid fact, Neer. We know that our Buffalardi launched successfully through Kil-Kol into Debordo space. That is solid and positive fact. Can these facts aid you at all, Neer Domyn?"

Further to Nyba's left, Prof Lyndyn abruptly spun his gray chair to face Domyn and exclaimed with his nasal voice, "And indeed that braid had closed as it should have. Your choice to deviate your launch trajectory was proven correct. We know now that some of Kil-Kol behaves as it should."

"Awright, yes, yes, Prof, you are right," Domyn agreed, stopping his nervous twitching of his chair, and then continued with sudden excitement, "Our Buffalardi and Wilchrison that created braid for its passage through Weznuski did function as it should. Yes, the braid worked as it should. It is not the Kil-Kol that's the problem. It's something unusual about or in the center of the Kil-Kol that's problem. Cap Bhiros said that their Buffalardi might be in center still. Why? He said that Khebol was very sure about that. Why do they believe their Buffalardi is in center of the Kil-Kol still?"

Just to the left of Prof Lyndyn's gray chair, Whyvvi, in her red chair, exclaimed hastily, "If Khebol believes so, then it must be so."

Beyond Whyvvi at the very end of the formation of chairs, Jamyk, with his full visor covering his eyes, swiveled his green chair and said, "Yup."

"Joculatus, portray the Kil-Kol sensor recordings from Fox Flash Alpha pertinent to their Buffalardi launch. Put it on ConCen holovision," Cap Nyba commanded. "Let's see what they saw nineteen days ago."

"Cap Nyba, your command will be executed in thirty-seven seconds," Joculatus reported, and then added, "estimated time until response from Fox Flash Alpha is three minutes, seventeen seconds."

"Thank you, Joculatus," Nyba said and then turned toward Domyn and asked, "Do you expect to see something specific in their recordings of their launch?"

Lifting the visor from in front of his right eye up over his tan cap on his forehead and scalp, Domyn replied, "Not launch itself, Cap. I'm more interested in Kil-Kol and if it is affected by the launch. If Khebol is correct, then the launch changed the normal action of Kil-Kol and produced present anomaly with these strange grav currents and twinings. Whyvvi, please watch your ongoing sensor reads of the Kil-Kol center. Something is going on there. Swyllo, get us an update on light brightness in and around the center also. I've got notion that it is all connected."

Before he finished his instructions, Domyn saw the area in front of and between the semi-circle of chairs on ConCen abruptly illuminate into holovision of LaOgres space with typical pale twilight gray. In the middle of this grayness, cloud-like, almost ethereal brightness shine. This was Kil-Kol of nineteen days ago. Well, it was at that moment, perfectly normal as Kil-Kol, Domyn noticed, just a vast region of bright spergits about as luminescent as moonlight on normal planet. There was no sign of the braid yet.

"Remember, boys and girls, this is a sensor recording made nineteen days ago during the passage of Fox Flash Alpha by this Kil-Kol," Nyba reminded hushed viewers on the ConCen.

In the center of the closest rim of Kil-Kol, barely visible spiraling of cloud-like substance appeared, and Lyndyn exclaimed in his nasal voice, "There, indeed, no doubt braid had started normally as usual when Fox Flash Alpha triggered Wilchrison of their Buffalardi. Now let us see what happens next. How long does a probe take to get through Kil-Kol? Does anyone remember that?"

Watching the swirling action of the braid extend into Kil-Kol, Domyn replied, "Several minutes, Prof, longer than we have before anticipated the reply from Fox Flash Alpha, which could be any moment now. Cap, I'm going back to Tier Three comm. I'm satisfied with what I've seen so far from this recording. Let's fast-forward this viewing until we see something unusual. I'll be watching with one eye. Please, everyone, be alert to anything unusual."

While he flipped the visor back down in front of his right eye, Domyn heard Cap Nyba command, "Joculatus, fast-forward recording three times normal speed. Lyndyn, it is our responsibility to watch most closely. Everyone else, your primary priority is your current function, right, boys and girls, and not watching this holovision. Let's be sharp, Blue Jayers! Let's find something useful."

"Cap Nyba, fast-forward will begin on holovision in seven seconds," Joculatus said and then announced in addition, "a sanbeam reception from Fox Flash Alpha is now arriving."

"Khebol, is it Khebol?" asked Whyvvi fervently. "It should be Khebol."

"Focus, Whyvvi, on your function. We need real-time data from your sensors," Cap Nyba demanded of the young woman in pink dionjocu. "In fact, Whyvvi, what does your zeta ray sensor reveal about the center of this Kil-Kol in our present time? Khebol believed that our problem may be related to the center of this Kil-Kol. What do you read now?"

Just before the Tier Three comm blocked out ConCen chatter, Domyn heard Whyvvi reply, "Nothing definite, Cap, no sign of Buffalardi probe or beacons, not even much spergit activity. There should be some reflected light at least as edges of braid path, right, Swyllo? The narrow probe braid channel should not eliminate spergit light..."

Then the incoming sanbeam comm triggered Tier Three restriction in his dionjocu hearing system, and Domyn listened to the mellow baritone voice of Neer Khebol in his earpiece say, "Wolf Streak, this is Fox Flash. I'm assuming that I'm talking to Domyn. We've received your recording of your sensor scans in previous comm. I've seen some of them to this point. I'm still watching as I speak, as I'm sure you are with our previous recordings. This time delay is nasty vulching..."

Silently Domyn agreed as with his left eye he observed the fast-forward replay of Fox Flash scan of the braid piercing Kil-Kol on holovision, and at the same time, saw in his visor over his right eye Khebol in the tan dionjocu continue to report, "...Your previous comm confirms to me that our first Buffalardi launch into center of Kil-Kol has not reached Debordo space. Your reception of my automated recording indicates that at least one of beacons has activated. Also, your scans and your observations suggest that probe is still actively braiding. If this is so, then something has blocked the probe's passage through the braid to the Debordo side of Weznuski. Apparently this blockage has trapped but not destroyed the Buffalardi probe or beacon..."

Yes, yes, Domyn muttered to himself, we've thought of that. Well, he'd almost voiced consideration to Cap Nyba, he reminded himself. Whyvvi's last report suggested the idea. Also, before Wolf Streak had been trapped in the null-grav anomaly, Swyllo had complained about a lack of brightness in center of the Kil-Kol quite time ago now. Why had he not seen this pattern earlier? Analyzing and

105

sifting through reports of his crew was not the same as maintaining sci-tech systems, he realized, and then forced himself to get back to his task.

When his left eye noticed a sudden halt of extending the braid on holovision, Domyn commanded hastily, "Joculatus, play pilot view from Fox Flash Alpha. Use the same time as the current point on holovision now. Whyvvi, Swyllo, we're looking for large physical blockage most likely somewhere near the far side of Weznuski in the center region of Kil-Kol. Focus on the spot where the braid stopped extending. Use your function sensor to the most precise level that you can."

In his earpiece, he listened to Khebol still, but the close and loud voice of Nyba overwhelmed the words of Khebol when she asked, "What do you see, Domyn? What are we looking for now?"

However, Domyn ignored this inquiry and instead focused upon the baritone voice of Khebol saying, "...doubt in my mind, Domyn, our first Buffalardi probe is active still and is energizing the cause of your problem. Somehow braid creation of Wilchrison has continued since we triggered it nineteen days ago. The small Flandecams of the probe have found a source of steady energy and are continuing to generate grav fields. The outer twining that is pulsing in your direction away from the trapped probe is most likely deflection of the braid off blocking mass. Why mass can withstand the braiding affect is unknown to me..."

While he watched Khebol draw a sketch of the theory being explained on the comm view in the visor over his right eye, Domyn saw with his left eye a change of scene on holovision as Joculatus played the pilot view from the Fox Flash Alpha. Though a central scene was receding rapidly in perception of the Fox Flash Alpha sensor read, there was a discernible change in grav flows and currents around passage of braid. With the eye now expecting the phenomenon, Domyn observed the subtle beginnings of the opposing grav current now trapping Wolf Streak Beta. The nasty things had started nineteen days ago. Somehow a tiny probe was getting energy well beyond its original supply. Somehow a small Wilchrison of Buffalardi was braiding still. Awe toxx, Domyn swore silently to himself, this was not cherp.

Meanwhile, a voice of Khebol was speaking still in his earpiece, "...launched second Buffalardi to forward edge of Kil-Kol. This did deploy into Debordo. This tells me that the peripheral rim of Kil-Kol is normal. The blockage is central only. Obviously this blockage is large enough to entrap probe. Remember, Domyn, braid for probe is narrow. The blockage may not be very wide. It would be larger than the braid for the probe and does seem to have some deflective property since the braid, or part of it, is being deflected. How this occurs, I do not know..."

In the holovision, Domyn observed the steadily expanding counter flow deflecting from the mysterious center. Had Chitir or Radhin realized what was being observed nineteen days ago? Could pilot of Fox Flash Alpha have recognized the beginning of the double opposing twinings that now trapped Wolf Streak Beta? Or had the pilot then been so focused on the forward flight of Fox Flash Alpha and probably a desperate attempt to launch the second Buffalardi before leaving Kil-Kol behind? Most likely Fox Flash Alpha had not time to do a routine comm with Wolf Streak Beta during that awakening. They must have been frantic, Domyn mused.

With his naked left eye, Domyn watched the holovision blank out for a few seconds and then return with a very defined portrayal of sensor read from Whyvvi's current position. The detail was more than normal for the sensor scan from just the perspective of Wolf Streak Beta in LaOgres space. In fact, Domyn realized, this highly defined portrayal could only result from at least two perspectives of a similar scene, two perspectives from almost parallax angles.

In his earpiece, Domyn heard the voice of Nyba override a deeper voice of Khebol, and she said, "Domyn, Joculatus has meshed reads of the Kil-Kol from both Fox Flash Alpha and Wolf Streak Beta. I've requested that he employ the common timeline and common parameters with central interest on most likely the position of the first Buffalardi launch coordinates of Fox Flash Alpha. Do you notice anything of interest? Does this new view help you any?"

In his earpiece, Khebol was also saying at the same time as Nyba, "...find your situation troublesome. We will do whatever we can to free Wolf Streak. We do not want another Kilczek-Kolrain memorial in Blue Jay history. Respond as soon as you can. I estimate three more exchanges unless Cap Bhiros decides to stop our flight progress and keep Fox Flash in range longer than normal. Awe be with you, Domyn. Tell Whyvvi that I may love her. Fox Flash ended."

Harshly kicking the pedal beneath his chair with his heel, thus ending his Tier Three isolation, Domyn heard abruptly the chatter on the ConCen, including Swyllo as she commanded brusquely, "Joculatus, mesh my energy reads with the same parameters as you just used with the Fox Flash Alpha energy reads."

"Damn, Cap Bhiros, his hastiness and recklessness may have doomed us," Cap Nyba mumbled in a low whisper beside him while she caught his gaze when Domyn spun his chair toward her, and then she added with some despondence, "That last bit by Khebol sure sounded a lot like good-bye to Whyvvi, don't you think?"

Flipping his visor up atop his cap on his head, Domyn stared at her, nodded in agreement, and then sighed, "Awe knows for certain that Khebol is not comfortable saying such things either of personal nature or of spiritual nature. And, well, that Bhiros is just Bhiros, hasty, rash, aggressive, daring, but I know that he will help all that he can. He's a Jayer captain still. He'll stall their flight progress if he must. Now what was on that holovision, Cap?"

However, before Nyba could respond, Whyvvi exclaimed excitedly from her red chair, "Look, Domyn, definite solid mass. It is larger than Wolf Streak, probably at least three or four times as large. It should not be there in Kil-Kol, but it is. It is right there where the braid is deflecting back around us. Right, Jamyk, you did correlate position with your current pilot view?"

"Yup," replied Jamyk in his green dionjocu while he slowly fluttered his gloved hands, which indicated to Domyn that the boy was monitoring the position of Wolf Streak Beta but not over-actively engaging the Flandecams with movement commands.

Therefore Domyn was stunned to hear the boy yell in a cracking rasp, "Moving!"

"What's moving?" Nyba asked sharply with suspicion in her voice.

"Wolf," Jamyk gasped, though Domyn observed still that the hands of the boy were not recklessly piloting the spacecraft, and then Jamyk blurted, "Us!"

Hastily Domyn flipped the visor back down over his right eye and triggered the view as pilot Jamyk received. The central twining associated with Buffalardi braiding was dominant in scene. Wolf Streak Beta had shifted toward this braid remnant. However, his eye could see no obvious movement or grav current streaming by view. What had the boy seen? Has he felt something with his uncanny espersense, Domyn wondered.

"Whyvvi, sensor read calibration now," Cap Nyba demanded urgently, and then with a steadier tone, tinged with just a subtle hint of excitement, asked "Can you confirm the movement of Wolf Streak Beta? Are we really moving now?"

"Moving," Jamyk repeated loudly, "yup!"

"Moving how? Where are we moving?" Lyndyn asked in a nasal voice heavy with skepticism. "Are you certain, my young man? It is not very likely under..."

While Prof Lyndyn sputtered, Jamyk lifted a green glove toward the holovision image of the combined sensor reads of Fox Flash Alpha and Wolf Streak Beta and mass in center of Kil-Kol and shouted hoarsely, "There!"

"Cap, we are moving," Whyvvi cried out with joy, "my zeta ray measurement is confirming that we are closer to that mass with each sensor pulse that I send."

"We're vulching moving!" Swyllo cheered. "We won't be snared in this nasty forever."

Domyn could not see any significant movement in his right eye visor, so he requested, "Cap, let's put Whyvvi's current view and time read on holovision. We've got what we need from recordings of Fox Flash Alpha now. Then we should end our transmissions to Fox Flash Alpha and give them time to respond."

"Joculatus, do as Neer Domyn has just stated," Cap Nyba commanded firmly, "Jamyk, can you fly a spacecraft yet?"

"Nope," boy in green replied and then reaffirmed, "Moving."

"The braid, the braid remnant is very slowly pulling us," Domyn shouted suddenly as comprehension engulfed his brain. "The function of the braid is to pull the mass through itself and thus through Weznuski space. Wolf Streak Beta is closer to pulling tendency of the original braid for the probe from Fox Flash than it is to pushing tendency of deflected twining on the back side of this null-space vortex. If we are inside the braid, Wolf Streak Beta will be shot forward as if we had braided ourselves. But this remnant was not designed to allow passage of a mass as large or as wide as this spacecraft."

"Does that mean that we are going to hit into that?" Whyvvi asked abruptly, pointing her pink glove at the dark center of Kil-Kol now in holovision. "Did we not decide that was a very large solid mass of something? Is it not much larger than us?"

"Moving," Jamyk rasped, "faster!"

Swyllo whined, "Vulch, yeah, we did say it was much bigger. That nasty blockage trapped probe that's making this braided vortex. And it is right in the center of this Kil-Kol. Now it will thrust us right into the very center. This is nasty!"

"Indeed what an ironic predicament," Prof Lyndyn murmured from his gray chair beside Nyba. "We are moving finally out of the trapped situation but now directly toward the likely collision with a much larger mass. What a predicament!"

"Moving," Jamyk yelled hoarsely, "faster!"

"Oh, vulch!" shrieked Swyllo

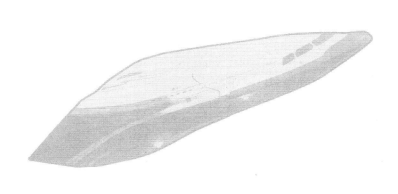

SPEC ONE: DOMYN THROUGH LAOGRES
CHAPTER 8

Jamyk rasped, "Moving!"

With worried anxiety in her voice, Whyvvi confirmed, "Yes, Cap Nyba, Wolf Streak Beta has increased velocity since my previous calibration read. We are going into that big nasty for sure and now much more rapidly."

"Can you confirm this increase in velocity, Joculatus?" Cap Nyba asked with a calm tone, and then as if an afterthought, ordered, "Joculatus, calculate the estimate of how much time that we have before the partial braid grabs us completely and hurtles this spacecraft toward that unidentified mass in the center of Kil-Kol."

"If we're in a braiding phenomenon, then we have only minutes, Cap," Domyn stated with certainty and also some anxiety, and then he continued, "Probably less time than the next comm with Fox Flash Alpha. We're on our own in this."

"Cap Nyba, I confirm increase in velocity of Wolf Streak Beta," Joculatus reported, "assuming the normal braid parameters, estimated time before seizure of this spacecraft by the alleged braid anomaly is nineteen minutes, twenty-nine seconds."

"Khebol and Fox Flash Alpha should be able to help us by then," Whyvvi exclaimed with obvious hope and enthusiasm in her voice. "Khebol will help us. I am sure of that."

"Vulch Fox Flash toxx! They are the ones who got us into this nasty mess," yelled Swyllo with an extreme shrill bitterness in her voice.

"This is not a normal braid phenomenon," Domyn sighed with exhaustion and then continued with some attempt at assured conviction, "Yet if we are now caught in thebraid or an edge strand of the braid, then it is the braid that was created to channel the probe. Narrow the braid! Not be a wide enough diameter to pull the spacecraft size of Wolf Streak Beta through as quickly as the braid designed to channel the probe..."

Shouting with hopeful confidence, Whyvvi interrupted, "We should have more time than the estimate of Joculatus. We should have time to get the comm from Khebol and Fox Flash Alpha."

"Maybe," agreed Jamyk, fluttering his fingers within his green dionjocu gloves in a pattern that mystified Domyn.

"But even if we get their comm, then exchange and time delay would be much longer than our most hopeful time estimate," Cap Nyba predicted. "Boys and girls, let's analyze this situation very quickly. Let's think of a strategy ourselves. We can't wait to hear from foxes. We don't want to collide with whatever that mass at any velocity equal to the pull of the braid."

"Vulch, we really don't want to be trapped in this nasty Kil-Kol. I can't stand LaOgres!" complained Swyllo now with little panic in her voice. "Vulching nasty LaOgres!"

In his earpiece, Domyn heard Doc Kymil suggest from somewhere off ConCen, "Cap Nyba, three crew members who were here to launch our recent Buffalardi are exhausted, physically and mentally. Do you not concur, Lyndyn?"

"No doubt, you are correct, dear Doc Kymil," Lyndyn affirmed in Domyn's earpiece and then continued, "Indeed, Domyn, you must be finding that your brain is functioning slower than you would prefer now. And no doubt, so are thinking processes of Whyvvi and Swyllo..."

"Yes, Prof and Doc, but we do need them now. We need their input now, not later," Cap Nyba interrupted and declared firmly, not letting fact that the medical advisers were much older than her daunt, which was something that Domyn often wished that he could manage to do.

Then ignoring the impulse to disclaim Prof Lyndyn's diagnosis, Domyn admitted to himself that he was very tired and befuddled. His mind was mystified with several factors and bits of data concerning the present crisis. However, he could not put them into any form of order or pattern. He felt that he was missing something simple. Awe help me clarify these tangled thoughts, he wished to himself. There was certainly something basic that was eluding his conscious mind just then. What was it? Damn, he was exhausted. Why could he not concentrate now with all this science related information, he mused as he yawned. His beloved crew and Wolf Streak Beta were in danger.

In his earpiece, Domyn listened as Prof Lyndyn continued, "...everyone has gone much longer this awakening without Saphyndenlairoum sleep than we are accustomed. Your mental awareness will be eroding soon if it has not already. No doubt, Domyn, you can feel that even now..."

"But, I must function, Prof. I must solve this now," Domyn interrupted with what he considered an appropriate counter argument and then commanded, "Joculatus, put the current pilot view on the holovision."

Cap Nyba reinforced the command, "Yes, Joculatus, do as Neer Domyn instructs. Whyvvi has velocity changed as predicted?"

Whyvvi reported from her red chair, "We seem to be moving a bit faster now, Cap. I wish that we could slow this pace. Jamyk, can you not do something with your pilot skills now?"

"Nope," Jamyk replied with some strain in his voice. "Try?"

"Not yet, Jamyk," demanded Cap Nyba stridently. "Don't make this any worse now with some foolish daredevil attempt."

On the holovision in front of the semi-circle of chairs, Domyn saw the same view as Jamyk the pilot. To the left of the displayed scene, he saw twining of red and purple threading away into the distance toward blackness in Kil-Kol. The rest of the holovision portrayed red representation of null-space. In the far distance, his eyes could see just vaguely a subtle purplish tinge, most likely representation of an-grav component of other twining creating the outer edge of this vortex of null-space. This null-space was preventing Flandecams from generating either posi-grav or an-grav fields.

Then suddenly he reminded himself that there should be some an-grav component to the nearest twining, and Wolf Streak Beta was partially into that twining now, so he asked hastily, "Jamyk, try it carefully and briefly. Try to make an-grav field now."

"Are you sure this is a wise risk, Neer Domyn?" Cap Nyba asked with suspicion.

"Don't make it any worse!" shrieked Swyllo.

"Yes, Cap Nyba, I am certain this is cherp move," Domyn promised with a stoic glance at her beside his chair. "We can't wait forever to try our speculations, can we?"

"I trust your speculations, Domyn," Nyba stated and then pivoted her blue captain's chair toward Jamyk and commanded, "Jamyk, do as Domyn requests. Try to carefully generate an an-grav field. Don't get careless or foolish, young man!"

"Yup," the boy in green dionjocu rasped when he acknowledged the order and his hands fluttered and his fingers twitched in the green gloves, and then he announced, "Yup... An-grav."

"We can power now!" Whyvvi cheered. "We should go now while we can. We should continue into LaOgres space and ride an-grav currents all the way to the Sexto system while we can."

"Nope," Jamyk rasped. "Weak."

Watching the reaction in the twining flows portrayed on the holovision, Domyn agreed with Jamyk, "No, the field is not strong enough to propel a spacecraft of size and mass of the Wolf Streak Beta. We can generate a field, but it is not of full strength for normal flight or to free us from this twining by itself."

Joculatus said, "Cap Nyba, the estimated time to full capture of this spacecraft by the braid anomaly is thirteen minutes."

"Oh, such vulching welcome info," Swyllo snarled sarcastically. "Will we be stranded here? Or will we be crashing into that blockage? Does anybody know?"

Prof Lyndyn peered at Swyllo and said with a soothing softness in his nasal voice, "Indeed at least, my young lady, artigence had recalculated that time to capture is more in our favor now. We may still have time to escape this predicament."

"Cap," Whyvvi cried abruptly with renewed spirit, "We did slow the velocity a bit when Jamyk tried the Flandecams to make some an-grav field. My most recent reads have revealed this to me now."

"Indeed that is good info, is it not, Swyllo? Now we may be able to give ourselves more time than just moments ago," Prof Lyndyn said with some enthusiasm and then added, "perhaps we may get enough time now to hear suggestions from Fox Flash Alpha again."

"Make sure that we don't lose contact with this inner twining, Jamyk," Domyn demanded as he watched the boy's fingers flicker and twitch inside the dionjocu gloves, "But keep punching that an-grav every so often to resist the pull of the braiding phenomenon. I trust you, Jamyk."

"Yup," replied Jamyk and continued with a slightly different hand and finger manipulations.

"Vulch, yeah!" Swyllo groaned, "Let's not get back into vulching lack of movement situation. At least we can move now. Not that I enjoy going toward that nasty, but staying here in limbo is vulching nasty. Don't do any silly toxx moves, little peener!"

After watching the glove manipulations of the boy in the green dionjocu, Domyn asked with some curiosity, "Did you just try posi-grav generation, Jamyk?"

"What vulch do you think you're doing, you toxx?" screamed Swyllo.

"Yup," Jamyk admitted, apparently ignoring Swyllo's outburst, and then the boy said, "Posi."

"Jamyk, don't get too independent," growled Cap Nyba. "Don't be careless with our gains now."

"Posi," the boy reiterated proudly, "yup."

"You can now command the Flandecams to generate some an-grav and some posi-grav fields, right, Jamyk?" Domyn inquired hastily, trying to keep others from ignoring and discouraging the achievement of the boy in this crisis, and then he said, "I assume that these fields by themselves are not strong enough to power a normal spacecraft flight, correct, Jamyk?"

"Yup," Jamyk rasped, "weak."

Cap Nyba spun her blue chair toward him and asked, "Neer Domyn, does this help us? Do we have time to do anything against the threat of this braiding twining pulling us into the mass of blockage in Kil-Kol?"

Was there time to do anything? Domyn wondered, what was the answer? It was probably something basic, something his tired consciousness should have considered by now. His brain was most knowledgeable of sci-tech theory and mechanisms on Wolf Streak Beta. Why could he not see any answer? Awe, stimulate my weary brain, help me to see the solution and to save my friends and craft, Domyn silently prayed, hoping the universe would take pity on his present stupidity.

"Braid," Jamyk rasped loudly and abruptly. "Debordo."

Cap Nyba asked with uncertain skepticism, "Are you suggesting that we pop into Debordo space now, Jamyk?"

"Yup," Jamyk replied, "soon."

"We should not do that," Whyvvi declared with conviction in her tone. "That would be counter to this mission. We would go off our schedule to Sexto. We might never get back into LaOgres space in these coordinates. We may never get back on the mission timeline. We should not do this. If we do not stay in LaOgres space, the trip will take several times as long in Debordo space. We all know this as basic space-time theory. Our velocity in LaOgres is many times faster than in regular space."

"Vulch, get us out of LaOgres," Swyllo cried out with fervor.

"Is this really a cherp notion, Neer Domyn?" Cap Nyba asked, glancing at him.

Before he could summon his will to give Nyba some response, a baritone voice bellowed from behind the semi-circle of chairs on ConCen, "Yeah, we must go now. We vulching must go soon if we want to avoid getting trapped again in that nasty vortex of toxx null-grav. Or maybe worse yet, colliding with that vulching nasty…thing…out there in the center of Kil-Kol will be toxx whipping. Popping is our best chance now."

"Yup," Jamyk agreed with Milyr as the lanky boy in the lavender dionjocu strode behind Domyn to the purple chair, and then Jamyk added in sudden silence, "Pop."

While he observed Doc Kymil return to her white chair beside him as well, Domyn suddenly realized in his exhausted mind, of course, that was the simple answer. Wolf Streak Beta could move out of this trap and potential collision by the braiding back into Debordo space. At least in theory, it could be done, Domyn reminded himself. Why hadn't he realized his earlier? Their recently launched Buffalardi had braided through the rim of this Kil-Kol and through Weznuski space into Debordo space successfully. It had not been affected by the anomaly in the center of Kil-Kol. Why had he not thought of this himself? With admiration and some astonishment, he glanced at the boy in green.

"Is this possible, Neer Domyn? Can we pop under our present circumstances?" Cap Nyba asked while she spun her blue chair toward Milyr and waved him to his chair, saying, "Join us again, Milyr. I hope that you've had some cherp rest. We will need you again soon."

While Domyn hesitated in replying to Cap Nyba's last query, Milyr plopped himself into his purple chair just beyond Doc Kymil, now in her white chair, and said, "Oh, I've been cherply rested now. Vulch, in fact while I was dozing under cherp relaxing massage of my favorite Doc, I suddenly came up with the idea of popping. I am vulching brilliant and primo, don't you think?"

"Argh! Oh, vulch, I can't believe that I'm going to say this, but yeah, Milyr, you and little peener's idea seems to be the best notion yet," groaned Swyllo as if in pain. "Oh, vulch, please let's do it. Let's just get out of LaOgres and this nasty Kil-Kol!"

"But what if we just braid into that giant mass?" Whyvvi argued. "We should fire our the Flandecams and head back along our intended course through LaOgres space. We have not lost much time yet from our scheduled journey. We can get back on the Blue Jay schedule once we get away from this Kil-Kol. Then we will be joining Khebol and foxes in Sexto right on schedule."

"Vulch, Whyvvi, we're not free from this twining trap yet. We can't fly Wolf Streak Beta as we normally would now," Milyr snapped at her as he reached behind his chair to the small compartment and pulled out a lavender cap and visor. "Not until we get free from this vulching clutch!"

"Whyvvi, what do your sensor reads tell you about our velocity and direction relative to the mass ahead in Kil-Kol?" Prof Lyndyn inquired in a calm nasal voice.

Joculatus reported, "Cap Nyba, estimated time to the collision is eleven minutes."

As Whyvvi mumbled the answer to Prof Lyndyn, Nyba asked with a loud and steady voice, "Neer Domyn, can Wolf Streak Beta do this popping now while in null-grav space? We always initiate the normal braid in either an-grav of LaOgres or posi-grav of Debordo. The braid channel pulls the spacecraft through Weznuski and null-grav space. We don't initiate in null-grav. That is why Milyr became caught in this vortex before because of the totally encompassing null-grav of this region. This is not like sending prongs of an-grav and posi-grav through the thin null-grav shield of this spacecraft when we fly through normal LaOgres space. This is a very substantial region of null-grav, and we're just barely moving through it now. Can we pop from here?"

Not desiring to rush into any commitment of speculation, Domyn let Nyba go on with her lecture of obvious gravitational science and braiding sequence, however, as his eyes studied red, purple, and now a very slight hint of blue patterns displayed in the holovision, he gained some confidence and said, "While we're caught in this twining or the partial braid, Wolf Streak Beta is connected to some an-grav component strand. Yes, Wilchrison may be able to create the braid for us to use to thrust Wolf Streak Beta through Weznuski space into Debordo space. Jamyk has been able to generate some posi-grav just recently. We have the potential to generate all three of the gravity fields that are required for making of the braid…"

Just then Milyr interrupted by blurting, "Vulch, yeah, we can, but we can't wait much longer. Even with the slowing of velocity of this craft, with every minute we wait, the twining pulls us closer to the full channeling force of existing the braid of the probe from Fox Flash."

"Yes, that's correct, Milyr," Domyn agreed, not at all offended by the other lanky young man's intrusion. "We do not have much time now. We must decide to do this very soon. We can't wait for the next comm from Khebol. Even though it may come within minutes, we just can't wait."

"Do you intend to aim the braid toward the periphery of Kil-Kol as you did with our Buffalardi?" Cap Nyba asked.

"Yes, that's only direction that we have any evidence of success," Domyn said.

"Let's do it!" Swyllo wailed from her yellow chair, "Hurry!"

"Pop," Jamyk called out with stress in is voice, and Domyn noticed sweat stains now showing from his underarms and back as the boy rasped again, "soon!"

"Cap, we are starting to increase velocity toward that mass again," Whyvvi reported and then sheepishly admitted, "I guess we should pop. I should not have complained before, Cap. I had thought that Jamyk had freed Wolf Streak Beta. Now I realize that he had merely slowed our inevitable movement toward that huge mass. We should pop. If our Neer and our pilots believe that we can pop, then we should pop."

Joculatus said, "Sanbeam comm from Fox Flash Alpha arriving."

On restricted frequency, Nyba asked in Domyn's earpiece, "Can they help us now?"

"Not soon enough under these time constraints," Domyn said to Nyba only on restricted audio feed, "I should not be distracted at this moment, Cap."

"Just in case they have something pertinent, Domyn, view the comm while the rest of us prep for emergency popping," Cap Nyba commanded of him, and then aloud to ConCen, she called, "Joculatus, what is the fastest prep time to initiate the emergency braiding sequence?"

Joculatus replied shortly, "Cap Nyba, emergency prep for braiding is twenty-nine minutes."

"Oh, vulch!" Milyr and Swyllo proclaimed together and then glowered toward each other.

"We do not have that much time," Whyvvi declared in a soft almost hushed voice.

"Indeed we must find a way to circumvent a normal routine. No doubt we can find the best way of shortening the procedure…" Prof Lyndyn began to say.

Then Domyn lost conversation on ConCen as he kicked in the comm and commanded, "Joculatus, put the incoming sanbeam on Tier Three again to my control. And Joculatus, check all of your program parameters to find way to shortening that prep time to the braid. Report any such protocols to Cap Nyba immediately."

In the earpiece, Domyn heard Joculatus respond, "Neer Domyn, the sanbeam comm is now on Tier Three. Manual pilot control with reduced safety protocols is option to shorten prep time to the braid initiation to estimated eleven minutes."

"Vulch, still too long! Awright, Joculatus, report this to Cap Nyba," Domyn ordered as he flipped the visor down from his forehead and in view of his right eye.

To his surprise, instead of the long narrow face of Neer Khebol, Domyn saw a round dimpled face of Chitir saying from beneath the green dionjocu cap and visor, "…Domyn, Radhin and I strongly urge you to pop to Debordo without delay. Tell Jamyk and Milyr to try the trick we used in the simulation on Steppingstone Tercero. Aim the braid for the rim edge of Kil-Kol. This may be your only chance. I am keeping this comm brief. I will repeat this comm for another three minutes to make sure that you get this. Hope to comm with you on Debordo side. We are trying to slow our departure from our current Kil-Kol to enable us to get another comm exchange with you. Cherp luck, Wolf Streak!"

When the image of Chitir began to repeat comm, Domyn said with a resigned sigh, "Well that was brief, wasn't it, Cap? I assume that you listened in. Did you hear Chitir's recommendation? Do you know about what he's referring?"

"Yes, I did, and no, I don't," Cap Nyba replied to Domyn and then to the entire ConCen stated, "Joculatus indicates that we can shorten the time to the braid if we go to manual pilot control of the Flandecams and eliminate redundant safety protocols. Do you anticipate any problems with this? Do any of your primary functions absolutely require safety protocols? This is no time to worry about any station bias. We need to know about all the factors. Domyn, are you with us again? Do you have an opinion about this suggestion from Joculatus?"

"The only difficulty with this lack of safety protocol would be skill and competency of our pilot. However, I have absolute confidence in both of our pilots to handle this challenge," Domyn declared loudly, gazing at Jamyk and then Milyr, and then with a more questioning tone, exclaimed, "Awright now, young lads, Chitir just told me on the comm that you might know of a procedure or trick, as he called it, that you simulated years ago on Steppingstone Tercero. He believes it will work in this situation. Do either of you lads know to what Chitir referred? I certainly don't."

Although his eyes were shrouded by the full visor of pilot, Jamyk spun his chair to look across the bridge at Milyr, who had gazed toward Jamyk at about the same time with a forlorn expression on his long face, and then Jamyk rasped, "Tell."

"If you know something that we don't, boys, be quick and inform us. Our situation is not getting any better," Cap Nyba declared with a surly tone.

"Argh!… we were just playing…experimenting really…with new maneuvers," Milyr stammered with strong guilt in his voice that even Domyn could sense in spite of the low volume audio of Chitir's comm still repeating in his earpiece.

"Indeed this is no time for keeping pup secrets, lads. No doubt we need any advantage that we can get, no matter how inappropriately it may have been discovered or learned," Lyndyn stated.

"Milyr, what did you do then? Chitir believes that it can work here," Domyn declared, and then with moderate impatience, growled, "Awright, speak now. It won't do us any good if you don't."

"Well, we...we...simulated firing the Wilchrison as it was extending through pre-generated grav fields. We did this manually to by-pass safety protocols of artigence there. We used four pilots. One operated Wilchrison, other three controlled Flandecams. Each had one of grav components of the braid," Milyr explained with slow, nervous pauses in his baritone voice and then added hastily, "We were just vulching pups then. We didn't to worry much about safety then."

Cap Nyba stared at the lanky young man for awhile and then asked in a firm, non-accusatory voice, "Milyr, how often was simulation successful? How well do you boys know it?"

Milyr raised his gaze to meet hers and admitted, "Once out of our five attempts. But first three were trials. The fourth failure was after we had succeeded, and we were not serious again. We didn't really know what we were doing until the fourth. It really worked...in simulator."

"Only one out of five? Vulch!" cursed Swyllo vehemently.

"What do you think about this, Neer Domyn?" Cap Nyba asked.

"Do we have any choice? It would give us much quicker sequence. Our time is getting short now," Domyn said, surprised at his own willingness to make such a hasty decision during this moment of crisis, and then he asked, "Joculatus, can you extend Wilchrison while the gravity fields are actively generating? Can you fire Wilchrison at the same time as these activated gravity fields are initiated?'

Joculatus said, "Neer Domyn, I cannot perform the operation that you describe at this time. All parameters of my present programming do not permit this activity."

"On Steppingstone Tercero, we controlled all pertinent functions manually. It required four of us, but we could do it without normal operation of simulator artigence," Milyr boasted though in humble, subdued manner.

"Did you reprogram artigence?" asked Whyvvi from her red chair beside Jamyk.

"Nope," Jamyk rasped.

"We requested manual operation of each function. artigence did not actively impede our efforts. Vulch, I don't understand how, but we accomplished our goal,"

Milyr said, nervously picking at his cap over his long narrow head and lightly tapping his double visor with his gloved fingers.

"Cap Nyba, manual operation is not really artigence free. The term is deceptive. The dionjocu functions must go through artigence still in manual control. Theprimary difference is elimination of programmed conscious control of artigence. The sci-tech is in full control of person operating mechanism. In sense the artigence becomes just another piece of mindless equipment for that duration. However, without conscious participation of artigence, some safety redundancies and procedures are likely to be by-passed temporarily. Somewhat as with human when conscious control is suspended," Prof Lyndyn explained from his gray chair beside Nyba.

"Pop," Jamyk rasped, "soon."

"Awe knows what's going to happen now, Cap, but we've got to go now," Domyn said with reluctance, and then more firmly, he asked turning toward the young man in the lavender dionjocu, "Milyr, will procedure be more efficient with two pilots now controlling the Flandecams?"

"Yeah, Domyn, I believe that little peener and me can handle chore this time. We did have three pilots all those years ago controlling three aspects of gravity, but we don't have that choice now, do we?" Milyr replied much more seriously than usual for him, and then he abruptly asked with some concern in his baritone voice, "But who is going to operate Wilchrison? We can't have Joculatus do that now if we go to purely manual protocol."

"Don't worry about that, Milyr," Domyn smiled at the young man just before turning back toward Nyba and suggesting, "Cap, I recommend that Jamyk generates an-grav fields from Flandecams one and two. Milyr generates posi-grav from three and four. I'll control and fire Wilchrison."

"What about null-grav? We need all three grav aspects, don't we for the braid?" Lyndyn asked.

"See all that red on the holovision, Prof? We're in null-space and that means null-grav. It's all around most of the spacecraft. Wilchrison will use that source for the null-grav strand of the braid," Domyn explained and then to himself hoped that he knew what he was talking about and could handle Wilchrison by himself without assistance of the artigence.

"Are you certain? Do we really want to try this almost untested procedure?" Whyvvi asked with definite doubt and some slight fear in her voice.

"The four best pilots in Blue Jay history have suggested popping, independently, on their own without consulting each other. That should tell us quite a bit about the likelihood of success," Domyn exclaimed and then to the young woman in the blue dionjocu bedside him, he said, "Cap Nyba, you will need to begin protocol for removal of safety protocols from this process and to transfer control from artigence to the pilots and myself."

"Oh my, and we do need to hurry, don't we?" inquired Doc Kymil, staring at the holovision.

"Then let's do it," declared Cap Nyba suddenly and decisively. "Joculatus, relinquish operation of the Flandecams one and two to manual control to pilot Jamyk. Relinquish operation of Flandecams three and four to manual control to pilot Milyr. Relinquish operation of Wilchrison to manual control to Neer Domyn. Are these commands acceptable to your programming parameters?"

For a few seconds, the artigence was silent and then responded, "Cap Nyba, I require concurrence from Neer Domyn of your commands. Then I require concurrence from medical officer indicating persons involved are healthy to perform the stated manual functions."

"I concur with cap Nyba's previous commands," Domyn stated hastily, wondering just how much time they had left before the partial braid seized the craft and hurtled them towards the blocking mass.

Doc Kymil acknowledged quickly, and carefully in her smooth melodious voice, "I concur that people assigned manual operation are of healthy physical and mental status. I also request that Bodacia monitor all personnel during upcoming operation."

"Doc Kymil, I am monitoring always," Bodacia stated from out of the air of the ConCen, and Domyn thought that he heard a hint of indignation in a female voice of medical artigence, but he could not concern himself about that now.

"Are we ready, boys, girls, and Milyr?" Cap Nyba asked with some nervous merriment, and then added more seriously, "Whyvvi and Swyllo, record all sensor reads from your functions of large mystery mass blocking the center of Kil-Kol. Let's get as much data as we can about that nasty thing. Perhaps the varying perspectives allowed by our passage through the braid will give you enough of a parallax view to give us a much better picture of what has caused all this nasty mess for us."

"If we do not hit it," groaned Whyvvi pessimistically.

"We're all Blue Jayers, Whyvvi," shouted Milyr as he snapped his pilot visor more firmly onto his cap and then pulled it down in front of his eyes and then continued with bravado, "We're the best vulching pilots in Blue Jay. Our sci-tech is best. We'll get by that nasty and then conquer it from the other side. We'll get out of this toxx clutch."

"First time that I ever heard you want to get out of a clutch," laughed Doc Kymil.

"Is everybody ready to pop Weznuski and get back to Debordo space?" Nyba asked in her steady but confident tone.

"Vulch, yeah!" retorted Swyllo. "Let's hurry!"

"Neer Domyn, this operation is yours to command. Boys, girls, and Jamyk, are you ready?" Nyba asked one last time.

A quiet hush fell over the bridge until Jamyk rasped, "Yup."

Awe, guide me, Domyn prayed and fired up the motor to begin to extend the Wilchrison.

In his mind, Domyn wondered if this was the correct action to perform at that moment. Was he doing the right thing now for his crew and his spacecraft? Would they survive this nearly experimental process? Awe only knows, Domyn admitted to himself.

"Does anyone need to go to latrine now?" Milyr asked with a chuckle from his purple chair.

"Yup," rasped Jamyk with a gasping giggle from a green chair.

"Indeed now I'm not so sure about these pilots. Perhaps we should invoke our Neer's most mystical universal deity now to save us from our own foolishness," sighed Prof Lyndyn.

"Now, people, let's not get any crazier than we normally become during these times of stress. We are the best crew in Blue Jay mission, aren't we?" Cap Nyba asked beside Domyn.

As their banter played through his mind, Domyn discovered that his task became less frightening for him. He let his large hands fit themselves to the lining inside his tan dionjocu gloves. He felt the joy of sci-tech that he was about to control with his own body and will. This was going to be more fun than he had believed at first when he suggested this foolish endeavor.

Then as the shaking began within his dionjocu gloves and sweat started to flow from his skin inside the gloves and the rest of his uniform, Domyn was not so sure about this attempt. His mind began to seek out panic and fear from deep in his subconscious. Could he overcome this internal challenge within himself in order to save his crew and his craft?

Domyn was not so confident then, and he muttered more aloud than he had intended, "Vulch, this is not as easy as I had hoped."

"Now you say this," Nyba whispered from the blue chair beside him.

From the far end of formation of chairs, Jamyk rasped hoarsely, "Nope."

Spec One: Domyn Through LaOgres
Chapter 9

"Posi-grav generation is confirmed," Milyr shouted in ConCen, "The field looks cherp to me. My huge Flandecams are performing very effectively. Vulch, this may actually work as planned."

"An-grav," Jamyk affirmed, "cherp."

"No doubt, Domyn, this might be the appropriate moment to pray to your universal metaphy," Prof Lyndyn chuckled with a hint of sarcasm in his nasal voice. "Indeed we could use helping of mystical assistance now. We do wish to arrive in the Sexto System eventually."

Ignoring the skepticism of the older mentor, Domyn focused his attention upon the view in his visor over his right eye. There he observed virtual representation of the outer surface of the Wolf Streak Beta surrounded by blue and violet gravity fields generated now by Flandecams operated by his two crewmates. Exterior to the violet an-grav field and blue posi-grav field existed a vast red field of null-grav occurring in the vortex now in Kil-Kol between the two entrapping twinings. This was going to be a challenge yet, he realized.

With his fingers inter-laced and hands clasped together in front of his chest, Domyn announced, "I'm extending the Wilchrison now. Keep your eyes focused upon your gravity field cohesion. If either of the two fields collapses, then we must stop this immediately. Do you lads understand?"

Milyr and Jamyk responded, "Yup."

Then while his two heels pressed down on the wide pedal beneath the front center of his brown chair, Domyn gradually pushed his entwined hands away from his chest. In the visor, he witnessed a bulb-like Wilchrison rise from the spacecraft. From all directions, skin of the spacecraft seemed to flow toward and upward following the Wilchrison. Very carefull, he held his nervousness under control to prevent any awkward shaking of his slowly extending arms and hands. That could easily misalign the aim of the Wilchrison.

Without wasting a moment from his concentration, Domyn knew from his many years of Blue Jay education and training that outer surface of Wolf Streak Beta was morphing into a tall pedestal shape to levitate the Wilchrison into position away from the hull of the spacecraft. There the Wilchrison bulb of about forty-seven feet in diameter could weave three gravity aspects and create the braid that would leap into Kil-Kol and then Weznuski space to form a tunnel-shaped pathway, which would pull Wolf Streak Beta through the braid and into Debordo space. At least, Domyn thought to himself, if everything went correctly as theorized and designed.

In the blue chair to his left, Cap Nyba asked, "Whyvvi, how is our inclination angle in respect to the path toward the periphery of this Kil-Kol?"

As he listened to this request, Domyn observed with his right eye the Wilchrison and its supporting morphing structure protrude away gradually from the hull of Wolf Streak Beta. Even though this morphing process was incomplete, he triggered the Wilchrison according to recommendation of Milyr and Chitir. Suddenly in his visor view, red, blue, and violet-colored fields began to swirl and twist in at first haphazard patterns beneath the Wilchrison. Within seconds a disorganized confusion of differing gravity aspects began to appear as colorful strands drawn toward the base of the bulb that was the Wilchrison. Each gravity field supplied a strand to this mixture. How Wilchrison allowed differing strands of opposing gravities to coexist in such a tightly confined space was still a mystery to Neer Domyn, but at that moment, he did not worry about this ignorance on his part.

From outside his limited attention, Whyvvi said matter-of-factly without any evidence of stress now, "Our inclination angle is not perfect for best peripheral trajectory. But it should aim our braid and then us significantly away from the blocking mass. We should be okay and should not attempt to reposition Wolf Streak Beta just to get that perfect inclination. Until the braid forms and begins to pull this spacecraft through Weznuski, we will need to stay in contact with this twining. If we separate now, we could lose ability to generate either an-grav or posi-grav or both fields."

"Yup," Jamyk rasped just next to Whyvvi, "contact."

"Just vulching make sure that you do, little peener!" yelled Swyllo shrilly from her yellow chair next to Milyr on the other side of the chair formation in the ConCen of Wolf Streak Beta.

While his concentration was teased by the banter of the crew, Domyn managed to force his concentration to remain on the view of his visor. But, he thought fleetingly, that he was glad not to have to worry about changing any spacecraft inclination just then. With a silent thank you to Whyvvi, he observed with his right eye the beginning of the three stranded braid organizing in space immediately outward from the Wilchrison. With time being limited and critical, he did not need any extra obligations. The procedure would not be successful if the braid did not form. Maybe Prof Lyndyn's sarcastic and brief prayer was enough, Domyn mused as a smile flickered across his face, but he chose not to say anything to the skeptical Prof Lyndyn.

"Posi-grav field is still cohesive and intact. There is no negation or disturbance now due to activation of the Wilchrison," Milyr reported proudly, and then with optimism in his baritone voice, added, "I guess our vulching notion to activate before full extension is working. Great primo pilots, are we not, little peener?"

"Yup!" laughed Jamyk from his green chair, "Huge!"

In his visor, Domyn watched the braid of gravity strands entwine into the unified whole and then begin a cyclonic pathway through the sparkling spergits of Kil-Kol. Almost immediately the width of the braid widened rapidly. Then, though he realized it to be an illusion to his eye only, the braided cloud-like substance of spergits seemed to race backward by his field of vision. In actuality he knew with great joy Wolf Streak Beta was now travelling through the braid. They were on the way out of the trap in the vortex of the abnormal Kil-Kol. Awspir, Domyn mused silently.

"Don't be such vulching toxx, Milyr! Or you either, Jamyk, you little peener!" Swyllo squealed from her yellow chair beside the figure in lavender dionjocu, "You're only as good as the power that I harvest. If I can't get enough cherp energy for those power-sucking Flandecams, then they will not generate your toxx grav fields. Remember that, you two vulching toxx!"

"Yeah, do not get infatuated with your cherp deed just yet," blurted Whyvvi sharply with a warning tone in her mellow voice, "If we should lose gravity fields in null-space, then the Wilchrison will not make the braid. Then we will be trapped in Weznuski null-grav space again. That would be worse than where we were before in Kil-Kol. Not even our sci-tech advances with these grav-propulsion systems have been able to initiate the braid from absolute null-grav space. Never in history of Blue Jay, right, Nyba?"

"Vulch, then the tiny tasty fem had better harvest a lot of vulching energy and keep it coming for us manly pilots," chuckled Milyr with what Domyn recognized as mock bravado in his nervous voice as his fingers twitched within the lavender dionjocu gloves to operate the Flandecams under his control. "Just keep it coming, tiny fem. We'll take all you can give us, right, Jamyk?"

"Yup," rasped Jamyk while he also worked his green dionjocu gloves with relentless effort.

Cap Nyba asked, "Swyllo, is energy supply a problem? Are we getting low now?"

"No, Cap, not at the moment. We should have more than enough for this trip through the braid," Swyllo reported with mild certainty in her gasping voice. "But because of lack of light reflecting from the nasty solid mass in the center of Kil-Kol, I believe we will be low when we finally pop out of Weznuski. That mass is like light sucking toxx. It just won't give me any light to use. Yet rest of Kil-Kol seems to be adequate to get us through this braid."

"Now that could be the worry, Swyllo," Whyvvi stated from other side of the ConCen. "We will lose light from this Kil-Kol eventually before we reach the other side of Weznuski space. You should get all that you can now while we are close enough to Kil-Kol light source."

"Yes, yes, I know that already. I'm doing my best to harvest what we will need," Swyllo griped.

"Just keep it coming to satisfy our vulching need," Milyr demanded. "That's what your duty is for this spacecraft, tiny fem, to satisfy our needs."

"Vulch, if this wasn't such a critical time, you toxx, I'd vulching kick your nads into your belly," Swyllo threatened as she spun her chair toward Milyr, "But we do need you at this moment, you toxx."

"Yup," rasped Jamyk with a hoarse gasp, "lucky!"

"That's right, we need to focus on our functions now," Cap Nyba declared with sternness in her voice. "We must all focus on our duties now, boys, girls, and Milyr!"

Well, Domyn thought, they were all correct in some sense. Now that the braiding phenomenon was thrusting Wolf Streak Beta through Kil-Kol and then soon Weznuski space, Wilchrison needed continuous generation of both an-grav and posi-grav fields by Flandecams. Flandecams were very important but also were very power inefficient. They ate much energy. However, he was confident in Swyllo to harvest light energy from what light source that she had available. He had confidence in the piloting skills of Milyr and Jamyk. He had confidence in the sci-tech of Wolf Streak Beta.

If he had any doubt or concern, Domyn abruptly realized, it was that they had never before braided across the twining such as one that had formed the outer boundary of pocket of the null-space, which had originally trapped Wolf Streak Beta. Now that twining was approaching. Did it have same properties that the blocking mass seemed to have which did not allow the passage of the Buffalardi braid from Fox Flash launch of nineteen days ago? Could this twining deflect their present larger braid and deflect this spacecraft back into null-grav vortex? Should he say anything to others? Did they need to worry about this concern? Was there anything they could do about it?

"Neer Domyn, can you give an estimate of time to reach Debordo space?" Cap Nyba asked in a normal voice just to his left, and then on a restricted frequency probably to him only, he heard in his earpiece her voice ask, "Do you believe that we should put this on the holovision? A view of movement through this Kil-Kol might give everyone hope."

While he listened to Cap Nyba's question, Domyn also answered his own doubts. Was there anything others could do about approaching the twining barrier? Should he mention it to them? He reminded himself that not everyone on the ConCen now was seeing this sight as he did in his visor. Yet did they need to see this now? Would this sight help others do their particular functions, or would it distract them now? No, perhaps not, he thought. Domyn had trust in his people. Even though this situation had not been rehearsed at Steppingstone training lesson, Domyn, his crewmates could do their functions. His crew was capable, no matter what they viewed.

"A normal passage through Kil-Kol and then Weznuski space requires about thirteen minutes. I don't believe this trip should be any different," Domyn replied aloud in the ConCen and then on a restricted frequency said to Nyba only, "It would not be a bad notion to put this view on the holovision, Cap. It is your decision though. But as I just recalled myself, half of us have seen this view already. You, me, and the pilots are all viewing this now. We might as well put it on the holovision. You are most likely correct about this sensation of travelling as being encouraging."

Holding his arms fully stretched in front of his broad chest and still clasping his tan dionjocu gloves together, Domyn locked Wilchrison into full extension mode about twenty-nine yards in front of spacecraft. With selected flicks of fingers within his tan dionjocu gloves, he commanded the Wilchrison to cruise mode. At least now he could rest and relax his large arm muscles. Well, as long as everything performed smoothly, he reminded himself, he could release his direct control. However, he realized that he could not take his attention from the braiding phenomenon portrayed in his visor.

To his left, Cap Nyba announced to the ConCen, "We'll put the advance pilot view on the holovision. Our energy supply seems to be strong enough for this luxury, doesn't it, Swyllo? Now let's not allow this holovision to distract us from our very important individual functions, right, boys, girls, and Jamyk? Joculatus, initiate holovision of forward pilot view as seen by Neer Domyn."

As a questionable twining barrier neared in his visor, Domyn heard artigence Joculatus respond, "Cap Nyba, initiating the holovision per view of Neer Domyn."

Almost immediately the three-dimensional portrayal of the scene in his visor appeared in an open area in front of and between the end chairs of the semi-circle on the ConCen. Domyn was astounded at once how much more powerful the view was in the full holovision compared to his one-eyed view in the visor. Perhaps he should lose the visor and just watch the holovision, he thought for a moment, but then realized that he had more tactical control with his dionjocu than the holovision and just then that was much more important for him. The others could enjoy the holovision, if they had time to spare from their own functions.

On the holovision, he did find sight more vivid. With pulsations of blue, violet, and red entwining into the huge cyclonic passageway through spergits of Kil-Kol, the thrust of the braid leaped ahead of Wolf Streak Beta. The spacecraft did not appear on the holovision or in his visor. He knew from experience that the view assumed forward perspective from the outer hull of the craft. Now without pause or slightest disturbance, the braid burst through purple and red representation of outer twining barrier. Then this man-made power jumped into a pure red of null-grav of Weznuski space. Kil-Kol center was now behind them.

Awspir, he mused silently to himself, that worry was proven to be frivolous, and then he said aloud, "Milyr, Jamyk, stay alert to your functions now. We can't lose grav fields now. We are in Weznuski proper now. We are the only source of an-grav and posi-grav now until we get into Debordo space. Keep close eyes on the conditions of your Flandecams. Vivacio, that is your primary function now as well."

The male voice of maintenance artigence Vivacio replied, "Neer Domyn, this is my function. I am always monitoring all systems of Wolf Streak Beta. Flandecams are operating within the programmed parameters as usual."

"We're on our way," Doc Kymil exclaimed in her upbeat encouraging tone from her white chair just to the right of Domyn. "Your efforts, all of you, have helped us get away from the most dangerous situation. You are all truly Blue Jayers this awakening."

"Yeah, we're going to be vulching legends now," boasted Milyr as he wiggled his fingers inside his lavender gloves, and then after a short laugh, continued, "Fems all over the galaxy will want to know us and cuddle with us. We'll be legends at every Steppingstone that we visit, right, Jamyk?"

"Yup," Jamyk rasped in his sweat-stained green dionjocu, and then added, "me!"

"Just continue performing your functions, oh, primo pilots, Milyr and Jamyk. We're not in Debordo yet," Nyba said with firm caution in her voice. "How is our trajectory, Whyvvi? Are we staying away from the center of Kil-Kol? Is there any sign that the mass in there is affecting our course?"

With a flick of his fingers, Domyn widened the view of his visor and consequently portrayal on the holovision. His optimism of their success began to increase. The concern of possible hindrance of twining was now proven false. Now the wide view revealed a dark mass at the center of Kil-Kol rapidly receding from the edge of the scene. The other hostile braid or twining was visible in the far distance and just as quickly fading from the scene. As his hopes celebrated, he knew the holovision portrayal would answer Cap Nyba's question.

When the ConCen fell quiet but for a flutter and rustle of dionjocu fabric, while others watched the holovision or performed their functions, Domyn replied for Whyvvi, "Looks like we are free of Kil-Kol, at least this end on LaOgres side. We'll put that unknown blocking mass behind us, Cap, and threatening twinings also. This is a very great achievement for this crew of Blue Jayers, Cap Nyba. The cherp testament to sci-tech and resilience of Wolf Streak Beta also, I believe."

"We'll be vulching legends for sure!" Milyr shouted with jubilation.

"Cherp! Anything to be away from LaOgres!" sighed Swyllo.

"We should have no trouble getting through Weznuski space now," Whyvvi predicted with assurance. "Our sci-tech is designed for this type of braiding passage. Now that the mysterious blocking mass has no effect on our braid, we should reach Debordo soon."

"Yup!" agreed Jamyk.

"Like I said, we'll be vulching legends," Milyr chortled with an exaggerated movement of his hands in emphasis, and then he hastily flicked his fingers in the lavender gloves and groaned, "Argh, I can't get careless yet. Sorry, Domyn, I've got that tiny nasty glitch under control. Don't worry!"

"Oh, you'd better be certain that you've got any glitches under control, you toxx," Cap Nyba snarled with real sternness, "You do not want to see my nasty side, do you?"

"Vulch no, Nyba! I suspect that would be very nasty for a primo guy like me," Milyr moaned.

Then with renewed calmness to her tine, Cap Nyba declared, "Let's not get giddy, boys, girls, and Milyr! We are not quite in Debordo yet. Once there we will need to very quickly plot our course back into LaOgres and perhaps recalculate a reasonable route to Sexto System. And I'd like to know still what exactly that blocking mass was and how it happened to capture the Buffalardi probe and keep the probe and beacon powered for nineteen years. We do have much to learn yet. Whyvvi and Swyllo, you've been recording your sensor read since this escape began, have you not?"

When sense of exhilaration and relief spread through the ConCen, Domyn did not feel he could criticize his mates. While his professional attention observed holovision, his own joy of success, even it was early to claim, lifted his spirit. Now with realistic reminders of Cap Nyba, he felt a true sense of accomplishment but not quite victory yet. Nyba was correct! The important work to be finished still!

Domyn had known that there could have been a problem with the exerted pulls of the double twinings. There could have been problem with blocking mass. There may yet be a problem with the appropriate level of energy according to something that Swyllo had said before. However, Domyn felt that the capabilities of this Blue Jay crew and their sci-tech had made a fortunate difference between total failure and now some success. He felt relaxed enough to give partial celebration to his own mental exhaustion. Perhaps, he grinned to himself, Prof Lyndyn's prankish invocation to universal metaphy had been useful as well.

"As you ordered, Cap, I put my recorder on continuous operation at the start of this ride," reported Whyvvi with a slight hint of irritated annoyance in her voice, "I do follow commands, Nyba. We should have a very complete picture of whatever my zeta sensors have recorded by time we pop into Debordo space. This I can promise you."

"Soon," Jamyk rasped with a panting breath as he waved his arms slightly and fluttered his fingers in his green dionjocu gloves, "pop."

"It had vulching better be soon," grumbled Swyllo. "I can't wait to get back into Debordo. The harvest of light energy is so vulching bad now that we are in true Weznuski space."

"Oh my, yes, it is not as exciting a view now. There is so much more darkness, so much more redness. Are we moving at all now?" Doc Kymil asked almost as if speaking for all others, "Where are the speeding lights now?"

Since the scene on the holovision was that of pilots and a Wilchrison operator, colors of grav-strands were visible still. However, Domyn realized that the density of multitude of spergits decreased very rapidly in true Weznuski space. The swirling of cloud-like Kil-Kol substance disappeared in this view of Weznuski space. To others this view might seem perhaps almost stationary, as if Wolf Streak Beta had stopped. He realized for half of the people on the ConCen there was no more visible streaming of lights from spergits.

"We do not often watch the holovision when we pop Weznuski, my dear Kymil," Prof Lyndyn explained with some tender patronizing in his nasal voice. "Braiding through Weznuski has become so commonplace in our Blue Jay travels that we've come to accept it as non-visual activity. Indeed, in truth, there is very little to watch. Therefore we Blue Jayers usually focus on other functions during our standard braiding procedures..."

"Oh now, my Lyndyn, you must remember that I've liked experience of watching spergit swirls rush past and then the first sight of stars as we return to Debordo space," Kymil sighed with genuine fondness. "Since our journey to the Quinto System on Turkey Trot Alpha when we were pups like these young people, you must recall how we loved to watch rushing spergits. Surely, Lyndyn, you must remember that!"

"Er... Umm... Indeed...my kind Kymil!" Prof Lyndyn stammered, "No doubt...in my memory... I can still feel thrill and excitement of those moments. Perhaps I've become so familiar with popping Weznuski that I've..."

"You are so vulching snagged, Prof," laughed Milyr.

"Yup!" Jamyk agreed while his hands in the green dionjocu gloves continued manipulating the Flandecams, and then the boy added, "Snagged!"

"No doubt it probably looks as if I may have forgotten some partial memories, however..." Prof Lyndyn began in a pleading tone, reaching slightly toward Doc Kymil who sat across the ConCen.

However, his try at salvaging his image before Kymil was suddenly halted when Swyllo called out tensely, "Cap, our energy reserve is falling much quicker than I had estimated. That vulching nasty dark center stole more light energy than I thought. We're getting low now."

While his eyes observed steady forward the progress of the cyclonic braid through the red of the null-grav in Weznuski, Domyn listened to Cap Nyba ask in a firm, calm voice, "Swyllo, are we critically low on power reserves? Now we need no more than three, maybe slightly more minutes to pop into Debordo. Is that about right, Neer Domyn?"

"That seems about right, Cap," Domyn responded hastily to ease Swyllo's immediate worry. "We need about 23 percent energy level to supply the Flandecams, Wilchrison, and other ship functions until popping. Then we should be able to begin to harvest light energy from whichever star system corresponds with other side of this Kil-Kol region of Debordo space."

"Vulch, we have 29 percent energy level now, and it is falling in spite of my continued harvesting, which is getting very scant," the small girl in yellow complained.

"Vulching find more then," snarled Milyr from his purple chair beside her. "Keep me supplied for my posi-grav. I need power for my huge Flandecams."

"I'm vulching doing my best! That vulching nasty Kil-Kol didn't give me what it should have. Now it is so far behind us that the very little free light is available yet on this side of Weznuski. Until we get into Debordo now, I can't harvest much free light. You should know that, you toxx!" shrieked Swyllo.

"Twenty-nine percent should be just enough," Whyvvi predicted and then suggested, "However, Nyba, we could shut down some of our less critical power usage until we pop into Debordo."

Domyn made his eyes peer intently at the holovision for the first hint of a distant appearance of the non-braid related blue that would signify approach of Debordo space. Was he relying too much upon this holovision now instead of his own visor? Nothing of this new blue showed yet on the holovision or his visor. Awe, well, it should not be too long of a wait now, Domyn hoped. Twenty-nine gave a reasonable buffer for necessary twenty-three that he was certain that they would need. Yet he was not totally sure as his eyes watched the holovision portrayal of red, blue, and purple braid of gravity strands swirl ahead of their course through Weznuski.

"Vivacio, power off all non-ConCen functions to the level appropriate for ship safety and minimal reacquisition," Cap Nyba called out loudly into ConCen, and then after a few seconds, added, "Doc, do we need Bodacia at this time?"

Doc Kymil responded with her melodious and gentle voice, "Health monitoring of crew has shown expected signs of exhaustion and low stress, but nothing that requires diligent and constant monitoring by Bodacia. I should be able to recognize any severe symptoms of more dangerous ailments. I'm certain my forgetful friend Lyndyn can aid me in this endeavor. I believe that we can let Bodacia rest now. We should be fine until we get into Debordo again."

"Indeed I can manage to do that for you, kind Kymil," Prof Lyndyn agreed smoothly.

"Vulch, you had better, Prof," Milyr snickered wearily from his purple chair.

"Holo," Jamyk gasped abruptly while he continued moving his hands in intricate patterns. "Off."

Of course the holovision used much energy, Domyn realized then. Why had he not thought of that? Why had Cap Nyba not thought of that? Were they both so exhausted that they were not mentally sharp now? He could view his function very appropriately with his visor, so could the pilots. None of them needed the full three-dimensional view supplied by the holovision. In fact pilots already had binocular view for their duties. The holovision was luxury at the moment. Thank you, Jamyk, Domyn thought silently to himself.

"Two very good suggestions from our crew, I'm impressed," stated Cap Nyba, "Vivacio, power down Bodacia to minimal level. Joculatus, turn off the holovision but keep recording the sensor reads from Whyvvi's sensors as pertinent to central mass in sear Kil-Kol."

Vivacio reported within seconds, "Cap Nyba, Bodacia has been powered down as directed."

As the holovision disappeared from between the ends of the formation of chairs on the ConCen, Joculatus reported, "Cap Nyba, holovision is now turned off. Recording per station of Whyvvi sensor reads are now of very minimal accuracy as this craft departs region of Kil-Kol. Do you wish for me to continue trying to perform this task, Cap Nyba?"

"If we can't get to Debordo space again this time, Cap Nyba, then those sensor reads won't mean much to us," Prof Lyndyn stated. "We do not want to get stranded here in Weznuski without power when we are so close to our goal."

"We should need adequate energy reserves after we pop, and we must pop out of this vulching space," Swyllo squawked in a high but determined voice. "We don't know for sure how strong a light of the next star will be in Debordo space that we enter, or if there will be a strong sun nearby. I will need some power just to harvest energy."

"That is very cherp advice," Cap Nyba agreed and then commanded from her blue chair, "Cease all recordings and sensor scans of previous Kil-Kol. That includes you, Joculatus. We'll have to be satisfied with what data we've collected to this time. How soon to be in Debordo space, Domyn?"

One-eyed view in the visor over his right eye showed still just a simple scene of the braided weave of red, blue, and violet strands amidst vast expanse of red, but Domyn could not let his people hear the negative possibilities, so he replied partially facetiously, "Not long now, Cap. With recent shutdowns, we should have adequate energy for our needs. Soon, very soon, I believe, that I'll see the blue edge of Debordo."

"Vulching hope so!" Swyllo whined.

"Oh, yeah, for once we agree about something, tiny fem," Milyr exclaimed.

"Yup!" Jamyk squawked in a hoarse voice. "Blue... Soon!"

"Indeed no doubt it may be time for another plea to your universal deity," Prof Lyndyn chuckled, but with a slight hint of conviction in his nasal voice, "What do you think, my kind Kymil? Can our sci-tech engineer's strange affection for metaphy be of assistance now?"

"Don't tease him, Lyndyn. I think expansion of one's belief is typically human and healthy. Perhaps my ability to see PEQA is more than merely a statistical probability but a gift from higher awareness," Doc Kymil declared from her white chair to the right of Domyn.

Then Domyn exclaimed much to his own surprise that his mind could create thought under these stressful circumstances, "Perhaps, Doc, statistical probability is a gift from universal awareness."

"Yup," agreed Jamyk in an exhausted voice from his green chair, "maybe."

"Oh, vulch, not you, too, now, little peener," Milyr groaned wearily as his hands continued their effort to control his Flandecams. "Next you know, I'll be the only one lusting for a clutch of sweet fems. I'm vulched for sure around this group of people."

"Nope," Jamyk laughed heartily and then added, "chitir."

"Jamyk, you peener of pup, wait till we get to Debordo. Your toxx is going to get nasty kicking," Swyllo screamed in what sounded like false anger to Domyn.

Grinning beneath the visor over his right eye, Domyn was almost certain that he could see the subtle blue of true Debordo space intermingling with the red of Weznuski now, so he retorted with some playful optimism, "Young pup, you'd be wise to avoid her clutches and be cherp to Swyllo. I believe that we'll be entering

Debordo soon. The last time I oversaw one of your tension release sessions, you could not run away from her...irritation."

In his earpiece on restricted frequency, he heard Cap Nyba ask with hope in her voice, "Do you really see Debordo space out there now, Domyn? Is it time to power on the holovision again? They all could use a cherp view now. Is it time?"

To Cap Nyba only, Domyn replied, "Not quite yet, we need to conserve our energy a bit longer. But I can see what does appear to be the edge of Debordo space now visible on this representation in the dionjocu visor. Of course this is only a representation and can be fooled by various minor nuances, so let's maybe go another two minutes, maybe less. Our two pilots may be seeing it sooner. Let's give others sure view of stars."

"That is a cherp notion," Nyba agreed. "We all need security of such a sight."

As he listened to her response in his earpiece, Domyn glanced at Milyr in the sweat-drenched lavender dionjocu. Then he turned his gaze to peer over toward the smaller boy in wet green dionjocu. To his surprise, Jamyk was already staring towards him beneath the double visor.

"Yup," the boy said grinning, "stars."

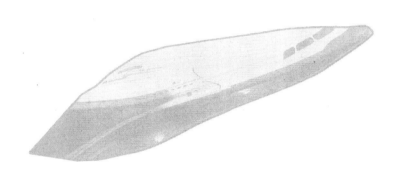

SPEC ONE: DOMYN THROUGH LAOGRES
CHAPTER 10

"Real space at last," Swyllo cheered, "Cherp! Vulching cherp! I'm so happy now I could even cuddle with you, Milyr, you toxx!"

"That is not a very cherp notion, Swyllo," laughed Whyvvi while she waved her arms and hands dressed inside her pink dionjocu uniform. "You would never know what nasty mutation has occurred to his manliness, or in this case, lack of manliness by antemgebemarzex."

"Ha, ha, fine fems, let's not demean a primo man like myself," the lanky young man in the lavender dionjocu declared while his fingers flickered within the lavender gloves, "I'm most a manly guy here in this region of space. That vulching antemgebemarzex can't hinder my strong and steady development to primo manhood. I'm here just for you now, fine bodacious fems."

"Pilots, I'm deactivating the Wilchrison," Domyn announced as his right eye observed many small points of light that began to sprinkle throughout the expanding field of blue now showing in his visor and also on the holovision. "We are in Debordo space again."

As last of red of null-space along rim the of the Weznuski faded from peripheral edges of the holovision, Doc Kymil sighed with true relief and delight in her voice, "Oh my, yes, those are stars, real stars twinkling in that field of posi-grav on our view. Oh, they are not of the Sexto System, yet they are stars. In not very many awakenings, we should be viewing the real location of Sexto stars."

"Pilot Jamyk, prepare to assume solo pilot function. Joculatus, prepare to resume standard pilot operation," Cap Nyba commanded briskly as she rotated left to right in her blue chair next to Domyn and then added, "Milyr, prepare to cease pilot function and then assume comm function. I want sanbeam comm sent to Fox Flash Alpha as soon as possible before they are out of range, if they are not already. Make it brief, but let them know our situation."

Holding his clasped hands out from his chest in correlation with the still extended Wilchrison, Domyn heard Milyr grumble something surly and unintelligible, so hastily declared, "Good idea, Cap Nyba, we need to inform Fox Flash Alpha what has happened with us. They need to know that we are okay and safe in Debordo space now."

"We will need energy harvest almost immediately," Swyllo stated tiredly as she flexed her small yellow dionjocu gloves. "Get us close to whatever light source is available as soon as possible."

While his clasped hands returned slowly to his chest, Domyn suggested, "Since we are low on energy reserve, we should take advantage of the forward momentum of popping from the braid as we gradually switch to normal flight in Debordo space. Pilots should use this momentum."

"I presume most of you are still viewing with your pilot visors," Whyvvi exclaimed loudly and with some excitement. "To my sensors, we are now within very strong sunlight from more than one source. This Kil-Kol region seems to be plunked between two stars perhaps in binary tandem."

"Vulching cherp, now that you say this, I do scan a strong light from many vectors," Swyllo agreed.

"Yup," Jamyk replied with a weary hoarse voice while his body gyrated mildly with necessary movements to pilot the spacecraft, and he rasped, "Yup, read gravity fluxes now. Milyr, now?"

"Vulching sure I read these two suns nearby us now," Milyr complained tersely. "This Kil-Kol must be abnormally strong to exist between binary stars in the same solar system."

Finally ending his primary view of the Wilchrison apparatus, Domyn observed on pilot view just what pilots were so enthused and worried about. From two directions, gravity forces pulled at Wolf Streak Beta. Somewhere in the near distance vortex of Kil-Kol would be evident on this aspect of Debordo space. This was very unusual for such Kil-Kol to be located so far inside the solar system but not completely impossible. Domyn smiled as he pondered that this was just another strange new discovery to credit to the legend of Wolf Streak Beta.

"Yeah, we are in so much sunlight now, I'm in cherp supply finally," Swyllo chirped in happiness. "Maybe now Jamyk won't gripe so much. Maybe you little one nad will burst into flame from vision of such strong sun gravity coming through your visor. Ha, ho, your smelly tiny body may toast away your grime and sweaty odor."

Bodacia said suddenly, "Swyllo, this possibility is not imminent for pilot Jamyk according to my monitor readings. Perhaps you should request assistance from Doc Kymil if you are observing some ailment of Jamyk that my monitor does not indicate."

"Oh my, Bodacia, ignore that recent comment by Swyllo," Doc Kymil commanded hastily. "There is no impending ailment to Jamyk. Swyllo was merely making a joke."

"Doc Kymil, please ignore my obvious moment of confusion," Bodacia said in a female voice.

"Cherp to be able to have you back with us, Bodacia. Please give Doc Kymil updated medical read on each of crew," Cap Nyba said to the medical artigence, and then to the girl in the yellow chair, she continued, "Swyllo, let me know as soon as our energy supply is on increase. We'll want to restart the rest of the operations, which we had shut down as soon as possible. I'm jovial that this will not take too long now."

"Ah, yes, I will set coordinates to the closest of the two suns," Swyllo reported in breathlessness.

"Swyllo, your coordinates have been relayed to pilot Jamyk," Joculatus reported. "Standard pilot operation is now established with pilot Jamyk. Pilot Milyr is now free of pilot function. All manual pilot operations are now ceased. Do you confirm, pilot Jamyk?"

"Yup," Jamyk called out in a throaty rasp, "Jocu."

While this chatter and the ConCen business occurred around him, Domyn switched his function back to view in his visor over his right eye retraction of the bulb-shaped Wilchrison, including morphing of the outer skin of the spacecraft back to its original formation, and he also heard Cap Nyba ask on restricted frequency, "Doc Kymil and Prof Lyndyn, what is the health and attention level of each of our crew? We will need to determine rotation of duty and rest soon. Domyn, that's your responsibility now, once you have finished with settling of the Wilchrison device. I've got something to supervise."

"Oh my, yes, Nyba," Doc Kymil agreed on restricted audio. "All of you young wolves are well past your normal awake limit and are beginning to experience some Saphyndenlairoum sleep deficiency. Do you not concur, Lyndyn?"

"Yes indeed, especially four crew members who began this marathon experience with previous Buffalardi launch back when we were in LaOgres," Prof Lyndyn exclaimed with conviction in his nasal voice. "We do not need readings from Bodacia to recognize this deficiency. No insult intended, Neer Domyn. You've all served beyond imagining."

"Don't worry, Prof. I'll be the first to agree that I'm exhausted and ready for my normal nineteen days of Saphyndenlairoum sleep. Before that I'll most likely take many drinks of nutrient and water," Domyn announced with a yawn as he finished putting the Wilchrison to bed inside the compartment within Wolf Streak Beta. "You won't need to force me to go to sleep now."

"Well, Neer, don't go to sleep just yet. And don't plan on going directly to your Saphyndenlairoum anytime soon. We need to get ourselves back into LaOgres space again and back on our mission journey to the Sexto System before any of us can return to the cycle of Saphyndenlairoum sleeping," Cap Nyba warned him on her restricted frequency, and then aloud to the ConCen, she asked of the lanky young man in the sweat-drenched lavender dionjocu, "Milyr, are you ready for the comm transmission to Fox Flash Alpha?"

Abruptly spinning his purple chair to face Nyba, Milyr replied with a mix of annoyance and pride in his voice, "Cap Nyba, I've sent sanbeam already…just like you ordered… The vulching foxes should get it soon. Like you wanted, I let them know where we are, our general condition, and then told foxy toxx to sanbeam us back. Is that okay with you, Cap Nyba?"

Hearing far too much disgruntlement, even some insolence in his tone, Domyn was about to growl at Milyr, but for some reason Nyba responded in a steady, calm voice, "Cherp, Milyr, that's fine. A hasty, short message will give Fox Flash Alpha more of an opportunity to return their comm if they have not gone out of range already. Now while we wait for the time delay and their reply, I've got even more difficult and important duty for you, young man."

"Ummh... Erhh! Yeah, Cap…" Milyr stammered more speechless than common for him, "What…do you want me to do?"

While Milyr murmured this, Domyn asked on restricted audio, "Prof, how is Milyr's stress status? He seems more irritable than I'd expect."

In his earpiece, Domyn heard Prof Lyndyn reply in a hushed nasal voice, "His brain scan shows elevated stress but nothing that I would worry about, certainly nothing unusual, especially considering tension and exertion his mind and body have recently experienced. You are all withdrawing from very intense anxiety. Irritation and excitement are equally likely to be a result. Each of you will react differently. I have not seen any sign from any scan yet to indicate a serious problem."

On restricted audio, Domyn quipped half-heartedly, "Maybe that is because we are all Blue Jayers, Prof. Perhaps we don't give in to stressful situations. Perhaps we overcome them. We are Blue Jayers after all. Don't you believe that should be the next step toward becoming universal awareness, Prof? Or am I getting too arrogant now myself, like our Milyr so often seems to do?"

"No doubt, young man, now I am becoming worried about your mental status," Prof Lyndyn chuckled with obvious merriment, and Domyn realized that the older man had appreciated subtle humor of his previous remark.

While he chattered with Prof Lyndyn, Domyn did listen to Cap Nyba say aloud in ConCen, "Now, Milyr, since you are allegedly our primary comm expert, I desire for you to sensor read this system of Debordo space for any trace of residue of electro-magnetic or perhaps sanbeam comm that could have remained from the passage of the spaceship through this space. Search this region. Find that residue. That is your special function now, young man. I'm confident that you will find the best means to negate the effects of the two suns upon any likely transmissions."

"Vulch, Nyba, that's just toxx duty! It's not vulching likely that any such comm traces are out there," Milyr whined, staring at her with his long face stunned and then scowling beneath the visor on his light purple cap mumbled sourly and bitterly, "Vulching that's impossible!"

"Awright, enough of that griping, Milyr," Domyn growled with a deep rumble from his throat, and then on restricted frequency, he asked, "Do you agree with Prof, Doc? Are there any signs of something in his vital reads or related physio condition?"

"Oh, I do not read any health difficulty yet, Domyn. All of his vitals are slightly in stress level, but that's only expected due to his recent traumatic experience, just as Lyndyn has stated," Doc Kymil replied on restricted audio.

As this conversation occurred on confidential frequency, Domyn heard Nyba's firm and calm voice say, "Maybe not, Milyr. You won't know until you search this region of space, will you? We've got time now. Let's discover if your talent for seeking out strange comm secrets is as cherp as you often claim. Start hunting, young man."

Then in confidential audio, Prof Lyndyn suggested with some earnest, "Domyn, perhaps you must be more watchful of Jamyk or Swyllo. Their past histories have shown that they often work their bodies and minds to their limits and then shut down suddenly. He may be cranky, but Milyr did have rest more recently. Do you not agree, kind Kymil?"

"Oh my, that's for sure. Our Milyr is very well-rested after his brief session with me in Med. In general he is in much better health at this moment than either Jamyk or Swyllo or even Whyvvi now. His body strength should be sufficient for few hours now that I insisted that he take nutrient and gave him my special massage," Doc Kymil said in Domyn's earpiece.

While he listened to their recommendations, Domyn also heard Milyr mutter in a low, almost hushed voice as the young man spun his purple chair to face away from others, "This is nasty vulching nasty! Why do I get these vulching duties?"

Again, before Domyn could admonish Milyr, Cap Nyba exclaimed in a lively, positive tone, as if nothing could bother her then, "There's our new destination, the energy rich binary star system not far away. Is that your best possibility for energy harvest, Swyllo?"

"Yes, Cap, that's where my receptors are now directed. Our energy level is slowly rising now. You may be able to restart more of our down systems," the young woman in yellow acknowledged with a weary voice.

"Very cherp, let's take advantage of that binary star pairing," Cap Nyba exclaimed with almost childish giddiness, uncommon to her, and Domyn wondered if perhaps she had not suffered some mental ailment after their recent experience, but her voice remained buoyant and authoritative as she declared, "Okay, boys, girls, and Jamyk, have we seen enough of this starry holovision with all this blue posi-grav background? If so, let's change it. Joculatus, put a sensor read from Whyvvi's recorded view on the holovision. Start at maximum magnification."

Then as a portrayal of distant stars sparkling in vast view of mostly blue posi-grav Debordo space disappeared from the holovision, Domyn wondered to himself, why was Cap Nyba in such a jovial mood? Why had she forgiven obvious insubordination of Milyr? Was she truly suffering from withdrawal from previous traumatic stress? Would he need to relieve her of temporary command?

As he thought this, Nyba declared with what sounded like mischief in her voice, "Let's see what you've been studying so silently for so long, Whyvvi. You'd been so quiet. I thought you'd fallen asleep. What have you been studying for our recent braiding flight?"

Then as the holovision returned now, showing a scene of Kil-Kol receding for Wolf Streak Beta's course, Whyvvi shook her head slowly from side to side and sighed with a sleepy tone to her voice, "I almost did several times, Nyba. My eyes are getting tired just trying to see something in this sensor read. I should be able to tell what it is, or at least what it looks like. My eyes must be too strained and my brain too exhausted. It is beginning to look all alike, space and Kil-Kol. And now the image seems blurred by double vectors of sunlight."

In his earpiece, Domyn heard Doc Kymil remind him and most likely as well, "She has been at the sensor function since before the Buffalardi launch. She is one of your original pre-launch crew, Domyn. She should be one of the first to rest, with you and Swyllo."

On the holovision, Domyn observed a region of dark starless space that was Kil-Kol in Debordo space. This was the same Kil-Kol that they had entered on LaOgres side of the Weznuski barrier of null-space. In Debordo space, Domyn remembered, Kil-Kol and atoms that composed it absorbed most of light and related electro-magnetic waves. For this reason, Kil-Kol appeared much same as dark matter, almost as black void in space, at least to human vision and most light sensing technology. Then as he observed a recording, a sight of sunnier lighted the Debordo space gradually glared into his visor.

"What do you have to report, Whyvvi, after all the eye strain?" Nyba asked with polite encouragement in her voice.

"Not much, I must admit. I should have been able to discover more," the girl in the light red dionjocu sighed apologetically. "But I believe that I can the detect section of Kil-Kol that is actually blacker than norm for a light-absorptive appearance..."

"Perhaps now you should dampen the harsh glare of two suns so close and filter our view as we had seen in LaOgres space," Cap Nyba suggested with a hint of merriment and perhaps knowing in her husky voice. "We have been and still are far too distant for any precise reads. The silhouette view may be just what you need now."

Domyn flipped his visor atop his tan cap over his scalp. He needed to get the three-dimensional view of holovision now instead of the one-eyed limitation of his visor. On the holovision, he observed vast blackness of Debordo space. Whyvvi had followed the recommendation of Nyba. Far distant dots of twinkling light indicated multitude of stars in this portion of the galaxy. Even though this portrayal was very accurate, he reminded himself that it was not the actual view as if he looked out the window at real space. This was a rendition by artigence Joculatus based upon sensor reads from Whyvvi's present station. In some situations, depending upon the type of sensor that she chose to employ, this portrayal could be far more precise than if he was looking out window. If she was using her zeta ray sensor now, as she had suggested earlier, then this should be a very precise rendition.

As he squinted at the holovision trying to see what Whyvvi described, Domyn listened to Cap Nyba in his earpiece ask, "Neer Domyn, have you decided yet who will serve as my transition crew while everyone else rests and eats? Remember I can function in any capacity. We must have a pilot, harvester, and one or more to recalibrate the navigational course with Joculatus for the Sexto System."

Aloud in the ConCen, Whyvvi continued, "...in LaOgres my reads definitely showed hard mass of specific volume. This mass was much larger than Wolf Streak Beta. Perhaps five times larger..."

In his earpiece, Domyn listened to Prof Lyndyn say, "Indeed, Cap Nyba, both I and Kymil can operate any function of Wolf Streak Beta as well. We'll help you do what must be done while others rest. However, there is no doubt that Jamyk and Milyr are our best pilots. Yet both should rest some..."

While Domyn tried to pay attention to both conversations and also study holovision showing many splotches of blackness and multitude of twinkling stars, he heard Nyba call out abruptly with authority, "Joculatus, do you have enough common points of reference in recorder sensor reads from both Wolf Streak Beta and Fox Flash Alpha involving all sensor and energy reads related to this particular region of space associated with phenomenon in center of the specific Kil-Kol through which we braided to compile the full three sixty portrayal in the three-dimensional view of anomaly? And if so, how much time will you need to do this?"

As his mind tried sluggishly to comprehend what Nyba had just asked of Joculatus, Domyn heard Doc Kymil suggest in his earpiece, "My advice would be to rest Jamyk first. My observations over the journey tell me that he is more susceptible to a sudden collapse from his currently over-stressed fatigue than Milyr at this moment. He has history of a shorter sleep cycle, so he should be able to regenerate much faster than Milyr. So I'd suggest that Milyr should function as pilot for the hours that Jamyk naps. Do you concur with that, Bodacia and Lyndyn?"

The artigence Bodacia said in her female voice, "Doc Kymil, I do concur that Jamyk has a much shorter sleep cycle than any other person on this spacecraft."

Prof Lyndyn replied after letting Bodacia respond first, "Cap and Kymil, I also agree that Jamyk needs rest earliest. Milyr is a young man now and can deal with extra effort as the pilot."

Joculatus said into the ConCen, "Cap Nyba, there are common points of reference in the sensor read to which you referred. My estimated time for compilation of these varied perspective views is three minutes, fifty-three seconds."

On restricted audio, Domyn asked, "Nyba, do you want Milyr as your pilot now considering his recent foul mood?"

Without taking her gaze from the holovision, Nyba replied in a whisper on the confidential audio, "For that very reason, Domyn, he must be my pilot now. I must show him that I have not lost confidence in his talents as a pilot. I have not assigned him meaningless duty now as punishment. In fact we may discover that he does not perform meaningless duty currently. We shall see."

"Indeed our young Cap shows much wisdom and bit of mystery also, does she not, my kind Kymil?" Prof Lyndyn exclaimed as normal discourse on the ConCen and pointing to the holovision for benefit of others not privy to restricted conversation.

Still unsuccessfully trying to discern some importance in the scene on the holovision, Domyn silently cursed his exhaustion and heard Doc Kymil agree, "Yes, she does. This compilation may reveal what our human eyes have failed to notice."

Then suddenly with awe in his voice, Milyr blurted loudly, "Vulch, this can't be happening. How did you know, Nyba? Are you vulching psychic or something?"

"Do you have something to report, comm primary?" Nyba asked firmly, still watching the present holovision, but Domyn witnessed a subtle turn toward Milyr and a slight shift of her hips toward the front edge of her chair. "Or are you being foolishly silly now, Milyr?"

"Yeah, Cap, there is definitely something here. I'm reading faint echoes of radio style transmissions bouncing around this system," Milyr exclaimed with excitement and surprise, "Some of these are echoing from that Kil-Kol. Vulch, how did you know?"

"Are you certain that these signal residues are not from our recent sanbeam transmissions with Fox Flash Alpha? There have been several in the last hours. All of the comms would have passed through this space no matter where they originated," Whyvvi remarked, twirling her red chair to stare across ConCen at Milyr.

"Vulch, Whyvvi, I know the difference between recent sanbeam residue and old radio echoes," Milyr groaned. "And these old vulchers seem to have enough continuity to them to suggest that they were possibly in the language descended from that of ancient colonials from Zerosolis System. Vulchers are even close to projected language evolution of our Blue Jay projection."

Silence on the ConCen for moments until Swyllo whispered, "You said some came from Kil-Kol? How can that be? The colonials had no braiding technology or grav propulsion, did they?"

"And signals may be in colonial language?" Whyvvi murmured softly, "Amazing!"

Joculatus in a deep male voice reported abruptly, "Cap Nyba, sanbeam transmission from Fox Flash Alpha is arriving. They are requesting full holovision reception. The compilation view of your prior request is prepared. Which do you wish on the holovision at this time?"

"Oh my, sanbeam request for full holovision, that is most unusual," Doc Kymil exclaimed. "But at least they had time to reply before going out of range."

Suspecting that such choice would be difficult for her, Domyn was surprised when Cap Nyba commanded hastily and decisively, "Joculatus, put the comm from Fox Flash Alpha on the holovision immediately. Milyr, prepare return the comm for them while we view their message. We may have time to update them with your recent discovery. That would be of importance to them as they go toward the Sexto System before us."

When new scene of Fox Flash Alpha ConCen appeared in space of the holovision, Doc Kymil murmured with a hushed voice, "Oh my, I'd forgotten just how potent the full holovision view of another ConCen can be..."

In the holovision, Domyn observed the full ConCen crew of Fox Flash Alpha. Almost like a mirror image, the Fox Flash Alpha semi-circle of chairs seemed to form a complete circle with the ConCen chairs of Wolf Streak Beta. The clarity of sanbeam transmission was the best that he had ever seen in his experience in Blue Jay. Very much as if they were all on the same ConCen, in the same common circle, all Blue Jay travelers on this mission were in one circle. Perhaps clarity was because the sanbeam comm did not have to return to LaOgres space through Kil-Kol as normal, he mused. But then he reminded himself that Fox Flash was most likely in LaOgres still.

In the few moments that his weary brain pondered this, Cap Bhiros said from the orange chair near the center of the holovision ConCen, "Praise Domyn's universal deity, you are out of danger for now. This whole crew cheered when we received your last comm. We'll keep this short. This will most likely be our last comm from this position. Khebol calculated that we would be out of range by the time you sent return comm..."

Cap Nyba commanded urgently, "Milyr, continue to prepare the short return comm for them. Transmit this very moment this comm ends. Maybe we'll have time to get them one more message."

"Yeah, Cap," Milyr replied while his right hand playfully reached out as if to grab Chitir, who seemed to sit is his green chair immediately next to Milyr.

"Don't disturb the holovision, you toxx," wailed Swyllo, "Spin around, you gangly vulcher. Stop blocking my view of Chitir."

The deep, steady voice of Cap Bhiros continued, "...have launched the second Buffalardi at this Kil-Kol and aimed it forward in the direction that our artigence calculates will best aid your computation for your new navigational coordinates and course to Sexto. We hope this will help you on your way..."

As he listened to the message from Cap Bhiros, Domyn observed the Fox Flash Alpha ConCen just as if they were there on Wolf Streak Beta. Beside Chitir, adorned in his typical green pilot suit, sat Carhel dressed in a pastel red suit in her deep red chair. Then Doc Thebon sprawled in his black chair wearing his characteristically black uniform with lightening silver stripes on arms and legs. Then of course was the captain chair with Bhiros wearing his bright orange uniform. Khebol, Domyn's engineer counterpart a in tan suit, was next in the brown chair. Beside Khebol sat Prof Hethep in her silver dionboda and gray chair. To her right, Emkhat in yellow of harvester primary sat tall in her chair. Finally Radhin in her lavender uniform sat on her purple chair not far from Jamyk.

Then Cap Bhiros turned toward his engineer with a wave of his orange glove and continued, "Khebol suggests that due to your necessary side trip into Debordo, your timeline will now be different than ours. Therefore we believe that this will be the last time that our comm exchanges will be possible until you pop into Sexto. We will pop into Sexto during our next awakening. We will have one Buffalardi left then to deploy there to reinforce the beacon chain back to Steppingstone Quinto..."

"No more comms from Khebol? That is nasty luck," moaned Whyvvi from her red chair on the Wolf Streak side of the circle.

"That is until we get to Sexto," Cap Nyba declared emphatically. "We will pop into the Sexto System. We will see these friends again, Whyvvi,"

"May universal metaphy hear your command, Cap," Lyndyn sighed.

"Yup," agreed Jamyk as he waved his green dionjocu glove at Radhin, whose image sat to his left in the holovision. "Again."

Domyn wondered to himself how the boy saw her when his full visor covered his eyesight. But then he grinned at his own foolish question knowing that Jamyk would know that someone was there beside him in the holovision. The boy was a rascal clown often but was not a fool. He did not need to literally see the existing image. Then Domyn scowled and wondered, why was he thinking of these inconsequential notions at the moment when he should be focused upon comm exchange. Apparently he was more exhausted than he had realized.

"...Streak Beta's legacy in history of Blue Jay will be legendary," Cap Bhiros stated. "Your deeds at that Kil-Kol will never be surpassed by any Blue Jay crew. You have done something amazing. Be very proud of what you have accomplished there. Our only chance to come close to your exploits will be to locate and contact colonials at Sexto. Let's hope that they do exist in Sexto. We can only hope that our deeds will be honored as much as yours..."

"What a lot of vulching toxx nasty!" laughed Milyr. "Does that vulcher believe what he's saying?"

"That does seem a bit nasty strange for normal Cap Bhiros," Swyllo agreed as she stared at the image of Chitir. "I wonder if he feels some guilt for his hasty pass at last Kil-Kol."

"...as we end this comm with our strong wish to see you again when you get to Sexto. Wolf Streak Beta, we salute you!" Cap Bhiros stated solemnly, and then as one whole crew of the Fox Flash Alpha stood from their chairs, silently stretched their arms towards the ConCen of Wolf Streak Beta, and then slowly clutched their hands back to their chests just over their hearts.

For the full minute of this silent tribute, the ConCen of Wolf Streak Beta was absolutely quiet also, until the holovision ended, and then Kymil whispered, "Oh my, I've never seen that done before. Do you young people realize how high an honor that was from the group of peers?"

"Indeed that is the highest possible salute that one Blue Jay crew can ever expect from the crew of their peers," Lyndyn murmured softly.

"Especially from Bhiros, Khebol, and Chitir, three of the most disrespectful clowns that I have ever known," Whyvvi exclaimed with slight chuckle.

"Yup," rasped Jamyk. "Clowns!"

"Let's not allow this to go to our egos, boys, girls, and Jamyk," Cap Nyba said in a subdued tone.

"Perhaps, Cap Nyba, after that salute, no doubt you could change that phrase to...men and women...now?" Prof Lyndyn asked rhetorically as he turned toward her with a smile.

"Indeed, Prof," Nyba grinned back at the older mentor, "No doubt you are correct about that. Okay, men, women, and Jamyk, we've got duties to perform now before we celebrate our new legendary status. Milyr..."

"Sending the comm already, Cap," the lanky young man interrupted in an unusually businesslike tone, "Should I sanbeam something to Blue Jay MisCom back on the Steppingstone Quinto as well?"

"At least begin preparing the comm. But don't send it yet. We've got some time here in Debordo before we plunge back through Weznuski and into LaOgres again. However, that's cherp thinking, Milyr. I can see that the rest did you some good," Nyba said with serious praise, and then she continued, "Joculatus, can you estimate time period to resupply our energy reserves and also prepare for plunge back to LaOgres?"

"Yes, Cap Nyba," Joculatus responded and then asked, "Cap Nyba, would you view the previously requested compilation of common recordings on the holovision now?"

"Cap Nyba, how soon until some of us can get some nutrient and some rest? I'll admit, I'm exhausted," Domyn inquired with another yawn.

"Yes, Joculatus, put compilation of anomaly in Kil-Kol on holovision now. Whyvvi and Swyllo, you've got our best eyes for solving puzzles. See what you can discover," Cap Nyba commanded, and then on restricted frequency, asked in earpiece of Domyn, "Neer, do you have a recommendation as to my transition crew for ConCen? I'd like your input before I relieve you of duty."

Domyn replied in a hushed voice, "If you can operate with Milyr as your pilot for the first part of your flight toward the light source and harvesting, then Jamyk and I can rest. Prof Lyndyn and Doc Kymil should be able to perform functions for Whyvvi and Swyllo. This would allow most of my Buffalardi launch crew some rest. Is this consistent with your thoughts, Doc and Prof?"

"Indeed we can perform duties, can we not, kind Kymil? It could be just like our journeys on old Turkey Trot Alpha," Lyndyn replied with enthusiasm.

"Oh my, yes, we can certainly do those duties, I am very sure. Those were journeys, my kindred spirit," Kymil sang with her melodious voice. "However, I should at least get our sleepy crew settled in Med before committing to the ConCen responsibility. Saphyndenlairoum sleep is not appropriate for this session of rest, so some sedative may be required."

"No doubt you are right about that," Lyndyn said. "Perhaps especially Swyllo, if she gets LaOgres anxiety. Possibly Jamyk also may be overly energized mentally, in spite of his physical exhaustion, to realize that he needs rest."

"Awright, that sounds logical to me," Domyn agreed, not at all upset with himself for letting others make decisions since he was just too weary for that kind of administrative duty.

Then aloud to the ConCen, Cap Nyba commanded firmly, "Milyr, prepare to take over pilot function. Coordinate transfer with Jamyk and Joculatus when you are ready. And how are you young women doing with your analysis of that holovision?"

"I have looked at this and the previous scenes for probably hours now," Whyvvi complained with a very frustrated groan. "This view now is much more precise and more definitive than before, but I just cannot see any specific phenomenon or pattern in center of Kil-Kol that means anything to me yet. I know there is a very specific mass and shape. I should be able to answer your request more accurately, Cap. I am sorry!"

"You are tired, Whyvvi. What do you believe that you can see in this new compilation, Swyllo?" Cap Nyba asked just to his left, and suddenly Domyn realized that he had not really comprehended the most recent view on the holovision, even though he had been staring at it directly.

As he finally admitted to himself that he was so distracted by his weariness that he had not paid any attention to the holovision, which was sure sign to him that he needed to get off the ConCen, Domyn asked feeling a bit guilty, "Cap Nyba, is it okay if I leave the ConCen now? I'm almost of no use at this time to you or this crew. I'm just too tired to think straight."

Before he finished his request, Swyllo groaned with frustration from her yellow chair, "Vulch, this view, this shape, I can almost recognize that anomaly as Joculatus pans around it from different angles. Can I cheat, Cap? Can I ask Joculatus to check history data files for comparison?"

"Why do you want to do that?" Whyvvi inquired suspiciously. "Do you know something now?"

"Cherp notion, Swyllo, I suggest you check historical Blue Jay mission files," Cap Nyba said with a hint of secret understanding in her voice as she smiled at Swyllo, and then when she turned her smile toward Domyn, Nyba said, "Neer, your idea of resting is also cherp now. Wait a few minutes for Jamyk to transfer his function with Milyr. Then you can make sure he goes with you and gets his rest. Doc, you'd better go as well to set up Med for our tired crewmembers."

"Joculatus, compare the silhouette shape of present anomaly with historical files of Blue Jay mission objectives," Swyllo commanded with authority in her high voice.

Whyvvi asked again with a tone of puzzlement, "What do you believe that you can see, Swyllo? I cannot really discern any logical pattern from this display yet."

When Domyn peeled off the light brown cap and visor from his sweating head, effectively breaking contact with Joculatus, he heard Milyr announce, "Cap Nyba, I now have complete transference from Jamyk. I am now a pilot. Joculatus confirms this."

Then immediately Cap Nyba commanded tersely, "Jamyk, go get some nutrient and some rest. You must behave as Doc Kymil instructs, little man. I'll need you healthy in about five hours maximum. Domyn, you go now as well and take this youngster with you. I'm putting you in charge of his resting. See that this rascal does get some."

"Cherp," Jamyk sighed, pulling off his green cap. "Rest."

Surprised at how readily the boy accepted his dismissal without squabble, Domyn rose from his brown chair and said, "Let's go, my friend. Time for some nutrient will be cherp for us."

"Yeah, Domyn, you can drink my share for me also," called Milyr in a jovial mood now that he was pilot. "That vulching antemgebemarzex will rot my nads. I might become like little one-nad peener. I don't want that if we're going to the Sexto System with all those colonial fems."

"One," Jamyk laughed as he stood up from his green chair and then emphasized with a spreading gesture of his hands. "Huge!"

"Argh! Hurry and leave the ConCen, you little toxx!" Swyllo squeaked with a giggle. "You're distracting me with your ridiculousness."

Then Joculatus reported, "Swyllo, within parameters of your request, there is a 79 percent probability that the anomaly has the silhouette shape of colonial spaceship Gullu Mette."

Walking toward the hatch with Jamyk leaning on his side, Domyn heard this and paused to turn back toward Cap Nyba as she asked with mild surprise, "Joculatus, are you certain it is Gullu Mette?"

"That's it," squealed Swyllo in excitement, "I thought that shape in the silhouette was vaguely familiar. That looks so much like one of the ancient colony ships that we are searching for on this mission. But is this possible here in this Kil-Kol?"

Joculatus said, "Cap Nyba, my analysis does not state that shape in Kil-Kol is Gullu Mette. My estimate of correlation of silhouette shapes based upon parameters given by Swyllo suggests that the chance of this match is 79 percent positive."

"The what? Did I hear you talking about one of colony ships from ancient times?" Milyr asked in obvious skeptical bewilderment.

"Gullu Mette, yes, now that you have mentioned the thought, I can see that shape in anomaly," Whyvvi shouted enthusiastically. "That was one of three great spaceships in which colonials departed the Zerosolis System over 500 years ago. Gullu Mette, here in our Kil-Kol. Milyr, you should pay attention in history lectures and briefs."

"Then should I put this discovery in my comm to Blue Jay MisCom at Steppingstone Quinto?" Milyr asked with a scowl and then grin as he inquired, "Is it important?"

"Go," Jamyk rasped, tugging on Domyn's arm,. "Tired."

"Yes, it's very important, if we can confirm analysis. But, Milyr, you are a pilot now. Prof Lyndyn can operate the comm function now," Cap Nyba decreed.

"Indeed I can, Cap Nyba. This discovery should be part of any comm we send. It is regretful that we are most likely too late to send this info to Fox Flash Alpha. This could be more meaningful to them than our escape from Kil-Kol," Prof Lyndyn suggested.

However, with his awareness totally exhausted, Domyn could not contemplate about the value of Gullu Mette at the moment. Let others debate about where to send any message now. He was so tired and hungry now that he did not care about Gullu Mette. Domyn was happy just to relinquish control of the Wolf Streak Beta to Cap Nyba. Awe guide her capable decisions, Domyn thought. Then he let Jamyk escort him from the ConCen.

The last comment that he overheard before the hatch closed was Milyr laughing heartily, "Vulch, Prof, if that's case, then instead of saluting us next time, those foxes will be sniffing our collective toxx!"

SPEC ONE: DOMYN THROUGH LAOGRES
CHAPTER 11

Only one more Saphyndenlairoum sleep cycle, Domyn thought, and then the last awakening in LaOgres space.

His feet pounded stride after stride on a dirt brown path. His lungs breathed heavily with effort of his running. His heart pumped rapidly, supplying his working muscles with energy and oxygen rich blood. Domyn felt vigorous and alive.

Beside him ran Cap Nyba in her blue JMO running suit. Her stride matched his in spite of her shorter stature. Perspiration wetness soaked her JMO and pasted it to her very feminine figure. Her heavy breathing coincided almost precisely with his. Her intermittent laughter revealed her own joy and ease.

Nyba exclaimed through panting breathes, "Surely this is so much better than our last awakening. I feel relief and excitement at our future now, Domyn."

"Awright, yes, so do I," he gasped while they veered around a left turn in the path between two tall hemlocks. "Our nasty experience during our last awakening, our escape back to Debordo, and then our return through Kil-Kol into LaOgres again, those trying moments are now in our past. That whole awakening was enough to fit into the entire journey. That last plunge through Kil-Kol and Weznuski space was a real wild ride, but we did it."

Beside him as they ran, Nyba panted, "Yes, and we did that around Gullu Mette... That was quite a wild ride, yet as you say, we did it. Our crew and our Wolf Streak Beta did it."

When a distant yipping bark filled air, Domyn glanced upward toward the small hill covered by short cedar saplings and scrubby mountain laurel bushes, and he joked, "That sure sounds like a fox... Do you think that could be a sign from Khebol...laughing at us?"

"Or maybe...cheering us...after their last comm during our last awakening," Nyba suggested with obvious mirth in her heavy breathing. "Something very special... Fox Flash Alpha sent to us when they gave us that standing tribute... from the heart, I believe."

Another short yipping bark accompanied a glimpse of reddish-orange movement in the mountain laurel, but then the hill receded behind them as they continued along the dirt path, and Domyn exclaimed, "Awspirational for me...to get such honor...from Blue Jay crew."

"Yes, that was something very special," Nyba gasped while they loped through the copse of yellow and brown colored leaves on trees unknown to Domyn, and then she continued, "Yet we must not...get satisfied now... We must go on to Sexto and finish our true mission. We must find colonials and two other giant colony ships that departed the Zerosolis System several hundred years ago."

Honking incessantly a large flock of geese flew in a characteristic vee-shaped formation far overhead, and Domyn glanced upward at them for a brief moment while he said, "Migrating? Up there, geese... They did migrate, didn't they? Nyba, you are our expert on ancient history. I don't remember those lessons very well... That was never really my interest... Those are geese, aren't they?"

"Yes, those are geese from the period just before... Despoliation..." Nyba huffed heavily of breath as they ran up the slight incline through trees now showing various colors of autumn, and then she continued, "The ancient files indicate that geese left colder climate...for warmer climate... This occurred so many centuries ago...before the horrible dark age...before they were gone..."

"Gone? You mean like most of the creatures...here in this program...that we view in this corridor...when we run for exercise?... Were they all sacrificed to extinction?" Domyn inquired while he turned in unison with Nyba around the gentle right bend along the cross-country trail in the corridor of Wolf Streak Beta, "Or could some of creatures of so long ago be restored on the planet again?"

Her voice either snorted, or was that a brief sob wondered Domyn, when Nyba replied, "Yes...yes...most were lost to the home world in the Zerosolis System...many centuries ago now... Most of creatures that we observe...here in this program...are extinct now... Despoilers were nasty toxx then... Vulching self-absorbed...with their battles for wealth...for power...for social and religious dominance... They were careless of their own home world... They were unconcerned about other people on their own planet... That is why...colonials left Zerosolis System...to find new home...new planet...new system in space...far away from despoilers of old world..."

Peering at his running partner, Domyn checked her stride and movements to ensure that she could not stumble at the fast pace that they were keeping now. She seemed under control physically as they raced along the rapidly bending path. Yet Domyn realized just how emotionally charged Nyba could become when these memories of her discoveries of ancient past involving the dark age that followed the horrid Despoliation on the home world of the Zerosolis System. Her almost obsession with the root causes of colonial exodus from the Zerosolis System was perhaps her greatest hindrance and yet her greatest motivation for her desire to complete the Blue Jay mission and find descendants of migrating colonials and a new planet for people to live a natural life once again.

Trying to encourage and tap into her positive determination, Domyn exclaimed with his own enthusiasm, "Awright, Cap...we're almost there...we're almost in the Sexto System...we're almost prepped for contact... Your leadership has brought us this far, and now we are almost there..."

Fluttering leaves danced and swayed as they fell in the air under the artificially generated trees, along the picturesque wall of the cross-country corridor, and Nyba gasped breathlessly, "Yes, we do plunge to Debordo space next awakening... Then we should be in Sexto... We should be there with foxes... Oh, I hope...we will find them there...and colonials...all those brave people...who left their known solar system...to search galaxy for another...place to begin to live again...I hope their descendants found one...I hope they found place better than...nasty world ancients created."

As a white-tail stag with impressive antlers stared at them from a group of crab apple trees for a few seconds and then leaped away into the forest with its white flag-like tail raised high on its haunches. Domyn panted, "We should find them, Nyba... You found Gullu Mette... Milyr found old radio signals in Debordo space nearby... These are sure signs that...colonials are not far... They should be in Sexto... That is about right...spatial distance through Debordo...assuming their propulsion hasn't changed very much...during intervening decades... since loss of Gullu Mette...to those colonials who continued...on farther into the galaxy... Ours should be a mission....to find them... Ours should be the climax of the Blue Jay project..."

"I hope so," Nyba panted and then loped along beside him in silence and also with a very fast-pace as she probably worked off some of her anxious anger and tension that she most likely felt while they had discussed ravaging symptoms of ancient times of Despoliation on the home world.

The flock of wild turkeys, frequently portrayed on this environmental program, trotted over the slight hill and approached within eleven yards of path. Their apparent lack of fear of human runners was unusual, Domyn realized, for this program, yet perhaps Khebol had reprogrammed the corridor display to give these creatures less flighty and skittish tendency.

However, this was thought of no significance, he mused to himself. Domyn sensed that Nyba might need to allow a flow of exercise to wash through her at that moment. He knew how she felt. He had experienced the sensation many times himself during years of the journey toward this upcoming climax to their Blue Jay mission. Awright, he mused, the next awakening should bring them to their goal. They should find their destiny in Sexto System if all calculations and long-range sensor reads had been correct. They should find colonials at last during their next awakening.

After they ran another nearly complete lap around the 200-yard course within interior diameter of Wolf Streak Beta, and warmth and humming vibrations of several Flandecams had bathed Domyn during his reflections, finally Nyba said, "Yes, Neer, we should succeed...this time... Milyr says radio residues...of our last Debordo space position...seemed to be less than...half century old... That is not that long ago...for colonial ship travel...in Debordo space."

"Awright, yes, you're right..." Domyn panted with encouragement. "That's about right for...colonials to be in Sexto now... Awspir, Nyba...we should find them for sure."

"Yes, that's about right for the time difference," Nyba said as they ran beneath the leafless trees under the graying sky of mackerel patterned clouds, "But I wish we knew more about Gullu Mette."

Around them the corridor wall and ceiling portrayed approach of the new season, winter season of northern hemisphere of the old home world, but Domyn relished the touch of chill on his heated body as he ran, and he said with praise, "You did well to find it... No one else could have... Our misadventure...had benefit at least... You did find Gullu Mette...and recorded sensor reads to study in future... That's a very cherp feat, Nyba."

"Still, well, I wish could find more... Sensors are not clear enough... Don't know how...beacon is working still... There's just not enough info," Nyba complained through panting breath. "Whyvvi is not sure how... Gullu Mette powers beacon... We wish we knew more."

"We know it's there now... We know residues of radio signals there... That's cherp info... That gives our mission hope... Blue Jay could succeed," Domyn exclaimed as a light cold breeze wafted over his mostly naked figure, except for his tan JMO running shorts at his waist and Clarinkevs on his feet, and this sudden cooling stimulated him to sigh. "This feels really cherp now... Don't you like this chill, Nyba? This makes me want to run for hours longer."

"Yes, this is my best time on these runs," Nyba agreed, and then after a few seconds of loping beside Domyn, she continued, "We will get time...to study sensor reads...now with Whyvvi and Swyllo... This awakening there is...no need to waste time with...comm to foxes... We are not in a common time cycle now... Foxes may have popped to Sexto now... I'm envious of Bhiros now."

Breathing deeply of cooler air with a hint of snow teasing his nose, Domyn said, "Be there the next awakening... Wolf Streak will pop the Sexto... We will get a share of glory... We are a legend already... Awe knows we will find more there, Nyba."

Low sun just above the mid-afternoon horizon was partially obscured by the mackerel clouds currently portrayed on the ceiling and walls of the corridor, and Nyba proclaimed, "Looks like winter is coming... It's almost time for me to go to my duty, Domyn... You do make sense about our chances... I hope you are right... We need to research more with Whyvvi and Swyllo... I want to study the sensor reads of Gullu Mette more fully... Are you ready for a sprint pace now, Neer? These will be my last three laps."

"Awspir, Nyba... I'm cherp to race," Domyn exclaimed as he heard a loud raucous squawk from some evergreen trees, and he asked abruptly, "Was that a real blue jay? Nyba, you know...was it?"

Laughter blended with her gulps for air, and she said, "Are you trying to distract me? Are you trying to get a head start on me? Are you getting as sneaky as Milyr...and little rascal toxx?"

When a shrill squawk pierced the air again, Domyn chuckled with honest denial, "Awe knows I wouldn't do that, Nyba. But did you hear that again? Was that a blue jay? You must know... Is Khebol sneaking some symbols into this program? That annoying squawk sounds like the noise of a blue jay... Serious, Nyba, I'm not trying to trick..."

Then the unique bird squawk rang out again and a flurry of movement stirred the evergreens that had lined the corridor for several strides now, and Nyba squealed with sudden delight, "Oh, yes...blue jay... I didn't know... Khebol had found one in the files… He must have added it…for our runs here… Khebol is such a cherp prankster… He can be just like a blue jay…annoying and cherp at the same time… But to see it just at this awakening…how cherp!… Oh, see, there it goes…how cherp…"

When his head turned slightly to observe the single blue-gray bird with black and white markings flutter from one branch to another, Domyn felt a sudden quickening of her pace on his other side, and he complained laughing as he saw her dash slightly ahead, "Awe cheat, Nyba… You cunning young woman… Trick me just like Khebol with the blue jay."

Then as she moved ahead of him while he laughed and struggled to get breath to keep up with her faster pace, she sang back, "Not cheat… I used my brain… And a pretty nature picture to distract you… Ho…ho…ho!"

Despite her stocky build and heavy footfalls, Nyba almost flew ahead of him. Her short legs seemed to stretch as they lengthened their stride. This young woman was full of surprises, Domyn thought as he attempted to catch up. Her blue JMO suit clung to her figure as second skin. Her distinctive pleasant scent wafted at him in her wake. She was running as if he were a demon chasing her, or perhaps from her inner thoughts and doubts about approaching climax to their Blue Jay mission. Domyn decided to allow her run for her own exhilaration. He caught up to her and then merely paced her at this nearly sprinting pace.

While they loped along the artificial cross-country course, snowflakes began to fall in in scenes on the walls and ceiling. Curiously, he mused, none actually existed in the corridor itself. Yet perhaps that would be much too difficult to create a program and mechanism to do that, he mused, and it would not be very consistent with the periodic warming spots near the Flandecams. However, this effect, which he enjoyed now as he ran, was joyfully winter as he could recall from the ancient archives.

The cold air current blew through the corridor, simulating the winter wind to coincide with the snowfall on the wall scenes. They loped side by side in the wintry scene. Their feet had the benefit of a solid, stable floor, so they had no worry of slippage that could have occurred in a real environment.

This pace was the fastest of any that he could remember of their many runs over this course during years on the Wolf Streak Beta. Nyba kept a brisk sprint. Nyba needed release, Domyn realized. He was willing to give her opportunity. She had made some difficult decisions recently. Most likely she would face many more in the Sexto System. He paced her silently, allowing her this freedom.

Other than the snowstorm around them, Domyn noticed very little of the visual environment. Their racing was much too rapid for reasonable scenery viewing. Occasionally a startled chirp or shrill cry of birds struck his ears as their passage triggered some programmed response from the artificial scenery. But even a hum and the heat of the periodic Flandecams barely stimulated his sense.

They loped along at their racing pace, kick that any cross-country runner would be proud to perform, Domyn thought as his awareness ignored the pain in his body and instead focused upon the thrill of this shared experience with Nyba.

Then abruptly ahead of them, he noticed a slender man jogging in gray JMO shorts, and Domyn yelled hastily, "Coming through, Prof."

Prof Lyndyn stepped to the side just quickly enough not to hinder runners, and the man called as they passed, "Racing, no doubt. See you on next lap…"

Words of Prof Lyndyn fell behind rapidly at the sprinting pace they ran. Why was Prof Lyndyn on this exercise course now, Domyn wondered. During the exercise period of Domyn, an older man of forty-seven years was normally busy preparing for his sessions with the other crew members or briefing with the artigences, especially Bodacia. Perhaps the man wanted the extra activity for his own health with an important plunge coming along on the next awakening. Perhaps he needed to observe or speak with them while they were on this course. Domyn was puzzled. This was not the routine.

Nyba spat through a puffing breath, "Let's race to Prof as our finish line, okay, Domyn?"

Suggestion surprised him slightly, but he agreed, "Awe why not? He'll be coming up soon again. This is a small circle at the pace we are running now. You did say race?"

"Bet your fat toxx!" Nyba gasped, and stunning Domyn, she somehow quickened her sprinting pace even more and gained stride on him.

"Awe damn, give me speed," he huffed from burning lungs as he tried to recapture his place beside her, realizing that this race had no more than half a lap to go based on the slower jogging pace of Prof at the prior position on route.

In a few seconds, he regained his position beside her. Nyba ran with extreme determination, faster than he had ever witnessed of her before. His body ached. His lungs burned. His heart beat as if it were coming out of his chest. Only a short distance to go, he reminded himself, but he would not surrender. He would pace her to Prof Lyndyn.

Then she shouted loudly, "Prof, stay in position. We are coming fast."

Their long strides gulped the distance. Their steps pounded into the floor. Their breaths seemed to come as one. Nyba and Domyn sprinted side by side. Then suddenly Prof Lyndyn was there just ahead around the next bend. In only seconds, if that, they streaked by the man. Domyn slowed his pace to a normal run but did not want to stop suddenly. Beside him Nyba did the same. They glanced at each other and grinned.

"Did we tie?" Nyba inquired tiredly.

"Awe, I couldn't tell," gasped Domyn.

"Cool down then?" Nyba suggested.

"Only...way...to...go," Domyn agreed.

"Now it's...right...season for that," Nyba gasped, waving her hand at the snowy scenario around them in the corridor, "Wonder if...colonials found...snowy planet...as home."

"Awright...guess...it is," Domyn agreed, slowing his exhausted legs to a fast jog, "Do you know...if snow...falls on ...home world...again yet?"

"A tie then...Domyn?" she asked again as she matched his slowing strides with hers, "From the last report...habitable regions...still in heated climates... Cold in mountains...and poles only..."

"Ask Prof...when we pass...him next," Domyn advised and then admitted, "But I guess...tie is best. We usually...work as...team most often...anyway, Nyba."

"Yes, ho, ho...tie, yes," she agreed.

"But, Nyba... we... ran...record pace tie! Pace set...by you, Nyba!" Domyn exclaimed with deliberate praise while they jogged along the wintery path through the corridor.

"By the both of us," she proclaimed. "We are a cherp pair of wolves. We can lead this pack well together, Neer Domyn. We will find a glorious planet of colonial descendants next awakening."

Then soon they jogged by stationary Prof Lyndyn, who called out as they passed him, "No doubt you two young racers are in cool down pace now. Do you mind if I join you? These legs of mine need more stretching and exercise than I've been allowing myself in recent awakenings. Don't tell Kymil please. She will goad me nasty if she finds out..."

As the man spoke this, Prof Lyndyn joined their jogging pace, and after awhile, Domyn asked, "Prof, who passed you first? Was the winner Nyba or me?"

"Don't worry, Prof," Nyba laughed while they jogged, "I won't be upset by your decision."

"Indeed, Cap Nyba, I try to tell you truth as I see it at all times. However, this particular event does not allow me any valuable opinion. When you ran be me, I was so overwhelmed by the effort that you two young people were exerting that I did not think to act as a judge or official. In all honesty, I cannot say who was first. I could not differentiate between your two forms as you flashed by me. I was just too…"

"That's okay, Prof," Domyn chuckled, wondering to himself how Prof could ramble like that without any hesitation of breath in spite of the jogging pace that they were setting for such an older man, so he said, "We have agreed already to call it a tie."

"Yes, tie," Nyba remarked. "Very robust and energizing tie. The best cherp feeling that my body has felt in a long time. I'm ready to go to work now."

Jogging in unison with the two younger people, Prof Lyndyn exclaimed, "Indeed this activity does tend to enliven the body and mental spirit, doesn't it? I'm feeling more vigorous than earlier this awakening. I'm almost ready to deal with a session with a difficult patient…"

"Jamyk?" both Domyn and Nyba asked abruptly and simultaneously.

"No doubt you youngsters must realize that I should not discuss such things with others besides individual patient. However, Doc Kymil did instruct me to forewarn you, Cap Nyba, that Jamyk had rather erratic sleep this past Saphyndenlairoum cycle. She is not confident that the boy can completely focus on the precision hand-eye functions this awakening. Apparently Bodacia interjected a stronger than normal sedative during sleep to calm the lad. Doc Kymil is concerned that the extra dosage may linger in his system longer that normal for Jamyk…"

Domyn interrupted, saying with worry as they slowed their jogging gradually, "I did notice him tossing and turning more convulsively at the end of his sleep cycle this time. He was also mumbling something in a frantic voice as well, but that I could not hear clearly. It was probably a dream."

"Damn that rascal toxx!" Nyba swore, breathing more rapidly than the slowing pace required, "I hope that he doesn't ruin my cherp feeling now. I'm too tired to make another run. I want my warm shower now."

Jogging beside her, Domyn said, "I wouldn't worry, Nyba. I've seen him twisted like a pretzel before when he comes out of Saphyndenlairoum sleep. It seems normal for the boy. Most likely Bodacia was trying to keep his reading within her programmed parameters. We all know that Jamyk can be difficult for her to monitor while he sleeps."

"Indeed do not worry, Cap Nyba. I am here to intercept the lad and observe him in activities other than normal psych sessions. I'm certain that I will determine if he is of appropriate perceptiveness to perform his normal functions," Prof Lyndyn stated as he paced them along the brown path that extended through the now changing scenes on the walls of the corridor.

Around them the scenery had changed gradually to a spring environment, but Domyn was attentive to his own pleasant exhaustion and anticipation of a hot shower, so he said, "That's cherp, Prof. We trust you to relate to the boy. I believe I like Nyba's idea of a warm shower and then right to work. I should have extra time this awakening to check the Flandecams with Vivacio."

As sunshine warmed the trail and forest alongside them while they continued their slow jog, Prof Lyndyn remarked, "I was hoping that you, Neer, could linger here with me to let Jamyk feel more comfortable. You are more of a peer and fellow athlete to him than I. I'm just a counselor. I could use your assistance just to make him more at ease."

"That is not a bad notion," Nyba chuckled, peering hastily at Domyn. "That should keep him off my scalp for some time. Perhaps, Neer Domyn, if you are successful in taming the rascal, then you can use him to aid in checking the Flandecams. Ho, ho, ho, I like that idea."

From behind them came a sudden raspy croak, "Pass."

Barely hearing footsteps and word of the boy now abruptly behind them, Domyn swerved aside inadvertently, taking Prof Lyndyn with him into the wall. Jamyk dashed past rapidly. His thin figure was dressed in the usual green JMO shorts and Clarinkevs. Domyn then realized that the boy had entered the course less than one lap behind them. Yet his pace was already near a full run.

Domyn yelled, "Jamyk, you should allow for some warmup. Don't start at the full pace."

However, the thin form raced ahead and cried out strangely, "Chitir…wait."

Not having stepped aside, Nyba was several steps ahead now when she paused and laughed, "I'm so glad that you two are going to handle this. I'm definitely heading for my warm shower now. He's all yours. I'll tangle with Gullu Mette in the tangled, nasty Kil-Kol any awakening rather than deal with that rascal Jamyk. Have fun counseling, guys."

Then Nyba disappeared through saplings of sumac and maple along the left of the trail. Domyn realized at that moment that she had stepped through the hatchway leading from the running corridor. From the angle which he looked toward the spot, Domyn could see only the simulated environment portrayed on the wall. Now he was alone with Prof Lyndyn.

"No doubt that the young woman is quite deceptive when she wants to be," Lyndyn declared as he pushed himself off the right wallm which displayed a scene of moisture dripping from newly sprouted tree buds and the first hint of blossoms opening. "Shall we wait for Jamyk to lap around again? I don't believe that we would catch up to him if we tried. He seemed quite energized when he passed us."

Notion of assisting with a counseling session as merely an observer and human pacifier did not appeal to Domyn at that particular moment. Yet as he walked to the hatch area where Nyba had vanished, he felt vibration and heard the hum of Flandecams above and below that area. Maybe Nyba had been cleverer than he had first realized. The idea of having Jamyk help him later when he checked the massive generators now seemed sensible and did appeal to his desire to work with the Flandecams. Perhaps he could struggle through the session here in the cross-country corridor. After all he enjoyed this exercise and company of Jamyk more than he liked to admit.

"We won't be able to slow his pace yet, Prof. Do you believe that you can keep up with him for awhile? I don't believe the sedative given by Bodacia has had any lingering effect, do you?" Domyn asked with a chuckle. "He certainly doesn't seem to be sedated now."

"Oh, indeed no, I'm in fairly good shape for a forty-seven-year-old, but not at that almost frantic pace that he was using when he passed us. I would recommend that we take the pace that would serve as a cool down for you and let the boy race around this course by himself for awhile until he uses his energy," Prof Lyndyn suggested and then perked his attention back along the way they had come and announced, "I hear him coming now. Decide now if you desire to run with him. He'll be here momentarily."

"Wait," a throaty wail hollered from beyond view back along the path, and then very soon in seconds, a slender figure in green JMO running shorts dashed around the previous bend behind them, and Jamyk yelled, "Pass."

Eyes of the boy were wide with intent. His face was serious with determination. Obviously Jamyk had no inclination to slow his rapid pace. He was racing away from or toward someone or something in his mind. Domyn could comprehend this nuance of behavior as he realized then that Jamyk's awareness of Lyndyn, and he was merely peripheral to Jamyk's inner motivation then. Domyn recognized this in a brief look that he got of the boy before Jamyk streaked by them and then dashed around the next bend in the trail of corridor.

"Awright, Prof, I guess we'll take our own pace for now," Domyn announced, walking rapidly along the trail. "Perhaps a slow jog will allow us to see more of the scenery as we go."

Striding alongside Domyn, Prof Lyndyn said with enthusiasm, "Indeed a brisk jog on the cross country trail can be very beneficial. Also, we may see some of the new changes that Khebol has made to our program in here. That lad can be quite clever and tricky sometimes. Perhaps he has coincidentally chosen some ancient flora, which the colonials stored in their banks of genetic options. We should discover this when we find the colonial habitation in the Sexto System."

Along the right side of the trail, robins flew from the tree branches to the dirty ground in the sunlight filtering through the treetops, and Domyn said, "Awe yeah, that Neer has magical way with these programs. Khebol is much more gifted at this type of sci-tech than I am. He's quite imaginative. I recall that geneticists of the ancient colony ships were just as clever and ambitious in their selections. If only they found a planet comparable to the home world before Despoliation."

"Oh, Domyn, don't be so modest. Your knowledge of this sci-tech of Blue Jay is almost legendary. Every spacecraft, every captain of Blue Jay would crave to have you as their Neer. You retain just as much knowledge as Khebol or any ancient colonial scientist," Prof Lyndyn exclaimed in earnest and then asked, "Should we speed our walk to a jog? I would not want you to get away from your planned routine because of my presence."

"Yes, I suppose we should. I do have some more energy in my body. Eventually we'll want to pace with Jamyk, that is if you wish to bond with him to get his attention during this exercise session," Domyn agreed, and then as he began to jog, said, "Let's go now, Prof. Jamyk will be lapping us again soon. I'm good for some more running in here, but not through all of this awakening."

Their suddenly quickened pace and louder footfalls startled some mourning doves from a hemlock tree portrayed on the left wall, and Prof Lyndyn laughed as he jogged beside Domyn, "Indeed this program has become very interactive with our presence over the recent years. Khebol and you have updated the program to become more responsive to our passage along the trail. When we first began our journey from Steppingstone Primero, these were but pictures of environments on the walls. Our old Turkey Trot Alpha did not have even those when Kymil and I were young pups like you. Now scenes seem alive and react to our presence. You have improved the interfacing sci-tech, Domyn. You are master Neer at every sci-tech design of Wolf Streak Beta. I'm indeed impressed with your advancement…"

Suddenly behind them, a croaking gasp of Jamyk shouted, "Pass."

Swerving aside toward the rabbit chewing on greenery of the forest floor not far from the trail, Domyn yelled, "Awe plenty of vigor this awakening, hey, Jamyk? You must have gotten restful sleep."

"Nope," Jamyk rasped as he dashed between them, and then called over his naked, bony shoulder, "Dream… Chitir."

As a glistening sweaty boy in green JMO shorts vanished around the next bend in the corridor ahead, and the startled rabbit hopped away into the underbrush, Prof Lyndyn exclaimed, "Now that is unusual, the boy will not often talk of his recent dreams after Saphyndenlairoum sleep. Perhaps your presence here now is allowing him some comfort to be more forthcoming with what he is feeling. No doubt, Neer Domyn, you may have more mystical abilities than we would assume for a sci-tech engineer…"

"Awright now, Prof, don't make me into some metaphysical magician. I'm just Neer. I'm just a mechanic who likes to play with this craft and these Flandecams," Domyn laughed, waving his hands upward toward the current of warm air flowing from the access port of the Flandecam presently over their heads as they jogged by.

"Oh, indeed you are an enigma to me, Neer Domyn," Prof Lyndyn sighed. "I've never understood how you could reconcile your interest, and perhaps even love for the absoluteness of mechanical and physical certainties with your obsession with obscure and often fantastic belief of a metaphysical being. This has surprised me always."

As they jogged at a slightly faster pace now by his own intention, Domyn responded, "Awe knows, Prof, I don't really need to reconcile those supposedly opposing concepts. To my way of thinking…two aspects of this universe… physical and universal awareness…have always existed alongside one another… Perhaps they are actually interconnected at some aspect beyond atomic quantum level on the microcosmic end and beyond the intergalactic infinity on macrocosmic level…"

"No doubt this makes some sense to you, Neer. Yet parallel existence of physical reality and metaphysical existence seems incongruous to me," Prof Lyndyn said while he kept a faster pace beside Domyn as they ran through the growing green branches of forest.

"Not for me, no, if we believe…universal awareness is…just as real and has been here…just as long as physical universe," Domyn said, now finding speaking and breathing becoming more difficult when tried simultaneously, but he did not wish to slow his pace for he planned to join Jamyk when the boy came by again, so he continued to talk and huff, "Two can coexist…just as we now know…three aspects of space coexist…or more recent acceptance…big bang and continuous creation do coexist… These…two opposing…views…were not compatible… several hundred years ago."

"Still, that is not easy for me to reconcile, Neer Domyn," Lyndyn said, panting along beside Domyn. "No doubt my brain organizes and thinks differently than yours. Perhaps I'm overly entrenched in scientific basis of my field of expertise. Perhaps I'm blinded by my own body of scientific knowledge…"

"Awright, Prof, you are our teacher…our mentor…our counselor…we listen to you… You don't have to agree with me…" Domyn chuckled, and then after a few deep breathes, continued, "I'll be running with Jamyk when he comes by next. Is that awright with you?"

While a yip of a fox barked through the air of the corridor as if this path was truly a portion of wilderness through which they ran, Lyndyn said, "Yes, indeed that would be good. No doubt you can get him into a relaxed attitude. He seems more forthcoming than usual already…"

"Can you tell that already, Prof?" Domyn inquired, surprised at the perception of this man after merely a few utterances by Jamyk during his momentary passes.

"Oh, yes, that rascal is normally very reluctant to reveal his thoughts so soon after the Saphyndenlairoum stasis sleep. His body and energy rise rapidly. Yet his vocalizations are lazy to reveal his inner thoughts and dreams," Prof Lyndyn said, and then with haste, added, "He comes again. Good counseling, Domyn! Trust you will speak wisely!"

Hearing nothing but sounds of their conversation, their footfalls, and noises of artificial nature alongside the trail, Domyn wondered how the older man could hear the footsteps of the small boy behind them. Perhaps those big elf-like ears, Domyn mused with a smile, but then as he glanced backwards over his shoulder, he saw Jamyk appear from around a bend in the corridor. When Jamyk ran into a spot of false sunlight shining through fake treetops above, his body gleamed with wetness of perspiration. His face was intently focused upon the effort of his racing pace.

"Pass," Jamyk gasped as he neared, "Domyn."

Domyn quickened his own strides and asked, "Awright, young lad, is it okay with you…if I run with you, my friend?"

"Yup," Jamyk grinned as he drew even, "run."

As he coordinated his steps and pace with Jamyk, Domyn heard Prof Lyndyn shout, "Don't wait for me. I'll keep this comfortable pace…"

Then the nasal voice was lost in the forest. Only thumping of footsteps and panting of their breaths reached Domyn's ears. Astonishingly to him, he matched cadence of his longer strides to Jamyk's shorter strides very quickly. They seemed to mesh as one runner in spite of their differing statures. Yet Domyn dismissed this observation as trivial, as he sensed the joy of camaraderie of running with his younger friend. This feeling had enthralled him whenever they had an opportunity to run like this.

While they loped side by side, spring scenes around them flashed by much too hastily for Domyn to notice much detail. They were loping at a fast pace, almost racing pace. However, Domyn felt no ill effects from his previous competitive run with Nyba. No, this pacing with Jamyk felt very relaxing, almost effortless, Domyn mused. Maybe he was in much better shape than he believed. Maybe he was not really fat after all, Domyn smiled. His stride matched the pace of the boy beside him.

Abruptly Jamyk rasped in a bewildered tone while tapping his head with one hand, "Chitir!"

Puzzled by this outburst, Domyn asked through panting breath, "What about Chitir? Are you missing him? We all miss Fox Flash. We should catch up…with them the next awakening…"

"Nope," Jamyk gasped harshly, tapping his head again, "Chitir!"

"You're thinking of Chitir… Yes, he's your best friend… I'm sure you miss him," Domyn gasped as he saw three gophers scurry away in his peripheral vision and then heard the bark of a fox ring through the scenery of trees and bushes.

"See!" rasped Jamyk emphatically in some frustration. "Chitir!"

Not sure how to interpret this, Domyn said, "Awe, yes, I get memories…of our comrades on Fox Flash…more often now myself… That's nothing to worry about… I'm sure we all…wish to comm with…them again soon…"

"Chitir!" barked Jamyk sharply and loudly while he tapped his forehead again without slowing his almost frenzied pace. "See! Hear!

On a small hill to the right of the trail, a flurry of orange-red attracted his attention for a second and then the bark of a fox yipped once just before Domyn replied, still befuddled by Jamyk's comments and points to his head, "I'm sure that we all miss them, Jamyk… Especially when we have…reminders of Fox Flash in this program…left by Khebol. That Neer is a true prankster…"

Then Jamyk exclaimed, "Khebol."

Pleased that Jamyk had apparently changed his focus from his worry about Chitir, Domyn said heartily, "Awright, that prankster…has put too many foxes in this program."

"Khebol," Jamyk giggled as he pointed before them as they rounded another bend in the trail and then to the left yelling with excitement, "Bear!"

There not far ahead ambled a big black bear. This was new, Domyn realized. Khebol had found archive files for display and activity of this black bear. The master prankster had added this scene since Steppingstone Quinto. From a thicket of dense hemlock saplings, two smaller cubs waddled behind the big bear. The sow looked at the runners and growled baring her long teeth.

"Nasty!" Jamyk exclaimed with a hasty laugh. "Run! Faster!"

Somehow the boy found another higher pace within his thin body and increased gait, and Domyn, surprising himself, matched the hurried acceleration and panted with breathlessness, "Awright…run faster…can do that…to race nasty bear…"

As they dashed, panting and laughing along the trail, Domyn saw the bear charge toward them as they passed by her location in hemlocks, and he heard Jamyk yell with enthusiasm, "Prank!"

Streaking past the growling bear not yards from the trail, Domyn panted heavily, "Awe damn…very real looking… Khebol master…seemed so real… I'm a bit scared…"

"Cherp!" Jamyk rasped, loping along the curving trail until the bear and her cubs were left behind. "Scary! Fun!"

"Awspir! Khebol has…given us…fear release…in fantasy… Awspir!" Domyn gasped with joy, amazed at a sense of vitality that flowed within him at that moment.

"Nasty!" Jamyk declared and then suddenly erupted into a frenzy of laughter so strong and uncontrolled that he stumbled to the corridor floor and rolled with hilarity.

Stunned by this sudden occurrence, Domyn loped past Jamyk several strides before slowing his run, and then turning back on the trail, he gasped with confused concern, "Okay? Are you okay?"

With his large hands splayed on his sweat-drenched knees and panting for breath, Domyn stared at the wet-skinned boy rolling on the false dirt trail until Jamyk laughed, "Prof! Bear!"

"Awright, yes, Prof is behind us! Bear is a new scene! Should fool Prof," Domyn huffed as he began to realize what had sparked the hysterically jovial laughter of Jamyk. "This should be...cherp fun to watch...when the bear runs at Prof."

"Big...bear!" laughed Jamyk, and tears streaked over his thin sweaty face, "Prof...small!"

Then from a distance behind them in the corridor, a nasal voice shrieked, "Aiyee! Khebol, you toxx! Run, faster, Lyndyn, you old man. No doubt kind Kymil will laugh at this."

Soon thudding footsteps approached, and then Prof Lyndyn flashed into sight from around a bend in the corridor. His bald head glistened with sweat. His face grimaced in fearful anxiety and determination. A slender, taut-muscled figure loped with purpose in gray JMO shorts. Domyn noticed at once that the older man was not about to pause with them for a moment.

"Run, young lads," Lyndyn yelled with frantic emphasis. "Now try to keep up with me. There's a vulching bear on my toxx."

Then when Lyndyn scurried past, Jamyk hopped to his feet and laughed, "Run!"

Then the sweating boy in wet green JMO shorts chased after Lyndyn. Peering briefly back down the trail just in case Khebol's prank would follow, Domyn groaned to himself, he was not really ready for another racing pace this awakening. Though after a moment, he whirled and followed the other runners. Awe give me strength, he grinned as he increased his pace.

When Domyn began to gain on his companions, he heard Jamyk giggle, "Bear... Prof."

Without slowing his pace, Lyndyn chuckled, "Indeed quite a shocking surprise from Neer Khebol. I'll have to remember to devise some diabolical prank for the lad before we see him again..."

"Bear," Jamyk laughed still as he pulled, even with racing Lyndyn. "Prof."

Gradually Domyn approached the other runners, whose pace was still competitive, and he panted breathlessly as he chortled, "Awe deliver us...from your pranks, Prof... Hope they're quicker...than your speeches."

"Yes, indeed that reminds me of a famous, or is it an infamous quote from before ancient times long, long ago," Lyndyn chuckled as Domyn moved alongside. "I remember seeing the file while Nyba was searching for her historical easy reading. I remember one particular line that seems to have some meaning to me now. The famous ancient hunter once declared upon returning from one of his hunts, 'Sometimes you catch a bear, and sometimes a bear catches you.' If not for my amazing speed, perhaps the bear might have gotten me this awakening."

"Prof," Jamyk giggled as he ran. "Fast... Bear."

In spite of the continuous laughter of the boy, he kept a pace. They all kept a racing pace, Domyn noticed. Glancing to the side, he watched for only moments the other two pairs of sweat-covered naked legs loping stride after stride and realized that his legs were matching theirs precisely. Each of them, in spite of their varying body heights and leg lengths, ran together. He and Lyndyn had adopted Jamyk's shorter stride.

As the three of them loped in unison stride for stride, side by side, for the first time in many awakenings, Domyn felt confident about the future. He felt truly free and relaxed. The stress and trauma of misadventure at the prior Kil-Kol were now in the distant past. With these two friends now, he was ready and enthusiastic about their journey into the Sexto System at the next awakening.

On the knoll of the hill, a red fox barked at him and then seemed to grin before departing over the crest.

Domyn smiled to himself and wondered if the tiny holographic creature knew something that he did not. Then he just kept his pace with his companions.

SPEC TWO: NYBA TO SEXTO
CHAPTER 12

On the final awakening prior to plunging through Weznuski space, Nyba stood in Med on Wolf Streak Beta.

As she watched the circular scanner descend along the torso of a light brown figure, she listened to Prof Lyndyn, who was standing beside her, remark with sincere amazement, "Indeed, Domyn, this scanner just barely fits around you now. Whatever happened to the little boy we started with so many years ago?"

On the far side of the Dionjossad pad, Doc Kymil, dressed in her white medical dionboda uniform with the one-eyed visor over her right eye, laughed briefly in her melodious voice, "He's a young vigorous man now. All well-toned muscle and thick strong bones, much like you once appeared."

"Now that goads me, my kind Kymil. It hasn't been that many years since I was his age," retorted Prof Lyndyn, grinning first at Doc Kymil and then with a wink to Nyba.

"Oh my, kindred spirit, it's been almost twenty-nine years now since our adventures on Turkey Trot Alpha," Doc Kymil announced with a smirk while the scanner passed down the tan-booted feet of her patient and then sank into the Dionjossad pad. "Your uniform is finely set now, Domyn, as usual. I wish that you and Nyba could instruct others to be more careful when they adorn themselves in their dionjocus prior to calibration with Dionjossad."

Domyn grimaced and then said with his normal deep, growling voice, "We have tried, Doc. Haven't we, Nyba? Guess they are pups still."

Watching Domyn step from the pad, Nyba declared proudly, "At least they seem very proficient in their technical functions. In fact didn't you have Swyllo and Jamyk help you check the Flandecams few hours ago? Just having them together was testing your patience I'm sure."

"Is there anything wrong? Are you worrying about efficiency of our Flandecams when we plunge through Weznuski?" Prof Lyndyn asked with a slight concern.

"No, this was just routine checks this time. The Flandecams were fine. But I needed help of our smaller pups," Domyn smiled sheepishly. "I'm too big to effectively fit into the work space accesses since our stop at Steppingstone Quinto. Jamyk and Swyllo can get in there with ease. You should remember, Prof. You helped Jamyk and me repair one several awakenings ago."

Prof Lyndyn nodded affirmatively and exclaimed, "Indeed now I remember. Jamyk was in the heated access fixing…coil. No doubt he and Swyllo can be useful at times when we big men don't seem to fit…"

To herself, Nyba mused, that rascal Jamyk is too often as small and as mischievous as a monkey. At this thought, she wondered how she had remembered this ancient animal of the Homeworld in order to make comparison. Perhaps she had studied archives for so many hours that much of the knowledge of the extinct creatures still haunted her mind. Very often as Jamyk haunted her present, she groaned to herself. Yet he was usually very skilled at his primary function as a pilot. She planned to have him as primary pilot during the plunge through Weznuski space and then the all-important pop back to Debordo space into the Sexto System. That is, she frowned silently, if the rascal could behave himself and not behave like a naturally wild monkey.

Chuckling merrily Doc Kymil proclaimed, "You are the big man? Oh my, my kindred spirit, I've never known you to be too big to fit into any tight situation."

"No doubt you goad me nasty again, my kind Kymil," Prof Lyndyn groaned comically, and then turning to Domyn, he suggested, "Indeed you would do well to praise them for their assistance earlier. The others of this young crew respect both you and Cap Nyba, although at many times you may not always think so by their somewhat unruly behavior and remarks. Our crew of wolves is well-trained to succeed in our mission to find the location of elusive colonials."

"We do have a very cherp but sometimes vocally annoying crew," Nyba agreed. "As long as they perform their functions correctly like the Blue Jayers that they are, perhaps we can allow some silly chatter and social foolishness on limited occasions. However, we must not let any pup-like behavior distract from our goal to meet at last the descendants of brave people who took flight many hundreds of years ago when our home planet was dying from a devastated natural resources and pollution of environment."

"Gratitude for positive achievement is a very good policy, Cap Nyba," a broad shouldered young man in tan dionjocu replied, and then added while ambling toward the door, "I have thanked them already, Prof. Your speeches and ramblings over these many years have had an effect on me. I'll see you in the ConCen. And you two older folks, try to behave yourselves in here. Keep an eye on them, Nyba, they can be childish themselves at times."

"Whatever do you mean?" Doc Kymil inquired with an amused grin as Domyn disappeared through the hatch and then she called hastily, "Domyn, send Whyvvi in next. I will set Dionjossad for her PEQA. Remind others to double check their dionjocu connections please, Domyn."

"Awright, Doc," Domyn's voice replied from the corridor, and then he bellowed loudly, "Whyvvi, report to Med now. Whyvvi, get to Med."

Glancing toward the white form, Nyba watched the woman of forty-seven years begin resetting the Dionjossad console for PEQA of the next member of Wolf Streak Beta. PEQA, or Physio Electromag Quantal Aura, was an identity link for each individual crew member in interaction with computer artigences of the spacecraft. Each PEQA was as individually distinctive as a fingerprint or retinal pattern. Nyba knew that Doc Kymil was one of extremely rare people who could see PEQAs, but her rare vision was not as precise as a Dionjossad device. This high precision calibration for each individual was essential for their respective interfaces with artigence computers of the spacecraft.

Knowing just how critical the interface calibration of Dionjossad was for proper link between the crew and spacecraft, Nyba asked seriously, "Did you scan anything unusual with Domyn? Is his PEQA in a cherp relationship with Joculatus?"

Doc Kymil wiggled a white glove on her left hand, twitching a small finger repeatedly as she readjusted setting on the device and responded, "His reading was very good, Nyba. His PEQA looks fine to my sight and meshed well with the Dionjossad interface. Neer Domyn has been a very steady patient since we first met him. His focus on this craft is still his primary concern. He seemed quite healthy medically... Lyndyn, how did he seem otherwise?"

"Mature, maybe more mature than we could have hoped considering he and this whole crew has experienced almost no real socialization with other humans other than infrequent meetings with other Blue Jay crews of Fox Flash and Lynx

Blaze for the past five years or more now. Of course there have been visits to five Steppingstones along the voyage, but those were short stays with little social time. Those were mostly Pulseball events and mission briefings, not much interaction with people. The millions of people back through the system of Steppingstones and the home planet probably know as much about us as we know of each other. The constant updates of our journey when we stop at Steppingstones no doubt provides people back home with more individual psychological profiles and personal interpretations of our crew by analysts than we determine here on Wolf Streak Beta. We'll just have to wait and see what occurs. Your crew, Nyba, is still young psychologically," Prof Lyndyn explained, and then with a sudden rise of optimism in his nasal voice, he added, "Yet indeed after his performance during our recent adventure in Kil-Kol, I should say that Neer Domyn is ready for any crisis. And so it seems are others. Don't you agree, Cap Nyba?"

"The whole crew performed exceptionally cherp in that crisis," Nyba stated bluntly. "We should be ready for anything the Sexto System has to challenge us. Wolf Streak Beta is a Blue Jay spacecraft after all. Let's just hope that Jamyk behaves like Domyn believes he can."

When a young woman in pastel rose dionjocu marched robustly through the hatch, she sang with enthusiasm in her husky voice, "Well, hi, Doc! Hi, Prof! Hi, Cap! We are almost there. I cannot wait. We should be successful this next pop into the Sexto System. We should find hidden colonials."

While Whyvvi strode automatically onto the scanner pad on the floor, Prof Lyndyn said with a smile and chuckle, "Indeed you're in a great mood this awakening, Whyvvi. Is there anything special getting you this energized more than usual?"

"Not really, Prof. I am just so excited about getting back to Debordo space and finally meeting our lost fellows after so many centuries. I wonder how they will have changed since their ancestors left the Zerosolis System. I wonder if they will be surprised to greet us. I am sure they will be overjoyed to learn that humankind has managed to survive Despoliation and horrible Dark Era after and then get back into space again. Those colonists started their journey so long ago. Can you imagine living on those giant colony ships for so many generations in space?" the young woman declared, waving her arms freely and with emotional excitement.

"Please, Whyvvi, keep your arms at your sides while Dionjossad scans you," Doc Kymil commanded, wiggling her fingers within her white gloves. "We want to get a precise update of your PEQA, so your interface with Joculatus will maximize your sensor function."

As the circular scanner ascended from the floor pad, slowly passing upwards along her well-shaped, athletic body, Whyvvi exclaimed, "Well, I am just so cherply ready, Doc. I cannot wait to read my sensors and see in the distance of space the first sign of their giant spaceships. When we discovered Gullu Mette, I knew that we would find colonials finally. Maybe they have colonized the planet by now and will have signals from land-based cities. Maybe they will have a gorgeous planet of pristine wilderness and untarnished beauty. Oh, be so cherp! We will be the best Blue Jayers ever when we discover them."

"No doubt you do remember that Fox Flash Alpha is ahead of us, Whyvvi. They have had a much better chance of making first contact with the colonials," Prof Lyndyn said with mild caution in his nasal voice. "Don't get your hopes up too much. Those foxes are very good Blue Jayers also."

"Well, don't be a pessimistic toxx, Prof. Do not dampen my mood. Cap Bhiros may be audacious, and Khebol is very crafty and lucky, but we are a better Blue Jayer crew. Fox Flash Alpha will need a head start…" she declared until the alarm whine sounded in Med when the scanner ring reached her abdomen.

Doc Kymil scowled motherly at the young woman and asked, "Did you forget to hook up your nutrition tube again?"

Rolling her eyes beneath the pink skull cap on her head, Whyvvi pouted with some dismay, "I just forget as usual. I should not be so forgetful, but I sometimes do. I am sorry, Doc. I will be ready for plunging and popping, really, Cap. I am so focused on our pop into Sexto. My mind is already speculating into the future. I do not seem to be able to help myself."

"Don't whip yourself over this, Whyvvi," Nyba said, consoling her crewmate. "You have done so much already for our mission by helping me identify Gullu Mette. You and I must still seek to unravel the mystery of how that great ship is still powering the captured Buffalardi beacon in that Kil-Kol. We do have some investigations yet to solve."

While Nyba said this, Whyvvi reached across her torso with her right hand and tapped a spot on the front of her left shoulder. An opening appeared beneath her hand. Smoothly, as she had done so many times before, she gripped the separating clothing at the opening and peeled the front portion of her dionjocu away from the other layer beneath and against her breast. With her left hand, she reached inside the separation just over her belly, fluttered the garment for a few seconds, retracted her hand, and closed the dionjocu flaps again.

As she finished this procedure, Whyvvi pleaded again, "I am so sorry, Cap. I will be ready. I expect that we will really find the colonials this time. When we meet them, we should learn so much of their advances in technology. We should learn how Gullu Mette is doing what it seems. I will try not to be so forgetful. I am so upset with myself. I should try to make my brain focus on the present and stop leaping ahead to future puzzles."

Observing Whyvvi's hand trigger melding the process that resealed the front of her dionjocu, Nyba said kindly, "Don't whip yourself. Like I just said, I expect that you will aid me in solving the Gullu Mette mystery. You are going to perform just like any other well-trained Blue Jayer, excellently."

"I have had one thought about that Gullu Mette situation, Nyba. I have wondered if they perhaps have mastered some form of power generation from light directly as we have. This might explain why the deserted ship could be taking power from the spergits around Kil-Kol just as Swyllo does when she harvests there," Whyvvi blurted as she aligned her arms alongside her torso and waist.

"That's a cherp possibility. I'll research some ancient history files to check if the people then on the home world just before the colonials departed from the Zerosolis System had begun researching light energy technology. They did leave before the downfall of civilization lost so much of the scientific knowledge of previous generations. We can only hope that their advances matched the renewal of technological trends after the Dark Age ended on our home planet. Perhaps you're not such a Jamyk after all," Nyba grinned.

Prof Lyndyn proclaimed, "Indeed perhaps that could be ancient truth. There is a certain body of suggestion that supports some divergent theories of a parallel development of separated human civilizations in which identical trend and technologies have been created independently..."

"No time for long-winded theories now, my kindred spirit," Doc Kymil interrupted while concentrating on the data that she observed in her one-eyed visor interfacing directly with the circular ring as it ascended up and then down the light rose-colored figure. "Whyvvi, your dionjocu looks just right now. Your PEQA reads just where it should. You're set to go now."

Prof Lyndyn said, "Indeed don't worry, Whyvvi. You have insightful notions. Your concentration on your analysis no doubt interfered with your attention to detail when you put on your dionjocu this awakening..."

After scanning the circle disappeared into recess in the floor, Whyvvi leaped from the pad and chortled, interrupting Lyndyn, "Cherp, I am so ready for this mission. We have to succeed. Do you want Swyllo next as usual? I will send her in if you wish."

"That will be just fine. See you in the ConCen later," Doc Kymil said, and then to Nyba and Lyndyn, added, "Oh my, she's got plenty of spirit this awakening."

Before Whyvvi had gone much beyond the hatchway, Nyba called loudly, "Whyvvi, make sure that Jamyk gets ready. We need him calibrated soon as pilot. Don't let him dawdle. Pilot function must have cherp interface with Joculatus."

Whyvvi yelled back, "I will try, Cap. But that little onad peener does not listen to me very often. But I will try to get his attention."

Nyba understood Whyvvi's pessimism regarding Jamyk. The toxx pup often seemed distracted and inattentive to his surroundings and wishes of others around him. He needed constant reminding and perhaps even...mothering? This was a distressing notion, she chided herself.

Then soon a short, slender girlish figure in a soft yellow dionjocu pranced into Med, and her high voice chirped, "Vulch, I'm ready. Let's get this over with. I've got more prep to do at my harvesting station. We'll need to collect as much energy as we can this time."

"You're all business this awakening, hey, Swyllo?" Doc Kymil greeted the young woman and escorted her to the Dionjossad scanner pad. "You must be looking forward to popping back into Sexto."

Stepping onto the pad and forming her body in an upright rigid posture, Swyllo replied, "Vulch yeah, I can't wait until we pop into some real space again. I hope I never enter toxx LaOgres space again. I always get a nasty feelings while we are in LaOgres. Creepiest feelings I ever get! They're creepier than listening to Milyr's toxx comments in ConCen!"

Nyba studied the feisty girl. She seemed nervous and anxious, yet full of energy. LaOgres travel often challenged the perceptions and emotions of spacers. Since Blue Jay crews spent so much of their existence in LaOgres space, this could become a problem. Over years of their association, Nyba had noticed that Swyllo's anxiety had gradually increased as they got closer to their goal of the Sexto System. Yet the girl had also dealt with the issue with increase of humor and more combativeness with both Milyr and Jamyk. At this moment, Nyba thought that she needed reassurance. Nyba counted on this girl to be ready for the important popping coming soon.

"I understand that you helped Neer Domyn inspect the Flandecams this awakening," Nyba said in a firm, encouraging voice, "Apparently he thinks well enough of your skill to trust his craft to your judgment. That's something you can be proud of, especially coming from our Neer Domyn."

As the scanner rose around her slight figure, Swyllo said somewhat acerbically, "Vulch, only because he's too giant-sized now to get into accesses. It is vulching tight in there you know, Cap. And that toxx humming and heat that thrums through the passageway. It's so nasty!"

"Remember that thrumming sound is a very good noise to hear, as I am sure you are aware," Nyba reminded the twitching girl on the Dionjossad pad, "It is a sign of our propulsion and protection through this LaOgres space. Those Flandecams are our lifeline to future success."

When the scanner ring paused above the line of Swyllo's small yellow-capped head, Doc Kymil announced, "Your suit and your PEQA seem all set, Swyllo. You did a good job of making sure all the dionjocu connections were properly attached. You've done much better than certain other people usually do."

"You're talking about that big toxx Milyr, aren't you, Doc?" Swyllo grimaced.

"No doubt you know your fellow mates very well, Swyllo," Prof Lyndyn chuckled and then said, "Indeed you have fit your suit just properly. Joculatus likes the correctly attuned dionjocu on a person with whom artigence must interact to perform the functions of this spacecraft. Of course I'm not sure whether the artigence can actually have likes or dislikes. Yet your correct adornment of your suit can only improve efficiency of your interaction with the artigence..."

Giving Prof Lyndyn a frowning look while the scanner traced back down around her yellow form, Swyllo retorted somewhat indignantly, "I know science, Prof. I can get along with Joculatus quite cherply. It's the nasty toxx LaOgres space that I don't like. I feel so helpless in here. I feel as if nasty space will just suck me away with its anti-gravity. I don't want to be split into trillions of spergits. That would be a nasty toxx like letting Jamyk win our Zapstik battles. I can't enjoy that. Yet he is less irritating than travelling through LaOgres."

"Indeed, my young woman, we won't be in LaOgres much longer. No doubt you'd better be getting to your station on the ConCen," Prof Lyndyn advised after the scanner ring recessed into floor.

Nyba proclaimed, "Yes, we will need your skill there soon. Harvesting light from the spergits around Kil-Kol is very important prior to popping back to Debordo space."

Eagerly striding from the Dionjossad pad, Swyllo looked sideways at Nyba, gave her a spritely glare, and then grinned as she strode toward hatch, "Cherp,

Cap, I'm okay. It is nasty in LaOgres. It will be vulching cherp to be back in real space again. I'll be able to relax then. Don't worry. I'll harvest a nasty supply of spergit light. Okay, you toxx colonials, here we come ready or not!"

Doc Kymil called to the disappearing form in yellow only a second before Nyba had intended, "Swyllo, send in Jamyk next. Make sure he gets the message. Cap Nyba will be blowing Flandecam if the boy doesn't get calibrated soon."

"Ho, ho, Doc, you know me so well now," Nyba smiled at the woman in the white dionboda.

Quietly Prof Lyndyn admitted, "Indeed my kind Kymil does seem to know each of us on Wolf Streak Beta so well since our days of youth on Turkey Trot Alpha. But then that was well before your time, Cap Nyba. Now don't tell anyone please, but I'm anxious in LaOgres as well. I can understand what Swyllo feels. It's unnerving to be in the aspect of space with laws totally different, even opposite to space humans had known for thousands of years. It's almost as unsettling as listening to Domyn spout about his belief in that silly universal awareness metaphy of his. That's unnerving!"

"Why, my kindred spirit, I thought you were always very tolerant and open-minded. I've believed always that you knew everything since humans could speak, read, and write. You've been my guy always. You've been so fearless," Doc Kymil proclaimed and then laughed merrily.

From the hatchway came a loud baritone guffaw, "Vulch, him fearless? Nobody in this crew would believe that, Doc. Prof is just too smart to be fearless."

Turning to witness the tall six-foot, six-inch lanky young man in pastel lavender dionjocu saunter lazily into Med, Nyba complained harshly, "I wanted Jamyk next. Where is the toxx rascal?"

Milyr grimaced at her sharpness and retorted with some resentment, "Vulch, little onad peener isn't ready yet. He's complaining about...something... I can't understand him."

"You can't understand him?" Doc Kymil groaned. "Then who will? You know him better than any of the rest of us. You seem to unravel his scant speech into meaningful phrases."

Feeling her anger swelling, Nyba tried not to project it to Milyr, so she grumbled while waving him toward the Dionjossad scanner pad, "Just get your toxx on the pad, Milyr. We can't wait now for Jamyk. I will probably kill him when I see him though. He's such a vulcher toxx rascal."

"Yeah, a real annoying toxx that little peener can be at times," Milyr laughed.

As her eyes followed movements of the tall figure onto the scanner pad, Nyba listened to Prof Lyndyn scoff abruptly, "I like that line, Milyr. 'Too smart to be fearless.' I'll have to remember that for some future instructional lecture."

"That's not vulching cherp, Prof. Don't let me give you any more ideas about your ramblings. They're long enough already," Milyr chuckled, and his eyes watched the scanner circle with an almost mischievous gleam, or so Nyba thought.

Suddenly, when the scanner reached to the top of his legs, an alarm whine erupted in Med, and Doc Kymil glared at the young man and demanded, "Did you…forget…to attach your urinal tube again? Isn't this getting a bit childish, young man?"

"Vulch, did I do that again?" Milyr smirked with a slight giggle. "I can never remember to do that. It's such a long way down there. Even my long arm has trouble reaching to tip…"

Still scowling over Jamyk's absence, Nyba commanded very emphatically, "Vulch, you can connect it yourself. You're too old to expect us to baby you. One Jamyk is enough."

"I don't look of you as a mother, Nyba. I'm just a young man. I can't always take care of myself," lanky Milyr pretended to humble himself. "Would you help me, Nyba?"

For a moment, Nyba desired to stalk over to him and reach her hand very roughly into his dionjocu and crudely attach the tube to his penis, but then her anger cooled. She found herself partially enchanted with his ridiculously adolescent behavior. Why was this, she wondered? His lewd facial appearance startled and yet tantalized her for a very brief moment. What was she thinking, Nyba scolded herself. She could not have such foolish notions now at this moment in the mission.

Her brief reverie was suddenly halted when Prof Lyndyn blurted more harshly than the man usually talked, "Fool, you can connect it yourself. You are too mature for this childishness, Milyr. You're not a whelp pup anymore. We all know that you are quite the young man now. We expect you to take care of yourself. Just hook up your dionjocu properly, Milyr."

"Vulch, Prof, don't get nasty on me. I'm just cherping," Milyr griped with a smirk as he tapped his left shoulder to release the meld of the garment. "I just hope my arm is long enough to reach way down there to put my manliness into the tubing."

As she witnessed Milyr extend his right hand into his dionjocu, Nyba struggled to keep a grin from evaporating her frown, and she warned, "If you cannot, then you had better hope that you don't have to relieve yourself in the middle of our mission when we are relying on you to send missives to either colonials or Fox Flash Alpha. You would not want to be sitting in an unpleasantly wet circumstances, would you?"

His long narrow face beneath the lavender cap grimaced almost in pain, and he retorted, "Ouch, that vulching hurt, Nyba. But I really worry about something else in the middle of the mission action. What if we see some bodacious fem on the holovision? She might be very lovely out here in the Sexto System. What if I erect and my manliness won't fit in the tube? What about that?"

"No doubt, boy, you know that antemgebemarzex in nutrient prevents just such sexual urges in inappropriate or even normal circumstances. You can't get the urge at this time. You're still too much on nutrient and antemgebemarzex," chuckled Prof Lyndyn, and then he laughed louder. "You can't get pud, Milyr."

Pulling his long arm from inside the dionjocu garment and sliding his hand up the edging of the soft lavender cloth to meld the suit, Milyr leered knowingly and asked, "Then why could I do it on Steppingstone Tercero almost three years ago when a young vivacious girl admired my form after the Pulseball game and wanted to see more? Or on the next stop at Steppingstone Cuatro with another young and willing fem?"

Annoyed with his remarks for some reason, Nyba ordered brusquely, "Be quick, Milyr. You've got to be in the ConCen very soon. We've got more crew to calibrate yet. Plunging into Weznuski space won't wait for your antics...or for Jamyk's either."

"Vulching, okay, okay, I hear you! I'm not that scrawny boy who started on the Blue Jay mission way back in the Zerosolis System. I'm a grown man now," he pouted in a more serious and hurt manner.

Prof Lyndyn said in a sober and almost fatherly manner, "No doubt we'll have to get together the first chance we get, Milyr. Just you and me, we'll talk between us men. I promise that I won't ramble. But now if Doc clears you, you're needed at your station in the ConCen."

During this exchange, a scanner had finished its ascent to above his capped head and then descended back to the floor without any further alarm, so staring into Prof Lyndyn's face, a young man said without joking for once, "I'll hold you to that, Prof. I'd like time with you, just us guys talking about manly issues. When we get the time then, okay?"

"Indeed, Milyr, that's my main duty in life. Now go find a way to communicate with those fellow humans whom no person from the Zerosolis System has contacted for over 500 years. You are our primary comm operator. Also, you will probably be the first voice and face from the Zerosolis System that colonists will hear or see. Milyr, you will be the face of Blue Jay soon," Prof Lyndyn declared.

"That's a frightening thought," Nyba said with a deadpan scowl.

Momentarily a seriously concerned expression masked Milyr's long face, but then as he realized her intended humor, he smiled and said, "That's not cherp, Nyba. You're nasty funny. I like Prof's vision better. That's who I will be really, the face of Blue Jay for colonial fems waiting in the Sexto System."

Prof Lyndyn laughed, "Indeed you must realize by now, young man, you can't nettle or goad our Cap Nyba. She is much too mature for a young man like you…"

"That's cherp," a tall lavender form chuckled on his way to the hatchway. "I like mature."

Suddenly, surprising even herself, Nyba yelled sharply, "Where are you going? Did Doc clear you to depart? Stay your toxx in here, young man."

Momentarily stunned and obviously uncertain, Milyr paused in his long stride and muttered, "Erhh, I… I'm okay to go, Doc, right? I'm cherp to go to my duty now, right?"

While Nyba silently scolded herself for stopping the departure of a young man before her and also wondering why she found herself longing for his presence a little longer, she listened to Doc Kymil say in a merry voice, "Oh my, yes, Milyr, go ahead. You're calibrated now with Joculatus. Your PEQA agrees with our artigence. Go do your function and help us all finish this long mission."

"That's cherp, Doc," he grinned, and then on his way through the exit hatch, he called back promising, "and Nyba, I'll tell Jamyk to get his skinny toxx in there now."

Gazing at his departing figure, Nyba did not say anything. She was hesitant to do so. She could not understand her current emotions toward the big toxx leaving her sight. At one moment, she wanted him to go to the ConCen as fast as possible for sake of the mission. Then within moments, she desired to have him near her, but for what purpose? Nyba was bewildered and agitated.

Nearby Prof Lyndyn sighed as he scratched his gray-capped head and then said, "You're all growing up too fast for me, Nyba. Seems that these last five years, or is it more now, while we were traveling from Steppingstone Primero to events of this awakening, have gone by too quickly. You were all young pups once. Now many of you think like young adults. It is...as you often say...nasty!"

Not feeling much like an adult at that moment, Nyba muttered as she stretched her right arm over his gray shoulder, "Considering that we all spend more than three quarters of time in Saphyndenlairoum stasis sleep, it is not surprising that time seems to leap by so rapidly for us. You have done the best that you can to prepare us for this critical climax of our mission, Prof. Without your social and psychological ramblings and your patience, this crew would lack whatever human perspective they have now. We would be simply organic robots filled with complex science and technological knowledge only. Is that what we wish to present to the colonials when we finally meet?"

"Oh my, Nyba, you have matured much more than you may realize," Doc Kymil said with her motherly smile. "You understand so much more than your days of experience would predict. You are truly Cap now, Nyba."

"Maybe, Doc, but I don't feel adult all the time, especially now. Perhaps I'm just nervous about the coming climax of our mission. After all that we have experienced so far in LaOgres and then in that nasty Kil-Kol with Gullu Mette, I worry what can happen next," Nyba admitted truthfully.

In an encouraging tone, Doc Kymil said, "We have a very proficient crew on Wolf Streak Beta. They can handle any aspect of the planned mission. Don't worry so much, Cap Nyba."

"It's the unexpected, unforeseen that can challenge any crew, even the Blue Jay crew. How can we prepare for the unexpected?" Nyba sighed and felt worry throughout her awareness.

"Cap Nyba, what can go wrong? The most unpredictable and dangerous unknown is LaOgres and Kil-Kols. We survived those dangers already. We'll pop into the Sexto System very soon. What can go wrong now?" Prof Lyndyn asked in an up-beat tone with a grin and snort for emphasis.

From down the corridor came a loud shout from Milyr, "Jamyk, you toxx little peener, why aren't you ready yet?"

Then Prof Lyndyn groaned and said, "Indeed perhaps it seems that the most unpredictable unknown is our own human behavior."

"No, Prof," Nyba scowled, feeling her temper rising as she snarled, "the most unpredictable unknown is Jamyk, nasty toxx rascal. Now what has he done?"

While she spun angrily to face the open hatchway leading from Med, Nyba heard Doc Kymil exclaim, "Oh my, I suppose we should go get him. Jamyk is the only one left to calibrate with Joculatus."

"And he may be the most important one as our pilot," Nyba grumbled, sounding somewhat like Domyn in her own ears, "That damn toxx rascal is going to regret getting me whipped."

Hastily marching from Med into the narrow corridor toward the crew quarters, Nyba felt her anger grow, and then from ahead around the corner, she heard Milyr hiss, "Vulch, little peener, what nasty toxx is going on with you? If Nyba sees you like this, she'll rip off your one nad and feed it to you. Do you hear me, Jamyk? Are you even paying attention to me, Jamyk?"

Then Nyba rounded the bend in the curved corridor and saw them. Milyr was standing slouched over in his lavender dionjocu. Beneath him on the floor of the corridor just outside Jamyk's room rolled little toxx. Sweat gleamed from his mostly naked body. He wore only his green JMO shorts and his green Clarinkevs. To Nyba his appearance suggested that the boy had just finished a long cross-country exercise run. Except that now he was squirming on the floor in some apparent anguish, not like Jamyk after the invigorating run. Something was wrong, or perhaps the toxx rascal was being foolishly childish again like was his habit so often recently.

"H-h-elp," Jamyk whispered in a raspy pained voice. "Ch-Chitir!"

Milyr yelled down, "What are you saying? Don't talk like this now. Cap will skewer you."

"I'm ready to do just that," Nyba growled, startling Milyr who apparently had not noticed her arrival. "Milyr, why aren't you in ConCen now? Neer Domyn will need you there now."

An astonished and perplexed look washed across his long face, and Milyr gulped nervously, "But, Nyba, I was trying to get this little peener ready. I know how much you…"

"Never mind that now," Nyba demanded. "You just get your toxx to the ConCen now. Report to Neer Domyn. Tell him that I'll be in Med for awhile until I'm sure this toxx is okay for duty. You will have to take pilot now. Inform Neer Domyn of the change. Damn, this little toxx is so annoying!"

"Are you sure, Cap Nyba, that you should go with us to Med? You really should be on the ConCen during this next plunge sequence," Prof Lyndyn advised.

"I suppose that I should," she agreed, but her intuition led her to say instead, "But I need to see that this toxx is taken care of in a way that satisfies me. Can you carry him, Prof? Do you need any assistance? What do you need, Doc, besides his dionjocu? Anything else from his room?"

Briefly other three people standing around gibbering boy on floor, peered at her like they were shocked or confused by her suddenly hasty and sharp orders and questions, but shortly Doc Kymil replied, "No, Cap Nyba, if you can bring his dionjocu and check for his...no, never mind his Clarinkevs will do for this chore and they are on his feet now. All I need is Jamyk in my Med. Lyndyn, can you carry him?"

"Do you need my help, Prof?" Milyr asked with concern in his voice that impressed Nyba, even though she was having a difficult time herself sympathizing with the toxx boy on the floor whose mumblings sounded like foolishness to her.

"No, you go to the ConCen as Cap Nyba commanded, my boy. You've gained new responsibility now as a pilot during our most important plunge operation of this mission. Go do your best," Prof Lyndyn said, "We'll try to have Jamyk sorted out by popping time if we can, won't we, my kind Kymil?"

"Oh my, I hope so," Doc Kymil replied with obvious consternation.

"Then I'll go to the ConCen. Take care of him. These mumblings are not typical of Jamyk, Cap. Trust me they may sound like his normal silliness, but I don't think so this time. I know him well," Milyr stated while he began to walk toward the main corridor.

Her eyes followed him until he disappeared around the corner. For such an often abrasive boy, Milyr had sounded actually concerned and empathetic toward Jamyk. Not the emotion which she was currently feeling, Nyba thought to herself. In fact, she mused, perhaps she might even, as Milyr had previously suggested, rip off someone's one nad and make him eat it.

Then while Prof Lyndyn lifted the sweaty boy into his arms, Nyba grabbed the green dionjocu off the floor and stomped after the man in the gray dionboda.

Yes, she thought to herself with some conviction, as her anger swelled within her, ripping off one nad seemed quite satisfying right about then.

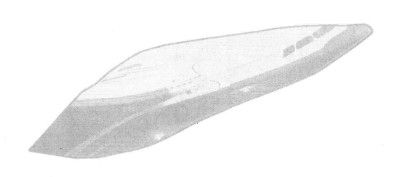

SPEC TWO: NYBA TO SEXTO
CHAPTER 13

"Kiblin!" Jamyk wailed forlornly and then in further anguish moaned with uncertainty in his cracking voice. "Chitir?"

Following behind Prof Lyndyn, Nyba saw the bald head of Jamyk loll downward over the straining right arm of the older man. The face of the boy was a mask of despair and bewilderment. When his slightly upturned eyes rolled in her direction, Nyba noticed a look of vacancy, as if the boy dreamed while awake. Yet as she carried his dionjocu draped over her shoulder, Nyba felt almost no sympathy for this rascal toxx boy.

"Hurt!" Jamyk gasped with spittle dripping down his cheek to blend with sweat and perhaps tears beading his face, "Chitir! Kiblin!"

His voice stressed with emotion, but his eyes stared blankly at the corridor. This corridor led to Med where she had not been long ago, where Jamyk should have been several minutes ago. This was not exactly where Nyba desired to be going at this stage of the upcoming plunging process, but this boy was her best pilot.

She observed the strained mouth gasp and mumble something incoherent. Nyba suspected that she needed to push or motivate Jamyk from this lapse of awareness back into the real world. This was if she actually believed that this was not some prank on his part. She was not so sure of the truth of this episode. Wolf Streak Beta needed him at pilot when they popped into the Sexto System, so that Milyr could be at comm where he would be much more valuable in his primary role of communicating to colonials. For the plunge into Weznuski, Milyr would do very well as pilot, but Jamyk would be better for pop. Nyba did not intend to let his foolishness interfere with the mission. She would make rascal do his duty. Jamyk would not goad her in this mission today.

"Pain! Fox! Chitir?" Jamyk rasped with a gurgle in his throat, and his head swayed side to side as if seeing some tormenting sight. "Hurt? Chitir?"

From not far ahead of Prof Lyndyn in the corridor, Doc Kymil ordered, "We will put him into the Borawinokev bed for now, Lyndyn. I need a brain and then full body scan before we can attempt to dress him in his dionjocu for calibration with Dionjossad."

"Indeed he sounds delusional, or at least entrenched in the past memory of the murder of Kiblin. He has never really gotten over that trauma of nearly three years ago on Steppingstone Tercero," Prof Lyndyn stated with breathlessness as he carried the slim boy in his arms. "No doubt he is ill on some level. His temp is very high at the moment. He is sweating profusely. Perhaps some kind of fever reaction…"

"Kiblin!" Jamyk sobbed. "Hurt!"

From just inside the Med entryway, Doc Kymil commanded loudly into the air, "Bodacia, prepare Borawinokev for patient Jamyk. You should quick scan for a bacterial or viral infection first. Then do special attention to the general brain scans."

As Lyndyn neared the Med entryway, Nyba thought to herself, it was a cherp choice to come here instead of going to the ConCen. Jamyk the damn pup was acting foolish and obviously clowning. She was sure of this. Domyn could handle prep for plunging. Here, Nyba could see that Prof and Doc were viewing only symptoms of illness or psycho-stress. She must keep them attuned to the reality of the boy's silliness or play-acting.

Loudly, perhaps more harshly than she had intended, Nyba demanded, "Just shake the skinny rascal out of his daydreams. Get him ready for duty. We need him at pilot when we pop into Sexto."

Twisting his torso slightly so as to clear the wobbling head of Jamyk through the narrow entry, Prof Lyndyn replied, "We'll do what we can, Cap. These episodes of memory confusion and possible hallucinations usually do not last very long for Jamyk. Although I do believe that Bodacia has reported that his recent Saphyndenlairoum stasis sleep has been more difficult than earlier on this latest journey through LaOgres. Perhaps there is something to the occasional speculation that LaOgres stimulates or enhances metaphysical behavior. Perhaps we should ask Domyn about…"

While the man in the gray dionboda rambled with his conjecture and finished stepping through the entry into Med, Nyba observed the dangling legs and long feet of the annoying boy in the arms of Prof Lyndyn. How skinny these legs were, she snorted silently, and how naked. Jamyk was wearing merely his green JMO shorts and Clarinkevs now when he should have been fully dressed in his dionjocu, calibrated with Dionjossad, and reporting for duty. Ho, ho, oh, not this toxx boy, she hissed sourly in her mind. This toxx would find any way to whip her existence.

"Ho, vulch this nagged nonsense, Prof," Nyba declared abruptly. "He's just being a nasty pup looking for special attention. Just give him a dose of some foul-tasting medicine and clear him from this foolishness. I want him at pilot soon for our pop into Sexto."

"No doubt you believe this, Cap Nyba. Yet I'm not sure that he's consciously controlling this behavior," Prof Lyndyn said while waddling to the Borawinokev bed along one side of Med. "Sometimes these episodes can manifest from deep hidden memories or stressful traumas subjugated in subconscious. I don't think dosing him up with pharmaceutical will get him into the appropriate condition which you desire for your pilot. Besides, indeed you have another well-trained pilot in the ConCen now. Milyr is proven an extremely capable of pilot..."

Sharply and loudly, Doc Kymil asked, interrupting Lyndyn, "Bodacia, is the Borawinokev set for Jamyk now?"

The feminine voice of Bodacia replied seemingly from the air, "Yes, Doc Kymil. We are ready for this difficult patient. All of my scans are prepared as you previously directed."

Barely listening to this exchange, Nyba responded, "Milyr is trained as pilot surely, Prof. Yes, I have confidence in that big boy's skills as pilot. However, I'd rather have him at comm. He is the best communications expert in Blue Jay. Milyr is the best squawker of Blue Jayer that we have on Wolf Streak Beta. He'll be the surest person to get our message to the colonials in Sexto System."

"Indeed that young man is a tremendous squawker," Doc Kymil began to say after turning to glance at Lyndyn with his slack human cargo, but then suddenly she paused with a startled expression and stammered with befuddlement, "Oh my...that...that's...very odd..."

Stepping past Prof Lyndyn, Cap Nyba tossed the green dionjocu to the nearest side table and inquired of the woman in white dionboda, "What's odd? What can go wrong now? What did Jamyk do now?"

191

Doc Kymil called into the air of Med, "Vivacio, darken lighting in Med to 5 percent illumination now. Everyone stay still for a few minutes please, so no one stumbles over anything. Lyndyn, please hold Jamyk a little longer."

"Indeed, my angel, I can hold his light weight for some time yet. But what did you see?" Prof Lyndyn asked breathlessly while he halted his attempt to place the boy into the Borawinokev.

The male voice of artigence Vivacio said from the darkening Med, "Doc Kymil, illumination in Med is now lowered to 5 percent of the norm. Is there a malfunction of equipment which I am unaware?"

"No malfunction, Vivacio, don't worry about your efficiency programs. I am performing a spontaneous experiment," Doc Kymil announced somberly for artigence, and then with more emotional bewilderment, she murmured. "His PEQA pulsated. I just witnessed it pulsate. PEQAs don't pulsate, yet I'm sure I saw it… Yes, there it goes again. I can see pulsation in Jamyk's PEQA…"

"Chitir!" Jamyk moaned. "Kiblin!"

"What is this nonsense, Doc?" Nyba demanded tersely.

Lyndyn's voice asked in the almost darkened Med, "A pulsating PEQA? Are you sure?"

"Hurt!" Jamyk gasped as if in pain. "Chitir?"

"Oh my, yes, Lyndyn, I can see his PEQA clearly as it contrasts with yours while you hold him closely," Doc Kymil said with wonder. "Definite pulsation as opposed to your steady glow. Not any regular rhythm though, it is just random bursts of differential PEQA intensity… Oh my!"

"Can rascal hear us?" Nyba asked with extreme doubt in her mind about the likelihood of these events. "Can he be causing this…this…naggedly weird thing that you believe you see? I think he's playing with us now. Not beyond his impish nature!"

While she expounded this opinion, Jamyk gasped forlornly, "Chitir…no!"

"No, Nyba, I can see PEQA pulsations from Jamyk only, not yours, not Lyndyn's. Just Jamyk is pulsating sporadically. This is not normal, even for Jamyk. PEQAs just don't pulsate in my experience. This is very rare and unique," Doc Kymil declared strongly not far from where Nyba stood in dimness, and the doctor ambled around the bed to the side opposite Lyndyn and Jamyk.

Prof Lyndyn sighed, "Indeed this skinny boy is slippery with sweat. Even through my dionboda sleeves, his skin is wet and very warm on my arms. My dear Kymil, may I set him into Borawinokev now? I don't want to drop him by accident. He is quite slippery now and getting more agitated…"

"Go ahead and drop him, Prof," Nyba suggested with satisfaction against her frustration. "The fall might jolt him out of this ridiculous foolishness."

"Yes, yes, Lyndyn," Doc Kymil said quickly, apparently ignoring Nyba's sarcastic comment, and then with firmness commanded, "Vivacio, return lighting in Med to normal intensity…now."

While the illumination gradually returned to normal in the room, Nyba grumbled to herself, now wishing that she had gone off to the ConCen to prepare for plunging instead of coming here to pamper this annoying little boy. Maybe Domyn would have been better here after all. No, no, she suddenly realized that the young man with his fondness to fantasize lately would most likely ignore his technical expertise and instead feed this foray into a naggedly weird metaphysical nonsense. Ho, ho, it was up to her to keep these medical professionals from going astray onto some pseudo-scientific path.

"Just put toxx rascal into bed and get your scans. Let's deduce his problem and fix it," Nyba demanded, barely controlling her irritation and keeping her tone professional.

"Hurt! Chitir!" rasped a wiggling, nearly naked figure in the gray arms of Prof Lyndyn, "Fox! Pain! Nasty!"

As Lyndyn gently set Jamyk's thin form into the hollow of the Borawinokev, which was almost a perfect fit for the boy's shape and size of his body, Nyba noticed the rank wetness of the crumpled green JMO shorts around his waist and glistening layer of sweat covering his body. In spite of her tendency to mistrust his motives, she felt a pang of sympathy for the boy. Her view suggested that this was possibly no play-acting on his part. His grimace of torment was as genuine as sweat on his flesh. Perhaps she had been wrong about him?

"Bodacia," Prof Lyndyn called out hastily to Med, "Please concentrate your primary scan on his brain. Be sure to scan all portions of the brain structure, including any unusual subconscious patterns of current occurrence…"

Interrupting Lyndyn, Doc Kymil added hastily, "Bodacia, scan priority for bacterial or viral infections throughout body. This has immediate priority."

"Hurt!" Jamyk groaned, writhing in bed. "Fox... Pain!"

"Damn, his constant wailing is giving me a headache," Nyba muttered.

"No doubt you are correct, Kymil. We should eliminate reasonable infections first. I'm sorry. You are the doctor here," Prof Lyndyn admitted humbly. "I'm just overly concerned about his state of brain function. Cap, here heeds her best pilot soon. How soon before plunging, Cap?"

Caught abruptly by his question, Nyba scolded herself for being so obsessed with this Jamyk situation, and then asked firmly, "Joculatus, what is the estimated time before braiding Weznuski?"

Bodacia said in her usual business-like tone, "Scanning now for bacterial infection, Doc Kymil."

At the same time, Jamyk gasped, "Pain... Chit!"

Joculatus replied after a pause, "Cap Nyba, estimated time to braiding Weznuski is forty-three minutes."

Forty-three minutes, Nyba grumbled to herself in dismay. She should be in the ConCen now prepping the crew for their most important plunge yet on this Blue Jay mission. However, she was here in Med with this rascally obnoxious boy. Why had she ever requested him as her pilot all those years ago on Steppingstone Primero? Yet she had, and now he was hers and the primary pilot of Wolf Streak Beta.

Briskly she stepped to the edge of the Borawinokev and looked down upon the sweat-drenched boy sunken into a recessed scanning bed exactly as deep as his body depth. His face frowned and grimaced. His breath came in sobs and snorts. His eyes fluttered and rolled. Jamyk appeared very uncomfortable and detached from reality at that moment.

"Jamyk!" Nyba yelled sharply and then again, "Jamyk!"

"Don't interfere, Nyba," Prof Lyndyn pleaded. "Let Doc and Bodacia handle this."

"Jamyk!" Nyba called firmly, shrugging off Prof Lyndyn's gentle touch on her arm. "Jamyk, we need you now."

Bodacia reported, "Bacterial scan shows negative. I am now scanning for viral infection."

"Yes, I confirm. I saw no bacterial presence that should not be there," Doc Kymil said, tapping the visor in front of her eye and then begged, "Nyba, be patient please. Let us do our work here..."

However, Nyba ignored the plea from the older woman and instead shouted loudly but carefully controlled, "Jamyk! Hear me. See me. Pay attention to me. We need you. Wolf Streak needs you."

"Hurt!" the squirming boy rasped, and then with uncertainty, he whispered, "Swyllo?"

At the same time Lyndyn asked in a voice much more adamant than common for him, "Joculatus, how much time before braiding Weznuski?"

Bodacia also reported, "Doc Kymil, viral scan shows negative. Would you prefer a full brain scan next?"

Concentrating her attention upon Jamyk's anguished face and last vocalization, Nyba asked with excitement, "Swyllo, yes, what can you do for Swyllo? Think about her. Can you hear me, Jamyk? Can you help Swyllo? Can you help Wolf Streak?"

Across the bed, Doc Kymil said, "Yes, Bodacia, start the full brain scan. Focus on overall firing patterns."

From Med around her, Nyba heard the male voice of an artigence Joculatus reply, "Prof Lyndyn, estimated time to braiding Weznuski is thirty-seven minutes."

The sweating face in the Borawinokev bed turned toward Nyba briefly and gasped through a garbled breath, "...Swyllo... No...hurt?"

Momentary glance from Jamyk peered directly at her before his head swiveled away again. Nyba was confident that Jamyk had heard her and had responded consciously with confusion but true intent. She did not understand to what he was referring about Swyllo now, but this was a change from his persistent tirade about Chitir and Kiblin.

Behind her she heard Prof Lyndyn suggest urgently, "Only thirty-seven minutes until braiding, Cap. Shouldn't you be in the ConCen now? We can care for Jamyk here..."

"Pain! Chitir!" the skinny boy cried out as his eyelids blinked frenetically, and his face still poured perspiration. "No...hurt!"

Ignoring Prof Lyndyn's obvious attempt to get her out of Med, Nyba commanded hastily, "Jamyk, hear me. See me. Come back to me. We can help Swyllo. We can help Chitter. Come back to me. That's an order, pilot."

"Oh my, what was that?" Doc Kymil exclaimed suddenly with startled confusion. "Bodacia, did you record that? Did you cause that?"

Bodacia reported, "No, Doc Kymil, I did not cause that response. This boy Jamyk is being difficult again. This patient has recent history of being difficult. I am not at fault for this sequence of scans. These are beyond parameters of my programming."

"Chitttterrr!" Jamyk screamed suddenly more violently than his prior outbursts, and his body arched at his waist and trembled spasmodically, "Pain! No...no!"

"Oh my, this is not normal," Doc Kymil cried with despair, and across the bed from Nyba, raised her hands to her visor, cupping the eyepiece and blocking the vision to her now closed left eye. "I saw flashes, rhythmic flashes, discharging throughout his brain. Not a pattern that I am familiar with in my experience as a doctor. Lyndyn, you must look also. You may put this into some perspective that I cannot. He is showing new brain activity to us now..."

"Perhaps Bodacia is incorrect. Or Borawinokev is malfunctioning," Lyndyn suggested, rushing to stand beside Nyba by the bed. "What is this flashing that you are seeing? I don't have my cap and visor at the moment. They are somewhere in here in Med, but I don't remember where at this time. What do you see? Is it more of the PEQA pulsating? Can you see that on the brain scan?"

Though her skepticism still haunted her, Nyba saw the tormented boy in the hollow of the Borawinokev bed, and she felt overwhelming concern for him as he listened to Doc Kymil try to explain, "Light flashes...electrical...light flashes, that's what it looks like. These sights are nothing like my PEQA vision. No, this is more like a shiny flash of light across his brain. I don't want to say...shine... No, I don't want to use a term that might lead us to consider Szczygiel Shines. This would be unprofessional. This would be foolishly hysterical..."

The hands of the older woman shook with either excitement or nervousness before her face. Nyba witnessed this unusual loss of calm professionalism in the doctor of Wolf Streak Beta. What could startle a steady woman this much, Nyba wondered. What was this shine that she spouted? This was a term that Nyba did not recall hearing...or had she once? Had Domyn mentioned such a term in one of his metaphysical discussions with Prof? How could Jamyk cause such turmoil?

Not sure about the possible memory about Domyn, Nyba tried to refocus her medics to fixing Jamyk, and so said firmly, "Let's discuss this science abnormality some other time. Help Jamyk now. Can this help fix Jamyk, so he can pilot Wolf Streak? We'll be plunging Weznuski soon. Then we'll be popping into Sexto not long after. We need this rascal ready to pilot. Let's go, people, fix Jamyk."

During her tirade, the perspiring boy squirmed in Borawinokev and muttered less violently than before, "Chit...hurt... No... Swyllo... No!"

Beside her Prof Lyndyn said with obvious skepticism, "Indeed the Szczygiel Shine sequence is very improbable. More likely there is some glitch in the system. Vivacio, check the current operational status of Borawinokev in Med. Please rush this diagnosis. Bodacia, stop the brain scan as currently performed. Instead prepare to scan the amygdale and hippo campus regions with special focus on the zachymatis area. Is that appropriate, Doc Kymil?"

Not waiting to hear Kymil's reply, Nyba stared at Jamyk's face and yelled, "Jamyk! Listen to me. Help Swyllo. Hear me. We need you. Wake up, Jamyk. Help Swyllo now!"

Doc Kymil sighed with resignation, "I guess that specialized focus for the brain scan is as good as anything. I don't know really where to check for this type of symptom. Pulsating PEQA and brain shines are not normal symptoms. I'm at a loss as to how to diagnose now. Bodacia, scan as Prof Lyndyn advised. It can't hurt condition now. Maybe we'll learn something."

Meanwhile Jamyk seemed to control his head swaying long enough to stare at Nyba and peer into her eyes when he mumbled with bewilderment, "Swyllo? Nyba? Pilot?"

"Yes, Jamyk!" Nyba exclaimed quickly while his attention was upon her. "We need you to pilot. Wake up out of this daydream. Swyllo needs you now. Wolf Streak needs you now."

Abruptly a male voice of Vivacio reported, "Prof Lyndyn, diagnostic check of Borawinokev in Med shows no malfunction. All scan recordings are within parameters."

With his eyes focused still on Nyba, Jamyk whispered, "Nyba? Pilot? Now?"

Groaning in apparent disappointment, Prof Lyndyn said, "Thank you, Vivacio… Then Kymil, my angel with gifted sight, your vision and Bodacia's recordings may be meaningful after all. No doubt this is confusing and a bit… crazy? Perhaps you are witnessing some undiscovered neural reaction to some just as an undiscovered phenomenon…"

Holding her attention upon Jamyk's wet face and haunted eyes, Nyba said, "Yes, Jamyk, you are our best pilot. We need you soon. Shake off this nightmare that grips you now. We need you alert."

Doc Kymil murmured in a soft voice, "I'm not sure what I see or how to interpret scans. There seems to be no current flashes of neural activity comparable to that which I observed not long ago. Bodacia, do you see any unusual neural activity patterns right now within scans of Jamyk's brain?"

While Jamyk fluttered his eyelids but retained his attention on Nyba's face, the boy whispered, "Pilot…now… Nyba?"

Bodacia replied, "Doc Kymil, my programming does not detect any unusual neural activity at this moment. However, there is high probability that activity beyond my parameters is occurring or has occurred recently. This patient, Jamyk, is difficult to diagnose and interpret within parameters of my programming."

Surprised at her own sympathy toward this usually annoying boy, Nyba smiled faintly at him and said calmly, "Yes, Jamyk. Soon we will need you as pilot. Swyllo will need you. Wolf Streak will need you. But Jamyk, now you have some time to rest. Now you have time to let Doc help you recover for your pilot duty. We will need you soon but not just now."

Across the Borawinokev bed, Doc Kymil said tiredly, "Thank you, Bodacia. Continue to monitor Jamyk's scans. Return to the full brain scan as priority. Record zachymatis activity on Tier Two and inform me if this activity changes or goes beyond your parameters."

"Nyba?" Jamyk gasped calmly but with exhaustion. "Pilot?"

Not knowing or caring if her action was allowed, Nyba reached her hand slowly to his damp cheek, and she said, "Soon, Jamyk. Just rest now. Get your strength back. Listen to Doc Kymil. She will care for you now. Just get rested now."

While Nyba had spoken these kind words, Doc Kymil walked around the bed to stand beside Nyba and then extended her white-gloved hand to Jamyk's forehead and said, "Very good advice, Cap. Yes, Jamyk, I can take care of you. Do as Cap Nyba has ordered. Rest and allow me to attach the nutrient tube for you. You've used a lot of energy and water from your body. Let's get some back into you. There's not that much there to start with, is there, my young lad?"

"Doc?" Jamyk blinked in doubt at Kymil briefly and then returned his gaze to Nyba, saying, "Nyba?... Pilot?"

"Yes, soon, little peener," Nyba grinned down at the frowning face, and then she said firmly, "I should go tell Swyllo and others that you will be ready soon, if that's okay with you, Jamyk? You will get yourself ready soon, won't you?"

As Jamyk's mouth opened to say something in a whisper, Joculatus reported in a loud voice, "Cap Nyba, estimated time to braiding Weznuski is twenty-three minutes, Neer Domyn inquires if you will be in the ConCen for this operation?"

"Perhaps you should be there, Cap Nyba," Prof Lyndyn suggested, "I think we can take care of Jamyk now. Your priority is on the ConCen now."

With his flushed cheek resting still on her hand, Jamyk rasped, "Nyba... Cap?"

"I should go to the ConCen for this important braid," Nyba admitted, gazing at the thin face in the hollow of the Borawinokev bed. "Don't you think I should be there, Jamyk?"

"Yup," he whispered, staring lucidly into her eyes. "Nyba...Cap."

"We'll nurse him back for you, Cap Nyba," Doc Kymil promised. "He'll be a good patient now, won't you, Jamyk?"

When his glance went from her face to Doc Kymil's direction, Jamyk gulped and gasped hoarsely, "Yup."

"Then, I'll be waiting on the ConCen," Nyba stated, backing away from the bed and turning toward the hatch to exit Med. "I will tell Milyr to practice his comm skills. Our best pilot will be there soon."

At the hatch, she paused as Prof Lyndyn approached her hastily, and then the older man said in a hushed voice, "Indeed, Cap Nyba, that was well done. I thought you were going to berate him or physically shake him out of bed, but you were very nurse-like. I'm proud of you..."

Interrupting him abruptly, Nyba snarled in a low voice, "I should have. I played game with him. Now, Prof Lyndyn, I expect you and Doc Kymil to get that toxx rascal healthy and ready to pilot this spacecraft. Our mission is important. We don't have time for you medics to play around with your naggedly ridiculous shine theories and pulsating PEQAs. Just fix him. Get him ready for his duty. Don't muddle his already whimsical focus with your speculations. I'm depending on you, Prof. Stick to your science, not that other foolishness."

For once, a man forty-seven years stared at her without saying a word. Nyba spun out the doorway from Med. Her face felt on fire. Her heart beat rapidly. She was surprised at her own ranting but not as much as her own recent empathy for Jamyk. This shocked her and fueled her temper as she stomped along the corridor toward the ConCen.

First Milyr and now Jamyk, she pondered in anger, why were boys becoming such a distraction for her now?

Damn boys, she grumbled silently as she stomped into corridor, they are all nasty toxx!

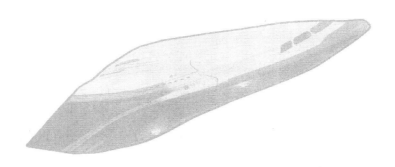

Spec Two: Nyba to Sexto
Chapter 14

Nyba strode toward the ConCen.

Over the conversations of four crew members in there, a distinct voice of artigence Joculatus announced through two open hatches, "Neer Domyn, estimated time to braiding is nineteen minutes."

Pausing just outside the first hatch, Nyba felt her temper heating her still. She did not want to enter the ConCen like this. She realized that she needed to cool her irritation. She needed to present a more captain-like persona to her crew. They counted on her for stability.

Damn that toxx rascal, she swore to herself. Yet was she angry at him or at herself for having experienced sympathy and concern toward him? Her thoughts were disturbingly bewildered. Not very Captain-like, she groaned silently, not at all like herself.

A warm current of air flowed down over her perspiring bald head. Nyba rubbed her hand harshly across her smooth scalp. Sweat slipped under her palm. Looking upwards she was reminded that maintenance access to the nearest Flandecam was directly above her just outside the outer hatch to the ConCen. Another was not far from her feet leading to Flandecam below this central deck on Wolf Streak Beta. Her head and hand were in flow of heated air pumped down from the working motor above. At this moment, she did not need any external sources of heat hitting her body.

Not a very convenient place to cool her temper, she scolded herself. Then another realization impinged upon her awareness. She had forgotten to bring her dionjocu cap with her. It was in Med still. Damn, she swore partly aloud in hiss. However, Nyba knew that she was not returning there now to get the cap and visor, not with Jamyk there still.

As was her normal foresightedness, she had another dionjocu cap in pocket in the back of her blue chair on the ConCen. But no, she decided, she could not walk into the ConCen looking unprepared, no, not as Captain Nyba. Her frustration challenged her attempt to calm herself. Damn that naggedly toxx Jamyk, Nyba growled to herself.

From the ConCen and hubbub of familiar voices, Joculatus announced, "Neer Domyn, estimated time to braiding is seventeen minutes."

As she heard this, she continued to feel a warm air current caressing her naked scalp. Enough time, she thought, yes, plenty of time. Nyba pivoted on her feet and stalked with heavy steps into the corridor to the left of the hatch as she faced it. She could go to her quarters and retrieve a cap stored there. Yes, she guessed, she had time for that. The walk around the circular corridor would give her opportunity to compose herself.

On her left as she stepped, Nyba passed quarters of Prof Lyndyn and then those of Doc Kymil. Her own refuge was next. She punched the door key harshly, heard a subtle pop of release and then pushed the hatch inward. She stepped over the seven-inch sill. Then after years of practice, she walked over and around the clutter on her floor. Her movement was purposeful. In spite of the apparent disorganized mess in her room, she knew exactly where the third cap was resting on top of one of her personal dressers. She knew where every item set in her room, though she had never been able to persuade anyone else of this. Nyba grabbed this cap hastily and stalked from her quarters.

Instead of retracing her route back to hatch to the ConCen, Nyba chose to proceed in the same direction that she had originally begun her walk. She passed Neer Domyn's quarters on her left. Then the toilet and shower section before she felt another downward flow of warm air. Pausing Nyba glanced upwards at another ladder maintenance access to another Flandecam. She was now exactly 180 degrees on the far side of the circular corridor from the outer hatch leading into the ConCen, which was within the wall to her right.

To her left, she noticed the entry to the gym facility where her crew periodically exercised themselves. No wonder Domyn liked going this route on his way to the ConCen, she pondered. Both Flandecams for his personal inspection, or at other times a gym for vigorous exercise, these were two of his most favorite past-times when not focused on his function in Wolf Streak Beta. She smiled to herself and thought the young man found his own calm and quiet in his past-times. Perhaps she needed to adopt more physical hobbies rather than her penchant for ancient history. However, at that moment, any remembrance of a horrid ancient history of Despoliation of the home planet just heated her anger further. She needed to relax now and calm her anxiety.

In fact, she thought spontaneously, perhaps she would have time to cut across the gym and enter the other longer circular running corridor, cross country trail with relaxing environmental pictured walls. A good, vigorous run would excise her irritations and emotions just now. Maybe there was enough time, she hoped, maybe she was not needed in the ConCen now after all. Her hand reached toward the door key pad to the gym.

Then with abruptness, she pulled her hand back and turned to continue her quickened pace along the curved corridor. Vulch, no, she realized, she could not forsake her role as captain of Wolf Streak Beta. The upcoming braid through Weznuski space would pop Wolf Streak Beta into the Sexto System. She would not let her own emotional frustrations hinder the climax of this Blue Jay mission. Nyba knew that she should be in the ConCen.

Yes, in the ConCen, she thought, and looked toward the curved wall on the right side of the corridor. Inside that wall was the Control Center of Wolf Streak Beta. Inside that wall now sat four of her crew nearly ready to begin the braid. They were relying upon her leadership. Nyba could not disappoint them. She needed to get her toxx to the ConCen, she smiled to herself.

On her left, as she walked quickly, Nyba went by Jamyk's quarters. The door was open wide as the boy had left it before his recent lapse into his foolishness. Her glimpse through the doorway revealed a well-organized neatness of his room. Such stark contrast to the random undisciplined nature of the boy's social behavior, she mused. If he could only focus his attention and behavior like that almost compulsively organized room, she wished, then he would not be such a naggedly toxx rascal.

When her hastened pace brought her back full-circle to the outer hatch of the ConCen, Nyba heard artigence Joculatus announce, "Neer Domyn, estimated time before braiding is eleven minutes."

Downward current of heated air from the Flandecam access dried partially the perspiration on her bald head. Nyba stood outside entry to the ConCen. She felt more in control of herself now than her previous stop there. With care she adorned her blue cap over her bald head. She smoothed the back and neck portion and melded this to the collar of the main body garment. Her dionjocu was ready. She hoped her mind and concentration was ready as well.

With a deep breath, Cap Nyba strode through the outside open hatch toward the ConCen of Wolf Streak Beta. She left her eyepiece visor up on her brow. She wished to view the ConCen with both eyes at that moment. Her primary goal was to focus attention of the crew upon the braiding procedure and not upon Jamyk's health situation.

When Cap Nyba walked through the inner hatch of the ConCen, she saw immediately the holovision portrayal of glistening Kil-Kol set between prongs of the semi-circular formation of chairs. Kil-Kol was larger than most previous Kil-Kols. A light reflected from countless spergits around periphery of Kil-Kol was very bright. Swyllo would be quite happy about that, Nyba thought. At least someone should be happy at this moment in their mission, she grumbled to herself.

Quietly, trying to be unobtrusive, Nyba sat into her blue chair, but her entry did not go unnoticed for Swyllo spun her yellow chair in Nyba's direction and asked in her shrill, demanding voice, "How is the little onad? Is toxx okay? Can he join us here soon?"

Groaning to herself, Nyba paused briefly to get everyone's attention and then said succinctly, "Jamyk is being treated. He should be with us soon. Now let's do our jobs and get on with this important braid. Neer Domyn, continue with command of this procedure. You are in command of the ConCen for a moment. However, I must ask whether we have scanned this Kil-Kol for possible obstructions. Whyvvi, have we?"

Before Whyvvi could report, Milyr blurted, "Is little peener okay? Will he…"

With abrupt authority in her voice, Nyba interrupted him and asked pointedly, ignoring him, "Whyvvi, have you surveyed that Kil-Kol for sign of obstruction? Answer me!"

The girl in a light red, almost pink dionjocu reported, "Yes, Cap, I have taken three sensor surveys with zeta rays so far from three different directional vectors as we approached this Kil-Kol. Sensors have revealed no obstruction. This Kil-Kol appears normal though quite large. We do not suspect any Gullu Mette in our path this time. We should have a clear braid."

From the brown chair to her right, Nyba heard Domyn's deep voice command, "Milyr, coordinate the final braid control with Joculatus. Prepare for the Wilchrison extension. I will final check the Flandecams with Vivacio. We initiate the braid in less than seven minutes. Let's get this right."

"That is cherp to hear, Whyvvi. That is a huge Kil-Kol. We should have more than adequate space there to channel the braid and get us through Weznuski space and back to Debordo space," Nyba said with optimism. "Neer Domyn, the braid prep seems to be very efficient. Sexto System awaits us, men, women, and Milyr. Our mission to find colonials is almost reality. Well down, Wolf Streak Beta."

While Milyr muttered something in a low voice, Domyn nodded his large head to her and then inquired into the air, "Vivacio, are our eight Flandecams still performing within the braid parameters? This is a final check before the braiding."

Two chairs to Nyba's left, Whyvvi spun her red chair to face Nyba and declared, "Cap, I should survey one more time through the anticipated route of our braid. We should be very thorough and careful this time. If colonials are in Sexto, then perhaps they have lost another colony ship in Kil-Kol. I should be redundant in my sensor search."

"Vulching, yeah," Swyllo squeaked emphatically from her yellow chair beside Milyr. "I don't want to get trapped in LaOgres anymore. I want to leave this vulching space as soon as we can and never have to come here again."

Vivacio, the maintenance artigence, reported, "Neer Domyn, all the Flandecams are within operation parameters for the braid protocols. I have informed Joculatus of this final check per protocol."

"Thank you, Vivacio, and well done this entire voyage," Domyn said, swaying his brown chair side-to-side in a frequent habit the young man performed when his excitement before plunging or popping needed release.

While she watched and analyzed this trait of her friend and crewmate, Nyba smirked at herself for starting to think like Prof Lyndyn and then said supportively, "Neer Domyn, the ConCen is ready for braiding. Your crew has prepped well. Braid when you deem appropriate. I'll enjoy the ride out of LaOgres. Swyllo, we do have adequate energy reserve for this journey, do we not?"

"Do you think that I would not collect more than we will need to get out of this vulching space?" Swyllo exclaimed with nervous laughter. "These bright spergits in this Kil-Kol provide me with plenty of light power to fill our reserves. We'll have more than enough. Let's just go!"

"Pilot control coordinated with Joculatus. We're ready to braid here," Milyr declared from his purple chair just beyond Swyllo in the formation of seats to Nyba's right. "I'll get you out of LaOgres, tiny fem. Just feed me that energy of yours, and I'll perform for you."

"Vulching toxx!" Swyllo swore but then giggled warmly. "Don't worry, I'll energize your mighty Flandecams. You just make sure that you and Joculatus get your braid pulses in synch."

"Of course, of course, tiny fem, I always get my pulses in synch with mighty Joculatus," Milyr crowed with a boyish brashness that sometimes offended, yet more often these recent months tantalized Nyba. "Perhaps, Domyn, we should extend Wilchrison, just for our tiny fem, hey?"

Suddenly stopping his nervous chair swaying, Domyn declared with authority, "For all of us on Wolf Streak Beta, we need to get out of LaOgres and go into the Sexto system. Joculatus, begin deployment of Wilchrison. Coordinate this with me. Coordinate pilot and the Flandecam functions with Milyr. Do you confirm, Cap Nyba?"

Knowing that entire crew, even three still in Med, were more than tired of the long almost one-year voyage through LaOgres space, Nyba said, "I confirm. Joculatus, Milyr, Domyn, the spacecraft is yours. Take us to the Sexto System. Begin the braid on your command, Neer Domyn."

"Cap, can we leave the holovision on?" Whyvvi asked.

"Swyllo, is that alright with you?" Nyba inquired, remembering the girl's aversion to LaOgres space travel and visualization of an-grav currents.

From her yellow chair, Swyllo answered, "In this case, I can make myself tolerate the nausea of watching LaOgres on the holovision. These sparkling spergits don't bother me so much as that vulching empty LaOgres. Let's just go."

"We'll try to give you a smooth ride, Swyllo, my tiny fem, won't we, Domyn?" Milyr promised, leaning slightly toward her and then announced more seriously, "Joculatus and I are prepped, Domyn."

"Then we are almost ready. Wilchrison will be extended in less than three minutes,"

Domyn said, and then turned to Nyba, adding more quietly, "Perhaps we should alert Med."

As he suggested this, she saw his eyes look at her. For a few moments, they held their glances.

Then Nyba nodded her head in affirmative. Apparently Domyn realized the necessity of not saying this connection to Jamyk in front of others at this time. He was truly a good crewmate and caring friend. The big Neer had fondness for the tiny rascal, and sometimes this was cherp for the crew.

With a rise of her hand, Nyba held out three fingers in sight of his vision, and after he nodded and turned his attention to his own function, Nyba whispered into the speaker in lining of her cap, "Joculatus, begin Tier Three comm with Med, exclusive to my control."

In her cap, Nyba heard Joculatus confirm, "Cap Nyba, Tier Three comm established with Med."

Domyn's voice said loudly with more enthusiasm than normal for him, "Awright, folks, this is our time. This is our mission. We are going to the Sexto System next. We have accomplished so much already, yet we can accomplish even more in Sexto. We are wolves. We are fast. We are streaking wolves. We can catch even the flashing foxes with a head start. We can find and contact colonials before our friends of Fox Flash Alpha. We are wolves of Blue Jay. We are best..."

In spite of her desire to listen completely to his emotional speech, Nyba did her duty as Cap and whispered into her speaker in her blue cap, "Prof Lyndyn and Doc Kymil, we are ready to plunge into Weznuski. You should take precautions as appropriate. We do not expect any problems."

After a few seconds of silence in her ear receivers, Nyba heard Prof Lyndyn's nasal voice say in a low, slightly hushed voice, "We are ready enough here, Cap Nyba. Jamyk is confused still and apparently worried about Chitir and Swyllo. He does seem to be able to converse with us now. His lapses into a panicked and bewildered dream-like state have not returned. Doc Kymil is not reading any unhealthy brain scans, at least nothing that concerns her usual medical expectations..."

In the ConCen, Domyn said, "Wilchrison is now fully extended. Milyr, activate your Flandecams into appropriate patterns. Joculatus, coordinate gravity flows to maximum braid potential..."

"Let's just vulching go!" Swyllo chirped impatiently.

Whyvvi exclaimed, "We should have an open and clear route. Nothing is blocking us according to my sensor reads presently."

Milyr announced in his baritone voice, "My huge Flandecams are generating strong gravity strands, all three aspects. We're ready to braid here."

Nyba said on Tier Three, "Prof, we are beginning to braid now."

In the holovision between and in front of the semi-circle of colored chairs, Nyba watched a multitude of sparkling spergits begin to swirl in the center of the scene. She knew this was a result of the braid formation as three strands of differing gravity aspects were woven into the braid by Wilchrison protruding from the fore curve of the shape of the Wolf Streak Beta. Slowly but inevitably, swirls of spergits elongated away into the vastness of the center of Kil-Kol. A funnel appearance much like that of a tornado took form. The velocity of movements of countless spergits, each less than microscopic dust in size, blended these spergits into a single brilliant white glow in the limited scope of her human vision. This glow lined the inner walls of the swirling funnel as it leaped outward into Kil-Kol.

Then suddenly with their spinning motion as a contrast perspective, the glowing walls seemed to flow rapidly toward and past her point of view through the holovision. Nyba realized the spacecraft was on its way through the braid. Wolf Streak Beta was now in reality, finally leaving LaOgres space and plunging into Weznuski space through Kil-Kol. At last, she sighed silently, they were going forward to the climax of their mission, their long and challenging Blue Jay mission. Wolf Streak Beta was now going to the Sexto System, or so she hoped based upon their navigational projections.

On her right in a brown chair, Neer Domyn reported, "Cap, the braid looks strong. Our velocity is within parameters. We are on our way. Awe thanks to our Blue Jay sci-tech!"

"Oh, what cherp light this is," Swyllo sang with obvious joy. "I can resupply our energy reserves easily almost as fast as we use it with this cherp light. Oh, what lovely little spergits!"

In her ear-piece, Nyba listened to Prof Lyndyn say, "…seems calmer now. We believe that we can have him ready soon. Was that subtle jolt Wolf Streak Beta leaping into the braid?"

Beside the yellow-clad girl, Milyr advised as his lavender-covered arms and hands waved and swayed before his tall torso, "Get as much now as you can, tiny fem. Remember these spergits usually only go partway through Weznuski before we leave them behind."

Quietly Nyba spoke into the speaker in her blue cap, "Yes, Prof, we are on our way inside the braid now. Everything appears cherp. Tell Doc that we'll be into Debordo space and Sexto before she can believe. Perhaps our little rascal will behave better once we are there."

Nyba observed Swyllo spin her yellow chair toward Milyr, and then the small girl squealed with feistiness in her shrill voice, "Vulching toxx, don't you think I know that? I'll do my job. I'll keep your energy coming. I know what I'm doing. Don't get nasty with me."

Milyr retorted, somewhat chuckling, somewhat bragging, "I certainly hope you do. I'm pilot with a big duty. I'll use a vulching hefty amount of energy feeding my huge Flandecams to move this wolfish spacecraft. Don't let me down on supply of your energy, tiny fem. My ability to keep up my power of these potent Flandecams is in your hands, tiny fem, oh, harvester of my energy."

"Argh! You're such a vulching toxx, Milyr," Swyllo laughed when she briefly swiped at his closest arm and shoulder with her right hand before pivoting her chair to face away from him. "But you do cherp flying to get us out of nasty LaOgres. My tiny hands will harvest as much energy from this streaming light as long as I can. Just vulching pilot us into Debordo space again. This is all I ask!"

"This is what we all expect of you, pilot Milyr. Just get us into the Sexto System," Nyba declared calmly but with firmness in attempt to foreshorten the inevitable verbal banter, which usually developed between the tall boy in lavender and the small girl in yellow, and then she continued in a more motivating tone, "We all need to see our mission have chance to finish, men and women. We on Wolf Streak Beta have accomplished and experienced so much more than our mission expectations. Yet we must not let ourselves become self-satisfied with what we have done already. We must continue to seek our Blue Jay goal of contacting the colonials. We can do this still. We are Blue Jayers!"

When Nyba ended this discourse, there was quiet in the ConCen, rustle of working dionjocu garments, but no conversation until after several seconds, Milyr exclaimed blithely, "Yeah, we are Blue Jay legends now according to Cap Bhiros. We are legends! Wolf Streak Beta is a new legend of Blue Jay. We are vulching primo legends of all time now."

From the opposite side of the semi-circle of chairs, Whyvvi retorted in her often analytically sarcastic manner, "Yes, we are now famous for getting ourselves out of a nasty situation, which we foolishly allowed ourselves to become entrapped. I am quite sure that our legendary status will be questioned in the future by historians of Blue Jay adventures when true accounts of our action and discoveries are more closely studied..."

Not liking where Whyvvi seemed to be going with this remark, Nyba interrupted her by saying, "Perhaps, perhaps yet we cannot ponder such concerns. Wolf Streak Beta has earned some recognition, if not fame, for our ability to recover from misfortune. We should take pride in our perseverance under crisis conditions. We can do so again. Our skill at discovering the identity of hidden Gullu Mette must not be dismissed as accidental. We should credit ourselves with this unexpected discovery of that super colony ship of ancestral colonials. You, Whyvvi, especially must take credit as our primary sensor operator."

"And also our clever idea to escape vulching Kil-Kol trap by deploying Wilchrison and braiding at the same time," Milyr boasted proudly while still working his hands and arms in piloting maneuvers. "And we did this manually. That's vulching unbelievable, at least to all Steppers and people back in the Zerosolis System. Only Blue Jayers can really believe that we could have done that primo impossible feat."

In her ear-piece, Nyba heard Prof Lyndyn say, "Indeed, well-stated, Cap Nyba. By the way, Doc says that Jamyk has responded very quickly now and is almost ready for dionjocu calibration."

"So humble, aren't we, Milyr!" Swyllo scoffed.

Nyba commanded into her speaker, "Prof, we're okay on the ConCen now. Let's make sure he's ready and healthy. Don't push his recovery. We've got several minutes before popping yet."

"That was a significant achievement, I must agree," Whyvvi said from her red chair. "We should be acclaimed for that maneuver. Also, as I recall more completely, Cap Nyba, you deserve much praise for realizing that colonials had at some time been in an uncharted system, had left behind radio residue signals, and had abandoned or fled from Gullu Mette trapped within Kil-Kol. Cap, your perceptiveness deserves legendary status."

"Well, awright, we can all agree to this," Domyn declared.

"Yeah, our Cap, best of Blue Jay," Milyr chortled with true enthusiasm, or at least that was what Nyba heard from the energetic young man in sweat-stained lavender dionjocu.

"No question, best Cap in Blue Jay!" Swyllo echoed cheerfully beside Milyr.

"Ho, ho, men, women, and Milyr, let's end this ranting foolishness, especially when Swyllo and Milyr agree about something," Nyba ordered half-heartedly, surprised at her own embarrassment, and yet her satisfaction of appreciation spoken by her crew. "We have serious popping into Sexto soon. This is our immediate next goal. Also, Whyvvi and Swyllo, we have yet to completely analyze sensor reads of Gullu Mette. I would like to find out how old the colony spaceship could continue to energize the Buffalardi beacon for several weeks now after it had been launched by Fox Flash Alpha. This information could be vital to us or to whoever is assigned to investigate Gullu Mette."

While her eyes observed a streaming light begin to fade from the scene on the holovision and a black spot in the far distance slowly expand, Nyba listened to Whyvvi ask, "Do you believe that Blue Jay MisCom will assign us this mission after Sexto? We should get that mission. We deserve this opportunity. We should be the best crew to study the trapped colony ship."

"I don't know. Maybe we will. However, more likely this next mission could go to Lynx Blaze. Blue Jay MisCom might believe both of us, and Fox Flash Alpha would be more useful in exchanges with colonials once we find them in Sexto," Nyba replied as she gazed at the approaching black spot in the holovision, and then with mild concern, inquired, "Whyvvi, this spot is just Weznuski space, is it not? We are not hurtling toward anything massive and dangerous, are we?"

"I don't see anything out there but empty Weznuski space and our braid," Domyn reported, tapping his visor.

"Same here," Milyr agreed. "Are you starting to sense things like Jamyk? Cap Nyba, you're not getting like him? This would not be cherp for the rest of us."

"Nope!" Nyba replied in as throaty a voice as she could manage with a snort, and then after pausing for several seconds of silence around the ConCen, she chuckled, "Ho, ho, men, women, and Milyr, even a captain can enjoy a joke now and then. If I ever get like Jamyk, then you should lock me in Milyr's quarters with all his many weeks of unwashed clothes. We don't need more than one Jamyk."

"Erhh! Argh! Cap Nyba, trapped in the squalor of this toxx would be nastiest punishment possible. We couldn't do that to you," Swyllo squealed with laughter as she squirmed in her chair.

"Vulch, yeah, Nyba, I would agree with tiny fem here on this," Milyr chortled and then with a scoff added, "I can't stand living in my own stink sometimes when I get behind in my laundry. Sometimes my room smells like rotten toxx."

"Perhaps you should clean more frequently," Whyvvi stated and then turned toward Nyba to say, "Cap, my sensor reads with zeta rays show simply a vacant space ahead in our course. We should be cherp until the popping into Debordo space."

Swyllo giggled in a hushed voice, "What vulch does rotten toxx smell like?"

To Nyba's immediate right, Domyn asked loudly, "Joculatus, what is our estimated time until the popping into Debordo space?"

Milyr snickered in his impression of a baritone whisper, "Oh, tiny fem, you really truly don't desire to know what rotten toxx smells like, do you?"

While she waited for a reply of artigence, Nyba scolded herself for her anxiety about this braid journey. Did she suffer still from a previous bad experience of two awakenings ago? Was memory of that trauma in Kil-Kol haunting her still? Would she be able to be strong and steady for her crew, for Wolf Streak Beta? Nyba despised herself for having these doubts now when the mission was so close to climax. What kind of captain was she becoming, fearful of memory?

She listened to Swyllo giggle, "Vulch, not really, if it's your rotten stinking toxx."

Then Joculatus reported over the ongoing banter, "Neer Domyn, estimated time to the popping into Debordo space is thirteen minutes."

"Thank you, Joculatus, this sounds about right by my calculations," Domyn agreed and then continued, "Joculatus, reconfirm navigational coordinates and vectors for entry into the Sexto System. Milyr, you should begin thinking about shut down sequence of fore the Flandecams soon."

As Milyr stopped his silliness with Swyllo and acknowledged the suggestion from Domyn, Nyba said on Tier Three, "Prof, we'll be popping in less than thirteen minutes. If rascal toxx can be ready about then, I'll be cherply happy, but don't rush, Doc. We will need our tiny pilot in perfect mental health and alertness. Milyr is performing chore cherply at moment. We don't sensor read any problems ahead. Just you make sure rascal is ready when you bring him to the ConCen."

"We're doing our best here, Cap Nyba. Since plunging into the braid, Doc claims his alertness has improved dramatically," Prof Lyndyn reported in his slightly nasal voice.

Thirteen minutes and then Wolf Streak Beta would pop into Debordo space and hopefully the Sexto System. Nyba sighed to herself while she watched the last of the shining spergits disappear from alongside the flow of passage of the spacecraft within the braid. Soon, very soon, they would near culmination of this long journey since leaving Stepping Stone Quinto almost a year ago. Wolf Streak Beta would be reaching the destination, which had been sought for more than five years by this Blue Jay crew and for more than a hundred years by the Blue Jay project. Nyba could remember only the diminished memories of her life before coming together with these people in early childhood. Everything else in her life had been Blue Jay and Wolf Streak Beta and these special crewmates…even rascal Jamyk.

"Just thirteen minutes, and we'll be at our journey's end," Nyba proclaimed with encouragement. "Just thirteen minutes, men, women, and Milyr, and we'll be able to comm Fox Flash Alpha. We'll be ready to fulfill our mission. We've done something no one else has ever accomplished. You should be proud of yourselves, my wolves, my men, women, and Milyr."

"Why does it always have to be me?" Milyr whined but with a slight chuckle and then laughed more boisterously. "But I'll be first to welcome the popping into Sexto."

"Awspir, to this fate!" Domyn laughed in his deep voice, making Nyba smile.

SPEC TWO: NYBA TO SEXTO
CHAPTER 15

"Are we there yet?" Swyllo asked in her shrill voice.

Nyba heard anxiety of doubt in the voice of the girl but also possibility of joyous success. These were the same feelings Nyba experienced herself. Were they out of Weznuski space finally and into Debordo space? Was Wolf Streak Beta now popping into the Sexto System? Was their long voyage of several years since leaving Steppingstone Primero about to reach climax?

Then the words of happy anticipation flowed from Domyn as he announced in his usual low growl, "Awright, I'm going to deactivate Wilchrison soon. Joculatus, do you confirm Debordo space immediately ahead of the current course of Wolf Streak Beta?"

When she heard this report, Nyba was confidently sure. Neer Domyn never miscalculated this procedure as the braid ahead left Weznuski and entered Debordo. He was skilled, as much as any sci-tech engineer in Blue Jay, with this use of Wilchrison. Nyba had trust in his knowledge and experience. His statement of entry into Debordo thrilled her entire being.

Joculatus reported, "Neer Domyn, Wolf Streak Beta will enter Debordo space in thirty-seven seconds at current velocity."

"Then I'll end the Wilchrison braiding then. Joculatus and Milyr, you should continue grav generation until our spacecraft is fully integrated into Debordo space," Domyn said.

"Vulch, I know that," Milyr snorted. "I'm not a complete toxx idiot!"

The ConCen was hushed for several seconds and then Domyn announced,

"Wilchrison off. We'll be coasting with our present velocity through the remnant of the braid. I can see real space in my view, Swyllo. We're there. We're in Debordo space again."

"We're back!" Swyllo cheered. "We're really back in real space. Oh, this is really cherp! I hope we never go into vulching LaOgres space again, never."

From Nyba's left, Whyvvi said, "Now that will be determined by Blue Jay MisCom. We should finish our mission objective here in the Sexto System. Then we will hear from Blue Jay of our next mission."

"Oh, Whyvvi, don't be such a toxx all time…" Swyllo started to complain.

However, Cap Nyba tuned out their conversation as she focused her attention upon Milyr when Joculatus reported, "Pilot Milyr, we can end the generation of the braid grav protocols. Do you concur? Are you prepared to pilot manually?"

"Vulch yeah, Joculatus, I'm a Blue Jay pilot. I'm the best," Milyr exclaimed in his usual boastful manner, but this time Nyba thought that she heard also relief in his anxious voice as well.

Joculatus said, "Pilot Milyr, you have full pilot function on manual now."

"No nastiness, Joculatus. I can handle this big Wolf Streak. You just help Domyn with his Wilchrison. It's probably time for it to come down and retract back into hull," Milyr chuckled and then added hastily with some unease, "Er, that's cherp with you, Domyn, isn't it?"

Typical Milyr, Nyba smiled to herself, always speaking his witticisms rashly, then trying to mollify his inadvertent victim with boyish charm. Not long ago, maybe recently as Steppingstone Quinto, she would have been irritated by such behavior. However, now Nyba felt tolerant, if not occasionally amused by his antics. The tall, slender young man was a good pilot, she reminded herself.

"…Opportune time to retract Wilchrison," Domyn was saying with a laugh beside her. "It did its job. Now we need to do ours, my friend. Cap Nyba, once Wilchrison is returned to its cradle, where do you wish for us to go?"

Slightly befuddled by his question, Nyba forced herself to end her observations of the lanky figure in the lavender dionjocu and asked in a hopefully steady, authoritative voice, "Have we confirmed that we are in the Sexto System, Whyvvi? And, Swyllo, how adequate are our energy reserves?"

Swyllo replied quickly, "Our energy supply is at 53 percent. Not that low considering how much Wolf Streak uses during the braiding and popping."

While she watched Whyvvi flickering and fluttering her fingers within the pink dionjocu gloves, Nyba realized the girl was trying to organize the complex data from her sensor surveys, so Nyba turned again to the other girl in yellow and said, "That is very cherp, Swyllo. You must have harvested a significant amount of light from spergits on the way through Kil-Kol. Have you found the nearest light source in this space for your next harvest?"

Slowly pivoting her yellow chair as she pointed one hand at the holovision, Swyllo replied, "At this time, our best target is that distant sun. It is the brightest light source according to my light sensors. There is a very large planet with much reflective light over there, but my surveys and my eyes like the sun as first choice."

"Then we'll go with your opinion, Swyllo," Nyba declared, and then as her glance turned toward the young man in the sweat-stained lavender dionjocu, she commanded, "Milyr, our current goal is that sun. Take us toward it. As we travel closer to that sun, perhaps our sensors will read more accurate data, so we can confirm our location."

Whyvvi sighed, "I am working as fast as I can. I should be able to portray the view of this system soon on the holovision. Have we surveyed any comm from Fox Flash Alpha yet? They should have left comm for us with their last deployed Buffalardi when they popped into this system."

Of course, Nyba reminded herself suddenly, comm from Fox Flash Alpha. Then her glance caught Domyn's beside her, and the large young man appeared as guilty as she felt at that moment. Apparently he had forgotten that basic post-pop procedure also. Though Neer Domyn had an excuse as he had been working Wilchrison. Cap Nyba realized that she had none.

Domyn announced, "I'm finished with Wilchrison. I can switch to comm duty while Milyr is at pilot. Cap, is that your wish?"

"Yes, of course we need that information," Cap Nyba declared, flustered with herself.

Why had she not ordered Milyr to search this space for Fox Flash Alpha's comm? Or why not electro-magnetic radio signals from colonials? This had been her plan. Milyr was her best comm expert. Yet Milyr was at pilot during this recent pop. He could not do both comm and pilot at the same time. Jamyk, she hissed in her mind. Why did toxx have to go nasty now? How soon before he was ready?

As her awareness seethed with her anger and frustration at her own forgetfulness and her agitation with Jamyk's recent bout of childishness, Cap Nyba listened to Domyn say succinctly, "Joculatus, I am switching to comm duty in two minutes. Relay any comm from Fox Flash Alpha or Buffalardi chain. There should be comm from their last deployed beacon."

While he peeled off his tan scalp cap and visor, Domyn rose from his brown chair beside Nyba. His large scalp and forehead glistened with sweat. Yet his movements were almost gentle and graceful. The big, young man seemed to remain calm, in control, even now while he changed with obvious haste from one duty function to another. For her, Nyba thought, man did this for her, for his Captain, to take some of the stress from her responsibilities.

Cap Nyba exclaimed to the crew in the ConCen, "It will be cherp to hear from Fox Flash Alpha again, won't it men, women, and... Milyr?"

"Yeah, Cap, I'm a man not whatever," Milyr complained with a hint of a chuckle.

Nyba was about to respond with a humorous quip until Joculatus reported, "No comm from Fox Flash Alpha is detected. No comm from Buffalardi beacon is detected."

Instead, after hearing Joculatus, Cap Nyba blurted with astonishment, "No comm? Not even from beacon? This is very strange."

"There should be a Buffalardi beacon out there. Cap Bhiros and Neer Khebol would have launched that last Buffalardi to complete the chain of sanbeam relays," Whyvvi expounded with absolute conviction.

"Maybe we're not in the Sexto System," Swyllo groaned. "Maybe, our side trip around Gullu Mette interfered with our navigation..."

"Vulch, Fox Flash Alpha might not be in this system," Milyr griped. "Maybe that toxx Chitir or perhaps Radhin got them lost. They're not as cherp as me and Jamyk at pilot."

"Calm down, men and women," Cap Nyba demanded in spite of her own anxiety. "Let's get our data before we assume wrong reality. Whyvvi, can you give us a portrayal of this system on the holovision yet? We could use whatever you have so far. Don't try to be perfect."

Beside her in his brown chair, Domyn finished adorning himself with his new cap and visor and said, "Joculatus, I am now a comm operator. Coordinate with me. Let's search this system for any residual sanbeam transmission. Then let's search for electromag radio signals."

Two chairs to Nyba's left, Whyvvi replied, "My sensor reads are not totally completed, but I should be able to give you something. Let me connect with the holovision. This will be a representation based upon my up-to-the-minute reads. I will need to delete our present view, Cap, in order to display a representation. Remember this perspective will not be the actual view as if out the window."

"Holovision is yours, Whyvvi, give us what you have found," Cap Nyba ordered with mild impatience escaping into her tone, and then to regain some authority in her opinion of herself, she added, "Joculatus, prepare to compare Whyvvi's representation with the long distance scans taken from Steppingstone Quinto before we began this latest journey."

That journey had begun almost year ago, Nyba reminded herself. The Quinto System was about twenty-nine light years away through Debordo space travel. Only the long chain of Buffalardi relay beacons stretching back through that vast distance connected Wolf Streak Beta with the closest human colleagues on Quinto. Such a long separation, Nyba thought, but that was the reality of inter-system space travel. Of course they were only a year or less away by LaOgres space travel, if she chose to return to Quinto System by that aspect.

Domyn exclaimed with excitement, "There are electromag transmissions bouncing all through this space, Cap. Definitely some refined or evolved radio-type residues are all around us, probably from the passage of colonial super ships. Maybe we are not alone here."

"Of course we are not alone. Fox Flash Alpha and Khebol are here somewhere," Whyvvi stated emphatically, then added with less emotion, "I will display representation, which my data can render now. I should remind everyone that this is only a representation, not a true view."

Then the holovision changed. The starry blackness of Debordo space with one yellow sun in the center of the scene that had been a view for several minutes disappeared. In its place appeared a starless blackness with several spherical bodies around a larger and closer image of same sun.

"There, Cap, this is data currently available from my sensors. I believe there could be other planets on far side of system. Even zeta rays require some time to travel there and back. I should get those longer reads soon. This is what I have discovered to this minute," Whyvvi reported.

In the holovision display before her chair, Nyba observed the large sun, quite brightly shining little right of the center of the three-dimensional scene. Yet this sun was not a sphere that dominated scene, and that surprised Nyba.

Apparently Domyn was also stunned for he commented in amazement, "Awspir! That looks larger than large gas giants back in the Zerosolis System. It's huge!"

To the left of the center rotated a very large super-giant planet of portrayed yellow, purple, and brown patches and bands of color. In her view, colors swirled in what could be massive weather systems. Yes, Domyn was correct, Nyba thought to herself, vastness of a gas giant reminded her of the holovisions of gas giants, which she had seen as a very young pup in the early institutions of Blue Jay education. Yet this new giant on their holovision dwarfed old gas giants in files.

"Yes, that gas giant is large enough for my sensors to create a more precise picture than the much smaller planets of this system. The diameter of this gas giant is almost vast enough to call it a mini-solar system just by itself," Whyvvi stated. "I should be able to create more detailed pictures of the other planets as surveys return."

"Vulch, I can remember how big those vulching giants of the Zerosolis System looked to me those many years ago in school and when we learned to space fly around the vulcher," Milyr exclaimed.

"We were all much smaller then, remember, you big oaf," Swyllo retorted. "Every moon and planet that we flew around looked big to us. And yet, vulch, that thing is almost as bright as the sun, at least according to my recent light sensors. Maybe we could go there to harvest reflected light."

Milyr scoffed as he interrupted her, "Vulch, tiny fem, you were not much smaller then than you are now. Everything looks big to you still."

Trying to ignore the developing by-play, Cap Nyba asked loudly, "Joculatus, can you find any correlation between this image on the holovision and scans taken on Steppingstone Quinto?"

Neer Domyn leaned toward her and reported in a competition against excited voices of others in the ConCen, "Cap, the comm surveys still reveal many electromag radio signals throughout this system. Most are residuals, some seem more recent. I'm not as skilled as Milyr at this, but I believe some may be very recent, if not current within a reasonable time span for radio wave travel."

Milyr was saying, "...getting closer to that big planet. I can feel and see a strong gravity pull from there. It's almost competing with the gravity of the sun. That sun is still our destination, isn't it, Cap? I'll take you where you want to go. Just let me know if we are changing..."

Then Joculatus reported, "Cap Nyba, there is a 67 percent correlation between this image on the holovision and the image compilation from the long distance sensors taken from Steppingstone Quinto."

"There is a 67 percent correlation?" Whyvvi asked with wonder in her rising voice. "Considering circumstances and comparing those long-distance sensors taken almost a year ago, this is a very high correlation. This must be the Sexto System. Nothing else is likely."

Trying to keep the gleefulness from her own voice, Cap Nyba said firmly with intended encouragement, "This is reasonable, yes, Whyvvi. Continue to update the holovision as more data comes to you. Work closely with Joculatus to give us the most accurate portrayal of this system."

"If this is Sexto, then where the vulch is Fox Flash Alpha?" Milyr asked in consternation. "Why don't we hear from them? Did vulchers get lost and go somewhere else?"

"That is a good question," Domyn agreed and then continued with his usual steadiness, "Cap, I can't get contact with the Buffalardi, which they should have deployed. This is not as planned."

"Are you certain that you are using the correct comm seeker? Khebol would have surely deployed the Buffalardi as protocol demanded. Not even Cap Bhiros is so reckless not to launch the Buffalardi," Whyvvi stated confidently from her red chair.

"Awe guides me, I believe so, but I don't have Milyr's special talent at communications. However, I have coordinated with Joculatus in my searches," Domyn admitted. "Yet I just can't get comm relay from the Buffalardi. Normally that chain of deployed beacons is very talkative, either from Blue Jay at Steppingstone Quinto or from Fox Flash Alpha via pre-recorded message."

"Yeah, that's right!" Milyr said while he waved his hands and arms directing the flight of the spacecraft. "Our reappearance in Debordo space would have triggered automatically any message left by Fox Flash. Remember how Khebol contacted us when we ran into that trouble in Kil-Kol with the toxx colony ghost ship? It should do the same thing now, if there is a beacon near this system."

As he spoke, Nyba marveled to herself at how knowledgeable he was at communications, even when he was doing other critical duty. He should be at comm now, not pilot. Damn, that Jamyk, she cursed silently. If the rascal was here to pilot, then Milyr could be working the comm function where she had needed him, according to her prior plan.

"Can we search for Fox Flash Alpha directly? Can we search for the beacon itself instead of comm signal?" Swyllo inquired from her yellow chair next to Milyr.

Nyba watched the long-legged form swing himself in his purple chair toward Swyllo, although he could not see her as he was using the double visor over his eyes, and heard him say, "Tiny fem, we shouldn't have to search like that. There should be a beacon there, and it should transmit to us on our arrival. Obviously vulching foxes have gotten their toxx lost. They may not even be here in Sexto. Maybe we got here before them."

Behind her a raspy voice said, "Nope."

Startled Nyba spun her blue chair around to face the hatchway. There he stood in his green dionjocu. His visor eye-piece was up on his capped forehead. Jamyk wore a pilot cap with a double visor. His expression seemed thoughtful, or as thoughtful as Jamyk ever looked. Nyba was unsure if she was happy or angry at his presence.

Slightly behind the boy stood Prof Lyndyn, and the man said, "Cap Nyba, he is ready for duty. Doc Kymil and I have both concurred on that. Jamyk is available for whatever ConCen function that you desire of him."

"Yup," Jamyk declared. "Ready."

While she stared at the green figure, Nyba heard Milyr yell with enthusiasm, "Yeah, little peener, cherp to see you again. Are you ready? We beat toxx foxes. We got here first. Do you believe that? We're vulching legends."

"Nope," Jamyk repeated and then pointing a hand and finger toward the holovision he added calmly and lucidly, "Chitir...there."

Grumbling under her breath, Nyba glared at the boy, then at Prof Lyndyn, and she asked with some sarcasm, "Sounds like more silliness to me. Are you sure, Prof? This is a critical time."

Domyn said, "Cap, we could use a pilot. Milyr could continue that function, but he is so much better at this comm duty than I am. We need our best comm person to unravel these mysteries we've encountered. We could use Jamyk at pilot now."

"Mysteries, what type of mysteries do you mean?" Prof Lyndyn inquired with interest, and as he stepped past Jamyk toward his gray chair on Nyba's left, he continued saying, "I really enjoy mysteries. What do we have now?"

"Prof," Nyba demanded forcefully, "are you sure Jamyk won't go back to his childishness like before we popped? I need a reliable person, not a toxx."

Prof Lyndyn plopped into his chair and said, "Indeed, yes, Cap Nyba, Doc Kymil sent him to the ConCen with her assurance. The boy is ready to function..."

"I could use rest, Cap," Milyr declared, interrupting Lyndyn. "My arms are exhausted from all this pilot duty. Comm duty requires less hand and arm action."

Swyllo giggled beside him and joked with a suggestive leer to her voice, "With all the hand and arm action you get when you're off duty playing with your Zapstik, you should be well muscled to do pilot duty. All that up and down and back and forth with your hands must be second nature to you."

"Yeah, ha, ha, you're very humorous, tiny fem," the sweaty figure in the purple chair scoffed. "This man can pilot longer, but Cap needs a comm specialist. That's what I am, a comm specialist, and of course, a vulching primo pilot, too!"

During this exchange, the boy in the green dionjocu stood there motionless, except for his steady breathing and gradually lowering arm. Nyba tried to study his face, his eyes, for any indication of his prior behavior, but she saw only his patience, which was unusual for him. She felt that he wanted to impress her with his reliability. Yet should she trust that? She did need Milyr at comm duty. She did respect the opinion of both Prof and Doc, at least most of the time when they were not astray with silly science fantasies.

Finally Nyba declared gruffly, "Jamyk, prep for pilot. Don't let me down. Don't let Wolf Streak Beta down. We are at a very crucial moment in our mission. We wish to succeed."

Then as she watched Jamyk walk past Prof Lyndyn in a gray chair and Whyvvi in a red chair, she heard Domyn say, "Milyr, when you get settled into comm duty, you might search system-wide for a total view of these radio transmissions. With your expertise, you may find some patterns that I do not. It will be good to have you at comm. I'm much better at some other function."

With her eyes staring still at Jamyk's thin figure as he sat into his green chair, Nyba suggested, "Domyn, search again for the Buffalardi signal. I don't like this that we can't find such a signal. It's not Blue Jay protocol. It's not typical of Fox Flash to fail in that simple procedure."

"I'll do my best, Cap," Domyn replied, swaying his chair side to side nervously. "Perhaps I can extrapolate a direct path from Kil-Kol behind us toward direction back to Steppingstone Quinto. The relay chain of beacons would have guided the latest beacon to align in that direction."

"Yes, that is what relays do, Neer. Do as you suggest. Try to locate that beacon or at least a signal," Nyba agreed and silently grumbled at the poor way this entry into the Sexto System had begun.

Buffalardi beacon should have located the Wolf Streak Beta once a spacecraft had popped into Debordo space. That was the automatic function of the last beacon to be deployed. A comm should have been received by now. Nyba slapped the chair in frustration. Had something gone wrong, she wondered. Had Cap Bhiros been too rash to find the colonials hastily and ignored protocol?

Seeking to soothe her anxiety, Nyba peered toward Milyr's chair, and with moderate firmness in her tone, she commanded almost reluctantly, "Milyr, turn

221

pilot function over to Jamyk. Joculatus, coordinate and confirm exchange. I hope that you are prepped, Jamyk."

"Yup," the boy reported. "Pilot...now."

Joculatus said, "Transfer of pilot to Jamyk is confirmed."

"Ah! I usually hate giving up pilot, but this time it's vulching cherp," Milyr exclaimed while he ripped off his lavender cap and arose from his chair. "I'm so vulching thirsty now. I want a dose of nutrient. My dionjocu couldn't keep me quenched fast enough."

"This must be cherping first. Milyr actually seeking a drink of nutrient," Swyllo chuckled, swinging her short legs out of his way as he hobbled on slightly stiff legs around their two chairs.

"It won't happen again, I hope, tiny fem. I need to be ready for all the colonial fems I meet. They'll be thirsty for me. One occasional drink of antemgebemarzex won't be enough to stifle my bodaciously magnificent manliness of myself," Milyr boasted with a laugh as he stumbled to a small alcove in the wall where he retrieved a cup of nutrient.

His sweat ran down his bald head into his long face. Nyba was surprised at the amount of glistening moisture. He had been working with much effort, just to pilot a spacecraft for her. His lavender dionjocu was saturated with wetness in spite of the automatic cooling function within garment. This young man was truly worthy, she mused to herself.

When the holovision blinked in her peripheral vision, Nyba shook off her unintended, lengthy preoccupation with the tall figure and said hastily with mild self-guilt, "Milyr, when you are ready, take over comm duty, so we can allow our Neer to use his sci-tech knowledge to solve our current mysteries. Do you need rest or change of dionjocu before you assume your new duty?"

After gulping down the nutrient liquid, Milyr said, "Cap Nyba, I'm fine to go to my duty now. I don't want to delay my search of radio signals and that elusive message from Fox Flash. Besides comm duty is much less strenuous than pilot. I can rest later. As long as tiny fem here can stand my stinking dionjocu a bit longer, then we are cherp."

"Argh! That's lot to ask of a colleague. But for the sake of our mission, I can hold my nose little longer," Swyllo laughed from her yellow chair next to the empty purple chair.

Attempting to avoid chuckling herself, Nyba nodded to Milyr and then swiveled her chair, perhaps more abruptly than needed, to peer intently at the updated display in the holovision. The variously colored orbs around the sun did not actually intrigue her, she realized. Her thoughts were on him still. Nyba wondered, what was happening to her now? Why was she not able to focus properly?

Whyvvi reported, "Two more planetary-sized bodies are now indicated on the far side of this system. I believe there are now eleven planets revealed. Some have moons, but precision of my sensor reads is too limited at this distance to get detailed images of smaller bodies even with zeta rays. However, positioning of these planets and moons correlates very highly with our long-distance sensors from Quinto. This is definitely the Sexto System."

"That monster gas giant is certainly impressive," said Prof Lyndyn in his nasal voice. "It overshadows every other body in Sexto. However, it does not look very inviting to human colonization. No doubt, like our gas giants of the Zerosolis System, it is not conducive to carbon-based life. The planet would not be likely a target for colonial terraforming. We should not expect to find our colonial brethren there..."

"Well, Prof, if my analysis of these comm signals is accurate," Domyn said, "then there was some transmission activity near it at some time. I'm not skilled enough to say when or how much. Hurry back to comm, Milyr. I'm revealing too much of my ignorance right now. Give me my big machines and spacecraft design. That's my specialty."

Nyba smiled to herself at the young man's self-criticism, hardly an opinion of anyone else in Blue Jay program, and then she asked, "Have you found any sign of the Buffalardi beacon yet? Or signal either? Even searching back toward Quinto direction?"

Shaking his big head negatively, Domyn replied, "Nothing. Unless my skills here are inadequate, I can say that my scans have back-tracked far enough to have found something, yet nothing shows. I must conclude that Fox Flash Alpha failed to deploy their Buffalardi that was scheduled for Sexto."

"Oh my, that sounds ominous," exclaimed Doc Kymil as she strolled into the ConCen. "From what I've heard while eavesdropping between arguments with Bodacia, you've got strange happenings here in Sexto. I guess no mission briefing can cover all possibilities, can it?"

"Yes, Doc, very strange," Nyba agreed, smiling a welcome at the sight of a woman in a white dionboda. "Cherp to have you on theConCen now!"

"Yet we are in the Sexto System," Whyvvi stated emphatically, but Nyba thought that she heard a hint of pessimism in the young woman's voice when Whyvvi continued, "We have found radio signals from colonial ships. We should hear from Fox Flash Alpha soon."

Back in his purple chair, Milyr slipped his new cap over his bald head and declared, "Joculatus, I am now at comm duty. Transfer comm to me. Domyn, you don't mind, do you?"

"Awspir, Milyr, that's the finest request I've heard this awakening. It's all yours. Joculatus, transfer comm to Milyr."

Joculatus reported, "Transfer of comm. To Milyr is confirmed."

"Ah, yeah, now let's see if we can get the whole system-wide scan on these radio transmissions. Let's see if we can determine some age and time delineation on residual traces," Milyr said, and the glee and enthusiasm of his voice amazed Nyba, not what he usually projected to others.

As she wondered about different attitudes of this tantalizing young man in lavender, Nyba heard Whyvvi say in confusion, "Cap, this is not as it should be, but my surveys are showing a small moon-like object leaving orbit from around the nearest small planet. Its trajectory might intersect with ours."

"Perhaps you should readjust your sensors for man-made objects," Domyn suggested.

"Do you think it could be Fox Flash Alpha?" Whyvvi asked with sudden optimism.

"Or maybe the colonials?" Doc Kymil inquired.

"Yup," rasped Jamyk.

Another unknown, Nyba complained to herself. This popping into Sexto was not proceeding at all as expected. Yet, she reminded herself, Blue Jay was searching for colonials. Why should she not expect to find them? Was she beginning to question her own leadership of this mission? No, that was almost as foolish as Jamyk's frequent silliness. She was a cherp captain, she told herself.

"Well, men, women, and Milyr, we are here to find the colonials," Cap Nyba stated, trying to put hope and confidence into her voice. "Perhaps we have found them or Fox Flash Alpha."

"Why does it always have to be me?" Milyr griped.

"Yup," rasped Jamyk.

Spec Two: Nyba to Sexto
Chapter 16

"We should deploy Buffalardi," Milyr said.

"Yup," agreed Jamyk.

While her eyes watched the blinking red dot in the holovision that represented an unknown object moving toward the current course of Wolf Streak Beta, Nyba stared first at the lavender figure at the far right and then over at the green figure at the far left, and with reluctance commanded, "Neer Domyn, launch the Buffalardi. We can't determine that Fox Flash Alpha did so. We need to send communication to MisCom on Quinto. We'll have to deploy our own beacon to finalize the relay chain. Your first priority, Neer Domyn, deploy the Buffalardi."

Young man in the tan dionjocu beside her replied, "Only thing to do. We've got at least three still in our inventory. They won't do us any good there. Joculatus, prep the Buffalardi for Debordo space deployment. Trajectory will be vector Quinto. No braid required."

Joculatus said, "Neer Domyn, the Buffalardi launch will be ready in eleven minutes. Course trajectory to Quinto is ongoing calculation. The Buffalardi can be navigated post-launch if necessary."

"I know that," Domyn declared with a growl. "Just have that beacon ready. I don't believe that I am annoyed with artigence, my own sci-tech. I must be tired."

"Oh my, Domyn," Doc Kymil soothed calmly, sitting in her white chair beside him. "Even you can get testy at times of uncertainty. You are human after all. You will do fine work this awakening."

Peering at Milyr in his purple chair, Nyba asked, "Milyr, do you have the comm prepped for the sanbeam transmission to MisCom on Steppingstone Quinto? As soon as we deploy the beacon, we must send a message to let MisCom know that we've arrived in Sexto."

"Vulch, Nyba, I thought you'd want me to start broadcasting to the colonials as soon as possible," Milyr said with defensiveness in his voice. "I have prepared a communication program ready to transmit on the frequency that we discovered around Gullu Mette and now here in Sexto. I thought that message to the colonials would be your priority from me."

"We don't know if they are out here, you toxx," Swyllo complained in her yellow chair next to the lanky form in a lavender dionjocu.

"There," Jamyk said with certainty.

"That's okay, Swyllo," Nyba said firmly and then continued trying to allow encouragement into her voice. "Transmit your colonial greeting, Milyr. That may have first priority now anyway, but also prep the sanbeam comm for MisCom. We must let them know our present situation."

Domyn announced, "Buffalardi launched, Cap. Beacon deployment should be in about seventeen minutes. Do you confirm that estimate, Joculatus?"

Joculatus replied, "Neer Domyn, I concur with your latest estimate. Buffalardi is travelling on the correct trajectory. The on-board Flandecam is functioning within parameters."

"Well then, Milyr, you have less than seventeen minutes to prep comm for MisCom. That should be plenty of time to do so and still monitor the Sexto System radio signals," Cap Nyba said with what she intended as a motivational challenge.

"Vulch, yeah, Nyba, it's me, the communications specialist. I'm almost smart at this. No challenge at all," Milyr chortled, flicking his fingers in short, quick movements as he worked his function within his dionjocu gloves in interface with Joculatus and Wolf Streak Beta.

Abruptly Whyvvi spoke from her red chair, "I hope that you got the right message. That unknown should be a human-designed spacecraft. It is definitely made of an artificial outer shell, not surfaced as any of the moons or planets of this system. Our unknown object should be our first colonial contact. It is certainly man-made."

"Could it be Fox Flash Alpha? Could it be Chitir flying toward us?" Swyllo asked hopefully.

"Nope," Jamyk blurted about the same time as Whyvvi.

The girl in the pink dionjocu gave Jamyk a glare and then replied, "No, mass, diameter, and shape are all incongruous with Fox Flash Alpha. And, Cap, before you ask, it is not super colony ship either. The mass is much too small for a colony ship like Gullu Mette."

"Oh my, won't it be exciting to see Cotto Rucci or Letta Vazza hovering in space," Doc Kymil exclaimed in excitement.

"Indeed that will be quite special," Prof Lyndyn agreed. "That sighting would make this long voyage so very worthwhile. Our hunt over the many years will be culminated with success. A century or more of the Blue Jay project to reunite two known branches of humanity across the vast light years of galactic distance will be finished. The moment of greeting will be historical and enlightening for all populations back in the Zerosolis System and on five Steppingstones. We will be…"

Interrupting Prof Lyndyn, Milyr exclaimed proudly with a grin showing on his long face covered by an only one-eyed visor, "Vulch, we should hear from them soon. I've used a program of language and dialect extrapolated from their time of exodus from Homeworld. Our Blue Jay linguistic prediction programs should provide us with a very close match to the present status of their language. At least we have current frequencies of their radio signals floating around this Sexto System to use as guide. I'm cherp on this, Cap Nyba."

"Very cherp, Milyr and Whyvvi," Cap Nyba praised, resting back into her blue chair. "I believe that this mission is starting to look more cherp now. How long before the beacon deployment from the Buffalardi, Domyn? I want to get the message off as soon as we can."

"Awe guides our probe, if the Buffalardi courses correctly, then deployment in about seven minutes," Domyn replied and then asked, "Milyr, did you get any result when you surveyed the system-wide for radio wave patterns?"

"Sorry, Domyn, I didn't get chance to read returns, but I'm primo cherp at this," Milyr exclaimed suddenly. "Vulch, I put reads on auto-scan. Joculatus has been recording them on Tier Two since I got distracted with this more important duty. I am primo cherp."

"Joculatus, show the surveys recorded on Tier Two onto my station," Domyn requested, and then after several seconds, he turned toward her and said with a smile, "Nyba, you've got to see this."

"Whyvvi, continue your sensor searches of that object. Expand as you can to include the closest planets to our course," Cap Nyba commanded while she adjusted one visor in front of her eye and then flicked the index finger of her right hand within her dionjocu glove.

From her red chair between Jamyk and Lyndyn, Whyvvi reported, "Surveys of the object are updating constantly with more precision, Cap. It is surely some humanly designed spacecraft with hull, which reads like a composite of metallic alloy, probably titanium-based, and some form of ceramic. It could be very like the materials that composed the original colony super ships."

While Whyvvi described this, Nyba observed the strange miasmic scene in her visor. More fluctuating than any gravity mix or light intensity scan, the sparkling eddies and currents of electromagnetic radio waves in the vast solar system threatened to overwhelm her brain. However, she fought initial confusion and optic overload. Soon her brain acclimated to view and allowed her to see some patterns of order. There was a pattern there, she realized. There were definite concentrations of electromag radio waves. Three of them, she noticed, three centers of the most frequent radio wave transmissions. This Sexto System was very talkative. Would they listen also?

"Neer, do you see three central points of dense activity?" Nyba asked in a low hushed voice, and then not waiting for his reply, she asked, "Should we put this data on the holovision in overlay with Whyvvi's chart of this system?"

While he swiveled his chair toward her and she looked toward him, they both remained silent in thought, but then Domyn nodded his big head and said, "I think that would serve us well, Cap. It could focus our decisions to the specific planet, area of space, or perhaps that object. We would need Joculatus to correlate all common points of reference. Perhaps we should go to the Full-Encompass as well. We will need to get a true perspective of how Wolf Streak Beta relates to these spatial bodies and radio wave environment out there."

"Well, Neer Domyn, as always you see the correct design for our needs. Take charge of it. Work with Joculatus and Whyvvi. Get me a working perspective, my friend," Nyba commanded with a smile at the large young man just to her right.

Then her gaze shifted slightly past Swyllo's yellow form toward the lavender figure further on her right alongside the now flickering holovision, and she asked, "Any signal return from the colonial ships, Milyr? Have you confirmed accuracy of our projected message with actual used in their radio residues? Talk to us now of your info. Don't keep new data to yourself."

"That is a vulching problem, Cap," Milyr complained. "So far all older transmissions seem to be degraded into gibberish now. Surely there must be some recent enough to be an audible reference of current language in use. But vulch, I can't find any that I can understand."

"Indeed that is strange," Prof Lyndyn agreed, sitting in his gray chair on Nyba's left. "Perhaps I can listen to your receptions of these residues, Milyr. Could you transfer just those radio transmissions to me? I don't want everything that you are coordinating at this time. I could not decipher the whole input as you can..."

"Just open your ears, Prof," Milyr said. "I can give you those radio transmissions now."

While the two men worked on this, Nyba let her attention drift toward the holovision. Now at the center was a blue dot, a representation of Wolf Streak Beta, she realized. Around this blue dot hung planets, sun, and a very slowly moving red spot. All these spatial objects moved within the three-dimensional globe-like grid as perspective to Wolf Streak Beta changed. Only the blue dot stayed in place. Everything moved around it. Still tech displays of Blue Jay held onto ancient supposition of the craft being the center of space.

Maybe humanity was not ready even in the present to acknowledge we are not center of the universe, hey, she mused silently in a cynical mood, remembering Despoliation of Homeworld, which began exodus of the colonials. Yet Blue Jay was trying to correct such a past mistake to bring humanity together again.

She had never felt comfortable with the slight dizziness and constant almost inverse vision one needed to understand this view. Nyba could not comprehend how pilots and Neers could acclimate to this visually challenging perspective of Full-Encompass view in the holovision. Perhaps that was one reason pilots were often a bit strange themselves, she thought, especially Jamyk, Milyr, Chitir, and Radhin. Yet they managed to cope with this unnerving perspective. Perhaps it was some unique attribute of the male brain, she wondered. But then she remembered that Radhin was a girl. Well, there are always exceptions. Then with a grin, Nyba mused, perhaps dizziness was the norm for pilots. All of the pilots of Blue Jay seemed a bit odd at times to her.

"Jamyk, pilot Wolf Streak Beta on smooth inclination without any hopping about or sudden spinning," Cap Nyba commanded more harshly than she intended. "Let's keep some consistency to this view while we try to read this system and radio waves in it. Where are those waves, Domyn? You've had enough time to get this together."

"Awe help me, just trying to be accurate, Cap. Here they are," Domyn said and his blue dionjocu gloves swayed slightly within her sight.

Then suddenly orbs on the holovision were entrenched within a sparkling miasma of silver and gold colored patterns. Briefly Nyba wished that she had not demanded this mentally confusing portrayal, but soon she overcame her discomfort. Just as she had observed not long ago on her visor, she saw three areas of highly concentrated radio wave usage in this solar system. The perspective had changed with the utilization of Full-Encompass, yet she did see still three distinct areas. Two large concentrations appeared to be toward inner planets of this system, perhaps even on far orbits beyond the sun. Now at least a third of these concentrations centered near the planet to their right from where the red spot had come.

"Awright, Cap, you were correct," Domyn said. "I detect three concentrations of transmissions. The nearest is that small planet in our octant two. This seems unusual since that little planet seems to be farthest from Sexto center. It's not a very strategic location for human activity."

"Long range zeta sensors do indicate that planet as the outer body of Sexto System," Whyvvi confirmed. "I am sure that you realize that planet is one from where the approaching object originated. My most recent sensor reads reveal with strong reliability that the object is some man-made spacecraft. And it is not Fox Flash Alpha…"

Nyba turned to Milyr and asked, "Milyr, any comm from that ship? Any reply to our broadcast?"

"Not yet, Cap," he responded. "I do have a sanbeam ready to send once we get the beacon activated. Erhh… Nyba, do you think I should use a sanbeam to try to contact those colonials?"

"We have not surveyed any sanbeam usage in this system, Cap," Domyn stated. "I do not believe that they have that technology. Do you know of any historical evidence or tale that such neutrino technology was available at years of the colonial departure from the Zerosolis System?"

"I do not," Nyba replied, and then swinging toward the gray figure at her left, she asked, "Prof, do you have an opinion on the likelihood of sanbeam tech in pre-colonial exodus years?"

Momentarily the man in gray seemed absorbed in his study within his dionboda cap and visor, but shortly Prof Lyndyn proclaimed, "No doubt your knowledge of that era is at least as complete as mine, Cap Nyba. I do not believe that neutrino research had advanced to useful technology until decades after the Despoliation had begun to wane. We all no doubt recall that ancestors of these colonials departed the Zerosolis System before the Despoliation was well advanced. However, I do believe that radio transmissions that sounded as gibberish to Milyr may be actually in some pattern. Although I can't determine what it means. No doubt it is not an anticipated language even allowing for several generations of modification..."

"I'll check it again when I get a chance, Prof," Milyr said. "Right now I want to be ready to receive any incoming comm. From somebody out there... colonials... Fox Flash...weird aliens...vulching anybody... Perhaps then sanbeam is not a cherp plan now, is it?"

Feeling a bit sorry for Milyr's disappointment, Nyba said, "At this time, Milyr, do not send by sanbeam to that unknown ship. Yet, as you get time, you can prepare such comm. Just in case we discover it could be useful. That was a good idea, Milyr. We should be able to comm with MisCom soon. Make sure you are ready to sanbeam that as soon as we can."

Domyn suggested, "Should be only a few minutes now before Joculatus confirms the Buffalardi beacon deployment and connection to the relay chain."

"This is heartening," Doc Kymil sighed, sitting in her white chair between Domyn and Swyllo. I'm starting to feel that we are alone out here in Sexto, so far away from our fellow humans at Steppingstone Quinto. I know that sounds foolish with a possible spaceship approaching, but this silence is annoying and frustration. Not even a message from Fox Flash Alpha. It's very unnerving."

"Vulch, I feel the same, Doc," Swyllo said. "I wish they would talk to us. Are you sure you are doing the comm right, Milyr?"

"Vulch, yeah, tiny fem..." Milyr grumbled sourly.

"Awright, people," Domyn growled in a firm voice. "We are doing everything as we practiced. We must be patient. There could be many explanations as to delay in responses from the colonials or from Fox Flash Alpha. We will be able to signal MisCom soon. Let's not get nasty uncherp now."

Satisfied and thankful by Domyn's intrusion, Cap Nyba refrained from barking out a harsher comment and instead smiled to herself as she listened to Swyllo inquire in shrill amusement, "Nasty uncherp? Neer Domyn, this sounds so...uncherp...when you say it."

As a few other people snickered and chuckled, Whyvvi said more stoically, "I do believe, Cap, the spaceship is heading for intersection with our course. More recent sensor reads indicate that the hull is definitely artificial and constructed very much as exteriors common to design of the colony super ships. There are many extrusions jutting from outer hull. Most likely this ship is of Hy-Fu propulsion design. Many of extrusions could be particle collectors."

"Indeed that would make sense. Hydrogen ion fusion propulsion was the way of those times, at least for pioneers willing to depart the Zerosolis System for exceedingly long voyages into the galaxy," Prof Lyndyn said, and then spinning his chair toward Doc Kymil, inquired, "Kymil, my kindred spirit, would you listen to these radio signals that puzzle Milyr? You have always had a good ear for sound patterns. This is one of many abilities which make you a very good doctor. I can transfer these sounds to you, so we won't bother Milyr at this time…"

Ignoring Prof Lyndyn's continuing comments, Nyba asked, "Whyvvi, did you ask Joculatus for correlation with files of the colony super ships? This is of importance, knowing if ship is of Hy-Fu propulsion. Perhaps outer extrusions can be correlated with files of the colony design also."

At the same time, Nyba observed the slow-moving red spot on the holovision approach the likely intersection point along the current vector of Wolf Streak Beta toward the sun. Her eyes saw other planets of this system, especially the super gas giant that almost demanded attention by its dominating size. However, she focused her observation to the gradually moving red spot. For a moment, locations and orbits of the planets was not of significance to her. This probable first contact with colonials captured her immediate focus.

To her left, Nyba heard Whyvvi report, "Cap, Joculatus and I have compared various file images of silhouettes of structure types of pre-exodus era. The correlation is high indicating that this unknown is of similar construction and design as super colony ships. It is not either Cotto Rucci or Letta Vazza. We know this due to the difference of mass, size, and silhouette configuration."

"If a vulching spaceship is colonial, then why don't they answer our comm?" Milyr asked in some frustration. "My signal to them is on the right frequency and should be close enough to their present language for them to know that we are trying to communicate. Why won't they answer?"

Meanwhile Nyba observed the radio wave representation on the holovision. Definitely, she realized, there was a concentration of waves near the small planet now receding in their octant two. She had no doubt that Milyr had read the correct frequency of those radio waves to signal toward that ship. He was very good at his primary duty. That spaceship should be receiving a message of Wolf Streak Beta. Then she wondered with growing concern, why did they not reply?

"Neer Domyn, shouldn't we be able to sanbeam with our recent Buffalardi by now?" Nyba asked in agitation, not happy with the pace of developments, and then as her gaze glimpsed Doc Kymil on the far side of Domyn, she added, "Doc, have you discovered anything from listening to Prof's radio transmission patterns?"

Domyn replied first, "Awe, yes, we should have received a deployment signal by now. It is possible that the Buffalardi needed to travel farther than we anticipated for contact with the relay chain. Remember, deployments from LaOgres were put out of sequence with a problem near Gullu Mette. This differential in timing sequence could have caused differential in distance spacing as well. Our recent Buffalardi would not deploy the beacons until reaching a pre-calibrated distance from previous beacon."

"Do you think the alleged differential in timing or distance spacing could explain our lack of signal from the last deployment of Fox Flash Alpha?" Nyba asked. "Could they have launched the Buffalardi, which needed to travel much farther toward the relay chain before deploying its beacons? Could those beacons be out of range to get a signal to us when we popped into Sexto?"

She watched his face frown in thought beneath the visor over his eye and then Domyn replied, "Awe only knows, perhaps, but I'm skeptical. Normally the range of activation of a signal is much more distant than the range of a beacon deployment. Our presence in Sexto space was long enough in time to have triggered a signal from a very distant beacon, or at least I think so. We don't know how far away the last established beacon is in space."

"Then it's cherp that we launched our own Buffalardi to complete the relay chain back to Steppingstone Quinto," Swyllo said.

"Maybe we should launch another," Whyvvi suggested. "We have two more in our inventory. They will not do us any service there."

While she listened to the discussion, Nyba watched the planets and overlaying radio wave images very slowly flow backwards in perspective to a blue dot in the center of the holovision. Only a red spot travelled in some conjunction with the blue dot. The two blinking colors seemed surely to be on intersecting vectors. How long before that occurred, she wondered, and is this the outcome which she desired at this time in mission?

Domyn said, "No, we don't want to launch another so soon. Let's give our Buffalardi the opportunity to align with the relay chain. It could be there any second now. It is still in easy range to serve as a sanbeam relay to Quinto. Just wait a short time more."

"Milyr, do you have that sanbeam prepped with the updated message?" Nyba asked the young man dressed still in his sweat-stained lavender dionjocu, and then before he could reply, she said, "Oh, I'm sure you do. Just be ready for an instant sending when we get the chance. Oh, yes, Milyr, did you think to include this recording of the holovision and some of Whyvvi's sensor reads of the other spacecraft? All of that would be of interest to MisCom. Do you have this ready?"

With confused petulance in his voice, Milyr reported, "Of course, Cap Nyba. I'm using a lot of Tier Two to get those recordings into short comm. But I don't guarantee such a short message now. Our data is growing fast while we wait for beacon activation. I may have to edit data records soon if we want a short, tight sanbeam. That's your decision of course, Cap Nyba."

"Do the best you can. Neer Domyn promises we'll have an active relay chain soon. I believe him," Nyba said with confidence that she hoped could encourage the crew. "You will be ready, Milyr. I know you will. Just as I know you've sent the best possible message to those colonials out there."

"If they are colonials," Swyllo retorted shrilly. "They seem to be ignoring us."

"Indeed their radio transmissions are on common human frequencies used during the time of the colony ship exodus," Prof Lyndyn said. "No doubt some advancement has been made in their communication technology, but unless they needed to overcome some catastrophic crisis, they would not likely develop any new sci-tech that much different from what had functioned in the past…"

"Oh my, these radio signals do sound very much like gibberish without comprehensible meaning," Doc Kymil stated while she cupped her hands over the cap layer over her ears to block out the filtered sounds from her hearing. "Yet there are sequences of repetition as I listen over time. There are patterns of gibberish. Much like listening to faulty blood flows or hampered breathing, if I listen long enough, some order can be deciphered from the disorder."

"You just used the term 'deciphered,' Doc. Are you thinking these radio waves could be in code?" Whyvvi asked from her red chair where she was very actively working her pink dionjocu gloves with her own sensor duty.

"In code? Why would they need to encode their transmissions? And most of these residual radio waves have been floating in this space long before we popped," Nyba asked with some disbelief. "Prof, Doc, does this make sense based on what you are hearing? Neer Domyn, does this make reasonable sense based on what we see on this holovision?"

Before anyone replied, Joculatus said, "Neer Domyn, our Buffalardi has deployed its beacons."

"Vulching cherp!" Milyr cried out. "Should I sanbeam to Quinto, Cap?"

"Of course," Nyba declared.

"Sanbeam message is sent now," Milyr reported with a sigh of relief, "Joculatus, confirm sending and then notify Cap Nyba of the reception by beacon."

Swyllo chirped in delight, "Finally we can send our message. Perhaps now someone to my right can be allowed to shower and put on some fresher clothes."

"Oh, no!" cried Whyvvi suddenly. "My sensors just picked up an explosion in space where our Buffalardi deployed."

"Can you portray anything on the holovision?" Nyba asked, startled by this development.

"No, Nyba, too far..." Whyvvi stammered.

Then Joculatus reported, "Cap Nyba, there is no reception of our sanbeam by beacons."

"Joculatus, is there confirmation that our beacons deployed?" Milyr asked hastily.

Joculatus replied, "Milyr, there is no confirmation that our beacons deployed now. The prior report of deployment was in error."

"Vulch!" Swyllo swore.

"Then we are still alone in this Sexto System," Whyvvi murmured in disconsolation.

"Nope," Jamyk rasped, pointing at the holovision, "them."

Nyba's eyes followed his pointing hand. The red spot was getting nearer. Was this going to be a cherp meeting, she wondered? Was her legacy as captain of Wolf Streak Beta going to be a cherp one? Nyba did not know at that moment, and her intuition was just as uncertain as her awareness.

"This is not cherp," Swyllo muttered sourly.

"Nope," Jamyk rasped, "nasty!"

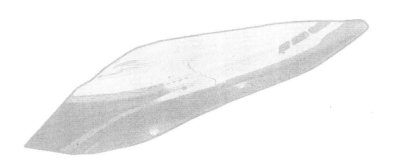

Spec Two: Nyba to Sexto
Chapter 17

"The Buffalardi beacons are gone," Domyn cried out with dismay.

"Are you sure?"

"Joculatus, confirm trace signal from the last deployed Buffalardi beacons," Domyn commanded from a brown chair to Nyba's right.

Briefly her eyes studied the octant three of the holovision as Cap Nyba attempted to see space where the beacons should be in position at the end of the relay chain stretching twenty-nine light years back to Steppingstone Quinto. Nothing, she observed, not even a recent flash of explosion reported by Whyvvi not a minute ago. Could Whyvvi have been mistaken?

Male voice of artigence Joculatus replied, "Neer Domyn, there is no trace signal from any Buffalardi beacons in this region of space."

"Vulch, didn't you say beacons had deployed? They should be there," Swyllo said in a high-pitched squeal, and Nyba heard a hint of fear in the girl's tone.

Also hearing agitation in the girl's voice, Cap Nyba declared as firmly as she could in spite of her own similar feeling, "Well, men and women, let's not allow this apparent problem discourage us. We have two Buffalardi in our inventory still. We can deploy beacons again. Yet first let's try to reason why the last exploded. Neer Domyn, has propulsion unit on the Buffalardi or beacon ever misfired or exploded on deployment?"

With his tan-gloved fingers working busily at whatever sensor search, which he studied at that moment in his one visor over his eye, Domyn said, "Cap Nyba, I do not recall any such mishap in deployment of the Buffalardi beacons in the

Blue Jay program since Turkey Trot's voyage to Quinto System. Prof, do you remember any faulty deployment history prior to your mission in Turkey Trot?"

As he said this, Nyba returned her attention to the blinking red spot on the holovision. An unknown object was moving closer to the course vector of Wolf Streak Beta. Whatever, or whoever, it was would intersect their route, perhaps in less than an hour. The object, maybe spaceship if Whyvvi's sensor reads were accurate, had not changed vector or velocity since its portrayal on the holovision. Were they colonials? Was Whyvvi's correlation with old files of the colony ships correct? Nyba wondered, if this was so, then why did they not answer Milyr's consistent signal?

"...no doubt in my memory that in the mission before Turkey Trot's journey to Quinto, there were no reported explosions of beacons after deployment by the Buffalardi," Prof Lyndyn was saying from a gray chair to Nyba's left. "Over decades Blue Jay has had very good record of highly precise and finely tuned sci-tech equipment. I do not recall..."

Interrupting him Nyba asked, "Whyvvi, did you record the explosion? Did you see any specific data on your sensor read that could tell us anything about what happened?"

"No, Cap Nyba, I am sorry," Whyvvi replied apologetically. "I was concentrating on getting more sensor reads from that spaceship out there. I did not think to track the beacons with specific sensors. However, energy release of the explosion was powerful enough to imprint on general sensor reads of this broad setting. That sensor program is in constant search as you requested..."

"Nyba," Domyn interjected abruptly, "any energy release of that magnitude would be much more powerful than the likely energy release of an accidental explosion of the beacon propulsion generator or beacon itself. Blue Jay beacons do not carry or store a large quantity of energy to cause such explosion, at least not enough to be picked up by a sensor search pattern diffuse enough to read the entire solar system. That would be too broad and too nonspecific for such a sensor read."

"Indeed such a search would not read small objects or small energy releases. No, no, only planet and moon, and oh, yes, maybe asteroids would show up on this large-scale sensor search," Prof Lyndyn agreed in his nasal voice.

"Then, oh my, that spaceship must be quite large to be read by the current sensor program," Doc Kymil stated from her white chair just beyond Domyn. "And I would think such a large ship would have adequate reception equipment to receive our signals. The radio waves local to this region of the Sexto System are consistently garbled, but in an organized pattern, if that makes any sense?"

"That's interesting, Doc, but I need to focus on completing the Buffalardi relay system and getting message back to MisCom. They need to know that we arrived at Sexto and may have found the colonials," Cap Nyba declared, trying not to discourage the older woman of forty-nine years. "Could you work with Prof on Tier Three to study that radio signal dilemma more thoroughly without distracting the rest of us? Perhaps Milyr could listen in should you need his expertise as long as he can continue his attempt to contact the spaceship out there."

"Of course I can, Nyba," Milyr called loudly. "I'm a comm expert! I can readily handle multiple conversations at once. And perhaps still pester the tiny fem here."

"Vulching keep those long arms to your work, you toxx. I need to keep harvesting light energy from that sun," Swyllo retorted from her yellow chair.

"That's an excellent recommendation, Cap Nyba," exclaimed Prof Lyndyn. "Don't you agree, my kindred spirit? We can focus on these strange radio signals. I believe some are now current. Yet they do not resonate with clarity. There is some interference or perhaps…"

"Prof, please go to Tier Three with Doc," Nyba pleaded with growing impatience as she worried about lack of communication capability with Steppingstone Quinto. "Now, men and women, we need to prep for another Buffalardi launch. I see no alternative but to attempt another deployment. We must complete that relay chain back to Quinto."

"We don't know yet why the last beacons exploded," Domyn said. "Now we are farther away from Kil-Kol and region of space most aligned with the existing relay chain. We will also need to calculate various trajectories that account for gravitational pulls of planets in this system. Our launching of the Buffalardi will be more complicated now than when we first entered Debordo space. Joculatus and I would need more time to calculate the launch trajectory."

"I'm certain that you and Joculatus are capable. We can perform a more complicated launch within the system. After all remember that we've popped through the nasty Kil-Kol around mass of Gullu Mette. We can do this," Cap Nyba stated more convinced as seconds passed that the message with Quinto must be finalized. "Swyllo, how is our energy supply? You've been harvesting busily since we popped. What's our status?"

"Almost 73 percent. Still long way from the maximum harvest potential of that sun, but we get good steady harvest as we approach. With Jamyk's steady course and not lot of wild zigzagging, like someone else likes to do, we're not using more energy than I collect," Swyllo reported with a snicker toward Milyr.

"Well, you are telling me that we are getting more than we are using since we popped into Sexto," Cap Nyba said confidently. "Then our energy supply is acceptable to make some vector maneuvers if necessary for a clear launch."

While she spoke, Nyba observed the holovision, which depicted a gradual shift in the relationship between the blue dot in the center, the red spot drawing closer, and the small planet they had passed upon entering the Sexto System. Now the planet was almost between Wolf Streak Beta and an area of space around Kil-Kol from where they had popped. Both the blue dot and red spot had flown closer to the distant sun of the Sexto System. Their paths were definitely on intersecting vectors.

For once Jamyk had kept Wolf Streak Beta on the course vector that she had commanded, Nyba thought in mild surprise, and then she asked, "Neer Domyn, will you need to alter our path to get the most effective launch trajectory for our next Buffalardi? Will that planet interfere with the launch?"

"Not unless its gravity is much stronger than normal for a planet of that size. A slight pull from such small planet is easy to account for in our pre-launch calculations," Domyn replied, but then with worry in his tone, asked, "But, Cap, do you think we should launch again before knowing why our beacons exploded? Is there a need to rush this action before we know more?"

Having been pondering this herself, Nyba was in doubt, yet her sense of mission protocol prompted her to state, "We should complete the Buffalardi relay chain back to Quinto. That should have been first duty of Fox Flash Alpha. For some reason, they did not, so now it is up to us. MisCom needs to know what's happening here in Sexto. I believe that we can do this, and at the same time, continue with our attempt to communicate with that colonial spaceship, which is our main mission."

"Vulch, we've been signaling them, Nyba. They just don't answer," Milyr griped from his purple chair. "The vulchers are just silent. I don't know why they can't hear us."

"Cap, we don't want to launch another and then lose that also," Domyn persisted. "We need to know what happened to our original beacons. We need to get a better sensor data of that region."

"How?" Cap Nyba asked, trying not to let her frustration show in her voice. "We are using zeta sensors now, aren't we, Whyvvi? How can we get more precise than that?"

"Reverse," Jamyk rasped from his green chair. "Back."

"Go back there? Abort our imminent contact with that colonial ship? Are you serious?" Nyba asked, hearing her own incredulous whine resound in the ConCen. "We can do both at once, I'm sure on our present course. Let's not withdraw from our mission, boys and girls."

To her right, a tan figure swayed his brown chair nervously, and Domyn said, "We would get a much clearer picture of what happened to our beacons, Cap Nyba. Milyr can continue communication attempts as we go. You said yourself that establishing communication with Quinto was most important. But should we launch blind, not knowing what happened?"

On the holovision, the red spot was getting closer. Kil-Kol region was out of the scene now. They should do all these activities at once, Nyba thought to herself. Why couldn't they, they were Blue Jayers? Why couldn't Domyn see that now? His suggestions were valid, she realized, yet her determination to proceed with the current course seemed right to her. Or, she abruptly wondered, was she resisting the alternative action because Jamyk had first mentioned it? Was she letting her mistrust of his competency cloud her own foresight and judgment?

Not sure of the answer, but confident of Domyn's expertise and reliability, Cap Nyba said with subdued authority, "Perhaps you are correct, Neer Domyn. Let's swing back there and get better data. Jamyk, change our route. Get your coordinates from Joculatus, who should have a precise record on his Tier Two recording. Don't make our flight change sudden or threatening to that other spaceship. We don't want to seem inhospitable to them."

"Yup," Jamyk rasped with mild relief in his creaking voice. "Jocu...confirm."

Joculatus said, "Pilot Jamyk, confirming the record of the beacon original coordinates with you now."

As she watched the boy's green dionjocu gloves flutter fingers and sway gently to the right, the scene on the holovision swirled gradually in the opposite direction. All planets on the holovision pivoted around the blue dot still in the center. The blinking red spot moved likewise and began to fall perceptively behind. The small planet revolved around the blue dot until it was the foremost object in the holovision. Jamyk's movements were subtle and controlled.

"Vulch, that's a nasty change of view, little peener," Milyr moaned yet with boyish delight in his voice. "Cherp go around, really vulching smooth ride as good as I could do."

241

"Oh, really? You big oaf, you are never cherp smooth," Swyllo grumbled. "This ride now makes my harvesting more troublesome, little onad. But I'll adapt and realign my hull collectors back to that sun. Just pilot as smooth as this big toxx thinks he is. Don't use up all my energy."

Thankful that spinning on the holovision had ended, and thus grudgingly was pleased with Jamyk's relatively smooth, as Milyr had termed, maneuver, Nyba inquired, "Domyn, would we be more precise if we changed the perspective away from this full Sexto System view to a more confined view? Whyvvi, do you have data enough to give us a clearer, more descriptive look at the other spaceship, if we go to a more confined view of this space?"

Replying first Domyn stated, "Yes, Cap Nyba, we will see much more accurate detail by narrowing our perspective. We don't need to see the rest of this solar system on our holovision for the moment. Whyvvi, I recommend adopting a perspective of the confined Full-Encompass that puts that spacecraft in the holovision as well as the Kil-Kol reference. Nothing outside that view sphere is important for now. Do you agree, Cap Nyba?"

"Yes, that is a cherp plan. Do it, Whyvvi. And get me a tighter zoom of the spaceship for viewing in my visor while the rest of you are researching the question of our exploding beacons," Nyba commanded as she flipped the visor down before her eye, and then another thought occurred to her, and she asked, "Whyvvi, you reported previously of sensing one explosion, didn't you? We deployed two beacons with that Buffalardi. Why was there only one explosion and yet we get no trace signal from any beacon? Neer, add that to your investigation."

"Awright, Cap, that's another mystery," Domyn responded. "Though it's possible both beacons exploded at the same time while very close together just after the deployment. We'll check that possibility if we can. Whyvvi, are you ready for some puzzle solving?"

When the holovision changed suddenly, Nyba saw on the far side of the blue central dot one planet against the blackness of deep space. Much larger in the holovision now than before, the planet showed a grayish, brown surface pock-marked with craters, which had smashed into low rolling ridges of mountains much like file pictures of Luna from the Zerosolis System before colonization by humans 300 years ago. No sign of cloud formation or icy poles, Nyba noticed, probably no atmosphere of consequence. Why had the colonial spaceship been in orbit around that planet? Why had that desolate orb been one of the centers of radio wave activity in the Sexto System? Not able to answer these questions at that moment, her frustration grew.

"Our companion out there seems to want to stay with us. Yet they will not return my comm," Milyr commented with unusual restraint, and then Nyba noticed his slackened shoulders sagging against the purple chair. "Vulchers just don't want to be friendly, I guess."

Observing his wet patches of sweat seeping through the dionjocu and sluggish movements of his long arms over the tops of his long legs, Nyba realized suddenly just how exhausted the young man had become. After a lengthy duration of flying Wolf Streak Beta, Milyr had then continued on duty as communication primary. The young man had been trying valiantly to contact colonials with varying signals and programmed strategies and at the same time work with Prof and Doc and also attempt to formulate a message to be sent to MisCom. All of his effort was for success of the mission, Nyba thought, and for her. Now his efforts were revealing his weariness, yet he continued still. Nyba was impressed with the lanky young man, as big toxx as he frequently could be.

"Milyr, put your communications on auto and send our originally programmed message to the colonials. I can see that you need physical rest. You can aid me with analyzing that spaceship out there. If they won't respond to us by some form of communication, then we'll have to study them visually with Whyvvi's sensors," Nyba declared, trying to relieve Milyr from his current duty without indicating displeasure toward him.

With a sigh of exaggerated relief, Milyr wiggled his lavender gloves a few more times, and then as he let his arms dangle down the sides of the chair, almost touching the floor, he said. "Thanks, Cap, even with my primo muscular body, my arms are vulching tired. I might be too tired to lift up my arm to cuddle with this young fem in the yellow suit beside me."

"Vulch, don't even joke about that, you toxx," Swyllo giggled while she turned her chair away from Milyr and moved her fingers and hands in concentration of her energy harvesting.

"Yup," snorted Jamyk on the other side of the three-dimensional holovision. "Toxx!"

Boy's comment irritated Nyba, but when she began to turn her glare at him, she noticed directly before her a large red spot portrayed on the holovision. Setting closely to her position at center of the semi-circle of chairs surrounding this side of the holovision, a red spot invited attention. Now with the confined focus of the Full-Encompass view, a red spot did look more like a spaceship. Like a small planet, a clearer silhouette detail could be seen now. It was no longer just a blinking red spot. It had followed the blue dot in the center of the scene.

"Follow," Jamyk said in a hoarse grunt. "Steady."

"Yeah, tiny onad, whoever they are, they seem to want us," Milyr agreed. "They changed their route to stay with us. Must be a ship filled with bodacious colonial fems who discovered we're here, hey, little peener? No doubt they desire our manly bodies."

"Big," giggled Jamyk, and then more seriously rasped, "doubt...good."

Then her visor flickered on, and Cap Nyba viewed a more detailed and enlarged spaceship as Whyvvi said, "I am sorry for the delay, Cap Nyba. I should have had this for you sooner. This is the most current data provided by my sensors. I do read residue trail suggesting that the ship uses some form of Hy-Fu propulsion still. But I cannot read which particles they use for fuel. Perhaps they still use hydrogen or separated ions or even spergits. I do not have that degree of precision yet. I would need to send other zeta ray sensor searches in order to concentrate for that degree of precision."

While Whyvvi reported this, Milyr chuckled across to Jamyk, "Yeah, onad, you're probably right. Any bodacious fems on that ship won't be cherp for us. We're such primo men..."

Ignoring the boyish banter, Cap Nyba said, "Whyvvi, stay on the sensor searches with Domyn. We need that data. This new info on the colony ship will give us something to study. Oh, yes, as soon as you can get reads of that planet. I want to know why the other ship was interested in it. Such info may be of importance. They had some reason to be orbiting that little planet. Let's try to discover why."

"Argh! Nasty of you, you toxx," Swyllo yelled to Milyr.

"Okay now, men women, and Jamyk," Nyba exclaimed partially in humor but mostly in annoyance at the increasing childish banter. "Let's focus on our functions. Milyr, get your thoughts off the fems inside of that ship and help me form some idea of its outer structure and capabilities."

"Straight," Jamyk declared soberly. "Line."

"Hey, yeah! That's right, Cap, if it uses Hy-Fu propulsion, then they must fly linear patterns forward only most likely," Milyr exclaimed enthusiastically. "Cherp read, little peener, but then the pilot would think of that. We can dance circles around them with our grav propulsion."

Heartened by Milyr's renewed spirit, Nyba pushed aside her initial disgruntlement over Jamyk's intrusion and said, "That is a cherp finding but for now. Let's stay on the straight trajectory to coordinates wherethe beacons deployed briefly. Hear that, Jamyk? No dancing around now."

"Yup," the boy agreed. "Straight."

"Cherp, let's not annoy them. They are probably confused by our sudden change in course. Right now they are following at a steady pace. At least they are not breaking contact. Milyr, prep your visor to receive Whyvvi's latest close-up of spaceship. It's quite interesting," Nyba commanded, peering at the very relaxed, lanky figure slouched into his purple chair.

His long, slightly square-jawed face turned toward her and his one exposed eye stared into hers as Milyr said almost languidly, "Hey, yeah, Nyba, that would be so cherp after seeing and hearing so much electromag signals. This will surely get me stirred into action. Anything for you, Cap Nyba!"

"I'm so glad, Milyr," Nyba said sarcastically. "I always try to stir you into action. It is my main duty as Cap. Now get that brain of yours to work and find out why they follow us, but don't talk to us."

"Maybe the women on that spaceship are telepathic and can read your mind, Milyr," Swyllo giggled. "Your few thoughts could discourage any sensible female from attempting an encounter with you. They probably already know what a big nasty toxx oaf you are."

"Oh, yeah, very funny, tiny fem," grumbled Milyr.

Before he could continue this banter, Nyba asked firmly, "Do you have a view on your visor yet, Milyr? Can you identify any structures that could be transmission arrays for radio signals that we've surveyed? Let's go, young man, help me here."

In her own visor, Nyba saw the overall cylindrical shape of the spaceship and numerous protrusions jutting out around the outer hull. This was typical, she recalled, of linear design of spaceships during the ancient century of Despoliation when solid state, nuclear, and eventually Hy-Fu propulsion were standard. Her interest of the past history of Despoliation was useful now, she realized. Linear design equated to linear movement just as Jamyk had recently suggested. This was consistent with the notion that this was possibly a colonial spaceship.

"Vulch, what a nasty-looking monstrosity," Milyr remarked. "That vulcher sure doesn't look as smooth and graceful as our Wolf Streak Beta on the outside. Some of those funnel-shaped things could be and old-style radar or perhaps radio transmitters. But I'm not sure. Technology of that era was very unsightly. Electromag radio transmissions could be coming from any of those ridiculous-looking prongs. Vulching ugly design, that is for sure."

"Ho, ho, that's big help, Milyr," Nyba retorted sarcastically. "Some of those wider extensions should be scoops for particulate matter in space to be used as fuel in Hy-Fu engines. There is a sign of some moving parts, there, do you see?"

"Yeah, hey, yeah, Nyba, look at those long prongs extending outwards," Milyr exclaimed with excitement. "Vulch, they look like they are erecting upwards from the hull, almost like our Wilchrison. No, wait…not erecting… Nyba, see the flash…those vulchers are launching…"

In her visor, Nyba observed one elongated extrusion move away from the spaceship, then another. A plume of incandescent propulsion trailed out the back ends of these objects. Gradually the launched tube-shaped projectiles sped away from the larger ship. Two, no, three, as there was another visible from behind the mastership, of these ancient rocket-like projectiles veered away into space from the mastership. Their velocity was much faster than the mastership.

"What vulch?" Milyr swore incredulously. "What are those things? Can we track them on the holovision, Cap? Whyvvi, are you reading those vulchers?"

"Awright, Milyr, enough, Whyvvi can read only so much focused data with her sensors. You know that," Domyn growled patiently but with firmness. "Cap, we can adapt our sensor focus to new objects if you wish. We've seen very little during our observation of space where our beacons exploded."

Too many differing variables on which to focus, Nyba complained to herself, and then with a mildly steady voice inquired, "Neer, what have you discovered so far? Do we know what happened to our Buffalardi beacons? Can we afford to alter the sensor focus to these new objects?"

"Awright, Cap, yes, let's track the new phenomena. We can't ignore anything that the spaceship does or launched. We can always get another survey when we get closer to the beacon location. I do have some data of interest, but let's search our friends out there for now," Domyn recommended.

"Whyvvi, reconfigure the sensors to search for objects of a smaller scale. You'll read the correct setting when you can portray new projectiles on the holovision… Jamyk, keep us steady on the vector toward the region of space where the beacons were destroyed. We still need to finish that investigation. We still need to deploy new beacons soon," Nyba commanded, glancing toward the pink figure and green form sitting side by side to her far left.

"Yup," Jamyk grunted hoarsely. "Steady."

As she spun her blue chair back toward Domyn on her right, Nyba heard Prof Lyndyn suggest, "No doubt Milyr should listen in on their radio frequency now to check for any ongoing transmissions. I'm quite certain that I am hearing signals passing from the big ship to those smaller ones. My communication expertise is not sufficient to this task. Milyr should be..."

"Yes, Milyr, do it," Nyba commanded, thinking how fortunate Wolf Streak Beta was to have such a gifted young man to perform these related challenges, and then she asked toward the other young man to her right, "Neer Domyn, what have you learned so far about our beacons?"

As she allowed her eye to peak at the present holovision and nearing the planet beyond the blue center dot, Nyba listened to Domyn report, "Well, there is a large residue of radioactive matter and energy signature in vicinity of where our beacons should be. There is nothing remotely recognizable now as possible composite from our beacons. Everything there was totally destroyed into elemental particles. However, definite high radiation covers that part of space."

"Our Buffalardi beacons don't use radioactive fuels or materials," Nyba exclaimed with certainty. "They could not have caused the explosion then. Do you know what could?"

"Not really," Domyn admitted. "However, Whyvvi did notice some unusual surveys from the planet out there. She can report more thoroughly on that than I..."

"She's busy at the moment, Neer," Nyba snapped abruptly. "You tell me what she found. I don't need all the science detail. Just give me simple info."

Before he replied, the holovision fluttered briefly and then familiar objects, a planet, red spaceship silhouette, and a blue dot were accompanied by three tiny red dots. These new arrivals to the scene were encircling the blue dot from behind. Their velocities had allowed them to gain position in three directions around Wolf Streak Beta's course. The larger red spaceship had fallen behind now. A distant planet had approached nearer. Nyba saw that the new red dots appeared to be holding similar distances from Wolf Streak Beta and now matching the velocity.

"What the vulch are they doing?" Swyllo chirped.

"Could be some escort of their greeting ceremony," Doc Kymil suggested. "Or perhaps they are wary of approaching us. We probably look quite alien to them. Wolf Streak Beta's appearance is nothing like any that the colonials have seen."

"Nope," Jamyk declared emphatically. "Fox."

"Let's not get distracted, boys and girls," Nyba demanded, annoyed with their constant tendency to get astray of her focus. "Neer Domyn, what did Whyvvi discover? Is it of significance to our destroyed beacons? Does it tell us anything about those people out there with us? Tell me!"

Whyvvi exclaimed forcefully, "Cap Nyba, I should report that information. I can now. This holovision can now go to auto-scan with Joculatus to continue the updating of surveys."

"Ho, okay, report," Nyba demanded bluntly and impatiently as she watched the three red dots remain fixed on the holovision in relationship to the central blue dot. "I see we've moved ahead of our former companion spaceship. They don't seem to want to go where we go now. Why?"

As the larger red mastership vanished from the outer arc of the scene, Milyr said, "Nyba, they are talking back and forth between the big ship and tiny vulchers."

"Okay, okay, Milyr," Nyba blurted sternly and then calmed herself slightly when she said, "Let me get Whyvvi's report. I want to know why that ship was orbiting the small planet... Whyvvi, what did you learn?"

"I do not know what they were doing there, but I do know that the surface of that planet is very strongly radioactive. There are traces of the most radiant elements throughout the surface crust," Whyvvi stated matter-of-factly from her red chair beside Jamyk.

"Critical masses, Whyvvi, what about critical masses?" Prof Lyndyn asked from his chair between Whyvvi and Nyba, who heard a tremor of concern in the nasal voice.

"I found no sign of any critical mass density. The entire surface is thinly spread with radiant elements. There was no indication of recent fission energy release," Whyvvi said while Nyba eyed the approaching planet and escort of tiny red dots on the holovision.

"Not on the planet," Domyn said. "But surely in space where our beacons had deployed."

"Vulching colonials were after radioactive materials," Swyllo declared. "There's no other reason to go around that nasty-looking planet."

"Why? Why would they use nasty radiants?" Nyba inquired and then said, "At the time of the exodus of their ancestors from the Zerosolis System, use of radiants was banned in much of the world after decades of Despoliation. Not even precisely designed nuclear fission reactors for energy production was permitted during that era after careless use of radiants for weapons had soured people on positive uses of nuclear energy. The colonial spacers would most likely have brought that revulsion with them into their journey. That is correct, isn't it, Prof?"

"Indeed most likely..." Prof Lyndyn started to say.

However, Whyvvi harshly interrupted his nasal drone to say, "We should not look for long-lost attitudes now. We just need to know that these people orbited the planet with radioactive elements. There are many industrial and scientific uses for radiants. This speculation does not tell us why or how nuclear explosion destroyed our beacons. There is no evidence that planet or that spaceship did it."

"Nope," Jamyk said, and then carefully pointing with a small hand gesture, said, "There."

His hand movement was hampered by his pilot function, but Nyba did see a slight gesture and looked toward the holovision. There, not far from the planet, was a fourth red dot. Perhaps it had been hidden by the planet, she wondered, or maybe its tiny size and distance had not triggered its appearance in sensor surveys creating the holovision. Whatever, she realized soon there would be four red dots around the blue dot, four ships around Wolf Streak Beta. That is, she reminded herself, if these were ships.

"Vulch, this doesn't feel cherp," Swyllo muttered sourly.

"The toxx vulchers out there are talking vulching ramble between them," Milyr announced in agitation. "I don't know what they are saying, but they are talking in their coded radio-waves. That big toxx ship is in talk, too."

"Did you get any idea about these probable encoded transmissions, Prof or Doc?" Nyba asked not at all comfortable with the developing situation. "Do you hear any sense of tone or manner, Milyr, in their transmissions? Can you interpret such nuances from what you hear?"

"Vulch, Nyba, I'm not Prof with his psycho-smarts or Jamyk with his intuition. This just sounds like nasty gibberish to me," Milyr griped with evident stress and disappointment in his voice, feeling that Nyba could empathize with the young man.

"Perhaps they worry about us going into a dangerous zone in this space," Whyvvi suggested. "We have not determined what did destroy our beacons. We do not know everything about this space. As we discovered in LaOgres recently, our knowledge about unexplored spaces is not always complete or accurate. We should not assume that we know everything about every region of space."

"Are you saying that some unknown spatial anomaly destroyed our beacons?" Nyba asked, trying not to let her own skepticism show in her voice. "And that these ships are here to warn us? Is that likely, Whyvvi? They won't or can't even communicate with us."

"Vulch, it does seem nasty unbelievable," retorted Swyllo.

The fourth red dot approached from the direction of the cratered planet. This brownish planet was near enough now to show its rotation in the holovision. The other three red dots shadowed the blue dot, their distance constant now from Wolf Streak Beta. This was annoying behavior, Nyba thought, especially since these other ships did not return comms. Why did they do this? What was their intention? If Whyvvi was correct and Wolf Streak Beta was in some naturally occurring jeopardy, then why did these people not communicate? Were they people at all, she wondered suddenly.

"Cap Nyba, those three escort ships have ceased propulsion," Whyvvi announced. "They are coasting now only."

Domyn spun toward her and said with wonder, "I'm surprised that they were able to make their fuel last as long as they did. At the velocity that they kept to pace us, those little ships must have burned all their fuel, whatever it was, just to get here with us."

"Hy-Fu propulsion can go a long way, Neer," Prof Lyndyn remarked.

"Yes, it can, Prof, yet those small ships could not have a large reserve supply, nor could they scoop much new particulate matter from space to resupply their need. Awe knows they must have wanted to get to this place with us badly. Those pilots were on a one-way trip. They probably used all their fuel just to catch us and keep up with us. They are stranded here until their mastership arrives," Domyn explained with some admiration in his deep voice.

"Vulching crazy nasty toxx, those pilots, hey, Jamyk?" Milyr chortled.

"Nope," Jamyk said with a strangely somber voice that surprised Nyba, and then the boy added with concerned conviction, "Danger."

"Yes, we should look for something in this space that could have harmed our beacons," Whyvvi insisted. "That could be very dangerous for us as well."

"We have sensor searched from a distance and found nothing," Domyn said.

"Let's magnify our immediate area," Cap Nyba commanded. "Whyvvi, set sensors on tight confinement for Full-Encompass. Use distance to the farthest ship out there, not including the mastership, as setting standard..."

"That should be the fourth one now getting closer," Whyvvi exclaimed as she began working her fingers within her pink dionjocu gloves.

"Yes, that makes sense," Nyba said a bit perturbed that the girl had interrupted her, and then she added gruffly, "Jamyk, keep our course steady. Ease back on velocity. Let's not dash ahead of our reads into something we can't see in time."

"Awe reasons that is a clever idea, Cap Nyba," Domyn agreed beside her. "The location of our deployed beacons is not much more distant than the orbit of the planet. We will be able to sensor search that region soon with much greater precision than before."

"Are we prepped for another Buffalardi launch, Neer, if we get the opportunity?" Nyba asked while she stared at the nearing grayish brown planet as if that orb of radiant matter was responsible for destruction of beacons, yet not trusting her intuition. "We need to finish the relay chain before going on with this mission. I am convinced of that."

"Well, we can be prepped very soon. I can have Joculatus restart the prep sequence while we investigate," Domyn recommended.

"Do that, Neer Domyn," Nyba commanded, but then she observed the holovision flutter into the newest confined view and saw s small round orb moving in space between one of the red ships and Wolf Streak Beta. "What's that? Where did it come from?"

"There's another one," Swyllo squealed, pointing at the holovision. "And another, vulchers are all around us."

"Four of them," Whyvvi exclaimed. "They are in a pattern similar to the positioning of those ships. They must have deployed those round things when they used up their fuel. Without a propulsion signature, they were too small to show up on our Full-Encompass view until we reduced confinement."

"What the vulch are they?" Milyr griped and then said, "Those vulchers are jabbering up nasty talk now in their vulching coded lingo."

"Maybe those newest orbs are some form of a communication device," Doc Kymil speculated.

"Indeed, Milyr, perhaps those are the things that you have been awaiting," Prof Lyndyn said.

"Whyvvi, do you read any propulsion or any composite trace?" Nyba asked, watching the tiny red dots close on the center blue dot, which was approaching the still planet. "Do you read anything about those things? Are we in danger? Or are they trying to communicate?"

Hesitantly Whyvvi stammered perplexed, "I...am...not sure. Radiant sign... but planet is interfering with all space in this region... Perhaps that is why..."

Suddenly Jamyk commanded emphatically, "Vivo...belts!"

Safety harness snapped across her waist and torso, pinning her to the blue chair. Around her Nyba heard a slap and snap of the other harnesses. Gasps of surprise and annoyance filled the ConCen. Then red dots on the holovision fell suddenly out of the sphere of view. The cratered planet was rushing toward the blue dot in the holovision. What was Jamyk doing, she frowned to herself.

As subtle tug of sudden change of inertia pushed her into her chair, Nyba cried out, "Jamyk, what are you doing? Where are you taking us?"

Joculatus reported in his usual matter of fact tone, "Cap Nyba, there are four nuclear explosions in the wake of Wolf Streak Beta."

"What kind of explosions?" Nyba shouted in disbelief at artigence, though her true annoyance was aimed at the form in green to her far left. "Whyvvi, quickly, long range search behind us. Find out what it's talking about. Jamyk, what's going on?"

"Hide," Jamyk rasped. "Fast!"

Joculatus reported, "Cap Nyba, an electromagnetic pulse wave will strike Wolf Streak Beta in ninety-seven seconds. This electromagnetic pulse could prohibit function of all electrical devices in or near the outer hull."

Whyvvi shouted in dismay, "Yes, Cap, I confirm. The explosions created multiple electromag pulses. They have converged on where we were just moments ago. Now the rebound wave will follow us until it dissipates."

"EM pulses only work in atmospheres," Swyllo retorted.

"Not these," Domyn exclaimed, tapping his visor with a hand. "Somehow they've modified the energy wave to remain cohesive in space. These people are smart techs."

"Smart toxx, you mean," Milyr whined. "This isn't cherp."

Joculatus said, "Cap Nyba, electromagnetic pulse wave will hit in seventy-three seconds at our current velocity."

"Vulching go faster, onad," Swyllo screamed.

"Kick it in toxx, little peener."

"Full," Jamyk rasped in effort, "speed."

"Oh, vulch!

"Awe, protect us."

"Indeed."

SPEC TWO: NYBA TO SEXTO
CHAPTER 18

The copper-colored, cratered planet approached quickly from the far side of the holovision. The red dots representing other spaceships disappeared from the scene as they fell behind out of the confined range of sensors. In their place appeared a curved, luminescent silver wave getting closer to the blue dot in the center of the holovision.

"Are you certain that the EM pulse is strong enough to affect our electronics and artigence programs?" Nyba asked, staring at the silvery arc on display before her chair.

"Awe yes, Cap, unfortunately," Domyn replied in worry beside her. "Intensity of that rebounding wave pulse is diminishing, yes, as it expands outward, but the power is still strong enough to do Wolf Streak Beta great harm. If it catches us, before it weakness substantially, it could interfere, if not deactivate our electrical systems."

"Fast," Jamyk yelled hoarsely. "Planet."

"Yes, that small planet should protect us from the full force of the pulse wave. Smart thinking, Jamyk," Domyn called across the ConCen to the figure in the green dionjocu. "At least its bulk should break up and interfere with cohesion of the pulse."

"Cap Nyba, the electromagnetic pulse will contact Wolf Streak Beta at current velocity in sixty-three seconds," Joculatus reported. "Present strength of the pulse could damage my interface with crew functions."

While she listened to both Domyn and artigence, Nyba battled her anger at Jamyk for jumping the spacecraft from their prior course without her command. Yet now as she heard the comments of others, she found herself understanding grudgingly that the rascal had most likely saved Wolf Streak Beta from severe damage. At first she had wondered if his sudden and arbitrary action had been another of his lapses into foolish mischief. Now Nyba was not so sure. This toxx rascal always caused her confusion and often grief.

"We should down all electrical activity on or near the hull. We should take artigences off-line as soon as we can," Whyvvi recommended from her red chair beside Jamyk.

On the holovision, the silvery arc swelled into the scene from one curved edge of the holovision to another as it closed on the blue dot, and Nyba listened to Milyr shout with obvious fear, "Faster, onad, vulching move this Wolf. It's all you, little peener. Kick this Wolf in toxx and get us away from the vulching nasty pulse."

Joculatus reported, "Electromagnetic pulse will contact Wolf Streak Beta in fifty-three seconds at present velocity."

"Can we pilot this craft with the Flandecams without Joculatus interface and outer hull systems?" Doc Kymil asked from just beyond Domyn.

"Yes, we can use manual control," Domyn exclaimed enthusiastically. "As long as we only shut down the outer hull functions and conscious programs of Joculatus, we can use manual control. Jamyk will need to interface with inner subconscious programs to pilot the spacecraft. It's the same maneuver we did to escape from the Kil-Kol trap, or at least very similar. But we need to hurry this transition, Cap. If the pulse hits us while Joculatus is active with exterior functions, it could damage him severely. We must seal the hull!"

"Well, then do it, Domyn, you are in command of this now. We don't have time to debate and give advice. Just do it now," Nyba demanded, and then to everyone else in the ConCen, she ordered, "Men and women, cease all exterior functions immediately. Close up our outer hull. Let's take Bodacia and Vivacio totally down. If that's not a problem, let's protect them in entirety. Doc, Domyn... any problems with this?"

"Oh, Bodacia can sleep through this threat with no trouble to us," Doc Kymil replied.

"Likewise for Vivacio," Domyn said hastily as his tan dionjocu gloves fluttered with his quick work with Joculatus and Jamyk. "Maybe sensors can keep one survey manually active to allow us to follow exterior developments. We would need to know what was going on out there. All other functions are not critical at this moment."

"Vulch, that's not cherp, Neer," Swyllo groaned. "I'll lose my harvesters."

"Sorry, for the moment, we don't need to harvest energy," Domyn blurted breathlessly.

"Just one sensor on manual," Whyvvi remarked. "Yes, I should be able to read our spatial region well enough with one manual sensor. If it is affected by the pulse, then I can eject that one system and seal the rest immediately. That should work for me, Neer Domyn."

"Then do it," Nyba demanded as she heard Joculatus call out forty-one second advisory. "Not much time before that thing is going to hit us. Let's do what we all know that we must and seal up Wolf Streak Beta. Just in case, our cherp pilot can't out-pace that pulse or hide us behind the planet. Now, men and women, let's protect Wolf Streak Beta."

"Neer Domyn, pilot Jamyk has total manual control of Wolf Streak Beta. I am going to sleep now," reported Joculatus.

Then as Domyn and Jamyk both acknowledged the exchange, everyone else busied themselves silently with their respective functions hastily. The activity on the ConCen was professional and expected of Blue Jayers, yet Nyba groaned as reality of artigence's last words invaded her calm. "Jamyk has total manual control." Her stomach seemed to knot in pain, or was that just her imagination? The little rascal seemed to dominate her awareness at that moment.

Her gaze watched a green figure at the far-left end of the semi-circle of chairs. His arms and hands worked steadily and systematically as he flew the spacecraft of very fast velocity toward the copper colored planet. Nyba would rather have Milyr at pilot now. She was probably thinking foolishly, she thought, for Jamyk had as cherp history as Blue Jay pilot as anyone. However, she felt more secure and comfortable with the other lanky young man in lavender dionjocu as her pilot. This did not always make sense, she mused, but that was how she felt, especially in recent awakenings.

While her eyes now stared at Milyr's sweating and slouching form in his purple chair, Nyba heard Whyvvi say in mild concern, "That EM pulse should overtake us in thirty-one seconds. All exterior seals read as being locked. All artigences are asleep."

Milyr turned his long face toward Jamyk and said tiredly with resignation, "Onad, it's all you. Kick this Wolf for all it can run. I know Wolf can do this and you can do this, my friend."

"Yup," Jamyk said calmly yet panting in his effort. "Focused."

On the holovision, copper-gray craters on the planet were distinguishable now as individual holes. The lack of any dust clouds or vapor clouds suggested almost no atmosphere. The rotational movement was negligible now that Wolf Streak was so close in near orbit and matching rotation with its velocity. So this is a planet that had attracted the interest of the other spaceship, Nyba pondered. What was their interest here? Would she survive to discover truth?

"Oh my, we won't get behind that planet in time, will we?" Doc Kymil moaned.

"No doubt that seems likely," Prof Lyndyn agreed in his nasal voice to Nyba's left. "That EM pulse is almost upon us. It does not appear to have lost much strength."

Older man of forty-seven years had seen what Nyba had noticed. The silvery arc did not look any less cohesive or threatening than it had just seconds ago. Now it was almost on the blue dot. Had she considered all their options? Was Wolf Streak Beta sealed and protected against that pulse? Nyba was not sure, but she had done what she thought was proper and had listened to wisdom of Neer Domyn. Her only reservation was her reliance of Jamyk as pilot. Yet circumstances had not allowed any other possibility. Now Wolf Streak Beta and this Blue Jay crew were in his skinny hands. She hoped the boy could do one of his fantastic saves now, just like in Pulseball.

"Full an-grav reverse thrust," Domyn yelled abruptly. "Posi-grav advance thrust. Use the planet's own gravity to pull us toward it faster."

"Yup," Jamyk retorted in distinct annoyance in his hoarse voice. "Already."

"Seventeen seconds to EM pulse contact," Whyvvi reported.

"Whip this Wolf harder, onad," shouted Milyr. "You'll get us there."

Planet was looming large in the holovision and approaching very quickly. The silvery arc was almost touching the blue dot. Nyba found that she was holding her breath. This was not very Blue Jayer, she scolded herself silently, not very captain-like, not very mature. Yet, she told herself, if Milyr could be anxious and worried, then she would not accuse herself so readily. He was as brave as Neer Domyn, as steady as Cap Bhiros, as reliable as Neer Khebol. For some strange reason, this young man had confidence in the boy at pilot now. Nyba could adopt this young man's optimism, almost.

"Awspir, Jamyk," Domyn exclaimed suddenly, "are you riding the wave with an-grav? Are you pushing against the concentrated energy of that pulse with our an-grav waves?"

"Yup," Jamyk replied with a gasp. "Riding."

"Vulching cherp, big nad," Milyr roared in enthusiasm. "That's so primo, Blue Jay cherp!"

"What is that about? Can the pulse hurt us now?" Doc Kymil asked.

Silvery arc on the holovision was now pacing behind the blue dot by only the thinnest separation, and that could have been only in her imagination, Nyba realized. A small degree of separation had not changed for several seconds now. Yet the planet rushed toward the blue dot. The EM pulse wave and Wolf Streak Beta were hurtling toward the cratered orb in tandem. Though still fearful, Nyba was awed by this sight. Even though it was a manually limited sensor representation, this view was astounding to her and a quite bit frightening.

"Jamyk, you will not crash us into that planet, I hope," she said matter-of-factly as she concealed her own anxiety. "This is no time for one of your foolish jokes. That pulse wave is only…what, Whyvvi, about eleven seconds behind us?"

"Crash?" Jamyk asked with annoyance and then blurted, "Nope!"

Whyvvi replied stoically, "Eleven seconds, yes, about that, but the time to impact has been holding steady for several seconds now. We should be able to ride this situation to extend our time before we need to get into orbit and let the planet buffer us from full impact of the pulse."

"Remember, Jamyk, you'll need to allow at least a forty-seven degree tangential when the pulse passes us to create the most effective deflection off our hull," Domyn said hurriedly.

"Yup," Jamyk rasped impatiently. "Focusing."

"Indeed you have done quite well at your focus now," Prof Lyndyn praised. "My sessions with you must have had some usefulness… But don't let me distract you now, my lad… Neer Domyn, what is that tangential reference you just mentioned. Are we in danger still?"

In spite of her usual preconception of Jamyk, Nyba had to agree with Prof Lyndyn's assessment of the boy's recent focus, but her own attention veered to Domyn when he replied, "Well, that EM pulse is still a danger. We don't know its actual strength. If it struck us broadside at anywhere near a ninety-degree angle, then the full impact of the pulse would be difficult to deflect from our hull. If we can meet the vector of that pulse's forward motion at a much lesser angle, then the reflective properties of our hull should deflect much of the pulse."

"Our hull can deflect such a pulse?" Swyllo asked in her shrill voice. "Then why did we run from it? Why waste time? We could sit there and laugh at vulchers."

"No, no, tiny fem," Milyr snorted. "You don't understand…"

"Vulch, I suppose you do?" Swyllo blurted.

"Belts!" Jamyk shouted sharply. "Ready."

Domyn yelled hastily, "Whyvvi, Jamyk, remember once we change course from off this riding vector, that pulse will catch us in less than eleven seconds. Be very alert to your manual systems. Be careful not to let that pulse enter any of our systems, even your manuals. If you read failure in your manual…"

Both responded loudly at same time, "Yup… Neer."

"Is everyone harnessed in?" Nyba asked, knowing that there could be a sudden shift of inertia or perhaps total loss of internal gravity.

"We won't need to worry about a nasty rough ride," Milyr cried out in anxious humor. "A Blue Jay pilot is driving this Wolf."

"Belts," Jamyk ordered. "Now!"

"Maybe the ride will be as smooth as your handsome, manly face," Nyba snorted with sarcasm and then added emphatically, "but if we lose electrical capability, then you'll have to deal with the loss of our internal gravity. Your gawky body will look quite fodish floating around the ConCen out of control."

Nyba saw his jaw drop momentarily while his eye stared at her and then his mouth reformed into a grin and Milyr said, "Nyba, you are cherp again. You're always watching out for my body…"

"Orbit!" Jamyk declared with a sharp croak. "Now!"

Then the brownish-gray cratered planet swung abruptly to the right of the holovision. The silvery arc of the EM pulse wave tilted in the opposite direction in relation to the blue dot. Nyba felt a slight inertial change as Wolf Streak Beta swerved into close orbit around the planet. The silvery arc followed the blue dot, though now at a different angle than before. She knew it would make contact soon. Could Wolf Streak get behind the planet enough to allow the planet to interfere with the pulse's cohesion? Could Jamyk incline the spacecraft enough to deflect the pulse?

"Move our toxx!" Milyr cried out in excited fear.

"Whyvvi, watch your one sensor outlet for the pulse invasion," Domyn ordered sharply.

"Yes, Neer," she replied somberly.

During this exchange, the planet turned in a steady but opposite rotation to its norm. Almost instantly Nyba realized that this was an illusion caused by the rapid velocity of Wolf Streak Beta, velocity much faster than the rotation of the planet. Since the blue dot in the center of the holovision was stationary in representation, other objects appeared to move around it. In the second that she realized this, Wolf Streak Beta had begun orbit around the planet. Not far behind approached the silvery arc.

"Contact is seven seconds," Whyvvi reported.

"Awe help us," Domyn sighed.

"Five."

Nyba watched the angle of the silver arc tilt in relationship to the blue dot. Part of the silver arc now struck the planet. Relentlessly the arc followed and gained on the blue dot. The arc continued to tilt. A subtle haziness rippled over the arc along its caress of the planet. Its cohesion was breaking down, Nyba realized with hope. Could they do it?

"Two."

Was a tangential tilt enough to allow the deflective qualities of the Blue Jay designed hull to reflect such concentration of an EM pulse? Could Jamyk keep Wolf Streak Beta in tight orbit? Would the planet hinder the power of the pulse wave? If the pulse hit and destroyed flight function, could the boy keep Wolf Streak Beta from crashing? Nyba pondered these questions in the last seconds.

On the holovision, the silvery arc caught the blue dot. Flickering interference distorted clarity of the holovision. A fluttering image dissolved in front of Nyba's eye. A sudden quiet seized the ConCen. No one spoke. No dionjocus rustled with duty activity. No hum of the Flandecams permeated background noise common to the craft. There was no background noise, Nyba thought abruptly in terror. Had she gone deaf suddenly? Had the EM pulse done any damage? Had Wolf Streak Beta suffered a system failure after all? She felt panic creep into her awareness.

Then with embarrassment, Nyba exclaimed almost in a hushed whisper, "Now I can see in the ConCen. We haven't lost that system. We haven't lost our internal gravity. Jamyk, the Flandecams, why don't I hear the normal hum?"

"Off," the boy replied wearily but with confidence. "Coasting."

"In orbit I hope," Milyr murmured. "Not in vulching freefall into that planet?"

"Yup," Jamyk said hoarsely. "Orbit."

Domyn stirred in his brown chair and asked, "Whyvvi, did you lose manual sensor when that pulse hit?"

"I do not know for sure," the young woman in pink dionjocu answered. "I turned off the sensor instant electric static revealed itself on my scan. I sealed the sensor system at the same time. I did not want to take a chance of the invasive EM pulse."

259

"Vulch, onad, are you coasting blind, too?" Milyr asked with a squeak in his normally baritone voice, and Nyba worried the same fear as she peered with anxiety at the boy in green.

"Nope," Jamyk replied with a tired sigh. "Port."

"Port window, are you serious? You're looking out the window to judge our orbit?" Nyba inquired in disbelief, not sure whether to praise his self-reliance or berate his foolish irresponsibility. "Argh, you rascal, you'd better be sure we don't lose our orbit distance and crash into that planet."

"Or perhaps worse, we might lose our orbit and get thrown out into space," Prof Lyndyn suggested in his nasal voice, which had a slight nervous tremor in it at that moment. "Wolf Streak Beta just barely made orbit. Our recent velocity could have been fast enough to reinstitute centrifugal force and shoot us into space again. Is that possible still, Neer Domyn?"

"Nope," Jamyk rasped. "Orbit... Cherp."

Domyn swayed his chair nervously but answered with confidence, "I trust Jamyk, Prof. The likelihood of re-engaging centrifugal force on Wolf Streak Beta is very small. Gravitational pull is more likely to be a concern without our Flandecams in operation..."

"We should be able to survey out again soon. The effect of the EM pulse has gone past us now," Whyvvi declared. "We cannot float in this blind condition forever. We should test my exterior sensors. We should test the Flandecams."

Young woman in the red chair was often opinionated and sometimes brash in her forwardness, Nyba reminded herself as she studied Whyvvi's upright posture but had been a source of optimism in Nyba's life. Whyvvi's obvious determination and Jamyk's almost boastful confidence stirred Nyba from her temporary fugue. She needed to be more captain-like, she scolded herself silently. She must not let this crew down by hiding in her own fears. Fears which she had not realized dwelled within her during the recent dash to safety.

"Well, yes, men and women, we must go on. We must be bold. We have a mission to complete. We have friends to find out there," Nyba said with rising optimism and determination. "Whyvvi, turn on your manual sensor at the setting which you viewed when the EM pulse hit us. Jamyk, prep the Flandecams for restart. Domyn, that won't require too much time, will it?"

Domyn replied, "No, Cap Nyba, especially if Jamyk just closed them down with an exterior seal and did not actually turn them off. Jamyk, you did just seal them, right?"

"Sealed," Jamyk sighed. "Cams…ready."

Meanwhile, the holovision sputtered for a moment and then reappeared with a normal clarity in front of and partially within the semi-circle of chairs, and Whyvvi exclaimed with excitement, "My sensor is fit. It did not take any damage. We should be able to go back to the exterior sensors with Joculatus awake and fully functional. We should be able to see out there into space again."

Now observing a remnant of the fragmented silvery arc moving into space well beyond the blue dot and a very close planet, Nyba asked, "Domyn, do you believe that there would be any residual EM pulse danger behind that wave front? Are we okay to get back to full capability of our Wolf Streak Beta? Can we start searching for any colonial ships out there?"

"The EM pulse was strongest at its wave front. There is not usually any strength following the single wave pulse. And remember, Cap, this wave was the secondary rebounded wave from the original focused convergence of the four nuclear explosions. We should be out of that specific danger now," Domyn explained and then added with less conviction, "Although we should be alert for aftershock waves. Sometimes those could follow such a strong frontal pulse. Of course we don't have much prior precedent involving the result of the convergence of four nuclear blasts either. However, I doubt if there would be any unified EM pulse power in any such aftershock waves. I believe that we are cherp to restart our external functions now."

"Vulch, we haven't felt any aftershocks," Swyllo squealed in frustration. "And I need to start harvesting light energy again. When can I put my system back into action? Without my harvesting, you others can't get your functions to work, remember that."

"You can get my function to work every time, tiny fem," Milyr chuckled while he sprawled his long form over his purple chair. "You can give me all your energy anytime."

"Well, boys, girls, and Milyr, it seems as if we are returning to the routine again," Nyba retorted with hesitant amusement and a glance toward the slouching lavender figure. "We have a mission to continue. We should launch the Buffalardi again. We should try to find some way to contact those colonials in a way that won't provoke them into trying to harm us. We should try to find Fox Flash Alpha. We certainly have much we should do. Perhaps we should get restarted."

"Indeed we must. Blue Jayers are forward thinking and advancing always. Blue Jayers are eyes and ears, and often the mouths of the human race out here in galaxy. We are forward scouts of Blue Jay. We are squawkers…" Prof Lyndyn declared with his nasal voice but then paused himself suddenly with a frown beneath his one-eyed visor and added, "Yet no doubt that other spaceship is out there still. We must be cautious. There is no doubt that those colonials, if they are colonials, are hostile to us for some unexplained reason. Cap Nyba, we must recognize this fact and not act recklessly."

"Very good advice," Doc Kymil remarked and then suggested, "Cap Nyba, our crew has exceeded the normal awakening span since Saphyndenlairoum sleep. We should attempt some rest and nourishment for the crew. At least we must take shifts resting, nourishing, and perhaps showering for some. The warm soothing shower of water can be very restful and invigorating at the same time."

"Vulch, yeah, I could go for that," Milyr moaned in what sounded like desire to Nyba.

"Oh, vulch yeah, you sure could," Swyllo chirped. "You stink worse than the black bear on the cross-country trail. I could use you to take a shower for my own effectiveness here on the ConCen."

"Tiny fem, you aren't so sweet yourself," Milyr chuckled, waggling his lanky arms at her. "But we stinking vulchers could go shower together, tiny fem. That way you can make sure I get cleaned. Hey, that's a primo idea, don't you think?"

"Vulch that idea, you toxx! Besides young wolfen bitches don't stink. We just have a sweet aroma, right, Cap?" Swyllo exclaimed with a giggle as she attempted to swat at his long arms.

With her eye peering into the holovision, Nyba noticed the absence of any red spots signifying hostile ships, so she commanded, "Unless Domyn believes it is unsafe, Whyvvi, expand your sensor search to the normal scan. Let's awaken Joculatus, Neer Domyn, carefully just in case of the residual EM pulse effects. We need to see what's out there in more detail now before we let the stinkers shower. Of course, Doc, you could begin feeding everyone a nutrient if you think that is vital now. I recommend starting with Milyr as he is most ravenous."

Domyn said, "I believe that the EM pulse danger is over now. We can awaken Joculatus and resume all external functions."

"Yeah, I could go for some cool nutrient now," Milyr admitted, and then with a big grin sat up and leered, "Maybe if I drink that vulching antemgebemarzex nasty stuff, tiny fem won't be afraid to shower with me. What do you say, tiny fem? That's a cherp primo idea, huh?"

Scene on the holovision expanded to show the vast empty space, except for the blue dot and disc of the planet on the right side of view. At a very extreme range of this new setting, the silvery arc of the pulse faded to nothingness. In the far, far distance twinkles of lights suggested other planets of the Sexto System. No red spots were visible. Not even the sun showed on the scene. Nyba realized suddenly that Wolf Streak Beta was now on the side of the small planet away from the sun and original position of the smaller colonial ships.

Abruptly an idea occurred to her, and she asked, "Jamyk, can you hold Wolf Streak Beta in orbit and also on this side of the planet? Can we stay out of view of the other ship for awhile longer?"

"Yup," he replied with certainty, but then after a moment, qualified his opinion by saying, "If... Jocu."

"Awright, Cap, we do need Joculatus back in action," Domyn said, waving his hands and flicking his fingers in his tan dionjocu gloves. "So far all his programs appear okay. I've awakened Vivacio's internal programs to help me check each artigence and systems of Wolf Streak Beta. Our Blue Jay sci-tech seems to have withstood the recent crisis very...cherply."

"Cherply?" Swyllo laughed. "That's nasty sounding from you, Neer Domyn. How soon before I can resume harvesting? Our supply must be lower now since we ceased external functions."

Yes, energy supply would be low now, Nyba thought, scolding herself for this bit of ignored reality, and then she asked hastily, "How much energy supply do we have, Swyllo?"

The small girlish figure in the yellow dionjocu swiveled her chair toward Nyba and replied, "Based on the last internal reading before we shut down the systems, our supply is about 47 percent. Our brazen pilot used a lot of energy during his wild race away from the EM pulse. Now we're not even on the sunny side of this planet. I can't harvest light until we get back into sunlight."

Hearing disappointment and agitation in Swyllo's tone, Nyba said with firm compassion, "Don't worry for now, Swyllo. We're going to rest for awhile. We all need rest. We need to catch our breath. We need to reevaluate. Even Wolf Streak Beta needs to recover a functional status. Does anyone disagree with this assessment?"

"Vulch no," Milyr chortled gaily. "I'm all cherp to go to that warm, soothing shower. And getting a cleaner dionjocu would be cherp, too. I'm ready to go now, Nyba. Just command me."

Whyvvi said from her red chair, "Our sensors are coming awake now. They read no other ships and no follow-up EM pulses. Yet we should set our Tier Two sensors to seek those small-scale nuclear orbs that did not show up on more long distant sensor settings."

"Well, then set that with Joculatus as soon as artigence is fully awake, Whyvvi," Nyba demanded, trying not to sound annoyed at the girl's reluctance to act with some self-initiative, but then Nyba recalled her own inner disgruntlement with Jamyk and his perceived rash decision to fly Wolf Streak Beta on his own initiative not long ago. "I have trust in your judgment, Whyvvi. That's a good idea. I'll take sensor function while you rest and get some nutrient. You've been at that a long time. And you also, Swyllo, and Milyr, you have all performed cherp duty recently. Now we need you to rest, relax, and try to recover in…oh, let's say about an hour… Does that seem reasonable, Doc?"

"Oh, yes, Cap Nyba, there's no reason to try for Saphyndenlairoum stasis sleep. hour of nutritional intake and relaxing rest and perhaps of sedative induced a nap in Med should revive our people," Doc Kymil prescribed with sure conviction in her motherly tone.

"Do you think recalibration with Joculatus is necessary?" Prof Lyndyn asked as Nyba watched Milyr arise from his purple chair. "With artigence awakening now again and lapsed time since previous calibration on Dionjossad, I wonder what the interface correlation is now."

"Awright, good thought, Prof," Domyn agreed and then said, "Joculatus, now that you are fully functional, how is the crew interface with your sensors?"

Joculatus reported, "Neer Domyn, this crew has a range of interface correlation between 73 and 89 percent."

"Seventy-three, isn't that low for maximum interface?" Nyba inquired and then on intuition, asked, "Joculatus, who has the lowest correlation now? And who has the highest?"

Joculatus reported, "Cap Nyba, Milyr has 73 percent correlation. Pilot Jamyk has 89 percent correlation."

Jamyk has the highest after his recent efforts to pilot, and before that his battle with his foolish daydreams? This was bewildering, Nyba convinced herself. This was unbelievable, but Joculatus would not lie or report false data. Yet thw stat for Milyr did make sense. Perhaps artigence was correct, she thought as she observed Milyr's sweating exhausted body stumble on wobbly, gangly legs toward the hatch. The young man had performed much strenuous activity in stressful conditions, she recalled.

"I'm cherp to go, right, Nyba?" he asked, pausing just behind her chair. "I could use some of that nasty nutrient, I'm starved. Then a cherp shower before getting into a fresh dionjocu. Maybe a cherp massage from Doc would aid my recovery."

"Don't goad her too much, young lad," Prof Lyndyn chuckled. "You don't want to see her nasty side. My kindred spirit is an angel most of the time, but when goaded, can be a demon."

"Oh my, Lyndyn, don't scare the lad..." Doc Kymil began to say.

However, Nyba ignored the woman's next words and peering at the young face with a bit of envy momentarily envisioned the lanky body standing in the warm flow of gentle waters, but then abruptly she declared, "Yes, Milyr, go rest for an hour, and you also, Swyllo and Whyvvi. The rest of us can monitor the ConCen functions while Wolf Streak Beta rests. Now go, all of you... Doc Kymil, will you need to assist them? Yes, yes, we should recalibrate, shouldn't we?"

"Yes, I should go with these young people. Recalibration is required," Doc Kymil agreed.

"Awright, yes," Domyn said. "I think we all should recalibrate with Dionjossad before we go anywhere out into the Sexto System. We'll want our interface as efficient as possible."

"I'll see to that duty, Neer Domyn," Doc Kymil smiled, and then in some amusement said, "I don't intend to be a pup-sitter for these young adults."

"No, I would hope you would not need to be," Nyba agreed as she watched the lanky young man saunter with tired legs out the hatch amidst the three women, and then she laughed, "Milyr, behave yourself in the shower. I don't want to hear of any inappropriate shenanigans or wild tales later during our voyage."

"Do not worry, Nyba," Whyvvi snickered. "We will make certain that he comes out clean and refreshed and ready to do his duty. You can rely upon us wolf bitches to nip any misbehavior from his person. I can guarantee this!"

"Vulch, that sounds nasty," Milyr griped.

"Sounds cherp fun to me," Swyllo retorted.

"Good luck, my kindred spirit. You may need it," called Prof Lyndyn.

"Yup," rasped Jamyk. "Luck."

"Awright, now, Cap Nyba, perhaps we can decide on our next move," Domyn said. "We can't stay in this orbit forever."

When her eye finally lost sight of his lavender figure, Nyba grumbled silently at herself for her distraction and then declared with authority, "Oh, Neer, we know what our next moves must be. We must launch the Buffalardi. We must harvest light energy. We must continue to attempt to fulfill our mission of contacting colonials. We must try to find Fox Flash Alpha. We have plenty to do."

"Awe help us," Domyn sighed beside her.

With a snort of slight irritation, Nyba chided, "We will do this on our own without any surreal aid. We are Blue Jayers after all. We can succeed in this universe on our own talents."

Then in the sudden quiet of the ConCen she wondered if she could manage the future without the tall young man in lavender dionjocu. Now why was she thinking this weird thought? Why had her mental reveries in recent hours found daydreams of Milyr so often? Almost as annoying to her as rascal Jamyk, Milyr had been only another male member of her crew prior to the Sexto System. Now his presence tempted her observations and contemplations. Why were Milyr and Jamyk so befuddling to her in these recent days? Jamyk, she could guess, but why Milyr?

With a grimace and unexpected intuition, Nyba glanced toward Jamyk's green chair. From under the double visor of pilot, his smirk faced her openly and silently.

SPEC TWO: NYBA TO SEXTO
CHAPTER 19

After over an hour of discussing the options of action with Prof Lyndyn and Neer Domyn, Nyba felt confident in her decision as she declared, "Well then, let's prep for the Buffalardi launch, so we'll be ready for that when we leave this hiding position. It's obvious to me that we must finish the relay chain and sanbeam communication to Steppingstone Quinto."

"Awright, Cap Nyba, the launch should not take long. Joculatus has prepped the Buffalardi in our launch port. We should be able to recalculate the trajectory coordinates soon," Domyn said from the brown chair on her right.

On her left side in his gray chair, Prof Lyndyn said, "No doubt we must consider the strong probability that the colonial spaceship that attacked us may also attack our Buffalardi. I'm sure now that the explosion of our original beacons was an act of the colonials. Perhaps that fourth smaller ship did the deed. It came from behind this planet well after the mastership set out to intercept us."

"Do you believe it is still out there waiting for us?" Nyba asked wondering with her weary brain if they had discussed this already but continued, "We have had no scan of them since tucking in behind this planet. They could believe that we were destroyed by their EM pulse or maybe their original nuclear explosions. We don't know if their sensor system can trace us at the speed of Jamyk's flying or in contrast to the energy release of those nasty blasts."

"Indeed we do not," Prof Lyndyn agreed. "However, we would be irresponsible to assume that they are no longer a threat. For whatever reason, they wanted to harm Wolf Streak Beta. We should not assume that their intention will be changed or abandoned so readily…"

"They would have backed away to avoid rebounding the EM pulse wave unless their tech has been shielded against such EM pulses," Domyn said, swaying his chair in a nervous or perhaps relaxing fashion, for now Nyba was uncertain of the reason this intelligent young man performed this habit when under stress.

"Yes, they did fall behind when we changed our original course vector as we headed back to the outer edge of the Sexto System," Cap Nyba said, glancing past Domyn to three empty chairs and daydreaming in envy about three other young people relaxing elsewhere in Wolf Streak Beta. "But at the time I thought that after they had launched their smaller speed ships, the mastership could not keep pace with us. Jamyk, what velocity were you using after we changed course but before the blasts?"

"Half," the boy in green dionjocu replied from the far left chair. "Potential."

"And the mastership could not pace us," Cap Nyba muttered almost to herself and then more vocally said, "They could have been pulling away then if they knew they were going to blast us. Those smaller ships used all their fuel to trap us with the fourth ship. They risked much in what appears to be desperation. They wanted us in a nasty way, but why?"

Domyn agreed with the conviction, "Yes, Nyba, I thought the same thing. I replayed a recording of the nuclear incident and confirmed to myself that their intention was to harm us. Their ship positions were almost a precise tetrahedron with four points of the weapon launch to aim original convergence of the four EM pulses right into us. That amount of power would have penetrated our insulated hull. To do that requires great power, even for EM pulses. As you remember, our Blue Jay hulls are designed and constructed to withstand and repel about five times worst dose of known cosmic range of electromagnetic radiants common to space travel."

"I do not understand why they would want to harm us," Lyndyn said in a nasal tone of confusion but then partially answered himself by saying, "However, colonials could have become wary of all other human contact. Their ancestors could have instilled suspicious trepidation in their descendants. The condition of human race on Homeworld in the Zerosolis System was quite negative when the original super colony ships departed. I can theorize the scenario where these present colonials could hate and fear humans from the Zerosolis System. Their history could be filled with bias against other humans…now consequently us in this spacecraft so different to their familiarity…"

"Yup," Jamyk rasped from his green chair. "Fear."

"Ho, ho, pilot, you just focus on your piloting duty," Cap Nyba declared as she fought her persistent worry that the boy would let his attention wander and put Wolf Streak Beta into jeopardy.

"Focus," Jamyk said with sincerity in his croaking voice. "Pilot."

"Well, make sure that you do," she blurted, glaring at his skinny figure in the green dionjocu.

"Awright, Prof, if your suspicions are accurate, then would the ingrained outlook explain lack of communication from them?" Domyn asked and then changed his focus to announce, "Cap, Joculatus has recalculated the launch trajectory for the Buffalardi. Several possible trajectories to be precise, as our possible movement should be considered. We can launch when you wish."

"Prof, do you have reservations still? Can we launch now? Or do you foresee a problem from the colonial mastership?" Cap Nyba inquired with mild impatience urging her to action, yet respect for the older man's opinion restraining her. "Are you getting any meaning from the gibberish in their radio signals bouncing around this space?"

"Indeed if this pattern of encoded signals is a sample of their cultural attitude, then I believe that they are a culture in conflict, or at least a culture with reason to conceal messages, which is most often a society at war or some political mistrust. Throughout human history, as you know, Nyba, most cultures have eras of unrest and rebellion. Every society has its dissidents, its rebels, perhaps even actual pirates or criminals. These colonials should be no different…"

"Well, I do know from my historical research that Homeworld, which they had departed, was a nasty planet heading toward a very nasty future. So much of the planet was embroiled in wars involving all types of biological toxins and chemical agents that leaders of nations and alliances and even private corporations were distracted from continuing ecological danger, which hi-tech civilizations of the Zerosolis System were racing toward unrestrained. Their own wallowing in their advanced technologies blinded them to their narcissistic ignorance of rape of the planet's ecology. But I'm getting astray of what we should be planning here and now. Prof, does your speculation tell us to launch or not?" Cap Nyba said breathlessly and very annoyed at herself for indulging in this long-winded lapse into her own personal interest of ancient history of Despoliation.

"Don't chastise yourself, Nyba, for having passionate interest in ancient history. Many great leaders often tried to look back in the history to find patterns to avoid in their own present times," Prof Lyndyn exclaimed, and then after a pause while he cleared his throat, he continued, "My point about these colonials is that if they are a group from the original colonists, then they could have historically biased a fear of either us, or more likely another faction of their own culture. They are unwilling to communicate with us, even though Milyr used a derivative of their language. They seem to need to keep their messages from the understanding of others. I find it almost impossible to believe that they have created this encoded system to keep us ignorant. They would not have known that we were coming."

"Foxes," Jamyk exclaimed. "First."

"Focus on your pilot function," Cap Nyba snapped and then restrained her agitation, which was as much toward Prof Lyndyn as it was Jamyk. "Keep us hidden from possible searching scans from our new enemies, pilot. That's your duty now... So then, Prof, if you are correct, then there could be other colonials out there that would welcome us. Hopefully we could complete our mission and make contact with them. Yet before we do that, we still need to deploy the last sequence of beacons to connect the relay chain with Steppingstone Quinto."

"Yes, Cap, this is logical," Neer Domyn agreed and then suddenly exclaimed with chagrin, "Awe, why didn't I think of this before? We could add the booster Flandecam to the next Buffalardi. This would increase its velocity for the first phase of the trip and extend duration of higher velocity travel. Our Blue Jay propulsion seems to be several generations ahead of what we've witnessed in their ships. Our Buffalardi could outpace any ships or weapons that they might launch."

Buoyed by his new enthusiasm, Cap Nyba said, "That sounds cherp. Do you think we can do this in short time? Is this something Joculatus and Vivacio can do mechanically?"

"No, Cap, I should go to do this type of modification myself. The artigences can advise me on physical design, but mechanics need to be performed by human hands and then checked by human eyes," Neer Domyn replied.

From her left, Prof Lyndyn sighed almost as if he did not want to speak, "No doubt you have a good idea, Neer, Domyn. Yet I must caution us not to decide our action rashly. Suppose colonials are at this time setting a trap for another Buffalardi? They were most likely waiting for us to launch our original Buffalardi. And yes, indeed that does presuppose that they may have known that we were coming as Jamyk recently suggested with his remark about Fox Flash Alpha entering the Sexto System first. The colonials may have destroyed the Buffalardi launched by Fox Flash Alpha. This would be an act of culture almost paranoid about other humans or aliens entering their space..."

"Ho, ho, no, Prof," Cap Nyba interrupted with increasing annoyance and disbelief. "That can't make any sense. They could not have that much fear of strangers. And your suggestion means that colonials would have made contact with Fox Flash Alpha and recognized them as enemies immediately. That seems very unlikely to me. There would not have been any warning of Fox Flash Alpha's entry into the Sexto System. There would not have been enough time after they entered to have this kind of negative interaction with colonials. I just can't believe people would act like this."

"Awright, Prof, Cap is making logical sense," Domyn argued. "How could colonials have known of our arrival, even if they had observed Fox Flash Alpha? Would they be paranoid enough to have a squadron of ships just waiting by this small planet on chance that some non-colonial spacecraft would enter the Sexto System? They probably do not know of Kil-Kol phenomenon or diverse aspects of space. These physics were discovered well after the colonial exodus from the Zerosolis System. They most likely do not know about LaOgres space or Weznuski space. How would they know to wait here for us to enter the Sexto System? Would they know the same physics as us? This would be some great coincidence. Did they know this knowledge before they left the Zerosolis System? They would not have, would they, Nyba?"

"Well, to my study of ancient history of the century of Despoliation and Dark Era centuries after that, I do not believe that multi-gravity physics had been discovered or researched before the colonials had left the Zerosolis System. Not until centuries of Dark Era that followed Despoliation did humanity resurrect studies and technologies that produced the discovery of multi-gravity physics. I believe that even Kil-Kol discovery was much later than the colonial departure," Nyba replied tempted to dive deeper into a conversation about the ravaging of the home world in the ancient era of great Despoliation, but her sense of Blue Jay priority prompted her to say, "But let's not get distracted by ancient history. Neer, you have thought of a way to enhance our Buffalardi to travel faster than the colonial ship or nuclear orb. Will this be enough to escape the pre-set trap, if Prof is right? We should consider all possibilities to ensure success, at least while we are safely hidden behind this planet. Our mission of contact with the polite colonials isn't so urgent for us to act recklessly."

"Awe, favor me, if I had precognition, Cap, I would know for sure. However, I do believe these modifications give us a better chance. I don't know how else to improve our odds," Neer Domyn sighed, and she could see his exhaustion on his wide face beneath the tan dionjocu cap and single eye visor.

"Launch," Jamyk rasped loudly. "Two."

The boy's harsh croak burst into the ongoing conversation, and Nyba was ready to scold him severely until she heard Domyn almost shriek in delight, "Awspir, Jamyk, yes, yes! That would enhance our chances of getting the last beacons into a chain. Awspir, that is a really cherp idea."

Bewildered and irritated, Nyba blurted almost vehemently, "What do you mean? How can wasting our last two Buffalardis help us? This is rascal foolishness!"

"Cap Nyba, we have no use for our extra Buffalardi..." Prof Lyndyn started to say.

However, a baritone voice behind the semi-circle of chairs startled Nyba as it declared, "Vulch, we could use it like a missile against those colonial vulchers if they get in our way again."

Spinning her chair, Nyba saw him stride into the ConCen. His face was grinning. His dionjocu was fresh and sweat-free. Milyr looked as handsomely cherp as he ever could, she thought. As he ambled between the two girls also entering the ConCen at the same time, his stature emanated authority, or at least, Nyba mused, in her opinion at that moment. He was a welcome spirit into the recent drudgery of conversation. Nyba smiled at him.

"We're ready for duty," Swyllo chirped, walking spritely toward her yellow chair.

"Vulch yeah, we're ready to start shooting something at those vulchers," Milyr shouted when he reached his purple chair. "We won't let them toxx try to hurt our Wolf Streak Beta."

Part of her awareness liked his notion of shooting back with offensive, if one could call the Buffalardi an offensive weapon, but that was not the Blue Jay philosophy and consequently not hers, so Nyba just ordered pleasantly, "All right, men and women, get prepped for your primary functions. Please do not interfere in our current conversation with your usual humorous quips. We are deciding some issue of importance to our immediate future."

"Cap, Doc says for the rest of you to get some rest and prep for recalibration with Joculatus," Whyvvi reported firmly as she sat down next to the wet-drenched green figure. "She seemed quite insistent, Nyba. Jamyk here surely should shower off his stench."

Yes, a woman would be insistent in this, Cap Nyba thought, for Doc Kymil was very protective of her Blue Jay family, yet Nyba asked in hope of getting reprieve now that Milyr was in the ConCen again, "Joculatus, what is my present interface with you?"

Joculatus responded, "Cap Nyba, your present interface correlation is 83 percent. This is within acceptable parameters for the normal function of captain."

"But it should be higher if we go into action again," Neer Domyn commented soberly.

"I'm okay for now," Cap Nyba declared thankfully. "Let's get this launch decision settled before you rest, Domyn. Why two launches? What benefit does it give us?"

"Two," Jamyk said. "Tracks."

"Vulch, you want to shoot both at once?" Swyllo griped.

"Not now, Swyllo, no comments unless they are useful," Cap Nyba stated in her authoritative tone and instantly felt sorry for the girl's puzzled pout. "Neer Domyn, if I understand Jamyk correctly, you are saying that two trajectories will give us a better chance of having at least one Buffalardi deploy its beacons properly. Does this take into consideration Prof's theoretical trap?"

"Yes, two differing tracks should confuse and maybe prohibit any hostile action against our Buffalardis. With modifications to the propulsion units that we discussed, our Buffalardis should have very good chance to deploy our last beacons," Domyn said, and his assured tone washed away her doubts with his certainty.

"Then you will need time to modify the Buffalardis, Neer. I'm afraid that this duty might cut into your rest and relaxation time," Nyba said with true sadness for the sweating big man beside her, so she asked, "Can you use Jamyk to help and make your work go faster? You both need to see Doc soon anyway. How much time do you need to do this modification?"

"I'm okay to take over as pilot," Milyr declared, and Cap Nyba noticed that he had pulled his double vision visor from the back compartment of his chair.

"Just hold yourself a moment, Milyr," Nyba demanded. "Well, Neer Domyn, we've decided on our action. How long before we can be ready?"

"With two of us sci-tech people, probably most of our hour of rest and relaxation," Domyn admitted. "We should get started soon. We don't know how much longer this site is sanctuary."

"Then you go now, Domyn. Start the process. As soon as Milyr has full pilot function, and I can release Jamyk, then I'll send him to you. Let's hope that he can find his way without getting side-tracked," Nyba commented with confidence in Domyn and much less in Jamyk, but the boy needed rest, and Milyr was back in the ConCen. "Jamyk, begin transfer of pilot to Milyr as quickly as possible. Milyr, you are my pilot now. However, before you get totally entrenched in the function, do you still have a prerecorded message for MisCom ready?"

"You know I'm always ready with my comms, Nyba. I assume you want to record this as an automated recording with our beacons to ensure this signal will be sent, just in case we get into any trouble and can't sanbeam ourselves live," Milyr suggested, and she noticed liveliness of his spirit and concentration following his rest and shower.

"That's cherp! Well then program it into both sets of beacons for an instant sanbeam to Steppingstone Quinto, just in case," Nyba ordered, watching his long fingers do their work within his lavender dionjocu gloves. "Once that's done or you can delegate the assignment to Joculatus, then take over full pilot function. Coordinate with Jamyk. I'm certain he can brief you on our recent position and strategy. I know I can trust you to hold Wolf Streak Beta steady."

"I'm always cherp steady for you, Nyba," Milyr grinned from his purple chair.

"Be steady in your duty also, my friend. This is a critical time," Domyn growled as he stood up from his brown chair beside Nyba and then announced, "Then I'm off the ConCen, Cap. Jamyk, meet me at the Buffalardi bay as soon as you can. And, my friend, grab a couple of nutrient cups before you leave the ConCen. We may not get any time to rest. Drink your meal on the go. I'll be waiting, don't let me down. The Buffalardi bay now, nowhere else, right?"

"Yup," Jamyk promised as his fingers and hands worked at the transfer of pilot function to Milyr, "friend."

"Awright, my friend," Domyn murmured as he waved to Jamyk and then stepped to the nutrient alcove at the back of the ConCen. "Whyvvi, keep alert for any small-scale objects on Tier Two. They could try to sneak something into our orbit from the low horizon of the planet. We might miss something like that…"

"Yes, Neer," Whyvvi said with some sarcasm. "I would not have thought of that myself."

"Go, Neer Domyn, get some rest, but first get my Buffalardis ready. We may not have much time," Cap Nyba commanded firmly, and then with a grin, added, "Now get your big toxx off my ConCen. Get out of here."

"Awright, enough abuse, Cap," Domyn smiled as he walked to the first hatch with a cup of nutrient in each hand. "I'll leave you young Wolves to control this craft and keep us safe."

Turning her attention back toward the holovision, Nyba observed almost an empty expanse in the scene, so she asked, "Whyvvi, do you need this holovision view setting now to search for the other ships? Milyr, will you need this Full-Encompass view for pilot duty?"

Milyr spoke up hastily, "Oh, no, Cap, I don't need this. I can see what I want in my pilot visor."

Whyvvi answered, "I should not find this view setting useful unless there are enough objects to sensor the read around us to make Full-Encompass relevant. I should switch to long distance zeta sensors and pivot them systematically around Wolf Streak Beta. I, too, will find my visor much more efficient."

"Vulch, then turn off this Full-Encompass and maybe the whole vulching holovision," Swyllo whined. "If I can't harvest any light now, we shouldn't be wasting what we have on luxury systems."

"That makes sense," Cap Nyba declared, trying to ease the girl's worries. "Whyvvi, switch to whatever sensor serves you best. I would like to know what's in our immediate region and then what's between us and Sexto sun. Swyllo will be getting surly nasty soon if she doesn't get a good light. We would not want to see her surly nasty."

"Vulch, no, you do not," Swyllo agreed with an evil sounding laugh. "You certainly don't!"

Joculatus reported, "Cap Nyba, transfer of pilot function to Milyr is completed. Milyr, you are now sole pilot."

Cap Nyba commanded hastily, and with some relief, "Jamyk, go help Domyn. Don't get lost on way to the Buffalardi bay. We need those modifications as soon as possible."

Then she returned her glance to Milyr in a clean lavender dionjocu and listened to his baritone voice say, "Remember, onad, don't get your little peener caught in the gadget. And don't forget to get some of that really cherp nutrient like Domyn said. After all the vulching antemgebemarzex can't hurt you too much, little peener."

"Nope," the boy giggled as he rose from his green chair and tapped his crotch. "Big."

"Argh! Not you, too, Jamyk!" Swyllo groaned.

"Just get your drinks and go help Domyn," Nyba demanded with a sigh of exasperation before glaring at Milyr and saying tartly, "You're no help. Focus on your pilot function now, you big toxx. See what you can do to get some sunlight for Swyllo to harvest without losing our protection behind this planet. Whyvvi, if he moves us into the higher orbit, then be alert for any other ships. We don't have any friends out there in Sexto, as far as we know…"

After he gulped down the drink hastily, Jamyk rasped loudly and firmly, "Foxes."

With excitement Whyvvi asked quickly, "Did you survey them? Did you get a signal from them?"

"No, this toxx rascal just thinks that he knows that Chitir is out there," Nyba muttered sourly, but then she forced her voice to become more optimistic and declared. "Yet of all of his foolishness, this hope for our friends in Fox Flash Alpha is useful. Continue to believe this, Jamyk. However, do it on the way to help Neer Domyn. Now get your scrawny toxx out of here."

"Cap," Jamyk nodded to her with a smile and then with two cups of nutrient, one in each hand, dashed out of the ConCen, and his raspy voice called back, "Foxes!"

From her red chair to Lyndyn's left, Whyvvi said soberly, "He surely keeps the ConCen lively."

"Vulching little onad is just a nasty toxx of time," Swyllo complained but then laughed abruptly, "But…he makes…a cherp target for my Zapstik sometimes."

"That's not what he tells me," Milyr chortled. "I hear you spend most of your time on the floor screaming for mercy. Always begging him not to hit you with his big stick…"

"Vulch, you toxx," Swyllo shrieked and then swatted at him from her yellow chair.

"Awright, enough, boys and girls," Cap Nyba yelled, trying to emulate Neer Domyn's deep growl but fearing that she sounded anything but like Neer. "Let's get on with our functions. We need to position Wolf Streak Beta for a run, no sprint away from this planet and at the same time launch two the Buffalardis. Swyllo needs to harvest. Milyr, you need to get her some sunlight from around this planet's horizon without letting our position be known to our enemies. Our attackers could be out there still. Now let's get to it, men, women, and Milyr."

For several seconds as the sound of rustling dionjocu sleeves filled the ConCen, no one spoke until Prof Lyndyn said in his calm nasal voice, "Cap Nyba, this seems a smart strategy if we can do it. Our launches and fast departure could catch colonials by surprise and allow both our escape and deployments to be successful."

Whyvvi asked, "So we have decided that other ships were colonial and are hostile?"

"Indeed evidence certainly leads to that conclusion," Prof Lyndyn stated. "Their encoded signals suggest that they don't want anyone listening to them or at least understanding them. This is a symptom of secluded culture, frightened culture…"

"Vulch, Prof, the main evidence is four nuclear weapons vulchers fired at us," Milyr exclaimed with anger in his tone and facial expression beneath the double-eyed visor. "That's all the evidence I need to know toxx vulchers don't like me."

"More reason to get me that sunlight," Swyllo demanded. "I feel useless here not being able to harvest. Hurry up and get us into better orbit, oh, so primo pilot."

"Vulch, tiny fem, you can always…" Milyr started to say with a sudden leer on his face.

"Men and women, do your functions," Cap Nyba snarled with intent this time as others were getting more annoying than usual for this pack of young wolves, especially Milyr with his comments to Swyllo, which were now beginning to bother Nyba for some unknown reason.

"Cap Nyba, my long-range zeta sensors are tracking something unusual in the inner orbits of the Sexto System," Whyvvi announced. "It is not a planet or moon. I do not believe its movement is consistent with an asteroid."

"What the vulch is it?" Milyr asked sourly. "Not another vulching attacker?"

"Just a pilot spacecraft, Milyr," Nyba commanded as she flipped her visor down before her eye and triggered the same view as Whyvvi's station. "Yes, that is different. Can we get zoom on this long-distance setting?"

Whyvvi explained, "My zeta setting is at max for this confinement. I am reluctant to go to ultra max because the time delay to get back to the close regional setting is longer than I like with potential enemies out there."

"Is Joculatus monitoring Tier Two close regional sensors for you?" Nyba asked, wondering why the other girl had not thought of this, and then said with authority, "If so then don't worry about your own supervision of close regional sensor reads. Let artigence warn us if anything shows. Your duty now is to search out the distant vistas of the Sexto System. Shoot your sensors to ultra max zoom. Let's see what's out there. We are looking for some friendly colonials."

"Friendly colonials?" Swyllo asked with sourness in her tone. "Is there such a thing?"

"Do you need me at the moment?" Prof Lyndyn asked in a bored nasal tone. "If not I should go to Med and recalibrate. I don't want Doc Kymil getting irate at me. That would not be pleasant."

"Are you sure you're going only for recalibration, Prof?" Milyr asked with a chuckle.

"Go ahead, Prof, we've covered what we needed to earlier. Get yourself refreshed," Nyba said, and then to the cocky young man in the purple chair, she asked, "Milyr, do you have Wolf Streak Beta in orbital position that puts sunlight on Swyllo's receptors? If you don't, then you'd best not be interfering with others functions or lives."

"Yeah, okay, okay, Cap Nyba," the young man retorted with a squeak in his baritone voice, and then after a few seconds, he continued with leer, "I like putting shine on her receptors."

Swyllo grumbled, "Vulch, you toxx, you're all talk. Get me my sunshine now."

As the man in a gray dionboda departed his chair to her left, Nyba turned her concentration away from the increasingly annoying puppy behavior to her right and instead into her visor and exclaimed in bewildered awe at what she saw, "Whyvvi, what is that? The shape is too abnormal for even an asteroid. You are right that it can't be planet or moon. Are you certain that it is in orbit around the Sexto sun and not moving on its own propulsion? What is that thing? This is now at ultra max zoom?"

"Oh, yes, Nyba, that is the best precision that we can get at this distance," Whyvvi replied, and then more hesitantly, she announced, "However, Nyba, I believe that the area of this Sexto System may be one of concentrations of electro-magnetic radio signals, which we discovered earlier this awakening. I am almost certain of this."

"Did you overlay the recorded survey on this scene to check that?" Nyba inquired, staring with one eye at the slightly elongated but very ragged-looking object. "It could be an asteroid after all. I've seen a few files of oddly structured asteroids. But you say this might be an area of radio signal usage?"

"I did not overlay the recorded survey on this view. I do not feel we have that kind of time," Whyvvi explained defensively. "However, my memory is usually very sure, Cap, you know that. I am wondering if perhaps…"

As the girl's words died away as if uncertain, Nyba felt irritated with Whyvvi for not speaking her new thought, so Nyba demanded with impatience, "Whyvvi, don't hold back. I need your opinion. I need your unique ability to see puzzles and patterns and ideas that the rest of us don't get right away. Like Gullu Mette in Kil-Kol..."

"Vulch, don't hint even that we are going near another place like around Gullu Mette," Milyr griped morosely. "I had enough whipping nastiness there..."

"Cap, Cap, that could be the answer," Whyvvi blurted suddenly, and then with excited hesitation, asked, "Do you think that it could be one of the other two super colony ships? Look at the silhouette irregularities, Nyba, it just could be..."

Could that be another super colony ship like Gullu Mette? Why not? There should be two more out there in the Sexto System, Nyba wished. Why should she be surprised to see one now in the distance of the Sexto System? This was why Wolf Streak Beta was here, she reminded herself.

"Whyvvi, run correlation with this image compared to file silhouettes of Cotto Rucci and Leppo Vazza," Nyba commanded, and her body shivered with a sudden thrill of anticipation.

"What did you find?" Milyr asked from his pilot station.

"We're not certain yet," Nyba replied with her attention on the strange-shaped image in her visor, and she wondered if she should put this on the holovision.

"Now don't lose your focus, you big toxx," Swyllo yelled. "I'm just now starting to build back our energy supply. Keep this Wolf Streak steady at this orbit. At least it's cherp sunlight here, even if it's so vulching far away. Keep us at this orbit altitude as long as you can."

"Don't get nasty, tiny fem," Milyr griped.

After listening to this exchange, Nyba decided that the view in her visor was fine, and she asked, "Whyvvi, anything yet on comparison with the files of the other colony super ships? Can Joculatus help with the analysis? No, forget that, artigence must work with everyone else now, especially Domyn and Jamyk with Buffalardis."

"It must be something cherp special, Nyba," Milyr said with unusual seriousness. "I don't hear you so excited and bewildered at the same time very often."

"Vulch, toxx head, even Cap can be human," Swyllo retorted. "Just stay in this sunlight."

Their off-handed concern warmed her spirit as she waited and then finally Whyvvi reported, "Nyba, I cannot tell for sure. The file images do not resemble what we see in this scene. I cannot turn this image without more points of reference as we did with Gullu Mette. There we had several viewing vectors, including those from Fox Flash Alpha. We may need Joculatus."

"Well, I suppose that this is important," Nyba remarked mostly to herself as she tried to justify another use of the already extended artigence, but artigence had done such a duty before, so she commanded, "Go ahead, Whyvvi, have Joculatus correlate this present image in as many variations as possible with file images. Let's hope the results are worthy."

"I will do what I can, Nyba," Whyvvi declared.

"Oh, yes, Whyvvi, why don't you give me the Tier Two close regional views away from Joculatus? That will take one task from his attention. I can watch that sensor. I'm not absolutely useless," Nyba commented, though at times she felt just opposite in her captain's chair watching everyone else working their functions.

"Vulch, Nyba, without your leadership, rest of us are useless," Milyr said with surprising solemnity in his tone at least to her ears.

"For once we agree, big toxx," Swyllo chirped.

Pleased and also embarrassed by their comments, Nyba was tongue-tied for several seconds and then saved by Whyvvi when the girl announced, "Nyba, correlations do not seem to help that much. Joculatus gives 31 percent correlation with Leppo Vazza and 23 percent correlation with Cotto Rucci. They should be higher or not existent. But these low intermediate correlations do not make sense. Also, one or the other of the colony ships should have no correlation at all. This just does not make sense to me."

"This is strange," Nyba agreed in a very real befuddlement, but then her intuition hit, and she suddenly had a possible answer, so she asked, "Whyvvi, why could this be? How could there be correlation for two ships yet only one object? This is a puzzle."

With interest Nyba watched the body movements and posture of the other young woman while Whyvvi contemplated enigma. Nyba suspected that other's brain was working furiously to solve the riddle. This was who Whyvvi was. Nyba had always realized. This was who Whyvvi had been since their first meeting so many years ago now at the beginning of their Blue Jay lives. Whyvvi and puzzles went together, and Whyvvi usually won.

"Vulch, this sounds like as much nasty useless data as gibberish we hear on the radio waves from the alleged colonial ships," grumbled Milyr. "I'm cherp that I don't have that duty now. Solving things isn't my best attribute."

"Really, do you have a best attribute?" scoffed Swyllo.

"I do get sunlight on your receptors, tiny fem," Milyr stated. "I'm good for that. I can't say much for your Chitir though. That toxx isn't even any good for clutching, is he?"

"Chitir could pilot circles around you…" Swyllo began to respond indignantly.

However, Nyba ignored rest of the girl's ranting when Whyvvi suddenly shouted with glee, "Oh yes, Nyba, it could be only be one reason. If two colony super ships were combined into one structure or closely bound in the same orbit, then we would get a distorted correlation that could not directly recognize each as a separate object. You knew that, did you not?"

"Ho, ho, yes, but I love watching you put these types of puzzles together with your brain," Nyba said. "Now that we know two super colony ships are there, we have a destination."

"You found two super colony ships?" asked Swyllo in surprise. "That's so cherp!"

"Yeah, but only if they don't shoot at us like the other vulchers," Milyr qualified.

"Well now, men and women, when the Buffalardis are modified, we will resume our journey," Nyba declared with joyous optimism. "That is if Swyllo has harvested enough light energy to supply our initial sprint and double launch. Can we be ready, Swyllo?"

"Oh, now you expect me to be ready," the girl complained but then admitted, "We'll be over 53 percent in a few minutes. This should be plenty until our primo pilot gets us out into clear space with a direct line to the sun of Sexto."

"This primo pilot can function very well for you, tiny fem," Milyr exclaimed.

"Then perhaps you should prep Joculatus with a sequence of updated trajectories that allow us a good shot for the double Buffalardi launch and then sprint to Cotto Rucci and Leppo Vazza," Nyba said, eyeing the lanky young man in lavender dionjocu.

"For you, Cap Nyba, I can do anything," Milyr smiled beneath his double visor.

As she glimpsed his leering grin, Nyba desired to retort that his mood was inappropriate for the ConCen, however, she did not and instead laughed, "Now, Milyr, just keep our flight steady above this planet and be prepared to dash us to our next goal when the time is right."

"My duty is to serve you, my Cap Nyba," he replied with a smile.

"And you do such a cherp performance at service, my man," Nyba laughed at him and yet she found her eyes lingering on his face and then his lanky figure in the lavender dionjocu.

Oh, yes, she thought to herself wistfully, he was becoming such a manly young pilot since popping into the Sexto System. She would need to remind herself from time to time just how much of a young man he was now and no longer a skinny boy who had left the Quinto System. Yes, he was now such a young man, Nyba mused.

Yet this feeling did seem very strange to her now. Perhaps she was ready for her own rest. Yes, that was it, she needed some nutrient and some rest for herself soon, Nyba thought.

However, her eyes lingered on his figure still.

SPEC TWO: NYBA TO SEXTO
CHAPTER 20

Stepping out of the pile on the floor that had been recently her blue dionjocu, Nyba felt a refreshing chill of cool air on her perspiring naked body. She reached to the small table beside her locker and picked up a cup of nutrient. She drank this quickly to get nourishment, which Prof Lyndyn had badgered her into taking when she had left the ConCen not minutes before.

That had been difficult a moment, Nyba recalled now, for she had been hesitant to turn her ConCen command over to Prof Lyndyn. Why? She did not know. Prof was more experienced than anyone on Wolf Streak Beta, except Doc Kymil. After all he and Doc had journeyed on the Turkey Trot Alpha the during Blue Jay scout to the Quinto System almost twenty-nine years ago. Either of the forty-seven-year-old veterans could command Wolf Streak Beta. Yet Nyba had felt reluctant and even guilty leaving the ConCen for her turn at resting.

If Domyn had been there, she would have felt better. However, he and the boy were not finished with modifications to the Buffalardis at that time. Nyba gulped down a second cup of nutrient as she walked toward the hatch to shower. Hopefully those two young men, if she could term Jamyk a man, would be returning to the ConCen soon. She needed to know that Domyn had finished his work, but more importantly, was supervising the ConCen while she was absent. Prof could do it, but she had more faith in Neer Domyn to get the young crew motivated to perform necessary tasks.

Then as she approached the hatchway to the showers, she heard Jamyk shriek from a persistent patter of water, "Chitir!"

Another deeper voice mumbled something incoherent to her ears, and Nyba paused before passing through the hatch. They were there in the shower. Apparently Domyn had finished with the Buffalardis and was now taking a moment to wash and refresh. Nyba could not find fault with this reason for his delay in returning to the ConCen. However, why did she feel uncomfortable suddenly about meeting them here, she wondered. Why did she pause her entry?

"Around," Jamyk called with a high squeak to his raspy voice. "Chitir!"

Domyn's growling laugh resounded more coherently this time from the constant splatter of water, "You mean that you are missing him, right, Jamyk? Sure, we all miss foxes."

"No," the boy's voice persisted stubbornly and loudly. "Here...now!"

Now well, she told herself, she needed to go in there and stop any rascal foolishness before it got any worse. The voice and tone of Jamyk reminded her of his lapse with reality prior to the plunge into Weznuski. She must go into the shower and set the rascal right, but Nyba hesitated still. Why not just stride in there, she scolded herself. This was crazy to hesitate out here, she grumbled.

Why was she feeling so self-conscious this time about showering with her companions? There was no reason not to do it for this was a normal routine for the previous five, or was it more now, years since they had been wolves together. No, she recalled, much longer than that since their meeting as very young children at the screening for Blue Jay potentials in the Zerosolis System. Communal bathing had always been routine, she told herself. Yet why did she hesitate now? What was different now?

Domyn said loudly with a slight chuckle, "Don't let Cap Nyba hear you say things like that, my friend. She will believe that you are crazy uncherp again. We all miss Fox Flash Alpha. I hope and want to believe that they are somewhere here in the Sexto System. But don't spout on about hearing Chitir here now in this shower when we both know that he is elsewhere. You'll get into nasty trouble."

"Yup," Jamyk squealed with a boisterous laugh. "Sexto."

"Awright, awright, I believe you. They are here in Sexto surely," Domyn laughed with a deep guffaw that infected Nyba with its simple, honest release of tension, and then a deep voice laughed again as he hollered, "Now stop beating on me with your silliness, you little peener, and finish. We're supposed to be resting and then getting back to the ConCen soon. With all this jumping around and swatting my toxx, how can you be resting? Awe only knows how you can keep up that kind of energy level all awakening."

Playfulness of these comments and jovial tone of Domyn's voice eased her own anxiety, so she strode into the shower and heard Jamyk giggle, "Play...relaxes."

"Awe grant me that kind of energy," the big young man chuckled, and as he pivoted around and saw Nyba, Domyn smiled in amusement and said, "Thankfully you're here now, Cap. This tiny monkey is beating me nasty. Maybe your presence will make him simmer down and behave somewhat."

With a grin to Domyn and then a quick scowl at Jamyk, Nyba retorted with mock seriousness, "Never has before, Domyn. This little rascal lives to goad me, I believe. However, boys, we do have a mission to continue. You do have functions awaiting you on the ConCen. I hope that you had the chance to relax and clear your heads. Your presence on the ConCen will be critical now."

"Yup," Jamyk rasped abruptly, ceasing his next leap at Domyn and spinning toward Nyba instead. "Rested."

"Ho, ho, it sure looks like you're rested," Nyba grumbled with earnest sarcasm, then while she tried not to let her eyes glance toward the smaller boy's crotch where only one nad hung, which had always attracted her curiosity, she said hastily and firmly, "I have left Prof Lyndyn in command on the ConCen. He forced me to take a break. But I realize that he's right. We all need to be ready for this next sprint of Wolf Streak Beta."

"Sprint," Jamyk said smiling as he danced in a pirouette circle in the splashing water at his feet. "Sexto...foxes."

"Well, enough of that, my friend," Domyn growled with more seriousness now and then continued in an affectionate tone, "Awe knows there is someone here very energized for duty. We're almost done here, Nyba. One more rinse and we can go for dryer. We should be calibrated in Dionjossad in no more than a few minutes later and then back to the ConCen."

While Domyn related this, Nyba saw for the first time in several awakenings that she could recall just how starkly different these two males were from one another. As they stood there naked, side by side in the falling steamy water, how oddly diverse they appeared to her. One was large, six feet tall, wide-bodied young man with a strong, sturdy stance. The other was barely five feet tall, scrawny, and fidgety as if he would fall apart any moment and shatter to the wet floor. Yet, she realized, after many years which this crew had journeyed together, just how close they were in spirit. Strange that she thought of this now, Nyba mused.

"Nyba," Jamyk rasped with a grin. "Cherp."

285

Not sure what this comment was about and suddenly feeling a warming blush creep into her face and chest, Nyba strode hastily into the showering water beside Domyn and declared, "Yes, I expect you boys to report to the ConCen as soon as possible. Now that you've finished modifying the Buffalardis, we should be ready to make our sprint and launches when I get there, which should be very shortly, I hope. At least this is my intention. Though this hot shower is tempting me to linger here longer."

Big body next to her blocked her glimpse of the giggling boy, and Domyn said in a solemn tone, "Awright, Nyba, we'll have everything ready for you. Take your own time to refresh. You deserve this as much as any of us. I know just how draining it can be to make critical decisions on the ConCen. I still remember the crisis during the Gullu Mette incident. That was a very nasty moment for me."

As warm, almost hot water gently pelted her bald scalp and forehead, Nyba heard sincerity in his voice, so she replied, "We all have done Blue Jay proud so far. I hope that people on Steppingstone Quinto and all the way back through light years to the Zerosolis System learn of accomplishments of Wolf Streak Beta. However, this may not happen if we don't deploy our beacons to complete the relay chain and get the message sent. This task has our first priority."

"We'll set it up by the time you're ready, Nyba," Domyn declared as he reached forward and punched a button to turn off the shower of water drenching his large body. "Awright, my little friend, it's time to go dry off and get into our dionjocus, some nice new fresh ones. We have work to do for our Cap Nyba. Hurry up, let's go. We must recalibrate with Dionjossad as well. Don't delay, Jamyk."

"Nyba," Jamyk said, looking at her through the space left by Domyn's departure. "Cherp."

In the brief moment that he dallied there in the falling water, Nyba thought that she witnessed sparkle in his eyes and glistening of his wet skin when the last of the droplets splashed against him, and then in embarrassed irritation, she hissed, "Go, Jamyk, don't be a foolish rascal please. You've got important work to do. Go with Neer Domyn and get calibrated with Joculatus. I believe that we will need your pilot skills again. Go now, you little toxx!"

When his thin arm reached out to punch the button to his shower, his eyes peered at her still, his face creased in a smile, and his raspy voice intoned soberly, "Nyba... Cap."

Then before the last drop of the abruptly ended shower fell to the wet floor, he was gone from her sight. Suddenly she felt alone and almost wished for his return. Now you are infected with foolishness, she thought to herself. Yet the sensation of loneliness remained with her in this communal shower with no other person as company. Strange feeling, Nyba told herself, especially as she was missing rascal Jamyk's presence. Very strange sensation, she mused again.

However, everyone had a function to perform, she knew, if Wolf Streak Beta was to continue their Blue Jay mission. Not if, she spat to herself in the falling water, but when we continue the mission. Just as warm water persistently caressed her body, the crew of Wolf Streak Beta would be persistent. In spite of setbacks so far, they would wash away doubts and frustration and pursue mission. Nyba felt this just as hotly as water bouncing off her bald head and tilted neck.

If she could only have a companion beside her now, she wished. If only the captain could have a special friend to ease the tensions of responsibility. She desired to have same foolish bond that Jamyk believed that he enjoyed with Chitir. Or perhaps that Swyllo appeared to share with Chitir. Or, she thought with longing, that Kymil had with Lyndyn. Or even an elusive bond between Whyvvi and Khebol. If she could have someone, Nyba longed in comfort of the hot falling water. But she was the captain with a lonely responsibility.

As showering water tickled her arms like massaging fingers, Nyba felt his hands stroke her skin. Long, slender fingers on long hands caressed the water into her skin. Her eyes closed as she tilted her face upwards into the full flow of the shower. His strokes travelled to her shoulders. Her torso shivered with the touch.

His scent filtered through the steamy waters, not as stinky rank as he had been during boyish growth, but now musky, pleasant, and alluring as a young man. Her nostrils flared and quivered with his scent and against the flow of droplets. His was a welcome scent of a welcome young man. His warm breath cascaded with the hot water down from his tall height to her neck.

Hands of gentle hot water flowed from her shoulders down over her breasts. Nyba shivered with sensation and thought of his long lanky fingers teasing her. Her mind envisioned a long face leaning down to the back of her neck and kissing her flesh tenderly. More trembling quivered down her waist and into her legs. She stumbled forward against the wet wall. With shaking legs, Nyba forced herself to stand more upright while leaning on the wall. The shower water flowed warmly down her back and buttocks. The warm feeling soothed away the trembling in her torso and legs. Nyba could almost feel him lean his lanky body against hers and stabilize her stance with his manly strength. Her mind felt his power, his support, and his firm companionship.

Oh, Milyr, she dreamed, if you could be here now with me, just as a very close friend. She could almost feel his presence. She could almost believe that when she turned around and opened her eyes, Milyr would be there with her. His smell, his voice, his figure, his strength, his eyes, his smile, all flowed from her memories to give her his presence there now in the hot shower with her. Nyba swam in the comfort and tranquility of his companionship.

"Cap Nyba," a voice called.

With a resurgence of controlled reality, Nyba pushed herself from the wet wall. She did not bounce into the male body behind her. Almost disappointed she turned in the falling water and tried to peer toward the hatch. Her eyes were wet with moisture. She was forced to blink her lids against the wetness.

"Nyba, are you in there?" asked Doc Kymil's melodious voice from out in the locker room. "Domyn said that you might be in the shower still."

As ecstasy of the recent daydream faded hastily from her awareness, Nyba exclaimed, "Yes, Doc, I'm finished now. I just need a moment to unwind. This seemed to be the only place and time to do that now. I'll be out soon. I'll meet you in Med to recalibrate. Do you have one of my dionjocus there? Or should I go to my quarters and get one?"

"I don't have yours in Med," Doc Kymil replied while she stuck her head through the hatchway. "I can go to your room and get one for you while you dry. You should get another cup of nutrient also."

"That's a cherp plan," Nyba agreed, turning to roughly punch off the shower. "It should save me some time in prepping. I want to be back in the ConCen shortly. We've got a mission to complete."

She must have appeared too rough with her body movement and acerbic in tone for Doc Kymil asked with concern, "Is anything wrong? Are you alright, Nyba? You seem…edgy for someone who is supposed to be refreshed and rested."

"Ho, ho, I'm cherp, Doc, just anxious about things that have happened and getting on with our mission," Nyba explained in a lame attempt at reasonableness but doubted that she could fool this wise woman. "Thinking about the colonials and their behavior is very disturbing."

"Oh my, Cap Nyba, you have important decisions to consider always. Being Cap is not easy. When we are now at culmination of our long mission, your choices must be even more difficult. I'm here, you know, if you need to talk about things," Doc Kymil said with her distinctly mothering tone, which suggested to Nyba that the woman was not fooled but would wait for Nyba to speak first.

Wiping loose water from her arms and torso, Nyba strutted to hatch and said, "I'll be dry soon. I will go directly to Med if you get my dionjocu."

"I will do that now, Nyba," Kymil agreed, and after a few seconds pause to peer at Nyba, the older woman departed chuckling, "Don't wait too long, Nyba. I know of one young man who would enjoy seeing you walk naked to Med."

Just what she needed to hear, Nyba told herself sarcastically. Then she entered the locker room and strode purposely to the drying cubicle. There she punched harshly another button with her fist. A blast of warm, dry air came from all directions within the small upright cubicle. She spun her squat sturdy body with agitated vigor, even though she knew that she could have stood still in the air flow. Yet the exaggerated movement felt cleansing of her temper.

Why was she nasty whipped? She should feel better now. Her body felt clean and invigorated now, but her mind…that was not so relaxed, she admitted to herself. But why? Was she goaded with looks from Jamyk just recently in the shower? Was she upset with her daydream of Milyr? That had seemed so very pleasant, yet she felt guilty. Nyba could not understand her feelings at that moment. The innocent button controlling the dryer took force of her agitation again.

Marching naked out of the locker room, Nyba headed toward Med. She did not care at that moment if someone else saw her. Why should she even care, she wondered? For almost two decades, this family of Jayers had lived, worked, showered, dressed, undressed, and played together in close quarters mostly on Wolf Streak Beta. What was the big concern about her nudity now? What had changed in her attitude just recently? Why was she so preoccupied during this voyage since leaving Steppingstone Quinto about her body and how others looked at her? She was Cap Nyba. They all respected her. She knew that. Why was she so nasty upset about this now? Her frustration swelled.

Door to Med was open, so she strutted inside, and Doc Kymil was there with a blue dionjocu draped over one arm and blue JMO suit over the other, and a woman said, "Here you go, Nyba, put these on. Let's get you calibrated. Your ConCen seems ready for you. Your crew seems excited to get on with our mission."

While she took a blue JMO one-piece body suit and pulled it up over her torso to just above her breasts, Nyba declared, "I'm more excited now myself. I need to get Wolf Streak Beta going forward again. We've been delayed too much already. There have been too many unforeseen occurrences."

"Life is like that, Nyba," Doc Kymil said soberly, and then reaching out an arm to give her a dionjocu, she added, "Here, let me help you stabilize yourself while you put your legs in. I often find that can be a challenging chore to do by oneself. Balance can be a tricky thing sometimes."

"I've noticed this recently. My body changes every time I wake up from Saphyndenlairoum sleep. I'm not always sure that I can keep acclimated in short periods of being awake. At least now I'll have plenty of time to get familiar with myself," Nyba said freely and then wondered why she had admitted this to Doc Kymil.

Grin spread over the other woman's face, and Doc Kymil exclaimed, "Oh my, Nyba, that's normal for young adults, especially your age. Although most people undergo these awkward stages few years earlier than Jayer, what you are experiencing is natural to some extent. The boys really struggle through this stage, but they try not to let us see this struggle."

Accepting Kymil's support, Nyba finally put her feet into the legs of her dionjocu and said as she did this, "Ho, ho, yes, boys have been acting like toxx this trip since leaving Steppingstone Quinto. Though Domyn is alright most of time. Jamyk is a nuisance for me. That Milyr, he's just...just... Milyr. I don't know how else to state that. Was Lyndyn like this when you were our age on the Turkey Trot Alpha? I can't imagine Prof acting like our boys do now."

"Oh my, yes, Nyba, he was probably worse," Kymil smiled, and Nyba was certain that she witnessed a twinkle in the older woman's eye showing beside the visor over half of her face. "Oh my, he was a nasty toxx then when he was younger and so brash. Yet I cared for him despite of his brashness. We have become kindred spirits over the years, my Lyndyn and me."

Not sure if she was entitled to hear this from Doc Kymil, not sure if she deserved the woman's trust and openness, Nyba steered the conversation back to the boys of Wolf Streak Beta by saying, "Well, our boys now can act like a complete toxx at times. Jamyk and Milyr goad me nasty at times. I can't wait for them to mature like Domyn seems to have recently."

"Jamyk will be several years yet. We must remember that he is two years younger than you other young folks on Wolf Streak Beta and also Fox Flash Alpha I believe," Kymil explained and then paused a few seconds, watching Nyba with penetrating eyesight, or so it seemed to Nyba, before continuing, "Now Milyr can be mature whenever he wishes. His body is as mature as he can be with the prolonged affect of antemgebemarzex. His social maturity...well, that is very unpredictable."

"That toxx doesn't act mature at all," Nyba blurted and then wondered why she had said that so vehemently since she did not really believe it, so after Kymil waited patiently, Nyba continued, "Well, he does on occasion do his duty very professionally. I often find his insight on the ConCen valuable. That is when he's not being toxx to Swyllo or Whyvvi."

Doc Kymil smiled and agreed, "Yes, lad had his childishly lewd moments, and then he gives you something of value when you need it. That is typical behavior of a young man who needs to impress and then to dominate those around him. I'm sure that Prof Lyndyn can explain behavior of the boys who try to be men. He went through the same toxx stage himself. I'm not certain that he has really finished with that stage yet. Milyr reminds me very often of a younger Lyndyn on Turkey Trot Alpha and also certain secluded places on Steppingstones."

"Erh, well, Doc, do you believe Milyr's wild tales of his exploits on Steppingstones?" Nyba asked hesitantly, not sure if she wanted an honest answer, and tried to hide her preoccupation on Milyr by adding, "I really mean to ask, most boys that brag like that, do they all have to tell tales of willing fems on Steppingstones? Did Prof ever do that?"

Doc stared at her with a penetrating gaze again as she asked this, and then after a few more seconds of studying Nyba, Doc Kymil replied, "Oh, I guess that is a boast for the boys who learn that they are at the age when normal boys become sexually active, yet know as Jayers that they must wait until effects of antemgebemarzex no longer inhibits their prowess. This delay in hormonal sexual maturity can be frustrating for anyone, boy or girl, especially when one had intellectual knowledge of what should be but not a hormonal urge to pursue. This affects us girls as well, I'm sure you know."

"Now I guess that could be. But I wonder about Milyr's tales," Nyba began to say as she tried not to reveal her persistent interest in the young man, or was it really jealousy now?

Then Joculatus announced, startling her, "Cap Nyba, Neer Domyn asks that you come to the ConCen now. There is a new sighting on the small planet below Wolf Streak Beta."

When she heard this message, Nyba hastened her pace and pulled up a dionjocu along her muscular thighs, made sure the crotch padding fit snugly, and then began placing her arms into the sleeves saying as she did this, "I'd better hurry. This could be another threat. Wolf Streak Beta may have to sprint away sooner than I had planned."

"Don't rush, Nyba. Your crew can take care of the situation if it becomes nasty. Just make certain that this dionjocu fits your new body form properly. You're not the little girl you once were," Doc Kymil declared as she aided Nyba's effort by holding up the collar of the blue garment. "Remember, attach the nutrient tube. We may not get many chances to get normal drinks of nutrient."

"Ho, ho, Doc, you don't need to tell me," Nyba snorted with annoyance as she reached her hand inside the garment and popped the tube to patch on her stomach, and then added, "My chubby body doesn't slide into this dionjocu as easily as I once did. But at least I don't have to worry about putting tube onto my… parts…like guys do. That toxx Milyr likes to make a big show of doing that."

"Oh my, yes, he does," Kymil chuckled, tugging the collar up Nyba's back and over her shoulders. "That young man needs to remind us women about his growth and manliness quite often. Yet that is not unusual for guys who are often less confident about themselves. We girls do mature on average more quickly than our guys, both physically and emotionally."

"This sure shows with our Blue Jay guys," Nyba laughed as she positioned her breasts into the supports within the inner lapel of dionjocu. "Guys from Wolf Streak, Fox Flash, and yes, even Lynx Blaze prove this to be so true. But they are Blue Jayers, and we love them all."

Joculatus announced, "Cap Nyba, Neer Domyn asks how much time before you can be at the ConCen."

Sensing that she should respond to this query, Nyba called loudly into air of Med, "Joculatus, please inform Neer Domyn that I should be there in about no more than eleven minutes… Well, Doc, that should give them something to go by, so they don't get nervous."

"Yes, and that's a good example," Doc Kymil said. "Our Neer is fully capable of supervising the ConCen and making decisions, yet he is unsure of himself and needs to often seek your approval. His body may be adult and quite manly, but his confidence is still somewhat youthfully indecisive at times, so unlike yours, Nyba."

"Ho, ho, and he is our most mature guy on Wolf Streak Beta," Nyba giggled but then thought otherwise and hastily added, "Now not including Prof Lyndyn. He is our most mature guy."

"Oh my, not always," Doc Kymil laughed and then more seriously asked, "How does the fit feel, Nyba? Did I select a dionjocu proper for your body now?"

Folding the outer lapel over the inner layer and melding two pieces together, Nyba noticed mounded bulges of her chest under her sliding hand and replied, "Oh, yes, these breasts seem to fit nicely into the support of this dionjocu. I guess that I'll need to get used to this now, won't I?"

"Yes, you will. You are a woman now and must accept benefits and disadvantages that go with this stage of human life," Doc Kymil said as she appraised Nyba from the front. "You are a shapely and well-figured young woman, Nyba. I believe that I can understand why guys are staring at you more often now than before when they were younger boys. You have matured. And so has their intellectual interest in your body shape. antemgebemarzex can't totally prohibit their natural fascinations with you young women. It's not that potent an inhibitor."

"Erh, is that why Jamyk stared at me in the shower? He has not been doing that so obviously before. The little toxx one nad, I'll beat his skinny toxx," Nyba grumbled in anger.

"Don't worry about that. It's a natural reaction for guys when they begin to mature and notice a difference between their bodies and us women. In many ways, this interest is complimentary to your value as a woman, although I'm sure that you would not see it as such, nor would they admit it as such," Doc Kymil explained, and then with a wave toward the Dionjossad pad, said, "You should get calibrated now, Cap Nyba. Your crew in the ConCen may need your guidance soon."

"Now I suppose they do. But I still get whipped thinking the little rascal is looking at my breasts. How would he like it if I stared at his one nad?" Nyba asked, hissing her anger.

"Oh, I don't believe that guys would even notice," Kymil sighed. "Sometimes I believe that they try to get our attention to their manly parts, as Milyr is always making innuendos. Another one of their low esteem issues, although I've never gotten Lyndyn to admit this."

"Erh, I get angry with that little one nad peener. After all it would be natural for me or anyone to glance at his crotch just because of his uniqueness with only one nad. But does he have to stare at my breasts? They are perfectly normal for a woman," Nyba retorted adamantly but wondered suddenly if she was really angered at Jamyk for this perceived invasion of herself, or her unresolved feelings for Milyr. "Why does the rascal have only one nad? How could he pass Blue Jay entry requirements with such deformity?"

During this discussion, Nyba did not notice that she had stepped onto the Dionjossad and the scanner ring had passed up and then down the length of her body and the dionjocu until Doc Kymil announced suddenly, "There, Cap Nyba, you are calibrated with good interface with Joculatus again. I believe that we should hurry to the ConCen now. Our men need our guidance now."

"Ho, ho, Doc, you snuck that by me," Nyba chuckled as they walked from Med and then she declared, "and I guess that you will not answer me about the little peener's one nad, will you?"

"Oh my, Nyba, you know that I do not like to discuss one person's health privacy with another," Doc Kymil explained solemnly, and then after a pause, almost whispered, "However, I sense that you could use some insight into Jamyk's background that could aid you in improving your relationship with the boy. Perhaps what I will tell you could explain some of his unpredictable behavior as well."

"I don't think anything can improve my opinion of him," Nyba stated vehemently. "But I would like to know about his one nad situation, especially if it explains his childish foolishness."

"Now, Nyba, you must not tell this to anyone else. Only Lyndyn and I know. Not even Jamyk knows unless he can remember events from his infancy," Doc Kymil whispered, gripping Nyba by the arm and halting their steps toward the ConCen. "Just a year after the birth, baby Jamyk had a very nasty infection in his testicles. The infection caused by unusual birth abnormality that almost killed him."

"So the rascal was born with two?" Nyba asked, wondering why the secrecy.

"No, he was born with three nads," Kymil said in a hushed voice. "Two had to be removed to save his life."

"Three nads? He was born with three nads? How could that be?" Nyba inquired, hearing her own bewilderment in her voice.

Doc Kymil pointed toward the ConCen, and as they slowly walked toward it, asked, "Have you heard of Bertrandando Postulate of Inevitable Genetic Mutation? It was taught many years ago in your early education before your Blue Jay voyage began. At least it was taught when Prof and I were of that young age."

Noises and voices could be heard from the ConCen now, but Nyba was intrigued by this revelation, so she paused again in the corridor and replied, "Yes, I can recall something about how natural evolution experiments constantly with genetic mutations to provide species with new patterns to enhance probabilities of survival against odd occurrences."

"Yes, that is a basic explanation," Doc Kymil said. "In general this postulate says that natural mutation will eventually cause at least one of any possible adaptation with growth of species. In several billion people, there is a probability that at least one will be born with three or even more nads, for purposes of our discussion. Of course this Bertrandando Postulate applies for every possible species mutation of various body parts and functions. But now we are talking about the boy's nads."

"Ho, ho, so Jamyk is a mutation. I always thought he was nasty strange," Nyba whispered with relish. "But three nads, how can that be a useful genetic mutation?"

"Oh my, Nyba, you must not say anything to anyone, even this trusted crew. I told you this in sincere confidence for your sake as a leader," Doc Kymil stressed seriously with her grip on Nyba's arm again. "In this mutation, three nads could very well be genetic advancement. The man with three nads could be more potent and sire offspring that could retain a mutated trait leading to an ever increasing population with this trait. We cannot be sure, but this could be nature's experiment to add a new survival trait into the human genome. Whatever Jamyk's trait is in his genetic make-up, nature may want it be become prolific in future. We do not know. I will not be so arrogant as to believe that I know if this is good or evil. I simply accept Jamyk as being what nature desires to add into the evolutionary future, just as I would with any of our Jayers."

"Jamyk, our toxx rascal, is a mutation template of advancement of the human species?" Nyba groaned in exaggerated despair. "That is enough for me to pray to Domyn's mystical entity for help. Jamyk is an advancement to our species? Oh, mighty entity, help us all!"

"Oh now, Nyba, it can't be that bad. We may not even know or see this possible trait from Jamyk himself, if it even exists. It could be recessive in his genes, if Bertrandando Postulate is even correct," Kymil whispered and then said cautiously, "Remember, Nyba, don't say anything about this to anyone. I trust you to be mature and prudent. Now we should get into the ConCen. Neer Domyn must be very anxious by now."

"Not a word," Nyba promised with true intent. "I don't want to remember this conversation myself. Argh, it's nasty just to think about."

Then she walked toward the outer hatch of the ConCen. Feeling Doc Kymil beside her, Nyba appreciated companionship, support, and now shared the trust of the older woman. They passed through the inner hatch and strode to their respective chairs. Busy voices and rustle of working dionjocu garments filled the ConCen. Her crew was performing functions of Wolf Streak Beta. Nyba was happy. Their mission was back on track or would be soon.

As she sat in her blue chair, Nyba asked, "What is this sighting on the planet, Neer Domyn? And are we ready to launch our Buffalardis?"

He peered at her for a moment with an uncertain frown on his wide face, but then replied, "The Buffalardis are ready to launch whenever you wish. Our sensors have found what seems to be a mining operation on the surface of this small planet.

It is presently located on the horizon as we approach. When our pilot adjusted our altitude and orbit in put us into better direct sunlight for Swyllo, ground operation showed on the sensors."

"How do we know it is a mining operation and not some other threat, such as spaceships capable of planetary take-off?" Nyba asked as she glanced over at Milyr when pilot was mentioned.

Whyvvi spoke quickly and with conviction, "Oh, Cap, I know. My locally confined sensors are very precise now. Our pictures of equipment and camp are very detailed. They are on the Tier Two if you wish to view them. You should be able to see the clearly tent-like structures and mobile surface machines creating some of the local dust but not too much for our viewing. I think the surface is very hard and does not create much dust with machinery usage."

As Whyvvi spoke, Nyba viewed the scene in her one-eyed visor. Definitely tents or similar housing or protection from the poor atmosphere down there showed on her view. Also, moving machines, some digging into planetary crust, some hauling material, some receiving this surface material for some form of processing, it all looked like a typical mining operation. So, Nyba wondered, was this the reason mastership of alleged colonials had been in orbit around this planet? Or had it been waiting on guard for Wolf Streak Beta or some other wayward victim? The answer to why they had attacked was still very much in doubt. Yet they had attacked, she realized.

"This does look like mining equipment. It must be nasty down there for miners. I wonder if they have any underground shafts," Nyba commented and then asked, "Have we scanned any transmissions from that camp going into Sexto space? Or have we picked up any signals from the ships to that camp?"

Prof Lyndyn reported, "No, Cap, there has been nothing recent on the radio wave frequencies in either direction. We may be the only spacecraft around this planet now. We've had no signals and sighting of any other, at least as well as I can determine this function."

"Indeed, Prof, I have trust in your skills, no matter which chair you sit in," Nyba smiled at the forty-seven-year-old man in the gray chair on her left, and then more vocally announced, "To all of Wolf Streak Beta, I say I have complete confidence in your abilities to do what we must in the future to fulfill our mission goals, and maybe more glories than we envisioned. Every person in the ConCen has proven to be a true Blue Jayer. We will succeed. Now let's get ready to sprint toward that combo of ships that could be Cotto Rucci and Leppo Vazza. Each of the three colony ships looked generally same in design and appearance but for subtle variances in outer hull constructions of towers and other spiky things sticking up…"

"What about our launches?" Domyn asked in some astonishment. "I was certain that you would wish for the launches to be your first intent."

"Ho, ho, Neer, don't worry. We are going to launch from this position and then immediately sprint for the target out there. Is there any problem with launch trajectories if we do that?" Nyba asked gazing into the face of a big young man in tan dionjocu sitting to her right, and she smiled to herself how different he looked now than he had less than an hour ago in the showers.

"Awe no, Cap Nyba, Joculatus has several vector trajectories planned. We can do it," Domyn said confidently. "We've got everything prepped and ready to go."

"Swyllo, I assume that our energy is sufficient for this challenging multi-task plan?" Nyba quizzed, looking past Domyn to the girl in yellow. "You realize of course that we will be heading directly toward your sunlight source as we make our sprint."

"That is cherp. We are about 67 percent now. Your multi-task challenge will use much of that, but I can get that back and more if we go into that sunlight," Swyllo chirped happily.

"Pilot, Milyr, are you ready to sprint us to the distant combo of ships? Are you capable of getting us there under reasonable the Flandecam thrust?" Nyba asked the long slender figure in lavender on the far-right side of Swyllo.

"Yeah, Cap Nyba, you know I can keep the thrust as high as you need it," Milyr grinned beneath his double visor of pilot. "These Flandecams really perform for my hands. Joculatus and me are in the very intimate interface now. Wolf Streak Beta is ready to sprint."

Peering over to her left toward the girl in the red chair, Nyba ordered, "Whyvvi, I'd like you to sensor search this region around this planet for any sign of other mastership. That will require putting our long-distance sensors on Tier Two auto search, but we have some time before we need a regular sensor read of the colony ships ahead. As soon as we do not need a rear view of this region, you can search ahead at the similar close confinement setting, so we are not surprised by any small ships or weaponry as we were last time."

"I should have no problem with doing this search, Cap," Whyvvi said but added, "This will not allow me to continue searching the planet's mining site. Do you want a sensor locked onto that site until we are safely away?"

This question puzzled Nyba for several seconds, but then in a moment of intuition, she demanded, "Give that sensor duty to Jamyk. And Jamyk, also be alert for any sudden radio or other comm transmissions coming from the mining site. They could attempt to signal other sips in orbit or out in this Sexto System. They could signal others of our presence or departure. Whyvvi, can you combine such functions into a single sensor setting for one auxiliary station to monitor?"

"I could listen for that…" Prof Lyndyn began.

But Nyba interrupted him hastily, "No, Prof, I need you to be very alert to any signals sent between any ships in space. No, we need separate surveillance on that mining site as long as it is a factor. Then we can adjust our priorities. Jamyk, I'm sure that you can handle this sensor function."

"Yup," Jamyk replied with ready energy. "Cherp."

Beside the boy in green, Whyvvi worked her fingers and hands within her pink dionjocu gloves and said, "Cap Nyba, we can program the setting as you recommended. I should have it prepped and at Jamyk's station in just minutes. Pay attention, Jamyk, when I set this up and transfer it to you."

"Yup," Jamyk said, spinning his chair around in a full circle and tapping his one-eyed visor as he faced Whyvvi. "Cherp."

"Just be ready, Jamyk," Nyba insisted more harshly than she really intended or so she wanted to believe. "Keep those eyes on your visor and those ears to your receivers. We can't be careless now and miss something. We could very well have enemies out there still."

Pivoting toward her, Jamyk smiled and rasped while tapping his head covered by a green dionjocu cap, "Sense."

His word made no sense to her, but Nyba decided not to give in to her irritation and scold the boy, instead she turned away from his stare and announced, "Okay, men and women, I hope Wolf Streak Beta is ready. Domyn, you are in command of the Buffalardis. Launch as you best determine the sequence. As soon as the second Buffalardi is launched, Milyr, you are to pilot Wolf Streak Beta toward the colony ship coordinates at a fast, steady pace. Do not go more than half the potential velocity without my command unless you determine a crisis developing before I can respond. Do you men understand this plan?"

"I can handle it, Cap," Milyr declared in an unusually deeper voice than he often used, she thought, almost a husky, sensuous voice to her ears.

"I'll need most of Joculatus while launching," Domyn announced as he flicked his fingers within his tan dionjocu gloves but not swaying his chair in his usual nervous habit, she noticed happily.

"Now then all stations are ready?" Nyba asked.

Whyvvi called breathlessly, "Now, Cap, I have sensor function for Jamyk ready. We are ready over here."

"Ready," Jamyk said. "Cap."

"Well, alright, Neer Domyn, launch the Buffalardis and let's begin this," Nyba commanded, and then with a glance toward the purple chair, she said, "Then, Milyr, it will be your turn to perform."

Beside her Domyn took control of the launching operation. His meticulous command in concert with Joculatus was impressive to witness. Nyba sat back into her blue chair and watched the big young man do his work. His hands seemed magical in their delicate precision. His domineering presence was a joy to be near. He was truly a mature man now, no longer a boy.

Soon her attention drifted toward the tall form in the lavender dionjocu. Shortly it would be his duty to perform. Milyr would be able to reveal his maturity as pilot, a truly manly function of Wolf Streak Beta. She had confidence that he would show his true capability. He was also a man and no longer that boy of long ago.

"Joculatus, prepare to launch the first Buffalardi," Neer Domyn commanded.

"Is my inclination okay for your launch, Domyn?" Milyr asked.

"At this angle toward the region of chain of relays, this is fine," Domyn replied. "Just don't take us out before I get a second one launched."

"Right, that's what our plan is, Domyn," Milyr replied with mild sarcasm, and then with more professionalism in his tone, added, "Don't worry, big man, I've got your toxx covered. I'll keep this Wolf steady for you, Domyn."

As Domyn grunted a short reply while his attention focused upon his function, Nyba almost felt moderate envy of the relationship that the two young men shared still after all the years of their companionship. Could she ever have such a tie with Milyr? Could she ever have more?

However, soon her mind wandered again. She found herself peering over at the small figure in green on her far left. She could suddenly only think of the evolutionary advantage of having three nads. Nyba glanced at Jamyk, then back to Milyr. How did this relate to Milyr, she frowned to herself. She wanted to focus her attention on Milyr's performance, but this distraction with the boy in the green dionjocu interfered. Again she turned her vision toward the lavender form.

Perhaps, she was wondering subconsciously, what it would be like if Milyr was a young man born with three nads? However, reality of the situation forced her to glance back to Jamyk, and she now cursed info, which Doc Kymil had shared with her. Of all boys, why did it have to be Jamyk?

Then abruptly she felt acceleration of Milyr's leap into space. The ride had begun.

SPEC TWO: NYBA TO SEXTO
CHAPTER 21

"Ship," Jamyk croaked suddenly. "Planet."

Fluttering her small finger on her left hand within her blue dionjocu glove, Nyba watched her view in the visor change from a long distant image of what Whyvvi had started calling Cotto Vazza to a shorter distant view of a small planet falling behind as Wolf Streak Beta sprinted into space. This was the scene which Jamyk now saw in his visor. There it was, a very tiny speck of gleaming light orbiting the copper-colored planet. For once the boy was alert and correct, she thought.

"Keen eye, Jamyk," Nyba exclaimed. "There is a ship there. At least they are not chasing us at this moment. Keep an eye on that as long as it stays in range of your sensor setting. Listen for any transmissions. They might signal another ship out here. Be alert."

"We're sprinting fast, Cap," Milyr said enthusiastically. "If they chase Wolf Streak Beta now, they won't even get to sniff our tail. I'm only going at half potential velocity. They can't catch us."

After reluctantly taking her glimpse from Milyr's active hand movements, Nyba asked, "Whyvvi, is there any scan from the aft octants showing other spaceships on your current setting?"

"Nothing on my sensor scans behind us," the girl in the light red dionjocu reported. "Should I stay at this setting? Should I continue scanning behind us? We have travelled some distance since the leaving orbit around that radiant planet. Jamyk has found only a ship in our aft octants."

It would have been Jamyk, Nyba thought sourly but did not let any of this disgruntlement show in her voice when she said, "Stay with the current aft octants view on your present confinement setting. Eventually as we move away, you should gradually adjust your zoom to keep that region in clarity for spaceships and smaller objects. Be patient, Whyvvi. I like having two eyes watching that region better than one. That's been our only threat so far since popping into Sexto. Let's keep our eyes there for awhile longer. We don't want to be surprised from behind, do we?"

"Okay, I can gradually widen my view. Maybe I will read something out there," Whyvvi said, although the pouting in her tone told Nyba that the girl was not optimistic about finding anything.

From beside her right, Neer Domyn said, "First Buffalardi has deployed the beacons by now. We are getting too far away to have positive confirmation. However, I have seen no explosion. This should tell us of success, but I'd really like to have a zeta sensor search before we get too far away."

Almost half an hour ago, Domyn had launched the second Buffalardi only five minutes after the first. Both launches had been good, and trajectories had seemed on course as programmed. No colonial spaceships had followed or fired on either the Buffalardi. Everything had proceeded as planned. Neer Domyn had been thrilled with the sci-tech of Wolf Streak Beta.

Now, perhaps they had completed the relay chain of beacons stretching back to Steppingstone Quinto, and Nyba said with a cautious praise in her tone, "You've done quite well in this launch, Neer Domyn. Let's see how our second Buffalardi travels. We have limited energy and should not spend excessively on zeta sensors unless we have cause to do so. Trust your sci-tech and launching skills, Neer. Most likely you have succeeded."

"Awright, Cap, if you are confident," Domyn replied. "I'll point the normal sensor toward that region of space near Kil-Kol as long as it is in range."

"We can afford to do that," Nyba declared and then asked, "Swyllo, you are able to harvest sufficient light now that we are in constant sunlight, aren't you?"

"Yes, this is cherp harvesting," Swyllo exclaimed with joy. "Especially with Milyr going almost straight toward the sun, this should be vulching cherp!"

"It's vulching easy pilot duty, too, tiny fem. Cherp luck for us, our destination is in almost exact line with the sun. Could not be more cherp," Milyr said from his purple chair beside Swyllo.

"Well, men, women, and Milyr, our mission is cherp back on track. We may be contacting descendants of colonials from the Zerosolis System in a few hours.

We can get there in a few days, right, Milyr?" Nyba asked hopefully while she changed the view in her visor to look at Cotto Vazza or whichever of the three colony ships was out there in the moment.

"Vulch, that should be cherp easy under these conditions," Milyr sighed, leaning back into his chair and letting his hands and fingers sway and flicker above his lap and thighs. "Little peener, you sure don't know how easy this flying is now."

"Ship," Jamyk announced loudly. "Follows."

"Yes, I see it also," Whyvvi agreed. "My sensor shows that it is the only one following now. My view is wide enough to see most of our aft octants region."

Nyba flicked back to Jamyk's view and asked, "Is there any sign that they or any other object have gone after the Buffalardis now? The spaceship must have stayed at the planet for some reason before chasing us again."

"Perhaps they stopped to collect their personnel from the mining camp," Doc Kymil suggested. "That radioactive terrain would not be very healthy for people over a period of time."

Swyllo retorted, "That assumes that vulchers in the big mastership cared about their miners. Remember they let their pilots in smaller speed ships use all the fuel and then stranded them in space where the nuclear explosions occurred. That doesn't seem very caring."

Whyvvi stated pragmatically, "They could have picked up their recently mined minerals at least."

"Very nasty vulchers," Milyr swore with disdain, and this showing of concern for strangers startled Nyba coming from such normally self-centered toxx.

"Well, they are chasing us again," Nyba declared with annoyance and then asked, "How is our second Buffalardi doing, Neer? Are the colonials paying any attention to that?"

"I see no evidence of any ship pursuit toward our Buffalardi deployment area," Whyvvi reported, but then qualified her statement by saying, "Yet I cannot sensor for very small objects like those orbs that trapped us earlier. Now even smaller speed ships would be difficult to read at this distance on this confinement setting."

"Nope," Jamyk rasped. "Chase... Wolf."

Domyn reported, "That's about what I keep sensing. No reads of any hostile action in the region of our deployments. Second deployment should be now at a different site. The alignment systems in beacons will position all these relay beacons in conjunction with those already connected within the chain back to

Quinto. We should be sending our auto message now or soon. We could try the sanbeam soon, if you wish to confirm the message, Cap."

"That would be cherp," Swyllo chirped. "All our fans in all Stepping Stones all the way back to the Zerosolis System will want to hear from us live."

"Vulch, yeah! We are legendary Wolf Streak Beta," Milyr sang in delight. "Our fans would want to hear more from us than our vulching dismal auto recording."

"Dismal? Is that the style of signal you sent, you toxx? Is that the image you gave to our fans?" Swyllo shrieked shrilly in obvious disappointment.

"Vulch, tiny fem, our situation at time wasn't exactly cherp. I had to send a basic truth for observers at MisCom who must decide the next phase of Blue Jay. I couldn't make up the cherp tale just to protect our image," Milyr complained. "They'll see that we are cherp legends anyway."

"Well, we're more cherp now," Nyba stated, trying to soften the young man's emotional turmoil. "As soon as we can, we will sanbeam the live report to Quinto. Maybe by then we will be able to report the contact of welcome from the colonials. Let's look toward this meeting with hope and optimism."

"Perhaps we will be able to report the reunion with Fox Flash Alpha," Whyvvi said with a sigh. "I would like to see and hear from Khebol and rest again and soon."

"Foxes," Jamyk rasped in agreement. "Sexto."

"Don't get him going, Whyvvi, or I'll make you responsible for him," Nyba declared in a light tone. "Yes, we may have cherp things to send in the sanbeam soon. I have hope as I look at Cotto Vazza. There is fulfillment of our mission. Perhaps we will become legends, hey, Milyr?"

"Vulch, in my opinion, we already are legends," Milyr crowed exuberantly.

Prof Lyndyn asked suddenly beside Nyba, "Did we try the sanbeam to the colonials? I don't remember that. Did we try that form of communication?"

"No, we did not," Domyn answered, wiggling his tan dionjocu gloves as he worked the sensors tracking the deployment region. "We considered doing so but reasoned that they probably did not have the sanbeam tech as science and research had not begun until after their departure from the Zerosolis System."

"Laser," Jamyk called out abruptly. "Ship."

"We could try laser transmission but that requires..." Domyn began to explain.

"From... Ship," Jamyk blurted insistently. "Comm."

His vehemence attracted her attention, so Nyba flicked to his station view in her own visor and saw a gleam of the spaceship following Wolf Streak, and then a subtle flash of light leaped past her vision, and she inquired, startled, "What was that? Was that a laser transmission?"

The flurry of hand wiggling and finger tapping from Prof Lyndyn to her left told Nyba then that the older man most likely understood what Jamyk was trying to explain in his usually short choppy fashion, and then Lyndyn exclaimed with interest, "Indeed streams of laser comms are flowing past us from that ship behind us. Good read, Jamyk. Good foresight on your part, Nyba, when you assigned this little monkey to special duty to watch that planet and mining camp for transmission activity."

Whyvvi asked, "Laser comms? Can we understand them? We should be able to receive and understand them. Laser transmissions are more difficult to encode. They are usually basic binary language not as useful for complex communications, at least in our experience. Maybe colonials have developed technology more advanced than we have in this field since their ancestors departed."

"That's right, yeah, Prof, can you read them?" Milyr asked. "If you can't, can you record some for me to study when I'm done at pilot?"

"Laser comms are not easy to receive without specific receptors. And we must be in direct line with a specific transmission. They are usually very narrow intensified beams of light," Domyn said.

"Oh my, be careful watching laser comms," Doc Kymil warned abruptly. "The intensity could damage the eye. We don't know intensities being used. We do know that these colonials do not have a high regard for their own people's safety. We don't have appropriate filters in place at this moment. Be very careful now viewing your visors until we get filters installed. You should stop using visors until we do so."

"This will make reading our sensors almost impossible," Nyba groaned in frustration. "How long before we can filter optics? Do we have to cease all the sensor scans?"

"Everyone, pause your visual sensor reads," Domyn ordered and then said loudly, "Vivacio, coordinate with Doc Kymil to filter optics on all visual sensor arrays. Priority repair."

The male-voiced artigence Vivacio responded, "Neer Domyn, I am coordinating with Doc Kymil. This type of function repair will require programs of Bodacia. Do I have authority to integrate with Bodacia?"

"Yes, Vivacio, you may integrate with Bodacia for this repair," Domyn replied and then turning to his right, said, "Awright, Doc, get us back in scanning function as soon as you can. Both artigences will work with your station."

Without word to others, a woman of forty-seven years of age turned her chair to face the wall and spoke in a low tone to invisible artigences. Her fingers and hands played their magic within her white dionboda gloves. Nyba was impressed by quickness and sureness of the woman. Yet this expertise and dedication did not surprise Nyba. Doc Kymil was a veteran Blue Jayer.

"Let's keep all other non-visual sensors active," Nyba ordered and then another idea came to her and she asked, "Swyllo, is our energy level good enough for the holovision Full-Encompass now?"

"Yes, I've been busy this entire sprint. I've actually accumulated a few percent more despite the steady drain from all of our active systems," Swyllo replied.

"Whyvvi, realign your sensor searches into Full-Encompass with the spaceship behind as the object focal setting. Change Jamyk's sensor search to the long distance zoom on Cotto Vazza. If possible make the object setting as small as useful. Perfect clarity is not necessary, configuration and movement are more important now," Nyba commanded glancing toward the girl in the pinkish dionjocu, and then shouted hoarsely, "Jamyk, I said don't look into that visor until filters are in place."

The boy spun toward her and gulped in guilt, "Yup... Cap."

At least he flipped his visor up to his forehead, Nyba was thankful and said more calmly, "Thank you, little peener, we can't afford to lose your keen sight. Did you see anything more while you were...cheating?"

"Nope," Jamyk pouted. "Ship."

"Prof, have you been able to get a specific vector for laser comms? They must travel the linear path from the sender to the receptor. We can perhaps determine where they are going," Domyn suggested. "We can get a benefit from Jamyk's observation still while we get filters in place."

Prof Lyndyn answered, "I'm sorry, Neer Domyn, my scans could just make out transmissions intermittently. We must be cutting across them while travelling."

"Vulch, cherp sighting, little onad," Swyllo squealed. "Too bad we can't see it now."

Suddenly, for some reason, Nyba felt oddly uncomfortable with a familiar nickname they had often used in reference to Jamyk. However, it had never bothered the boy before. Why not, she wondered. Was the boy inured to its use? Did he ignore its negative connotation to his manhood? Did he care about that? Or did he feel it sign of comradeship? This was an inexplicable boy, Nyba reminded herself. Why was she pondering this now when the mission had just hit another nasty snag?

Then the holovision alighted in front of the ConCen and very little showed at the moment. The central blue dot representing Wolf Streak Beta was there of course. The red spot in aft octants not far in front of her chair was there again. Off to the far arc of the spherical display was the copper brown planet. On the opposite outer arc of the holovision, a crescent edge of the super gas giant shined with intensity. Due to the setting, Nyba had instructed, Cotto Vazza and distant Sexto sun were not in display. These two special objects were getting steadily closer, Nyba knew, but were several days away at the present velocity.

Then she remembered that Jamyk's current view would be region of Cotto Vazza. She went to look in the visor but suddenly stopped herself. The filters were not in place yet. Perhaps no laser signals were travelling to that direction or from it, but she was not going to take a chance for the whimsical peek ahead at the sight far away. Doc Kymil would have filters ready soon. Nyba could wait. She had developed some patience over the years dealing with this spirited crew.

"Prof, are you getting any new radio signals coming from Cotto Vazza direction?" Nyba asked as she peered over at Jamyk and caught him peering at her with his hand on his visor and impatient set to his thin face, or at least that was what she interpreted.

Prof Lyndyn replied, "No doubt I could be, but I'm little out of practice with this sensor system. I'm afraid I am not as capable at this as Milyr. There are so many residual radio wave signals in the Sexto System that determining the new transmissions is too precise for me. I do believe that I was getting laser messages from that direction before Doc ordered us from looking. I hope I didn't hurt my eyes."

"That's not cherp," Milyr said. "If vulchers ahead of us are signaling with toxx behind us, then that's not cherp. Unless they are trying to scare them from chasing us, that's possible, right?"

"Vulch, Milyr, you big oaf, anything is possible right now," Swyllo chirped.

Abruptly Doc Kymil declared breathlessly, "Filters are in place for all stations. We can use visual sensors again for laser signal detection. These filters are safe for five times the normal laser intensity that we are familiar with in our Blue Jay experience. Obviously we do not know exactly the intensity of the colonial laser comms, but I doubt if these in use as signals are very intensive. That would be a waste of power for colonials. In the Sexto System by themselves, I would guess that power is a rare commodity and very valuable."

Domyn suggested, "If intensity was much higher than Doc has indicated, then laser would be of the weapons caliber. This would be a waste of precious power out here in Sexto."

"Weapons, do you think colonials have laser weapon tech?" Nyba asked suddenly concerned, and then partially answered herself, saying, "Well, now I recall some history files of Despoliation just before their ancestors departed the Zerosolis System. There was research and some limited development of laser weapon tech prior to Despoliation. But this was not the focus at that time when people of the world were playing around with bio-toxins and chemical agents as weapons of mass destruction. However, we should be alert to the possibility of some type of laser tech. They have used ancient nuclear weaponry already."

Whyvvi stated bluntly, "Their technology of weaponry may appear ancient to us, but it is harmful still. We should not become arrogant with our Blue Jay sci-tech and ignore what these colonials use against us. Modern humans can be killed by stone to the head still."

"Vulch, I wish Blue Jay had given us some vulching weapons," Milyr complained. "I feel toxx naked out here in Sexto against them with no weapons."

"Blue Jay is a scout mission, search and contact mission. We are not hunters," Whyvvi declared and then added with a flourish of her pink gloves, "Jamyk, now your long-range sensor is ready. Filter and all should be safe for your viewing Cotto Vazza."

"Cherp," the boy croaked and flipped down his visor. "Look."

Domyn spun his brown chair toward Nyba and inquired, "Cap, should we sanbeam the updated message toward our deployment region now? We are still in acceptable range but not for long."

Not certain that this was useful at this time, Nyba decided, "Let's trust that our auto recording is enough for the moment. We must be careful not to attract colonial attention to that region of space now. We do not know the capability of their sensors to track such a sanbeam or just an energy trail. Our best communications person is at pilot now. We have much to focus upon now here, Neer. Cease your sensor function on the deployment region. Perhaps you would better serve Wolf Streak Beta by putting your attention to aiding our pilot functions and maximizing conditions of your Flandecams. Does this sound reasonable?"

Nyba was not surprised when the young man grinned beneath his visor and answered, "Awright, Cap Nyba, this is the function that I can do. Much more my department than watching long distance scans. I can interface with Vivacio and do a current diagnostic check on our Flandecams and other pilot systems. We'll want to be well-prepared should we have to make any defensive maneuvers."

"Vulch, Domyn, don't be diagnosing me as part of the pilot systems," Milyr chuckled from his purple chair. "I'm vulching cherp as I am."

"Argh! I'm not so sure about that," Swyllo giggled.

"Awe only knows about that truth, my friend," Domyn exclaimed with humor. "But I'll leave diagnosing you to the expertise of Prof and Doc. I don't need a headache."

Watching the holovision during this banter, Nyba saw the red spot follow steadily, just as it had several hours ago during their first contact. The small planet had disappeared from the scene. The only other body visible was the crescent edge of the super gas giant. Cotto Vazza was still too far ahead to be in this confinement setting. A hint of vague light shimmered at the forward arc of the display, probably reflection from the gas giant, Nyba thought. The crescent of the gas giant imperceptibly moved along the outer arc of display. This was the only indication of movement around the blue dot, Wolf Streak Beta. Yet Nyba realized that they were advancing toward the distant Cotto Vazza.

Glimpsing Jamyk lift his hand to wiggle his visor, Nyba was spurred to check his view. She flicked the small finger on her left hand in her dionjocu glove. Her visor switched from a scene of the gleaming spaceship following them to the murky vague shape of Cotto Vazza ahead. Her view was sprinkled with a shimmer of hazy subtle lights, much like the look of spergits in LaOgres space. What was this? Was this the same reflection that showed on the holovision Full-Encompass? Nyba glanced back at Jamyk. His body posture indicated unease.

"Pilot," Jamyk blurted as if giving a command. "Veer."

"Vulch, what do you want, little peener?" Milyr asked. "No time for vulching around. I'm a busy pilot."

"Veer," the boy requested stubbornly. "Across."

"Side to side, vulch, that will slow our flight," Milyr declared. "Do we want to do that?"

"Cross," Jamyk persisted. "View."

Then suddenly Nyba understood as she watched the view in her own visor with one eye and the holovision with the other, "Ho, ho, yes, Milyr, give us a better parallax view by zigzagging back and forth on a forty-three-degree course from our X-axis course to our Y-axis course, then to our Z-axis course as Wolf Streak Beta advances. This straight forward view does not give us enough contrast and depth to get a cherp look at what's out there. Do as he asks. We can afford a delay. The ship behind us is not gaining, and you are using only half our potential velocity, correct?"

"Yeah, I'm only using half the thrust, Cap," Milyr admitted, and then with sudden renewed spirit, chortled, "Vulch, yeah, this flying straight is getting boring. Dancing side to side sounds like cherp fun. How far off course do you want me to go?"

"Domyn, what do you suggest for this?" Nyba asked, turning toward her best sci-tech advisor and also watching the cloudy dark image of Cotto Vazza behind the vague shimmer of sparkles in her visor.

"If we are using zeta rays as our sensor, then about deviation of about seven arcs to side from our current straight line should give you enough parallax to see more depth and contrast for your long-distance scan," Domyn reported. "Vivacio, confirms that our Flandecams are working within parameters, so should have no problem with Milyr's crazy piloting."

"Hey, vulch, Domyn, I'm not a crazy toxx flyer," Milyr claimed sourly.

"Veer," Jamyk insisted. "Begin."

Hearing the boy's persistent concern, Nyba felt her own intuition nag at her awareness, so she ordered, "Milyr, start your dance now. Use recommendations of Neer Domyn. Get your toxx into this dance now."

"Vulch, okay, okay, Cap Nyba," Milyr grumbled, but with a trace of humor, added, "I'll move my toxx anyway you demand. Wolf Streak Beta will follow my dancing toxx."

"Do it," Nyba demanded bluntly. "But continue to advance also as I said before. We have hostile chasing our toxx."

"Vulch, I don't like hostiles chasing my toxx," Milyr moaned.

"Cap Nyba, I'm intercepting more laser transmissions from our friend following us," Prof Lyndyn announced. "These comms are directed somewhere ahead of us. There is not enough info to decipher their meaning. Our limited laser receptors are not suited for interpretation of the pulses used by this colonial technology. But I can say that they are signaling to someone ahead of us."

Swyllo griped in her shrill voice, "This doesn't sound cherp. I'm getting a nasty feeling about these colonials. Their sense of greeting has not been vulching cherp."

As Milyr skillfully swerved Wolf Streak Beta to one side, Nyba observed the crescent of the super gas giant bulge slightly into the holovision. The red spot moved off toward the opposite octant. A shimmering curtain ahead seemed to stay constant. Did that mean it was a reflection of light caught on their zeta sensors, she wondere.? Or was it something else with an endless width as she perceived it now? Perhaps a special cloud of some kind, she wondered.

"I scan continuous laser comms as we move across this way," Prof Lyndyn reported. "Many individual comms, each narrowly beamed as predictable for a tight laser signal. I scan so many. Domyn, does this make sense? Am I reading this right?"

In her visor, Nyba watched the shadowy image of a distant Cotto Vazza move very slightly to one side of the original track, and she asked, "Jamyk, does your keen eye see anything different yet? Do you see that cloud-like sheen between us and Cotto Vazza? Am I seeing things with my tired eyes?"

However, Jamyk remained silent as he raised his right hand to cover his exposed eye, and instead Nyba listened to Whyvvi say, "Cap, that spaceship behind us is gaining very slowly. They must have increased velocity when we changed course. That is what they did last time prior to their attack."

"Veering to Z-plane now. See if this new angle helps your parallax," Milyr said. "Don't worry about those vulchers, Whyvvi. If they get too close, I can increase my thrusting forward velocity and sprint faster away from toxx."

"Follow the plan for now, pilot," Domyn demanded in his deep growl. "Our sci-tech systems are functioning very well. Just keep us on the planned dance, as you called it."

"Awright, no problem, big man," Milyr chuckled, lowering his voice more than the common in imitation of Domyn's growl, and Nyba appreciated the young man's attempt to keep the stress level low in the ConCen.

"Roids," Jamyk yelled. "Ahead."

At this outburst, Nyba focused her attention back to the visor and saw only more sparkles of glinting light, so she asked, "What do you see? Jamyk, it just looks like space dust in a cloud in front of us. Can you zoom closer? Whyvvi, does his station have that option now?"

The girl in the light red dionjocu replied, "Not as originally programmed. Jamyk has only what I gave him when we made his station subunit of sensors. I am putting zoom capability into his station now. It should be there in less than a minute."

On the holovision, the red spot swung in another direction relative to the blue center dot. The crescent of the gas giant almost fled from the arc of display as Wolf Streak Beta travelled further away in a new swerving course as Milyr zagged. Only the shimmering curtain of sparkles remained constant and slowly approached closer. Nyba tried to compare this holovision Full-Encompass view with the long-distance view in her visor, but this only gave her a beginning of a headache. Vulch, she swore to herself.

"Roids," Jamyk repeated in earnest. "Ahead."

"Asteroids, belt of asteroids?" Prof Lyndyn asked. "Is this what you think that you see? Is this possible, Neer Domyn? Does an extrapolated model of the Sexto System predict a belt of asteroids at this orbit around the sun?"

"Veering down to the new X-plane," Milyr shouted. "Vulch, onad, this is cherp fun. Almost like fooling with training simulators back on Steppingstone Primero. Vulching cherp!"

"Just pilot Wolf Streak Beta," Nyba demanded with a surly edge to her tone as she viewed an approaching cloud-like shimmer, and with new a angle, began to see what could be small rock-like shapes floating in the vast belt of space. "Those could be asteroids, small asteroids between us and Cotto Vazza. However, there does not seem to be any large ones as I would expect from a random nature of size formation in a normal asteroid belt."

"Awe only knows, Prof, I don't remember that kind of info about an extrapolated model of this system," Domyn murmured in guilty disconsolation. "My mind was always paying attention to design, mechanisms, and hard sci-tech, not sensor models and extrapolations. We could ask Joculatus to search the mission parameters for that info…"

"Vulch, not a cherp idea," Swyllo gasped just beyond Doc Kymil on Domyn's right. "With all this sensor function and this Full Encompass holovision and this zigzag flying, we are using more energy than I can harvest. We don't need to add any more assignments to Joculatus. That artigence uses much of our energy supply every time we give it something else to do. We must learn to be more frugal with our energy usage, Cap. I mean it. I'm not just vulching goading you."

"Is it getting critical?" Nyba asked while she observed the seemingly endless expanse of small rock-like objects ahead.

"Not severely yet, as long as we can get cherp sunlight still, we'll be okay. I can keep supply at moderate levels. However, we should not waste what energy we have on systems of luxury," Swyllo lectured in her strained voice and then suggested, "Perhaps we are at a point where we may want to conserve what we have and shut down some of the non-critical functions."

Fascinated by the approaching vastness of the shimmering belt and Cotto Vazza beyond, Nyba commanded, "Neer Domyn, take charge of shutting down the non-essential systems for the moment. Let's conserve Swyllo's energy supply. I need to focus on this possible threat."

"Awright, Cap, I'll do that," Domyn agreed, although his tone did not sound enthusiastic to Nyba, and then she heard him ask, "Doc Kymil, is Bodacia necessary now? Do you think Med systems are necessary now?"

Doc Kymil began to reply, "Oh, I think we can..."

However, Nyba tuned out the woman's comments and instead became absorbed within her own visor. With the most recent veer in Milyr's new zigzag course, more detail became obvious to her eye. The objects were all quite small, at best no more than a hundredth of mass of Wolf Streak Beta, at least to her estimate through the visor and sensor system. Yet expanse of the belt seemed unlimited. Wolf Streak would need to detour a very great distance to find way around. Beyond this belt in the far distance set an obscure image of Cotto Vazza. This was her destination. She did not want to detour away, especially with the colonial spaceship already having demonstrated hostility chasing behind. Nyba was resolute in her destination for Wolf Streak Beta.

"Anything new, Jamyk?" Nyba asked the boy sitting erect in his green chair, and she wondered suddenly why she had started to value his contribution more than previous times, yet she continued by asking, "Does your keen eye see anything of interest?"

"Small," he replied somewhat distracted within his visor. "Shiny...apart."

"Yes, that's what I think," Nyba announced, peering into her visor and also noticing with her exposed eye how close the massive belt was now to the blue dot in the holovision. "Those rocks are quite far apart. There could be room between them. And none of them are very large, not even close to being a serious threat to Wolf Streak Beta with our composite hull and deflective shape."

The holovision swayed back and up as Milyr made another zigzag change in their course vector, and Whyvvi said in earnest, "Cap, I think that I have found some smaller ships behind us. As the parallax improved and the colonial spaceship gained closer, several smaller flashes of glitter started showing on my sensor reads in our aft octants. I think that we have more company behind us."

"Vulch, now doesn't this seem familiar," squawked Swyllo.

"Vulch, not those toxx again," Milyr griped, "When can I just kick it in and sprint forward again, Nyba? Do you have enough view now to let me get back to the straight ahead thrust again?"

"Nope," shouted Jamyk. "Zoom."

"Wait a little longer, Milyr. Let's give this little rascal some leeway. He's been cherp right recently, for change," Nyba declared, and not really believing that those comments had spoken from her own mouth, "Jamyk, do a zoom of your zeta rays if you must."

In her visor, she observed objects suddenly leap toward her. Their small size and wide apart spacing seemed confirmed by this new view. Yet the zoom did not stop at the belt but jumped into distant view toward Cotto Vazza. Why was rascal looking out there with the zoom, she wondered. Was he having another lapse into mischievous foolishness after being so dependable recently? Then very tiny twinkles around Cotto Vazza gleamed back at her eye. There was movement there, she was certain, slow, steady movement of very tiny glitters, almost like twinkling stars, spreading away from the dark mass of Cotto Vazza.

"What are those, Jamyk? Can you guess? Can you see those star-like things moving around Cotto Vazza?" Nyba asked, mesmerized with him in this common shared vision.

"Ships," Jamyk said uncertainly. "Maybe?"

"Perhaps they are ships to help us against pursuers," Prof Lyndyn suggested. "We have considered the possibility that there are conflicting factions in play here in the Sexto System. Maybe these new things which you are seeing are repellent to colonials chasing us. Even if they do not know us, they might be at odds with those chasing us…"

"There are real ships coming behind us," Whyvvi declared with impatience from her red chair beside Jamyk. "Those are real ships. They are gaining on us. This is starting to feel much like before the EM pulse incident. We should focus our interest on those ships behind us, Cap Nyba."

As her eye watched the extremely distant view around Cotto Vazza, Nyba shrugged off her fascination, yielded to logic of Whyvvi's comments, and then agreed, "Yes, you are right. Milyr, return to your straight vector toward Cotto Vazza. That super colony ship could be sending protective escort for us, as Prof suggested. Let's get far ahead of our pursuers. We know how they treat guests. Our best future seems to be ahead with Cotto Vazza. Domyn, view Jamyk's scene of asteroid belt ahead. I need your opinion."

"Awright, Cap Nyba," Domyn replied, "Jamyk, give me your best zoom view of this alleged asteroid belt. Nothing more, I just want to see the belt. Milyr, you are on your own for the moment."

"Ha, vulch, isn't that what all Steppingstone fems say?" Swyllo smirked beside the lavender figure. "Oh, primo man, you're on your own, toxx."

"Vulch, yeah, tiny fem," Milyr laughed while he moved his hands in synchronization with his piloting. "But only after a long, long, session as I showed them how I pilot this huge Wolf Streak Beta with powerful thrusts of my massive Flandecams."

While she tried unsuccessfully to ignore Milyr's comment and Swyllo's shrieking comeback, Nyba watched the asteroid belt approach quickly toward the blue dot on the holovision, and then peering toward the tan figure beside her, asked, "Neer, can we fly Wolf Streak Beta through that belt without damage? Is our composite hull solid enough to withstand a collisions of those rocks?"

Domyn hesitated a few seconds while he viewed the scene in his visor, and as his expression frowned in concentration, he replied, "Our hull is very tough and can withstand most incidental contacts with masses no more than eleven feet in diameter, assuming their velocity is not high in perpendicular contact to our hull. Some of these objects seem close to that limit. But, Cap, I'm not sure these are truly asteroids, or at least some of them. Too many are very smoothly shaped and not as ragged-looking as normal asteroids."

"Can we go through that belt of whatever?" Nyba asked bluntly with authority.

"Decide quickly," Milyr hollered. "We're going in soon."

"Awright, if our pilot can avoid hitting the big ones, then I think there is enough clearance to work with," Domyn said with some reservation seeping from his voice. "But we don't know how deep this belt is, do we? We could be in there…"

"Decide now," Whyvvi cried out. "I think the smaller ships have just punched in their speed thrusters or something like they did before. They are moving toward us very quickly now."

"Nope," Jamyk croaked. "Veer."

His voice was shouted over by Milyr when a lanky young man yelled, "What do I do, Cap? We're there in seconds."

In a moment of decision, Nyba heard his baritone voice crack in uncertain fear, so she commanded, "Keep going straight, pilot. Our destination is super colony ships. I have faith in your skill to get us through and quickly!"

"Vivo," Jamyk yelled. "Belts."

Suddenly safety harness snapped across her lap and torso, pinning her arms to her chest, and Nyba complained, "We could have done that ourselves, Jamyk.

Is everyone okay? Let's get comfortable for this wild ride. Sensor functions should continue with your specific views. Swyllo, you should continue with your harvesting if we are questionable on energy supply. Domyn, you will be able to guide our pilot, won't you?"

"Of course, Nyba, but at this sprint and dance, he will need to make most of the course maneuvers on his own," Domyn said as he repositioned his arms through his harness. "Also, we will not be able to seal our hull to provide solid protection for the various sensor, harvester, and Flandecam units positioned in the exterior hull. While these systems are active, they will be open to collision damage. Our pilot must try to avoid these rocks."

"I have faith in Milyr," Nyba declared, peering over at the frenetically moving arms and hands of the young man. "And I believe in our Blue Jay sci-tech to repair damage if necessary."

"That's cherp, Nyba," Milyr shouted with a sudden grunt of effort as his arms jerked left. "We are in the belt now. Hang onto yourselves, everybody. This won't be my usual smooth entry. In fact this could get nasty rough."

Despite artificial gravity within Wolf Streak Beta, Nyba felt a torque of inertial change sway her body within the harness, and she asked with partial control of her nervousness, "Do we need this Full-Encompass holovision anymore?"

"It is a luxury now, Cap," Swyllo chirped.

Prof Lyndyn gasped as Wolf Streak Beta swerved in another direction, "For me this view of all these little rocks swaying and dancing in obnoxious patterns is disturbing. Feel free to turn it off."

After the blinding light flashed over the display scene and the holovision blinked off, Nyba grumbled, "Who did that? I didn't order this off. That sudden switch off could damage the system..."

"Vulch, what was that?" Whyvvi screamed, ripping visor off her pink cap.

"Lasers," Jamyk shouted hastily, flipping his own visor up to his forehead. "Weapons."

Swyllo screeched, "Vulch, vulch, vulch, my harvesters are going off all around this craft. I can't get enough to work now for harvesting..."

"We're in the laser mine field," Domyn announced, wiggling his fingers in his tan dionjocu gloves. "All around Wolf Streak Beta. These objects are weaponry, mines is an ancient term. They are hitting our hull systems with pinpricks of laser beams very highly intensified."

"Lasers," Jamyk rasped. "Melt...parts."

"Vulch, I can't avoid beams and all those objects," Milyr complained, now panting with his work effort and growing terror.

"A laser beam should not do much damage to our hull," Prof Lyndyn said.

"Not one or two," Whyvvi said, regaining some of her usual calm. "But if we get struck by many, then damage to our open exterior systems could be significant."

"Seal hull," Nyba ordered hastily. "Cover our outer apparatus panels."

"Vulch, the Flandecam Three just lost the outer component, I think," Milyr yelled while his body swayed with his moving arms and hands trying to fly the spacecraft. "I can't get a full thrust from Three anymore. Its ability to generate a grav field, which I need, is weaker now."

"More of my harvesters are gone," wailed Swyllo.

"It's like getting stung by an entire hive of bees," Domyn explained. "We're taking hits all over our hull. Many of exterior panels of our systems have been stung already by lasers. I am trying to seal the rest but, the systems are sluggish. Vivacio, seal hull."

"Another Flandecam has been hit," Milyr screamed in desperation. "I'm losing full control of grav generation from the Flandecams. I think Joculatus has lost some exterior sensors. Our interface is getting nasty shaky."

"Vivacio, reply," Domyn ordered firmly and loudly.

Vivacio stuttered, "Neer... Dom...not able to seal...hull...outer...not responding...in parameters..."

"Joculatus, cease all exterior functions, except interface with pilot Milyr," Domyn commanded.

She should have been angry and upset with his presumption of her authority, but Nyba trusted her Neer to know what to do to safeguard his spacecraft. No, she convinced herself, this is not her time to be leader. This was his time. So Nyba sat back in her blue chair and watched her young crew of wolves do their jobs as they had been trained. Although this situation had never been anticipated by Blue Jay, they would do their best under these terribly nasty and unforeseen circumstances. They would do okay, she wanted to believe. They were the best of Blue Jay.

"Pilot," Jamyk yelled. "Full...speed."

"Vulch, what do you think I've been doing?" Milyr cursed as his recently changed dionjocu started to show very wet sweat stains. "Don't nip my toxx, little peener."

"Joculatus, report," Domyn shouted with an edge of concern in his deep voice.

"Manu," Jamyk croaked. "Jocu."

Then the boy unfastened his harness and jumped up from his green chair. Without falling during the next sudden swerve, Jamyk clutched his chair and moved around to the back. Nyba saw him reach into the compartment in the back of the chair and then pull out a new visor. As the boy stepped back to the front of the green chair, she saw that it was a double visor, visor of pilot. Then sitting down again, he snapped this to his green dionjocu cap.

"Nyba, I can't get Joculatus' primary level programs to acknowledge," Domyn groaned in some worry. "He is probably already automatically switched to manual. His exterior functions could have been severely damaged by the earliest multiple strikes by these lasers."

"Just like bees," Doc Kymil moaned. "They are lethal in swarms."

"Are we in the mine field still? Are those things attacking still?" Nyba asked now frightened.

"Vulchers are still out there," Milyr shouted in desperation. "I can see them in grav views, especially their intensified light tracks. But don't worry, my eyes don't receive actual laser light itself. There's a vulching load of them out there."

"Milyr," Jamyk shouted. "Help?"

"Vulch yeah, I could use some help, little onad," Milyr screamed, flailing his arms. "I think Joculatus put me on manual without telling me. This Wolf spacecraft moves like an old Swyllo chased by the ugliest vulcher on Stone. Can you take some of the Flandecams? But then how can we coordinate movement with two minds? Maybe we can't do this."

"Which Flandecams are faulty now, Milyr?" Domyn asked hastily.

"Three and five, I think. There are some others with nasty damage, but they function," Milyr reported, and Nyba heard relief in the voice of the young man as Neer Domyn took part in pilot decisions.

"Are we flying blind?" Nyba asked, trying to battle her own fear and stay involved with the ConCen activity as everyone fought to save Wolf Streak Beta.

"Except for our pilot, yes," Domyn declared. "He doesn't need to worry about laser damage to his eyes, just his Flandecams."

"Two," Jamyk rasped. "Pilots."

"Vulch, yeah, Domyn, give us a way to work this with two pilots on manual. This is too nasty for even a primo pilot like me to handle alone," Milyr demanded.

"It can't be that far to get through this belt, or is it a mine field?" Prof Lyndyn interjected.

"Just plow through the vulching rocks or mines," Swyllo cried out in shrill panic.

"This would be a simple thing to do," Whyvvi agreed calmly. "We would need baffle or a plow on our front to do this."

"Awe thank you, Whyvvi, you're a genius," Domyn suddenly exclaimed. "That's what we need, a baffle on our fore. One solid an-grav field should push objects away before we hit them. It may even deflect or bend light in lasers. At least an-grav can bounce those vulchers out of our path."

"Yup," Jamyk agreed. "Smart."

"One of us just pushes an-grav in our fore octants," Milyr shouted in excitement. "I'll do that. Then I can believe I'm actually attacking vulchers."

"Yes, that's cherp," Nyba said, peering at the quivering figure in lavender dionjocu. "Do it, pilots. Wolf Streak Beta is in your hands again."

"Jamyk, are you ready to take over the rear drive thrusters?" Milyr asked. "I can't wait to bash these vulchers with my an-grav bursts."

"Yup," Jamyk replied with a flurry of hand and finger movements in his green dionjocu gloves. "Rear...thrust."

"Will this work, Neer?" Doc Kymil asked.

"It's our only chance now," Domyn replied.

"Ready, little onad?"

"Yup," Jamyk rasped enthusiastically. "Go!"

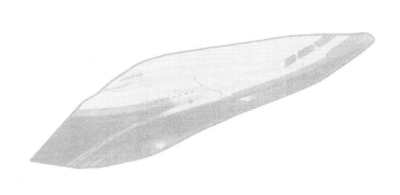

SPEC TWO: NYBA TO SEXTO
CHAPTER 22

"Yeah…yee…hah, we got through!" Milyr cheered.

Domyn growled, "Don't stop yet, pilots. mines will continue to fire their lasers at Wolf Streak Beta. We don't know limit of their range. Put some distance between us and them, straight ahead, keep going."

"Should I continue an-grav forward?" Milyr asked in a tired creaking voice, "I get no gravitic images of lasers or objects now on our fore octants. Should I switch to posi-grav?"

Sighing in disappointment toward the lanky form in the purple chair, Domyn declared, "Awright, Milyr, what do you think? You're a good pilot. You know the answer already. You don't need my permission to do an appropriate maneuver."

To her left, Nyba listened to Prof Lyndyn ask with concern, "Won't this increase our chances of crashing into something? Without an-grav buffer as a cushioning shield, won't we be risking collision? Is this wise at this time? Are we not blind without our sensors functioning? We must not become reckless…"

In exhaustion and frustration, Domyn said, "Trust me, everyone, I can see pilot views. There is no hazard between our position and Cotto Vazza, which is days away yet at maximum velocity. There is nothing to crash into out there now."

"Vulch, not much chance of max velocity now," Milyr grumbled, and Nyba heard despair and perhaps even subtle fear in the young man's voice as he continued, "Most of the Flandecams are at low generation now. I really don't want to see the damage diagnosis report. I will probably cry like a vulching young pup."

Was this all her fault, Nyba wondered. For over one hour, maybe two, Wolf Streak Beta had fled through the mine belt. Countless laser burns had pricked the outer hull of the spacecraft. Her pilots and Neer had worked desperately to get the craft into a clear and safe space. She had never before been so proud and astounded of their efforts. Her young men had been amazingly persistent and tirelessly determined. Despite continuous strikes of multitude of lasers from the mines, young men had swerved, bounced, and sprinted Wolf Streak Beta through the threat.

"Cry if you will, Milyr," Nyba said with compassion and then continued in complete honesty. "Yet I will not be any less proud of what you, all of you, have done to save Wolf Streak Beta. Our pilots and our Neer have just added another tale to the legend of Wolf Streak Beta."

Swyllo squealed in mild irritation, "Vulch, in doing this legendary feat, they have used most of the energy. Our level is below 31 percent. I can get a very few of my harvester panels to function, and unfortunately most of those are currently on our aft curve away from the sun."

"Roll?" Jamyk asked hoarsely. "Milyr?"

"Yeah, we can roll Wolf Streak Beta to put our aft to fore, just for you, tiny fem," Milyr said in a much more sympathetic tone than Nyba had expected from the usually acerbic young man, at least in his vocalizations to Swyllo.

Domyn declared, "I do not see any problem with this. Harvesters should have priority for the next several hours. As soon as we are out of range of lasers, we can roll this spacecraft. For the moment, I'm detecting some lingering hits on our aft still. We'll also need to do a damage diagnostic if we can get Vivacio to perform. Does this plan sound right to you, Cap Nyba?"

While this conversation had taken place, Nyba had been only half listening as her mind replayed memories of Milyr's frantic physical maneuvers and Jamyk's cries of warning whenever he was about to make a sudden veer in their course during the recent escape out of the mine belt, so a question from Neer Domyn startled her, and she stammered, "Aw...that...is cherp... Neer,... We all...trust your judgment. Take charge of this recovery."

"Awright, Cap," Domyn replied slowly, hesitantly himself as if he did not welcome responsibility, as if he felt same disappointment and shame as she did at that moment.

Then scolding herself for her own weariness and reluctance to resume her command, Nyba said with stronger authority in her voice, "Neer Domyn, there is no one in the Blue Jay project better prepped and capable of diagnosing Wolf

Streak Beta's condition and then beginning to repair our problems. I would not trust Khebol himself to fix our Wolf Streak Beta rather than you. Neer, you are our best. Now take charge and help our Wolf. Our mission is now over. Our safety is not assured."

"Neer," Jamyk rasped from his green chair. "Cherp."

"Vulch, somebody do something," Swyllo complained. "I'm not goading now, toxx do something. Our energy level continues to drop. I can't harvest a cherp sunlight with most of my harvesters malfunctioning, probably melted all around our hull."

"At least you can get some sunlight," Whyvvi exclaimed, working her fingers inside her light red dionjocu gloves. "I am having difficulty finding sensors that will function adequately to the survey either long distance fore or short distance aft. Perhaps if we roll Wolf Streak Beta, then my sensor station will benefit also. I deduce that those exterior operations, which were active when we entered the mine belt, were most severely damaged by lasers burns. Hopefully those units not active then will be in a better functional condition now. We should roll now if we can."

Domyn sighed, then sat more erectly in his brown chair and said, "You have a good point, Whyvvi. Unfortunately I have not received acknowledgement from either Joculatus or Vivacio. My guess is that their safety shut down feature put them into sleep mode and made all stations manual. Please check your specific functions to confirm this. Everyone should do this now. If sensors and energy find this condition, you must determine which of your individual units are working now. We may not be able to repair on the exterior hull without Vivacio and Joculatus in awake mode, but at least we will know Wolf Streak Beta's capabilities. For now each of you should check to discover your specific operational functions."

"Neer Domyn, no doubt you would like me to continue to monitor the communication function," Prof Lyndyn stated almost rhetorically in Nyba's opinion.

"Yes, Prof, we will need to know which of our communication alternatives are available," Domyn said, and then with a sudden twist toward a man in gray added, "And, oh, yes, Prof, if any reception is functional, we could really use the current info of how those colonials are transmitting and to where. We may not understand coded messages, but we can know where they come from and where they go."

"Indeed a very insightful suggestion," Prof Lyndyn murmured and then uncharacteristically for him went silently to work, wiggling his fingers within his gray dionboda gloves.

When she noticed this activity in the dionboda gloves, Nyba suddenly remembered the recent coordinated program between Bodacia and Vivacio and Doc Kymil, and so she asked with worry, "Doc Kymil, how is Bodacia? Is artigence awake and in the functional status?"

Before Doc Kymil replied, Domyn announced loudly, "Awright, everyone, we are now going to roll the spacecraft 180 current Y-axis. Whyvvi, Swyllo, be ready with your opposing units. I hope we improve your situations. Are you ready now? This won't adversely affect your current diagnostic checks, will it?"

Both girls replied in unison, "No, Neer, go ahead."

"Belts, fastened, everyone," Domyn ordered. "Our artificial gravity seems stable, but we won't know for sure until we roll at least once."

"Let's do this, Domyn," Milyr laughed with an attempt at gaiety. "It'll be cherp fun if we find gravity is not functioning perfectly. It's cherp fun floating around."

"Awright, no foolishness," Domyn growled and then commanded, "Pilots, roll Wolf. Only roll 180 now. Don't get us spinning uncontrollably."

"Ready, Jamyk?" Milyr asked with a little smirk. "On three."

"Yup," Jamyk rasped and then quickly yelled, "Three!"

Despite her experience of so many years of space travel, Nyba half-expected to feel abrupt and nauseous spinning-sensation like some wild Steppingstone amusement ride. This notion was ridiculously foolish, she chided herself. Her intellect informed her that regardless of the position in space of Wolf Streak Beta, only up and down was determined by artificial gravity at her feet. Her feet were down always, no matter rolling or tilting of the spacecraft. Of course this was when artificial gravity was functioning properly, she reminded herself again.

"Easy there, onad," Milyr shouted. "Too much thrust."

"Ease," Jamyk rasped. "An-grav."

"Okay, okay, vulchers don't handle so well now," Milyr griped.

"Ease," Jamyk repeated with a panting breath. "Cherp."

"Yeah, we're stable now," Milyr cheered. "How's yours hanging?"

"Cherp," Jamyk sighed and then asked, "Swyllo?"

Swyllo chirped, "That's a slight bit better, now I've got more functioning harvesters. However, I don't have very many, maybe less than 23 percent and not all on the same arc of our hull. I'll struggle to keep our energy supply at this level unless we stop the most energy usage."

"This is not likely," Whyvvi stated. "Our sci-tech functions depend on the constant flow of energy. We do not have the option of using any other energy source at this stage of Blue Jay. We are a scout craft designed for specific task and mission…"

Not liking where the girl was taking this lecture about limitations of mission, Nyba interrupted Whyvvi and asked, "Do you have any reliable sensors? We should know what's ahead of us and of course if our pursuers have come through the mine belt after us?"

"Oh my, do you think they would come through that mine belt just to chase us?" Doc Kymil asked, and then as if suddenly remembering some forgotten comment, said in startled embarrassment, "Oh, yes, Cap Nyba, I never reported to you about Bodacia. I'm sorry. I can't get her higher functions to respond. Just like the other artigences, Bodacia is in partial interface in manual mode. My guess is that her connection with Vivacio when we were investigating…whatever we were doing…had never disconnected. When Vivacio lost conscious function and digressed to manual, so did Bodacia. I'm sorry, Cap Nyba."

"Vulch, we don't need Bodacia now," Swyllo retorted. "Unless it can fix my harvesters. We need Vivacio and Joculatus. Where are the vulching artigences when we need them? Toxx take this sci-tech!"

"I really miss Joculatus," Milyr complained. "This pilot function on manual is very complicated and almost impossible with two pilots when we try to fly normal. It's nothing like the time in Kil-Kol when we could each concentrate on one specific task. This is vulching much more difficult."

"Yup," Jamyk agreed. "Uncherp."

Trying to ignore these pilot complaints, Nyba turned back to Whyvvi and asked again, "Do you have any useful sensors? Can we search the mine belt? Can we search ahead to Cotto Vazza?"

To her right, she heard Domyn command, "Awright, my pilots, good job with the roll. But stop complaining about the Flandecams. Let's find out what we do have and power capabilities of each individual generator. Milyr, you are aft now. You keep whatever propulsion you can generate to fly this spacecraft forward. Jamyk, you test your fore Flandecams very slightly. Find out what we have on the fore arc now. Short bursts only, so you don't interfere with Milyr's thrusting."

From the red chair to her left, Nyba heard Whyvvi report, "I have two sensors now aft, which can search the intermediate range with no zoom capability. Cap, I am searching now as wide an angle as I can. I do not know if you can view my sensors now in your visor with Joculatus in sleep mode. This function sometimes must be programmed before digression to sleep."

"Just tell us if you see anything, Whyvvi," Nyba demanded impatiently. "I don't care now if I see it or not. Besides Swyllo wants us to conserve energy. I'll not use my visor. I have reliable people to report me the information. I'm tired of micro-managing."

Apparently her tone had hardened as she spoke for after she finished this tirade, the ConCen was very silent of conversation for almost a minute until Doc Kymil said in a confident tone, "Yes we have very capable people on Wolf Streak Beta. Cap Nyba, I have no useful medical function at this time. How can I help?"

Peering past Domyn's tan figure, Nyba gazed at Doc Kymil for several quiet seconds and then replied with a slight smile, "I think you just did. Doc Kymil, could you help Whyvvi by taking fore sensors and checking ahead of us? I would like to see Cotto Vazza. Whyvvi, on manual mode, can you delegate that function to Doc's station?"

Whyvvi replied in a subdued manner, "I should be able to do this assuming link between three artigences, which was active in her station at the time of digression was not compromised during the damage by the laser stings. I will try to transfer a long-distance sensors to Doc. I do not know how many, if any, on the present fore arc will function."

"Do what you can, Whyvvi. That's all any of us can do," Nyba exclaimed trying to put encouragement into her tone, and then to everyone in the ConCen, she said, "All of us have recently passed a nasty terrible crisis. We can do our best to continue. We are Blue Jay wolves."

"Indeed, yes, Cap Nyba," Prof Lyndyn declared with optimism stirring his nasal voice. "We are living Blue Jay wolves. Although our Wolf Streak Beta is injured, our Wolf is alive still. Although our artigences are damaged, they are alive still. Although our enemies, for whatever reason, have attacked us twice now, they have failed. We are going still..."

"Yeah, Prof," Milyr interrupted. "But we're limping nasty awful. I never believed Wolf Streak Beta could ever be hurt like this. It is just too vulching unbelievable to me."

So this off and on discourse continued for almost a day while they struggled to find slim chances to fix the limping spacecraft. Cap Nyba tried to provide uplifting optimism with her words of guidance and direction of certain repair notions that she had expertise. But mostly this time was a domain of Neer Domyn to command the wolfen crew. The spacecraft lumbered forward toward Cotto Vazza still as her priority destination. She held hope that colonials likely there would give aid and protection from any that might chase still. She demanded that one pilot rest, Jamyk first, and Swyllo rest while Whyvvi work for two hours more before switching crew again. Domyn claimed his stamina was cherp to stay his duty as Neer. Kymil and Lyndyn gladly took turns at latrine and nutrient shifts. Nyba tried to stay course, but felt exhaustion of the responsibility of command wearing.

"Do you think Wolf Streak Beta can die?" Whyvvi blurted suddenly when she returned from one of her rest sessions and then added hastily in her analytical voice more than actual trepidation, "I mean to say could Wolf Streak Beta actually shut down totally?"

Entering the ConCen behind her, Milyr groaned in befuddlement, "Now why do you ask this toxx question now? We didn't talk of this only a moment ago."

Whyvvi declared emphatically, "You would not have any useful opinion of this matter. So I waited until we were with some people with smart brains and logical responses…most of the time."

"If Wolf Streak Beta shut down, what happens to artigences?" Swyllo asked in a tone of concerned despair while she moved her hands furiously to work the few harvesters at her control. "What happens to our functional control without Joculatus? Can we function within this craft if artigences stay asleep or even die?"

"Vulch artigences, what about us?" Milyr moaned yet still performed his function as an aft pilot.

Seeing that her crew was busy at their respective functions, Nyba did not try to end this topic. Some intuition, some sense convinced her skeptical mind to allow this exploration at this time, as long as no new threat appeared and they continued toward their destination. As she wished to peak ahead to glimpse Cotto Vazza, Nyba also wondered if perhaps she would like an answer herself to this question, if there was one. What would happen to them? Would they just die like the spacecraft?

So she asked, feeling very out of place and very out of character, "Domyn, can artigences have what you often call iotas of awareness? Can they be parts of your universal metaphy?"

The silence now in the ConCen was more profound than after the earlier tirade at Whyvvi, until of all people Jamyk volunteered his short opinion by saying, "Yup."

Domyn hesitantly replied, "I… I…have never…considered this before, Nyba. I don't have a clear definition in my head for the concept of iota of awareness. If Jamyk believes that artigences can have iotas of awareness, then I cannot disagree.

A universal awareness, to me, is so infinite that only it knows who or what can be made aware by iota. This is beyond me."

"Can Milyr have an iota of awareness?" Swyllo giggled while she worked. "If so it doesn't show very often unless these iotas are not required to have any intelligence and cherpness."

"Ha, ha, tiny fem, one of these awakenings you'll wish for me and my spark, and I won't be there for you," Milyr chuckled, flapping his lanky arms in pilot patterns in the chair beside her. "You'll miss me nasty then, won't she, onad?"

When the boy did not respond with his usual short witticism, Nyba peaked toward the green figure and saw him leaning forward in his chair with both hands upon the dionjocu cap. His arms quivered down to his shoulders as if he was forcing himself to focus on some vision in his visor. Nyba hoped that he was not about to become Jamyk rascal now. Perhaps he was actually checking his Flandecams as Domyn had ordered. Although, she recalled to herself, this boy could usually perform his function and sling jibes with others, as well as anyone.

"Jamyk, did you find something interesting?" Nyba inquired, trying to keep her concern hidden and her voice normal. "Is there anything Domyn should know about your Flandecams?"

"Hurt," he rasped in a forlorn voice. "Not...cherp."

"Vulch, we know that, little peener," Milyr declared. "I've got the same problem. If Swyllo here could get me some more energy, maybe I could fix some of the inner components."

"Nope," Jamyk whined as if crying. "Not... Swyllo."

"Vulch, yes, it's not my fault, you big toxx," Swyllo retorted. "Let me do my job. I'll get you as much as I can. What you do with it is up to you."

Some unexplained compulsion, yes, compulsion, she decided, forced Nyba to continue staring at the hunched form in the green chair, and she asked, "Are you okay, Jamyk? You're not going to become a foolish rascal suddenly, are you?"

However, his mumbled response was hidden by Doc Kymil's excited voice when she cried, "Nyba, we have one sensor capable of the long-range zeta search on our fore arc. I can see Cotto Vazza now. It is not very clear, but I can see it. It is there still between us and the sun."

This distracted her from watching the boy, which was becoming disturbing to her anyway, so Nyba turned her attention to Doc Kymil and said with optimism, "Well, at least we have the sensor working ahead of our track. Now we can see our destination. Whyvvi, what is going on behind us? Are your limited sensors giving us anything yet?"

Whyvvi replied, "My sensors show no ships on this side of the belt. Perhaps they cannot pass through. If they could, then they should have appeared by now."

"Indeed if your idea that Cotto Vazza was sending aid to us is true, Cap Nyba, then the colonials behind us would be wary to get too close to this space. The mine belt could be a territorial border between two factions. Our damage from the laser mines could have been unintentional if they were placed there against hostile colonials," Pro Lyndyn speculated.

"Unintentional or not," Domyn growled, "we have been damaged. Have you surveyed any comms of any type since we came out of that mine belt?"

"No, Domyn, I have not, though communication receptors were partially damaged like every other system with exterior components on the hull..." Prof said.

But his comments were cut off when Doc Kymil blurted excitedly, "Cap, were there many twinkling lights moving away from Cotto Vazza when you were viewing before?"

Her memory was hazy now about occurrences just before the laser mines, but Nyba recalled a small scene and answered, "Maybe, I don't remember exactly. Some star-like twinkles around the big colony ships. Is that what you see?"

"Yes, I can just barely see. The sun is almost behind Cotto Vazza and is a hindering clear view. Many lights quite long the distance from Cotto Vazza. Perhaps eleven times the length of super colony ships," Doc Kymil gasped in wonder.

"That far now?" Nyba asked in surprise as her memory played a vague vision in her awareness. "They were much closer before, right, Jamyk? If I could remember correctly, but you must recall what they looked like, Jamyk?"

Turning her chair to peer at the boy and noticing his slumped form still, Nyba was about to say something to him but then Swyllo hissed critically, "Vulch, is this a really important use of our energy? Our supply is dropping steadily no matter how much I collect now. Do we need to keep these long-distance sensors running? Is this luxury use of our energy helping us?"

With annoyance Nyba snapped back more harshly than she had intended, "Of course this is critical. That's our destination. The closer we get, the better sunlight you can get to harvest. Stop whining, Swyllo. Do the best you can with the harvesters that function. Our sci-tech is a valuable use of energy. Our mission requires it to succeed."

"Hurt," Jamyk mumbled just loud enough to reach Nyba's ears. "Swyllo."

Nyba whirled toward him to chastise his comment, but suddenly Doc Kymil blurted very unlike herself, "Vulch, what was that?"

Only a moment later, Swyllo shrieked in despair, "My sunlight, it's gone. I can't find any sunlight with my harvester sensors. It's vulching gone."

Domyn leaned toward Doc Kymil and asked quickly, "What do you see? Tell me."

While Swyllo continued to wail incoherently next to Kymil, Nyba was able just barely to hear Doc Kymil reply, "I don't know. It is just vast blackness all around the spot where Cotto Vazza is or was. It's as large as the twinkling lights had been from colony ships. It's totally blocking sunlight just like an eclipse."

"My sunlight is gone. I can't get energy now," Swyllo wailed.

"We've got to move into some sunlight, Cap," Domyn insisted. "No matter how much we use in energy, we must move this spacecraft into sunlight. No matter what strains we put on our Flandecams, we can't stay in this position on this course vector without sunlight. Our energy supply will run out. We must move to fill our reserve."

Move, yes, she agreed, but to where, and then she thought she heard a croaking voice mumble in exhaustion, "Gas...giant."

However, she was not sure, and her mind was bewildered at that moment, so her voice asked of its own, "Where, Domyn? Do we go back? Go ahead? Go where? Where will we fly into light? Give me advice now."

Domyn declared in a confident tone, "We cannot move ahead unless the blockage vanishes. We can't rely on this to happen. If we go back, we do not increase our chances of getting into light..."

Then Whyvvi remarked loudly, "Yes, Jamyk, you say our goal. We should travel toward the super gas giant planet. Reflected sunlight serves our harvesters almost as well as true sunlight. We should go toward that planet harvesting something as we move until we travel beyond the shadow of whatever has stolen Swyllo's sunlight."

"Awright, let's get going," Domyn demanded with enthusiasm. "This group of wolves will not be trapped so easily. Pilots, prepare to change course vector... Cap Nyba, on your order of course."

"Do it," Nyba snapped, feeling a throb begin in her left temple just behind and below her eye, "Domyn, take command. You understand our needs in this situation better than I. I need to rest my brain a bit. You take command."

His expression of fright scared her, but Nyba nodded her assurance toward him and leaned over to pat his wide arm through a tan dionjocu. Neer Domyn could do the job, she knew. Her sudden headache was very unusual for her. It sapped her confidence, stole her decisiveness. Intuitively she glanced over toward Jamyk's slouched green form and wondered if the boy had a similar ailment. What were odds of two such different people getting the same illness at the same time, she wondered between pounding throbs. It was almost more terrifying to think that she had sucha close tie with the rascal. Nyba shivered within her sweaty blue dionjocu.

"Jamyk!" Domyn was shouting boisterously, and this stirred Nyba back to some vague attention.

"I can pilot solo, Domyn," Milyr declared. "It will be more efficient with one pilot now. Let the little peener rest. You know how he burns out sometimes after a long, strenuous effort. Let him rest. We will need him later, I am quite sure."

As she thought that she heard Doc Kymil ask her if she felt ill, Nyba did hear Domyn agree, "Awright, Milyr, you take solo pilot. Our course is the shortest distance toward that super gas giant. Keep our inclination such that Swyllo gets the maximum number of harvesters exposed to reflected light from that planet."

"I'll take care of your needs, Swyllo," Milyr bragged loudly, then his voice and her reply receded into the background of Nyba's awareness, which was drawn uncontrollably toward the green form leaning back into the green chair as if he were asleep, yes, sleeping...like...the...little...

...As a sleepy haze gradually lifted from her awareness, Nyba heard Whyvvi shout emphatically, "Yes, Neer, there are five or six, no, at least seven small speed ships leaving the mine belt and heading our way. They appear to be the same type as we encountered during the first skirmish with these colonials. And, Neer Domyn, there was no sign of laser fire from the mine belt when the ships came out. Apparently these ships had a free pass through the mine belt."

Before the young woman finished her statement, Nyba felt wide awake. This was not normal for her. Usually when she napped, she awoke groggy with a mild but lingering headache. Now she felt perky, cherply refreshed. This was very welcome, yet disconcerting in its strangeness. Well, she thought to herself, what in recent hours had not been weirdly strange from her prior years of experience and expectation. This entire trip into Sexto had been...uncherp... and very strange.

Neer Domyn said beside her in his brown chair, "Awe damn help us! At our slow crawl, we can't outpace them this time. Is there any read of nuclear orbs?

And also, can you determine whether they are tracking into any pattern yet to enclose our position as they did last time?"

"No, Domyn, these ships are too far away at this time to calculate any specific pattern of deployment. The orbs would be too small to show on our present sensor confinement setting. I do not believe I should attempt to change this setting. With our low energy supply and inconsistent interface with our sleeping Joculatus, I might lose what sensor capability that we do have," Whyvvi said with obvious concern in her weary voice.

When she glanced to her left toward the young woman, Nyba was attracted to the slouched green figure in the green chair. Jamyk was asleep still. His arms were splayed over the side of his chair. His skinny legs were spread out straight in front of his chair. His body was very still, yet his head swayed side to side and incoherent mumbles gurgled from his mouth and throat. This was uncherp, she thought, that they should fall asleep at the same time. However, his slack form and swaying head did bring worry to her awareness.

From her right, Nyba heard Swyllo gripe, "It won't matter soon. Our energy supply is being used by the Flandecams just to get us this close to the gas giant. I can harvest barely half of what we use. This reflected sunlight is useful but is only about half the strength of true sunlight. Vulch, where is direct sunlight now?"

"Swyllo!" Jamyk shrieked, suddenly sitting erect in his chair and staring toward the girl in yellow.

His abrupt outburst caused Domyn to pause, and then a deep voice growled, "Just collect what you can. Our priority now is to get away from those speed ships."

"Swyllo?" Jamyk repeated in bewilderment and then unhooked his harness and stumbled across the void where the holovision would normally be displayed and asked, "Hurt?"

As the boy fell to his knees only a yard in front of Swyllo's chair, the girl hissed, "Keep away, little one nad. Don't bother me now. I'm working. Don't be toxx."

"Little peener, you're awake finally. Sleeping almost two straight days isn't you, toxx onad!" Milyr yelled with relief and joy while his hands flailed with his effort to pilot the spacecraft. "I thought I'd have to save us all by myself. Not that these Flandecams have much left to give us. Vulching colonials and their vulching laser mines stung our hull operations really nasty foul."

"Two toxx days, we slept for two days?" Nyba muttered, perplexed with fright and shame.

Yet Jamyk was focused only upon Swyllo at that moment and rasped again in uncertainty, "Swyllo... Hurt?"

"Get away, you toxx," Swyllo demanded with a bitter squeal in her voice, "Get away, or I'll kick your one testicle up into your scrawny throat. I'm too busy now for your vulching playing."

"Awright, Jamyk, get back into your chair," Domyn commanded. "This ConCen has critical duties to perform. Put your toxx back into your chair, pilot."

"Jamyk, do as Neer Domyn ordered," Nyba demanded as her voice croaked hoarsely from her recent sleep, and she blushed inwardly at the embarrassingly frail tone of authority, which she presented to her crew at this moment and silently mused amazed that Domyn kept command alone for two days.

"Cap Nyba, cherp to have you back with us," Prof Lyndyn said from his gray chair to her left.

Nyba watched the boy as he suddenly seemed to notice activity and others in the ConCen besides Swyllo, and Jamyk arose from his knees, stared at her, and said, "Cap... Nyba."

Then while he returned to his chair, Milyr chuckled, "Vulch, this strange act was a bit weird to me. But yeah, it's cherp to have both of you awake. We can use some help or at least motivation."

Hearing both temporary happiness but also overriding despair in his voice, Nyba peered toward Milyr and declared, "Well, I'm awake now, young man. Don't you let me down! Now, Neer Domyn, what is our situation? How long was I asleep?"

With a smile on his wide face and definite relief in his tired voice, Domyn reported, "Cap, you were out as long as you needed. So don't whip yourself. You are human after all. Now Wolf Streak Beta is in nasty condition. Milyr is flying us on at best three Flandecams..."

"Not really that many," a lanky young man in sweat-drenched dionjocu interrupted. "All of these are partially damaged. I'm beginning to believe the super gas giant is pulling us toward it with strong gravity more than I am propelling us with our Flandecams."

"At least we are moving," Whyvvi said matter-of-factly and also in obvious exhaustion.

"Can I see your sensor view in my visor?" Nyba asked, flipping the visor down from her forehead but seeing nothing but blank darkness before her eye, she sighed, "I guess not. I hear that our energy supply is critically low. How low is it?"

"Vulching bad!" Swyllo retorted sourly while her small form slouched tiredly in a yellow chair.

"Yes, we're under 23 percent. The harvest intake is not strong. We can get some from the gas giant, but our usage is surpassing this intake. Our level continues to drop," Domyn reported and then slumped wearily in despair against the back of his brown chair.

"Why isn't sunlight from the Sexto sun helping now? We should have travelled back into direct sunlight by now. We've moved off of our original course vector for over two days, haven't we?" Nyba asked in confusion, now feeling as if her sleep had left her behind the situation.

"Yes, we have," Doc Kymil replied. "However, the blocking mass around Cotto Vazza is acting like eclipse that moves as we move. It is blocking sunlight still. Before we ceased my sensor search in that direction, I was able to record movement of this blocking mass. For some reason, it moves through space at velocity, which keeps it between the sun and us."

"Vulchers are doing it on purpose," Swyllo screamed angrily.

"This accusation would suggest that they know of our harvesting procedure and are preventing us from performing this function. Why would they do this? How would they know to do this?" Lyndyn asked as his sweat-soaked gray dionjocu gloves lifted the visor up upon his brow.

"Or perhaps Cotto Vazza could be in orbit that coincidently parallels our current vector," Whyvvi said and then added, "Do you recall, Nyba, how we had speculated that perhaps the colonials had created light absorbing technology roughly similar to Blue Jay tech. This could explain how Gullu Mette had continued to power trapped Buffalardi beacon by taking light energy from spergits around Kil-Kol and then channeling this energy to the beacon. Perhaps similar technology is at work around Cotto Vazza. Maybe they are collecting sunlight for their own use."

"What the vulch does that mean to us now? How can this help us now?" Milyr griped sullenly.

Whyvvi replied indignantly, "For some people like you, maybe nothing about this makes sense. But Nyba and Domyn can understand that maybe Cotto Vazza is harvesting sunlight just like we do. Maybe the super colony ship is repositioning in orbit to stay closer to us. Maybe it does not intend to harm our progress. This could be unintentional."

"Whyvvi, I recall our discussion, and your theory makes logical sense, but it doesn't help us now," Nyba declared. "Even if Cotto Vazza is not an enemy, the effect of the blocking curtain is just as bad. We need to shut down all our systems that do not involve flying to safety and of course continued harvest of whatever light we have available."

"Awright, Cap, this makes sense," Domyn agreed. "We have already shut off all exterior functions from hull to Circum Two, except pilot functions and harvesting and limited sensors. Now also, all artigences are at manual mode, which is a minimum mode that allows our dionjocus to interface with them to perform operational functions outside the craft."

"And you say that we are losing energy still," Nyba reaffirmed, and then with a deep breath and hasty silent prayer to whoever would listen, she commanded, "Turn off all the systems beyond Circum One. All systems! We do not need any of those luxuries now, not even artificial gravity or lighting beyond Circum One. Is Whyvvi's one sensor critical now? Does the surveying approach of those colonial speed ships help us now?"

"Only if they release nuclear orbs, and we need to divert our course," Domyn replied.

"Erh… Domyn, I'm not sure how much we could maneuver now," Milyr admitted sheepishly. "I'm doing well to keep Wolf Streak Beta flying away from the mine belt toward the gas giant. As I said before, that super giant is doing more pulling on us than our Flandecams are doing propelling us."

"Do we need our artigences on manual mode?" Whyvvi asked. "Can we shut them down completely and secure their base programs into Wolf?"

"Vulch, without manual Joculatus, I can't pilot with my dionjocu," Milyr complained bitterly.

With great reluctance, Nyba commanded, "Terminate Bodacia and Vivacio to base mode into Wolf. Shut down all power to systems beyond Circum One, except pilot interface and harvest interface. Do this now, no more discussion. Our time is getting short."

"Awright, Cap Nyba," Domyn acknowledged, and Nyba knew that he realized also at this moment that Circum One was a corridor immediately around the ConCen, a corridor where their quarters were located.

"Milyr, you are our only external sensor now," Nyba said. "Whatever your visor can see or read of gravity eddies and other related energy surges is all we have to guide us. No pressure on you of course. Just get us into orbit around that gas giant. Quickly before the colonials decide to launch more weapons at us. Swyllo, harvest as much as you can."

"Vulch, Nyba, I always do that," Swyllo hissed in annoyance.

"All discretionary systems beyond Circum One are off, Cap," Domyn reported.

"Without Joculatus at manual mode for my station, my exterior operations will not function through my dionjocu interface," Whyvvi declared.

Doc Kymil suggested, "Cap Nyba, now that these dionbodas and some of the dionjocus are not usefully functional, perhaps we should change into McAnderwikes instead. There is a possibility of losing internal gravity, or worse, crashing or other potentially injurious harm to our bodies. These interface garments are not designed for bodily protection, but McAnderwikes are quite protective."

"We should do that," Whyvvi exclaimed.

"Awe knows that you are wise, Doc," Domyn said. "Our McAnderwikes with their titan-flex fabric can protect us from almost any physical blow short of destruction of this craft. These dionjocus are not made for that function. Our rooms are in Circum one. We can change to our McAnderwikes."

"Then do it. Everyone but Milyr and Swyllo, go now," Nyba ordered brusquely, not allowing anyone to disagree. "Quickly, men and women, we don't know how much time we have. I want everyone inside the ConCen as soon as possible. We may need to seal Wolf before this is over. Now hurry and please get our McAnderwikes for us. I'm staying here now."

"Get my JMO please, Whyvvi," Swyllo called out tiredly.

"Awright, as you command," Domyn said, getting up from his chair. "Let's go, everyone. That includes you, Jamyk."

After a flurry of rustling dionjocus and sloshing sound of caps being peeled off sweating, bald heads, Nyba watched the last one leave through the inner hatch, Jamyk or course, and she yelled, "Jamyk, go right to your room and get back here pronto. No side trips this time."

Suddenly the ConCen was quiet and seemed almost empty to her. Though of course, Milyr's presence was filling to her awareness. Yet Nyba realized what she had suggested just minute earlier. They might have to seal Wolf. This was a drastic and frightening thought. At the moment, the ConCen was the central heart of Wolf Streak Beta functions. Should the worst happen, then the ConCen could become the final escape pod of the spacecraft. ConCen would become Wolf. Nyba's body and spirit shivered at what this might portend.

However, as captain, she must consider all possibilities to secure and save her people who were the true heart of Wolf Streak Beta. Perhaps she should order the raising of emergency control console next, she pondered. With Joculatus basically down, only the truly manual controls for emergency console would serve the ConCen. At least those controls would give them a rudimentary sensor and communication functions again, as well as pilot station. How soon now before Milyr lost what little interface he had with the subconscious program of Joculatus? Could she gamble on that tenuous pilot contact? Could she rely upon limited energy supply to be powerful enough to raise and activate the emergency console if she waited? Nyba hated to think of these worries and crisis, which had brought them to her.

Then Prof Lyndyn reentered the ConCen with a blue garment over his arm and said, "Cap Nyba, here is your McAnderwike. Doc Kymil said it should fit you well enough."

"Thanks, Prof, did she remember to send JMO for me?" Nyba asked, taking the garment and also as she stood from her blue chair, "Milyr, how soon before we are in orbit around the gas giant? Can you tell if our velocity is increasing with the pull of that planet?"

Prof Lyndyn muttered in a forlorn voice, "No, I don't believe she thought of JMO."

In exhaustion Milyr replied more forcefully, "With its gravitational strength, we could begin orbit any time, Nyba. But I'm worried about pulling up too soon and letting those vulching colonials get an easy shot at us."

"Yes, I've considered this myself. We should get as close to the atmosphere as we can. Perhaps we could even get into the upper atmosphere and confuse their tracking sensors. Did Whyvvi discover any info about that giant planet while I was asleep," Nyba inquired while she opened the front of her dionjocu.

Prof Lyndyn answered instead, "No, Cap, when we stopped communication function because there was no longer any purpose in that, then I undertook some of her duties as Domyn insisted that she focus on the mine belt region. After Whyvvi set my station to a new sensor function…"

Swyllo griped interrupting him, "At the cost of some of our precious energy."

"Indeed this was unfortunate, but I was able to learn some basic facts about the planet. There is a very deep, turbulent atmosphere almost five times the atmosphere of the old gas giant planets of the Zerosolis System. I believe that I read several dense patches within this stormy atmosphere. Some of these seemed to be almost solid, but the accuracy of the sensors was poor then. There seemed to be much sulfur dioxide, methane, and related obnoxious gases similar to the gas giants of the Zerosolis System. Somewhere deep inside this voluminous gas atmosphere of many different densities of layers, I believe there is a solid and very strong center of gravity..."

"This is not a bad sensor reading for Prof with the poor sensor system," Whyvvi chuckled as she cut across the semi-circle of chairs to her own red one. "I could give you only rudimentary sensor capability at the time."

The young woman was dressed in her blue McAnderwike and seemed more relaxed than before when she had sensor responsibilities, and so Nyba declared, "Well, yes, he did as cherp a job as you do under such nasty conditions. Now I need your opinion, both of you, without a lot of verbal discussion. Do you think that I should raise the emergency console now?"

Whyvvi replied hastily, "Yes, you should."

Before Prof Lyndyn expressed his opinion, Domyn's deep voice said, "Definitely, Nyba, and don't hesitate. It cannot hurt what little function we currently have available. And... I'm reluctant to suggest this...but...perhaps we need to consider the manual separation of Wolf...if situation gets much worse with our low energy supply..."

"Indeed this is a dire and radical possibility," Prof Lyndyn agreed in a very displeased tone. "If our situation becomes that terrible... I don't know..."

Manual ejection of Wolf from Wolf Streak Beta? This scared Nyba just considering it. If they lost most of the remaining power though, she realized, then Wolf may not be able to disconnect from a much more massive structure of the spacecraft. The manual ejection system was a redundant backup just for this last option for ejecting Wolf. If Wolf could not eject, then any serious calamity to Wolf Streak Beta could destroy Wolf and the people inside. It would not be a very functional escape pod, she thought, if they could not eject from the spacecraft proper. These thoughts bothered her more than she wanted to admit.

"Neer Domyn, I believe that you are correct. We will need to prep the manual ejection system," Nyba agreed reluctantly as she finished undressing from her blue dionjocu. "Do we have the adequate energy to raise the emergency console now? And do we have enough power to also set the ejection charges from here now?"

"Vulch, not both," Swyllo complained.

"Yeah, I agree, if you want to save enough to go into the controlled orbit around the gas giant, then we can't do both raise console and set the ejection system from our current functions," Milyr said and then added with an exaggerated breathless effort, "Especially if we try for the very tight orbit against the strong gravitational pull. It is vulching strong, almost more than even my muscular arms can handle…"

Abruptly Domyn asked, "Strong enough to pull us the rest of the way? Can we turn off Joculatus totally and steer from the emergency console?"

"Vulch, that's nasty scary!" Milyr cried out.

"If it can save any of my energy supply, then let's vulching do it," Swyllo declared shrilly. "We don't need your lazy toxx flying now anyway. You can't steer us anywhere, can you?"

"Once I stop pilot function with Joculatus," Milyr grumbled and then muttered the rest under his breath, and Nyba was certain his thoughts were not cherp.

"Raise the emergency console, Neer Domyn," Nyba commanded with firm decisiveness. "I believe we have no other choice now. Prof Lyndyn, I need you to supervise the team to set ejection charges around this ConCen, perhaps soon to be this Wolf."

Domyn paused in his activity to say, "Nyba, manual charges are in the access ways to the Flandecams. Prof may not fit into those crawl shafts. I know that I don't anymore. Only Jamyk…and maybe… Swyllo can do this task now."

"I'm vulching busy with my two remaining harvesters," Swyllo called out.

"That won't matter soon, Swyllo," Nyba said. "And young woman, you need to stop to put your McAnderwike on. I don't want you endangered just to get another 1 percent of energy harvested. Get ready to cease harvest function… No protest, girl."

Swyllo's mouth was caught open in planned response, but Nyba's stern demand stopped girl's the retort, so instead she said calmly, "Yes, Cap Nyba. I'm shutting down the harvest function now."

While this exchange occurred, the floor of the ConCen slid away in front of Nyba's chair and disappeared beneath the forward curve of the ConCen. Then as hydraulic hum filled the room, a console of old-style monitors, push-button keyboards, hand levers and knobs, and even foot pedals, all this lifted from the hollow beneath the floor above which not hours ago the three dimensional holovision had once displayed its scenes. We have come to this, Nyba mourned silently. Wolf Streak Beta would be controlled by the tech of many centuries ago, but it could be controlled.

"Vulch, will I have to pilot us with that?" Milyr groaned in pessimistic anguish.

"At least it will use our energy more slowly," Swyllo declared.

"Prof Lyndyn, you should take your recruits, your little monkeys, and set those charges," Nyba commanded, standing naked in the ConCen behind her blue chair. "We may not have much time. I'm sure the colonial ships have closed considerably as we have lost our velocity. They may launch weapons at any time as before. I don't know how much time you will have to finish the job. Do it quickly, just in case Wolf must be sealed and ejection occurs."

"Vulch, tiny fem, you'll be outside Wolf while you do this. Be careful and fast," Milyr advised in honest concern. "We don't want to lose you, tiny fem."

"You toxx, you just won't have anyone to goad then," Swyllo giggled as she stood up from her chair and ripped the yellow cap from off her head. "What will you do then, hey, big peener?"

"Where is Jamyk?" Prof Lyndyn asked, pausing by the hatch. "He should be back by now. And Doc Kymil, where is she?"

As she reached for her McAnderwike, wishing they had thought to bring her JMO for underneath, Nyba listened to the emergency console lock into place with a distinct thud and click, and then Domyn moved quickly to one of the two seats and said, "We should get this operational while we have adequate power to interact with Wolf Streak Beta. I'll need Milyr as soon as possible."

"Why vulching me?" Milyr whined. "I don't even have my McAnderwike on yet. I haven't had the chance."

"Stop whining," Domyn growled. "Shut down your station now. Get your clothes changed, and get your toxx into this other seat. We've got prepping to do. We'll need both of us manly guys here if we must fly this old system totally manually. Only our bodies have enough muscle to wrestle this Wolf into orbit if we lose the spaceship itself. Now get your toxx moving."

"Vulch, okay, Domyn! Can I have time to get dressed into my McAnderwike, or must I fly this thing from my bare toxx?" Milyr grumbled in irritation and perhaps fear as Nyba heard emotions in his voice and knew she felt the same anxiety.

"Just change your suits, Milyr. You have time," she said calmly, pulling the blue pants up her bare legs and waist. "But please hurry, we need you."

"Where's my McAnderwike?" he yelled in anger, but then as his eyes glimpsed toward Nyba as she stood behind her chair still naked but for a partial covering of an unadorned garment, Milyr paused momentarily and then smiled slightly to say, "Well, I guess I'm not the only one who has had to put dressing on hold while all this has played out. I'm sorry, Nyba and Domyn. I don't try to be toxx on purpose. I guess it just comes out naturally without my awareness."

Just then Jamyk rasped as he entered the ConCen and tossed a blue garment toward Milyr, "Milyr... McAndy."

"Vulching thanks," Milyr mumbled as he grabbed the blue garment from a thin hand and disappeared out the hatch.

"Jamyk," Nyba shouted in anger, "where have you been? We're in an emergency here..."

As she said this to the boy, Jamyk turned to Swyllo and gave her a blue garment in his other hand and in a soft voice said, "Swyllo... McAndy."

Then Doc Kymil returned through the inner hatch and said breathlessly, "I forgot to send your JMOs, Nyba, so I went back. Also, I got these tethers. I'm not sure why, but he pointed to them and told me to bring them. But if you are contemplating any activity outside the ConCen, we should plan on possible loss of artificial gravity. Tethers could be useful in this situation."

Grateful for the JMO piece and so peeling down the pants again, Nyba lost her anger at Jamyk and Kymil for their tardiness and said in a decisive way, "Well, we are going to set ejection charges manually. Prof is going with Jamyk and Swyllo to do a chore. Perhaps extra precaution is a good idea. If you use tethers, Prof, someone else should go with your team to assist with holding or fastening."

"I'll go," Doc Kymil volunteered immediately. "These older arms have some tough muscle in them still."

"No doubt they do," Prof Lyndyn exclaimed and then commanded in his nasal voice, "Let's go, team. We have an important job to do. Now where's Swyllo?"

From outside the outer hatch, her shrill voice cried in annoyance, "I'm here trying to get into my McAnderwike without this big toxx oaf bothering me. You big oaf, don't be such a toxx. Can't you stand up on your own?"

"Milyr!" Nyba yelled about as loud as she had ever. "Hurry up. Get your toxx in here."

"Coming, Nyba," a baritone voice called, "But my toxx is still bare."

"We'll meet her out there," Prof Lyndyn said. "We'll move quickly now, troops. We've got four sections with two Flandecams each. The manual ejection charges are positioned with the Flandecams. We'll do this closest to the hatch last. Just in case of last-minute trouble, then we'll be near the hatches to the ConCen. Let's go, team."

As they left the ConCen, Jamyk paused looking at her and then with a smile said, "Nyba... Cap."

Then he twirled and followed the others through the hatches. For awhile Nyba stood peering out the hatches after the departing figures. Was she doing the right action, sending them on this mission? It seemed to be a drastic ploy setting ejection charges, she thought, but circumstances had come to this. Had she led her crew of wolves to this disaster? Was this horrible situation her fault? Nyba could not answer herself. The only image imprinted still on her recent memory was Jamyk's smile.

As she stood clutching the JMO suit in preparation to adorn it, with an anxious deep voice, Domyn asked in fright, "What are those? Whyvvi, come here quick. Look at this monitor. Are these dots what I think they are?"

His startled tone forced Nyba to abort dressing and step toward the console to look over his shoulder, and she heard Whyvvi gasp, "Oh, no, those look like the nuclear orbs we experienced before. They must have launched them awhile ago. If this picture is standard magnification, they are only...about...seven minutes away from distance that they exploded last time."

Pointing to six pictures on the monitor bank in front of the empty seat, Domyn said, "I count at least five visible orbs heading toward us from multiple vectors. They did not wait to align around us in a precise pattern as last time. I think they plan to catch us against atmosphere this time. Full power blasts. No, precision the EM pulse strategy this time."

"Less than seven minutes? Can we make a tight orbit around that giant before then?" Nyba asked breathlessly, pulling on her blue JMO suit. "Will it be enough to protect us behind that huge planet?"

"We can't get enough of the planet between us and these orbs. We can't outpace the EM pulse like we did before. And most likely just nuclear explosions will do severe damage to Wolf Streak Beta this time," Domyn said in resignation.

"Will that turbulent atmosphere give us any protection?" Nyba inquired, hoping in desperation for any chance while she hastily dressed into her McAnderwike.

"I don't believe so," Domyn stated. "Our Blue Jay sci-tech can protect us only so far."

"Should we call others back in and seal the ConCen now?" Whyvvi asked. "Will we be safe inside? Will Wolf resist the power of those nuclear explosions?"

"If separated from the spacecraft proper, Wolf could withstand the EM pulse if completely sealed," Domyn announced. "But I'm not confident of survival if the close nuclear blast or several were added to the EM pulse. The combination would most likely be too much."

"Need my help, hey?" Milyr asked, plopping into the empty seat next to Domyn, and then after a glance at the console, blurted, "Vulch, are those what I think they are?"

"Awe help us, my friend, I don't believe they are greeting gifts," Domyn sighed tiredly. "Those nasty things are only maybe five minutes away from range at which they exploded last time."

"Can we use our Flandecams still with this old piece of toxx system?" Milyr asked.

"I believe that the controls will operate the Flandecams on standard bursts but only at current directional vectors," Domyn said. "Why? What are you thinking?"

"I'm thinking that we load up our fore with as much posi-grav as we can generate and let two bodies draw each other together. I don't think we need to worry about the nice perfect entry into a nice perfect orbit, do we?" Milyr asked.

"Just a stone going into the pond, hey, my friend?" Domyn chuckled. "Why not? Do it, Milyr."

"How do I use these antiquated controls?" Milyr groaned as his hands hovered over the console.

"Some pilot you are," Whyvvi said sarcastically.

"Awright, close your eyes, remember back to basic pilot school and push some buttons," Domyn suggested. "Just don't cause us to stop just yet."

"Well, now, Neer, you're a big help," Nyba scoffed in resigned humor, not knowing how else to let her mind deal with the situation, then turning to Whyvvi, she ordered, "You should tell the others to hurry. Their time is much less than we thought. Please hurry, Whyvvi. I want them all back inside this Wolf as soon as possible. We will not let our crew be harmed."

"Vulch, I hope I'm doing this right," Milyr groaned as his hands worked buttons, levers, and knobs, "I don't want the tiny fem to come back in here and tell me I'm doing it all wrong."

"Awright, Cap Nyba," Domyn chuckled in fearful irony while working his hands over the console. "At least if Wolf Streak Beta blows apart on entry or because of nuclear blasts, the colonials will believe that we are destroyed and may not stalk us anymore."

"Well that's a clever plan, if we are alive afterwards," Nyba agreed sarcastically, and then suddenly thought to herself, perhaps if Wolf was sealed and survived the destruction, maybe there was a chance, a very slim and unpredictable chance for her wolves to survive…somehow.

Yet what would happen afterwards, she wondered.

"Vulch, I'm doing something now. Our velocity just increased several fold. We're hurtling toward that very nasty giganormous planet down there. I don't think that I could stop us now," Milyr shouted. "We are vulched for nasty sure this time."

Nyba ran hastily to the hatch and yelled to her crew, "Hurry, my friends, you don't have much time. Between colonials and Milyr's piloting, I think we are in a nasty toxx vulched."

No specific response came from an echo of the corridor. Merely gasping shouts of indistinct commands from Lyndyn and Kymil and one or two squeals of anger from Swyllo flowed to Cap Nyba as she waited a few moments for her wolves to appear before she ducked back into the ConCen to go to her command chair behind the two manly pilots.

Before her Milyr yelled with a creaking voice, "I think we are about to hit the atmosphere."

Domyn murmured in a hushed voice, "Awe, help us."

Nyba agreed, but her spirit of survival laughed loudly, "I suppose we could just surrender now."

"Vulch that's a foolish idea," Milyr groaned from the seat at the pilot console.

"I guess I must agree with you," Nyba proclaimed dismally. "The colonial track record of sympathy is not very encouraging to me."

"Like I just said," Domyn exclaimed breathlessly. "Awe help us!"

Surprising herself Nyba said aloud before witnesses, "I must agree finally with you, Domyn, wholeheartedly. I can now disavow my skeptical view...for this moment."

Milyr laughed, "Vulch, Nyba, you are Cap after all, aren't you?"

Maybe, she mused silently, but she sure got them into one big vulching nasty mess.

"I believe I will let you take over that role, my young man," she retorted.

Then the first explosion shook the spacecraft from outside.

SPEC THREE: LYNDYN AFTER SWYLLO
CHAPTER 23

As a blue form pushed past him, Lyndyn heard Jamyk squeal in an emotionally cracking voice, "Swyllo…out!"

"Just…need…to…set…charge…" Swyllo gasped in the narrow access space below the corridor.

Then when the boy dove into the access, Jamyk's body blocked Lyndyn's view. A safety tether followed the thin form and snapped taut against Lyndyn's shoulder and arms. His own grip on Swyllo's safety tether slipped few inches, but he clutched it hastily again, his gloved fingers and hands straining against the pull of Swyllo's slight weight, but more so her vehement stubbornness to finish the job. Behind him Lyndyn felt the body of Kymil bump him as she grasp hold of Jamyk's tether.

"Out," Jamyk shrieked. "Now!"

In the survey view available around the two small figures, Lyndyn saw in horror a structure of access around the ladder and platform below Swyllo begins to disintegrate. Wolf Streak Beta shook violently, probably due to the shock wave of recent external explosions, Lyndyn thought. Scattered fissures in structure glowed with the light of the fireball. The Flandecam, colonial missiles, perhaps balls of lightening outside, Lyndyn was not certain from where this light and intense heat originated. His attention at that moment was on pulling Swyllo to safety.

"Jamyk, Swyllo, now. Don't resist our pulls," Kymil commanded frantically.

"One…more…switch…" Swyllo stammered breathlessly, and then the hatch below her suddenly fragmented into countless pieces, and the access became a suction tunnel as air pressure vented outward into thin atmosphere through multiplying fissures in the disintegrating outer hull of Wolf Streak Beta.

In the next few seconds, Lyndyn observed a flare of an orange-red explosion just below Swyllo. A shock wave momentarily counter-acted the air pressure venting and threw Lyndyn backwards into Kymil. While his eyelids blinked spasmodically against the force and flare, he felt the tension of a safety tether cease suddenly. Through the after-effects of the flash, debris, and his own autonomic tears, Lyndyn observed Swyllo vanish.

She was no longer there in remnants of the access workspace of the Flandecams. A bright blue-white flash surrounded Jamyk and the spot where she had been only a moment ago. As Kymil pulled in hastily, a tether still connected to Jamyk, the boy's body seemed to go limp. Fortunately the blast had thrust Jamyk back towards them. His scrawny form flew upwards in the tunnel.

"Get back here now," shouted Whyvvi from the nearest hatch. "We will be sealing Wolf in less than a minute. You must come now. Hurry!"

As Jamyk's limp form seemed to fly feet first at him, Lyndyn heard Kymil yell in noise and fury around them, "Grab his feet, before the escaping air pressure pulls him away again."

With his conscious mind numb from the sight of Swyllo's sudden disappearance, Lyndyn obeyed the woman instinctively and reached out to grip the small blue boots. Then another red-orange explosion flashed off to the side of the former access tunnel. Wolf Streak Beta shook again. The death throes of the great spacecraft, Lyndyn's mind cried. His exhausted and cramped hands continued pulling at the legs and then waist of the obviously unconscious boy, perhaps dead boy. Beyond where he could imagine seeing Swyllo's face still, breakup and fragmentation of the outer portions of Wolf Streak Beta quickened with renewed force.

"We've got to get him behind the next hatch," Kymil shouted. "It will close soon. Nyba can't wait, or Wolf will be compromised. Hurry, Lyndyn, let's go!"

Vacuum pressure began pulling at them again. Lyndyn clutched the thin body against his chest and stepped quickly after Kymil. Fortunately they needed only five paces to get past the outer hatch of the ConCen. Lyndyn was grateful that Jamyk weighed so little. Even in partial gravity now, the weight would have seemed a great burden against the escaping air pressure. Also, he realized the burden to his awareness after the disheartening occurrences of the last few minutes.

"Are you in?" Nyba shouted from inside the ConCen.

Whyvvi exclaimed with her head sticking out the inner hatch, "Yes, they are inside the outer hatch. Close it now. Hurry!"

Then a metallic thud and click of the closing hatch sounded behind him. The equalization of air pressure lightened his burden, at least his physical burden, for the vacuum pressure no longer pulled at his back. To his own surprise, Lyndyn found himself thanking Domyn's metaphy at the sound of the hatch sealing. Then, just as startling, he considered swearing at the same metaphy for the loss of Swyllo. Despite his current confusion, his intellect berated himself as hypocrite, or at least psychological weakling.

Shaking these spurious thoughts from his mind, Lyndyn carried Jamyk onto the ConCen. While walking toward a green chair, he observed frantic activity on the ConCen. Inside the original semi-circle of chairs, Domyn and Milyr sat at the emergency console. Their blue McAnderwike suits revealed sweat stains down their backs and in their arm pits. Obviously, as Wolf Streak Beta broke apart piece by piece, a chore of flying the spacecraft with the ancient system had become more physically trying, even for two strong young men.

"Seal Wolf inner hatch before we lose energy to do so," Nyba commanded from her blue chair behind the emergency console. "Whyvvi, check the manual lockdowns to make sure we are positively sealed."

Rushing past Lyndyn, Whyvvi asked with concern in her voice, "Is he okay? Where is Swyllo?"

"I'm sorry to report, she's gone," Lyndyn stated with remorse while placing Jamyk into his green chair and removing the McAnderwike helmet.

"Gone? What do you mean gone? Is she...dead?" Milyr asked hesitantly.

"Oh my, I must confirm that, yes," Kymil murmured in sorrow as she bent over her young patient to look at his facial features. "At least this one is still alive."

"Vulch, she's really dead?" Milyr murmured, and then after a few seconds, asked in a hushed voice, "Is Jamyk okay? Is our little peener hurt?"

"Focus on your function, pilot," Nyba commanded urgently. "We've got to make this flight appear random and haphazard as if a result of the explosion vectors. We don't want to look like this piece of debris is under a controlled flight. Whyvvi, are those manual locks set and checked?"

"I am working on that now. I should be finished in just seconds," Whyvvi shouted.

"Jamyk was near Swyllo when the explosions hit," Lyndyn said wearily, standing over the boy in the green chair. "There was a blue-white flash as if lightening had surrounded him and then he was unconscious. But Swyllo was just...gone."

Doc Kymil said as she looked over her patient, "From my present observations, he did not suffer any burns or electrical strikes. I don't see any direct signs of blows or physical trauma."

"If he had, McAnderwike would have moderated trauma," Domyn announced, gasping with exertion as his hands flicked the switches and punched buttons on the ancient console.

Whyvvi reported with mixture of determination and emotion in her sobs, "Locks set, Nyba, hatch is now secure... But... Swyllo...not here anymore?"

"What about lightning? Vulching, lightning is all over this atmosphere out there. Even vulching blue balls of lightning if that's what they are, zipping around us, goad me nasty," Milyr whined, breathing heavily with his exertion.

Constant flashes shone through the large window above and in front of the emergency console. It was viewport of Wolf compiled by several interconnected clear plasti-glas tubes that extended from the ConCen to the hull of the spacecraft for a moment at least, Lyndyn reminded himself. A flicker and distortion occasionally hindered this view now as portions of this viewing system where destroyed near the outer hull. This disturbance began to make his consciousness slightly dizzy.

From outside swirls of thin yellow-purple clouds churned in the viewport. Some of the movement was due to uncontrolled spinning of Wolf Streak Beta as remnant of the spacecraft fell lower into the thin atmosphere of the super gas giant planet. In fact slight spinning through nauseous colors disturbed Lyndyn's stomach enough, so that he looked away quickly from the window. Instead he returned his sight to Jamyk's young face.

"He seems to be breathing regular for a sleep pattern, a normal sleep pattern," Doc Kymil stated after lifting his eyelids gently and leaning her ear close to the boy's mouth and nose. "He's definitely in some form of unconscious sleep, perhaps a coma. I can't be sure about that. I really hate not having my equipment, my dionboda, and Bodacia to help with diagnosis."

"Should we try to wake him?" Lyndyn asked, also feeling at a loss without sci-tech dionboda sensors and views that he had relied upon for his entire Blue Jay experience. "I don't see any signs of electrical shock damage to Jamyk or his McAnderwike. This is probably not lightning damage. But no doubt, strong stress and very close proximity to the explosions would have contributed to unconsciousness. Do you think he may have a concussion, Kymil? If so we should not let him stay asleep, should we?"

"If that was the situation, then I'd agree with you, Lyndyn," Doc Kymil said but then added as she wiped perspiration from around the eyes and nose of the boy, "Yet since he was already asleep when he came in here, and since his sleep seems to be normal to the limited observations that I can make now, I do not want to change his condition. Let's let him stay as he is for now. I'll watch closely."

As he spoke with Kymil, Lyndyn also listened to Domyn's report, "Outer hull and the two Flandecams are now seriously damaged, Cap. If my recollection of our situation just before this damage is accurate, that leaves us with only one partially functioning Flandecam. This could explode from the blasts outside or stress of the weakening structure of the spacecraft. I expect this Flandecam and the rest of the outer hull could be gone soon to these explosive forces and low atmospheric pressure pulling at what is left of our inner pressurization."

"Are you certain that we have no further chance at the effective Flandecam operation?" Cap Nyba asked.

"Once we lost our artigences and our external energy generation, our Flandecams could not function as designed. Our situation is getting worse, Cap. We can't expect to use our sci-tech as designed without the right amount of energy. I hate to say this, but Wolf Streak Beta is dying," Domyn groaned despondently.

Whyvvi weeping said, "Then maybe we will be joining Swyllo soon."

"Not as long as we are alive still and have our Wolf," Cap Nyba stated emphatically. "It's time to blow the escape charges and separate this Wolf."

"For what?" wailed Milyr. "To go where? We have no vulching thrust for propulsion anymore. We can't fly anywhere without the Flandecams of Wolf Streak Beta."

"As long as we're alive, as long as this Wolf can protect us, there is a chance," Cap Nyba exhorted her crew, and Lyndyn was astonished at her conviction, at her perseverance to go on, to keep trying to survive despite of the horrible sequence of tragedies suffered recently by Wolf Streak Beta.

"A chance for what?" Milyr continued irately. "We're vulching in toxx nastiness now!"

"Awright, enough, Milyr, that's enough," Domyn growled sharply. "Be pilot now. Do your duty. We're counting on you. I'm not strong enough to control this spacecraft by myself."

"Sorry, big man," Milyr apologized. "I'm vulching angry about losing Swyllo."

"We all are," Nyba stated and the ConCen fell quiet.

After taking the blue glove from the thin wrist and getting a pulse of the boy, Kymil said softly, "Lyndyn, I'm not sure if he has a concussion, probably not. His eyes look clear, appropriate pupil reaction, and his pulse is within norms for a seventeen-year-old male. His skin is not extremely clammy, just perspiration wet. Breathing seems normal. I just don't know for sure. However, his PEQA seems strong, and that is one thing that I can diagnose without Bodacia."

"Under our current conditions, perhaps he is better unconscious than alert," Lyndyn murmured. "Not much he can do for us at the moment. This may be the best we can do for him. Secure him in chair and let McAnderwike protect him from whatever happens next."

"I believe that everyone should secure themselves into a chair," Cap Nyba ordered with a tired sigh and then added, "I guess, men and women, it no longer matters which chair we each take. The dionjocu interfaces no longer apply. If you've ever had a desire to try someone else's chair or vantage position, this is as cherp a time as any."

"I must stay near Jamyk. So I'll have to take your chair, Whyvvi," Kymil explained.

"Yes, you should, Doc. That is so much more important now," Whyvvi declared from her standing position behind the two young men at the console. "I have always wanted to sit in that purple chair. Something about it always attracted me. Probably it was the view. This should be quite interesting now through the window. I shall take your chair, Milyr."

"Most likely because my toxx was always in it," Milyr chortled from his current position at console. "All you fems seem to want my chair, or is it me?"

As she approached the purple chair on the far-right end of the original ConCen formation, Whyvvi paused at the vacant yellow chair and stated in a solemn tone, "No, I think that I always wished to be closer to my best friend on Wolf Streak Beta. And that was not you, Milyr."

"Vulch, you wish…" Milyr began until he glanced toward Whyvvi, saw where she stood, then suddenly ended his retort and turned his attention silently to the console.

For a few moments, the ConCen was very quiet until Cap Nyba said in a low calm tone, "We have a chance still, people. Fox Flash Alpha should be out there somewhere. Blue Jay will be sending another scout craft, most likely Lynx Blaze to the Sexto System if they do not hear from us again. If we can hold on long enough, help is possible still. I believe that strongly. I hope that you will also."

"Awe let's hope that my universal awareness can hear what you say, Nyba, and can effect some miracle for us," Domyn muttered, and Lyndyn silently echoed the same thought, even though he did not believe that there was such entity to hear the words, but he was desperate himself at that moment.

As his attention was drawn briefly to the view out the window, Lyndyn was surprised to hear himself suggest, "In that mess around this huge planet, it will be difficult for our friends to find us wherever we rest. The same atmospheric conditions that hide us from the attackers will obscure sensors of our friends. Cap Nyba, we should not disregard the choice of surrender to our attackers if that is our only option at some future time."

"Thus far the colonial ships have not been very receptive to talking with us," Whyvvi stated. "Does not surrendering require some form of communication?"

"Yeah, they are not very cherp at talking," Milyr exclaimed as he worked his pilot console. "Yet our mission was to contact the colonials. Blue Jay never said vulchers would greet us with loving clutch. Although that has always been my dream as I anticipated the bodacious fems of the colonials."

With his sight diverted away from the spinning scene in the window, Lyndyn agreed, "That is true, Milyr, at least the first part of your comment. However, we cannot be certain that those attacking spaceships were controlled by colonials. Although that is most likely the scenario, we are not certain. No doubt Cotto Vazza could have totally different intentions toward us. They are very likely descendents of the original colonials..."

"Not now, men," Nyba interrupted. "Let's just get further into this gaseous soup. I'm blowing Wolf loose now... Is everyone harnessed in? Thank you, Wolf Streak Beta, for your service."

Suddenly the ConCen shuddered. A crack thudded around the outside of the enclosure. In a window, the spinning effect increased, so Lyndyn had to avert his gaze again. Just before doing this, he saw large and small pieces of Wolf Streak Beta move rapidly past view. The purple-yellow gaseous clouds and blue-white lightning churned with spinning view. Now without looking, he realized that Wolf, which now contained the entire surviving crew of Wolf Streak Beta, was descending in a very haphazard route lower into the atmosphere of the large gas giant.

When he peeked with a side-long glance at the window, Lyndyn witnessed a few bluish-green balls of possible lightning shoot past and heard Milyr complain,

"Vulch, those blue balls of lightning seem to be trapped by our wake. I can't seem to get them out of my view. Strange nasty behavior for ball lightning, don't you think, Domyn?"

"Well, very unusual if they are lightning," Domyn replied, panting with his physical effort to help pilot recently freed Wolf through a scattered cluster of remnants of Wolf Streak Beta. "However, patterns of physical phenomena in this gas giant may be unique in our experience. We're not in the Zerosolis System now. We must not be close-minded to new forms of spatial formations. Scientists did not know all there was to know about the gas giant planets of our Zerosolis System when we left many years ago. We should not assume that we have a template of knowledge to analyze this new Sexto System with complete accurate insight."

With a nervous chuckle, Lyndyn exclaimed, "No doubt you have borrowed one of my many lectures in past sessions. That sounded so much like me, Domyn. But I agree with you now. This monster planet is at least three times as large as the largest of gas giants of the Zerosolis System. We may discover many new spatial phenomena here…"

"Well, gentlemen, don't get lost in your speculative discussion," Cap Nyba interrupted firmly. "Just watch out this window and on your radar screens on your monitors. We would not want to strike something large and solid while you are discussing spatial theories."

Gasping with his frenetic arm movements, Milyr retorted, "Vulch, those nasty little blue balls are the only phenomena close to a solid mass in this atmosphere. And they seem to stay clear of us, unlike real lightning, even as they dance all around us."

"A new behavior for ball lightning should not be so surprising in a complicated atmosphere like this. And, Milyr, the color is more accurately called…aqua," Whyvvi proclaimed in a saddened voice.

"Aqua, blue, green, does this matter now? They vulching goad me just by being out there," Milyr complained. "Vulch, where are we going? Do we have a plan, Nyba?"

"Cherp question, pilot," Cap Nyba stated calmly with only slight anxiety reaching Lyndyn's ears. "We have not had any hostile attack since the recent nuclear blasts at the outer edge of this atmosphere. Perhaps our ploy of playing dead has fooled them. Stay alert. Let's descend bit more into this cover. Watch for anything threatening."

Sitting in his own gray chair next to Kymil in Whyvvi's red chair, Lyndyn tried to focus his attention on the two chairs to his left instead of the dizzying scene in the window and asked, "Kymil, how is our patient?"

"Still stable, as for my limited readings with my own senses," the woman replied in a gentle but forthright manner that had always attracted him, "I can say that his PEQA seems very healthy. At least I can see PEQA on my own. Don't need dionboda for that."

"That is indeed a good sign, my kind Kymil. Jamyk is lucky to have you here to nurse over him," Lyndyn said, hoping to encourage her confidence in her natural abilities now that their reliance on sci-tech was apparently over.

"You're so nice, my kindred spirit. I'm so glad you are with me still. I was so afraid when we were with young ones setting charges. Any one of us could have been killed with Swyllo," she murmured in a low, hushed voice leaning toward him.

"No doubt Domyn's metaphy has some other fate for us," Lyndyn chuckled half-heartedly.

"What is that?" shouted Whyvvi, suddenly alerting Lyndyn to the other conversation in this newly released Wolf.

Reluctantly looking out the window, Lyndyn felt immediate unsettling in his stomach as he saw the nauseating purple, yellow, brown miasma of churning gases. Frequent lightning flashes highlighted and further blended distressing color mixes. The occasional aqua sphere, no wider than about a yard or two, flew past the window. However, it was rounded, almost solid appearance of yellowish-brown spot in the lower left corner of the limited viewport field that caught his attention. Surprisingly this spot did not nauseate his stomach as much as the rest of the scene. Relief at last, he wondered.

"We're getting a gravity pull toward that direction," Domyn announced. "It started to be noticeable less than minute ago. Do you feel it, Milyr?"

"Yeah, Domyn, it's pulling us that way and is the same direction as our random vector after breaking up with the rest of Wolf Streak Beta. Although it's strange that much of the debris scattered in other directions. Vulch, I can't figure this out. Fly random, as explosion blew us, is what we did," the lanky young man explained with frustration and guilt in his voice. "Vulch, but we're still heading for that thing, whatever it is."

"We're not putting blame on anyone, Milyr," Cap Nyba said and wistfully continued, "I wish that we had your sensors still, Whyvvi, to search that anomaly and get a better read of what it is and how strong the gravity pull."

Spinning the purple chair to face Nyba, Whyvvi asked, "Gravity should be strongest from the center of this gas giant, should it not, Neer Domyn?"

Domyn replied, "Normally yes, Whyvvi. But we have limited knowledge of elemental composition of the center of this planet. Of course we have no real sense of our navigational vectors at the moment. It's possible that the spot ahead aligns between us and the planet center. If that's true we could be drawn toward both at this moment."

"Vulch, with this spinning and toppling, I can't see exactly where we're going. And with double gravity pull possible, we could begin travelling much faster," Milyr exclaimed in some mild anxiety. "Can't we morph into glider-shape, Nyba, and begin some controlled flight? Vulching, that spot is not even in our view now, and we are rushing toward it blind. Not very cherp, is that?"

When the spot had swung out of view, Lyndyn had averted his gaze hastily from the sickening swirl of nauseating colors, but now he felt compelled to enter this discussion and advised, "Cap, we will need significant amount of energy to morph Wolf. If we wait too long, we may not have the minimum energy level required for morphing. Without a glider-shape, we will have no ability to control or direct our course. Am I not correct, Domyn?"

"Awright, yes, you are correct, Prof. So far we've been using small bursts of thrust to temper our movement, but without morphing to glider, we really can't fly this Wolf. Morphing does require minimum availability of energy. If we want to go to that spot, we won't need to morph. Seems like the anomaly has a strong tug on our course," Domyn explained.

"Vulching too strong! If we don't morph, we'll strike that toxx nasty at very high acceleration," Milyr complained with mounting nervousness. "If we don't morph, I won't be able to fly this Wolf properly. Vulch, I'd like to know how soft or hard that anomaly is."

"What does your radar show?" Whyvvi asked.

"Radar, why it shows me that we're going towards it," Milyr snorted. "What else would it show?"

With some smugness to her tone, Whyvvi stated, "Radar is the ancient form of sensor. You should be able to read some physical characteristics of anomaly with your radar images."

"Vulch, I'm pilot," Milyr grumbled. "I'm just doing my best to keep us in some control of our freefall into this wild atmosphere."

"Whyvvi, take a look at the screen. See if you can read any information from the echoes," Cap Nyba suggested in her decisive voice that Lyndyn had come to recognize over the years of this association. "Pilots, perhaps we should morph to glider now. We'll need a steadier Wolf for Whyvvi to unbuckle from her chair. Also, perhaps morphing would help to keep this anomaly in our view on a consistent basis. Domyn, can you perform morphing with Milyr while still handling pilot functions?"

"No problem, Cap," Domyn announced. "We're doing very little flying at the moment. We are falling and toppling mostly now. Morphing would allow us to fly better. Awright, Milyr, prep to morph in what…one minute?"

"Yeah, sounds cherp to me, Domyn, one minute from…now," Milyr replied with much more optimism and enthusiasm in his voice and body movements. "Vulching it will be much better having control now. I hate this flying out of my own control like this."

"Once we morph, our flight pattern will begin to appear organized and self-directed to anyone still searching region," Cap Nyba reminded everyone. "It is possible that the hostile attackers are searching still. We should be prepared for defensive flight."

"To where would we flee?" Lyndyn asked softly but not intending to put any emotional burden on the crew continued, "That spot perhaps? What little I've seen of it, it appears to be denser than the surrounding atmosphere. If we get behind it, perhaps it may conceal us better than the rest of this gaseous mess. Indeed now that I think further on this, the course toward it would appear probable to any other observing intelligence with gravity sensing systems. Yes, Cap Nyba, even directed flight toward that anomaly would seem almost random to any logical observer at a distance."

"Perhaps," Domyn said as his blue-gloved hands worked over the old-fashioned buttons and switches on the console. "It will have to do. Milyr, are you ready?"

"Ready, Domyn. Morph Wolf…now," Milyr declared holding his steering control tightly. "I've got rear flaps. Maybe there is enough atmospheric resistance out there to catch them when they extend."

"Pray, we have enough energy to complete this morph," Domyn exclaimed.

Whyvvi declared solemnly, "Whatever energy we have, we have Swyllo to thank… You served us well, my friend."

"Yes, she did," murmured Kymil, and in his mind, Lyndyn saw the young face smiling beneath the yellow cap.

Then watching the two pilots perform their functions, Lyndyn envisioned in his mind the external transformation powered by Swyllo's last efforts. Wolf was normally a small duplicate of Wolf Streak Beta. About eleven yards in diameter at its center, Wolf would look like a circle from top down view and oval from any side view. During morphing the external skin would elongate to form wings along the horizontal axis perpendicular to the forward-facing position of new Wolf. These wings could perform flight movements similar to a winged glider, assuming enough atmospheric density to allow wings to catch air friction or draft. Very ancient, very basic, Lyndyn pondered, but appropriate at the moment. The two young men at the console would handle pilot duties.

"When you get flight maneuverability, stabilize Wolf, so we can keep that round anomaly in our view. But, men, let's try to keep our general movement as if randomly attracted by that anomaly," Cap Nyba commanded. "We're hiding still from possible hostile forces."

"Is it my imagination, or does it show curvature of the spherical spatial body?" Whyvvi asked while staring intently at the window. "As we topple about, I am sure that I observe varied perspectives to suggest that anomaly is spherical, not just a spot of denser gases."

"It's a vulching ugly mixture of color," Milyr groaned, and then his back and shoulders tensed suddenly. "I've got draft, enough vulching draft to glide this Wolf. I can stabilize Wolf for you, Whyvvi, if you want to look over my shoulder at your old-fashioned sensor screens."

"That's first," Nyba said with a subdued chuckle. "Milyr actually asking a woman to look over his shoulder. Go ahead, Whyvvi. Maybe your trained eyes will read something of use from those old radar screens. That is, if you are willing to work that close to Milyr."

While Whyvvi carefully unbuckled her harness, Lyndyn was thankful himself that Wolf was no longer toppling as it descended toward the yellow-brown anomaly. The reduced visual movement and increasing size of anomaly allowed him to watch the scene outside the window with less stomach distress. Yes, he was certain there was definite curvature to spot of the dense gases. He realized that the spot was possibly a planetary body, moon? A moon inside the thin outer most atmosphere of this huge gas giant, was that possible, he wondered in surprise.

"I believe it is moon," Domyn announced in a low hushed voice. "Whyvvi, can you read solidity of that...moon? Can you at least confirm for me that it is a moon, that I'm not seeing things?"

With her hand on Milyr's chair, Whyvvi leaned over his shoulder, peered at the two radar screens on his console for a few seconds, and then commanded,

"Bounce some more radar probes at it, Milyr. Do several in a rapid-fire sequence. Can you do this without hindering your pilot control?"

"I can help with controls, Milyr," Domyn said. "Morphing is completed. Wolf is now a glider and will stay that way unless we somehow get a massive infusion of energy."

"Okay, big man," Milyr acknowledged, and then with a punch of his blue-gloved hand, added, "Rapid-fire bouncing, Whyvvi, just as you ordered. Vulching cherp, having you breathe down my neck for once. It is very strange having you stand taller than me."

"Not so cherp, inhaling your stink at the moment," Whyvvi teased without changing her position over his shoulder. "There, see the subtle difference in the spacing of echoes compared to the spacing of your bounces. To me that tells us the body is solid mass. Yes, Domyn, probably moon. But shoot another sequence, stinky. There is something odd about the last return pattern?"

"Stinky? Just the aroma of man doing tough duty in a stressful situation," Milyr exclaimed as his hands danced over the console, "Vulch, I might just bottle an essence of myself as new fragrance of perfume for our next Steppingstone visit…"

A silence pervaded Wolf suddenly, and Lyndyn realized that they would perhaps never see Steppingstone again, so he exclaimed to break the pessimistic quiet, "Never a bad idea, Milyr. Perfume is always in short supply on Steppingstone. With all those steppers living closely packed together, perfume would be a very good product. Especially one derived from the essence of a handsome, vigorous, hard-working young man. Don't you believe, my kind Kymil?"

Before Kymil could answer, Whyvvi declared, "I do not know about that, Prof. That last bit of description was a tad over-done, I believe. But I can tell you that the surface of this moon is most likely some type of liquid. Between radar echoes and visual cloud-like thin atmosphere of this moon, which I can now see in the window, yes, the surface should be mostly liquid."

"Whatever it is, it is coming at us fast," Milyr reported. "I get increasing acceleration as we approach. Do you confirm, Domyn?"

"Confirmed, that moon has a strong gravitational pull," Domyn agreed. "It may be as strong as that of the home world in the Zerosolis System, if my memory is correct."

"A liquid surface there on the moon inside the atmosphere of the gas giant, is this possible?" Nyba inquired mostly to herself, just barely loud enough for Lyndyn to hear, and then more vocally she continued, "Any chance we can glide around this moon into orbit?"

"An orbit, possibly, but for what reason, Cap?" Domyn asked, flipping a few switches and watching the monitors on the console in front of him. "Will we evade attackers in orbit or be more visible to them? This outer atmosphere of the gas giant is lightly clouded and turbulent but not very useful as concealment. Once we go into orbit, we lose the random-piece-of-debris effect that was your original ploy and very wise gambit at the time."

"Can you read any other data from the radar screens, Whyvvi?" Cap Nyba asked and obviously revealed a sign of stress at last, Lyndyn thought, and not unexpectedly after all the young woman had tried to lead her crew and spacecraft through recently.

"Very little, Cap. It seems as if the liquid ocean-like surface has some depth to it. The colors of the atmosphere suggest gases, such as sulfur dioxide, methane, ammonia, gases common in the gas giants of our historical knowledge. No obvious sign the solid land in limited expanse that our radar surveyed or we can see from this window. Probably there are various oxides due to a prolific number of electrical storms in the thin atmosphere of the moon. Very much like lightning storms in this layer of the atmosphere through which we fall now. Perhaps an unusual friction of two atmospheres so closely entwined causes these numerous lightning storms…"

"Not a vulching inviting moon, hey?" Milyr groaned, interrupting her. "Surrender doesn't sound so bad now. At least we'll be safe in our captivity and hopefully well-fed and nurtured."

"No doubt you hope by bodacious fems, hey, stinky?" Whyvvi laughed, and then more in character, said stoically as she gripped Milyr's shoulders and briefly massaged the straining muscles of the young man. "Do not worry, my stinky comrade. I am here to protect you."

"Now, men and women, we're all here still. As long as we are alive, we have a chance," Cap Nyba declared. "Cherp sensor reading, Whyvvi. If there's nothing else that you can read from the radar, you'd better harness-up. We'll take Wolf into orbit. Our attackers would need better sensors than those in the Blue Jay craft in order to sense craft as small as our Wolf as it orbits this moon. I believe that risk is minimal. I believe that Fox Flash Alpha will have adequate sensors to survey us. Remember, Jamyk had a belief that foxes were out there in the Sexto System. We must also believe. Let's prep for low orbit around this new strange moon."

"Indeed, Cap Nyba, that makes excellent logical sense," Lyndyn praised the young woman sitting beside him but wondered to himself if he had heard a trace of irritation in her voice after she had witnessed Whyvvi knead Milyr's shoulders.

"Yes, it does," Domyn agreed. "Yet I am concerned at how quickly we are accelerating toward the moon. The gravity there may be stronger than I thought."

"Prepare to make orbit entry," Nyba commanded. "Everyone must be harnessed and wearing our McAnderwikes. Is Jamyk ready, Doc?"

"He is asleep still. I did see a sign of REM sleep not long ago. His eyes were moving under his lids, a good sign. At least his brain is functioning," Kymil replied with more optimism than concern in her voice. "His PEQA is very strong, much stronger than normal for him. I assume that is a good sign."

"Don't worry, my kind Kymil," Lyndyn smiled at her. "You would know if anyone's Physio Electromag Quantal Aura was inappropriate. You have your sight still, even without our sci-tech."

"My kindred spirit, Lyndyn," she sighed with hope seeping into her tired voice. "We are all worried. This situation can only bring out anxiety and fear in our minds. You of all people should understand this inevitability. This Wolf is ripe with an odor of fear, and I'm glad there is fear here now. Fear gives us strength and determination to survive and to do what we never before believed could be done. My kindred spirit, Lyndyn, sometimes you can be a lame toxx!"

"No doubt I certainly can be," Lyndyn agreed, ruefully grinning at her.

"That moon is getting quite large in our window," Whyvvi stated with emphasis.

"Acceleration is increasing," Milyr reported with anxiety.

"Can you counter with a reverse thrust?" Nyba asked.

Domyn answered with stressful concern, "I'm not sure if we can make orbit. Our Wolf does not handle very effectively with just impulse gas bursts. Our course is too steep for orbit, Cap. Our acceleration is too fast for correction with the old controls that we have now."

"We're vulching going to crash!" Milyr exclaimed, even as his hands buzz in activity over the console. "At least maybe we'll hit some of those vulching blue balls swarming around in the vomit-looking air around this moon."

"That is aqua, big peener," Whyvvi snorted from the purple chair.

"Does it vulching matter?" Milyr retorted with some weary irritation.

"Atmosphere is coming up soon," Whyvvi reported, and Lyndyn was amazed how she could read this using her eyes only and view out the window.

However, the whole scene in the window was of the moon now. A thin outer layer of atmosphere of the super gas giant was pushed off view by a disc of the approaching moon. A cloud covered, storm-riddled, yellowish brown colored gas atmosphere leaped up at them. A very inhospitable place to crash upon, Lyndyn thought to himself. His stomach was not nauseated now, but the rest of him was terrified.

"Will our hull survive heat reentry?" Nyba asked abruptly.

"Our titanium-justimmonium alloy should withstand heat," Domyn replied, but Lyndyn heard some doubt in the deep voice of the engineer, or maybe he only imagined that.

As the first of the yellow-brown clouds rained against the window, Milyr turned toward his former purple chair and asked in tremor and grin, "Hey, fem, do you really think I'm a big peener, or were you just teasing my ego?"

"Oh, sure, you big peener, I would never tell you a lie. The truth is so much more cherp," Whyvvi declared sitting in his purple chair, and then added softly but audibly as she turned to the vacant yellow chair beside her, "Do you not think so, my friend?"

To Lyndyn's surprise, Milyr murmured, "Yeah, I think she would."

"No orbit now, Domyn?" Nyba asked as clouds wet the window port.

"Don't see how now. Every vector is wrong. Our Wolf just doesn't have the sci-tech to do it," Domyn replied in as defeated a tone as Lyndyn had ever heard from the big young man.

"Can we thruster to slow our descent?" Whyvvi asked.

"Our impulse gas bursts are not strong enough. We're in total freefall. The only thing we can do is to try to steer this Wolf into flatter trajectory to moderate the crash down," Domyn suggested.

"Vulching tough to do that at our pace of falling," Milyr griped while wrestling with the old-fashioned steering. "But us big peeners will try, right, Domyn?"

"Argh!" growled the big man battling his own steering system and punching buttons.

Whack!

"What happened? Where is our view?" Whyvvi shrieked.

When Lyndyn glanced to the window, he saw only a purplish coating on the window, and heard Milyr ask in agitated annoyance, "What the vulch is that? Now I can't see to pilot. Vulch, this is toxx!"

"We need an ancient device called... I believe...a windshield wiper," Nyba laughed with hysteria tickling her voice.

"Milyr, just hold the trajectory that we had," Domyn ordered. "We're blind, but we were heading for a definite splashdown on this moon. I guess it doesn't matter where we land, only how hard. Everyone should recheck their harnesses. This time there will be gravity to affect our inertia. This time we will feel the hit."

"Awright, big man," Milyr chuckled through his terror and challenged, "Race you to the surface."

Leaning toward Kymil, Lyndyn said softly in low nasal voice, "No doubt Jamyk did foresee this was going to happen and decided to sleep through it all. At least that's what Domyn might believe."

"No, my kindred spirit, our Neer would believe that his universal metaphy had gifted Jamyk with a trait of survival," Kymil whispered.

"Indeed, my Kymil, you are truly wise."

"You're such a toxx, Lyndyn, my kindred spirit," Kymil whispered with a chuckle.

Then Wolf splashed into some external liquid, and the force of impact knocked Lyndyn into unconscious darkness.

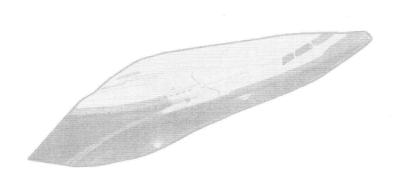

SPEC THREE: LYNDYN ON WYLLOS
CHAPTER 24

Clouds and fog, smoke and steam in various shades and contrasts of white and gray swirl and churn gently up and down, back and forth.

Laughter sings in the distance.

Two human figures appear through the rolling tumbling mists. One is bright yellow. One is sparkling green. They run and chase after each other in gay merriment.

As they approach closer, long thin blue clubs are visible in their hands. Frequently they halt the chase to playfully pummel each other with blue clubs. Continuous squeals of joyful laughter and soft thuds of blows suggest no harmful contact.

Then running and chasing continues. The figures move closer. Now the yellow figure is obviously a naked female. The green figure is a naked male. Both are bald and smooth skinned. Both are giggling with joyful gaiety.

Now quite close, they pause for a frenetic exchange of blows with their blue clubs. After several dazzling strikes and counterstrikes, the green male knocks a blue club from the hands of the yellow female.

Flashes of blue-white lightning in the distance silhouette the figures. The female form kneels before the male form. Then she lifts her hands upwards towards the male. With his club now vanished, he reaches toward her hands. Between their extended hands now glows the blue sphere, small at first, then expanding slowly to about one foot in diameter.

The green male takes the glowing sphere. The yellow female arises and steps away a few paces. Then the green male tosses the blue sphere to the yellow female.

She catches the blue sphere. At that moment, another glowing blue sphere appears in the hands of the green male. They toss these blue spheres back and forth between each other. Never once is there mistake or drop. Their timing and teamwork are precise. They move closer in the billowing cloudy mist.

Now as they approach closer, their individual faces are seen more clearly. They are familiar. The yellow female in recognized as Swyllo. The green male is recognized as Jamyk. They both wear smiles of enlightened contentment.

A third glowing blue sphere appears. They juggle three spheres with precision. Despite increasing wind, roiling clouds, and distant lightning, they approach closer without misstep or fumble. Juggling three spheres, they approach nearer.

Then staring toward the observer, Jamyk tosses the blue sphere in that direction. The glowing blue sphere hurtles towards the dreamer…

…With a sudden start, Lyndyn awoke just before his mind caught the blue sphere. His extended hands bumped arms of someone warm and alive. His eyelids fluttered as they tried to open. Through the blur and haze of awakening, he saw a face, a very kind and welcome face.

In spite of darkness around her, her face shone in his vision, and Kymil smiled, "My kindred spirit, you are awake at last."

"Awake?" Lyndyn questioned, trying to clear his mind and memory as his eyes scanned hastily the immediate vicinity. "Where's Saphyndenlairoum? This doesn't feel normal."

Her eyelids squinted with concern as she asked, "Do you remember what happened? Do you know where we are? Answer me. Let's get your brain working, Lyndyn."

What happened? Where were they? Two naked figures throwing blue balls, what was reality? Kymil was reality. Her face, her manner, her concern, her gentle touch on his arms, these were reality. No, Saphyndenlairoum meant that this was not a normal awakening. Why had he been asleep outside Saphyndenlairoum? What had happened?

Then suddenly his memories awoke, rushed through his awareness, and he said in a throaty gasp, "A crash…knocked out? Are we alive? Indeed we are alive. This nagging discomfort in my back and neck could be felt only if I were alive. I'm certain death would be without sensation…"

"Oh my, let's not talk of death," Kymil declared abruptly. "We all survived the crash. Now we must discover a way to stay alive, my kindred spirit. Now about those pains, where are they? How is your body movement?"

Trying to wiggle and flex his shoulders and torso, Lyndyn felt the restriction of a safety harness over his body and then realized that he was in a chair still and replied, "A little sore in my shoulders and chest where this harness straps me. I probably thrust against it on the splashdown. My neck hurts, but I can move it up and down and swivel."

"Good, good," Kymil murmured as she unsnapped his helmet from neck support and lifted it from his bald, sweaty head. "These McAnderwikes have proven to be so much more useful than the mere athletic uniforms as they had been designed. I believe that Nyba's decision to dress each of us in our Pulseball McAnderwikes prevented many serious injuries."

From not far away in the dimness of Wolf's lighting, Nyba acknowledged, "Thank you, Doc, it's cherp to believe that at least one of my decisions turned out to be correct. Yet I recall that you came up with idea first."

Hearing a trace of self-doubt in the young woman's voice, Lyndyn was glad when Kymil said in encouragement, "Cap Nyba, don't ridicule yourself. You have been forced to make very difficult decisions recently. The previous circumstances could not have been rehearsed or even predicted during your training on Steppingstones as we journeyed here. At least we are all alive still."

A momentary silence in Wolf, and then Nyba's voice sighed from darkness, "Not all of us, Doc. Swyllo is gone."

"Yes, oh, how I miss her," Whyvvi moaned from somewhere beside Nyba's voice.

Swyllo was gone? Yes, as his brain replayed the memory of the small blue-clad girl in the disintegrating access space of Wolf Streak Beta, Lyndyn remembered. Swyllo, yellow girl, young woman who tried to stay until the final switch had been thrown was gone. Swyllo, spirit of intensity when she was alive, was now lost.

As a flutter blinked his eyelids and moisture clouded his vision, Lyndyn remarked, "No doubt, Nyba, we will feel her loss. You must know that she was determined to save us when she was in that access way. Now in her honor, we must survive. You must lead us to that survival."

"Don't know!" Nyba muttered in exhausted disconsolation. "Can we do anything now?"

"Of course we can," declared a more confident Whyvvi from the dimly lighted Wolf. "Swyllo wants us to go on. She would goad you, Nyba. You have made important decisions since splashdown already. Do not get discouraged, Nyba. You are our Cap."

Now that his eyes had cleared away the sleepiness and adjusted to the dimly lighted surroundings, Lyndyn observed the yellow-brown scene of tumultuous clouds churning above the window port. Flashes of lightning flickered frequently in the stormy atmosphere above. An aqua sphere glowed as it flashed by the window.

But for him, a worst new observation was the roiling ocean of wavy liquid that rose and dipped just outside the window. Occasional drops splattered upon and then flowed off the window. His stomach felt upset. His brain began to register a horrible sensation of imbalance as Wolf swayed with action of the choppy liquid.

"Ugh, uh…oh, how I miss steady firmness of artificial gravity on Wolf Streak Beta and all Steppingstones," he groaned, closing his eyes again and sitting back into the chair. "Are we buoyantly sound? Is this Wolf ocean-worthy? We won't flip over or sink, will we?"

"Is it your inner ear equilibrium again?" Kymil asked. "I thought that we had controlled that ailment after our voyage in Turkey Trot. That was…how many years ago now?"

"Almost a lifetime," Lyndyn replied as many personally fond memories played through his mind in a flash, and then he hastily forced himself to focus on the present reality to say, "No doubt the recent crash may have jarred something in my head. With all that empty space in there, I'm not surprised… By the way, is it really as dark in here as my eyes are seeing? Or am I having sight problems as well?"

"Just sit there and let your brain and body acclimate to these new and different environmental factors. We are all used to security and stability of artificial gravity of the spacecraft. Now we must get used to real motions of the lively moon. All that empty space in your head may allow too much room for your tiny brain to bounce around," Kymil chuckled. "Don't worry, your eyes are correct. It is dark in Wolf. Cap Nyba chose to save energy by not using internal lights."

"Another wise decision," Whyvvi declared.

"We seem to get enough light from sun of the Sexto System through double atmospheres above us to allow us to perform basic movements in here," Nyba explained from a seat at the emergency console just in front of the regular semi-circle of chairs of the former ConCen, "Although I'm not sure if this is day or night on this moon. There is some light, but it is not bright now."

Focusing his eye sight into that portion of Wolf, Lyndyn was able to partially alleviate the discomfort of the churning atmosphere outside. Though the window did tease periphery of his vision. Some low console lights illuminated the hands and arms of two women sitting in pilot seats of the console. They both wore their McAnderwikes with helmets and gloves.

Then suddenly a realization occurred to him, and he asked with worry, "Domyn, Milyr, are they okay? Did anything happen to them? Where are they?"

"They are fine. A bit bruised and very tired but as healthy as we can expect after our recent ordeal," Kymil replied, gently feeling his neck and upper back with her well-trained hands.

"Asleep," stated Whyvvi. "The boys used all they had to get us down safely. They should sleep for awhile. Not much that they could do for the moment anyway. They got us down through this stormy atmosphere and managed to crash land Wolf right side up on this very wavy ocean of whatever. They deserve sleep."

While his eyes noticed finally a lanky form of Milyr in his regular purple chair at the end of the semi-circle of chairs, Lyndyn then remembered the purplish obstruction that had struck the window during the wild descent, so he asked, "What happened to the purple thing that blinded us? How did our young men land this Wolf while blind?"

"We do not know," Whyvvi answered. "The boys managed to land without sight. Who knows how! They did not."

"The purple whatever, blanket thingy, just seemed to melt into liquid after the splashdown. Whatever it was just rode down on Wolf's window and hit the ocean with us," Nyba said.

Kymil's fingers and hands withdrew from his neck and shoulders as she said, "Your movement seems fine. I don't feel any swelling. Nor do I feel any excess heat as fever. But move carefully until you try out your muscles and joints, especially your neck. We do not have our Blue Jay sci-tech medical equipment any longer. Our med supplies are limited to old-fashioned first-aid. You know as well as I what that means, my kindred spirit."

"Indeed we must be more careful in our risk-taking," Lyndyn agreed. "Is it my imagination, or is it very hot in here? I thought these McAnderwikes had a built-in coolant function like our dionbodas."

"They do, but they are not strong enough to counteract very hot temperatures. McAnderwikes are designed to temporarily cool the body of an active athlete during short duration of competition. We are asking them to keep us cool a much longer time. McAnderwikes are not long-term as cooling device anyway," Whyvvi explained.

"Yes, I remember that now," Lyndyn said as he carefully turned his neck to peer at the large sleeping form of Domyn in his regular brown chair set slightly out of the dim light through the window. "So it is just unusually hot in here? Is there a problem with Wolf's air conditioning?"

"We can't afford to be using that with our very small amount of reserve energy, Prof," Nyba declared sternly. "We will have to get used to the natural temperature of this moon. Whyvvi, what was your last temp reading?"

After briefly bobbing her head closer to the dimly lighted console, Whyvvi replied, "Internal temp is now 103 degrees. External temp is still climbing slowly. Now it is at 137."

"Is that the air temp outside?" asked Lyndyn in serious worry. "I hope that was Fahrenheit."

"Yes, Prof, that 137 is the air temp at the peak of Wolf and is Fahrenheit," Whyvvi confirmed. "Ocean temp below is fluctuating but averages 117. This is certainly quite hot for us."

"Oh my, yes, very nasty hot for us," Kymil agreed. "However, for now this Wolf is our best environment. At least we can survive in this heat in protection of our Wolf. Although I must agree that it will be very uncomfortable. We have limited supply of nutrient, slightly heated of course. We have breathable air supply…"

Nyba interrupted abruptly, "That air supply is breathable as long as our energy reserve keeps the air purification system working. We must be very conserving with our energy usage. We have limited supply only and no equipment to harvest more. I hope Fox Flash Alpha can find us in time."

A sudden groan and mumbled words sounded from behind Kymil, and Lyndyn said in surprise, "Jamyk? Is that Jamyk? I'd forgotten about him. How's he doing?"

When his attention was led to the chair to Kymil's left, the window scene of tumultuous clouds, lightning, and tall rolling waves of yellow-brown liquid caught his sight. The scene reminded Lyndyn with visceral force of the situation around Wolf, their refuge for the foreseeable future. His stomach rebelled momentarily, but he tried to convince himself that it was merely hunger pangs. Not with much success, he realized. However, his concern for the boy overwhelmed his feeling of nausea.

Lyndyn was grateful to be able to focus on her words when Kymil replied, "Jamyk has been dreaming quite often since the splashdown. He has not awakened. His vital signs, those which I can monitor under these conditions, are acceptable."

"Isn't this longer than the normal length of time for him to sleep? Isn't his sleep cycle normally very short compared to the rest of us?" Lyndyn asked with worry for Jamyk but also with encouragement for his own memory improvement since awakening.

"Oh my, I'd say not by very much yet. You were not unconscious for very long, Lyndyn. Jamyk has not been asleep as long as it may seem to you," Kymil explained while she tested his forehead and neck with her hands. "However, if he does not awaken soon, I might attempt to awaken him. I'm uncertain still about whether to do that or not. Forcing him awake, I am not sure. He has suffered trauma that I have no expertise or history to use as a guide…"

As she stated this, a mildly luminescent flash passed before the window and attracted his attention, so Lyndyn inquired, "What was that? Did I see that, or am I hallucinating?"

"Oh, you mean the aqua balls?" Whyvvi said with familiarity. "They go by every now and then, one or two at a time. Not as many as Milyr claimed to see when he was steering Wolf before. We do not know what it is yet. With all the lightning jumping cloud to cloud out there, things could be a random ball lightning or some other electrical phenomena that we do not understand yet."

"Indeed I feel like the events have jumped by me. I'm trying to catch up with everything that's happened since we crashed," Lyndyn said despondently, and then with guilt, continued, "I'm sorry, Kymil, to have interrupted you. Your concern for Jamyk is much more important. Please forgive me."

"Now, Lyndyn, don't worry. As a matter of fact, there may be a link between Whyvvi's electric balls and Jamyk's situation. You did say before the crash that you saw possible lightning glow during the tragic experience on Wolf Streak Beta. Electrical trauma may have affected the electro-neural activity of his brain in a way that we are not familiar. We just don't know," Kymil explained, patting sweat from the boy's face with a tissue from first-aid.

"This whole trip is becoming a sequence of new nasty toxx happenings," Nyba declared with annoyed amazement. "Our original Blue Jay mission seems to have exploded in our faces."

"Do not give up yet, Cap Nyba," Whyvvi said.

As his eyes observed splatters of liquid strike the curved window and slide off into the ocean, Lyndyn asked with renewed interest, "But you say that the boy has been dreaming? And that his vital signs are healthy?"

"His temp is up a bit warmer than normal for him. I can't be sure if it is because of the fever or this environmental heat. He has been in and out of REM sleep a few times. The stages are not as long or as consistent as REM would normally cycle. More like an erratic sequence of on-REM, off-REM stages. That concerns me because it is reminiscent of a difficult stage which Bodacia had reported during his stasis sleep," Kymil stated while she nursed the boy and at the same time managed to keep her partially seated balance against the roll and sway of Wolf.

Then Lyndyn noticed for the first time that Kymil was not harnessed to the chair, and he blurted anxiously, "Kymil, be careful. Should you be doing that without your harness? You could be thrown about Wolf in these swells. Be careful!"

"Don't worry, my ocean legs are much quicker to adapt than yours. My short, stubby legs are very strong and steady. My big toxx sits firmly in the chair without a harness," Kymil chuckled and then added, "Besides Nyba and Whyvvi assured me that Wolf may sway and dance but will not capsize. That is right, ladies?"

"Right, Doc," Whyvvi replied as Nyba grunted.

"I worry still," Lyndyn murmured and then his eyes saw another aqua spot move across the scene and the ocean liquid splashed on the window. "At least Jamyk does not have to deal with that vomit-like view of ocean. Does this sporadic REM stage resemble a strange difficulty Bodacia encountered periodically during his stasis sleep in LaOgres?"

"Not exactly, yet Bodacia did record some periods of non-REM dream states that she termed post-REM. However, each was a single added period to the normal cycle. These now appear to be more sporadic, more like random sequences of on-REM, off-Rem. No, this is new and unusual, even for Jamyk," Kymil said with motherly concern, and Lyndyn was sure he heard some professional curiosity in her tone as well.

The bald head of her young patient turned side to side and a garbled raspy voice mumbled something unintelligible, but Lyndyn was sure Swyllo was mentioned. Kymil paused her nursing until the boy became still again, then began to dab the moist face with tissue. This time after wiping his face, she carefully raised the naked eyelid over his left eye. Then she did the same to his right eye.

"How can you see in this dim light?" Lyndyn asked.

"There is enough light at this position for me to see what I need to see," Kymil suggested and then added, "Also, my PEQA sight can often give me subtle variances over repeated observations. Sometimes these sensitive aural variations can at least warn me of dramatic change. However, at the moment, his PEQA is very healthy, more so than common. It doesn't give me any variance, but at least I can assume a healthy PEQA equates to a healthy patient."

"But he is unconscious!" Whyvvi exclaimed bewildered. "How can he be healthy?"

"Unconscious but safely asleep," Kymil said with some trepidation in her voice, noticeable perhaps to Lyndyn alone. "There is something going on here that is beyond my experience, even with PEQA sight. At least I have not witnessed any PEQA pulsations yet."

"If you believe Jamyk is stable and not in any immediate danger, then that's good enough," Nyba declared firmly. "Let's hope that we don't get any foolish PEQA pulsations."

A steep wave tilted Wolf at a sharp angle, causing Lyndyn's stomach to threaten regurgitation. With great determination, especially with manly pride in jeopardy with the women in attendance, he controlled his natural response. Toxx inner ear dysfunction, he swore to himself, and gripped his chair tighter with both hands. Just his luck to have both a balance problem and a nauseating scene attack his senses at the same time. Maybe he should pray to Domyn's metaphy for some relief, Lyndyn wondered momentarily, but then decided that was only for believers like Domyn.

"Do we have any idea of what this environment is like outside?" Lyndyn asked, trying to squelch burp. "Besides looking like liquid vomit or really unhealthy urine, do we know anything about out there? What is this liquid for instance? Or perhaps what clouds are composed of besides gases?"

"Oh my, Lyndyn, since awakening you are beginning to sound more like Milyr," Kymil teased. "Except for lack of vulgarity, of course, thankfully you do use graphic color so like he often does."

"Whyvvi, what have you discovered?" Nyba asked. "We know it is very hot, too hot for us as equipped. Can you deduce anything else?"

"I cannot say for certain. With basic instruments and probe analyzers embedded in the outer skin of Wolf, I have found the ocean to be on the acidic side. Our analyzers cannot determine the exact acid. It may be new acid unique to this moon, or possibly a mixture of acids. Whatever it is, strength would burn our skin in a relatively short time. Whether we can extract pure water from this acid ocean is very unlikely given our limited sci-tech now."

"Will the hull of Wolf withstand this acid ocean? Will our window?" Lyndyn asked in sudden anxiety as his eyes stared at the terrible scene beyond the window for a few seconds before his brain reminded him of his dislike for the nauseating view.

"Neer Domyn would know about that more than anyone else. But I do believe that the outer hull composite of the titanium-justimmonium, or Justix I believe, withstood the most severe tests in the Zerosolis System, including some on the gas giants there and also the sister world of very intense heat and vapor. Our hull should be resistant for awhile to corrosion caused by this or any acid ocean," Whyvvi stated.

"Should be? Suppose this is an unknown acid, which we could not test," Lyndyn complained as Wolf wobbled again with the action of waves outside, and the ocean acid sprayed over window. "And what about this window, will it hold?"

Beside him Kymil leaned toward him, patted his arm, and said with confidence, "Relax. Don't worry. The engineers and designers of our Blue Jay spacecraft were very skillful and thorough. I'm sure that they made a safe and very sturdy Wolf for us."

"Yes, Prof, you've probably forgotten, but you yourself taught us years ago about Justix and diamond matrix, Justinex design of all the windows for the Blue Jay project. Nothing this clear has ever been created by humans with strength and endurance of this Dijustix composite. Not even a vacuum of space and pressure differences can break this Justinex," Nyba stated.

"No doubt you are correct," he sighed with a burp-like gasp as his stomach challenged his self-discipline again. "If we could only stop the wave action, then I'd be happier."

With one hand working some buttons on the console, Whyvvi waved the other hand at the scene out the window and said, "That is what we have landed into. From the limited sensor reads during our descent, I would say this entire surface is the ocean of this liquid. The atmosphere above is constant turmoil of storms, wind, and lightning. My suspicion is that this moon is very active geologically, which contributes to the disturbed weather pattern. Also, this shallow atmosphere interacts with major, though thin atmosphere of the gas giant planet. I do not imagine there is ever aperiod of calm on the surface of this moon."

"So no doubt we will have to get used to this," Lyndyn groaned with literal distaste in his mouth. "I won't be taking in much nutrient for awhile. I am surprised how Domyn and Milyr can sleep through this constant wobbling."

Kymil explained, "They were very tired. I gave them a sedative to help them get rest. However, fortunately sometimes natural need for sleep of young men their age can be of use."

"And sometimes they are just lazy toxx!" Whyvvi laughed.

While his eyes watched the splatter of large droplets strike the high curve of the window, Lyndyn, though repulsed by the exterior motion, felt obligated to support the manly honor of his comrades, so chuckled, "Maybe once in a while, but without their determination and strength, Wolf might have been splattered in pieces across this ocean. After a wild toppling ride, we endured up in this atmosphere to glide this Wolf to a safe and upright landing is quite remarkable."

"Milyr has always bragged about his ability to get straight and on course when he needed to," Whyvvi laughed briefly, and then her tone became more serious as she added while staring at the window, "That is not cherp! This is odd that those last sprays did not flow off the window like others have before. What is the difference now?"

To Kymil's left from the shadowed chair, Jamyk stirred and mumbled something incoherent. His garbled words mixed with a groan of discomfort. Lyndyn felt a swish of Kymil spinning her chair toward the unconscious boy. Doc Kymil would be loyally attentive to the needs of the lad. This was one of many attributes of her personality that had attracted his interest over the many years.

Reluctantly peeking upwards at the window, he saw what looked like rounded triangular splatters of slightly iridescent orange liquid, and he asked, "Don't those splatters have too much uniformity of shape and size to be random ocean spray?"

"Yes, they do," agreed Nyba as more iridescent orange shapes landed on the curved window. "Those are not random ocean spray."

As Jamyk moaned in the dim light, Whyvvi exclaimed with anxiety, "They are not random and are not flowing off. It looks as if they are sticking to the outer surface. Not cherp! I do not like this."

More and more triangular-shaped orange things smacked onto the window. The number grew quickly and a pattern of attachment spread in rough concentric circles from the original splatter. Lyndyn found blockage of the atmospheric scene by these things eased his stomach discomfort. However, his mind warned him that growing coverage of the exterior of the window could not be good. Louder and more restless moaning by Jamyk reinforced his own anxiety. Was he becoming more like Domyn, Lyndyn wondered. Was he beginning to believe in Jamyk's feelings of espersense?

"This is definitely not cherp, Cap. I always feel threatened by unexplained physical phenomena. This is really unexplained. Not cherp at all!" Whyvvi muttered.

"Doc, can we wake Domyn? I'd like his opinion and his sci-tech thinking," Nyba said.

From near the disquieted boy, Kymil replied, "Yes, Nyba, the sedative was weak. It should not hinder his awakening. He has rested enough for moment."

While the women discussed and then attempted to awaken the large young man, Lyndyn stared with growing trepidation as hundreds of slightly rounded triangular orange shapes seemed to individually pulse. Very weakly, almost beyond his visual acuity, but yes, he was certain that he saw things pulsing, slowly in independent random rhythms. Collectively the vision began to reawaken his stomach upset. Toxx, just cannot win, he swore to himself, averting his gaze quickly.

Nyba, now out of her chair, standing with legs wide-spread to brace against the sway of Wolf, shook Domyn roughly by the shoulder and called loudly, "Wake up, Domyn. Wake up."

"Oh my," Kymil exclaimed from near Jamyk's chair. "Look at that. Oh my!"

With annoyance he peered again at the window, observed twinkling star-like cracks appear in the window beneath some of triangular things, and announced, "Cap, Whyvvi, look at this. This is not good. Our Dijustix composite is cracking. No doubt those things did not read design specs for Wolf. They should not be able to cause those cracks."

"Not cherp! Vulching not cherp!" Whyvvi yelled with fear. "If the window shatters, the atmosphere outside will most likely be poisonous to us. The acid ocean liquid will be corrosive to us. What should we do, Cap Nyba?"

A fleeting glimpse of an aqua ball streaked behind hundreds of rounded triangular things pulsing and cracking the window. Lyndyn wondered, why would he notice a passage of an aqua ball at a time like this? His attention shifted immediately to Nyba still shaking groggy but muttering Domyn. Then Wolf swayed abruptly, causing Nyba to stumble forward into Domyn's lap. At least this helped to rouse and begin to awaken the young man.

From the chair to his left, Lyndyn heard Jamyk writhe and groan more frenetically than before.

A peek at the window revealed fissure-like lattices spreading between the star-like cracks, and Lyndyn listened to Whyvvi wail, "Not cherp! We must do something!"

Still groggy and half-asleep, Domyn muttered, "Do…some…what…going…on?"

Pushing her squat form up from the big lap, Nyba shouted nervous and flustered, "We need you, Neer. window…is cracking…an emergency."

"Wha…wha…em...gency?" Domyn mumbled, pushing the young woman to standing position.

Whyvvi exclaimed in a subdued, defeated tone, "As Milyr is often saying, we are vulched!"

Another glance upwards, and Lyndyn saw fissures begin to descend downward into seventeen inches of Justinex window thickness. This was the best, unbreakable, shatter-proof composite that Blue Jay had ever created. The cracks and fissures slowly, inevitably spread into the window. How long would that hold, he wondered.

Then to others, Lyndyn said, "Yeah, we're vulched!"

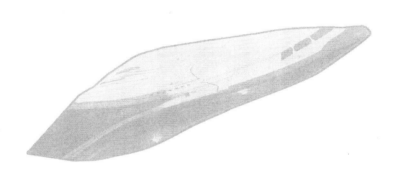

SPEC THREE: LYNDYN ON WYLLOS
CHAPTER 25

"Wake up, you lazy toxx," yelled Whyvvi.

Lyndyn watched her shake long lanky legs side to side at the knees and heard Milyr mumble in a dreamlike sleep, "…so good…more…do more… Swyllo…so good…"

"No, you toxx! Wake up! It is an emergency!" Whyvvi hollered, punching the long legs.

Then Lyndyn's view was blocked by Nyba's squat form when she staggered to a standing position against the swaying of Wolf and commanded forcefully, "Neer, your Wolf is in danger. We need your ideas now. The window is cracking."

"Cracking? Can't be! Justinex should hold against any pressure from the inside or outside," Domyn asserted from his chair in the darkened Wolf.

"See for yourself, cracks in the window. Not from pressure, Domyn. Something has attached to the window and caused cracking," Nyba shouted in an anxious voice. "Is there anything we can do? We need your knowledge and ideas, Neer Domyn."

Milyr's voice muttered from the far side of the semi-circle of chairs, "No… don't…go… Swyllo…"

His line of sight partially blocked by Nyba's form, Lyndyn turned his gaze forward toward the window slightly and was greeted instantly with an unsettling glimpse of tumbling waves of yellow-brown color just outside the window. As had been the circumstance since his awakening recently, nauseous sensation hit his stomach. He closed his eyelids hastily but not before seeing the ocean liquid splash on the periphery of the window. When this acid liquid flowed off the window, some of the orange triangular shapes seemed to wash away with it. At least he thought so.

"Nasty toxx! It is me, Whyvvi... Swyllo is not here. Get your lazy toxx awake," Whyvvi shouted, and then Lyndyn heard a slap against human flesh, probably Milyr's thigh by thesound.

"Hey...what...hitting me?" Milyr groaned sleepily.

Domyn's deep voice growled, "Awright, damn, Justinex is cracking. What are those things?"

"Does it matter right now?" Nyba yelled in stress as she toppled backwards against the empty seat by the manual console. "Think, Neer, can we do something to reinforce the window?"

In spite of the unsettling of his stomach every time he glanced at the wavy ocean and pulsating iridescent triangles, Lyndyn forced himself to stare at the edge of the window again. Had he witnessed things wash away with ocean splatter? Or had he imagined it in his very brief last glimpse?

From his left, Kymil called out, "Everyone should get into the chair and harness up again. I don't want to have to treat anyone for injuries in this constantly bobbing and tilting Wolf."

With his attention focused upon the window, Lyndyn ignored her demand and viewed the border of the window where he saw a clear band of Justinex with no triangles closest to the ocean splashes. Other than this border edge, the window was covered on the exterior with iridescent orange triangles. None overlapped each other. Beneath hundreds of these things, fissures and cracks continued to splay downward into the thickness of the window. Another more voluminous splash of ocean acid struck the window. Lyndyn observed as flow of this splash carried away those few triangles in its path.

"Acid liquid of this ocean is washing them away," he yelled in his weary voice with mild excitement. "Look, they can't withstand the acid of this ocean."

"Yes, I saw that also," Kymil exclaimed from a chair to his left. "But there are hundreds still breaking into the window. How long can it hold?"

Domyn's large form stood from his chair and almost leaped to the pilot console as another wave swayed Wolf, and he announced, "I'll take the pilot seat. Milyr, get your toxx into the other."

"What do you think we can do?" Nyba asked, dodging his hurtling form and then jumping toward her normal blue chair, captain's chair.

"We should send this lazy toxx out the hatch with a mop and bucket," Whyvvi yelled, still trying to awaken Milyr. "He can wash nasty tri things off the window."

"Wash windows…no vulching way… This toxx doesn't wash…windows," Milyr exclaimed with emphasis, and Lyndyn thought he heard a click of a harness being unhooked. "I'll be the pilot…not vulching window washer. That's not for this primo handsome pilot."

On the window where the ocean splashes had recently washed away some of the triangular orange things, Lyndyn observed more strike suddenly and fasten immediately, so he said despondently, "The ocean acid is only a temporary solvent. New things are attaching after the acid flows away. Now indeed I wish waves were larger and splashier. No matter how sick it made me…"

"Awright, yes, Prof, perhaps more splashing, bigger waves," Domyn exclaimed suddenly with renewed enthusiasm. "I believe that we can do something here."

"Whatever we do, we don't have much time. Those cracks are getting deeper," Kymil declared with stressful worry in her voice, and Lyndyn felt sadly impotent to hear her fear and not be able to help her from his harnessed sitting posture in his chair.

Yet he managed to say as he moaned with distress, "Argh! If I have to become sicker to save Wolf, then I believe that I could stomach that…"

"Vulch, just don't vomit in Wolf," Milyr suggested hurriedly as he arose from his regular purple chair with Whyvvi's support and then fell toward his pilot's seat at the console. "Prof, just stick your head out the hatch and gurg out there."

"I just may do that," Lyndyn groaned after Milyr's movement had tricked his eyes to glimpse the roiling ocean surface and churning storm clouds showing through the narrow band of the unblocked window. "This persistent up and down motion combined with that obnoxious churning scene outside is not settling my insides any time soon."

"No, you won't," Kymil demanded firmly. "Just keep your eyes closed. Buckle your harness tightly. No sticking your head out the hatch, my kindred spirit. If you wish, I can give you a mild sedative. We have a few left still."

Nyba asked sharply and hastily, "What do you have in mind, Domyn?"

Waving a big hand toward the window now almost totally covered with round-cornered orange triangles again, Domyn said, "Like Prof said, we need more splashing. If this ocean liquid is a useful wash for those things, then let's make bigger splashes. How much energy reserve do we have, Cap?"

"Not very much, and we should use it carefully. How do you intend to make bigger splashes?" Nyba asked with suspicion.

"Rock Wolf," Domyn stated. "With short thruster bursts, we should be able to rock this Wolf into a wave to get maximum splash on the window. It should wash off many of things."

"But not capsize us, right?" Whyvvi interjected in panic only a moment before Lyndyn was about to open his mouth with same worry.

"Probably not," Domyn speculated as his hands began to work buttons and switches on the console. "The built-in stability of Wolf, especially now that it is morphed with wings at our sides, has to this moment kept it buoyant and oriented to our perspective and to our gravitational needs. However, if ocean acid is a problem for these things, then turning Wolf upside down to put the window into the ocean might not be a bad idea."

"Urgh!" belched Lyndyn as he listened to startled gasps from the others in the dimly lighted Wolf.

"Nasty, idea, Domyn," Whyvvi declared sourly.

"Not a great health benefit on our systems either," warned Kymil. "If we must hang upside down in these chairs and have the gravity of the moon pull our blood into our heads for any long length of time, then I don't know how well we will react."

"Better than having those things break seventeen inches of the Justinex window and flood Wolf with gases and acid from out there," Domyn countered. "But if we don't have enough energy reserve to thrust, it doesn't matter, does it?"

"There seems to be some energy for a couple of thrusts," Milyr speculated, peering down at the vaguely lighted console before him. "And I've always enjoyed a rush of blood to my vulching head once in a while. It can be really vulching stimulating!"

"It's your decision, Nyba," Domyn said. "Do we thrust a couple of times to see what happens?"

As Nyba hesitated, Kymil leaned towards Lyndyn and asked in a whisper, "Do you want a sedative?"

"Nyba, we shouldn't wait too long if we are going to try this," Domyn said with impatience.

Briefly peeking at the expanding lattice of fissures in Justinex window, Lyndyn understood their plight but tried to respond bravely, "No, my kind Kymil, someone else may yet need a sedative for some more vital reason. No doubt I'll manage whatever happens."

Sounding confused and uncertain, Nyba said, "Even if we use limited thrusters, we'll use up much of the energy reserve. I don't know, Domyn. We can't be sure if it will be successful."

"You are, Cap," Whyvvi shouted abruptly, sitting next to Nyba in Domyn's brown chair. "Nyba, you must make a decision."

"Milyr, on order I'll fire the left forward thruster for a second," Domyn commanded. "You be ready to steer the flaps to get our top into the wave. Be ready to counter the thrust on your side, if necessary. We are not attempting to capsize this Wolf at this time."

"Okay, Domyn, but we won't have time for discussion once we start this. I'll have to do some of this on my own," Milyr complained with slight self-doubt in his voice reaching Lyndyn's ears.

"I trust your judgment and your skill, Milyr," Domyn declared and then asked impatiently, "Nyba, do we do this or not?"

Nyba replied with uncertainty, "I'm worried about using our energy that we need to keep the air purification system working. I don't know. It's so difficult now to know what to do."

"If we do nothing, those vulchers will eat through the Justinex window and kill us anyway," Milyr griped. "Vulch, Nyba, let us have a chance to do something, vulching anything!"

While Milyr spoke, Jamyk mumbled a sound from a chair on the other side of Kymil. With his eyes closed, Lyndyn did not see her movement, yet he felt a spin of her chair and her body as Kymil turned to her younger patient. Her other patient, he mused suddenly. Yes, Lyndyn had to agree, he himself had recently become patient for Kymil. Now Kymil had two to attend, two to nurse. Embarrassment and self-annoyance attacked his image of himself. Lyndyn felt horrible.

"Then do it. Rock Wolf," Nyba commanded with some reluctance in her voice. "Our situation can't get much worse."

"Everyone harnessed in?" Domyn asked loudly.

"In case we turn over," Milyr chuckled.

"Vulching toxx, you had better not!" Whyvvi swore with dismay.

"Awright, now remember, Milyr, our goal is to tip this Wolf into the wave to get more ocean splash on the window," Domyn stated emphatically. "We do not intend to capsize Wolf on this attempt. Do you understand?"

"Yeah, I do, Domyn. Tilt into the wave. No tipping over," Milyr replied seriously and then added hastily with slight levity, "At least not purposely."

As Wolf leaned to the right with left side rising sharply due to the motion of the wave outside, Lyndyn wondered if he should lock his chair into a non-pivoting position. His eyelids remained tightly closed against the stomach disturbing sway and roll of scene partially displayed through the large window. Then as a pull of gravity moved from his buttocks in his chair to his back against the chair, Lyndyn realized that the chair had spun quickly. He was glad not to have seen the movement. Maybe he would let the chair pivot with the pull of gravity as long as his back was always down. No doubt. If he did not see swinging of his environment around himself, then perhaps unsettling sensations would not bother his stomach. As he gripped the sides of his chair, he could only hope.

"Firing one burst now," Domyn shouted loudly.

"Let's wash this window," Milyr cried out boisterously.

As gravity pulled at his back and head, Lyndyn felt a sharp upward angle of Wolf almost on its side, and heard Whyvvi yell, "Vulch, we are on our side. Hold us steady, you guys. Do not tip us over."

"Look, the wave's coming faster and steeper. It's going to hit," Nyba declared with a squeak in her voice, but Lyndyn forced himself not to open his eyes and peek out the window.

Before she finished, Lyndyn heard a thud of liquid force of the ocean slam at Wolf. Almost instantly he felt the chair and floor shudder with impact, impact that he realized, without actually seeing, was much more intense than sprays and splashes he had witnessed earlier. But then, he recalled, that is what they had hoped would be the result of this maneuver. He longed for a peek at the window, but his brain and stomach warned him against such a foolish venture.

Instead he gasped, "Is it working? Is the acid liquid of this ocean washing away those things?"

Then as Wolf fell suddenly back to its original, somewhat horizontal rolling position and gravity seemed to pull more at his buttocks than his back, Lyndyn heard Kymil murmur with both excitement and anxiety in her tone, "Oh my, what a ride. Yes, Lyndyn, it seems to be washing away things. At least where ocean liquid strikes, those things are washed away. But so many more cover the window. Will we be able to remove those things?"

"Let's try that again from the other direction," Domyn shouted. "Milyr, thrust comes from your side next time. The one second burst, no more. Let's not waste our energy."

"Yes, we need our energy reserve to power the air purification system, or we will be without appropriate oxygen," Nyba declared with obvious worry. "This maneuver had better succeed. You won't be able to do it many times again."

"Looks like another mighty huge wave coming," Whyvvi hollered as Lyndyn listened to the conversation with his eyes shut and his hands checking the tightness of his chair harness.

Feeling a tug of gravity on his back again and sensation of Wolf tilting as his feet skidded along the floor when his chair spun, Lyndyn belched and gasped, "Hang on, Kymil. I hope your harness is well-fastened. The young men are giving us another ride…"

"Vulching huge wave, Domyn," Milyr yelled in excited terror. "Should be a big vulching splash. We should wash the vulchers right off this window cherply. I'll try to time burst at our peak tilt. Should be…thrusting…about…about…now… I'm thrusting now!"

A shudder trembled through Wolf, and a loud splatter of liquid sounded above his head. His body drawn by gravity strained against the back support of the chair. His internal sense of balance, in spite of his dysfunction, felt a moment of almost weightlessness as momentum of the rising chair and floor battled with a pull of gravity. Then the gravity of the moon recaptured its domination, and Lyndyn felt its pull on his body.

"Vulch, I can't pull flaps against this force," Domyn swore, panting. "Milyr, help me quick."

"Oh my," Kymil squealed beside Lyndyn.

"Counter thrust…counter thrust…" Nyba screamed.

"Too late," Domyn and Milyr yelled together.

"What's happening?" Lyndyn asked, hearing panic in the young vices, and then his weight fell against the restraining harness and away from the chair.

Beyond intellectual control of his brain, his eyelids opened wide to view the darkness deeper than that, which Wolf had endured moments before. Lyndyn could not see the window at first until his eyes adjusted to observe the iridescent orange triangles sliding along and floating away from the dark space above his head. Or was that below his head, he pondered as his brain acclimated to a new feeling of gravitational pull.

"Vulch!" Milyr cursed with sheepish embarrassment. "Sorry, everybody!"

"You toxx!" Whyvvi shrieked in near perfect imitation of Swyllo's shrill voice.

Then as blood bounded in his temple and his own acid bile oozed into his esophagus, Lyndyn realized suddenly he was upside down. Wolf had capsized. The view out the window was of the ocean, not the unsettling atmosphere of this ugly moon. The nauseating yellow-brown churning clouds were not in sight, but rocking and swaying of Wolf was evident still.

"Will Wolf's buoyant design return us back to normal in this choppy ocean?" Cap Nyba asked in serious anxiety. "Can we correct this nasty situation soon?"

With his form visible in the faint illumination of the console, Domyn answered from a seat not far in front of Lyndyn and Nyba, "Possibly, Nyba, but I would not rely on Wolf's flotation and buoyancy traits to automatically right our position. With wings extended, Wolf's shape as glider may work against this."

"Is anybody hurt?" Kymil asked in a concerned and shaken voice. "Is everyone sure of their safety harnesses? Make certain harnesses are tight. Everyone knows, I hope by now, that we are upside down. This is a very dangerous situation."

"Yes, everyone, do not unhook your harnesses," Domyn declared hastily and with authority. "We are not in space any longer. The gravity of this moon will drop anybody into what used to be our ceiling. This includes the Justinex window. We do not know what would happen if one of us smashed into that window after it has been weakened by the actions of those orange things. We must be careful."

"Vulching nasty if we break the window from inside and let that acid ocean into Wolf," Milyr groaned. "After the trouble we had to protect it in the first place, breaking the window ourselves would be vulching nasty irony."

"Toxx, what do you know about irony? If you had not flipped us over, then we would not need your vulching irony," Whyvvi complained.

"Just trying to do my duty," Milyr snarled. "So I vulching made a mistake."

"I did not hear anyone claim injury," Kymil announced. "I assume everyone is fine for the moment."

As a trickle of bile seeped down into his esophagus, sending heart burn-like annoyance into his chest, Lyndyn attempted to sound confident and positive, so he said with a slight sigh of relief, "Indeed, my Kymil, at least this position gives me a more stable and steady view to alleviate my nausea. Although I would suggest that we not hang around like this for very long. This inverted flow of blood to our brains is not healthy if allowed to continue for a long length of time."

"Yes, you are correct," Kymil agreed. "Nyba, we must get back to our normal perspective reasonably soon. If not we should plan how to get out of these chairs and right ourselves without injury to us or the window of Wolf."

As she spoke this, Lyndyn felt continued swaying of Wolf, which was most likely on the ocean surface still. Yes, as Wolf bobbed, he thought that he saw once glimpse of a yellowish light shine dimly through the edge of the curvature of the window. Very few iridescent triangles could be seen now on the window. The disappearance of the strange and hostile things was hopefully enlightening to their emotional perspective but also darkening to the physical lighting of Wolf. But apparently Wolf was on the surface still. They had a chance to turn Wolf topside or the window up before reverse blood flow affects the intellectual thinking of their brains.

"Domyn, you said Wolf's shape was hindrance to turning us over," Nyba said hastily, obviously battling rising anxiety. "Can we morph back to Wolf's original shape?"

"Not enough energy, Nyba. Morphing requires a high energy output. We haven't had that capability since we morphed to the glider shape. That was the last possible morphing for Wolf," Domyn explained in a subdued and exhausted voice.

"Yeah, and our best energy harvester is gone now," Milyr muttered mournfully and then abruptly shouted, "But Swyllo would not give up. Why should we?"

"Do we have enough energy to do anything?" Whyvvi complained despondently. "Can we do anything with what energy we have left, thanks to Swyllo's effort?"

"We could thrust again," Milyr declared. "Vulching waves are still rocking Wolf. A burst of thrust and Wolf's normal buoyant characteristics might turn us back over."

"More energy usage? Is this what you're suggesting?" Nyba sighed in dismay.

"We can't wait for a chance wave," Milyr said impatiently. "My head is starting to hurt being upside down. We've got to try something."

"I agree," Lyndyn gasped, trying to hide a belch but afraid the sour taste in his mouth might have revealed itself. "We need to right Wolf. If we cannot, we must anticipate gradual impairment of our thinking abilities. Then, very likely, we will experience an increase in mild hallucinations, or for some of us, unconsciousness."

"We could all end up like Jamyk?" Whyvvi asked with agitated fear in her voice.

"Y…yup…" muttered a raspy voice, then a sequence of nonsense sounds, a few deep breaths, and then sleepy mumbles.

"What the vulch was that?" Milyr croaked startled and befuddled. "Is he awake, Doc? Vulching scared me nasty!"

"Let's not get off our discussion for some foolishness," Nyba demanded with some annoyance in her trembling voice. "How can we flip Wolf back to our normal perspective? Milyr, you suggested it. What did you want to try?"

"Vulch, Jamyk scared me," Milyr exclaimed. "Little peener is always unpredictable."

"Like toxx friend of his," Whyvvi said emphatically toward Milyr. "A big toxx friend!"

"Awright, enough! Focus people. Milyr, focus," Domyn scolded. "If we thrust, we cannot be sure we'll turn over. But your point about buoyant flotation characteristic of Wolf is a sound one. This time it will be working in our favor."

"Thank you, Neer," Nyba declared sharply. "I thought we had gone foolishly astray."

"Erh, maybe a longer burst of thrust?" Milyr asked half-heartedly, and then suddenly swore in irritation waving at the window below, "Vulch, the toxx blue balls are back. Can't we get away from them? Vulching goad me nasty!"

Peering down at the window, Lyndyn observed a few aqua spheres float past in the ocean below. In the liquid, strange spheres seemed to give off a very faint glow, almost like orange iridescent triangles of before. Not at all like some form of electricity or lightning, Lyndyn mused, now that he studied the phenomena in the ocean setting. However, this was not important now in this critical moment. Was he losing rational intellect already? Lyndyn wondered if his brain was being affected by abnormal blood flow and pressure in his current inverted position. What about the others?

Then from darkness beyond Kymil's chair, Lyndyn heard a sudden rustling of McAnderwike fabric and a raspy croaked mumble, "...elp...ahh...cum...ahh... elp...cum...erhh..."

"Vulch, I wish he'd stop doing that," Milyr griped.

"We do agree about something," Whyvvi declared.

"He is still asleep, isn't he, Doc?" Nyba asked with annoyed concern. "We don't need any interference just now from the toxx pup. I hope he stays asleep for awhile."

"Yes, I think Jamyk is unconscious still," Kymil replied.

"Jamyk acting weird in here! Blue balls moving out there. Blood flowing to my head," Milyr grumbled in mock humor. "Vulch, we really need to thrust soon, Domyn, to get back to some form of normality."

"Has there been any kind of normality recently?" Nyba asked rhetorically and with disgust.

"Yes, I believe that we can thrust to turn Wolf upright," Domyn agreed finally, yet his words and tone seemed forced and strained to Lyndyn's hearing.

Was Domyn feeling light-headed already? Was their best engineering brain starting to show a sign of confusion or indecision? Was Domyn's incredible will being tested by this unique situation? Could the young man will his intellect to counteract the negative process in his brain? Could he focus long enough to correct difficulty, to find an answer, to perform an action? Lyndyn was not sure. Lyndyn doubted his own analysis at the moment. May Domyn's universal metaphy help them all, Lyndyn thought and pleaded unconsciously.

"Hey, big man, what do you want me to do?" Milyr asked.

"Not the same way as last time," Domyn muttered almost to himself. "It's too risky with a low energy supply. We must flip on the first try."

Watching the aqua sphere pause now in the darkness beyond the window and then drift off out of sight quickly, Lyndyn listened to Milyr argue in frustration, "We will use some energy to turn Wolf. There is no alternative. We can't do it without some energy expense. But we can't wait forever."

"But the air purification process..." Nyba started to debate in a very stressful tone.

Milyr interrupted with more irritation, "Won't do us much good if we all go light-headed or crazy sitting like this. Vulch, we need to do something now."

"Sounds like it is happening already," Whyvvi snarled. "Boys cannot take pressure, huh?"

As bile soured his mouth and sent heart burn through his chest, Lyndyn could hear panic entering the argument, so he tried to concentrate his encouragement and persuasion on the young engineer as he said, "Domyn, what is it you are thinking? Your knowledge is of most importance now. Your ideas or intuition must be followed. You are in charge at this moment. But you cannot wait."

"I'm captain," Nyba shrieked from a chair beside Lyndyn. "I'm Cap! It's my ship."

In spite of fear and reluctance to let go of his grip on his chair, Lyndyn reached over with one hand, grasped her closest arm firmly, and shouted forcefully, "Not now, Nyba, not at this moment. Not for this threat. Let Domyn do what he must."

"We could... We could..." Domyn stammered hesitantly from a faint glow of the console.

"No, I'm captain. It's my decision," Nyba screamed, shaking Lyndyn's hand away.

"Yes, Nyba is Cap," Whyvvi protested with unusual vehemence.

"We must thrust harder next time, Domyn," Milyr said loudly. "Maybe we thrust twice as hard, just enough to flip Wolf in one attempt. We can't stay like this belly-up. It's not safe."

"Twice as hard...one shot..." Domyn muttered. "Need steep wave... Wait for steep wave."

"Do not vulch us again," Whyvvi shrieked. "Listen to Cap Nyba."

"We can't wait, Domyn. My head is throbbing. My eyes are losing focus on our console buttons," Milyr yelled in desperation. "I don't want to do it by myself."

"You have to do it soon, Domyn," Lyndyn commanded in a rarely used voice of authority that his older age and respected position within this crew allowed to him. "Domyn, you are leader now at this moment. Do what you must. Our health and Wolf's security are at stake."

"Elp...cum...y-y-yup...elp..." croaked a raspy voice in garbled sleep from the darkness.

"No, don't!" Nyba screamed in anguish.

"We must, Domyn, big man," Milyr demanded. "We must thrust twice as hard on our first shot!"

"Twice...twice..." Domyn murmured, and then Lyndyn thought the young man would give up and withdraw his consciousness into the safety of his mind where he did not need to make a decision.

"Yeah, Domyn, twice thrust but can't wait," Milyr yelled.

Mumbles and frenetic rustling of McAnderwike fabric resounded from Jamyk's unseen form.

Then suddenly Domyn commanded with exhausted certainty in a moderately confident voice, "Yes, awright, Milyr... You fire forward thrust for one second. I'll fire reverse thrust for one second. We must fire the same time. Thrust on my command."

"But energy," Nyba wailed. "We will need it."

"Prepare for another vulching ride," Milyr declared boisterously.

Watching another aqua sphere drift by the window, and then gently spitting sour bile from his mouth, Lyndyn gasped, "Do it...men...soon...as...you must."

Whyvvi pleaded with intense fear seething from her voice, "Do not vulch it this time."

"Umm...elp...ahh...um...elp...cum..." mumbled Jamyk from darkness again, and Lyndyn wondered very briefly if the boy was aware of activity in Wolf at this moment.

Then as his weight shifted back into the chair and he closed his eyes, Lyndyn listened to Domyn command firmly, "Milyr, ready...on my word...now!"

"Oh, vulch!" screamed Whyvvi. "I am not ready to join Swyllo yet."

"Power off," Domyn shouted hastily. "Grip steering. We can't let Wolf roll over too much...must end...window up."

Lyndyn's chair pivoted sharply. Gravity tugged against his back. His feet slid across the floor during the chair spinning. Lyndyn clenched his eyelids closed and his fingers tighter into the chair sides. Around him Lyndyn listened to cries, swears, and pleading of others. Fear reeked in the confined air of Wolf. But he realized it was a fear of purpose, fear of hope.

As Wolf toppled heavily around him, Lyndyn felt a sudden impact with the ocean surface and heard Milyr yell through stressed and strained breathes, "With you, big man. I've got my flaps under control... Vulching nasty ride, hey?"

His buttocks squashed downwards into the chair, and then the chair began to spin another direction, so Lyndyn wailed, "Not again!"

"Don't worry, Prof," Domyn gasped breathlessly. "Think we can handle it this time."

"Just pendulum momentum, Prof," Milyr laughed raggedly but with relief and joy in his voice. "Vulch, we can get Wolf under control now. What a nasty ride! Are we not the best primo pilots in Sexto, big man? Vulching cherp!"

Light-headed and dizzy despite his closed eyes, Lyndyn gripped his pivoting chair while the motion continued while he listened to Kymil say with controlled mirth, "Oh my, yes, you did fantastic. Seems cherp to see that ugly yellow sky again. Especially in proper perspective with gravity at my feet and my sight turned upwards. Oh, my people, don't be alarmed if you feel dizzy for a few moments. That would be normal under the recent circumstances. Does anyone feel any other ailments? Lyndyn?"

With a sour acid taste in his mouth and throat, Lyndyn leaned toward her voice and admitted in a sheepish soft voice, "Indeed I could use some water to wash out my mouth. Stomach acid found its way up, or was it down, my esophagus."

"I thought that I got a whiff of that odor," Kymil said, her tone smooth, soothing, motherly as her hand patted his left arm. "My brave kindred spirit, I'm proud of you. You were so steady."

Peering spasmodically toward her voice, Lyndyn allowed his vision to clarify against the dizziness of his blood redistribution back to normal and then glimpsed her smiling face behind the protective shield of the McAnderwike helmet. "No, Kymil... I'm afraid I was anything but heroic or even useful. My stomach was a constant distraction. I can't even look out the window now without getting a sick sensations. I'm not a brave spirit at all."

While he spoke this, Lyndyn heard Domyn shout wearily but purposely, "Don't let go yet, Milyr. Let's settle Wolf into as buoyant a float as this turbulent ocean will allow. We're getting control, but let's finish this wisely. Take no chances now, my friend."

"That's cherp for me, Domyn. Notice the gorgeously clear view through the window? Are we not cherping nasty window washers, Domyn?" Milyr laughed.

"Just lucky, you window washer," Whyvvi griped but with a chuckle tickling her voice. "Just toxx the window washer, just like I thought."

As a packet of liquid appeared in Kymil's hand from the dimness in Wolf, Lyndyn struggled to disconnect his McAnderwike helmet and remarked loudly for the whole crew, "You all did very fine work recently. All of you! We have had a continuous sequence of horrible situations that have required extremely difficult decisions. As Cap Nyba likes to say, men and women, you have kept us alive so far against the trying conditions. We and Wolf are alive still. Our situation is not hopeless. Keep your intellect active and your actions appropriate to our survival. You are Blue Jayers."

"Awe wills that we can do that," Domyn sighed and then added, "I hope!"

Nyba agreed, though somewhat sullenly, "We could use help. We are almost out of our own options. We are almost out of energy to power the systems in this Wolf to keep us alive."

"That may be true, Nyba, but it is always cherp to see a clear window. No more trings," Whyvvi stated with relief and elation.

"No more what?" Milyr squeaked with his usual baritone voice cracking on the final word.

"Trings…trings," Whyvvi declared emphatically, "I've decided to term phenomenon…trings. I could not keep thinking of those little triangular things as such. I needed a new but related term. I decided on…trings. For less observant of you, Milyr, that is short for triangular things."

"Trings?' Milyr winced while his shoulders and arms strained with the gradual rocking motion of Wolf. "Vulch, that's best that you could do? Trings?"

"Sounds good enough for me," Domyn agreed, working at his own side of the pilot console. "What do you think, Cap Nyba? Can we accept Whyvvi's term for little nasty things?"

As he sipped water into his mouth and swished it around, Lyndyn heard Nyba respond with some apathy, "Okay with me. Whatever you decide, Domyn, you're in command. It is cherp to see no…trings…on the window now. But our situation has not changed that much, we are on this nasty moon still."

About to spit out his mouthful of cleansing water, Lyndyn realized that he should not soil the interior of Wolf. They might be doomed to live in here for awhile, he thought. Besides diluted acid in his mouth was from his own stomach, so he swallowed his mouthful. Indeed, he thought, watery liquid felt good as it washed down his throat and esophagus. He sipped another mouthful.

"Trings...not a bad term for a new and different phenomenon," Kymil commented as her eyes stared at Lyndyn, probably scrutinizing his condition like a mother would her child, he thought.

"Perhaps we should put Whyvvi in charge of naming all the new weird phenomena we'll find in Sexto?" Milyr said jokingly as he stretched his torso and shoulders across the back of his seat. "Vulch, I sure could go for a cherp massage about now. Any fems interested?"

Sitting to the right of Lyndyn, Nyba exclaimed, "We don't have time now, you lazy toxx. But your first idea seemed cherp to me. How about you, Domyn? Should we make Whyvvi our permanent officer of new terminology for phenomena here in Sexto?"

"Now, Nyba, you do not have to do this. I do not want responsibility," Whyvvi pleaded, perhaps falsely according to the nuances of her voice and tone to Lyndyn's ears.

"Okay by me, Cap," Domyn replied with a hint of humor. "But you are Cap. It is your assignment prerogative."

Gulping down his second mouthful of cleansing water, Lyndyn saw a splash of the ocean flow from the window with his peripheral vision and then said firmly with a slight scold to his tone, "Nyba, you are Cap. We all rely on your judgment. Don't carry a grudge because of what happened recently. Behave as Cap. What's your most important concern now at this moment? As Cap what do you believe that we should focus upon at this time?"

For several seconds, Wolf was almost silent. Only the thrashing of McAnderwike fabric and mumbles of a sleeping, dreaming boy reached Lyndyn's ears. That is, he reminded himself, it was silent inside Wolf. Outside Wolf was quite another story. Apparently his hearing had relegated the constant splash and thud of heavy ocean waves against the outer hull to his subconscious awareness. Now in the quiet inside, he could hear the noise of the turbulent moon outside Wolf. Noise and sights, thunder and lightning, splatters and clouds, all intruded onto his senses now. He wished that he could tune out these obnoxious stimulations, but he was not going to complain in front of this young crew now.

In a hesitant, slow manner, Nyba's soft voice declared, "Our Wolf position seems to be stabilized. Thank you, guys, for your efforts... Now how is our energy supply?"

Several flashes of lightning and a rapidly flying aqua sphere crossed his vision through the window as Lyndyn waited in the hot wetness of his McAnderwike. Continuous splashes of ocean splatter resounded on the window. Jamyk garbled something from his chair on the farther side of Kymil. Everything seemed almost exactly how it had been before the incident with the orange trings, except that nasty things now had a name, Lyndyn mused.

Finally Milyr responded, "Cap, from what I can see here on the console, our energy supply is very low. But that's not really any surprise, is it?"

"Vulching nasty," swore Whyvvi beside Nyba in Domyn's brown chair.

"How low? Could we fire a thrust if needed?" Nyba asked, her voice exhausted but mildly calm.

As Domyn's large form leaned toward Milyr's portion of the console, Milyr replied, "No, probably not, Cap. The supply is too low. What do you think, Domyn?"

"I agree. Wolf's energy is too little now for thrusting," Domyn stated with resignation in his deep voice. "Without more energy, we cannot fly or move Wolf any longer."

"We can send Milyr out there with a paddle," Whyvvi quipped sardonically.

"Vulch no!" Milyr griped and then waved at the window, cursing, "Vulch, all that electricity out there and we can't make power. Vulching nasty!"

"Awe damn ironic, isn't it?" Domyn exclaimed. "We're sitting in an ocean of immense thermal energy under the sky of a potent lightning energy. Yet we don't have sci-tech now to harvest any. I guess Blue Jay never envisioned this scenario."

"Maybe we will be struck by lightning," Whyvvi said in a dejected but humorous tone. "I still like my notion of Milyr out there with a paddle."

"Lower power," Nyba whispered beside Lyndyn, and then louder ordered, "turn off all systems, except life support. Be sure to keep power to the air purifier. If we can't do anything with Wolf, except hide in here, then that's what we'll do for now."

"What about the sanbeam to Fox Flash?" Whyvvi yelled suddenly.

"Not enough power for the sanbeam transmission," Domyn declared.

"What about the standard message to whoever gets it?" Lyndyn asked. "Even hostile colonials would be a good option about now."

"A communications attempt would use much of our energy," Domyn predicted. "We could send a short message, but leave almost nothing to power the life support. We have had no indication that anyone is out there close enough to respond if they receive our comm."

As splatter struck the center curve of the window and the ocean churned in his squinting sight, Lyndyn averted his gaze hastily and suggested, "A simple, old-fashioned cry for help, like ancient SOS perhaps. No doubt the colonials would have some lingering memory of the old code. We know Fox Flash does. This could not hurt us to try."

"Vulch no!" Milyr yelled suddenly and loudly, and Lyndyn was surprised at the young man's strong vehement disagreement.

But then he heard Whyvvi scream, "Trings...the trings are back."

"Oh my, no!" Kymil wailed more profoundly than normal for her usually calm demeanor.

"We can't topple Wolf anymore," Domyn declared with dismay.

Lyndyn stared up at the continuously growing numbers of orange trings as they struck and attached to the outside of the window. As the previous encounter, the trings pulsed with an iridescent rhythm. Cracks and fissures began forming anew to join and extend into the lattice of before.

"Send a signal to anyone out there immediately, Milyr," Nyba commanded.

From the darkness beyond Kymil, Lyndyn heard Jamyk mumble a garbled, dream-like sequence of nonsense, "elp...mmmhh....elp...alllmmm...cum....elp...."

But Lyndyn's eyes stared reluctantly and fearfully at the hundreds of orange trings attacking the window. His brain told him that this time there was absolutely nothing that this crew of Wolf could do. Their survival was out of their hands.

"I don't suppose that you could ask your universal metaphy for some assistance now, Domyn," Lyndyn inquired. "I think we need help."

The big man sighed, "I don't think it works that way, Prof. I think that we are supposed to use our freedom of choice to get ourselves out of danger or to prevent ourselves from getting into it."

"Well, that is not much help in this situation," Whyvvi declared.

"We could hope that Fox Flash will hear our cry for help," Kymil murmured. leaning closer to Lyndyn's left arm, and he extended this towards her for comfort, both hers and his.

A voice rasped in the dark, "...cum...elp...cum...elp...ahhh...esss...elp..."

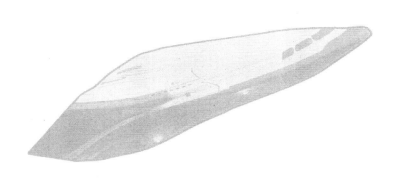

Spec Three: Lyndyn On Wyllos
Chapter 26

"Nasty trings!" Whyvvi wailed. "This should not be happening to us. Why is this happening?"

"No doubt our luck has been nothing but bad," Lyndyn exclaimed while his eyes stared at the increasing patch of trings covering the outer surface of the window to the front and top of Wolf.

"Bad luck? Vulching terrible nasty luck since popping into the Sexto System!" Milyr whined, sitting at his pilot console not far in front of and to the right of Lyndyn.

"Now we have almost no power. We can do nothing," Nyba moaned beside Lyndyn. "There is nothing that we can do to stop those things from shattering our window and letting poisonous air into Wolf. Nothing we can do, is there, Domyn?"

As he continued to stare at the window, now almost completely filled by the iridescent orange triangular shapes, Lyndyn listened to Domyn mutter in disconsolation, "No, Nyba, our sci-tech and energy is almost gone now. Wolf can do nothing but serve as a shell against the toxic environment around us. Perhaps we could try a short electrical charge through the hull. Perhaps that might dislodge them. But for how long? Would an electrical charge bother the trings? Whatever they are, they seem to thrive in an atmosphere of constant and strong lightning..."

"No, Domyn," Nyba interrupted. "What little energy that we have must power the life support system."

As a tring coverage of the window alleviated his stomach distress since they blocked the view of nauseating churning yellow brown clouds from his sight, Lyndyn said with some slight confidence and hope, "There is hope still. Our signal for help may have reached Fox Flash Alpha. Or perhaps the colonial ship has received it and is looking for us now. As long as Wolf holds integrity, we have a chance to be rescued. We must not give up all hope. I do not believe that our mission or purpose here in the Sexto System is meant to end like this…"

"Vulch, Prof, our Blue Jay super-resistant Justinex window won't hold long enough for help to arrive," Milyr complained, and Lyndyn observed a fissure spreading gradually downward into the clear structure of the window. "Some toxx in Blue Jay never considered the moon like this when they designed our Justinex composites. Won't do us any vulching use now when it shatters."

"If that window does shatter, then we will not last very long breathing that toxic atmosphere of this moon," Whyvvi declared in a trembling voice, and then after a sudden slap of hand against her chair, she added, "We should have been supplied with self-contained emergency suits to protect us from the poisonous airs and other hazardous environments."

"Vulching short-sighted of Blue Jay MisCom," Milyr griped vehemently, squirming in his seat at the console. "Maybe those types of suits would have had better air conditioners. I feel like I'm vulching cooking in this McAnderwike now. It's vulching nasty hot in this suit!"

Feeling slightly dizzy from the swaying of Wolf on this wavy ocean of acid liquid, Lyndyn sighed, beginning to sense desperation of the young crew around him, "Indeed it is very hot in here but not as bad as out there. Wolf may protect us yet. Aid must be on the way by now…"

"Ahh…cum…elp…umm…elp…ahh…cum," murmured Jamyk from the far-left chair of Wolf.

"Damn, I wish that he would stop doing that. It is getting on my nerves," Whyvvi complained loudly. "What does it mean? Is he having a dream or nightmare? Whatever it is, it is toxx annoying."

"Does it really matter, hot fem?" Milyr groaned. "We're going to die soon. I don't see how any other future could happen for us now. We're too far away from any help from foxes or the vulching colonials who were trying to kill us anyway. But worse yet, we'll never get a chance at a real sexy adult life…vulching unfair!"

Watching the cracks and fissures inexorably spread through the Justinex window, Lyndyn listened to Nyba sigh tiredly, sadly, "I'm sorry! I wish that I could have led Wolf Streak Beta better. I wish that I could have saved you all. I'm sorry."

Beside him Lyndyn heard Kymil say with her usual firm conviction, "Cap Nyba, you have been an ideal captain. This entire crew has performed as the best Blue Jayers ever. This has been due to your example and your determination. Don't believe that you have let us down. Few, if any captains, could have gotten their crews through the strife that this crew has endured. Yet we are still alive. There is a chance still. Your leadership has given us this chance."

"I should have done better. I should have made sure we had emergency self-contained suits. I should have insisted," Nyba sputtered as her voice weakened and finally ended in soft sobs. "I...should...have...saved... Swyllo...and all...of us."

From the pilot chair in front of Lyndyn, Domyn's deep voice said, "Not your fault, Nyba. Blue Jay had gradually come to rely upon the strength and endurance of the spacecraft like Wolf Streak Beta and our pod Wolf to be our emergency protection. We in Blue Jay have become so confident in our sci-tech that we have eliminated much of the redundant...baggage...our ancestors required."

"Vulching bit arrogant, don't you think?" Milyr snarled. "We could use that baggage now. Blue Jay sent us out here, how many light years from our closest human assistance? And now we are going to die like Swyllo. Vulching toxx back on Quinto can't help us from that far away."

"We should have had emergency equipment," Whyvvi stated bluntly with emotion.

"Probably would not help us in this situation," Domyn tried to explain, but Lyndyn heard a tremor of fear in the big young man's voice and then a gulp in his gasping stammer, "The acidic ocean...and possibly...acidic atmosphere...would corrode most of...the emergency ...available not as durable as... McAnderwikes...against blows..."

"We are going to die!" declared Milyr. "Nothing your great and all powerful metaphy can do for us, is there, Domyn? We could use some vulching help just about now. Hey, you out there, are you listening? Can you give us some aid? Will I ever get real sex? Come on, primo power, can't I get a break here? All those bodacious fems in those vulching colonial ships, they'll miss me."

"Damn, trings toxx!" Whyvvi cried out in dismay. "See you soon, Swyllo!"

"Elp...elp...elp...ahh...cum..." garbled Jamyk's raspy voice in dimming lights.

In spite of inevitable fear spreading through Wolf, young people had tried to stay calm, had tried to consider options, had tried to keep their terror from affecting their behavior. Quite extraordinary, Lyndyn thought to himself. He was very proud

397

of his young associates. Perhaps their Blue Jay training had been more valuable than ancient equipment for their survival. Perhaps Domyn had been correct that emergency equipment would not have been useful. Although, Lyndyn mused, too bad that such young people were going to perish, unless benevolent metaphy actually did become involved in their plight and find a way to save these people. But was that not slightly presumptuous and hypocritical of him to even think such a request?

Whack!

"Vulch, what was that? What now?" Milyr yelled in startled panic.

As the sensation of a sudden uplifting of his body against the harness reminded him of his recent experience of hanging upside down, Lyndyn felt his own fear and panic surge heat throughout his body. Then momentary sensation passed. His weight settled back downward into the chair. Around him he felt Wolf stabilize its swaying motion in persistent action of the turbulent ocean surface outside as if a giant hand, Lyndyn mused momentarily, had pushed down on Wolf. No, that was his imagination reacting to his sudden fear, he realized.

"Did you do something, Domyn?" Nyba asked abruptly.

"No, Nyba, but look there, the window has darkened. I can't see the yellowish light from the atmosphere," Domyn replied, suddenly alert to the new condition of his Wolf. "It seems as if Wolf isn't rocking as much. Something has blocked light from above."

"This Wolf is definitely not rocking as much," Lyndyn echoed emphatically. "Indeed trust me, my insides tell me so. Wolf is much more stable now. I thank your metaphy, Domyn. I hope this condition stays awhile."

"The lightning flashes are much dimmer now," Kymil said. "And see there, a dark purple ring around the edge of the window where there had been no trings close to the ocean."

"I believe something had struck us from above," Whyvvi shouted. "That would explain the sudden downward push we just experienced. But will this help us with our tring problem?"

Gazing upwards toward the darkened window, Lyndyn observed a pulsing of iridescent orange trings, and he gasped uncertainly, "Am… I…imagining this… or has the frequency and brightness of the trings decreased?"

"It may be a symptom of your stressed health and this extreme heat," Doc Kymil suggested with worry in her tone. "Perhaps you need another drink of water."

"No, Doc, I see it also," Domyn yelled with enthusiasm. "I hope this is good for us."

"Yes, the trings seem to be fading," Nyba stated much more optimistic than she had been before. "Maybe we do have a chance to survive now."

"Vulch, anything is improvement on this toxx moon," Milyr blurted sourly.

"Is this one of those purple things again?" Doc Kymil asked almost hopefully.

"However, will this…this purple…blanket…save us?" Whyvvi shouted with some doubt. "Or will this new thing make everything worse? Will this cause pressure outside to shatter the Justinex? Or will it help stop the trings and then seal the cracks?"

"Vulch, fem, at least let's have a more cherp outlook for the moment," scolded Milyr. "One nasty crisis at a time. Get rid of the vulching trings first, right, big man?"

Domyn declared, "Considering that we have no control of the situation outside Wolf, we'll have to accept whatever happens. Awe alone knows what will or will not help us get a tiny bit of luck in our favor. We can only look at this as cherp for us. Our own optimism may be our only tool now, but it may persuade the universal chance to grace us with cherp luck."

"I'll agree to that request," Lyndyn attested while observing the fading pulsations of the orange trings. "My scientific psychology can be overwhelmed by your metaphysical universal awareness at this moment. My desire and belief are flexible and adaptable as the situation demands, especially when facing death. I will admit that I can be a toxx hypocrite at times like these."

"Oh my, that is an unusual admission from you, my kindred spirit. You are mellowing in your old age," Kymil teased with some subtle mirth indicating to Lyndyn that her spirits had been lifted by the sudden recent new circumstance.

Believing that the mood of young people could use brace of a humorous by-play, Lyndyn countered with feigned annoyance, "Old age? Why I'm not even in my prime, especially for a Blue Jay spacer. I'm not even a complete forty-seven, still very much in my youth."

Whyvvi exclaimed with cautious joy, "Cherp, the nasty trings are disappearing. They appear to be harmed by that purple blanket covering our window outside. In fact I believe that the trings are being absorbed by the purple blanket thing. This is cherp for us now."

With his eyesight confirming Whyvvi's observation, Lyndyn said in mischief, "No doubt, my kind Kymil, if my memory is correct, are you not a few months older than me, old lady?"

"Why yes, I am, young man. And I'm quite more mature as an adult than a certain youngster whom I know very well and care about," Kymil declared, and Lyndyn believed almost that he could see her smile not far away in the increasing darkness.

"Whyvvi, or Milyr, since you two are at the console, what is the hull temp above and below Wolf now?" Nyba requested with her voice and tone hinting at more confidence now.

After Milyr's head leaned down toward the weak illuminations on the console, he answered, "Getting hard to read these gauges, but I think the top is 123 and the bottom is 113. Vulching feels like 200 in this McAnderwike."

Kymil chuckled seriously in her mothering voice, "I think that you'd be dead, Milyr, if it was that hot. What is the internal temp in Wolf?"

"Too nasty hot!" complained Whyvvi. "I am sweating my toxx off in this suit."

Milyr's baritone voice giggled, "You wish you were hot, young fem. And I thought you fems only perspired and did not sweat, or was that just Swyllo? Too bad we need these McAnderwikes for protection. I would love to shed this blue skin for the sake of my own comfort. My skin is vulching on fire, or at least feels like that."

"Milyr, answer Doc's question," Domyn commanded with a growl. "What is the temp in here?"

"Too vulching hot!" Milyr replied. "Actual temp seems to read about 103."

"That sounds cooler than my skin at the moment," Lyndyn said, and then with a sigh of mock contentment, added, "Indeed just quoting a perceptually lower temp makes me feel cooler."

"Do not try any of your psychological trickery on us, Prof," Whyvvi laughed. "I know hot when I feel it. This is vulching hot. For once I agree with this nasty toxx of a boy."

"In case anyone else is interested still," Nyba announced with slight irritation in her voice, "the trings have dissolved into the giant purple thing...blanket thing... covering Wolf's window."

Lyndyn peered up at the darkening window. Hardly any light from above seeped through the blackish purple window of Wolf. A little light filtering through the darkened window revealed to him the diminishment of cracks and fissures caused by the trings. Was it lack of light that showed this lessening of cracks or was Justinex being mended? No, not mended, Lyndyn corrected his thinking, for that would entail some similarity to living function from either Wolf or that purple blanket. He was sure neither had the capability, neither could be a living thing.

"Does it seem as if fissures are disappearing?" he asked aloud. "Does anyone else see this?"

"Well, I don't see them as vividly as they once were," Domyn admitted. "But available light from outside is getting less than just moments ago. It's almost as if we were sinking farther from the surface."

"Sinking?" Whyvvi yelled with panic edging her voice. "Is that purket pushing Wolf under the ocean surface?"

"Purket? Is that another one of your weird terms, Whyvvi?" Milyr laughed disdainfully.

"Yes, you worthless toxx, and it makes very cherp sense, too," Whyvvi responded more in control of her fear suddenly when her choice of new name was challenged. "I will call that thing a purket. You can like it or not, but it is a purket now, not purple thingy or purple blanket thing, just a purket. Is that okay with you, Cap Nyba?"

"Yes, that makes some sense," Nyba said with more of her calm authority in her voice than just minutes before. "I believe we could be sinking also, for Wolf has stabilized now with much less rocking. I don't believe that we are on the surface now. The ocean would not become suddenly less turbulent. That does not seem to be a trait of this moon, as you stated earlier."

"And the top temp above has dropped since earlier," Milyr added as he interrupted Nyba. "The temp at the top of Wolf is getting lower and closer to the temp beneath Wolf. Vulch, I agree, we are sinking."

"Is that necessarily bad?" Lyndyn asked rhetorically. "I, for one, find this situation much more comfortable. My insides and my head like this lack of motion very nicely."

"It's still vulching boiling in this McAnderwike," Milyr complained. "I used to love putting this on for battle in a Pulseball competition or for kicking some toxx in practice on Wolf Streak Beta. But just now, this is too vulching hot. I'm roasting my nads off in here."

Kymil agreed seriously, "Yes, Cap Nyba, I'm becoming concerned that the confined body heat within these McAnderwikes will become a health risk soon. Even if the temp levels off in this Wolf, we may not be able to disperse our body heat efficiently while inside these suits. They have performed very well to protect us from physical trauma when we crashed, but now in this heat, I'm concerned."

But her comment was obscured as Whyvvi wailed, "We are sinking. How can that be good? We will be much more difficult for Khebol and Fox Flash Alpha to find. We do not know what we are sinking down toward. This could be worse than the trings. And what is a purket? Will it continue to be cherp for us or suddenly started dissolving Wolf like it dissolved the trings?"

As he listened to her worries, Lyndyn realized that what was less nauseating for him could make others more terrified, so he said with an assuring tone, "No doubt this is troubling to you. However, we must recognize that submerged or on the surface, we are in a hostile environment. Wolf can protect us in either, so it matters not which we are in. While submerged it appears that the trings cannot harm Wolf…"

Whyvvi interrupted, "However, Prof, we should not trust this purket to stay useful for us. We do not know enough about it. We do not know what it can do to Wolf."

"That is true, yet to this moment, it has been useful and not harmful. We can do very little about it anyway," Lyndyn stated in his professorial lecturing voice. "However, more importantly, as we sink lower into this ocean, lowering of the external temperature can be healthful for us inside. A new stability should allow us to move from these chairs. I know my toxx is certainly numbly sore. I'm sure that Doc would agree physical exercise can't hurt us at the moment. We must assume that our time is not over. We must plan on keeping our health adequate for whatever future we have."

Kymil agreed quickly, adding, "Yes, that is true. I am worried that our McAnderwikes while serving to protect us recently are now merely enclosing us in heat generating…cookers. Yes, that may be an appropriate metaphor. We may cook inside these clothes without coolant systems functioning. Milyr is correct. We should undress out of these McAnderwikes. We need to lower our body temps soon."

"But what about swaying and rocking around Wolf, will that begin again? What if we suddenly rise to the surface again?" Whyvvi asked with genuine anxiety and logical stubbornness.

"We have been very steady and stable for several minutes, fine fem," Milyr stated as the click of his harness reached Lyndyn's ears. "I am not hesitant to follow Doc's recommendation. I'll take my chances rather than cook in this vulching McAnderwike."

Whyvvi snorted, "You should wait for Nyba's decision, Milyr."

"Why, I'm vulching hot. My actions won't hurt anyone else. Doc has given instructions," Milyr stated, slowly standing from the pilot seat at the console.

"Nyba, what do you think?" Domyn asked from the dimly illuminated console.

"When you get up…don't move very…quickly or suddenly," Milyr gasped as if in pain. "Unless you are healthier now than me… Muscles and joints are very stiff right now. Move carefully."

Cap Nyba said with hesitant resolution, "If Doc thinks that we should undress, then we should perform the most beneficial behavior now for our survival. It's not as if we are shy creatures and haven't been living with each other for most of our lives. If circumstance changes and we need protection of our McAnderwikes, then we can put them back on. With any health issue, Doc Kymil has authority. Let's get out of these McAnderwikes. They have done their duty for us."

"Sound judgment, Cap Nyba," Milyr sang with relief and enthusiasm as his tall figure in the low illumination of the console staggered momentarily while he worked his legs into shape and regained a standing balance. "Oh, vulch, this is going to feel cherp to my skin."

Several other clicks reached Lyndyn's ears as harnesses were unfastened, and he whispered to Kymil on his left, "Thank you, at least we will be comfortable as we wait."

"Wait for…rescue? I'm sure that's what you meant, my kindred spirit," she replied and then commanded with a chuckle, "Now, Lyndyn, move slowly as Milyr suggested. Remember your recent bout with imbalance. And your toxx is numbly sore, is it not?"

"Doctor, most of this elderly, forty-seven-year body is numbly sore," Lyndyn said, wincing as he stood up slowly. "At first opportunity, I may seek a therapeutic body massage from someone well-skilled. Do you know of anyone qualified to perform that health service?"

"If you are fortunate, perhaps we'll be rescued by Fox Flash Alpha soon. I understand that Doc Thebon is quite skilled at that medical treatment," Kymil said quite stoically but undoubtedly with a smile in the darkness. "His hands have been finely attuned to the human body over the years."

"Hmmn! Not who I had in mind," Lyndyn groaned in disappointment as he held the back of his chair while glancing around the darkened Wolf to observe most of the young people stretching and twisting their bodies carefully, slowly releasing the tautness of stiff muscles.

Only Jamyk, still in unconscious sleep, and Whyvvi remained in their chairs. With a series of snaps, he disconnected the helmet from his neck guard. The relative coolness of the air outside the helmet felt very good on his sweating bald head. Oh, yes, he grinned to himself in pleasure, this was definitely a very good idea.

"Oh! That's so much better," Milyr chortled in apparent ecstasy. "Vulch, I never thought 100 degrees plus could feel so cool. It's vulching cherp refreshing!"

When he glanced over at the tall figure in the dim illumination of the console, Lyndyn saw a young man tear open his chest fastenings. His helmet was already on the chair seat, just barely gleaming in a very low light. Then the lanky figure shook and twisted in attempt to allow McAnderwike to slide to the floor as gravity pulled the clothing downward. Yet obviously, as Milyr struggled, the tight uniform clung to the young man's sweating shoulders.

"Vulch, I need help," Milyr complained as he flapped open the chest lapels of McAnderwike back and forth probably to create some air flow. "Will anyone give me a hand? Whyvvi, you're closest."

"Sorry, you lazy toxx," Whyvvi exclaimed in a suspicious tone. "You are not going to fool me into undressing you. I am wise to your sneaky tricks, you toxx. Swyllo and I learned about you long ago."

"No, no, not now," Milyr griped while he tried to wriggle the fabric from his shoulders, "Really I'm not vulching tricking now. I must be too sweaty or too muscular to get this thing off myself. Really, Whyvvi, this is no trick!"

"Well, sure seems like nasty trickery, Milyr!" Whyvvi scolded and then added, "Besides, if you are sweaty, then you are stinky, too."

"Didn't bother you before," Milyr retorted with hurt disappointment in his voice.

"Argh! Hmmn! That was before," Whyvvi stated with a laugh.

Then Nyba exclaimed calmly but forcefully, "Now, men and women, let's be adults. Step over here, Milyr. I'll help you. Now that I can stand up on my own, I'll help you. Is everyone else okay? Anybody else need assistance?"

Lyndyn had learned that his McAnderwike had stuck to his narrow shoulders just like Milyr's. He was about to request aid when he felt a tug at the neck of his garment. Without turning he realized that Kymil had seen his predicament and acted. As slightly cooler air washed across his sweating body, sending shivers of goose bumps over his skin, an incredible relief was almost as sensual as good sex. Yes, that was what it felt like, he thought, and only Kymil could assist him with that. At least that was the vision that he had frequently dreamed during the years of their shared voyage on mission to the Quinto System aboard Turkey Trot Alpha. But that was so many years ago now, and their shared love had swelled so much since then.

Twisting slightly toward her, Lyndyn murmured, "Thank you, my kind Kymil. As usual you can foresee my every need before I can."

"Oh my, don't be such a lame toxx, my kindred spirit," Kymil chuckled.

"I might need some help, too," Domyn announced, squirming beside his seat in darkness.

"Step around here then," Nyba demanded. "As captain I'm responsible for the safety of my people. Tugging on McAnderwikes is about as easy a chore as Cap can get... Stop wiggling so much, Milyr. I have to reach up to get at your collar, you tall sapling."

"What's sapling?" Milyr inquired as he turned his back to Nyba's reaching hands. "Did you just insult me? Or was that a sexual innuendo about my primo body?"

"No, Milyr, nothing of the sort. A sapling is a young tree, sometimes just not more than a twig with roots in the ground. But usually quite tall and spindly without much branching," Nyba explained patiently as she positioned her hands on the upper neck and shoulder portion of McAnderwike in preparation of working the garment down his lanky torso.

"That's a cherp description of this toxx!" Whyvvi giggled as she finally unbuckled her harness. "He is tall, skinny, with not much more than a twig and with almost no lower branching. Ha, ha, don't you think so, Swyllo, my friend? Oh, yes, of course you do... He is such a toxx, is he not?"

"I resent that slander to my primo body, but I will ignore your silliness in honor of our missing friend," Milyr said with a pretended affront in his tone so easily recognized by Lyndyn, and then as Nyba peeled the garment down his tall figure, the young man sighed emphatically, "Oh, yeah...that's cherp... Feels like diving into a reccing pool back on Steppingstone Quinto... Oh, yes...so much cooler now... Thanks, Cap Nyba, now my vulching primo body can breathe at last."

"Milyr, you toxx!" Whyvvi shrieked with startled gaiety. "You are not wearing your JMOs. You toxx! You are vulching naked."

"What? I never wear JMOs in McAnderwike. It's much too nasty irritating and binding," Milyr explained with emphasis as he stepped his naked figure from the jumble of clothing at his feet. "You should know that from seeing me in locker rooms on Steppingstones when we dress before and then shower after our Pulseball games. Why such a reaction now, young fem?"

"I try not to notice at those other times," Whyvvi stated with feigned dignity.

"But in this darkness, you notice? I wonder what that means," Milyr chuckled.

As she performed same disrobing sequence for Domyn, Nyba said in a relatively Cap-like professional tone that impressed Lyndyn, "Milyr, you and

Domyn here are much different now than you once were. You are truly men physically. Even dreaded antemgebemarzex in our nutrient couldn't stop that transfiguration. Yes, and we women do notice change. We may not talk about the subject as much as you do, but we do notice, don't we, ladies?"

"I try not to, but it is hard sometimes not to notice," admitted Whyvvi, standing and gripping her chair for support. "But this toxx is so obnoxiously annoying when he is dressed, I do not particularly like to see him worse when he is undressed. Milyr, you are such a toxx."

"Oh my, yes, we do notice," Kymil agreed with her melodious voice slightly huskier than normal. "Including times when not on duty as your doctor. Now is everyone feeling cooler now? I'm most concerned with you men, for your bodies, though stronger, are more inclined to harm by overheating. Domyn, you are the biggest male here, how do you feel?"

At her question, Lyndyn turned his gaze towards the two young men standing near the emergency pilot console in center of the former ConCen. Their glistening sweating bodies were just barely visible in very dim illumination from console gauges and screens. Now as a limited light at the surface of the ocean waned as it was blocked by the deepening liquid above and the purket on the window, this console light was the only illumination in Wolf. Was that flicker on the console?

Domyn's deep voice answered, "Much better but still hot inside. I could use some water or nutrient. My muscles feel like I've just come out of stasis sleep. They are stiff and tight."

"Nutrient? Vulch, not me," declared Milyr, walking away around to the front of the console. "No more of that damn antemgebemarzex for me. I'll go thirsty before I take that again."

"Nutrient sounds good to me," Lyndyn exclaimed, glad to have a more normal stomach sensation and hint of appetite. "We should keep our stamina high. We've been using up much of our adrenaline stamina and also our stored body energy supply during the recent stressful days. Soon we'll become lethargic and feel so run down that we may give up. Nutrient for everyone, Doc, do you order?"

Doc Kymil agreed, "We must keep our bodies and minds strong in this crisis. We must be prepared to assist Fox Flash Alpha in our own rescue."

As she slipped out of her McAnderwike with help from Domyn, Nyba commanded, "Okay, then nutrient for all. Whyvvi, can you help Domyn get our drinks from the dispenser? And, Doc, what about Jamyk? Should we get him out of his McAnderwike? He is an annoying rascal, but I would not want to see him suffer with heat prostration."

"Oh my, yes, I'd almost forgotten about him. What an awful doctor I am!" Kymil scolded herself.

"Is little peener okay?" Milyr asked in genuine concern as he almost ran around the console to Jamyk's chair. "I haven't checked on the lad, some friend I am."

"You've both been responsibly busy recently. You should not feel guilty. If he was aware of what was going on around him, then Jamyk would understand you both had vital duties to perform. That's if he was aware. It often sounded like he was in some dream insulated from our reality. At least he has been quieter since this purket attached to our window," Lyndyn said while he assisted Kymil undress from her McAnderwike.

"We should keep close watch on this purket. We should be aware whether it begins to harm our window. Although thus far it seems to have repaired Justinex, but we do not know why this has occurred. There may be another nastier development to follow," Whyvvi speculated while she opened the front of her uniform as far away from Milyr as she could get in Wolf.

As Lyndyn gratefully inhaled Kymil's sweet womanly scent, he listened to Milyr click open Jamyk's harness and then ask, "Doc, we should undress him, right? He's got to be as hot as we were."

"Yes, we should. His smaller body should be just as hot. Sometimes boys his age cannot dispel their body heat as effectively as you men do. You may sweat like rutting bears, but it does help you cool your body and expel much of your internal heat. Younger bodies, smaller bodies are not as efficient. Go ahead, Milyr, get him undressed. His metabolism is usually much higher than the rest of us. I would guess that he is very warm now not being able to release his stored body energy with his usual strenuous activity."

"You mean, Doc, his usual annoying mischief," Nyba laughed as she kicked her discarded garment under a seat at the console, and Lyndyn observed a slight reddish glow of the console lights dimly shine on her blue JMO suit covering her squat torso.

"Hey, Nyba, he's my friend. Don't always goad him with those remarks," Milyr complained as his hand reached to unsnap the helmet from the neck guard and then suddenly swore, "Vulch, he's hot. I can feel it through the clothes. Vulching one nad must be boiling in there. No wonder he was making such tormented sounds before. Vulch, he's damn hot, Doc."

"Then get him out of that McAnderwike, Milyr. Let's get his skin exposed to this slightly cooler air in this Wolf," Kymil suggested.

As Milyr's long singers unsnapped the helmet and pulled it from the boy's head, Jamyk abruptly mumbled, "Swy...lo...lo."

"Vulch!" Milyr exclaimed startled and leaning back with a helmet in his hands. "He is asleep, right, Doc? I'm not bothering him now by doing this, am I? I don't want little one nad getting nasty mad with me. He may be small, but he can get nasty vicious when he gets goaded."

"Oh, I think he's asleep, probably just dreaming," Kymil chuckled. "You're doing him a favor by taking off that cooking attire, Milyr. You may be saving his life."

"Nutrient, Doc, Prof?" Whyvvi asked, handing them each a container of liquid. "How is this little peener doing? And who is the bare toxx nurse here. I do not recognize that ugly toxx. Oh, it is Milyr, self-absorbed egotistical toxx! What a shock, he is aiding someone for change."

"Yeah, yeah, fine fem...make fun of Milyr!" the lanky young man chuckled while peeling the top half of Jamyk's McAnderwike from the thin, slack boy's arms and shoulders. "I think you just can't stop ogling this sexy, manly body. My manly shape must be goading you something awful, fine fem."

"No, no, nurse Milyr. I do not find that skinny sapling of body either sexy or manly, is that not right, Swyllo? In fact the only manly form in my sight at this moment is the little boy in the chair in front of you. He is so much manlier than you are, Milyr," Whyvvi teased with a giggle while she turned to vanish into the darkness of the back of Wolf.

"Ha, ha, fine fem, very funny!" Milyr said sarcastically. "Don't try to goad me into deserting my friend here by making me jealous. If I had to choose between his friendship and your fine body, then I'd have to start drinking that vulching nutrient to ensure that I could resist your bodacious form, Whyvvi. But I would never desert my best friend here, even for such a fine fem."

As his large figure in tan JMO shorts came out of the darkness, Domyn asked, "Is Jamyk awright, Doc? Is the lad going to get healthier soon?"

Kymil replied, "He seems to be okay, Domyn. My new nurse reports the boy's body temp is very hot. However, all other vital signs seem okay, as well as I can determine. We should be able to cool him now that he is undressed. Do you have some nutrient for him? Get that into his system and he should be as healthy as an unconscious boy can be."

"Do you know why he's still sleeping? Have we tried to awaken him recently?" Domyn asked.

"No, and that does worry me," Kymil replied, stepping to kneel beside the thin glistening body with green JMO shorts, color barely discernible to Lyndyn's eyesight in the poor light of Wolf. "I'm not sure whether to try to wake him, but I do not like this prolonged sleep for him. It is not his norm to sleep for so long. He is normally the first and fastest of us to awaken."

"His skin is very hot, Doc. But he is sweating freely," Milyr reported as he finished pulling the jumbled McAnderwike from Jamyk's feet and tossing it aside. "Hey, little peener, do you hear me?"

When Jamyk did not reply, Lyndyn stepped behind Domyn toward Jamyk's chair and advised, "Let's try to get some nutrient into the lad. You should take some also, Milyr. Show him how to do it."

"No, no more of that vulching nasty!" Milyr declared, settling back on his haunches in front of Jamyk's chair, a faint glimmer of the console lights glinting off his wet back. "Give my share to Jamyk. You like the nasty drink, right one, nad?"

"There is plenty of nutrient drink. We don't have shares," Nyba sighed, sitting in her captain's chair. "You must drink, Milyr, for your own health. We want you to stay alive and healthy for our future. You must drink some nutrient now. I want your manly body to be nourished when Fox Flash comes to rescue us. Think of all the vixens on Fox Flash that will mourn your withered manliness if you die."

"Oh, yeah, Nyba, that will really motivate me. Vulching vixens won't get near me, will they?" Milyr inquired with a slight snicker to his voice. "And if I refuse, are you going to punish me?"

"We could throw you out the hatch," Whyvvi suggested with a stoic calm.

While he helped Kymil and Domyn trickle the nutrient into the mouth of the sleeping boy, Lyndyn heard Milyr chuckle, "Oh, vulch, that makes sense. How do you plan to do that without filling Wolf with acid from this vulching ocean? Really well-planned, fine fem!"

"You only punish yourself, Milyr, by not keeping up your stamina and strength," Nyba said calmly. "You will need that stamina and strength when we are rescued."

"Rescued? Nyba, do you really believe we'll be rescued?" Milyr asked in a suddenly agitated tone as he arose from his knees and walked hastily between the window and console.

"There is always hope of that," Nyba stated.

While listening to this, Lyndyn felt a hot flesh on Jamyk's arm and asked, "Kymil, isn't he too hot still? Feels like a fever, but he hasn't contacted any virus in here to trigger a fever. What's going on? Is this normal for this young lad to be so much more affected by these surroundings than the rest of us? What could be causing this long sleep and this very heated flesh?"

Kymil brushed his arm when she bent over to check Jamyk again and replied, "I'm not sure. That's correct that there should be no fever. This long-lasting comatose-like sleep is beyond my experience. I believe that we need to cool his temp, but I don't know why he's so much hotter than the rest of us. I'm sorry, but I just don't know."

"Maybe we could fan him," Domyn suggested.

"Or bathe him with vulching nutrient you all want to sterilize me with," Milyr snorted half-heartedly, pacing against the darkened purple window. "Give him my nutrient if it will help him. I don't mind sacrificing that for my best friend."

Strolling behind Milyr along the curve of the window in front of Wolf, Whyvvi giggled, "Not much to sterilize from what I can see. Not much of a sacrifice…"

"Vulching…ha…ha…" Milyr chortled, walking away from Whyvvi toward the other side of the console nearer to his regular chair. "It's too vulching dark in here to see anything. You only wish you could see my manliness, fine fem. Don't goad me now. You won't like me when I get whipped!"

"Well, now making your toxx whipped does sound like cherp fun," Whyvvi laughed loudly.

Watching the vague form of Whyvvi move along the window in slow pursuit of Milyr around the pilot console, Lyndyn heard Kymil say, "Perhaps nutrient is cooler than his body temp and can serve as an external coolant. We could try that for awhile. That's not such a silly notion, Milyr. We don't want the rascal to actually die on us, now do we? How is our temp in here now?"

"Milyr, what is our internal temp now?" Nyba asked as the young man neared the empty pilot seat. "While you are there, Milyr, report the outer hull temp as well."

Milyr leaned his gleaming bald head down toward the faintly glowing console and said, "It is vulching hard to read these gauges now, Nyba. I think the inside temp is still over 100. I'm not certain about the hull temp, but it looks like the top and bottom temps are about the same and hotter than in here. We're losing lights quickly now, Nyba. Gauges are difficult to read."

As he peered toward Milyr, Lyndyn asked abruptly, "Are you still sweating, Milyr? I know I am and Jamyk is. I can feel us. How about you, are you sweating?"

"Vulch, Prof, what's that about? Of course I'm sweating. Have been for hours," Milyr replied in bewilderment and slight annoyance. "I'm sweating my nads off still like before."

Lyndyn announced matter-of-factly, "I can't see the reflected gleam of your sweat any longer. The console lights are fading fast. If we need to check anything that requires those lights, we should do it now before Wolf is totally dark in here."

Domyn stood up beside Lyndyn hastily and inquired, "Whyvvi, can you see into the window? Can you see well enough to determine the status of fissures caused by the trings? We haven't checked on that for awhile."

Halting her pursuit of Milyr around the console, Whyvvi turned toward the large curved window and exclaimed in some disappointment, "I was having such fun, Domyn, chasing this naked toxx... Well, let me look... It is hard to see...but I cannot see any cracks in Justinex, I think fissures have been repaired somehow. I am not totally sure though. The light here is very poor."

Walking quickly and closely to the window, Domyn said with satisfaction after a brief inspection, "Yes, awright, it looks solid here, too. I believe that Justinex has been sealed or mended or whatever we want to call it by that purket that dissolved the trings. By the way, the window is very hot to the touch. I guess we won't be getting any relief from heat any time soon."

"Oh my, then I'd better start bathing Jamyk with nutrient while it is still cooler than air temp," Kymil stated almost to herself, and then she asked, "Lyndyn, would you get more nutrient for me? I will need as much as you can carry please."

"No doubt, my kind Kymil, my useless old body can do this task. You will do what you can for the boy," Lyndyn replied and turned toward the back of Wolf.

As he did so, his gaze witnessed the tall lanky figure of Milyr suddenly vanish beside the console, and he heard a baritone voice groan, "Vulch, our console power is gone. We're in black dark nasty for sure now."

Pausing in his steps toward the hatch and the back wall of Wolf, Lyndyn heard Nyba ask almost hesitantly, reluctantly, "Neer, does this mean that we are completely out of energy reserve now?"

The deep voice of the big man answered from the darkness, "Yes, Nyba. Awe help us, this includes a life support systems as well. It seems as if our Wolf has begun to quit."

"Including the air purification system?" Nyba inquired with despair.

"Yes, Cap Nyba, that system is done now," Domyn announced from darkness near the window.

"How long do we have with cherp air?" Whyvvi whispered with uncertainty.

"Awe hopefully we can have maybe two hours with this many active people and this relatively small confined volume of air," Domyn replied in a hushed pessimistic voice.

"Two hours for rescue?"

"Vulch, I guess it's too late to go off nutrient now. Won't have any need for my manliness now."

"Milyr, come sit by me. Domyn won't mind if you use his chair. Now, before you fall over the chairs. That's an order, pilot."

"Vulch, it's dark in here!"

"Swy...lo...elp... Swy...cum...elp..." a raspy voice mumbled.

"Oh my!" Kymil moaned as her hand found Lyndyn's in the darkness.

SPEC THREE: LYNDYN ON WYLLOS
CHAPTER 27

"I am afraid," Whyvvi admitted humbly from the darkness.

"So am I," Domyn said. "Follow my voice. Come to me."

"Domyn, you should never say that you are afraid," Whyvvi scolded as her voice moved somewhere between the pilot console and window. "You should be brave always. I need you to be brave. We all need you to be brave."

Slowly stepping away from the nutrient dispenser and carefully carrying two cups in each hand, Lyndyn paused in complete darkness and said, "Whyvvi, most often bravery is accepting your fears and then overcoming them."

"Still trying psychological trickery on me, Prof?" Whyvvi asked in a trembling voice. "You are as sneaky as clever Swyllo...used...to be."

Closer than Whyvvi's voice, Nyba said, "Here, Milyr, give me your hand. I'll lead you to Domyn's brown chair. You really should sit down and conserve your energy. Your muscles must be getting stiff just standing there in the dark for several minutes. Come here, young man."

Using voices to orient his steps, Lyndyn cautiously walked toward the left side of Wolf where he had left Kymil and Jamyk not long ago, and he listened to Domyn say, "Go ahead, Milyr, sit in my chair. I'm staying here with Whyvvi. We're pretending to be brave."

"Don't say that!" hissed Whyvvi, and then Lyndyn heard the slap of a hand striking solid flesh.

"Ouch! Awright, enough of that! You are definitely getting like Swyllo!" Domyn declared with a pained chuckle. "Here, clutch to me. I'll be brave for you, if that is what you wish of me."

Whyvvi sighed shortly, "I feel better already. However, I really miss Swyllo. I wonder where her tiny iota of awareness is now. Do you know where that could be, Domyn, my big brave philosophical engineer? Where could her awareness be now? Can we go there with her if we do not get rescued from this Wolf in time? Can we go there together, my brave man?"

"Oh my, those words have such romance to them, don't they, my kindred spirit?" Kymil sighed.

"I do not know for sure. I would like to believe that she is near enough to help us rejoin universal awareness with her if we…do…not…" the big man's voice whispered and then gradually dropped below Lyndyn's hearing.

Instead, as he approached Nyba's chair, he heard Milyr admit grudgingly, "Okay, okay, Nyba, I'll sit down. But I can't see a thing now in this vulching blackness. Where's your hand?"

Then Kymil called out softly, "This way, Lyndyn. Follow my voice. I can see your PEQA to guide you in this darkness. I will take care of you."

Turning toward her voice and brushing against the chairs between Nyba and Jamyk, Lyndyn gradually found his way. Since the console lights had gone out, inside of Wolf was as dark as a moonless, starless, midnight. No reflective surfaces, no dim light sources, not even a window provided any trace of sunlight from the Sexto System star above this moon. Obviously Wolf was submerged deep into the acid ocean. No doubt a purket on the outside of the window was blocking what little light reached this depth.

"Oh! No, not there, you toxx, that's me on my chair," Nyba yelled scornfully.

"Vulch, I'm sorry, Nyba. I have to feel my way in this darkness," Milyr apologized.

"Yes, Milyr, now you've got my hand. Just swirl your skinny toxx a little to your left. You should be able to sit it into the next chair," Nyba said, guiding his movements.

Lyndyn heard naked flesh slap heavily into the chair and Milyr groaned, "Ugh! Vulch, this chair was closer than I thought. Ah, so this is what Neer's view looks like. This looks so cherp here!"

"Awright, my friend," Domyn scoffed with an abrupt chuckle, "usually you could see so much more. Someday after we get out of this, perhaps you'll see the real view in daylight, hey?"

"Oh, that would be cherp," Nyba exclaimed in feigned gaiety. "Milyr next to me for real!"

"Vulch, Nyba, is that any way to talk about my primo self now that you've invited me here?"

"One more step, Lyndyn," Kymil directed from her position beside the chair in which Jamyk sat sleeping still, though with restless movements and noises in the dark.

"I'm coming carefully with cups of nutrient, kind Kymil, for our patient," Lyndyn said tiredly.

As he carefully stepped, Lyndyn heard Milyr ask with doubt, "So Domyn, do you still believe we'll get out of this vulching mess? Doesn't look cherp from my view, I'm afraid."

"Of course we'll be rescued," Nyba asserted boldly. "That's the plan. We behave as if we will be rescued. Until we are all dead and mere iotas of awareness, we will plan to be rescued."

"Vulch, then I'd better stop drinking the nasty nutrient and vulching antemgebemarzex," Milyr declared. "If I can keep my manly dreams alive, then maybe I can motivate myself to survive. That's my vulching plan! I'm not a stupid toxx to ruin my nads if I have a future."

"Any motivation to survive is useful motivation," Lyndyn said while he knelt beside Kymil and handed her two of cups of the nutrient. "No doubt everyone should restrict movement as much as possible. We must calm our bodies, slow our metabolisms. Conserve our breathable air for as long as we can. This is one time where we would be wise to settle somewhere and be lazy. No one should be alone now, my young friends, not at a time like this."

"Yes, and talk as little as possible," Kymil suggested, and Lyndyn heard a splatter as she plopped a cup of the nutrient onto Jamyk's chest. "Has everyone taken nutrient recently? We must keep up our body nutrition and water. Air is not our only concern."

"Milyr?" Nyba inquired emphatically. "Did you get your drink? Did you get one for me?"

"No vulching way," Milyr retorted. "Not in my plan."

"Your plan has little chance of success, you toxx," Whyvvi yelled from in front of the console. "Your dream of wild endless sex with colonial fems is not reality unless you survive. You need nutrient to survive. Your super large egotistical concept of yourself is not enough to sustain your manly body."

"She has a valid point, my friend," Domyn agreed from near Whyvvi's voice.

"Ahh, vulch, she just wants to ruin my nads with vulching antemgebemarzex," Milyr argued.

"Drink some nutrient," Nyba commanded. "How much worse can it be for your manliness now?"

"Not in my plan. Vulching nasty toxx will ruin my manly dreams," insisted Milyr adamantly.

"Perhaps your manly dreams can happen in spite of antemgebemarzex," Nyba suggested with a much more feminine tone than her normal authoritative voice. "I could help you perhaps."

"What…what…what do…you mean, Nyba?" stammered Milyr, sounding suddenly unsure.

Grinning to himself at the young man's sudden befuddlement, Lyndyn chuckled as he said, "No doubt, Milyr, you may get more than you could dream from the young ladies of this Wolf. Be careful how you respond now… My kind Kymil, does this resemble a dying man's wish scenario? Or am I reading too much into Nyba's words?"

Nyba stated with a snort, "This manly toxx believes that he is a dying man."

"Uhm…erh…vulch, aren't we all?" Milyr stammered. "We can't get out of this now."

As she splashed another cup of nutrient onto Jamyk's chest, Kymil replied, "Oh my, yes, in a way we are now in a dying man's scenario, my kindred spirit. How we spend time remaining is of importance to us now in these moments. This is one time when the present is most important."

"But what about conserving air?" Whyvvi whined. "We need this air to survive."

"Oh, yes, that is also important. However, as air becomes stale and we pass out, will stretching our time to another eleven minutes be of any value?" Kymil asked while she and Lyndyn swathed nutrient liquid over Jamyk's torso with their hands.

"It would give Khebol and Fox Flash Alpha those extra minutes to rescue us," Whyvvi argued.

"Possibly," Lyndyn conceded. "This is a choice you must make, my young friends. How do you spend what could very well be your last hours? I'm not trying to frighten you. This situation can do that itself. In my mind, it is a matter of quality of your existence now in these minutes. Only you can make that choice for yourself. You are adults now, my young friends."

"Yes, that is true," Nyba said suddenly, and with her usual decisiveness declared, "And at this moment, my choice is to get out of this wet clinging JMO. If Milyr can be totally free, then so can I."

With that declaration, Lyndyn heard her stand up and peel with a sloshing noise her full torso JMO down her body to the floor, and as her sudden quick movement unbalanced her stance, Milyr arose hastily to support her, exclaiming,

"Vulch, Nyba, be careful. If you move too sharply, you could trip or fall in these clothes in this darkness."

"Oh my," Kymil chimed with a mischievous tingle in her voice. "What a nice cute couple you two make standing there together. I never noticed that before."

"Vulch, you can see us?" Milyr asked in startled disbelief. "How? It's vulching black in here."

"Oh, you forget, Milyr, my PEQA sight," Kymil explained with a laugh. "I see the PEQA glow of everyone, even when normal visual range of light is absent. In a way, at this moment, you all appear as glowing ghosts shaped in your normal physiques. Oh my, it's quite a sight, very fascinating!"

"We look like ghosts?" Whyvvi wailed. "That's not cherp! A very nasty depiction, Doc, but, oh, can you see Swyllo? Is her iota of awareness anywhere around here?"

"No, my dear, I don't see Swyllo," Kymil chuckled as her hands brushed Lyndyn's while they continued to cool Jamyk's skin with liquid nutrient.

"Actually if Doc Kymil sees our PEQAs, then we can't be ghosts. PEQA corresponds to living beings, not dead ones or iotas of awareness, correct, Kymil?" Lyndyn explained and then hastily added, "Yet not that I actually believe in such metaphysical silliness. I'm too pragmatic for that."

"Oh my, yes, I see PEQAs from only living beings. And you, my young people, are still very much alive. Your PEQAs show quite strongly now. In fact my vision detects two very well-matched PEQA couples on this Wolf at this moment," Kymil exclaimed in her matronly mature voice, a voice Lyndyn was well aware of during their long acquaintance in Blue Jay since their travels on Turkey Trot Alpha.

"Are you suggesting...?" Milyr squawked in disbelief until Nyba slapped some part of his flesh.

"This JMO is getting annoying," Whyvvi declared, interrupting his cry and then asked, "How about yours, Domyn? Never mind, it is saturated wet. I will get it off you. You just lay there."

As the big man grunted in a deep growl, the other young man asked a bit modestly, "You can see my physique? How do I look? Am I healthy, Doc?"

"You feel fine," Nyba announced.

"You look very manly, Milyr. You will no doubt like to learn that PEQAs always look larger by about five inches per body surface. You look well filled out by my PEQA vision, Milyr. Perhaps what you'll look like in middle age," Kymil said, pouring another cup of nutrient onto Jamyk and some of splash wetted Lyndyn, who was enjoying the way she teased and led the lanky young man with her words.

"Does everything look bigger all around?" Milyr inquired sheepishly.

"Oh my, yes, Milyr, all of you looks larger. PEQA does not discriminate against any body part or shape," Kymil laughed. "Believe me that you are a handsome young man, at least according to your PEQA. The rest is your making and the young woman who will have you in her clutches soon."

"Then I must look like really fat nasty," Nyba whined forlornly.

"You don't feel fat," Milyr exclaimed. "Are you the young woman who will get me in her clutch?"

"No, no, Nyba, your PEQA glow presents you as squat, yes, but very fit, very vigorous, very powerful," Kymil said hastily, and good recovery, thought Lyndyn. "Forget your shape. Help Milyr."

"If I look large and filled out, then Domyn must look...giganormous," Milyr laughed.

"Giganormous?" Whyvvi wailed in dismay. "Where did that come from?"

"Yeah, fine fem, he's more than gigantic, more than enormous," Milyr explained. "If you can term the trings and purkets, then I can term my big friend...giganormous."

"Vulch, Milyr, that's ridiculous," Whyvvi yelled but then momentarily changed her mind and agreed abruptly, "But yes...now I sense...that Domyn can be termed...giganormous... You are truly a big man, my Domyn...giganormous is very appropriate..."

"Ugh! Awright, that's enough," Domyn complained with a throaty huff from the darkness, but Lyndyn was unsure if the young man was referring to the questionable label or something else.

"Now, Milyr, can I persuade you to drink some nutrient to strengthen your stamina?" Nyba inquired with determination in her husky voice. "Come on now, young man, I'm your Cap, remember."

"Erh...uh...it's not...on my plan," Milyr argued. "But let's sit down again and come to an understanding. I'll be willing to see your point of view, maybe."

"No, my toxx is pained of sitting. We'll just lie down on the cushioned floor near the hatch. We can stretch out, roll around like pups again. We can get to know each other," Nyba suggested.

"Uh...erh...you are Cap," and Lyndyn was certain he heard a gulp in Milyr's voice.

"Yes, I am. Now remember, Milyr, our discussions concern your drinking nutrient. Keep that in mind. Don't try to get away with anything else. I am in charge here," Nyba demanded firmly.

"Uh…choice, Prof said it was about choice," Milyr quipped as he stalled and then asked, "Prof, you are mature. What would you choose to do in your last hours? Suppose you and Doc were alone."

"Milyr!" Nyba scolded impatiently. "That's nasty rude to Prof. Besides we can come to an arrangement between the two of us here now. Are you worried that I'm too much Cap now?"

With no hesitancy, Lyndyn stated, "Indeed. There's no nasty here, Cap. Under these circumstances, both Kymil and I will choose to serve you young people. Don't you agree, Kymil?"

"No question, my kindred spirit," she admitted, clasping his hand over Jamyk's hot torso.

"Milyr?" Nyba demanded harshly. "Is that necessary now? Can't you focus on me now?"

"But… Prof, what if you two were alone? What if we were not here as your responsibilities, then what would you elders believe?" Whyvvi asked from beyond the console near the window.

"Are you asking if we'd finish our lives having sex?" Kymil inquired patiently, swabbing Jamyk's torso with nutrient, and Lyndyn helped her as he grinned and was reminded of her often blunt, unexpected comments.

"Well, yes," Domyn answered in his deep voice. "My friends are trying to be discreet and respectful, but the subject comes up once in awhile when you are not around. If we're in our last hour, then we'd like to understand your relationship better. You two seem so…wonderfully together always."

"No doubt I am certain that in recent years, as your bodies and knowledge have matured in spite of inhibition of antemgebemarzex, you have wondered if we ever found a way to enjoy sex while under Blue Jay restriction," Lyndyn suggested with a slight chuckle.

"Awright, well…yes," Domyn replied with a low huffing gasp to his breath as Whyvvi giggled.

Kymil laughed politely, with gaiety, "Oh my, yes, my young friends. There are always means and situations when an inhibitor cannot prevent enjoyment of the shared act. You have to work more vigorously to get your…parts…to work as nature designed when you don't have a flush of hormones to force your bodies into the act. But if you really love your partner, if you really care about your partner, acts of sex, even without hormonal persuasion, can be enjoyable. The key is shared bond, almost spiritual bond between two partners."

"We have to have a spiritual bond?" Whyvvi asked with sudden concern and disappointment in her voice. "Do I have to really believe in universal awareness ideas?"

"And like and love our partner?" Nyba groaned in despair.

"Oh, now I'm hurt," Milyr moaned sarcastically. "You don't love me? What a surprise!"

Laughing in spite of his nasal snorts, Lyndyn said, "Indeed you don't realize this, but no doubt you all have deep bonds with everyone on Wolf Streak Beta and most likely Fox Flash Alpha as well. We don't view spiritual as the religious term or even deep psychic sensation. No, my young friends, spiritual bonds are those between very close friends...of very, very close friends..."

"Yes, and over time these ties can become very strong and very deep, no matter how they are ignored or refused by each other. I'm certain everyone here deeply misses Swyllo...and everyone here, especially you Milyr, cares deeply about Jamyk. Even you, Nyba," Kymil said, then stopped herself and added, "But we are talking too much. We should be conserving our air by not talking as much."

"Did they just dodge our question?" Milyr asked.

"Doesn't matter, you toxx," Nyba demanded. "Come back here with me. Let's test Prof's theory. Let's study if we have enough spiritual bonding between us."

Whyvvi asked demurely, "Are you up for the experiment, my big engineer?"

When neither the young man answered aloud, Wolf became silent, and Lyndyn turned his attention to Kymil and her patient, "How's he doing? Is this bathing helping any?"

"His temp is high still, but I don't feel any skin clamminess for a boy his age during normal sweating," Kymil replied. "I think the slight coolant effect of nutrient is helping, but I have no readable thermometer to use as a check."

"There's none in first-aid kit?" Lyndyn asked, the patting wet skin on Jamyk's shoulder.

"Oh, yes, they are there but are not readable in this lack of light," she responded, taking his hand and placing it on the boy's neck. "Give me your opinion of his temp. I'm concerned that my touch sensation may be acclimating to his temp and cannot be trusted now."

"No doubt, that is the least I could to help our little rascal now," Lyndyn whispered.

While he felt the skin on Jamyk's neck, Lyndyn heard Nyba whisper from the darkness, "...To touch man...never...thought... I would..."

Milyr's attempted whisper reached his ears more clearly, "I don't mind being your experimental specimen. Oh! Such hot soft hands for a scientist captain..."

"Indeed Jamyk's temp seems hotter than mine and environment in this Wolf. That means it's hotter than he should be. But you are doing everything you can to keep him cooler," Lyndyn told her, and then added with an almost silent whisper near her ear, "Do you believe that we were right pushing others in the sex direction? Do you think they know what to do? Is it appropriate now?"

With a merry chuckle, Kymil whispered, "Don't worry, my kindred spirit. They've seen enough sex education holos since they entered early puberty. I'm sure they've learned some things on Steppingstones in spite of Blue Jay supervision. We did, don't you remember our days on Turkey Trot? They may be novices in practice, but natural instincts and just old-fashioned play will guide them to some enjoyment in the little time they may have left. And besides, can you think of any better way to share your last hours of life with a friend?"

From the darkness, Nyba's voice rose slightly as she exclaimed, "Oh...see antemgebemarzex hasn't totally inhibited you... Oh, that's what...feels...like..."

"No doubt seems you are correct," Lyndyn sighed. "Yet I'm having a disturbing time now accepting that this could be our last hour alive. You are so calm going about your duty with this boy, as if there is going to be a future for all of us. You are amazing, Kymil. You are angel of warmth for these young people... and me."

Nyba's voice whispered, "Oh...yes... I...spiritual...bond...you..."

"Bond maybe... like we do... I'm vulching hotter now...but it's cherp," Milyr moaned softly.

"Oh my, Lyndyn, I have to believe that we do have a future. My very being is for all of you here. You most of all, of course," Kymil whispered, then softly giggled, "We never did answer them about what we would do if we were here alone, did we?"

"Not directly," Lyndyn whispered close to her ear. "Yet they seem to have grasped the general suggestion, haven't they? Would be nice to share each other physically one more time, wouldn't it?"

"Oh my, yes, it would. A physical joining certainly reinforces our other connection, my kindred spirit. Just being with you like this with the shared concern and empathy for this young boy and all others is almost as joyous as coupling," Kymil murmured, stroking his arms. "Almost."

From darkness, Nyba demanded in a hushed voice, "Now...nutrient...you... promised...if...we could stimulate...something...bonding...promised... Milyr."

"Oh, Nyba, do I have to?" whined Milyr in a low voice.

"You...deal...you...performed..." Nyba whispered adamantly.

"You are vulching tough," Milyr groaned softly, and then as his knees thudded on the floor, added, "See if I can find dispenser and then reach it."

"You are Cap, Nyba," Whyvvi cheered vocally suddenly from the darkness near the window.

"Vulch, she is," agreed Milyr ruefully. "This stubborn fem got me to drink this nasty stuff again."

"You didn't hear us, did you?" Nyba asked with alarm in her tone. "Everything, the whole time?"

"Milyr could not whisper if he was mute. Such a big toxx with a big mouth," Whyvvi exclaimed, giggling. "So apparently antemgebemarzex does not make a male totally nonfunctional."

Milyr groaned suddenly, "Whoa! Vulch! Dizzy."

Then Lyndyn heard a body topple heavily to the floor, and Nyba screamed, "Milyr, are you okay? You spilled nutrient all over us, you big toxx. Are you okay?"

"Uh...oh...dizzy suddenly when I turned from the dispenser," Milyr stammered. "But I'm cherp on the floor now. Vulch, that was weird. That was scary nasty."

"Air is getting stale... Carbon dioxide...is building up," Domyn gasped from the darkness near Whyvvi. "Us bigger men will be first, right, Doc?"

"Yes, Domyn, as your larger size needs more oxygen, you'll feel effects of the stale air soonest. Just lay still. Take it easy. Move as little as possible. Try not to talk much," Kymil stated.

"I will cuddle with you, Domyn. You are not alone," Whyvvi murmured. "When Khebol and Fox Flash Alpha get here, I will order him here first with oxygen for you."

"We should all limit movement as much as possible," Lyndyn instructed. "We have a hope of rescue still. Your universal awareness metaphy hasn't forgotten us, has he, Domyn?"

"No...of course...not, but...I'm not sure if...it works that way...and not sure if...it is he...not sure...haven't thought...that far ahead...yet...just pray...maybe get help.... Just believe...we are all...connected ..." Domyn stammered breathlessly.

"Of course we are. Now, you big men, rest quietly and save your breath," Kymil commanded with motherly authority.

Nyba declared, "Whyvvi and I will make them stay still. I don't want you dying on me now that I truly know you, Milyr. Now that we have a spiritual relationship, I intend to hold your bond close."

"Spirit...uh...what..." Milyr stuttered.

"Doc said to be silent and lay still," Nyba asserted firmly and then chuckled maliciously, "Would you rather that I squeeze or be playful?"

"Argh!... Ahh!... Playful," Milyr croaked hastily with a panting breath. "Don't...hurt...me...bonder."

"Then lay still and shut your mouth," Nyba commanded. "You're in my hand now."

"Oh my," Kymil exclaimed abruptly with a startled voice. "My eyes must be suffering already."

"Why? What's happening? Tell me, Kymil. Your eyes are the only useful ones in Wolf now," Lyndyn said, gripping her wet shoulders in his hands.

"Oh my, another!" she declared almost as if astounded. "This is not possible!"

"What do you see? I see nothing. It must be the PEQA sight," Lyndyn remarked, worried for her.

"His PEQA just flashed twice. Like, like, pulsations I saw in LaOgres. Maybe and shine," she whispered in uncertainty. "I must be suffering oxygen deprivation, Lyndyn."

Lowering his voice to a nasal whisper, he asked with doubt, "A Szczygiel Shine? Through PEQA? How likely is that? You should be one of the last to be affected by oxygen deprivation. Do you have a headache? How's your respiration? Do you have any other visual pain?"

Nervously, not at all the steady professional woman he knew, Kymil muttered, "I... I feel fine in all my normal vitals. I checked myself out just a few minutes ago. But, Lyndyn, I did see what looked like Szczygiel Shine pulsate into his PEQA. That sounds crazy, but my vision registered it. Either it happened or my vision is a problem now. I'm scared."

"Don't worry," Lyndyn said calmly as his mind buzzed with frantic worry, and his stomach felt as if it rose into his chest, and then he asked, "What about my PEQA? Does it look normal to you? What about the others? Check your PEQA sight with your memory of our PEQAs."

"Is Doc okay?" Whyvvi asked with obvious concern.

"Just checking her vision," Lyndyn explained with a slight lie. "Because of the air situation."

As her head turned just above his hands, still grasping her shoulders, Kymil replied with some confidence, "You look normal... I can see Nyba and Milyr. They look normal together. And now Jamyk's PEQA is as it has been since the awful time with Swyllo. Perhaps I imagined it, or my brain is starting to be affected by lack of oxygen. However, I should withstand that deprivation longer than you."

"Do you believe that your PEQA sight is stable now?" Lyndyn asked with hope rising in his heart. "No other visual flashes elsewhere? Inside Wolf? Outside Wolf? Anywhere?"

"No, Lyndyn, my normal vision shows everywhere as darkness just as I'm sure yours does," Kymil responded, then after a pause added, "Though several minutes ago, I thought I saw one of those aqua spheres glow just outside the window. But I didn't think anything of it. When I looked again, it was gone. That I thought was my imagination. Maybe this was, too. I should not see those aqua spheres unless they do have some strong form of iridescence or are living beings, but that is not likely."

"Indeed, as long as you feel fine, I'm satisfied with imagination as the answer. I've never been one to believe Szczygiel Shine as a natural human phenomenon. I certainly do not believe that one could be seen shining through the PEQA. That is almost absurd, not that I'm accusing you, my Kymil," Lyndyn said hastily once he realized what he had just suggested.

"Shine...saw shine?" Domyn asked weakly from the darkness in front of the console.

"No one, Domyn," Lyndyn said, trying to quiet the gasping man. "This is just a scientific discussion. Not at all useful at this moment! We're all starting to suffer oxygen deprivation. We all need to get settled and relax. Just rest now, my friend. Let Whyvvi comfort you."

"Was it about Jamyk?" Domyn asked meekly.

"Ja...Jamyk..." rasped a voice near Kymil. "Wake."

"Oh my, he startled me," Kymil exclaimed, shuddering beneath his hands.

Then the boy's legs wiggled against Lyndyn's legs, and Jamyk croaked hoarsely, "Swyllo?"

"Don't try to get up," Kymil insisted. "Stay in chair for now, Jamyk."

"Swyllo? You?" the boy rasped.

"No, Jamyk, it is me, Doc Kymil," Kymil said, gently bumping against Lyndyn to get closer to the boy, no doubt to inspect her patient as thoroughly as she could in this darkness.

"Your legs will be unsteady now," Lyndyn said, but the kicks he felt showed him the boy had energy. "Don't rush it, Jamyk. You've been unconscious for some time now. Go easy, please."

"Swyllo here?" the wriggling boy persisted, and his impatience was evident and determined.

"No, Jamyk, Swyllo is...gone now...she died," Lyndyn stammered, suddenly realizing the difficulty of speaking fact.

"Jamyk…is… Jamyk…awake?" Domyn stammered with a panting breath.

"Could have picked a better time," groaned Whyvvi sardonically from the darkness near Domyn.

Trying to position himself in front of the chair more squarely than he was, Lyndyn prepared himself to catch the boy if he was to stumble forward in a rush to stand, and Lyndyn said with emphasis, "Slow down, Jamyk, you'll find breathing is difficult now. We're low on oxygen. Take it slowly."

"Domyn…alive?" Jamyk asked, slipping from his chair into Lyndyn's arms. "Milyr…alive?"

From the darkness near the hatch, Milyr moaned with a heavy panting breathlessness, "Vulch…yeah…little…peener….spirit…bond…now…get… .you…soon."

"Jamyk…bad time… Breathe…hard….dizzy…tired…sleep….maybe," Domyn gasped.

"See… Domyn… now," Jamyk insisted, pushing against Lyndyn with surprising strength for one just awakening from a near comatose state. "Go to… Domyn."

Kymil brushed Lyndyn's arm and said, "Okay, Lyndyn, you might as well guide him there. With possible limited time left, we can't refuse. They are close friends."

"Where's Domyn located? I myself need guidance," Lyndyn complained, trying to hold the slippery squirming boy.

"I'll take him," Kymil volunteered. "I can see Domyn's PEQA clearly."

But as they attempted to reposition themselves, Jamyk wriggled free, escaped Lyndyn's grasp, and shortly was saying from the darkness near the window, "Good, Domyn alive."

"Argh!... Don't…hug…so hard," Domyn stammered. "Can't…breathe…easy."

"I…love… Domyn…alive," Jamyk wept with obvious gulps from the darkness.

With a hint of a gulp or maybe a soft sob, Domyn murmured, "Love…you… too…friend."

"Sorry, Kymil, I just could not hold him. He's so full of stored energy it seems," Lyndyn explained.

"I'm surprised how he just ran straight to Domyn, avoiding console and Whyvvi. He went straight to Domyn in this blackness. He doesn't have PEQA sight," Kymil said with amazed confusion.

"Probably keyed in on the voice," Lyndyn replied but not convinced with his own answer.

Whyvvi yelled in annoyance, "Do not get so pushy, little peener, but it is cherp to have you awake again. We were all very worried about you."

"Cherp... Whyvvi alive," Jamyk rasped.

"Ugh! Do not hug me, you smelly toxx," Whyvvi complained in the dark.

Jamyk gasped, "Cherp... Whyvvi...bond Domyn."

"Don't know...how long...left now...friend...sleepy..." Domyn sighed, his deep voice fading.

"Help get...good air," Jamyk sputtered. "Help out there."

"No, there's only ocean out there now," Whyvvi stated tersely. "Only atmosphere is high up there somewhere and that is poisonous to us."

"Get air...help there," Jamyk mumbled insistently. "Soon...help."

"What help, Jamyk?" Lyndyn asked, wondering if the boy was really awake or perhaps actually walking in his sleep and still dreaming, or maybe hallucinating due to lack of oxygen. "Kymil, guide me to him please. I can't see anything, and my balance is always questionable in this darkness."

While Kymil gripped his arm and escorted him a few steps, Jamyk mumbled, "Out there...help waits...soon help...get air."

With a very weary weak voice Domyn gasped, "Listen...to...him... listen...to..."

"Domyn!" Whyvvi screamed suddenly. "Domyn, don't! Get out of the way, you little toxx."

"What's going on?" Milyr groaned.

After a moment, Nyba stammered, "Is...is...every...one okay? What's happening...over there?"

"Vulch, Doc, I think Domyn passed out," Whyvvi cried out in panic.

"Domyn alive..." Jamyk rasped. "Sleep...now."

"Sleep sounds good to me, too," Milyr yawned loudly. "But...I've...got to see...my little peener...help me up... Nyba please...spirit...bonder."

"Vulch, Milyr, you are too heavy now for me. I'm weak and dizzy myself. Let him come to us. Jamyk, we're too tired. Get your skinny toxx over here," Nyba commanded.

"If you're not...too weak from...you sleep," Milyr added, panting breathlessly.

As the thin form bumped into him, Lyndyn advised, "Slow down, Jamyk. Let Doc lead you to them if you must go there. Console and chairs are in the way. Don't move too fast. You'll get dizzy."

"I'm cherp," Jamyk croaked, but then said, almost as if he were appeasing elders, "Doc, help me please... Need to see...friend Milyr."

"What about Domyn?" Whyvvi whined. "We have lost my friend Swyllo already. I do not want to lose Domyn, too."

"As long as he's breathing, he is stable. What he needs is better air. We'll all need better air soon... Jamyk, give me your arm. Please don't rush me."

"Get air...." Jamyk asserted confidently. "Help...come."

"What help?" Lyndyn asked in frustration, wondering why and how this boy was now able to put more than a word or two together into phrases and also why he seemed so adamant about help coming. "Fox Flash? Colonials? What help, Jamyk?"

As his voice moved away in darkness, Jamyk replied hoarsely, "Foxes... Chitir...far away."

"My little peener," Milyr exclaimed in a husky gasping voice, "I'm vulching... glad to ...hear you... Can't see you...get your toxx...over here... Vulch, you're ...talking so much...now."

Jamyk giggled, "Milyr...little peener?"

"Ha!" Nyba laughed tiredly. "His mind is still sharp...for recently comatose sleeper. And just what Swyllo might say as barb."

"Hey...not...what I...meant," Milyr protested weakly, breathlessly, then grunted in the darkness, "Ommph...don't jump...on me...toxx."

"Love you...big toxx...cherp...you alive," Jamyk exclaimed with a cracking voice.

"Me, too...little toxx...you smell like...vulching nutrient," Milyr stammered, panting heavily.

"You smell...odd now...Milyr," Jamyk said with confusion. "New...stink..."

"Don't answer, Milyr," Nyba warned, "if he's lucky...and we are rescued soon...he can find out...for himself. Our rascal can get his own bonder."

"Nyba smell...odd," Jamyk stammered, "But...cherp...alive."

"Oh, you sticky rascal," Nyba whined. "Don't hug me. I don't like you that much."

"Like, Nyba," Jamyk croaked. "Help soon...help friends."

"I hope so...you...are...right....so...tired...hard...breathe..." Milyr whispered.

Hearing the young man's voice trail off, Lyndyn arose from his kneeling position beside Domyn and Whyvvi, but before he could speak, his sense of balance suddenly spun in his head. Dizziness attacked his equilibrium. He felt himself begin to fall. Automatically his hands and arms reached forward and caught against the front of the console.

Whyvvi cried out nearby in the darkness, "Prof, what is wrong? Are you okay?"

As his eyes saw the false mist of yellow-white stars, he thought he heard Jamyk mutter, "Cherp, Nyba bond Milyr."

Lyndyn was afraid that he would pass out, but his intuitive sense caused him to lower his head onto the top of the console, which was only about waist high. Consciousness wavered for a few seconds but held alert. However, his medical training told him not to move suddenly now, not to attempt to stand up again for awhile. He realized that he, too, was suffering oxygen deprivation.

From the muddled darkness around him, he heard the young woman shout again with more alarm, "Prof, are you okay? Doc, I think Prof just collapsed."

He could not let himself go yet. The young people needed him. He was not ready to relinquish his last awareness yet. He would probably never wake up. He was not ready to join Swyllo yet. The air was getting dangerously toxic now. If he went into unconsciousness, Doc Kymil would be left alone to help the young wards. He had to stay awake.

Then hands were tilting his weight backwards, and he heard a familiar voice say, "Let his head hang down, just don't drop him on it. He's air-headed enough already."

"Okay, Doc," another female voice replied. "It is cherp that you said that and not me. He can probably hear us."

"Y-y-yes, I can," Lyndyn stammered. "Thank you, ladies. Never passed out, Kymil. But I was very close and very dizzy. Looks like I'm going out soon, too. Sorry to leave you alone."

Another raspy voice said nearby, "Get air...soon help."

Jamyk? Yes, Jamyk had awakened just recently and could not stop asserting that help was coming. But from where? How could the boy know? Was Jamyk hallucinating? This toxx dizziness and lack of quality air made his thought process more confused, more scattered than normal. Would he be able to assist anymore?

"Try to stay with me longer, my kindred spirit. If Jamyk is right, I'll need help with this crew. Both Milyr and Nyba are now unconscious like Domyn. The rest of us can resist the inevitable only so long. We'll all be out within minutes..." Kymil was saying.

"Don't worry," Jamyk said confidently in his boyish cracking voice. "Help outside."

"Where? How can that be? We have heard no signal," Whyvvi protested vehemently but also gasping for air herself now. "Fox Flash has a sci-tech that could get a signal to us from the high orbit. The colonials could easily rap on the hull. We have heard no signal."

"No Fox Flash," Jamyk rasped again. "Far away."

"How's your dizziness now, Lyndyn?" Kymil inquired, leaning arm around his slumped shoulders.

Her simple touch enlivened his will and brought a smile to his face, so he said, "With you near, it can be endured. With you near, nothing can bother me. Not even almost certain death so close upon us can spoil the joy of having you near."

"That sounds so cherp," Whyvvi exclaimed wearily. "I should go to Domyn and hold him and say something like that...even if his is asleep now. Thank you, both of you, for all you have done for me and this crew... Thank you for being who you are... And you, too, Jamyk."

After that the young woman vanished from his awareness into the darkness. But soon another arm coiled behind his back and a hot sweaty head leaned against his side opposite Kymil. It had to be Jamyk. No one else felt so bony. The boy nestled tightly for sometime as they all sat silently in the darkness of Wolf.

Finally Jamyk said with a soft sigh, "Trust me...get help."

Surprised at the unusual number of words the boy had spoken, Lyndyn whispered weakly, "What? Do what? Jamyk, are you feeling okay?"

"Now yes...must do soon...before no air," Jamyk said, revealing his own fight for oxygen had begun. "Trust me."

"What must you do? Wolf can do nothing, no signals, not anything," Lyndyn gasped, feeling light-headedness attack again.

"What can we do, Jamyk?" Kymil inquired with puzzlement in her voice. "Wolf is but a shell now. We have nothing left but our feeble brains, and those are fading quickly."

"Trust me," the boy murmured against Lyndyn's side. "Believe me."

Then Jamyk swung his other arm around Lyndyn's chest, and with a thin arm behind, engulfed him in a tight hug for several seconds. As the boy performed this, his head bobbed into Lyndyn's side a few times. Lyndyn thought he heard very soft sobs but was not sure. They could have been gasps for oxygen. Yet the bald head felt hot against his sweating skin.

Abruptly Jamyk released his hug, slowly stood up, and rasped with a true gasp for breath, "I...must do now...before no air."

"Do what, Jamyk?" Lyndyn asked meekly.

"Bring help," Jamyk replied, and his footsteps moved into the darkness and then Lyndyn felt bony arms encircle Kymil with a hug, and then he whispered, "Thank... Kymil...save us."

"Oh my, my young man," Kymil gasped with a heavy gulp and then asked, "Save us how?"

"Open hatch," Jamyk answered, releasing his embrace and backing away hastily.

"No, you can't," Lyndyn tried to yell, but his weak breath would not allow that but only panic.

He felt Kymil stand up cautiously and heard her exclaim, "No, Jamyk, the ocean outside is acid."

"Trust me," the hoarse voice said farther into the darkness. "Only way."

"Is he...serious...opening...hatch?" Whyvvi complained in a feeble battle for air.

As clicks and whirls of the manual release of the inner hatch sounded in his ears, Lyndyn tried to shout, "No... Jamyk...it is not real...this is an illusion... Kymil, stop him..."

As her footsteps thudded around the console, she gasped, "No...stop...kill us... Jamyk."

Lyndyn listened in terror as the inner hatch swung open with metallic sounds that he had heard so often during his journey. Was this journey now about to end? He attempted to rise, to give chase, to help Kymil, but he had no energy. Her frantic gasps quickened and then he heard her stumble and fall upon the fleshy body.

"Stop... Jamyk...no!" she called out in the darkness of Wolf.

"Believe...trust," the boy rasped from the wall inside the only corridor between the inner and outer hatch now, only one keeping the acid ocean out.

"Vulch.... I never...planned to...die... like this..." whined Whyvvi breathlessly. "Swyllo? Are you there? Are you waiting for us? Or can you help us now?"

Then the sounds of the outer hatch opening struck his ears. Darkness deeper than the interior of Wolf threatened him.

Just before he lost consciousness, Lyndyn heard Kymil scream, "Oh my... he's gone."

Blackness!

SPEC THREE: LYNDYN ON WYLLOS
CHAPTER 28

"Are we dead?"

"We really should be dead now," the young woman's voice said.

"Is this after-life? Are we iotas of awareness now?" another young woman asked.

"Then where is Swyllo to greet us?"

As consciousness awoke, he realized that he felt neither heat nor cold on his skin. Then he wondered if he was even in his skin, in his body. No temperature sensation, was he dead? Was he some bodiless spirit, was he an iota of awareness? What was an iota of awareness?

"Oh my, I believe that we are alive," an angelic melodious voice chuckled.

The voice soothed his worry. The voice was somewhat familiar. The voice came from not far away in the vague yellow dimness before his eyes. Yes, he now felt his eyes move beneath the sleepy fluttering lids. Both hearing and sight sensations stimulated his consciousness. He was most likely alive, Lyndyn admitted to himself.

"Why do you think that?" the woman's voice asked.

"We really should be dead," the other declared. "The acid ocean should have killed us."

Acid ocean? What acid ocean? Where was he, Lyndyn wondered. What had happened? Why was he not awakening in saphyndenlairoum? Then he suddenly remembered the distressing, nauseating sensation that had attacked him sometime prior to sleeping. Nausea due to the ugly churning atmosphere and turbulent swaying waves in acidic ocean had disturbed him. Yes, there had been the acid ocean, he recalled now, and the hatch had been opened to this lethal acid ocean.

The angelic voice murmured nearby, "I believe we are alive because in afterlife, these sleepy males would not find it so difficult to awaken as they do in life. I'm certain that universal metaphy, or whatever Domyn wants to call it, would have cured the men of their habit of sleeping late."

As a feminine voice chuckled with gentleness that comforted his confused awareness, Lyndyn moaned briefly and moved his head. Yes, he felt his head swivel and nod slowly on his sore, stiff neck. Soreness, stiffness, movement, all sensations of bodily existence, his brain registered to his awakening consciousness. So he was alive. Indeed somehow he had survived the acid ocean.

"Oh my, this old timer is awakening finally," the angelic voice said, and then as fingers stroked his bald head and kneaded his stiff neck, the voice continued, "My kindred spirit, don't move too suddenly. You've been asleep for quite some time. Awaken slowly as if from stasis. You do remember saphyndenlairoum and the awakening sensations of that experience?"

Lyndyn tried to answer with dignity and lucidness, but his mouth could manage only, "In...eed...mem...ber...soooo...eepy...my...kin...mil."

"That's certainly not our Prof talking," giggled the young woman. "Sounds much more like Jamyk."

Jamyk? Jamyk? The acid ocean should have killed them, Lyndyn recalled with breathless terror. Jamyk opening the hatch, yes, he processed his memories, some intact some partial, some not committed because of trauma, but he could recall Jamyk opening the hatch. His brain analyzed his recent situation automatically and quickly. The oxygen deprivation, darkness, fear, the boy going to the hatch, sounds of the hatch opening, then he could remember nothing but blackness.

Yet he did remember enough of the events just before losing consciousness to ask now, "Alive? How? Jamyk...acid...how?"

"I'm not sure. I blacked out almost immediately then," a familiar angelic voice, his Kymil, replied. "But don't worry about that now. Let's get you fully awake. Let's make sure you are in reasonably good health. I believe that we will have plenty of time to discuss other things later."

While her hands massaged his neck and shoulders, Lyndyn fluttered his eyelids against sticky sleep and yellowish glow of light. Only off-colored yellow light, not intolerably bright, greeted his eyes. Above, below, in front, all around his eyes saw only one shade of yellow, no, not really yellow, more like darker golden, honey golden yellow. Not at all like Swyllo's bright yellow that had been vibrant in her chair and subtle in her clothes. Suddenly sadness afflicted his awareness at the memory of her death.

Then as he reminisced of Swyllo, his mind returned to his prior concern, and Lyndyn asked, "Jamyk? Is he here? What happened?"

"He is not here," Whyvvi replied. "He was gone when we awoke."

"Gone?" Lyndyn inquired surprised and worried as he sat up with Kymil's warm support at his back. "Is he dead? Have we lost the boy now just like we lost Swyllo?"

"We don't know," Nyba replied in a subdued almost painful tone, "I don't remember much. I passed out before anything of that happened. Last thing I recall was the rascal trying to hug me... I yelled at him... I said I didn't like him that much... I was toxx."

Hearing her voice trail off in discomfort, Lyndyn sensed that she felt guilt at her treatment of the boy, so he said in compassion, "It's not your fault, Nyba. Jamyk was acting strangely if my memory is correct. I had a feeling that he was saying good-bye, as if he thought that he must do something drastic to save us. But I myself was suffering lack of mental awareness at time, so my thoughts may be inaccurate... I did not do much to help him at that time either."

"I guess your mind is back to normal," Kymil suggested with laugh. "Your speaking habit has returned back to normal, even though I instructed you to talk very little for awhile."

"For Prof, that was relatively brief," Whyvvi giggled.

"Mmh! Now what does that mean?" Lyndyn feigned annoyance but then more seriously asked, "What about Jamyk? I seem to remember you saying something as I passed out. Did you see something then, Kymil? Do you remember?"

As he asked this, Lyndyn turned himself around, carefully kneeling on the warm soft surface. The golden yellow light was there behind Kymil as well. The first view of her since his awakening stirred him, especially with the honey golden lighting behind her. Her smile, her glittering eyes, her pert little nose, her perfectly proportioned feminine body naked before him, everything attractive to him about her sang to his mind. She was his angel in this golden idyllic! Then he laughed at himself for this metaphor of such a silly metaphysical notions.

Then a scowl of confusion distorted her face, and Kymil said with uncertainty, "My memories are...shaky... I, too, was having difficulty breathing. My eyes were tired and only my PEQA vision was somewhat reliable. I'm not sure what I saw or if I saw anything significant."

When he sensed an almost uncontrollable urge to reach out to her discomfort and soothe her turmoil with embrace, Lyndyn instead simply held her hands in his and encouraged, "No doubt it was a tough situation, my kind Kymil. But I feel and know that your remarkable memory and concern for all of this crew will allow you to recall eventually with confidence whatever you can. You are most reliable of all of us. You are the core of our Wolf Streak Beta family."

"Oh my, Lyndyn, don't start being a lame toxx," Kymil laughed and her hands gripped his firmly.

Whyvvi said hesitantly, almost shyly, "I do remember something, Doc. At least I think I do. I should remember better, but I think I heard you say something like 'he is gone.' Does that make any sense to you? Does that help you remember?"

With her warm hands still in his and her face with its puzzlement staring at him, Lyndyn said in confirmation, "Indeed that seems to stimulate memory in me also. Not much of one but something. Anything, my kind Kymil, do you recall anything, perhaps a vision of Jamyk in the hatch area?"

"Not any memory just before falling unconscious. Sorry, Lyndyn, my short-term memory probably did not activate neural stimulation due to trauma and oxygen deprivation. I'm sorry," Kymil apologized humbly with dissatisfaction in her tone and on her face.

"Don't stress over this. Even a doctor with rare PEQA sight is not immune to trauma and stress of what we have been through in this journey," Lyndyn said affectionately while gently rubbing her hands with his fingers. "That memory is not vital to us now. Perhaps caring for these here now is much more important. Are all our ladies in good health?"

After asking this question, Lyndyn cautiously rose to standing position, allowing Kymil to assist and steady him. At the same moment, he felt the soft cushion of the honey golden surface beneath his feet. Soft yet firm enough to support his weight, this surface was also just about the same temperature as his feet. At least, he thought, he could feel no significant difference in warmth or coolness. It was just comfortable, almost like human flesh.

Standing with him, Kymil replied with an attempted smile on her face, "Still I want to remember... But maybe if I don't focus on it now, yes, that always seems to work for me. As much as having your presence to stimulate me, my kindred spirit..."

"Now, old folks, do not forget that us young people are here still," Whyvvi exclaimed with true embarrassment. "All that clutching kind of talk about stimulating this or that is not for us to hear. Please not while we are around. It is uncomfortable enough with none of us having any JMOs or other clothes. We really do not want to see you act like that. You are older people now, not pups anymore."

For the first time since awakening, Lyndyn noticed that the young woman was correct. All six people in the honey golden enclosure were naked. Not a single piece of any type of clothing was to be seen. He saw the surface of the golden substance all around and six people. No clothes, no furniture, no equipment, nothing but remaining humans from Wolf Streak Beta. Six naked humans inside the strange golden...bubble?

"Is everyone okay health-wise?" he asked, peering down at the forms of Domyn and Milyr lying on the soft golden floor. "Are our men hurt? Are they okay?"

"As far as I can tell without my dionboda, we are all fit. Healthy as we can expect after our recent problems," Kymil replied. "Even our sleeping young men seem to be okay."

Slowly striding over the cushioned floor surface around the sleeping young men toward a side of the golden enclosure, Lyndyn asked, "Have they awakened yet? If not, do you think we should try to awaken them? Is this anything like what Jamyk had recently experienced in Wolf?"

While he hesitantly touched the curved inside of the enclosure and felt the same soft, cushiony warmth as the floor, Lyndyn listened to Kymil respond, "No, our boys have not yet awakened since we were in Wolf. And, Lyndyn, I think that we've been asleep at least as long as the saphyndenlairoum cycle."

With his hand pressing against the soft inner substance on the side, Lyndyn was sure that he could feel a solid unyielding structure beyond the soft layer, but her statement caused him to turn hastily, and he asked, "More than the stasis cycle? We've been asleep more than nineteen days? Is that possible? How can you know?"

Nyba chuckled, "Our young men told us."

"How did they do this? You said they haven't awakened," Lyndyn asked, instantly aware of the sudden giddy merriment passing between the three women.

"Normal medical ethics would not permit me to divulge personal secrets, not even to you, my kindred spirit. But under our present circumstances, I guess some personal secrets become well...exposed," Kymil stated, trying to retain a professional demeanor yet not succeeding very well in the presence of the younger giggling girls.

"What are you talking about? What could you have hidden from me all these years?" he inquired. "I thought that I knew everything about each of our people on Wolf Streak Beta."

Stooping over Domyn's face-down prone body, Whyvvi announced exuberantly giggling, "Look here, Prof. Our big muscular man has a tail."

"A what?" Lyndyn grimaced in disbelief, squatting down beside the girl who waved her hand at a spot at the base of Domyn's spine and just above his buttocks, and there he observed a tuft of hairs.

From beside Milyr's lanky figure sprawled face-up across the golden floor, Nyba giggled very heartily, "If you think that's strange, see what this toxx has got. And I can tell you it wasn't there when we were in Wolf."

Walking over the warm floor, Lyndyn paused to glance down at the prostrate young man. There not far below Nyba's finger was a line of curly hair between Milyr's navel and his crotch. Lyndyn's brain instantly informed him that such rare mutations to the attempted hairlessness procedures of all Blue Jay spacers were possible. It was likely that some crew members in a given mission period could have rogue hairs sprouting from their skin. After all humans were naturally endowed with hairy skin of various degrees, and to expect the Blue Jay project to totally negate this natural genetic trait was arrogant.

However, at the moment and more importantly, these hairy mutations were not just humorous growths but a true means to measure a passage of time without convenience of mechanical timepieces. These hairy growths provided them with definite time separation between the time they were in Wolf and now. These hairs needed certain time to grow to this visible stage. Kymil was right. They had been asleep for some long period of time.

"Indeed if we've been asleep for at least the stasis cycle," Lyndyn exclaimed, "then how can we have survived in this small...bubble...without recycled air? How could we survive without nutrient infusion or water? This makes no logical sense..."

Interrupting him curtly, Whyvvi declared as she sat beside Domyn and rubbed his broad back, "We must have passed some waste matter during sleep also. We did not see any around when we woke up. There should be some signs of natural human life activity and bodily functions here."

"That is another mystery. But there is not doubt that the hairy growths of our boys tell us that we were asleep at least nineteen days and possibly more," Kymil restated with conviction.

As he heard Milyr groan and mumble in his sleep behind him, Lyndyn watched Kymil's facial expression to confirm confidence in her voice, and then said, "It seems that you are telling me that this bubble has performed functions of saphyndenlairoum for us collectively. We should discover as much about this bubble as we can. This is our world for the moment. Until we can get out, if we chose to leave, we will live in here. Wherever here is…"

"That's very disheartening. We have journeyed over twenty-nine light years from our last inhabited Steppingstone. We have lost contact with our closest colleagues in Fox Flash Alpha. We have been attacked and rejected by colonials, as far as we can tell anyway. This is disheartening," Nyba said with disconsolation and a trace of anger.

"And we lost Swyllo and Jamyk," Whyvvi mourned.

"And I lost Wolf Streak Beta," Nyba admitted solemnly as she absent-mindedly traced her finger along the hair line on the abdomen of Milyr. "I wish I could have done better as captain for you."

"We lost Wolf for this, this bubble," Kymil murmured. "This very comfortable bubble that can function like saphyndenlairoum… However, will it prove to be a golden bubble of hope or a glorified tomb? We do not know yet, but you are correct, my kindred spirit. We must learn about this bubble."

"But where is this bubble? Where are we now?" Lyndyn muttered almost to himself while taking a few steps back to the curved inside of the bubble. "And did you notice, Kymil, an almost touch deprived feeling in here. I could not feel the floor while I was laying on it. This side surface feels the same temp as my hand. Is anyone else feeling this temp sensation? Am I imagining again?"

"Lyndyn, your touch sensation is accurate," Kymil replied, walking toward him. "We've all commented on that while you were asleep. This surface and most likely the air temp in this bubble is almost exactly the average human body temp. We've noticed no deviation either up or down, just about our normal body temp as compared to my own skin. Since I have no other device to measure the temp or any other physical characteristic in this bubble, I must rely upon my own senses."

"Nasty not having our sci-tech anymore," Nyba complained.

"Yes, we should have our Blue Jay sci-tech to study and analyze this new situation. But we do not even have a shell of our Wolf any longer," Whyvvi griped as she massaged the shoulder and neck muscles of Domyn's still sleeping body.

Not even Wolf any longer? All Blue Jay sci-tech was now gone, Lyndyn realized. All devices, the Dionjossad system, the Flandecams, three artigences, the holovision, the sanbeam transmitter and receptor, the zeta sensor system, and now even the Wolf escape pod, all had been lost to them. All their clothing, JMOs, dionbodas and dionjocus, McAnderwikes, all was gone now. They were as naked of their sci-tech as they were of their clothing. The only remnant of Wolf Streak Beta of Blue Jay was now them.

"We may not have our Blue Jay sci-tech with us, but we have our Blue Jay training and knowledge in our brains. That no doubt is something," Lyndyn exclaimed with as much encouragement as he could manage in his own slightly depressed state of mind.

As the big man lying beside Whyvvi turned over, his deep voice grumbled, "That…training…is based on…the sci-tech…and its…functionality."

"Do not move too quickly, Domyn," Whyvvi warned with concern as she tried to catch his rotating torso in her hug. "You have been asleep for while. Your body will need to go slowly at the moment. Let me help you."

While he contemplated Domyn's critical comment, Lyndyn pinched and plucked at the soft pliable surface of the bubble with his fingers and then abruptly exclaimed, "I can see my finger through this…stuff… Look here, Kymil, do you see this? It looks transparent."

Beside him, brushing against his raised arm, Kymil peered closely at the pinched material in his fingers and agreed, "Oh my, yes, I can see clearly through it. I see your finger. I wonder if it is all transparent. If it is, where is the color coming from?"

"Awe damn, it sure looks like the same yellowish-brown color of the acid ocean out the window," muttered Domyn with grogginess to his voice. "But this can't all be a window. And there's too much brightness in Wolf. What's happening? This doesn't look right now."

"We are not in Wolf," Whyvvi explained, leaning against his shoulder and back as he sat. "The Wolf is gone. You probably heard us talking about that just minutes ago, remember? All of Wolf Streak Beta is gone. Except us, of course, we are here still."

As he moved around inside of the bubble, studying the inner surface, Lyndyn heard Domyn reply with a groan, "Ugh! Yes…of course… I did hear you. This is just too much to accept right now. No more sci-tech? That's been my whole life…until now."

Lyndyn declared almost harshly, "No, Neer Domyn, your life was as a scientist, engineer, a man who could use his scientific training and knowledge to learn about and study science around him. I could use your skills now to help me study our current habitat."

"Awright, Prof, engineer and scientist needs tools and sci-tech to observe and measure his world and his science," Domyn mumbled pessimistically, "I have none of that now. Our sci-tech is gone. What is there for me to do now as engineer? My usefulness to Blue Jay is limited now."

"You are not useless to me, big man," Whyvvi declared sharply.

"My friend, you don't need your sci-tech to investigate our present environment. Just use your eyes and hands and that engineer's brain. If your scientific brain can rationalize about metaphysical awareness, then you can no doubt study this very real physical setting with me," Lyndyn prompted the young man firmly and hopefully with encouragement.

"Awright, Prof, I'll play for now. But you cheated with that metaphysical awareness line," Domyn replied, sighing slightly. "Awe well, my eyes tell me that this coloration looks just like the ocean on that moon before Wolf capsized and then submerged. This is just brighter than I remember, as if stronger sunshine. Yet my brain is still addled and sleepy. I may be confusing a memory of what was with what I can actually see now. Am I starting to sound too much like you, Prof?"

"That's a sure sign of being addled," Kymil laughed, following Lyndyn around the inside of the bubble, and then she called out, "Nyba, how is our other sleepy man? We should probably wake him now. More sleep will put him off our normal stasis cycle, or at least more than we would like."

"Not...asleep..." mumbled a hoarse, baritone voice. "Vulch...just...laying here...on top of this...cherp warm...young fem...trying...to feel...this soft... warmth...maybe mams... I'm laying on."

"That's interesting," Nyba declared loudly and sharply as she sat by his side, and then her hand patted his belly as she said, "Seems as if only your mind is dreaming of the young fem. Your manly body looks like just a lazy toxx! Rise and shine, my spirit bonder, and that's an order, pilot."

Watching the young man's eyelids open suddenly and widely, Lyndyn grinned to himself as he listened to Milyr stammer, "Erh!... Uh!... Nyba?... I thought... I was lying on you...in Wolf... What's going on here? Where are we? It's so bright now... We can see...everything?"

"Now yes, we can see everything of you, my spirit bonder," Nyba giggled, patting his belly.

"Well, yes, where are we? That is what we should be attempting to discover, you toxx," Whyvvi scolded and then stated with assurance, "At least Domyn has some reasonable ideas. Do you?"

With sleep in his voice still as he lay prone looking up from the floor, Milyr said, "Domyn always has reasonable ideas. Even if he's asleep, his brain can think so much faster than mine. I'm a very simple vulching man, young fem. Surely you must know that by now. Take me as I am."

"Hm! Not now," Nyba murmured. "There are more immediate actions we must perform now. Just get your toxx fully awake. We need to learn about our new situation."

"We're not vulching dead yet?" Milyr asked and then continued with a smoother tone and grin, "I was sure I was in heaven with you, Nyba. Are you sure all this golden light isn't heaven? And you are my own vulching personal angel?"

"If this were heavenly after-life, Milyr," Whyvvi exclaimed with firm conviction and merriment, "then I am sure that Swyllo and Jamyk should be here instead of your nasty toxx."

Milyr began with a cracking voice and real dismay, "Jamyk is not here? Where is he? He's not dead, is he? Oh, vulch, if I lost my best little peener friend…"

While only partially listening to the banter of the young people, Lyndyn continued his walk around the bubble. Each pinch of soft pliable surface revealed a transparent substance. Then with a press of his fingers, he felt the hard and hot solid surface beyond the inner surface. Golden patterns like designs of snowflakes seemed embedded and sometimes wavering within the soft surface. But his eyes were not sure which surface held these patterns. Yet they were beautifully intriguing, even to his pragmatic mind. Lyndyn mused laughingly at himself, were they the handiwork of some universal metaphy? Was he becoming infected with Domyn's philosophical disease?

Then as he plucked at another area of the inner surface, snowflake patterns departed suddenly, and Lyndyn thought that he observed aqua spheres float beyond the golden substance, and he exclaimed loudly, "Indeed, Domyn, you may have been right that this could be the acid ocean around us again. I think I have seen familiar things move outside our bubble. But I've not had much confidence in my eyesight recently. I could use some other younger eyes to confirm my observations."

"Awright, Prof, I'm not very optimistic just now, but I can try," Domyn muttered.

"Vulch, I need to urinate now really nasty strong," cursed Milyr abruptly. "I sure miss saphyndenlairoum at a moment like this. Usually don't have this vulching nasty sensation after awakening from stasis. A sweet piece of sci-tech just takes my fluid away for me. Vulch, I miss that."

Whyvvi yelled emphatically and hastily, "Do not just release anywhere, you toxx. This is not communal waste pail! Find a secluded spot."

"Vulch, what do I do?" Milyr shouted in frustration. "Didn't anyone else need to urinate after awakening? Vulch, it must have been a toxx nutrient you made me drink, Nyba."

"That was over nineteen days ago, Milyr," Nyba stated. "You have processed that nutrient through your system many days ago. Just walk over to the bubble side and release there. This bubble should absorb your urine. At least it did that for the rest of us. But you are a nasty toxx, maybe not."

"Very funny, Nyba! Vulch, nineteen days ago? That's a full stasis sleep cycle. We were out that long? How do you know?" Milyr asked in disbelief as he began to sit up.

When her hand reached toward his lower abdomen, Nyba chuckled, "Why, my young man, this cute hair showed us. You have such a cherp trail of curly hairs for a very uniquely rare trait of Blue Jay specimen. My own special Jayer, Milyr, you are a big toxx with a hairy belly."

Glimpsing the tall man peer down to his belly where Nyba's hand pattered, Lyndyn grinned as he listened to Milyr stammer, "Uh!...erh!... Vulch, we have been asleep for awhile. That's just my real manliness trying to escape the evils of vulching antemgebemarzex... Now where's latrine?"

"Here, over here is good enough," Nyba laughed, taking him by hand and leading him to a side away from the others surrounding Lyndyn and his inspection.

Beside Lyndyn now, Domyn said, "I do see some movement outside this bubble. Almost like a liquid current flow and small objects floating within this flow. There, did you see that? Was that something larger, something green?"

"Vulch, don't look, Nyba," Milyr complained boisterously. "I can't do it with you staring."

Kymil agreed, "Yes, Domyn, I did see those green objects. They seemed to glow with a similar iridescence as the trings."

Nyba laughed from the far side of the bubble, "Why now, don't be so shy, my manly male. This is your dream come true, is it not? Everyone will be naked perhaps for the rest of your life. Get used to it. Privacy will be very rare from now on. Now do your thing, you big manly toxx."

"Trings! No more trings," Whyvvi said emphatically while standing next to Domyn whose hands tested the bubble substance. "Please do not mention those toxx tiny nasty trings."

"Whoa! Vulch!" Milyr shouted abruptly in dismay and jumped away from the bubble side. "The vulching blue balls are back. Nasty things are right outside the bubble here. Vulch, guy can't urinate in peace anywhere. Vulch!"

"Just don't go on me," Nyba shrieked laughing.

Smiling to himself at Milyr's predicament, Lyndyn pushed on the soft inner layer of the bubble until his hands could feel the harder solid surface beyond, and then after a few seconds, said, "Quite hot, hotter than our environment in here. It is most likely the acid ocean, Domyn. You were right before. I believe that this bubble is somewhere in the acid ocean on the moon where Wolf crashed."

Following Lyndyn's technique of pushing against the bubble surface and then peering intently and closely at the golden colored layer, Domyn announced, "I believe that you are correct, Prof. All our recent observations suggest that this bubble is in the yellow acid ocean most likely on the moon of that super gas giant. How we got here from Wolf is still a mystery. But at least we are alive."

Whyvvi murmured in a hushed quiet voice, "I almost would prefer that we could be truly dead and in this peaceful after-life in the golden bubble with our best friends. Of course I would hope that Swyllo would arrive soon. But that is just a wish and only if this was a heavenly place."

"Vulch, Whyvvi, if we were dead, we'd be nothing but corpses. Vulching rotting corpses, light years away from any other friendly Blue Jayers to honor our legend properly," Milyr sneered. "Is that how you want to end? Is that what this Blue Jay trip has accomplished?"

"You toxx! Death does not have to be just corpses," Whyvvi yelled angrily. "I believe there has to be more. I believe that Swyllo is somewhere, still waiting for me. We must be more than just these bodies of organic construction. We just have to be."

"Perhaps we are just as we appear now," Domyn suggested. "Yet our awareness is reality…"

However, Milyr interrupted rudely and snarled with emotion, ignoring Domyn, "No, fine fem, we are these gorgeous bodies now. We should make use of what we have now as long as we are alive. There is nothing more after we die. So don't vulching rush your wish for death! I want to do things, some vulching joyous things with my body before I die."

"Like vigorous spiritual bonding?" Nyba inquired, standing against Milyr's lanky frame.

"Erh…yeah…that would be a cherp priority," Milyr admitted.

"So you believe that Swyllo and Jamyk are just gone totally from this universe. That they have no after-life! That they do not matter anymore," Whyvvi blurted angrily.

Lyndyn, sensing that she was close to weeping or hitting Milyr, whichever seemed more emotionally releasing at the moment, abandoned his investigation of the bubble and asked loudly, "Domyn, what does your philosophy of universal awareness have to say about death and after-life?"

In momentary hesitation before Domyn spoke, Milyr retorted with obvious indignation and feeling, "Of course they vulching matter. I really miss them, especially my cherp friend little peener. I miss him very much. But I can't do anything for him now. Vulch, I still hope he's alive somewhere. I still hope to see him again. I do vulching care about Jamyk….and Swyllo."

Kymil asked with a gentle murmur, "Then you have faith that he is alive still?"

Swinging his long arms in agitation, Milyr paced away from the bubble edge and whined, "Did anyone see him die? Has anyone seen his body? Vulch, no, I don't think so. He could be alive. You didn't see him die, did you, Doc?"

"I'm not sure what I saw. My memory is still repressed. But, Milyr, I don't recall his death. That's hopeful! Believe that he may be alive. I wish to still," Kymil said passionately.

"So do I!" Domyn said with conviction.

"Let's hope that your universal metaphy hears you, Domyn," Lyndyn exclaimed and then added, "Indeed if we were somehow rescued and put into this bubble chamber somewhere in the acid ocean on the moon of the gas giant, then perhaps Jamyk's bizarre behavior in Wolf had more meaning than I had believed. Perhaps he is somewhere rescued as we are. The little rascal has always been very unpredictable. Perhaps your suspicions of his espersense have been more truth than fantasy, hey, Domyn?"

"You are starting to sound too much like me," Domyn growled but benignly in his deep voice.

"Rescued? But who or by what?" Nyba asked, waving her hands around nervously. "Certainly not by Fox Flash Alpha. This is not Blue Jay sci-tech. Who could have rescued him or us?"

"No, this is definitely not Blue Jay sci-tech," Domyn agreed, still attempting to peer through the bubble to the outside. "In fact I doubt that this is colonial construction either."

"Vulch, then what is it? How did we get into this bubble from Wolf?" Milyr asked, flailing his arms in the center of the bubble and gesturing toward the yellow surroundings. "If we were rescued, then for what purpose? We seem to be in the nasty acid ocean still. The only difference now is that we're trapped inside this bubble and not Wolf. But we're still trapped!"

"Oh my, Milyr, we do have adequate air now. I'd consider that improvement since Wolf," Kymil said in her sensible calming tone heard so many times before by Lyndyn since Turkey Trot Alpha.

"Awright, yes, and we've determined that we are alive and not in the after-life," Domyn reminded others just seconds before Lyndyn was about to say the same comment.

"Yeah, I guess that's better than being a corpse," Milyr admitted grudgingly. "But a vulching corpse would not feel anything. Would the corpse be afraid? Would the corpse miss his friends?"

"Scientifically speaking the corpse of a once living being decomposes after death. All research indicates that corporeal feeling and consciousness ceases with the death of the body," Lyndyn said but then continued, somewhat surprised by his own next words, "Yet our very scientific-minded engineer theorizes that there is…spirit…component to living existence. Now this may exist beyond the organic confines of the body. Is that not so, Neer Domyn?"

As everyone became silent suddenly, Lyndyn hoped that Domyn would not be too embarrassed by the pointed question and his abrupt placement as the center of attention, but he said confidently, "I have little doubt that there is an iota of awareness associated with every individual life-form. This iota of awareness enters the body at birth, energizes awareness of the individual during the lifetime of the body, and then returns to universal awareness at the death of the body. I do believe that the iota is eternal both before and after the lifespan of an individual body. It must be as it is a component of universal awareness that exists throughout infinity of the universe."

Whyvvi asked solemnly after the young man had finished and others were very quiet, "Then an iota of awareness of Swyllo is out there somewhere in the universe? Perhaps she is already nagging at universal awareness to help us. That is a very cherp way to believe, my big man, for Swyllo's sake….and for Jamyk, and any other friends maybe from Fox Flash who have died in this Sexto System."

"Yeah, it is," Milyr agreed with a sigh and then more vehemently said, "But, vulch, I still want to believe Jamyk and Fox Flash are still alive somewhere. We'll meet him again, I hope, in this life."

"Yes, we all do I'm sure," Nyba stated, walking to the tall young man and embracing his lanky torso in her arms. "Let's hope they are alive. Now let's make sure that we stay alive."

Trying to keep the young minds focused on Domyn's interesting and positive theory, Lyndyn asked, already knowing the answer himself from prior discussions with the big engineer, "Domyn, where does your iota of awareness go after death? Does it go directly to universal awareness or does it have other duties for metaphy in let's say some form of reincarnation for example on the occasion?"

"Vulch!" shouted Milyr, interrupting Lyndyn abruptly. "Now I'm seeing vulching purple balls. That one looks like it is in the bubble wall. Vulch, this is a nasty toxx!"

Following the direction of the frantic young man's pointing arm and finger, Lyndyn turned and saw a dark violet spot about one foot in diameter on the side of the bubble surface. Then his peripheral vision noticed another to his left about halfway up the side. The violet spots were midway on the inside of the bubble surface.

"There's another," yelled Nyba, waving her arm overhead. "What are they?"

"Over there, too," Whyvvi cried out frantically, and Lyndyn followed her gaze to his right.

"What the vulch?" Milyr hollered, leaping into the air and staring down at his feet where Lyndyn observed another spot starting to protrude from the golden floor. "The vulchers are all around us."

With fascination Lyndyn watched the violet spot about one foot in diameter gradually protrude into an elongating and flexible cone, then shortly a longer tube, and then it lengthened into a very narrow tendril-like appendage. He could not see all the violet spots at once because many were not in his direct sight. But those that he saw all extended from their anchor points on the golden bubble. Each now almost tentacle-like protuberance waved slowly into the interior of the bubble. The lighter purple extensions appeared to be groping toward Milyr.

"They are almost like our morphing technology," said Domyn with awe of the engineer.

"Vulch, they are coming at me," shouted Milyr, moving to one side of the bubble where no tendril flailed from the side.

Yet when he stepped away from the center of the bubble, the undulating thin tips of the almost lavender tendrils veered after him. Lyndyn could not be sure, but he thought that he counted six lavender tendrils. Smooth, slowly waving, these six tendrils inexorably aimed for Milyr.

"Vulch, they are after me," the lanky naked young man screamed, trying to dodge and run from the flailing tendrils. "Vulching toxx, this is not cherp!"

As he pushed past Nyba and shoved her toward two undulating tendrils, she screamed, "Watch out, Milyr, but don't push me into them instead. I'm not ready to sacrifice myself for you yet."

"Vulch, I'm doomed. I hope they don't want to eat me. I hope I'm not their next meal," Milyr yelled, frantically ducking under the lasso-like twirl of tendrils "What a vulching way to die. I am dinner for these toxx vulchers. I won't even get to be a corpse."

Partially trying not to laugh and yet fearing likely a danger to his young ward, Lyndyn peered intently at the weaving tendrils as they attempted to enclose around Milyr. Would he lose another of the young Jayers now, Lyndyn worried.

SPEC THREE: LYNDYN ON WYLLOS
CHAPTER 29

"Go away, you vulchers," shouted Milyr in panic. "Leave me alone. Don't eat me."

As he saw long lavender tendrils swaying round the tall young man, Lyndyn cried out, "Don't let those things touch you, anyone. We don't know if there is acid on or in them. This whole moon environment had been toxic to us. Be careful."

Waving his hands and arms defensively around his head, Milyr ran a few paces across the center of the bubble floor to the opposite side and hollered frantically, "Vulch, go away. Stop chasing me. I taste like a nasty toxx. Don't eat me!"

When Milyr passed between the other naked young people, flailing tendrils paused briefly and then redirected their aim toward Milyr's new position. Lyndyn noticed that light lavender tendrils, all six of them, maneuvered slowly, meticulously above and around himself and others. Their aim seemed to be exclusively Milyr. Their paths seemed to avoid contact with any other person.

"Maybe that is exactly what they like to eat, nasty toxx," Whyvvi joked, though her voice was serious and her hands punched at the snaking tendrils, yet missing them.

"These things are avoiding the rest of us," Kymil said. "These whippy things seemed focused on Milyr only. Perhaps the rest of us are safe from this attack."

"Indeed perhaps we can protect him," Lyndyn suggested, turning to follow Milyr's movement. "Milyr, get in between us. Everyone else let's form a human shield around him."

"If I stand still, they'll vulching get me," Milyr protested and then whined, "I don't want to be eaten to death. That is a vulching nasty way to go."

447

Quickly striding behind Milyr and punching at his buttocks, Nyba demanded with urgency, "Do as Prof says. Move between us. Those things aren't after us… I hope. Let us surround you."

"Hurry then," Milyr squealed. "That one just brushed my arm. And another vulcher is just above my head. Hurry, chase them away."

As he saw others enclose around Milyr's jittery lanky figure, Lyndyn ordered, "Everyone, keep your hands and arms waving, especially over your heads. Milyr's taller than us. We'll need to defend some of the space above. Wave your arms. If those tendrils won't touch us, then we can shield Milyr. If we can keep this up long enough, then maybe tendrils will give up their intention."

"Hunch down a little, you tall toxx," Nyba commanded while she swatted at the lavender tendril coming in from the right side. "Try to be shorter for once. Tallness isn't always useful."

"Vulch, there's too many of them," Milyr wailed. "I'm a vulching target just standing here. They are coming from all directions. I'm vulching toxx food for those vulcher nasties."

"Do not panic, you toxx," Whyvvi said with panic in her gasping voice. "Trust us. We will protect you. We do not want any strange alien thing getting your toxx before we get our chance to kick it."

"Squat down lower," Nyba ordered loudly with authority. "Shrink down, make yourself shorter, you tall toxx. Don't run out of our circle. Let us help you."

With Nyba at his backside, and others forming a tight human wall around him, Milyr groaned with fright, "Vulch, I never thought shrinkage would ever do me any good. But, vulch, right now I wish I was a little peener like Jamyk."

"Keep waving your arms," Kymil shouted. "I think it's helping to confuse or block their intention. We have a chance to succeed doing this if we don't tire too quickly."

Yes, that seemed to be the situation, Lyndyn thought. Six tendrils, protruding from six almost precisely geometrically spaced positions around the spherical bubble, now swayed above and around the huddled humans. The memory of tutoring Jamyk and Swyllo about protective circling of herd animals, such as wild buffalos, flashed suddenly into his mind. Indeed that was exactly what they were now trying to accomplish, protect a member of their human herd. Apparently the maneuver was proving successful, for the swaying tendrils slowed their persistent movements around the group of naked humans and ceased their attack upon Milyr for a moment.

"I hope that they do not decide to go after someone else now," Whyvvi muttered.

"How long will those vulchers wait?" Milyr asked, now kneeling low within the protective group.

"Who knows? We do not know why they want you," Nyba said, tiredly waving her arms over his head still. "Why anything would want your stinky toxx, not even Domyn's universal metaphy knows."

"Hopefully not long. My arms are getting tired already," Whyvvi complained. "Maybe we should just let them have him... Then they will not need to eat us... But no, then there would be no easy toxx to make fun of and ridicule like our favorite toxx, Milyr."

"Oh yeah, you're a big help to my self-esteem," Milyr muttered sourly. "My ego is so vulching restored now. I feel so vulching wanted."

"Yes, you toxx...by those purple thingies," Whyvvi exclaimed as she chased the two tendrils aside with her swinging arms.

"Let's just stay tight, herd," Kymil said with encouragement. "We've stopped their attack. I believe we have them buffaloed."

"We have them what?" grimaced Whyvvi with a squeak in her voice as Lyndyn suddenly stared in puzzlement at Kymil since he found it quite a coincidence that she would have a similar metaphor in her mind at this hectic time as he had recently thought himself.

"Buffaloed," Kymil explained, still waving her arms. "It's an ancient expression that means that we have them fooled or confused but at least pausing in their efforts. Like a herd of buffalos protecting their young from predators."

Curiously in spite of the continued defensive flailing of his arms, Lyndyn asked, "How did you revive that particular memory at this time? This seems very strange under these stressful moments but also very appropriate. What made you think of this notion?"

"Oh my, it just appeared on my tongue as I spoke," Kymil replied, panting with her effort. "From nowhere or no train of thought, it just seemed to be the right thing to say now."

"Is that vulching useful now?" Milyr wailed from beneath them. "Those vulchers are still there. After me, I guess, just trying to eat me. Vulch, I'm not ready yet to be a mutilated corpse."

"Just relax, be patient. I'll protect you, you ugly toxx," Nyba stated. "This is working. I believe that we've...buffaloed...them. That is so cherp, Doc!"

Indeed this ploy was succeeding at the moment, Lyndyn thought to himself. Very strange that Kymil had remembered a similar old memory. Yet they were a kindred pair, Kymil and himself. Maybe not so strange after all that they would recall a coincidently appropriate memory. They had served together on Turkey Trot on voyage to the Quinto system and had shared a common experience. Perhaps not so strange, he convinced himself.

"Cherp?" Milyr squealed. "Nothing about this vulching situation is cherp."

"Now, my big man, don't worry. I'm here. I'll guard your skinny toxx," Nyba promised, bending over to embrace his head and shoulders against her chest.

As he witnessed her caring gesture, Lyndyn said, "We'll all protect you, Milyr. If Swyllo and Jamyk could sacrifice themselves for us, then we cannot do any less for each other. We are a family of sorts. We will need each other to survive this trial and whatever future destiny we may have."

"Oh my, look. I believe the tendrils are withdrawing," Kymil whispered.

"Vulch, I hope so," declared Milyr still within Nyba's embrace.

Turning his attention to the nearest tendril, Lyndyn observed the lavender protuberance retract with a gently undulating motion into a fatter tube shape, then a purple cone, and finally a dark violet spot on the golden surface of the bubble wall. Several other tendrils within his sight withdrew in the same manner at the same time. The tendrils seemed to be as coordinated in retraction as they had been in extension. Slowly, so as not to dizzy himself, Lyndyn turned around to check the other violet spots. They were all six back on the bubble surface. Then they were gone.

"Oh my," Kymil exclaimed in excited curiosity, "I'm sure that I just saw a green sphere outside the bubble where that tendril had been located. Yes, there's another moving away from that other dark spot. They are out there in the ocean."

Hastily Lyndyn followed her line of sight, but his eyes did not see anything in the golden ocean outside the bubble, so he asked, "Are you sure? My eyes don't see anything. But you've always had a better observation power than me."

"I thought that I saw something moving," Whyvvi stated. "But I could not describe it."

"Vulch, I don't want to see any of those toxx vulchers again," Milyr grumbled in despair.

"Actually so did I up there on top of the bubble," Domyn said enthusiastically. "Up there where there is a better light. I'm certain that I saw a greenish object depart from the bubble."

"Now we're seeing green balls," complained Milyr, sitting with gleaming sweat covering his body on the golden floor. "Vulch, I'm glad that's over. I hope they don't come back."

"If they do, I'm here," Nyba promised, releasing her embrace from around his neck and standing up. "Prof, do you think that it's safe to separate now and to move around again?"

"Maybe urinate?" Whyvvi inquired in desperation. "This excitement has triggered my system."

"I believe that we're safe for the moment," Lyndyn speculated while he walked close to the bubble inside layer, "We should know what to watch for now. Those spots and tendrils moved very meticulously and somewhat slowly. We should have adequate time to regroup our...herd...if we must."

"Vulching cherp!" Milyr exclaimed, rising slowly to stretch his long legs. "Vulch, I've got to cate something nasty after that experience. The vulching fecal toxx is ready to run right out."

"Do you want me to hold your hand?" Nyba murmured with a giggle.

"Vulch no! The man's got to have some dignity," Milyr grumbled. "Even a vulching toxx such as my primo self must do some personal things by myself. Now where's the private spot?"

"Maybe you could pull and pinch the inner layer around your skinny toxx and make one," laughed Whyvvi. "But do not worry about me. I am not intending to watch while you cate. I have my own dignity. You take that side. I will take this side... Just watch out for the purple spots."

"Thanks a lot!" Milyr snarled. "That really helps my system. Vulching purple spots, just what I want to plunk my toxx onto. This is getting to be so nasty vulching toxx now!"

Yet Whyvvi's joking suggestion lingered in Lyndyn's mind. How flexible was this inner lining of the bubble? Could it be plucked away from the more solid outer layer and reformed? Could this allow them to design something to defend against the tendrils? These were questions for Domyn, their man with the best engineering mind. When he glanced toward the big young man, Lyndyn was surprised to see Domyn peering at him already from a few paces away. His large fingers had already begun pinching about the foot of the inner layer from the normal curve of the bubble wall.

Domyn nodded once to Lyndyn and announced, "Whyvvi may have an idea. There does appear to be some elasticity to this substance. But how much we could ply away without damaging this inner layer, I don't know. I'm certain we do not want to hurt this inside layer. I'm sure it's keeping our environment at this comfortable and stable status."

"No doubt I believe that you are right to be cautious. We would be foolish to destroy our own sustaining environment just to keep Milyr's eating private," Lyndyn declared with a grin. "Yet careful study could provide us with some advantage or some defense."

Domyn fingered the substance, gently pulling another few inches out from the wall and said, "I'm not sure if we need a defense, Prof. I felt that those tendrils were being extra careful not to contact anyone but Milyr. If the intent was very aggressive, then they could have knocked the rest of us out of the way and taken him. Those tendrils did not behave that way. They demonstrated very little aggressiveness for having such a focused intent. I'm in doubt if they are truly dangerous."

"You are starting to think like me," Lyndyn grinned. "I had the same thought myself. Herding protection succeeds only if the predator is very wary of the herd's collective strength or is sympathetic to the herd. I'm not certain though if the tendrils can be wary or sympathetic. This supposition assumes the tendrils to be living and aware beings. That I doubt very much at this time."

Flexing the transparent soft substance from the bubble wall in his hands, Domyn agreed, "Well, you are probably right there, Prof, likelihood of any organic carbon-based life on this moon is very remote. Those tendrils and green balls are most likely some physical inorganic phenomena. I'm not ready to consider them benign. This bubble...well, I'm not sure... Like you said before, we should be very cautious how we treat our habitat. It is our only livable environment now. We'd be absolutely foolish to degrade this habitat for the sake of short-term defensive capability."

Nyba's voice laughed as she walked towards them, "That looks like something Jamyk would grab a handful off the wall and throw at someone like a splatter bulb. I can easily envision the rascal doing that to any of us now, even in this ridiculous situation."

"Sounds like him, but I would hope that he would be more considerate now after our recent series of devastating events. Even a self-absorbed rascal like him or Milyr should be able to see that playing around with one's only environment just for self-gratification is a disaster waiting to happen," Domyn sighed. "Only fools would do such a deed."

"No doubt you believe, as I do, that this bubble, or at least this inner layer, is somehow providing and sustaining our breathable air from the toxic ocean outside. Otherwise we would have suffocated long ago in our sleep," Lyndyn stated, taking a light grip of the wall substance and feeling warmth and elasticity.

"That is only a reasonable possibility," Domyn agreed. "This bubble is somewhere submerged within the acid ocean, not too deep to block out that light from the sun out there but deep enough to stabilize against the wave action of the ocean surface."

"Thank your metaphy for that," Lyndyn smiled, thinking how wonderful his lack of stomach distress had been since awakening in this bubble.

"Awright now, Prof, I'm not convinced yet that universal awareness actually controls or responds to the actions of individuals or even communities. My ongoing theory of this universal awareness that permeates this reality parallel with physical aspects, such as spergits, quarks, atoms, and larger masses relates only to my belief that there is such awareness," Domyn said, and then with a chuckle said, "Awe help me, I am starting to sound like you, Prof. I'm rambling on about nonsense."

"Not at all, my friend," Lyndyn smiled. "When you ramble, at least you know what you are talking about. You can support it with your reputation as a Blue Jay engineer with a vast body of knowledge within your brain. I, as my kind Kymil will often say, am speaker of endless ridiculous ramblings from a very empty head."

Carefully releasing a collection of the inner layer substance in his hands, Domyn chuckled, "Oh, I do not believe that she is very serious when she teases you about that. No, Prof, I think that is one of many ways that she and you show your mutual love for each other. But don't worry. I won't divulge your secret to others."

"Not much of a secret now, my young friend," Lyndyn smiled sheepishly, knowing that so much had been revealed during the hour just before the end of Wolf. "Yet I thank your metaphy for giving me my life with my Kymil. I myself may not really believe in that metaphysical nonsense, but that doesn't mean that I won't use it on occasion when it suits me. I admit that I am a hypocrite."

"Awright, Prof, don't berate your opinion. I often find myself calling upon such a single all-knowing awareness during moments of uncertainty or danger. However, that is not how my theory of universal awareness has progressed in my mind. I have merely convinced myself that my own iota of awareness is one of an infinite number that compose universal awareness. Whether sensations and experiences accumulated by infinite iotas combine to generate a single collective conscious awareness is still very much in question within my own mind. Yet perhaps it is at this point that logical thought no longer satisfies the problem under consideration and instead faith, or at least reasonable belief, must take over in absence of the physical or mathematical data," Domyn expounded while his fingers idly tickled a substance of the bubble wall.

"You are talking more and more like Prof," Nyba laughed from behind the two men.

"And rambling on and on just like him also," Kymil added while walking over to stand beside Nyba. "Have you two men discovered anything of significance about this inner layer or truth of universal awareness perhaps?"

Slightly startled by her sudden statement and approach, Lyndyn laughed at himself for his own preoccupation in the recent discussion and then aloud joked, "Just that it is very comforting to fondle and very conducive to speculative discussion."

"Awe well, that surely seems to be true," Domyn laughed heartily. "Yet we've also decided not to disturb or try to manipulate this layer of our environment. After all we know so little about this bubble. We don't want to harm it accidently. This bubble is keeping us alive."

"Oh my, very wise understanding…" Kymil started to say.

"Vulch, more purple spots," swore Milyr frantically.

"Sneaky nasty toxx," Whyvvi yelled. "I did not see them approach. We should be more observant next time. Should we herd together again?"

"Vulch, never mind, next time I want to get by this time without being lunch for vulchers," Milyr exclaimed, hopping into the center of the bubble floor and spinning around trying to watch all directions at once. "Where's my vulching herd? Where are my guards to protect my godly body?"

"Awright, wolves, let's huddle around this skinny pup," Nyba commanded. "But I don't want his toxx this time. Someone else can cover his toxx."

"My toxx, my vulching manliness, don't be fussy, help me, protect me," Milyr whined spinning around, trying to watch all directions at once. "I vulching don't desire to be snack for these toxx."

Observing dark spots prominent on the golden walls of the bubble, Lyndyn suggested, "Let's move away from the center this time. There is a spot near the bottom center. Set our herd over here between these spots where none have appeared. Let's make it more difficult for those tendrils on the far side."

"I agree," Domyn said, gripping Milyr by the arm and tugging the lanky young man toward the area where Lyndyn stood, "The precise geometric spacing this time is similar to the last attack. I think whatever triggers this activity requires some order, some sense of geometric precision. If we move our herd off-center, then we may disrupt this precision."

While they formed around Milyr, Lyndyn watched the spots protrude just as they had before. Slowly the spots became cones. The cones became slender cylinders. The cylinders thinned to become elongated, flexibly wavering tendrils. Gradually this change occurred before his eyes. The extending tendrils again came from six spots around the sphere of the bubble.

Domyn shouted as he positioned himself almost against Milyr's figure, "I'll take the front. I'm almost as tall as Milyr. I can defend that critical direction better than anyone else."

"Good idea," Nyba exclaimed breathlessly. "Let's get into our tight group and keep our arms moving overhead. That worked last time. Who's covering his toxx?"

"Not I," declared Whyvvi. "The nasty spots can have that part."

"Oh, ha, ha, young fem, this is no joke," Milyr grumbled, squatting low within the group.

Taking position to the left of Domyn Lyndyn stared at the meticulously lengthening tendrils now aiming their tips toward the herd. As before darkness of the spot lightened which each stage of extension. However, now the thinned tendrils seemed to look different than prior attack. What was it, Lyndyn wondered. Why do tendrils look slightly different than before?

"If you put your toxx against the bubble, Milyr, we won't have to cover your back," Kymil advised as she stood behind Lyndyn. "That will allow us to be tighter around the front."

"Vulch, just keep them away from me," Milyr pleaded, backing toward the closest side with no darkened spot extending the tendril. "I'd like to stay alive in case Jamyk is going to return. And I don't want to be a snack for these nasty toxx vulchers."

"Watch your toxx for any new spot that might develop behind you," Whyvvi warned with a giggle. "Yet I think your toxx is safe now. There are already six spots on the bubble. What a shame!"

"Vulch, just what I needed to hear," cursed Milyr despondently.

Was color different? Was that really lavender? Lyndyn could not be certain. The yellow golden light through the bubble made colors appear odd to his eyes. Yet he was certain that he noticed color in the thinning tendrils was other than a violet shade.

While Nyba and Whyvvi screamed at the nearing tendrils, Lyndyn asked over his shoulder, "Kymil, what color are the tendrils? I don't trust my eyes now."

"Green, no, that's not right... That's memory vision. Where did that just come from?" Kymil grimaced in frustration. "No, now they appear...yellowy purple... no...more like sandy purple...maybe light brown... I'm not certain. The general lighting in here is confusing."

Watching the approach of six tendrils from various spots on the bubble, Lyndyn peered intently at the swaying tips to discern true color. For some subconscious reason, his mind told him that color meant something. Was that really tan coloring in the six small bulb-like tips drawing closer to the herd? Did that really matter, or was his brain wandering again?

As the tendril tip from the top of the bubble paused above the group of naked, defenseless humans, Domyn called out, "Keep those arms moving overhead. I think we can repel these again."

The tendril tip from the floor had stopped its forward movement right in front of Domyn at the head of the herd, Lyndyn observed tendrils from the sides pause about waist high, not a yard from the front of the herd. Why were they waiting? Lyndyn wondered if they would push aside the human barrier to get to Milyr. It seemed as if the tendrils awaited the slow arrival of the tendril from the farthest spot. Then would they attack aggressively this time?

"Vulching nasty toxx, why can't they leave me alone?" Milyr protested.

"Get away, you ugly nasty toxx!" Whyvvi shrieked, punching at the nearest bobbing tendril.

Purple? No, not the purple of lighter lavender, Lyndyn observed, more like a light tan, hard to tell in the golden light. Yet tips, yes, tips suddenly reminded him of splatter bulbs that Swyllo and Jamyk would throw at each other during stress relief sessions. The image of their joyous faces as they splashed each other with splatter bulbs flashed into his consciousness. The two young pups had included Domyn in the most recent session back in LaOgres travel. This strange memory, though only a few seconds in his consciousness, overrode all current thought. Then his mind returned hastily to the situation, and he realized the tendrils were brown and not purple. Brown was Domyn's color on Wolf Streak Beta.

"Back away, Domyn," Lyndyn yelled loudly. "They are here for you this time. Get behind me."

"Erh, what? Are you sure?" the big man stammered in sudden bewilderment in his voice.

Striding in front of Domyn, Lyndyn pushed the young man behind him and shouted in an urgent nasal voice, "Yes, get into the center of our herd. Quickly… do it now."

When he stepped forward, Lyndyn felt a gentle swish of flowing air as the tendrils closed in around the space where Domyn had just stood. The sudden and brief brush with some tendrils across his flailing arms sent shivers through his naked flesh. Yet he felt no other physical harm. In fact the tendrils recoiled at contact more emphatically than he did. All six pulled back and swayed in the air in front of and to the side of him.

"Oh my, Lyndyn, are you hurt?" Kymil cried out.

"No, no, I'm fine. Just keep a tight group around Domyn. I'm sure he was the target this time."

"Vulchers wanted a bigger meal," Milyr quipped with nervous relief in his voice. "Not this skinny toxx anymore… Sorry, big guy! I know what it feels like."

"Will they come after us instead?" Whyvvi asked with worry, yet she held her position at Domyn's front right. "What do those things want? Why should those toxx chase us?"

"As long as they back off, I'm happy," Nyba declared.

"And happier if they leave," Milyr added, still squatting down inside the herd. "Right, Domyn?"

"I should believe so…yet I'm not sure they are here to eat us," Domyn said, his voice a mix of confusion and relief. "Just before Prof pulled me back, I sensed a very brief feeling of comradeship like we always experience when we practiced Pulseball with Jamyk back in Wolf Streak Beta. My mind was awash with the fleeting memory. Very bizarre, but I felt a feeling even while trying to guard you."

"Vulch, I got no cherp feeling. Those things just give me vulching nasty quivers. I'm sure they just want my manly body as a meal," Milyr retorted.

So Domyn had a sudden memory flash also, Lyndyn pondered as he watched the hovering tendrils alertly. The six protuberances snaked and swayed in the air above the bubble floor. Their goal had, now obviously, been Domyn. Why had the young man experienced such a memory flash during this incident? Why had he himself experienced a similarly related memory about Swyllo and Jamyk? Were their brains suffering some ailment, some neurosis, some espersense? No, that last was just imagination, Lyndyn convinced himself. But other possibilities were worrisome. Could these memories be triggered by appearances of the tendrils?

As he considered these possibilities, Lyndyn heard Kymil ask again with genuine fear, "Lyndyn, are you sure you are not hurt? I'm certain those tendrils contacted your skin. Do you have any sensations of pains, itching, or any discomfort?"

"I am fine. Those tendrils only brushed me. The touch was no different than the inner layer of the bubble. Soft and warm! I got no sensation of acid," Lyndyn replied calmly while he studied the swaying tendrils closely. "Is everyone else okay?"

"I'll be vulching cherp as soon as those toxx tendrils leave," Milyr declared. "I'm not at all cherp with my toxx against the bubble side. What if other purple ones come in behind me?"

"You big toxx," Whyvvi yelled as she waved her arms overhead. "This time they were after Domyn and almost got him. But all you can do is worry about your ugly toxx."

As Milyr grumbled an incoherent retort, Lyndyn noticed six tendrils begin to wither back to the spots of origin on the bubble, and so he said hopefully, "Looks like the tendrils are retreating once more. Apparently our herding protection maneuver has worked again."

"Watch closely as they disappear," Kymil commanded. "I'm certain that I saw something outside the bubble last time. You young people with better eyes, watch closely."

"I'll observe the top of the bubble," Domyn volunteered. "I think that I saw something last time. These tendrils are annoying and intriguing at the same time."

"I will follow this one on the right," Whyvvi said with some trepidation in her voice as she stepped slowly from the group and toward the shrinking tendril. "You did say that these nasty toxx will not chase after any of the rest of us, did you not, Prof?"

"Yes, indeed I believe you are safe from those brown tendrils. But, everyone else, let's not break apart our herd until we see the spots go. Whyvvi should be able to get a good view closer to the spot. But, Whyvvi, don't get too close. Don't take any chances," Lyndyn warned, admiring the young woman for her brave curiosity.

Nyba exclaimed happily, standing beside Domyn and Milyr, "We buffaloed those things again, hey, men and women. We're getting cherp at this herd protection behavior."

Observing most of the tendrils retract into the dark colored spots on the bubble, Lyndyn said with frustration, "Yes, but I wish that we understood the purpose. Are they a threat or not?"

"How did you know they were after Domyn?" Nyba asked.

That was a reasonable question, Lyndyn thought, how had he known? His sudden action had seemed absolutely correct when he stepped before Domyn. Somehow his brain had processed the rather dubious input and ordered him into action, and action was not his strong talent. Yet could he tell the others of his momentary flash memory of Swyllo, Jamyk, Domyn, and splatter bulbs? Would they understand? Would they believe? Did he himself believe? Then there was the color of tendrils, and he had not known for sure what the color was at that time.

However, it made a logical answer, so he stammered, "In…in…deed… some…how… I guessed once Kymil confirmed the color of the tendrils to be tan or brown rather than violet. I guessed that tendril color matched Domyn's Wolf Streak Beta color, just as earlier the violet tendrils matched Milyr's Wolf Streak Beta color. But in reality, this connection was pure speculation. We were lucky."

"Well, Prof, maybe you have more espersense than you want to believe," Domyn said with a chuckle. "However, those tendrils are gone now. There was very definitely a dark shape about the size of one of those spots outside the bubble up there at the top. I am positive that it was not the spot itself. It was more greenish, but the colors are difficult to make out in this yellowish light."

"I can confirm Domyn's observation," Whyvvi said from near the one curved side of the bubble. "I got view of one near here. The dark green object outside seemed to discard the dark spot into the ocean before moving away from the bubble. I am certain that my eyes are adjusting to the golden light. This time I saw everything outside much clearer than earlier."

"Indeed, my young wolves, we have learned and deduced new information about our situation and environment without any Blue Jay sci-tech. With just our brains, we have learned something," Lyndyn praised, glad to switch the subject from his own role of the recent event.

"But we need to know so much more," Whyvvi protested. "We should be able to discover what those tendrils and green objects are and what they are doing to us. Do they want to hurt us?"

"Yes, you are correct, Whyvvi. Scientific observation and deduction are a never ending process," Lyndyn reminded his young wards in his tutorial voice. "Only very foolish succumb to the fallacy that their scientific knowledge is the absolute end of discovery process."

"Does that include espersense and Szczygiel Shines?" Domyn asked with a slight laugh.

"No doubt, even this old man can have the right to believe foolishly," Lyndyn smiled at the big young man. "However, after recent events and without sci-tech equipment, we must use what we know we have and perhaps even what we foolishly deny that we may have."

"Enough of this science philosophy debate," Nyba demanded tersely. "We've got to stay focused. Prof, you said that you knew the tendrils were seeking Domyn because they were brown. And that was deduced because they were purple when they sought Milyr. If this is so, how could the tendrils know or adopt the color of the intended target? How could this knowledge of our codes be known?"

"That is a question that I can't answer now," Lyndyn admitted sheepishly. "But I'll accept any suggestion that any of you might have."

"We should be able to reason this out," Whyvvi said emphatically. "Only the crew of Wolf Streak Beta and Fox Flash were familiar with our individual color codes. I think that we can eliminate Fox Flash Alpha at this moment. The chance of their presence on this moon is very low. This tells us that only Wolf and we have that information. We think Wolf is gone, and besides, no person but one of us could access what little computer records may be left in Wolf, if any. I believe that we can say Wolf was not the source of that information for the tendrils. That leaves just us and the information in our brains and memories."

"If you are right, then vulch, things are taking it from our brains," Milyr exclaimed with alarm. "Vulchers were in my brain...reading my brain!"

"Not much to read," Whyvvi scoffed.

"Erh...vulch, you are so nasty funny," Milyr retorted sarcastically.

"Or perhaps someone else is giving this information to the tendrils, or more likely the green objects using tendrils," Kymil almost whispered suddenly. "Oh, my...green tendrils... I've seen the green tendrils before."

"Green is Jamyk's color," Domyn blurted.

"Are you certain, Kymil?" Lyndyn asked, tenderly gripping her arms in his hands. "When did you see this?"

Her eyes were wide with anxiety as she replied, "The Wolf...before blacking out...at hatch...after he opened it...green tendrils came in and took him...he was gone... I remember now."

"But there was no light in Wolf. How could you see the other than the PEQA glow?" Domyn asked.

Yes, how she could have seen the green tendrils with no light, Lyndyn wondered. Yet he knew Kymil very well. She was very reliable. Her past memory of that last hour in Wolf could have been activated easily by recent discussion. Or perhaps her suddenly activated memory was caused by some espersense link with Jamyk, if he was alive still. No, that was foolish imagination again, he thought. Yet he himself, as well as the others, here now in this bubble had reported the unusual memories in the past hours. Could living Jamyk using espersense be the cause? No, that went against all his prior education and experience as the Blue Jay psychologist.

"But I'm certain that I saw the green tendrils take him through the purple cover across the hatch," Kymil insisted. "Yes, Lyndyn, the purple covering was illuminated or iridescent. And, oh my, no ocean flooded into Wolf... This is too vivid a memory to be an oxygen-deprived hallucination. I'm positive this is a true memory. The purple cover kept the ocean out. The green tendrils took Jamyk out the open hatch. He may be alive just like us but somewhere else."

"Or, Doc, maybe the green tendrils ate Jamyk and absorbed his knowledge somehow," Milyr suggested. "But I vulching hope not. Not even the little peener should die like that."

"This is terribly difficult to believe. I'm sorry, Doc, but I'm not ready for this," Nyba exclaimed dubiously, and her nervous shifting of her feet and legs reinforced her uncomfortable feeling.

"Yet the tendrils did come for Milyr and Domyn, specifically two males," Whyvvi said logically. "If they come again, I am glad that I am a female. Oops! Sorry, guys, that was heartless."

"Why would tendrils orient toward the males first?" Domyn asked and almost immediately then suggested, "Maybe because Jamyk is in another bubble and in need of some repair or attention. It would make sense that whatever has him would need one of us to analyze and compare with Jamyk, physiologically, psychologically, or something."

No doubt there was some scientific logic in Domyn's suggestion, Lyndyn realized. That is if one accepted observations and memories of Kymil as fact. Yet he would also have to accept the possibility that Jamyk and they themselves were in the care of intelligent and aware beings. Here on the poisonous, toxic moon, this notion of living intelligent alien captors was difficult for Lyndyn to accept. His scientific training told him this was foolish to accept. He was uncertain of what to believe.

"But we were vulching asleep for a very long time. We could have been compared and analyzed then. Why wait until now to come for us?" Milyr asked, glancing around the bubble in anxiety, probably checking for dark spots on the bubble wall, Lyndyn thought.

"For all that we know, we were," Domyn declared. "Maybe that's why we are alive still, to serve as specimens to an intelligent investigation. From what little I remember of the last moment in Wolf, I recall Jamyk repeatedly saying of help coming as if he had a connection to someone or something outside Wolf. We must not dismiss that as absolute foolishness or delusion from his mind."

"That is correct. I remember that now," Whyvvi agreed. "But I thought then he was just being Jamyk, a little peener toxx. He seemed to be in one of his nonsense states then."

"But why come back for more analyzing and probing?" Milyr asked with a slight crack and squeal to his questioning voice. "The vulchers had plenty of time while we were asleep."

"That is it," shouted Whyvvi excitedly suddenly. "You were asleep. Any observer studying us could not get complete analysis unless they tested you awake as well as asleep. They need you awake to finish the comparison. This makes logical sense to me."

"I still think vulchers are trying to eat us one by one," Milyr retorted bitterly.

"And indeed that speculation is just as likely as any other at this time. We have no real evidence to support any proposed hypothesis over any other," Lyndyn stated. "We just can't scientifically deduce or judge any hypothesis trying to explain the actions of the tendrils. Our limited observations are based on questionable, possibly hallucinatory visual sightings. Our speculations are fueled by a lot of imagination. Our experiences on this moon have not been particularly positive..."

Domyn interrupted him and said, "Sounds like we are at the point where our decisions will have to be based on belief, trust, and faith. That's not very scientific, is it, Prof?"

"You might as well include espersense on your list as well," Lyndyn said, surprising himself. "Yet if that is what we have to work with, then perhaps it cannot be ignored."

"I see movement outside," Kymil announced abruptly.

"Yes, I see them also," Nyba confirmed. "The things are spreading around the bubble. I believe more tendrils are on the way. Prepare yourselves for another buffalo herding maneuver."

"If so watch for color as they elongate. That seems to be our best guide to the potential target. Unless we wait for the tendrils to reach out for someone," Lyndyn advised, but in his own thoughts, he reasoned that most likely he would be the next target, being one male yet to be sought.

"I can see with certainty that the objects are spherical and dark green," Kymil said.

Green, Jamyk's color, Lyndyn mused. Should he assume this had significance to their prior speculations? Were the objects acting in some form of concert with Jamyk? This was much too far-fetched for his life's experience to contemplate. Yet Domyn had suggested that perhaps the situation called for trust and faith rather than scientific deduction. Could he have faith in the opinion of Wolf Streak Beta's prime science engineer?

As his eyes observed the dark object outside the bubble attach and form a blackish spot in the side of the bubble, Lyndyn said loudly, feeling his adrenaline rush, "Tendril time again. Let them attach and reveal their locations before choosing our defensive position. Be alert to any change."

Beside him Kymil said, "I am certain that I just witnessed the green sphere take something from the ocean. I think the green things make or use something else to form the tendrils, almost like a tool."

"I saw that also," Whyvvi confirmed. "That is very odd. Inanimate objects should not do that."

Using a tool? Manipulating the environment? Those were traits of aware life, Lyndyn thought. Should he add this observation to the speculation that some living entity was working in concert with living Jamyk? Did he trust this data? Did he believe this possibility? His own consciousness nagged at him that he must resolve this debate soon. Yet this dilemma was so far away from scientific analysis that Lyndyn could not force himself to accept the resolution now.

"Here they come. Vulchers better not be after me again," Milyr protested. "Sorry, guys, but I can't help but feel this toxx way. I'm such a selfish toxx!"

"I can't blame you," Domyn said, and then pointing his hand and arm, commanded, "There, let's cluster there between those spots. They have all attached. We know their positions. Let's herd there."

Following Domyn's pointing finger, Lyndyn agreed, "Good position. Herd there. Men, stand in the center until we determine who will be the target."

Watching dark spots meticulously elongate into extending tendrils, Lyndyn noticed a black spot lighten in color to dusky gray and then gray-silver toward the tip. His heart rate quickened in his chest and temples. His breaths came shorter and more frantic. However, he also felt more curiosity than panic. Lyndyn stood his ground at the front of the herd with other men behind him. Why was he doing this, he wondered. Why was he not backing into protection?

"Oh my, Lyndyn, the tendrils are grayish," Kymil exclaimed with much worry in her voice. "They are after you. Get behind us. It is our turn to protect you."

Still he held his position, in spite of the rising terror. In less than a second, his conscious awareness considered and reconsidered all previous discussions and speculations. His eyes observed the slowly approaching silver gray tendril tips. Faith or scientific certainty, belief in Jamyk's resilience, in espersense, in Szczygiel Shines, or instead in practicality, observable data, known science, what should he use to make the decision? This was difficult, he thought in desperation.

Domyn stepped in front of him and commanded, "Get behind me. It is my turn to protect."

Yet did he want protection? Lyndyn saw tendrils sway before Domyn. Those tendrils had been persistent but not aggressive nor harmful. Should he trust Whyvvi's logical presentation of the benign entity trying to help Jamyk? Should he believe in his recent flashes of memory relating to Jamyk? Should he accept Kymil's remembrance of the last hour in Wolf and the green tendrils taking Jamyk?

"Get down, Lyndyn," Kymil screamed obstinately. "I can't cover over your head."

Kymil, then others, would they become targets next? If no one accepted contact with the tendrils, would they become aggressive in the future? If their purpose was benign, would they give up and not repair Jamyk? Would reason to keep humans alive in this bubble become unimportant and the bubble destroyed? Could he accept the implication that the tendrils were an aspect of the living entity? This was just too much for him to consider just at that moment. Yet he tried.

"Don't let vulchers eat you," Milyr yelled from behind him.

What did he believe right at this moment, Lyndyn asked himself. Was Milyr right about danger? What did he feel inside his awareness inside the fear of the unknown hovering tendrils and uncertainty of their purpose? They could not go on herding together without knowing the purpose of the tendrils. That gnawing unknown and anticipation of attack would be as bad as an aggressive physical assault. Lyndyn realized they needed more data about the purpose of the tendrils.

Beside him Kymil tugged on his arm and shouted, "No, Lyndyn, get down. Let us guard you. I love you. Don't take any silly chances."

Yes, Lyndyn realized, he loved her as well and all the others of Wolf Streak Beta. He could not let them continue this existence under this constant anxiety. Then a flash of vision of the yellow girl and the green boy playing catch with a blue ball over-rode his awareness. This was no memory of actual experience, he knew immediately. Yet the image was familiar. He had viewed it sometime before recent now. The green boy had a smile on his face. The vision felt very warm, very comfortable. Then a true memory of bony arms hugging him around his torso engulfed his consciousness. Lyndyn accepted what he must do, though that acceptance did not lessen the terror of the unknown.

As he pushed his way past Domyn, Kymil yelled in her own terror, "No, Lyndyn, don't take the chance. I can't lose you now, not yet, my kindred spirit."

Domyn grabbed at him, but at that moment, Lyndyn's arms were much stronger than the big young man, and Lyndyn said calmly, in spite of his internal fear, "Don't worry. I love all of you. Stay away now. I must do this. Do not interfere."

"No, Prof, you don't know what the vulchers will do to you," Milyr shouted.

Then once he was alone away from the herd, six tendrils surrounded his standing body.

"Get away, Prof. Run back here into our group," Whyvvi screamed.

Slowly, smoothly, six tendrils entwined his form, encasing him from head to toe. The fluid movement very briefly caused his vision to blur with a trace of dizziness, but he fought that sensation and stood in his upright position.

"Awe protect him," murmured Domyn from outside the shimmering enclosure of the weaving gray tendrils.

Lyndyn was meticulously engulfed in a cocoon-like wrap.

Kymil moaned distantly, "Oh my, Lyndyn…"

Then his awareness slept.

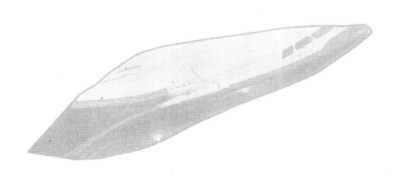

SPEC THREE: LYNDYN ON WYLLOS
CHAPTER 30

Awareness flooded his consciousness abruptly. Hushed voices seemed loud to his hearing.

"I hope he is alright," someone whispered.

"Vulchers, maybe the toxx things ate his brain," the baritone voice of a young man declared.

"Don't say that. He was courageous to go to them," the hushed voice of the woman exclaimed.

Bright yellow light hurt his eyes through closed eyelids.

"Yes, he was brave. But I hope that he is alright. I hope that he made the right choice," a familiar voice murmured with obvious concern.

"That's one vulching choice I won't make. Not without a vulching overwhelming amount of guarantee of safety. Not me," the young man retorted.

His skin felt wet with sweat. His back lay upon the warm soft surface. No, that was incorrect, he realized with a heightened sense of touch. There was more than one surface beneath his body. One was level, warm, and pliable. The other was rounded, warm, soft, and yet with a feel of bone within. This second surface was a thick leg. His acute senses instantly informed him. He was lying across a heated thigh of someone. Arms and hands stroked his torso and arms as they supported him.

"Not even if your friend has done it?" the voice of another woman asked with sharpness.

"For a friend, would you do it for a friend?" inquired the woman again.

"If I was sure, maybe I would! If we knew for certain what we were doing. I'm not a vulching coward," the young man grumbled.

A scent, a familiar pleasant scent from a memory of more than a year ago tickled his noise. This sweet aroma was of a woman that he recognized as his beloved Kymil. Yet this aroma that he inhaled was more than her normal scent. His now acute olfactory system sensed her pheromones, as well as her normal pleasant scent. His sensitive nose was recognizing consciously what would normally be only subconsciously noticed. Yet this was quite stimulating. The totality of her presence tantalized his body.

"Oh my," her breath sighed across his forehead. "I guess effects of antemgebemarzex have worn off, my kindred spirit. Are you aroused from your sleep? Do you hear my voice?"

As his body reacted naturally to stimulations of her touch, her voice, her scent, her spirit in a way, it had not since the last visit to Steppingstone Quinto, Lyndyn mumbled, "Yes...yes... I hear...my Kymil...and I feel your presence....even without...my eyes open. Every sense is amazingly sharp at the moment...Um... so, too, is supposedly an inhibited bodily function. Please roll me over...the pups...should not see...me like...this..."

"Too late, Prof," called Whyvvi rather loudly to his currently sensitive hearing. "You are rather amazingly impressive for an old forty-seven-year-old man, do you not agree, Nyba?"

"Now, Whyvvi, forty-seven isn't old," Nyba giggled. "Maybe over the hill but not old. But any man who has the courage of our Prof must have a lot of manhood, with or without antemgebemarzex. I'm proud of you, Prof. I'm goaded and worried as nasty hell but still proud."

"Why worried?" Lyndyn asked puzzled. "Why do you call me courageous?"

"Oh my, you don't have to act humble. What you did was very brave, perhaps foolish as well," Kymil scolded in her mothering tone while she swiped sweat from his face.

"Did what? And why am I sweating so much after just sleeping? This bubble hasn't made me sweat this heavily yet," Lyndyn complained. "And why is that yellow light so bright now? I don't remember it being so bright before I went to sleep..."

"Don't you remember the vulching tendrils grabbing at you?" Milyr asked, squatting next to Lyndyn. "The vulchers were totally surrounding you. We couldn't see you at all. Only those nasty gray tendrils were there around you. Did they eat part of your brain? Is that why you seemed confused?"

"Tendrils were around me? Eat my brain?" Lyndyn asked more to himself as his mind tried to make sense of his situation and recent memories. "I really do not recall the tendrils around me. I do vaguely remember grouping together to defend against the tendrils…and many questions in my mind about Jamyk, about tendrils, about faith, about trust, about science…"

"That is enough memory for the moment," Kymil demanded. "You have undergone something with which we have no previous experience. We have no historical past to predict how your memory, short-term especially, might be affected. In our own medical operations and procedures, anesthetic compounds are often known to suppress memory. I would not worry about loss of memory now. It is most likely temporary. As long as you know where you are and recognize us, I'm satisfied."

"Will the same thing happen to Domyn?" Whyvvi asked suddenly alarmed.

"What about Domyn?" Lyndyn asked, trying to reconcile his current state of highly functioning senses with his discomforting feeling of not knowing everything present around him.

"We tried to argue with him and stop him, but Domyn followed your example and let the next brown tendrils take him," Whyvvi explained stressfully with a wave of her hand behind Lyndyn's prone position on Kymil's lap. "He is there inside those tendrils. He has been like that for some time."

When he tried to sit himself up and peer around his shoulder, Lyndyn felt unbelievable exhaustion within his body and groaned in pain, "Uh! I feel…so… weary…physically…as if I've…just played three Pulseball games in a row. Every muscle is sore. I can't move without aching."

"Milyr, use your manly muscle and take hold of his feet. Spin the elderly wolf around," Nyba commanded and then asked, "That is alright with you, Doc, isn't it? And you, Prof?"

"If Lyndyn agrees," Kymil said. "Seeing Domyn's experience might stimulate your memory, my kindred spirit. Perhaps you can tell us of your experience inside the cocoon."

"Do it. I'll try to help, but I'm so tired," Lyndyn complained. "I feel as if my body has performed every possible physical movement and function a person could do. I'm tired right down to my cells, if that is possible."

"Vulch, Prof, not every part is tired," Milyr laughed, looking at Lyndyn's crotch while lifting his feet. "I'm so jealous now. I feel like a vulching pup toxx, Prof, being so jealous. And you did it without any help and just lying there. You overcame vulching antemgebemarzex. You're a legend!"

"Maybe you should have accepted the purple tendrils, you toxx," Whyvvi quipped while she helped Kymil grip Lyndyn by the shoulders and arms.

Nyba laughed loudly, "Now my spirit bonder doesn't need any help from a weird cocoon."

"Do you think the tendrils caused it? I think our Prof is just the randiest man in the Sexto System," Milyr declared with admiration. "And hopefully antemgebemarzex is wearing off for all of us. Not having vulching nutrient since we left Wolf may make all of us friskier. Vulch, I can hope!"

"Oh, you just wish that would happen for yourself," Whyvvi said in mocking distaste.

"Everybody ready?" Milyr asked. "Let's spin this randy bear around, so he can tell us what's happening with Domyn. Maybe, he'll become…energized…like Prof. I bet you'd like that, huh, Whyvvi? You must be feeling something for the big guy yourself."

When they picked his sore body off the warm floor and began to reposition him, Lyndyn saw immediately the tan tendrils protruding from the golden bubble. The light tan color was just barely visible to his sight against the very bright yellow light from outside. No wonder he had not noticed the tendril that his peripheral vision should have observed before, he thought. His attention had been focused on the young people before him, and of course lovely Kymil. But now he saw the geometrically spaced spots with the extended tendrils.

"Perhaps, Milyr, if you had gone to the purple tendrils before, you would be energized," Whyvvi retorted as she grunted helping to lift Lyndyn's torso with Kymil while Milyr carried the legs. "But no, when they came seeking you, you ran away and hid behind us again. Even after witnessing Prof bravely let them take him, you were afraid."

While the tall young man glowered and grumbled, Lyndyn followed the tendrils with his eyesight to the light-brown cocoon-like structure formed by the joining of six tendrils. This image stirred a fleeting memory in his consciousness. Vaguely he recalled the gray silver tendrils swarming around his body but nothing after that until waking in Kymil's lap. This light brown cocoon was quite large, over seven feet high, and easily five feet wide at its mid-height. Domyn was inside that cocoon.

"When they came for you, Lyndyn, you went away from our protection and allowed the tendrils to surround you," Kymil explained with some distress still in her voice. "Do you remember that? Do you remember how it felt like inside your cocoon?"

While he stared at the smoothly writhing tendrils forming a tan encasement, Lyndyn replied, "I have some memory of the tendrils closing around me. I remember a discussion about Jamyk and whether he related to these tendrils somehow. I remember deciding that we needed to know for sure if these tendrils were benign or harmful. I do not remember anything while inside the cocoon. Yet I do know for certain that every part of my body feels sore and exhausted. Strangely my awareness is sharper than ever before. My senses are very…sensitive…"

"We could see that, Prof," Milyr smirked. "That's why I'm so vulching envious."

"Indeed…erh…no doubt…you are all mature enough to allow me my human reactions, especially those that the man finds difficult to control in specific circumstances," Lyndyn declared with embarrassed dignity and tried to change the focus of his audience by asking, "Now Domyn is inside that cocoon, correct? How long has he been like that? For that matter, how long was I in the tendril embrace?"

"A tendril embrace…oh, that sounds so cherp," Nyba exclaimed. "So much cherper than Milyr's idea of those tendrils eating our bodies and absorbing our brains! I like the notion…a tendril embrace. And since you seem unharmed and in reasonably good health, I think you have shown that tendrils are here to help us and not eat us."

As the tan cocoon moved about two yards to one side, Lyndyn heard Kymil say, "Obviously we have no real accurate time calibration now, but I would guess that the gray tendrils had you at least an hour, likely more. When they unwound from around you, they laid you on the bubble floor gently. You were asleep by the time we could walk to you. I saw no sign of bodily harm, and your sleep seemed appropriate. That was…oh…maybe three hours ago."

His eyes watched the tan cocoon move around in a circle of about seven feet, and Lyndyn asked, "Did my cocoon move as one? Or is Domyn struggling to get away?"

"This is the same activity as yours was, Prof. The cocoon would move sometimes, bounce up and down, and spin around, actually laid down once. We didn't know what was happening. We were afraid for you," Nyba admitted. "But then when you were released, and Doc said that you appeared in cherp health, we were so happy. I recall even Milyr cheered slightly."

"Until the vulching purple tendrils reached in after me, then I was worried," Milyr protested. "Not long after you came back, vulching green balls appeared outside the bubble and sent in more tendrils after me. I didn't know what to do. You were still unconscious. I couldn't ask you how you felt."

471

"No doubt my unconsciousness was a bit unnerving to you all," Lyndyn sighed wearily.

"You know, that makes sense," Whyvvi stated abruptly. "Oh, I mean about the way a cocoon moves around like this. If the green balls are seeking information about how a male human functions in order to help repair Jamyk somehow, then they would have to study your movement techniques, how your bones and muscles and neural system combine to function when you walk, jump, run, lie down, do push-ups, whatever activity your male body is capable of performing while awake. If we are the first humans green balls have encountered, then they would have to analyze every aspect of our body behavior. Maybe they will even study how you defecate, Milyr?"

"Vulch, that's one function I'll gladly do on them, but they will not get me into one of those cocoons willingly," Milyr promised adamantly.

"If you are correct about the green things attempting to aid Jamyk, or if we are right that they are actually studying us, we now know more because of Lyndyn's risky gamble," Kymil said with some pride, yet also some skepticism. "However, we cannot be positive in our conclusions yet."

"Indeed you are, as ever, our anchor to reality, my Kymil," Lyndyn sighed and then with a groan added, "However, Whyvvi may be correct. I can surely testify that my bodily movements must have been tested based on soreness and aches throughout my body. I feel very good, like after a vigorous workout, but do need some recuperation time. Now you said that the tendrils came for you again, Milyr? They do seem to have you as their main focus, don't they?"

"Vulchers, yeah, toxx came for me again," the lanky young man answered. "But I wasn't sure if you were okay at the time. I'm still afraid they might have bad intent on my manly person."

"Do not be such a toxx," Whyvvi protested. "Think about your friend Jamyk. What if we are correct that we could be helping him as well as ourselves by cooperating with the green balls and their tendrils? Think about Jamyk instead of just your own toxx."

"But we just don't know yet," Milyr declared, and Lyndyn noticed the young man glance nervously at the tan cocoon.

"But they come for you more consistently than anyone else," Nyba said in her steady captain's tone that had been absent for several hours. "I believe you have something that is needed for whatever purpose. If it is to save a crewmate, then I have trust in your loyalty to help that crewmate and friend. I believe that you can be the young man that I would like you to be."

"Uh...erh... I want to be...but I also don't want to be eaten or have my brain sucked out," Milyr stated, staring still at the light brown cocoon holding Domyn. "Let's see what happens with Domyn. It's cherp that Prof came out okay. Let's see about Domyn."

"Oh my, yes, Lyndyn did return to us in rather fine shape for an elderly forty-seven-year man," Kymil laughed in her matronly melodious tone. "Yes, indeed he has shown some new life since coming out of his cocoon. Milyr, you may take notice of certain manly recovery that you often envy."

Grumbling beneath his breath, Lyndyn hoped his prior sexually aroused situation would be forgotten by now, but then trusting Kymil's quick grasp of the situation, he chuckled with embarrassment, "Indeed my old body did seem to respond to your charms notwithstanding the evil affects of antemgebemarzex. The tendril embrace must enhance some manly traits perhaps?"

"Vulching antemgebemarzex, I hate that stuff," Milyr attested, turning toward Lyndyn to say, "But, Prof, you are a man who can defeat even nasty stuff. You're a vulching legend!"

When the young man's wide eyes stared at him, Lyndyn gazed into the young eyes, held them as if with special power, and whispered almost silently, "To be a man, you must behave like a man. Once you behave like a man, manliness comes upon you."

With their eyes locked in a common gaze still, Milyr replied with merely mouthing of his words, easily heard by Lyndyn, "I want to be a man. I want to behave like a man. I want to help my friend, yet I am afraid."

Lyndyn replied in their almost silent conversation, "I was afraid also. Fear does not make you unmanly. Facing fear and doing what you must in spite of fear makes you manly."

Milyr mouthed silently, "Manly deeds can be hard to do."

Lyndyn agreed in a whisper, "Yes, indeed they can. Yet results can be worth the risk."

Then as Milyr nodded in agreement and consequently broke the gaze connection, the young man said in a normal voice, "Yeah, my cherp friend Jamyk is worth the risk."

"What was that about?" Whyvvi whined with bewilderment.

Seeing a startled expression on Kymil's face, Lyndyn asked, "What?"

"You tell me, kindred spirit," Kymil quizzed him with concern in her voice. "You and Milyr were just staring at each other for a couple of minutes at least. No words, no sound, but I thought I saw your lips move. Are you feeling okay?"

"I thought you men were going to fight or something foolish over antemgebemarzex or some other silly man behavior," Whyvvi exclaimed, her voice slightly distressed.

Then Lyndyn realized that no one had heard their conversation. This was odd, he thought. He was certain that they had whispered but not so low as to seem speechless. Was this another weird espersense experience? Why was he thinking of this psychic nonsense again? Yet the women seemed genuinely assured that they had heard nothing. He was certain that Milyr and he had talked.

Turning to look back at Milyr, Lyndyn listened to the young man mutter, "Little peener again. He's got to be alive still. Vulching too many weird one nad type occurrences have occurred now."

"But what was happening?" Nyba insisted in some confusion. "Shouldn't we be concerned for Domyn now? Why this obsession with that rascal? Milyr, you should be rooting for Domyn's safe return. We all suspect the green balls will be back for you eventually."

"No doubt, of course, Nyba," Lyndyn agreed and then added, "Don't worry, Milyr and myself were just experiencing a male bonding moment. It was a man thing. Nothing you ladies need to worry about..."

"Vulch, yeah, this was just a manly thing!" Milyr said with a sheepish grin. "I just needed a lesson from one of the best Blue Jay legends, my own personal role model, someone who has defeated the dreaded antemgebemarzex. Thanks, Prof, for a hard lesson in manly truth. I think I will be ready if my time comes. Yet I can't claim to be fearless. I'm too much a toxx to be fearless."

"What did you do to him, Prof?" Whyvvi asked in amazement. "That does not sound at all like toxx Milyr that we all know and ...love?"

"Just manly maturity," Milyr exclaimed with a bit of aloofness to his manner. "Nothing you fems could understand."

"Oh my, look, the tendrils are releasing Domyn," Kymil said, stepping toward the unraveling cocoon now lying Domyn on the golden floor of the bubble.

Not yet capable of getting himself off the warm floor, Lyndyn was satisfied to sit up and lean his torso and shoulders on his arms behind him. Quietly the six tan tendrils separated and swayed their way slowly back into spots on the bubble. With his acute vision now adjusted to the bright yellow light, he could see the green spheres outside the bubble while they were still connected to the brown spots. This was more clarity than he had previously, he realized.

"How is he?" Whyvvi gasped, perhaps holding her breath. "Is he breathing?"

Beyond the green spheres, Lyndyn saw floating odd shapes and sizes of small to tiny objects silhouetted in light from the sky above the ocean surface. Perhaps the ocean had cleared, sunlight had increased, his eyesight had improved dramatically, or all of the above, he thought. As the green spheres disconnected from the bubble exterior, spots were discarded into the ocean. Then he followed two spheres within his line of sight. The two were joined by others until all six spheres grouped together, and as one form, dashed off into the yellow ocean.

From beside Domyn's prone still body, Kymil reported loudly and professionally, "He is healthy. He has a good breathing rate, good pulse, and sweating freely just like you had done, Lyndyn. He is asleep. I can't find anything to indicate that he has been harmed by the tendrils."

"Can I hold him?" Whyvvi asked hesitantly.

"I am certain that would be fine," Kymil said standing up. "Just keep the dripping sweat from being inhaled by his breathing. Obviously he had quite a workout in that cocoon."

"She likes his sweat," Milyr chortled with a slight sneer. "I believe perhaps more than she used to like Khebol's manly fluid. I wonder what ever happened to Khebol as your true passionate interest, Whyvvi. We haven't heard about him for some time now. Perhaps he's too far away for clutching?"

"Oh, you vulching toxx, Milyr, can you not leave me alone even for awhile?" Whyvvi wailed. "Domyn just had a nasty experience and might need my help. Do not act like a nasty toxx just now. Your nads would not like me if I got angry. My fingers are very strong."

"Young man, my friend, I think that you should heed her warning," Lyndyn smiled while he continued to observe the activities in the ocean outside the bubble. "No doubt you still have ambition to be manly someday, do you not? That would be difficult without cherp nads."

Hastily backing away from Whyvvi sitting beside Domyn's form, Milyr agreed with serious conviction, "Erh! Yeah, Prof, as usual your advice is very sound. I'm sorry, Whyvvi, I guess I become toxx when I'm anxious or even scared. I'll try to be more cherp to you."

"Why would a big tall man like you be anxious?" Nyba asked, striding against his side and taking his hand in hers. "You know that I can soothe any anxiety that you may fear."

"Not any, my Cap," Milyr admitted. "I'm certain the vulching purple tendrils will be back for me. I'm not certain I can do what I think I must. I don't have nads to be like Prof and Domyn just yet."

"Now, my young man, as Cap, I order you to be a man and do what you believe you must. Only you can know in your mind and in your heart what you must do. However, I can assure you, Milyr, my pilot, my friend, my spiritual bonder, that your nads are just as fearless as those of Domyn and Prof Lyndyn. This I believe for certainty."

"You do?" Milyr asked in surprise.

"Of course, you big toxx!" Nyba exclaimed, slapping his buttocks once.

"Ouch! Some friend you are!" Milyr griped.

While Nyba tried to encourage Milyr, Lyndyn continued his observations outside the bubble. This new sight was so much clearer and stronger than the eyesight that he had lived with for his entire life. Hopefully this enhanced vision would remain for a long time to come, but he doubted that. Yet while he had it, Lyndyn watched many small, almost feather-like objects float through the yellow ocean. They acted similar to plankton on the home world. Could these feathery objects be a life-form indigent to this toxic moon? Was it possible that the green spheres were a life-form that could live in this poisonous environment? That seemed far-fetched to his scientific experience and body of knowledge, Lyndyn mused. Could he convince himself to believe beyond his limited knowledge?

"Has anyone seen anything outside this bubble besides the green spheres and dark spots that make the tendrils?" he asked to anyone in general.

Kymil knelt down behind him with her warm knees against his lower back and her hands on his shoulders, and she replied, "We've been preoccupied since you showed some crazy behavior when you went into the tendrils. Our first concern has been the well-being of themen in this bubble, crazy as you are."

"Indeed that is no doubt true. I believe we must learn more about this moon, more about the ocean and the things in it. Do you see those delicate feathery things out there?" Lyndyn inquired, leaning back a little into her gentle hands.

"I can see general substance drifting in the light rays as they shine into the ocean. I can't quite make out individual shapes or patterns though. Those smaller things do not have the same visible iridescence as the green balls or the trings had earlier. It is very surprising that you can. You have always relied upon my eyes to see that detail in the past. Apparently your experience in the tendril cocoon had had more than one benefit," Kymil exclaimed with a subtle laugh.

"Don't start that again, my kind Kymil, please," Lyndyn said in a hushed voice. "Let's not distract pups or ourselves with my personal issues. I'd much rather turn my attention to our situation regarding our survival and our possible future."

"Oh my, yes, I just like to tease you, my kindred spirit," Kymil giggled quite unlike herself. "After all our Blue Jay journeys, I don't get to see the real you very often. This is a very wonderful sight, my Lyndyn, the real you, especially with my PEQA vision."

Groaning and mumbling to himself, Lyndyn wished she would not of this, but then his attention was abruptly diverted by the approaching cluster of the green spheres, and he whispered, "More tendrils coming, I believe. Don't startle Milyr. He has a tough decision to make soon. I'm sure they come for him. Let's wait until they show themselves."

"I'm very amazed that you can see those green spheres. If not for their luminescence, I don't believe that I could see them at this moment," Kymil admitted. "However, regarding Milyr, there is not much we can do to shelter him now. You and Domyn are not able to defend in our herd. Just we three ladies do not make a very large herd for a tall guy like him."

While he observed a cluster separate into the six spheres and deploy in a now routine geometric pattern around the outside of the bubble and wondered why he did not see the luminescence that Kymil had mentioned, Lyndyn whispered, "Please try to protect, if he can't go to the tendrils."

"Of course, what else would we do? Those spheres are beginning to attach now. They have taken hold of the other entity that forms the tendrils. This has no iridescence, but I can see those tools well enough," Kymil stated in a soft voice to Lyndyn only, and then more loudly, said, "Milyr, I believe that your time has come. Are you ready, young man?"

"Ready? For what? Oh, vulch, I see them now," the lanky young man swore. "Vulch, I don't know. I admit I'm scared like a pup."

"Maybe they didn't come for you," Nyba suggested in an obviously half-hearted manner, "But if they did, just be the man that I want you to be. Show us the quality of your nads."

"Yeah, you really believe in me that much, huh, Nyba?" Milyr retorted. "This is me, a toxx oaf!"

When dark spots began to elongate into the six tendrils, there was little doubt that they had come for someone. Lyndyn noticed the greenness of the spheres showing through the gold of the bubble and dark violet of the spots. Although he could not detect the luminescence described by Kymil, his enhanced eyesight did allow him to see so much more than before his encasement in cocoon. But would this ability help their uncertain situation? He had no answer as he witnessed the purple tendrils begin routine protrusion into the bubble from the six precisely spaced spots.

"Vulch, what should I do? My herd is vastly depleted. If this is for Jamyk, then I should help him. I don't know. I'm scared to be eaten. But I want to be a man. What do I do?" Milyr danced, fidgeting around in the middle of the golden floor with Domyn laying on one side and Lyndyn on the other.

"Do what you want," Nyba demanded firmly. "It is your decision now. We will try to defend if you wish. You must choose your actions, my spirit bonder."

"Do not include me in the herd this time," Whyvvi snarled. "Let this tall toxx take care of himself this time. If you want to be a manly toxx, then do something about it besides whine."

"Vulch...vulch... I should do it," Milyr jittered about as the six lavender tendril tips slowly approached his position. "This is vulching hard to make myself do. Was it hard for you, Prof?"

"Of course, my friend, I had terrible fear but found a way to ignore that fear," Lyndyn exclaimed, trying to attract the young man's gaze. "For your friend, Jamyk, you can ignore fear. And perhaps you can do this also for manliness?"

Then Milyr turned his eyes toward Lyndyn, and grinning, yelled, "What vulch! For Jamyk and for manliness!"

"Be brave, my spirit bonder," Nyba sighed "Let your cherp heart rule your fear."

Lyndyn watched the shaking naked young man strut into the midst of the six lavender tendrils and let his lanky body become enclosed in their entwining embrace. A very tall lavender cocoon of writhing tendrils formed around Milyr. Very soon the young man was totally covered and lost to sight.

"He is very brave," Nyba murmured as she sat against the side of the golden bubble gazing at the lavender cocoon. "I wasn't really sure if he would make himself do that."

"About time," Whyvvi snapped churlishly. "He should have allowed this embrace hours ago. Maybe Domyn and Prof would not have had to risk their lives then."

"Most likely we would all be targets of the tendrils, or more correctly, the green balls that are using the tendrils. If your speculation about recuperating Jamyk in contact with these green balls is correct, Whyvvi, then I would guess all males in this bubble would be needed as specimens eventually," Lyndyn explained, watching the tall cocoon.

"If just you men are specimens for study, why would they need to keep us women?" Kymil asked abruptly. "I just thought of that. Why did they save us women? There must be more to this than just repairing Jamyk. If he is alive still, and that is only a speculation."

"Indeed you are perceptive as usual," Lyndyn acknowledged, letting her settle his head against her torso as she massaged his arms from behind. "We have only our own suspicions that this tendril activity is based around Jamyk. There is some logic to our assumptions, but at best, we are guessing still...."

"We may be guessing, but we are still alive," Whyvvi declared from the other side of the tall cocoon. "I believe my speculation about Jamyk is our most logical so far. Much more logical that Milyr's ridiculous 'they are going to eat us' theory."

"That was a bit melodramatic and silly," Nyba conceded. "Or at least that seems to be the case now after we have witnessed some fairly decent treatment from the green balls and tendrils."

Yes, but the young man was afraid at the time, Lyndyn thought. He himself remembered his own fear. If not for unusual memory flashes relating to Jamyk and Swyllo, he probably would not have allowed the green spheres to embrace him. No, he could not ridicule Milyr for being afraid.

In a hushed voice, he inquired, "Kymil, did you find it strange that several of us had memories of Jamyk during the original tendril attacks? For us as scientists to put credence to such memory flashes as evidence seems strange. Did you feel that way also?"

"I don't really remember my feeling of those moments, except for my fear for you when you stepped out of our herd," she whispered, embracing him. "Yet I do recall how many of us had related memories coincidentally pop into our minds under stress. The disconcerting part for me was when we started to talk of these memories as evidence in our investigation. In spite of our science methodology, we still let our sensations guide our decisions. It was very unscientific of us, my Lyndyn."

Laughing suddenly Lyndyn agreed, "No doubt Jamyk has always bewildered my scientific approach. Since I first met the rascal, he has befuddled my perceptions of science of psychology..."

"Yes, oh my, Lyndyn... My visions of Szczygiel Shines or pulsating PEQA... We always thought those false...but do you suppose? He did score extremely high for a human on the zachymatis testing. You don't suppose that he is one in a billion?" Kymil murmured in hushed astonishment.

"Our Jamyk, who can't remember to suit himself before popping? Who chases Swyllo around with splatter bulbs for fun? Jamyk, one human who might possibly have a true rare espersense ability, is this possible? That does sound farfetched and highly unscientific," Lyndyn chuckled with disbelief in his voice, yet silently he wondered could such Jamyk convince unwilling Milyr from afar to step into the tall lavender cocoon now in center of the bubble?

"Oh my, Lyndyn," Kymil whispered with sudden mystery in her manner. "Remember how he went on about Chitir and Fox Flash Alpha in danger just before popping into Sexto? Don't forget how irritated Bodacia artigence without emotions would get at times with him in stasis sleep. We never thought these single incidents had meaning. Now I'm not so sure. Now if we put them all together, perhaps we have pattern of…some form of…what should I call it…espersense… Sounds crazy, doesn't it? Ye, some of that could explain his very unusual behavior at times."

"No doubt, to my scientific orientation, yes, my Kymil, it does definitely seem crazy," Lyndyn agreed while resting on her lap and torso. "Yet in spite of our loss of our Wolf Streak Beta sci-tech, we are alive still on this poisonous moon. Our science and technology aided us as long as possible, but we are well beyond that now. Our current existence has long outlasted any benefit of our Blue Jay sci-tech. That in itself might lead me to accept something other than my science for our present survival. Perhaps some espersense from Jamyk or maybe some aid from a life-form so alien to our existence that we cannot accept it as reality, I don't know. My problem is going through that hatch now that I've opened it. I'm still stuck in Wolf mentally and am afraid to come out the hatch into this new reality."

"And I along with you," Kymil sighed. "That is such a huge step for people trained like us. We have seen signs along the way but did not trust to believe them. Now that belief is more difficult yet very compelling, is it not?"

However, before he could reply, Lyndyn heard Nyba exclaim, "I believe the tendrils are leaving. They seem to be done with Milyr. This time was much quicker than Prof or Domyn."

"Yes, Lyndyn, that was much faster than your experience in the cocoon," Kymil confirmed to him, "Apparently the green balls did not like or need him as much as you, my model of a man."

"No doubt the green spheres have learned much about our physiology and anatomy from Domyn and me. Remember that they had us while we slept also. Most likely Milyr served as the confirmation of the prior results," Lyndyn speculated. "Of course Milyr has his own unique psychological makeup that may be closer to Jamyk than we have suspected. Perhaps that was what interested the green spheres most about Milyr. They did want him persistently..."

Whyvvi interrupted joking, "Maybe he tasted bad, or if they were absorbing his brain, they did not get very much. Oh, Swyllo would like that barb!"

"I just hope that he is not hurt. I hope that they were gentle," Nyba worried, cautiously advancing toward the untwining tendrils.

As the lavender tendrils unraveled from around Milyr, his body appeared laying on the golden floor. Lyndyn watched Nyba stride purposefully through the retracting tendrils to the lanky figure. The naked chest rose and fell with obvious breath. A sleeping form rolled slightly to one side. Milyr was alive. The young man's greatest fear of being eaten by the green balls had not happened. No doubt Milyr rested peacefully within his sleep. Lyndyn felt momentary pride and sympathy for the young man.

"Is he okay?" Whyvvi asked honestly, sitting beside Domyn's large sleeping form.

"He seems to be healthy physically," Nyba replied. "I'm not as gifted as Doc at this without any sci-tech med gadgets, but I'm sure he is fit. Of course, for his mental state, we'll have to wait."

"That was not very cherp before," Whyvvi quipped.

"Damn, girl, give the man some credit. He did do a brave thing. He has been a valuable crewmate on this disastrous journey into the Sexto System," Nyba scolded angrily. "What will you do if the tendrils come for you next now that they have tested all the men? What will you do?"

"They should not come for us. Should they? They do not need to analyze the women. Do they?" Whyvvi asked with sudden concern edging her voice.

While he watched the violet spots drop from outside of the bubble and the green spheres regroup into their cluster, Lyndyn replied, "We don't know if they will come to test you ladies. We have only our own speculation as to the purpose of the visits. Perhaps we will never see them again."

Observing the cluster spheres move away into the yellow ocean, Lyndyn was struck by his own words. They really did not know. Anything could be possible. Even Milyr's fear of being eaten was possibility still. Could their hopes for a happy outcome have skewed their speculations to positive slant? Was Jamyk really alive and reaching out to them with some espersense? Or was this joyful fantasy that they had all created to give themselves hope for a pleasant future? Looking out into the poisonous acid ocean surrounding this golden bubble, Lyndyn wondered and not confidently suddenly.

"If they do come for one of us, then we will not have much chance to avoid the tendrils," Kymil said with resignation as she hugged Lyndyn vigorously. "Our men are all currently defenseless themselves after being weakened by their cocoon experiences. We would not be able to use our herd defense now. Fortunately what little evidence we have about actions of the tendrils seems to indicate benign intent...so far!"

"Maybe the green balls are female," Whyvvi exclaimed suddenly. "Maybe they go for males only. This could be. We do not know, but it makes logical sense."

"I'd put that hypothesis in the same category as Milyr's 'they are going to eat us' theory," Nyba said disdainfully while checking Milyr's body thoroughly, no doubt for any sign of harm.

Outside the golden bubble, tiny feathery structures continued passing through the acid ocean. Their passage was revealed by strong rays of sunlight filtering down through the ocean above the bubble. Then Lyndyn saw what looked like a straight unwavering line above the bubble. Was that a real vision? Highlighted by sunrays, it was there angling away and upwards from the bubble. Then he lost sight of it. Pivoting cautiously he peered up through the top of the bubble. Was that another straight line on a different angle from other side of the bubble? He could not be sure. He lost sight again as the ocean currents eased around the bubble and feathery floaters vanished from the acid liquid. Where had they gone suddenly? He needed their help to give his vision perspective.

"What is that?" Whyvvi shouted abruptly. "Vulch, is that red? Is that red cluster coming for me? Nyba, did you foresee this? What should I do?"

As he refocused his eyesight into lower depths as indicated by Whyvvi's waving hand, Lyndyn heard Kymil say, "Oh my, not likely. tendrils were used by green clusters only thus far. color never revealed itself until tendrils entered bubble. What you see is something else. And, it seems to have glow to it like trings, although a different shade of orange-red."

"Oh, I hate the trings," Whyvvi muttered. "I hope this new thing is not just as bad."

"I believe that we all agree to that," Nyba remarked emphatically. "Yet this is a rather rosy beautiful color. Maybe it is friendly."

"Maybe it won't come to this bubble," Lyndyn suggested, however his keen eyesight noticed subtle change in the red-orange object's course, now directly toward the bubble.

All around the outside of the bubble, the ocean seemed abruptly empty. No green spheres, no feathery floaters, just the golden bubble, the bubble with six defenseless naked humans inside. An unknown object stimulated a natural fear reaction within him. He was certain that he was not alone.

"It is pretty to watch," Nyba exclaimed.

"So are many of the deadliest fish in the marina sanctuaries back on the home world," Kymil exclaimed with anxiety, "I do not particularly like that obnoxiously loud orange-red color. It gives me shivers."

While the red-orange mass approached, Lyndyn saw that it was very likely at least as large as, perhaps larger, than the bubble. That was why he had seen it from so far down in the darker ocean depths. He did not see the iridescence that Kymil had mentioned, but his eyes were different than hers. With an almost star-fish appearance, the massive thing moved closer. Its red almost artery-like patterns lined mostly the orange mass. Undulating...arms...or very thick tentacles... protruded from all sides of basically spherical center mass. Like the three-dimensional starfish, Lyndyn thought, five, six, maybe seven or more arms waved in the acid ocean as thing drew nearer.

"I do not like this," Whyvvi whined. "It does not look so pretty close-up."

"Those red marks look so much like scarlet blood arteries. I hope it does not suck blood," Nyba groaned, embracing the sleeping Milyr as if to protect him.

Whatever it was, when it reached the bubble, one, two, no, three of the extended arms wrapped onto the outside of the golden bubble. The other arms flailed in the yellow ocean but could not bend to reach onto the bubble. The swaying arms reminded Lyndyn so much of the tendrils of the green spheres. Yet he knew this was different. He silently wished he could call upon Jamyk or someone with an espersense cry for help. Might as well ask Domyn's metaphy for an aid, Lyndyn chided himself.

"Oh my, see that?" Kymil gestured toward the point on the bubble where one orange arm clung.

At that point, the bubble began to shrivel within its outer surface. A trail of red fluid seeped within the structure of the golden bubble. Then seeping became a stream branching out like a river spreading into the delta. Lyndyn watched helplessly in horror as the red stream pulsed into the hard-outer layer of the bubble.

"This is not cherp, men and women," Nyba declared with a trembling voice.

"Can we do anything?" Whyvvi asked, sitting next to Domyn's big sleeping body.

Then Lyndyn observed the other arms secrete red fluid into the outer shell of the bubble. At each of these three points of the arm attachment, the outer shell began to shrivel. At the same time, red fluid continued to flow into the shell itself. The shriveling effect began to follow the flow of red fluid. The golden bubble was harshly discolored now. The golden bubble appeared to be dying.

"We need some help," Kymil whispered.

"No doubt we do," Lyndyn agreed.

Their only livable habitat was dying.

SPEC THREE: LYNDYN ON WYLLOS
CHAPTER 31

"What is happening?" Whyvvi screamed. "Is that blood shooting into our bubble?"

Staring in fascinated terror at the scarlet red liquid pumping from the giant star-shaped thing now into both of the golden layers of the bubble, Lyndyn answered, "Not as we define our blood but perhaps something similar to this star... thing...here on this moon. Whatever it is, it seems to be harming our habitat. This can't be good for us."

"We've got to do something. We can't let our bubble die," Nyba declared with frightened certainty. "And our men are still too weak to do anything to help us."

"Oh my, not blood, more like a toxin to our bubble," Kymil suggested as she backed away from the gradually shriveling inner layer of their bubble habitat. "That red liquid seems to be killing our bubble."

Yes, Lyndyn thought in panic, this was most likely. The three arms radiating from the rounded center of the large star-shaped thing had clamped onto the outside of the bubble. From the tips of these arms, the scarlet red fluid pulsed into the structure of the bubble. These three tips were spaced apart, one slightly toward the top of the bubble, another about waist height on the rounded side, third about knee height on the opposing side. From each of these tips, thickening arms lay against the outside of the bubble back towards the large rounded center of the star thing.

As the flailing other arms of the monster swung beyond in the yellow ocean, Lyndyn was silently grateful that those others could not bend to reach the bubble, although they were trying, and he shouted with rising terror, "Let's hope the other arms can't connect with our bubble. Yet there is very little that we can do against

485

this threat… Try yelling and waving your arms at it… Maybe noise or activity can chase it away… I don't really have any other suggestion…"

"Go away, you nasty bloodstar," Whyvvi screamed, trying his suggestion by rushing at the orange-red thing and waving her arms frantically. "Get the vulch away from here."

"Bloodstar?" Nyba questioned, following Whyvvi's example with her arms waving and hollered loudly at the ugly thing, even as she asked between shouts, "Where…did you…get that?... Nasty bloodstar!... Go away…. Sounds like …good term…for you,…you vulching toxx…bloodstar… Go away."

While the young women attempted to frighten…bloodstar… Lyndyn rolled onto his stomach still too exhausted to stand. His new perspective allowed him to trace the arms back to the center more clearly than before. There on the rounded, pliable center between junctions of the arms, he observed the neon pink, wrinkled…mouth-like maw attached to the exterior shell of the bubble. The mouth in the armpit, he groaned at his own metaphor, as he watched branches of the red fluid extend through the orange body of bloodstar. Some of these branches connected maw to the arms contacting the bubble. Some spread back to disappear beyond his vision into the center of the very massive body of bloodstar. They all looked horribly fearsome.

"…Away, you bloodstar! Get away from here," Whyvvi continued to shriek, jumping and waving her arms at the thing. "Oh, I wish Swyllo was here… She always knew how to handle…nasty toxx like you, you vulcher toxx bloodstar."

"This doesn't seem to be chasing this thing away," Nyba panted, still punching at the air towards bloodstar. "What if it doesn't hear us?"

"Or if it doesn't see us either?" Kymil asked through a gasping breath beside the two younger women. "We are merely assuming that it is alive with senses like ours. What if that assumption is wrong? Will we be able to scare it away with these tactics?"

"You can't do much else yourselves anyway," Lyndyn declared, trying to battle the forlorn pessimism creeping into his consciousness, but so as to somehow encourage the women, he said, "Give it your best shot like in the last seconds of Pulseball match when trailing by the goal. Wolves never give up trying. Swyllo would not. Jamyk would not."

"But…we do…get tired," Kymil gasped.

"Vulching bloodstar, go away," Whyvvi screamed.

A groan from the large prostrate body of the young man a few paces from him caused Lyndyn to glance toward Domyn. He saw the young man stirring from his sleep. Then a movement from above caught his visual attention. A single droplet of moisture fell from the bubble where one of the tips of the bloodstar arm gripped onto the bubble. When a droplet splattered onto Domyn's thigh, Lyndyn heard a sizzle of seared skin and saw a wisp of vapor. Another groan sounded from the young man.

"Kymil," Lyndyn shouted urgently, "move Domyn quickly. There is a leak of acid above him. Hurry! His flesh is being burned."

However, his cry was drowned out by the yelling of three women, so Lyndyn struggled to crawl towards Domyn and shouted again, "Kymil, move Domyn... Nyba... Whyvvi..."

Another droplet fell and sizzled into the large thigh, and Domyn cried out in agony. Apparently his sudden loud cry and Lyndyn's movement made the women aware of the situation. Just as Lyndyn touched Domyn's side, three forms dashed by him and dragged Domyn's big form away.

"Oh my, that must be painful," Kymil moaned with concern.

"Vulch, he's heavy," Nyba complained, panting for breath.

Then while Lyndyn paused to rest on his hands and knees, droplet splashed less than a yard in front of his face. A trace of splattered liquid leaped onto his hands. The tiny drops burned his flesh on his fingers. However, his visual focus oriented on the center of the original droplet, there a golden layer of the bubble smoked and sizzled just as Domyn's flesh. The acid of this ocean could harm this inner layer of bubble.

"The acid ocean is leaking inside our habitat," he blurted. "Our bubble is definitely being hurt by this bloodstar. Be careful of the acid droplets..."

"What can we do, Prof?" Nyba asked in controlled panic. "What can we do?"

What could they do, he pondered. Was there nothing that they could do any longer to safeguard themselves or this bubble? Had they finally run out of options? Were they totally at the mercy of the environment of this moon and whim of their captors? Yet this feeling had attacked him before, Lyndyn remembered, in Wolf, when he had been certain that they were out of breathable air with no way to survive. Yet they had survived. Somehow Jamyk had saved them, Lyndyn admitted to himself. That had to be the only explanation... Jamyk and his green balls.

"Jamyk," Lyndyn yelled loudly, spontaneously, "we could use some help again..."

As he rolled away from the acid landing spot, Lyndyn noticed a sudden silence in the bubble and glanced up to see the women staring at him in shocked surprise, so he grinned sheepishly and muttered, "Nothing else seems to be working for us now. I thought a cry for help might work. When all our logic fails...rely on hope... and desperation...perhaps!"

Kymil smiled at him and sighed, "Why not? We have been at the mercy of this bubble and whatever saved us last time when we should have died. When hope is the only tool we have, then we should use it."

"Ah!... Hurts..." mumbled Domyn, stirring on the floor now laced with the thin scarlet red streamlets within the layers of the bubble.

"Domyn...wake up... Domyn, are you okay?" Whyvvi whined, hefting his upper body from behind against her torso and chest. "Oh, you are so heavy, my big man."

"How bad are his burns?" Lyndyn asked, glancing over at the thigh of the young man but not having the proper angle to see the damaged skin.

As another acid droplet sizzled into the soft, shriveling layer of the bubble behind him, Lyndyn crawled on hands and knees away from the splash and towards others while Kymil replied, "Some skin burns and reddening starting. However, there is nothing that I can do. I have nothing to swab him. Now I miss even the simple old-fashioned first-aid kit."

"Where are those green balls?" Nyba complained in a shrill voice. "They kept coming after you men before frequently. They were very persistent. Where are they now?"

"Damn things probably do not need us anymore," Whyvvi wailed, holding Domyn in her arms tightly. "For all we know, they could have sent this bloodstar to finish us now that their study of us seems to be finished. Like most specimens, we are now dispensable."

"What...what's all shouting?" Domyn mumbled, and then when he tried to move, cried out, "Argh! That hurts... What's happening?"

"Perhaps you would have been better off to have stayed asleep, my young friend," Lyndyn said with winded breath as he reached others. "Our situation is as severe and dire as we have seen recently. Our bubble habitat is being destroyed by that bloodstar. The acid ocean is starting to leak into this protective sphere..."

"That's what struck your thigh, Domyn," Kymil explained with compassion. "I'm sorry it hurts. I can't do anything to relieve your pain. I'm sorry."

"Bloodstar? Acid ocean?" The young man stammered in obvious befuddlement.

"It's a long story," Nyba sighed despondently, and then admitted, "The short version is that you woke up only to die soon. I should probably be with Milyr. At least he gets to sleep to his death and not be eaten as he had feared. He's a lucky toxx!"

Death? Yes, Lyndyn agreed to himself, this seemed the only logical future. The bubble was badly shriveled now, only about 71 percent of its original volume remained to protect them. The bloodstar had been able to attach two more arms to the smaller bubble now. The scarlet streamlets were visible around the entire circumference of the bubble. The yellow gold light from outside was dimmed by the increasing presence of red fluid. The mouth-maw had widened and now opened to about a two-foot diameter. If that broke through, it could inhale or absorb one of them whole. Now he was thinking like Milyr, Lyndyn laughed at himself in terrified horror.

With true desperation, Lyndyn leaned back on the hardening floor, faced upwards, and bellowed, "Jamyk...you little peener... We need your help...now!"

"What is that about?" Domyn asked in obvious confusion. "Is Prof finally going insane?"

"That's another long story. The short version is that our Prof is going truly crazy. He's beginning to believe the foolishness of Jamyk's myth," Nyba exclaimed with irritation as she held Milyr's upper body in her stout arms.

"No doubt I'm starting to feel that way," Lyndyn agreed, watching the scarlet streamlets thicken in the bubble walls. "Yet if you have ready access to your universal metaphy, Domyn, please go ahead and invoke some assistance. We need it from any source. If not then our iotas of awareness will find themselves long way from the Zerosolis System when we die."

"Oh my, die, we may die soon," Kymil wailed with weary dejection. "I'm getting tired of that feeling. How many times have we felt that certainty in the last days? It's too much for me now."

Rolling his form against hers, Lyndyn reached up and pulled her tightly to him with his arms and murmured, "Here now, my kindred spirit, clutch with me now. If we are to end this physical life now, then let's end together... Oh, Domyn, will our iotas of awareness stay together afterwards?"

"I...do not know... I'm sorry...but I like to believe so... I do believe that all iotas of awareness are merely miniscule parts of the universal awareness. Perhaps they reunite when they are released by these temporary bodies. I try to believe that strongly...sometimes," the big man stated holding Whyvvi.

"We should end together," Whyvvi exclaimed with conviction. "Our iotas should go on together. That is the only right way for the universe to be organized."

"No doubt one more time won't hurt," Lyndyn said more matter-of-factly than he felt and then yelled almost hysterically, "You rascal, Jamyk. We need vulching help."

Then the bubble was silent, except for the heavy breathing of the six humans. His enhanced vision searched through the red streaked bubble wall into the yellow ocean outside. Yet he saw nothing. Perhaps Whyvvi had been correct, again. Maybe the green clusters had no more use for them alive. Maybe they were being put down, tossed aside, as so many of the experimental animals on which his science of psychology had been constructed so many centuries ago. Were they now nothing but experimental specimens? Was he insane or naïve to believe in living Jamyk? For comfort Lyndyn nestled with his Kymil.

Her sparkling eyes locked with his, and her pert mouth murmured, "I love you. Our iotas may stay together forever, my kindred spirit."

Lying on their sides, chest to chest, he replied, "And I love you, kind Kymil. May Domyn's universal awareness keep us together, in spite of my frequent disbelief in such metaphysical notions."

Then with his neck aching, he let his head settle onto the now hardening bubble floor. Heartbeats thumped in his ear. Their two heartbeats, he realized and smiled. Thankful for his acute hearing, Lyndyn wallowed in the joyful sound of their beating hearts, almost pumping in unison. As long as he was with his Kymil, he was ready for death.

While he was thinking that, he was also thankful for having known and listened to the young engineer with an almost strange philosophical belief beyond science. Lyndyn's acute hearing detected subtle hisses, swooshes, and chimes, almost like faint music, in addition to heartbeats. His first thought was of red toxin flowing through the bubble layers, making hydraulic noises with its flow. He was angered at intrusion. He wanted to die hearing just the heartbeats. However, the chimes, hisses, and swooshes became louder. These new musical noises seemed to come from the ocean outside the bubble.

"Do you hear anything?" he asked the beautiful angel before him.

"No, my kindred spirit, only our hearts beating as one," the angel sang in reply.

However, his ear on the hard red-streaked floor heard strange noises louder, perhaps closer. Was the bloodstar creating these sounds with its assault on their bubble? Why had he not noticed these noises before? Yet noises were really there, he was certain that he was actually hearing them. But from what or where did they originate?

Raising his head from the bubble floor, Lyndyn listened intently. His eyes searched around the bubble near the bloodstar contact. He could see very little movement of maw or arms of the bloodstar that would account for these new noises. These sounds were much too musical in nature to be from the bloodstar, he mused. A very faint trace of sound, not related to breathing or occasional movement of person, reached his presently keen hearing. What was it? Where was it emanating?

"What is it, Lyndyn?' Kymil asked puzzled. "You seem suddenly distracted, even alert."

Then suddenly a movement in the ocean outside the bubble attracted his attention. A dark green object approached. Another followed close behind the first. His vision was hampered by the scarlet streaks in the bubble wall. Yet, yes, he was confident that he recognized the now familiar clusters of the green balls. Two, no, more followed. Clusters of green quickly moved toward the bloodstar. This time the clusters did not separate as they had when they had formed the tendrils. Were they here to help the bloodstar or to protect human specimens in the bubble or to observe only?

"We have our green balls back, everyone," Lyndyn announced, feeling the others should be informed of the changed situation…for good or for bad.

"About time; I hope that they kill that bloodstar," Whyvvi stated with hatred and relief.

"If that is why they have come," Nyba sighed. "Then I'm agreeing with you, my friend."

Watching with fascinated curiosity, as well as hope, Lyndyn observed the green clusters surround the bloodstar. Then his ears heard a swooshing noise and his keen eyes saw what looked like shiny silver sprays shoot from the clusters toward the arms of the bloodstar attached to the bubble. He could not be sure, but he thought that he counted at least seven different clusters. Their movement and continual spraying interfered with his accuracy of observation.

"What are those green balls doing?" Kymil asked, leaning against his back for either comfort or to support him, Lyndyn could not be certain, but he was grateful for her touch. "Lyndyn, I can just barely see them out there because of their luminescence, but I cannot see activity clearly through this red liquid in the bubble."

"The green clusters are squirting something on the bloodstar," Lyndyn said, and then as he observed the action, he continued, "Indeed I believe the bloodstar is letting go of the bubble… Yes, yes, the arms are pulling away. The bloodstar is thrashing at the green clusters. It seems not to like that silver spray. It is backing away…"

"I hope they kill it," Whyvvi spat. "For dripping acid on Domyn, I hope they kill it."

"Doesn't appear as if that is the goal," Lyndyn reported. "The green clusters have left an escape route behind the monster. They are continuing to spray at the bloodstar as they chase it away. Forceful mercy seems to be their intent…"

"Oh my, at least they chased it away. At least this shows that they may want to keep us alive. This is hopeful," Kymil exclaimed nervously, kneading his shoulders with her fingers.

"But is our habitat destroyed?" Domyn asked wearily. "Can it recover its prior health?"

Glancing around Lyndyn wondered the same question. All around the bubble, red streaks existed still. The inner soft layer had shriveled and hardened during the attack. The bubble itself had decreased to about half its original size. Droplets of acid liquid from the ocean continued to periodically fall from the highest leak. They were still in considerable danger. What would the green clusters do now?

"Are we going to be able to live in here now?" Nyba inquired gazing around at the damaged bubble. "Can this bubble keep us alive like this?"

"Just watch out for the acid leak," Kymil warned. "Our bubble has changed size. Make sure that you stay away from under that leak. I do not have any medication to repair that type of burn now. I suppose that we are lucky that only one leak occurred during the attack."

"Damn right! And that big mouth could have swallowed us whole if it broke through the bubble," Domyn said in Whyvvi's arms. "Even my fat toxx would fit into that thing!"

"Now, Domyn, you should not believe you are fat. You are just a really big man," Whyvvi said tenderly, stroking his arms and shoulders. "Does the burn hurt very much?"

"Only when I try to move," Domyn said with a wince.

"That was a really big opening if it was a mouth," Lyndyn agreed. "But thankfully the green clusters chased it away…"

"Maybe we have Jamyk to thank?" Domyn smiled, gazing at Lyndyn.

Staring back into the young man's eyes, Lyndyn nodded and said grinning, "Perhaps my insane hollering had some effect after all. Or maybe your universal metaphy has some other destiny planned for us. Perhaps, my big friend, it is not our time to rejoin the infinite collection of awareness."

"Awe well, we will never know until it happens," Domyn sighed in exhaustion. "Prof, were you this tired when you awoke from your sleep after the tendrils? I'm so listless and tired."

"Indeed I am still almost useless here for much physical effort, righ,t Kymil?" Lyndyn declared.

"Oh, yes, you lazy toxx, if I keep mothering you, you'll most likely lay on this floor until our bubble pops, if that's what will happen next?" Kymil responded in both mirth and then worry.

"I want to know what will happen next," Nyba demanded firmly, and then when she peered up toward the ocean surface somewhere above, she yelled, "Vulch, you little rascal, what can you do now? We are still trapped in this dying bubble. Can't you do something for us now for a change, you rascal?"

Glancing upwards in reflex to Nyba's action, Lyndyn saw sunlit feathery objects floating by in the yellow ocean. The appearance of these feathery things eased his concerns at least about return of the bloodstar. Usually small life returned to the sea only when danger is less likely. Yet, he reminded himself, this was not the environment of the home world. Those feathery things were not likely a life-form. He should not assume similarity to the original home world conditions. Perhaps danger had not left.

"It's contagious," Kymil smirked. "I refer to our swelling acceptance of notion that somehow Jamyk is behind our survival and is intervening still. Are we all going insane, I wonder. To be accepting such fantasy that is so unlike our sci-tech experience as Blue Jayers is very unusual. Are we all becoming so like you, my kindred spirit, a slight bit crazy with your mental conflict between science and fantastic philosophies?"

Domyn stated emphatically from his position on the floor in Whyvvi's embrace, "Awright, well, if we do, then I won't complain. I can't think of a better role model for any Blue Jayer than our Prof."

Pleased but also embarrassed by sincerity of the tone and praise of the young man, Lyndyn pretended in ignore the comment and instead muttered to himself while looking up into the yellow ocean, "I thought that I saw something before the bloodstar attacked. I wonder if I can find it now."

"You elderly bear of a man, you can't fool anyone with your humbleness," Kymil laughed, gripping his shoulders and biceps. "We know you thrive on our compliments."

"Um! Well, no doubt, if any of us resembles a bear, it would be our big man Domyn," Lyndyn chuckled, yet still trying to avoid uncomfortable recognition.

"I'm much more like a gopher or woodchuck...or maybe on a really good day... a wolf. But certainly I'm not a bear!"

"Okay, my elderly wolf, I can accept that," Kymil giggled, no doubt relieving her stress with humor and hopefully, Lyndyn thought, helping others with their anxiety.

As the younger ones laughed, Lyndyn smiled and continued to peer upwards and said in attempt at a seriousness, "I did see something up there, before the bloodstar attack. Of this I am certain. It was some kind of straight line. Actually two...one about there and another about there..."

Then abruptly his eyes noticed a descending purple thing. It was like a blanket but much larger, big enough to cover this bubble. Slowly it fluttered from the surface above down toward the bubble. Yes, he realized those were green clusters around the edge of the purple blanket. Where had he seen the purple covering? His memory recalled the purple covering over the tring damaged window of Wolf. Kymil had mentioned a purple covering over the hatch when Jamyk had opened Wolf to ocean. This high awareness of his mental faculties was no doubt from experience in the cocoon of tendrils.

"I believe that we have a repair crew on way," he announced nonchalantly to the others.

"A repair crew?" Whyvvi inquired surprised and then suddenly more hopefully asked, "Do you mean Fox Flash Alpha? It should be Fox Flash Alpha. They should have noticed our signal for help by now. It must be Khebol and foxes."

"Not Fox Flash Alpha, our green clustered hosts are bringing the purple cover for our bubble," Lyndyn announced. "Just as they had for our damaged Wolf during your tring attack."

"They were not my trings," Whyvvi retorted. "I just termed them. That is all. I hate the trings. Is this new arrival a purket?"

"Well, don't worry about whose trings they were," Domyn murmured, patting her arm. "We may have some aid now. We may have a secure bubble again. Let's hope that is case. If it is one of your purkets, then the green clusters have come to help us."

"That is better than dying," Whyvvi conceded. "These green balls have been cherp for us."

"Don't be shocked when light dims," Lyndyn advised the others while he observed the green clusters bring Whyvvi's purket over the top of tbe bubble. "They are up there now."

Suddenly yellow light ended from above. The dark purple, almost violet covering capped the top of the bubble. Part of this covering flowed between the green clusters to encompass the entire outer surface of the bubble. As visible light dimmed into the violet range, Lyndyn found his keen vision was not as sharp, but he did witness the green clusters release the covering and back away. Hisses and whooshes blended with what sounded like faint chimes and clicks to his sensitive ears. What was that sound, he wondered. Yet that did not seem so important just then, so he tried to view the damaged shell.

"Our repair crew?" Nyba asked with optimism. "Is this activity outside now?"

"Indeed it appears to be," Lyndyn replied with a yawn. "The green clusters did bring a purket."

"Are you exhausted from all that sitting and watching that you have been doing, Prof?" Whyvvi teased more gaily now that the bubble seemed to have assistance. "My purket has come to our rescue."

"I know how he feels," Domyn said, still barely able to sit himself without Whyvvi's support.

"And my tall man is still asleep," Nyba said, peering down at Milyr. "Guess men can't handle the few tendrils, eh, Whyvvi?"

"Oh! That sounds so much like something that Swyllo would say," Whyvvi quipped.

"No doubt, young lady, you have no idea of how exerting an experience in the cocoon can be," Lyndyn said tiredly. "And now that I have time to relax and think about it, how hungry I am suddenly. When did we eat last? I don't recall eating much, if anything, since Wolf and our nutrient."

"Awe well, since you mention that, I'm famished myself," Domyn admitted. "Is there nothing to eat? Didn't our hosts learn about our need to eat when they studied us?"

"I am a little hungry myself," Nyba said. "This is frustrating not getting fed. How can we do tricks for the green balls if they don't feed us?"

With his eyelids starting to feel heavy, Lyndyn hastily scanned the bubble to confirm that the green clusters were in fact engineering the repair of the bubble. His awareness quickly ascertained that the leaking had been stopped. Also, the streaks of red fluid seemed to be thinning. Yes, his eyes could just see red liquid flowing from the bubble shell into the yellow ocean, partially visible along the lower curvature of the bubble. The texture of floor on which he sat seemed to be regaining some of its original softness. Their bubble habitat appeared to be regaining health. Thank you, green balls, he silently praised, we appreciate your diligence and protection. However, what about food, he growled.

"Indeed, if there is no food or nutrient available, then perhaps this elderly wolf will curl up and nap. Wake me if you can summon Jamyk with some tasty morsels," Lyndyn smiled as he yawned, settled his head onto Kymil's chest, and fell asleep again...

...Oh, heavenly tasting, he dreamed. A thick syrup flowing down his throat into his slowly filling stomach was so much better than nutrient. His mouth suckled on a warm teat. His tongue tasted luxurious flavor. If this was not real, Lyndyn thought, then perhaps it was remnant of a glorious dream. Yet it was so enjoyable nourishing himself by suckling on a warm teat. He did not want to wake.

"Take it easy, Lyndyn," Kymil instructed through the mist of his awakening. "You haven't taken in food or water for some time. Don't overfill your stomach."

Her voice sounded so close to his ear. Her breath tickled his lobe. Her scent, so tantalizing, filled his nose. Her hands on his back supported his weight forward. Then he gradually opened his eyelids and saw nothing but golden honey yellow. No, that was not right. Immediately in front of his eyes, he viewed the golden liner of the bubble. In his mouth, he felt a teat from which he did now truly suckle. Then his awareness coordinated with his brain and senses. He was feeding from the bubble. This was no dream. A surprise of this fact ruined his enjoyment, so he stopped suckling and leaned back from the bubble wall.

While her grip supported him and yet allowed his backward movement, Kymil said, "There now, my kindred spirit, do you feel better with a full stomach?"

Still groggy and confused from his nap, Lyndyn stammered in confusion, "Erh...full...stomach? We got food? How? I was sleeping, wasn't I?"

The professional patience in her voice filtered through even his current state as she replied, "Yes, you were asleep. While you slept, we discovered how to feed in this bubble. Obviously, before we awoke for the first time, we must have fed during our long sleep. There had to be way of feeding. Actually Milyr is the hero who discovered the secret."

"He is awake now? How long did I nap?" Lyndyn asked, looking around in the well-lit golden bubble. "Wait a moment, why is the light so bright again? Where is the purket covering of the green clusters? Did I dream all that? The bloodstar? The green clusters coming to help us?"

"Awright, Prof, that's enough questions," laughed Domyn in a deep growl. "Many changes have occurred while you slept. You don't have to do everything yourself, you know."

"I still don't believe the vulching bloodstar story," Milyr protested, lying on his back with his head and shoulders against Nyba's side. "That is just too vulching unbelievable."

"Let's tell Prof about the food first. I like that story," Whyvvi giggled. "How did you discover the secret of getting fed, Milyr? Tell us please."

"Um! Erh! Not something I can say in front of respected ladies. It's a man thing. Let's just say I did finally get an idea," Milyr sputtered uncomfortably.

"Yes, you did. It was an interesting discovery. A very useful discovery, I should say," Kymil exclaimed in a positive congratulatory manner. "We could have eventually starved if you hadn't come across the technique. Well done, Milyr."

"Yeah... Erh...any sensible man...um...person could have figured it out," Milyr said.

"Oh, I think a man would definitely think of the method that you discovered before a woman," Nyba declared with a chuckle. "Especially the way you formed the golden substance..."

"Awright, well, we are not explaining this very well to Prof at the moment," Domyn announced abruptly. "Perhaps we should inform him of the other new conditions about the bubble. Us men can get together later and talk of Milyr's discovery privately."

"Indeed, let us move along. What happened to the bubble? Did the green clusters repair it already?" Lyndyn asked, stunned at how healthy the golden bubble appeared now with no red streaks, no shriveled skin, no acid leaks, no evidence that the bloodstar had attacked.

"That's an easy answer," Kymil responded. "Yes, the purket covering repaired the bubble in less than half of your sleep cycle. Oh, and by the way, that is how long you were napping, one of your sleep cycles."

"Then that was about four to four and a half hours," Lyndyn estimated. "And the entire repair was finished in less than two hours? Very quick reconstruction crew those green clusters hire. Was there any recent reappearance of the bloodstar? I did recall that monster correctly, didn't I?"

"Yes, you did. We've seen no sign of the bloodstar since the green balls chased it away. Those clusters have been appearing more regularly now. I believe they are guarding us from the bloodstar," Domyn suggested. "Though that fact makes me a bit uneasy, if they believe we need guarding."

"I really don't believe your bloodstar story," Milyr reiterated again. "That's so vulching nasty!"

"Then tell us about your feeding discovery," Nyba teased.

"No, that's okay, maybe I can begin to accept your bloody star tale," Milyr muttered sourly.

Laughing with Nyba briefly, Whyvvi then said, "This guarding is a really cherp change in behavior of the green balls. We should be much safer now. We can also assume the green balls are helping us just as I reasoned hours ago. Maybe it was days ago. I have lost my perception of the time passage. Yet now I finally feel safe, at least until Fox Flash Alpha can rescue us."

"Indeed recent events do support your hypothesis partially. Although we have no real evidence to indicate that Jamyk is at nexus of this situation…" Lyndyn began to say.

"Awright, Prof, let's not get onto that subject right now. Let's get to the really cherp new discovery, or at least really interesting discovery," Domyn interrupted.

The young man was obviously anxious to tell him something, so Lyndyn asked with puzzlement in his voice, "What is this new interesting discovery? I thought feeding was good enough for me."

"Oh my, you ravenous wolf, you and your stomach," Kymil sighed.

"Remember the sightings you thought that you had seen recently above the bubble?" Domyn asked rhetorically and then almost immediately went on explaining, "Awe well, when the purket was removed by the green balls, I saw something like you had described. Then the green balls traced along one line. Their course through the ocean to surface allowed me to focus my eyesight and attention along that line and then back again to the bubble. Actually there is a line of some strand-like material. And one of the lines attaches right up there."

Following Domyn's pointing finger, Lyndyn peered upwards to see a very faint discoloration in the bubble layers and asked in surprise, "What is it?"

"We think that it could be our air intake system coming from the surface," Domyn stated with excitement. "And, Prof, there are two more of these lines and valves, one here and one over here."

Again Lyndyn followed the young man as he pranced around the bubble pointing at two additional locations. No doubt, he convinced himself, if Domyn could step so lively after his tendril cocoon experience, then so could he. Yet Lyndyn arose cautiously to allow his legs and feet to get their balance after having been inactive for several hours now. However, he did manage to stand. He did stride to where Domyn now stood beneath another slightly off-colored spot on the bubble.

"How did you see that? I can just barely see the difference myself and I have enhanced…" Lyndyn was saying but then stopped suddenly before continuing, "Of course you must have the similar enhancement of your senses after being in the cocoon. Is that correct? And you also, Milyr?"

"Awe well, yes. I thought it was just me being more rested than before," Domyn said. "I didn't think it was unusual. I never suspected to be more sensitive to everything."

"Vulch, so that's why everything seems so clear, every sound so sharp, every touch so…" Milyr exclaimed, letting his voice trail off abruptly.

"It wasn't so nasty being in the tendril embrace after all, was it, my tall man?" Nyba exclaimed.

Before Milyr could reply, Domyn said abruptly, "But the really important finding is that all three openings or valves, I believe, are connected to the surface by a line or tube that you had originally noticed. See how evenly arranged these three valves are placed? I believe that they also act as rigid cable supports that stabilize the position of our bubble. This stabilization would keep the bubble at relatively constant depth in the ocean to control the temp in the bubble. It is a clever design by our hosts."

Staring upwards into the ocean, Lyndyn could just barely follow line to surface, and he said with admiration, "Very well done, my young friend. Your deductions seem very reasonable and based upon relatively solid observations. However, what leads you to assume that the tubes are designed for air exchange?"

"While you were napping, we lifted Kymil up to the one," Domyn grinned with pride. "She isn't that heavy, and Nyba and Whyvvi are strong ladies, since I was too weak at the time."

When he turned to look at Kymil, she nodded her head affirmatively and exclaimed, "Yes, there was active air flow coming in through the valve. It is very fresh oxygenated air. Somewhere in that tube, there must be a device or membrane that filters out gases toxic to us and allows those necessary for us to pass in. The designers of this system have learned much about our needs."

"No doubt, if you are correct, then this new data and everything that we've experienced since entering…no…being placed in this bubble suggests very strongly of an intelligent living system of which this bubble is just a portion. Those green clusters or balls or whatever could very well be intelligent, non-carbon-based living beings. This could be a truly amazing discovery, or at least speculation," Lyndyn stated. "If we could only get this info out to Blue Jay or Fox Flash Alpha, then this would be fantastic."

"Vulch, we thought escaping Kil-Kol trap and finding the lost colonial spaceship would be our glorious achievement. Now we find this. Vulch, we will be more than legends," Milyr gloated from his back on Nyba's lap.

"Only if we are found by someone in Blue Jay and can get our newest discovery known to humanity," Nyba cautioned in her firm voice of reason. "We're still trapped here."

"Awright, well, if the green balls continue to help us and keep us alive, at least we have chance of rescue," Domyn declared hopefully. "That's better than just a few hours ago."

"I told you several hours ago that we should be confident. This entire circumstance is cherp for us because it is cherp for Jamyk. I have logical reasoning for this and also a strong feeling," Whyvvi stated. "Although I will trust my logic more than my feeling."

"For once I agree with you," Milyr said with a grin, surprising everyone, especially Lyndyn. "My discovery of feeding was based on a recalled dream memory involving our rascal Jamyk and myself discussing...erh...um...well, manly talk. My point is that this connection with Jamyk makes me feel strongly with your speculation, Whyvvi."

"Now considering that shape of floor on which you were feeding was well-rounded and about hand width across..." Nyba began with a giggle.

"Vulch, don't go there please, my Cap," Milyr blurted in embarrassment. "I think everyone gets the vulching picture now. We're all adults here now. Vulch, we don't need to play with this now."

Feeling and scenting Kymil at his side, Lyndyn peered at her face. She was looking up at him with a pleasant smile. He grinned back. For the first time in several days, Lyndyn felt secure and comfortable for himself, for his Kymil, and for their young friends.

Thank you, green balls! Thank you, Jamyk. Thank you, universal awareness. The future, Lyndyn thought, at least had a decent forecast now.

He hugged Kymil closer.

SPEC THREE: LYNDYN ON WYLLOS
CHAPTER 32

"Urinating is vulching annoying," Milyr complained.

Smiling at the tall young man standing beside him on his left, Lyndyn said, "No doubt, though you like feeding and drinking that fills your stomach. But then this enjoyable activity will eventually require elimination of your human waste by-products. You can't have good without annoying. Life just doesn't happen like that."

"Awright, I think that we were much too reliant on our former Saphyndenlairoum to perform functions and clean-up after while we slept," Domyn exclaimed, standing to the right of Lyndyn.

While they conversed, the three men urinated into cup-like formations that they had gouged with their toes in the pliable golden layer of the bubble. Behind them on the far side of the same bubble, the three women were most likely performing the same bodily function, Lyndyn thought. Now that their habitat bubble had begun feeding them at their wish, they had found these bodily functions could not be postponed forever. They did not have Saphyndenlairoum sleep stage anymore to service some of these functions. Urinating and defecating were necessary life processes and were now more frequent. Yet, he realized, their need for privacy, at least gender privacy during these very personal moments, haunted their social behavior still. Or perhaps, Lyndyn mused, not so much privacy but maybe some same-gender bonding.

Then as the last of his stream was absorbed into the bubble and then expelled by the bubble out into the acid ocean, Lyndyn said, "We can't be too dissatisfied with our situation. The green clusters are providing us with a place to live in this acidic environment. They have given us means to nourish ourselves. This habitat takes care of the removal of our wastes. The green clusters have apparently assumed role of our guardian against the bloodstar. Indeed I believe that we are as well off under our present circumstances as we can hope to be."

"I agree," Domyn said. "Since the loss of Wolf Streak Beta and then Wolf, we are fortunate to be alive at all on this deadly moon in this toxic gas giant planet."

"Vulch, I would rather be in my old life on Wolf Streak Beta," Milyr grumbled.

"On that we no doubt all agree," Lyndyn stated, staring through the golden bubble wall not more than one yard in front of his eyes and raising his hand to point. "It seems that the green clusters have definitely assumed role as guardians for us around this bubble. That's the third pass by this view since we walked over to here. I can see another cluster drifting farther out from our bubble. I wonder if those things sense that the bloodstar is a threat still."

"Are you acknowledging that the green balls are some form of intelligent life, Prof?" Domyn inquired. "The chance is very tiny, almost nonexistent, that the carbon-based organic life-form as we know on the home world can survive in this acidic ocean or poisonous atmosphere of this moon."

"Since we have only our observations without the benefit of hard, measurable physical evidence at this time, then I would say that the circumstances of our safe habitat, our rescue from Wolf, and apparent behavior of the green clusters would suggest actions of intelligent life. Even I, as indoctrinated in my scientific knowledge and bias as I am, must concede that not all intelligent life must be carbon-based or have some common physical basis common with life we have know on the home world in the Zerosolis System," Lyndyn admitted with great personal difficulty. "We must be wary of limiting our perspective with excess of scientific arrogance."

"Vulch, I've heard you say that many times before," Milyr said. "But I don't feel comfortable about the possible intentions of those green balls, whether they are intelligent life or not. I still don't vulching trust them. Maybe they keep us as pets or something besides specimens to study. Vulching makes me very nervous with them outside all the time."

"Too bad that you slept through the bloodstar attack and then our rescue by the green balls," Domyn stated. "I am very sure the experience would have changed your current perspective."

"Bloodstar? That's not in my memory," Milyr declared. "To me it doesn't exist."

Suddenly Whyvvi's voice exclaimed loudly from behind them, "If you manly guys stand there like that much longer, we might begin to believe that you are doing something besides urinating."

"Um! Erh!" stammered Milyr. "Just nating, that's all. And deep discussions about our present situation here in this bubble, right, men?"

Grinning as he turned to face the women now standing in the center of the bubble floor, Lyndyn quipped, almost surprising himself with his comments, "Indeed a very serious discussion. Besides, if you are hinting at what I believe that you might be suggesting, then, young lady, you need not worry. With three such gorgeous and playful young ladies populating this golden bubble, any sane man would trust them to control the natural urges of all concerned. We men are mere toys…"

"Now, ladies, I don't know if we've been praised or insulted," Nyba interrupted and scowled at Lyndyn. "Prof, I am very shocked at you now."

"Oh my, my kindred spirit," Kymil laughed in her melodious voice. "Are you sure that you and Milyr have not just experienced personality transference? You have not expounded like that in quite some time. Not since our own younger years on Turkey Trot."

"Hey! I don't expound by myself like that," Milyr protested. "I'm a real man. I don't need to expound to relieve my stresses. I'm me. Prof is an expounder."

"I must agree with you, Milyr. You are much nastier ridiculous," Whyvvi chuckled. "Now what were you really doing for so long? That was not a competitive manly event, was it, guys?"

"Awright then, if you insist on knowing our manly secrets," Domyn chortled with gaiety and melodrama, and then paused for emphasis before continuing, "we were talking about how unusually so beautiful and…yes…bodacious…the shape and size of …the green clusters are to us men."

While Domyn stood with his cupped hands slightly extended in front of his chest and grinned widely, the expressions of the three silenced women went from amusement to bewilderment, then to amazement as they realized that this was their stoic Neer who had just used this innuendo. Lyndyn was surprised himself at Domyn's sudden relaxation of his usual manner. Then he just laughed deeply in his nasal snorts, and tears trickled from his eyes.

Nyba finally joined the laughter and sputtered, "Oh… I see… did this skinny toxx…tell you how…he discovered …feeding technique? Is that the manly secret?"

With a frown, Whyvvi asked puzzled, "Were you really talking about our…
you know…whatever you men call them. Domyn…you would not talk about…
would you? I do not believe that you are so like this obnoxious toxx here, this
Milyr toxx. You would not…would you?"

Gazing into Kymil's eyes, Lyndyn sighed with contentment, although he was
surprised at how freely he and Domyn had suddenly begun talking with sexual
innuendo, and said, "If this is the substance of our dialogue, then I guess that we
are no doubt feeling secure. We all feel less threatened at this moment than we
have in several…days?"

"Yes, and this is such a nice feeling," Kymil agreed, stepping to him and
embracing him, and then whispered into his ear, "Playful woman? Be careful of
what you dream."

Hugging her form tighter to his own, Lyndyn whispered, "Dreams may be all
we have now. Perhaps we should not wait. We don't know what we have as future,
my kind Kymil."

Feeling her embrace strengthen slightly, Lyndyn inhaled her comfortable and
compelling scent. She had been his dream always. Since their first meeting when
they were very young pups before qualifying for the Blue Jay project, he had felt
that she was his future. His spirit bonder, as they had told the young people on
Wolf when the end had seemed near. Through their adventures on Turkey Trot
through Steppingstones and LaOgres on the long mission to the Quinto System to
be amongst the first people to scout there, they had shared their lives. Then back
to Steppingstone Primero to educate themselves in their present primary functions,
they had shared their lives. Then years later as mentors to this current crew of Wolf
Streak Beta, they had shared their lives. Always with the future intent of finally
being a couple once Sexto had become part of the Blue Jay realm. Perhaps then
they could settle and begin family…children perhaps?

"Is this the right time? Is this an appropriate situation?" she asked in a hushed
voice. "We have responsibility yet, my kindred spirit."

Yes, responsibilities, Lyndyn reminded himself. But how could he aid these
young friends now? What options did he have under their current circumstance?
Could Kymil and he actually do anything to give these young people a future? Oh,
indeed how he wanted at that moment to flee his obligation and enjoy his time
with Kymil. Perhaps their future was this present. Was there any real probability
that those in this golden bubble had a significant future? Was there anything in his
control that could give them a future of merit, a future of meaning? Oh, he wished

that he could just be with Kymil. Did they not deserve a joyous time alone after all these years?

Then a sob disturbed his concentration, and he heard Domyn ask in as sympathetic tone as his deep voice could manage, "Whyvvi, what's wrong? Are you hurt?"

The young woman sputtered through tears with her head resting against his big chest, "No…just… Swyllo… I was just…so sad… Swyllo could not be here… now…to feel this way…that I feel with you… She should be here… She should have had the chance to have a big man like you as I do."

"That's okay, you can miss her now," Domyn murmured, continuing his embrace. "Her spirit or iota is with us as long as we remember her. Her life had meaning as long as we ourselves continue to have meaning and accomplish deeds of value with our lives. She is not totally gone."

"But if we die soon. If we lose meaningful lives, what will become of Swyllo?" Whyvvi wept.

"I believe her iota of awareness is already serving the universal awareness in some role. If we die, then our iotas will do the same. I believe that we will rejoin Swyllo in awareness of universe. Our iotas will meet together again," crooned Domyn just loud enough for Lyndyn to hear.

"I wish we could leave something for someone to remember her. Just something…or…perhaps a name…for something to honor her memory," Whyvvi muttered into his chest.

"That is a cherp thought. We haven't named this bubble yet. We haven't named this moon or gas giant planet that it orbits. Whatever you believe is best, Whyvvi. You are our certifier of new terms as decreed by Cap Nyba days ago in Wolf," Domyn said firmly and soothingly.

"I will… I will think about it," Whyvvi mumbled. "Hold me tighter, my big man."

Thinking about Swyllo, Lyndyn thought, he had not dwelt on the death of the young woman. Yet he excused himself, for his attention had been on so many other critical occurrences since that horrible sight. Now as he hugged Kymil for support, and yes, courage, he allowed his memory to recall the vision of the last moments of Swyllo in the very narrow access ladder in Wolf Streak Beta. Her determination to throw that last switch, to fulfill her duty for her crewmates, moved him to tears. Her unplanned sacrifice to give her fellows a chance to go forward to their destiny moved him. As tears trickled down his nose and cheeks, Lyndyn understood Whyvvi's feelings.

"Name this yellow moon for her," he suggested, glancing into the round face of the young woman in Domyn's muscular arms. "Her spirit was feisty, tempestuous, unpredictable but also had a heart of honest concern and regard for her friends. Does that not seem much like this moon?"

With a snort, Milyr quipped, "She was certainly heated and annoying as this vulching moon."

The wide eyes peeked at him, and Whyvvi replied, "Yes, Prof, I agree. I should honor her memory by naming this yellow moon for Swyllo. And I believe that this golden bubble could represent her caring heart. Yes, her heart, which could care for even such a toxx as Milyr and her arch rival… Jamyk."

"Awright, that sounds wonderful and typically logical from you, Whyvvi," Domyn exclaimed, and then holding her apart from his chest with his large hands on her arms, he asked, "Now what name do you plane to use… Swyllo?"

"No, that does not sound or picture right to me," she replied, peering up into his face. "I want to make a name that we will know refers to her, but others outside our wolf pack would not recognize the immediate reference… Let me think of this some more, my big man. With your support, I will term it."

"Awright, if we are going to name this moon, then we must survive and find a way to contact someone to let them know of this new name. We must live on to bring Swyllo's legacy to awareness of the rest of humanity," Domyn declared loudly with enthusiasm and confidence.

"What new name?" Milyr blurted abruptly, halting his kiss to Nyba. "Who's naming this vulching moon? Do we really need to name this horrible moon? Can't we just plan to vulching leave it?"

"According to Cap Nyba, Whyvvi is the official termer of the Wolf Streak Beta crew," Kymil said in a steady motherly tone. "Do you intend to challenge that decree, Milyr?"

Glancing down at Nyba's face, the lanky young man hastily replied, "Of course not; if Cap said so, then that's the way it is…. Vulch, would I want to stress my brain with a chore like that? Would I want to bother thinking up names that will never become known to anyone but us?"

"So you don't believe I can lead us out of this crisis?" Nyba snapped with her voice rising slightly as she lifted her face from his narrow chin.

"Um! Look, Nyba, we're not really in a very cherp situation here on this vulching moon. I mean in terms of getting our word out to someone. Vulching Fox Flash Alpha could be gone now. The colonials just aim to kill us. Who could we tell?"

"You don't believe I can be a cherp Cap?" she said with a defiant stance and her arms suddenly pulled from around him and crossed in front of her chest. "Is that what you think?"

"Erh! No, no, Nyba…it's nothing about you. You are the best Cap in Blue Jay. You are my spirit bonder. I believe in you," Milyr protested with a squeak cracking his voice.

"Oh, really? Why are you always so negative?" Nyba inquired, stepping back a pace out of his long reach. "Can't you do or say anything optimistic for once?"

"Vulch, Nyba, you should know, for you I would if I really felt optimistic… I would for you," Milyr retorted with a trace of desperation in his voice. "You are the best Cap."

"Anything optimistic? Anything positive? Anything for the benefit of everyone here?" she pressed firmly, holding her stance. "Would you really, Milyr, for the benefit of all of us?"

"Of course, Nyba, I would. I'm vulcher toxx most of the time. But, vulch, I do care. I do have loyalty," Milyr declared, taking one step toward her and reaching his long arms out to her.

"Then you have confidence that we will survive? You have belief that we will get beyond this bubble sometime? You have belief that Wolf Streak Beta can have a future through us and our actions?" Nyba persisted, still poised in her authoritative stance.

"Vulch, Nyba, I want to believe all those things," Milyr groaned with his hands extended toward but not clutching her form. "It's very hard to accept all that, but if you say it, I'll try to believe it."

"And you will try to say positive statements, hopeful statements. You will try to do helpful and hopeful things for this crew. You will try to act less of a toxx," Nyba insisted, brushing away his hands, even as her face began to lose its scowl.

"Of course, I always try to do that," Milyr pleaded desperately. "Although it's against my nature since I am a toxx. I admit that. What can I do or say to convince you, Cap Nyba? Tell me! Command me! I am your obedient crewman. I am a Jayer."

"Very well, as your Cap, and if you really believe me to be your spirit bonder, Milyr, answer this one question honestly," Nyba demanded with a grin abruptly appearing on her face. "What were you thinking of when you discovered the feeding method of this bubble?"

While Whyvvi snorted abruptly with merriment, Milyr's face gaped slackly, and he sputtered, "Argh! That's not fair… Um! I…can't…"

"Very well, I guess that shows just how serious your intent really was, or in this case, was not," Nyba sighed as she started to turn her back to him. "If you really don't care…"

"Um! Vulch! Truly I don't want to offend you… It is just man talk… You might get the wrong impression…" the tall young man muttered in despair. "I need you to respect me, Nyba."

"Oh, whatever you have to say could not be worse than my current impression of your alleged loyalty," Nyba hissed with intensity. "You other ladies won't be offended by manly talk, will you?"

"I could use cherp ridiculous manly talk right now," Whyvvi chuckled still close to Domyn. "Besides this lame toxx should be used to saying really nasty ridiculous things by now. He's cherp at it."

"Argh! Um! This is embarrassing," Milyr stammered. "Domyn? Prof? I don't know."

"Doesn't bother me, my friend. I'm becoming comfortable with myself now," Domyn said.

"Do what you must to feel yourself, man. Do what you must to impress yourself. Perhaps it will be enough to impress Cap Nyba," Lyndyn said with calmness. "It is your story. Tell it or not."

"Milyr, now how did you think of how to feed from our bubble?" Nyba asked firmly, pointedly.

"Okay, vulching okay… Don't condemn me for what I'm going to say," Milyr grimaced as he nervously jittered about on the balls of his feet. "I was still mostly asleep on the floor. I was dreaming. My dream was about time probably on Steppingstone Cuarto because Chitir was there. We were talking about…well…about…girls…um… .their…erh….their…mams…yeah, girl's mams. Me, Chitir, and Jamyk were wondering what it would be like…like…to…to….vulch…to suck on girl's mams! There, are you happy? I hope you are not vulching angry at me now. We were just pups then."

Momentarily Nyba, Whyvvi, and Kymil glared at him with scowls as if to pierce his manhood from his body, or so Lyndyn hoped Milyr would believe. Then suddenly all three glanced at each other and broke out in laughter. It was a deep belly laughter that had them clutching their stomachs and shaking their heads. The young man's expression froze into a pained scowl and his long jaw dropped open, yet no words came out for once.

Finally, with some gasps of breath, Kymil exclaimed, "That's cherp! Don't be embarrassed, my young man. That was only natural behavior for boys of your age then. Even Jayer boys inhibited by antemgebemarzex would wonder those questions. Isn't that right, my Lyndyn?"

"Indeed most natural to have those kinds of boyish questions and share them with peers," Lyndyn smiled, patting the tall sweating young man on the shoulder. "What intrigues me more is that memory was another involving Jamyk at the time when we were hungry and seeking food. This is very fascinating, very coincidental perhaps. But, my friend, that took some manly nads to tell that to the ladies. Maybe someday they will divulge what they talked about at that young age when they discussed us men. What they found naturally attractive to their young imaginations about boys."

"Now, you elderly wolf, don't try to start any gender battles now," Kymil chuckled, squeezing his wrists within her strong grip. "We have other things to focus upon now."

"Awright, well done," Domyn praised. "And hopefully you did not offend the ladies here."

"Not at all," Whyvvi laughed still. "I needed to hear something silly like that. I needed to watch this toxx squirm for awhile. Thank you, Nyba. And thank you, Milyr. A cherp treat! Swyllo would like it. I am sure wherever she is now, she is rolling over the ground with joyful laughter. Thank you, you toxx! We all needed this release."

"I suppose that you would not wish to name which girl was the topic of conversation those years ago on Steppingstone Cuarto?" Nyba asked with a sly smile. "Knowing you, Chitir, and Jamyk, as I do, one of the Blue Jayers must have attracted your interest then. Is that not so?"

"Um! That was a long time ago, Cap Nyba... Do you really want me to stress my poor memory for a name?" Milyr asked sheepishly. "All the Blue Jay girls were cherp then just as you are today. I could remember for you, you know, if you insisted."

Staring at him a few seconds, Nyba then said with a grin, "No, I think you should be able to keep some of your boyhood secrets, my spirit bonder... For now!"

"Cherp! Thanks, Nyba," Milyr said with some relief, then somewhat humbly yet with a tease in his tone, he said, "Now that I've made a foolish toxx of myself, perhaps someone else can reveal this naming of the moon secret. Surely you've had time to consider your new moon name, Whyvvi."

With a triumphant smile on her face, Whyvvi said, "Actually I have. But we were having so much cherp fun with you that I postponed my announcement. I have decided to name this moon... Wyllos... That is W-Y-L-L-O-S. It is an anagram of her name, easy for each of us to recognize her name within, yet alien enough for anyone else to accept for this alien moon. What do you think? Am I not a cherp termer of moons?"

"Not bad… Wyllos… It sounds good," Domyn said, wrapping big arm around her shoulders.

"That's really cherp, Whyvvi," Nyba exclaimed. "Swyllo would be pleased."

"Better than trings," Milyr scoffed jokingly, and then more seriously stated, "Yet indeed that is remarkably very… Swyllo. I am amazed at how professional you are at this new assignment… No doubt, you have anticipated this naming for some time now… Perhaps your subconscious had been working at this thought for some time now. Finally you have had a moment of relaxation in which to let your thought come out into the reality of our situation…"

"Awright, enough," laughed Domyn. "Milyr, you don't have to sound like Prof to get your view across to us. Just be your toxx self."

"Okay, its vulching cherp, Whyvvi," Milyr declared with a grin.

"Now that's sincerity," Nyba said, striding to Milyr and hugging him around his narrow waist, then slowly sliding her hands down to his buttocks, "I knew that you had potential within you."

No doubt, Lyndyn thought to himself as he scanned the acid ocean outside the golden bubble to see regular patrols of the green clusters drifting by and around the bubble all of Blue Jayers in this bubble seemed to feel safe now. The previous conversations were about insignificant trivial topics compared to the prior hours or days since awakening in this bubble. This feeling of security would aid the young people as they decided how to deal with their circumstance. This habitat was life-sustaining but not life rewarding, not invigorating. For the young people trained for Blue Jay space exploration, they would soon find themselves bored and frustrated with their limited existence.

"What is floating around in that absent-minded head of yours, my kindred spirit?" Kymil inquired, softly hugging him again. "I know that vacant look of deep thought on your handsome face. What concerns you now? I was hoping that you could relax and feel playful."

"No doubt you know me well enough to see into my mind better than anyone with espersense," he murmured. "I am merely thinking about what we do next. What we focus our attention upon to keep our brains active. We don't want to become just…pets…or specimens…or caged attractions for our hosts. Humans need some challenge, some activity upon which to focus our intellect."

"Don't worry about that now," she said softly in her melodious voice. "Let's not waste first and thus far only period of calm and security. Even Blue Jayers need recreation time, especially nineteen-year-olds, or...forty-seven-year-olds."

"I suppose you are correct, my reliable Kymil. I must be getting delusional to see threat in peace. No doubt we all need some time to relax and make silly conversation," he exclaimed, squeezing her tenderly. "Perhaps we can fantasize about our dream on the future Steppingstone Sexto like we once did as young pups on Turkey Trot."

"Oh my, yes, those memories are cherp when we were young like these people," Kymil giggled in a low voice. "What was that...a whole lifetime ago... or longer? Such a long time! I feel so old."

"Yes, a long, long time ago," Lyndyn chuckled, quietly holding her head against his throat. "We're so old at forty-seven, too old to cuddle like young ones do."

"Oh my, I don't believe so after your reaction coming out of the tendril cocoon," Kymil murmured. "And I must confess some longing for you at the sight. You were very attractive coming out of that tendril embrace, my elderly wolf."

"Not in front of the pups," Lyndyn scolded with feigned concern. "Yet your closeness is warming to my heart. I am tempted strongly to act very much like a youthful wolfling."

"But, my kindred spirit, are you not the best role model for their upbringing, according to Domyn. Are you not the older brother who instructs his younger lads on how to be manly?" she said impishly, teasing him as if they were back there years ago on Steppingstones during the voyage of Turkey Trot, and he was very, very tempted to react as he had so many years ago then.

"Yeah, Prof, show us how you can give her a manly kiss," Milyr chortled as he embraced Nyba less than five feet away from Lyndyn and Kymil. "Doc deserves your best. She is Blue Jay's best women's role model. Give her your best, Prof. You may not get very many chances again."

"You are absolutely correct about Kymil being a role model," Lyndyn agreed solemnly and then inquired with some surprise of his own action, "My kindred spirit, may I kiss you?"

"Oh my, yes, my kindred spirit," Kymil murmured, turning her face toward his. "Let us show these young people how role models do it."

"Oh, do you really have to do that here now?" Whyvvi complained sourly.

"Now, my young lady, they deserve the same happiness that we enjoy together," Domyn said.

511

Then without thinking or planning or worrying about proprieties, Lyndyn and Kymil kissed gently, slowly, kindly, neither seeking dominance, neither seeking advantage, just shared a kiss of love between them.

When she pulled her head away after their lips parted, Lyndyn was certain that he observed glittering stars in her eyes, but then Kymil said suddenly, looking upwards past his head, "Oh my, that is so beautiful up there on the surface of the ocean. It is so bright, so sparkling, and so beautiful. Did we make that vision with our kiss?"

Spinning around to look in the direction that Kymil now gazed, Lyndyn paused and blinked momentarily as his still keen eyesight was dazzled by the sight. Still a distance away, he saw a vast gleaming white light, floating on the ocean surface. At least he assumed that was where it floated. The brilliance of phenomenon was so strong that the whiteness almost flowed through the darker yellow ocean to this bubble. Not knowing the actual distance of the brilliant thing from the bubble, he could not determine the magnitude of the sight. However, it was vast and very slowly approaching.

"That is so cherp," Nyba exclaimed. "I really love the way it floats and bobs with the motion of the waves. That is so cherp!"

Lyndyn had begun to notice the same effect as Nyba. His enhanced vision had been hindrance at his initial sighting of this phenomenon for the brilliance baffled his perception. But now he observed that indeed vast spread of thing undulated with the action of the waves. If not for the whiteness of the thing and its brilliance, he may never have seen it. Gradually the gleaming mass approached.

"Such pretty glitter," Whyvvi said breathlessly. "It should not be here on Wyllos. It is much too delicate looking, much too...gorgeous to exist on Wyllos where the atmosphere is stormy and the ocean is turbulent. That glitter is just so out of place. Yet it is so cherp!"

"It is so vulching bright," Milyr complained, turning his glare away after one brief peak. "Now I wish my eyes were not so sensitive. Vulching cocoon, I knew it would hurt me somehow."

"But it did help you overcome antemgebemarzex," Nyba whispered in a husky voice. "Perhaps that can happen again? My tall, big man, can you perform as your Cap demands?"

"Vulch, don't get me excited, Nyba," Milyr protested with a gulping chuckle but then admitted in his baritone voice, "Yet I'm really vulching liking you at this moment, my spirit bonder."

"Oh, yes, I can see that," Nyba exclaimed. "Let's move over here."

As glitter floated closer waving with the surface, Lyndyn was certain that he observed what looked like silver- gray raindrops or maybe dew-shaped droplets descending like a rain storm downward from the phenomenon into the yellow ocean depths. Obviously these were not rain drops, which would not sink in this ocean. Whatever the rain or dew drop substance was, it was denser than the acid ocean. Yet millions of tiny droplets filtered downward from the underside of the vast glitter. This mass continued to undulate as if it were part of the ocean surface. It was no doubt very shallow in its own depth but extremely widespread in its girth.

"Oh my, see that green cluster?" Kymil reported, clutching his sweating arms with her own wet palms. "It suddenly veered from its patrol course and headed toward that thing."

"There goes another," Domyn said breathlessly. "I hope this is not another threat. But I can see many green balls moving away from around our bubble toward that...thing. Whyvvi, clutch to me... I'll protect you. Awe yes, I'll protect you if there is danger."

"I name it glitter," Whyvvi announced quickly as she nestled into Domyn's chest. "Let us just call it glitter. That should save everyone from trying to think of what to call it... I am thinking of something else now, my big man. And you are the center of my feelings now."

"Awright, well, yes, that makes sense," Domyn mumbled, and Lyndyn heard undisguised uncertainty in the young man's voice. "I, too, am just now feeling something unusual. You look so cherp...to me just now, Whyvvi."

"Then your vulching glitter is luring all of our green balls to it," Milyr protested, shading his eyes under a long lanky hand, and Lyndyn thought that he saw glistening sweat on the young man's arm.

As he suddenly realized that he, too, was sweating profusely in this bubble that had kept their temperature very stable for so long, Lyndyn also observed the green clusters separate into single balls as they moved near to the dew storm under the glitter. They were not rising to the surface or to the glitter itself. Instead individual spheres dashed about in almost frenzied, hap-hazard manner in the dew storm beneath the glitter. Every cluster broke apart, sending individual balls into this frenzy. At the same time, he felt similar unfamiliar roiling within his own stomach and loins.

"Oh my, I feel so strange," Kymil said, gripping Lyndyn's arm in hot sweaty hands and pulling him to her. "I have not felt this since ...since... Quinto."

513

His heartbeat had increased just moments before she said this. His nose inhaled her womanly scent as it had when he had first come out of the cocoon. His loins caught the heated blood flow, and his body reacted with complete manly vigor, no hint of any antemgebemarzex residual inhibition. Her eyes caught his gaze. His hands clutched her body to his. She was obviously equally anxious and ready for arousal. This was normally completely natural for two adults, his intellect informed him, but this sudden urgency was also totally beyond his self control. Feeling her heated body move to his, he realized that she was in exactly the same state. They were not in control. This was not natural sensation this time.

From his peripheral vision, Lyndyn observed Nyba grab at Milyr as she cried out, "I need you now. I want your manliness now. Whether your toxx is ready or not, I need you, tall man."

"My toxx isn't ready, but the rest of me is stimulated. Vulch, you don't have to command me twice," Milyr yelled breathlessly. "Vulch, I dream about this all the time. But usually I'm in control. Not this vulching time. Be easy with me, my Cap. I'll be cherp for you. But is this how it should happen, so suddenly? I do not feel in control. But vulch this feels really cherp."

"Just get your toxx down here with me. Let's just let biology take its own course," Nyba gasped. "I'll show you how to be manly, you big oaf."

"What's happening, Lyndyn?" Kymil moaned as they went to the floor totally out of self control. "I just must have you now. It's my only thought now. This can't be the result of our prior talk. Coupling with you now is my only desire. Nothing else matters to me now. This is not normal."

"Indeed, my kindred spirit," Lyndyn groaned as he fell atop her hot body. "Our natural drive to mate is overwhelming all my conscious desires and intellect. I can't help myself, yet I'm glad it is you."

From somewhere in the bubble, Domyn breathed heavily with what sounded like a sob, "I need you, Whyvvi, now. I don't understand this, but I must have you now. Don't hate me for this."

Whyvvi gasped with a strained attempt at her normal logic, "I feel the same suddenly. This must be related to the green balls out there... They seem to have instinctive drive to the glitter... They may be affecting our internal desires on a sensual level that we cannot reason...only react... I need you, my big man. Don't fight this... Don't hurt yourself... Let go, my man."

"Don't talk now. If we can't control them, let our urges guide us," Lyndyn groaned as his body and mind drove him into copulation with Kymil. "If we...try to fight it…it could…be dangerous…to our health… Everyone…follow your urges… Don't fight…this… Don't worry…about logic…or reason….now."

While he let his body have its way, his intellect continued to battle for some foothold of control of his own mind and actions. Yet self control was very, very difficult. This sudden urge to copulate was much more than recreational sex, much deeper than shared intercourse with a consenting partner, his beloved Kymil, much stronger than the primal need to mate. This was pure procreation at a very deep level, perhaps almost cellular level. This urge was a much stronger drive than his own wishes, his own dream of being a father someday, or his love for Kymil. He was certain that this uncontrollable urgency to procreate was stimulated by other than his own body and brain, his own gratification and his own subconscious. This urgency was coming from outside of himself.

"Yes, you big man…my Domyn… I will have…you now," Whyvvi exclaimed from another part of the bubble, "Oh, yes…what …glorious sight…to see…your face…with that…pretty glitter…up there…above… You look…so cherp…against that…glittering whiteness."

"Awe help me… I love you…now, Whyvvi," Domyn's deep voice rasped. "I must love you."

"Awright…my big man…do not worry for me," panted Whyvvi. "Do what you…must…do not hurt…yourself…to save me…. Release yourself…to your…emotions."

Listening to the heavy breathing and moans around him, Lyndyn realized that this urgency to procreate was affecting all of them at the same time. This was beyond any reasonable probability as a chance event. No doubt the appearance of glitter and frantic behavior of the green balls in the dew storm had somehow caused this procreative drive in each of the humans. His intellect tried to fight this urgency, but his emotions demanded his action. He copulated with his Kymil.

"Again…Milyr…again," screamed Nyba.

"Could…not…stop…anyway," Milyr panted.

With swelling sensual passion, Lyndyn groaned, "No doubt this is …not within…our control."

Kymil cried out, "Vulch, let it happen…my spirit… Don't analyze…now… you will…hurt."

"You…tell…him… Doc."

As grunts and moans emanated from bodies not far away in the bubble, Lyndyn felt the trembling of his body at his sudden ejaculation. His fevered intellect hoped that he could control himself to break this urge. He did not desire to mate with his Kymil in this manner.

"We...do...not have...any control," she panted beneath his sweating figure.

From haziness beginning to fog his senses, Milyr screamed, "Yeah...yeah... this is...so...cherp."

The notion to stop his sexual activity seemed insane to his inner primal male ego, which naturally drove him to seek sex as often as possible, yet Lyndyn realized with what little thread of true responsibility remaining in his awareness that this continuous unending urgency now forcing his actions was hazardous to his health and certainly his beloved Kymil as well.

"I... I...can't...stop... Forgive me..." he gasped into the wild-eyed expression of the woman beneath him, and his brain faintly considered the possibility that this fervent sequencing of sexual stimulation was no doubt being controlled by some external force.

This was not healthy. This was not enjoyable.

Somehow he must try to stop.

SPEC THREE: LYNDYN ON WYLLOS
CHAPTER 33

Rivulets of hot salty sweat flowed from his bald head into his eyes and mouth. Lyndyn shook his head vigorously in an attempt to remove this irritating salty nuisance. However, just as an internal urge to mate with the woman lying beneath his feverish body was beyond his control, so, too, did the annoying sweat cling to his face and eyes. This was not enjoyable at all. With Kymil it should be.

When he tilted his face upwards in forced passion as his sweating body rode atop Kymil, his eyes noticed the glistening white brilliance of the glitter almost directly overhead the bubble now. Most of his consciousness was absorbed with sexual urgency, but a fraction of his awareness observed the frantic swirling of the green balls within the falling dew drops beneath the vast undulating glitter. In the second that he could make his consciousness comprehend this observation, Lyndyn saw that the green balls were absorbing the dew drops frantically as if they, too, had no control of their behavior.

"My man...you are...my man," gasped Whyvvi amidst almost bestial growls and grunts of a large young male over her, "My only man... My big man..."

From somewhere else outside his procreative obsession, Lyndyn listened to another female voice squeak with husky satisfaction, "But...my tall...big boy is... so cherp...right now... Oh, Milyr...you are...so cherp...Is ...this...the ...way... you...dream?"

"Vulching...no...way...so much...cherper," Milyr's baritone voice huffed with much strained and ragged breathlessness. "This...is...cherper...than...any...dream..."

517

As his own body pushed beyond the normal limits of exertion, Lyndyn listened to some of these comments, but his conscious focus was tied to his unwilling rutting with his beloved Kymil. He hoped that his actions would not hurt her, yet he could not control himself. Was this overwhelming primal urgency coming from the green balls as they performed their own frenzied dance within the dew storm beneath the glitter? Was their physical compulsion linked to some strange espersense which was dragging human captives into procreative frenzy?

With as much will as he could muster, Lyndyn moaned in a faint whisper, "My Kymil... I will try...to stop this... We must...try...to overcome...someway..."

Her eyes stared up at his, and her mouth moved, but her words were so soft that he could not hear them. Lyndyn felt a flush of panic that very briefly forestalled the sexual compulsion as he worried that he might have hurt her. But then as her body entwined with his in passion, his brief freedom from compulsion was gone.

Could compulsion of the green balls be forcing the urgency driving him now, Lyndyn wondered in a second of clarity in his mind. Then his awareness fell back into power and ecstasy of compulsion. As his body forced itself on his Kymil, his mind fought the urge long enough to wonder if the green balls were somehow generating a psychic field of this procreative urgency that had trapped humans. Yet he could not concentrate on this thought for compelling urgency overwhelmed his intellect and his self-control.

As she writhed within this compulsion along with him, Kymil's eyes widened abruptly, and she tried to gasp, "Blood...blood...stars...up...there..."

"Blood... I do...not....focus...what...you...say," he panted through sweat and spittle flowing from his face and mouth, but her terror stung his awareness long enough to fight the urgent compulsion. "Blood, are you bleeding...my love? I am....sorry."

Kymil shook her head violently side to side, and with a tortured grimace gasped, "Blood...star...I...see star...blood..."

Her fear seemed to give his mind a weapon of emotion to fight compulsion. Lyndyn could think more clearly for a few seconds at a time now. Blood? Was she worried about bleeding due to this crazed forceful activity? Did she see yellowish stars that often precede loss of consciousness? What was she saying? Was he hurting her with his unbridled thrusts and heavier body? Could he stop himself now that he had moments of clearer conscious awareness?

Somewhere in the bubble, Whyvvi shrieked in true fear, "No, oh, no... It is...back."

Weakly as she moved still with sexual urgency beneath him, Kymil gasped with a moment of lucid fear, "Bloodstar...here...now!"

His conscious mind struggled to comprehend her. Her obvious terror fed his strength against sexual compulsion. He was able to begin to make his mind focus on her words. Had he heard...bloodstar? Yet his brain and body kept returning his conscious awareness to procreative urgency. Yet her face of fear stimulated his deep love and concern for her, and Lyndyn forced his mind to fight his own brain long enough to consider other thoughts and visions.

From not far away, he heard Milyr's cracking baritone voice gripe, "Vulch... blood...on ...the...floor... Are you...bleeding...my... Cap?"

"No...hot...so hot...red...up there...red in my...eyes...can't...see...glitter... shine...all...red," Nyba moaned, her voice sounding exhausted to Lyndyn's ears.

Then through the sweat and salt streaming around and into his eyes, Lyndyn noticed scarlet red streams flowing within the floor of the golden bubble. His eyes noticed the beginning of shriveling of the soft inner layer beneath Kymil's back and head. In a brief moment of rationality allowed his consciousness, he realized that the bubble had been attacked by the bloodstar again. The damage had spread surprisingly quickly this time since the bubble was smaller than the prior attack.

"Blood...star... Domyn...a bloodstar..." Whyvvi screamed with breathless gasps.

"Can't...resist...must...have...you now," the big man growled in desperate frustration.

Red fluid flowed down within the curved side of the shriveling bubble. This was impossibly ridiculous, Lyndyn griped silently. He needed to halt this intercourse to defend against the bloodstar. They all needed to stop and defend, if they could. Yet though he could think clearly for a few seconds once in a while, a very deep primal urgency of his desire to mate prevented any long duration of rationality. However, his mind recalled terror on Kymil's face and his own strong concern for her safety, so he forced himself to wallow in this vision as long as he could.

Perhaps the green balls could help, but no, they were just as trapped in this compelling urgency. With a hasty glance upward, Lyndyn briefly observed the undulating thin mass of the glitter moving away over head. Could the green balls free themselves from their compulsion in time to help this bubble? If not, what could he do? Yet his thoughts faded and his consciousness fell under the desire of procreation again.

"Vulch... I'm...so...hot...burning...up...inside...so hot... You do...this...to me?" Milyr stammered through his breathless exertions. "Dizzy...seeing... glitter...stars...vulch."

Nyba moaned with desperate weariness, "My man...try...to stop...slow... your...self...if can...too hot... Hurt...you...manly...body... Milyr!"

As Lyndyn listened to the young couple complain of their over-heating bodies, his strong concern for their safety wedged its way into the powerful compulsion hampering his conscious thinking, and he found a foothold for himself, his true self. His mind almost dreamed of a scene of red and purple and green and blue splatter bulbs splashing around within his limited vision. A smiling Jamyk and grinning Swyllo wavered within the mists of this vision. Their hands were graceful and persistent as they pelted each other and him with colorful splatters. Then abruptly the dream was gone. Yet his mind stayed under his conscious control for a few more seconds.

In these seconds, Lyndyn gasped with exhausted breathes in a weak nasal voice sapped as much as his bodily strength by his vigorous exertion, "Jamyk... Jamyk...need help.... Can't protect... Kymil."

"I know...," her voice whispered meekly below his body, and then she shivered with another orgasm, yet her body was not allowed to rest by compulsion, and she sought his exertions again, clutching at his sweating heated form.

"Green...cluster...compulsion...make us...do this...uncontrolled...primal... " Lyndyn panted as he stared down at her tormented face.

What could he do? His brain and body prevented him from reasonable action. He could merely continue his mating behavior. Yet in his few occasional moments of rational thought, he realized that he must stop this urgency overwhelming his rationality. How could he intervene between irrational urge and his self-control? What was more basic than a mating drive? He had been able to use his fear and worry for his beloved Kymil before, but this had been very temporary. What was more primal than love for his Kymil?

"Green balls...help us," Nyba yelled with a hoarse breathless voice. "Milyr... try...to...stop."

"Too...strong...this....force...dizzy...can't...breathe...hot...very....hot... vulch...whoa...stars..." the tall young man's voice faded weakly, and then in the peripheral vision, Lyndyn saw movement of a long body collapsing onto a female body beneath.

"No... Milyr...no...don't...die... Milyr," the young woman wailed, "Please... Milyr...don't...so...big."

Then between the prostrate couple and him, splatter of a liquid landed and sizzled on the red-streaked golden floor of the bubble. Acid, the ocean was starting to leak into the bubble. As this realization pumped intense fear into his body and mind, Lyndyn found that he could concentrate on this event with some reasonable attention. The bloodstar had been attached to the outer shell of the bubble long enough to begin working one of its tips into the outer shell. The leak had been started.

Nyba's forlorn squeaking voice groaned, "Milyr, don't...die... Wake up...so heavy...need you...tall man... Wake up... Help me...so heavy...can't move..."

Another splat hit the bubble floor between his position and Nyba's. The ocean was beginning to seep in. The red fluid was already well on its way to infiltrating layers of the bubble. Shrinkage of the inner layer had already begun. What could he do, Lyndyn wondered in panic. Was his recent vision of Jamyk and Swyllo meant to help him or to encourage him, but how? His mind shimmered between alert awareness and confused sexual urgency. And urge to procreation was starting to win the battle again. Against his own will, his body copulated with his beloved Kymil again.

Kymil peered into his eyes with exhaustion and terror and murmured in anguish, "Must stop...kindred...spirit...must...help...pups... Desire you...but must...stop...compulsion...too strong."

"Yes...we...must stop this...must defend...some way," Lyndyn gasped as he futilely tried to cease his sexual assault on this special woman to protect her, but he could not against the compelling urgency.

Another splat and sizzle stung the bubble floor. Only pure chance had positioned the leak so as not to fall upon his back or Milyr's back. His mind wandered again with his bewildered consciousness flitting toward a vision of another splat, series of splats, but these were of many colors, many patterns. These splats adorned the skins of his young pups, Jamyk and Swyllo, as they playfully pelted each other with splatter bulbs. They included him in their amusement.

His vision was of joy and playfulness. Yet once he recalled the accidental blow which had dropped Jamyk to the floor of the gymnasium. It had been unintentional, but the blow of a splatter bulb to one nad of the boy had been very painful to the lad. Now in his confused and hazy mind, Lyndyn remembered agony on the boy's face. Yes, pain had ended play then.

Pain, sudden pain, nothing was more primal than pain, his mind tried to consider. Then another splat and sizzle fell between himself and a couple of young bodies prone on the bubble floor. Pain, sudden pain of acid splat would be terrible, Lyndyn thought as he thrust into Kymil again and again. His brain was locked on this mating urge, yet his mind contemplated pain. Then another droplet of acid bit into the soft golden floor, and the inner layer convulsed ever so slightly. The bubble had felt pain. If the bubble could feel pain, would it scream in pain as Jamyk had long ago, Lyndyn's mind foolishly tried to contemplate. Was he going insane in his battle to wrench control away from this sexual compulsion, which gripped his brain and body?

Another splash of acid splattered into the bubble. Again the bubble convulsed slightly. His mind dreamed of Jamyk's agonized face as the boy lay crying on the gymnasium floor. Pain, what is worse than pain? Yes, pain, as elemental primal force as any, Lyndyn suddenly agreed as his mind focused with clarity upon vision of Jamyk's pained face. Pain should be more primal to the sense of self-preservation to the individual than a mating drive. In this sudden moment of lucidness, he realized that pain was his only answer against this sexual compulsion.

While in this moment of lucid control of himself, partially against directives of his brain and loins, Lyndyn ceased his sexual motion and flopped down on top of Kymil. Slowly with a shaking, twitching hand and arm, he reached out toward the path of the acid droplets. His body insisted that he resume his sexual activity, and his loins began some movement to accede to this demand. Yet his awareness struggled to move one hand. Working against his own muscles and brain, his arm stretched out with the power of his will and vision of the scrawny face of the boy.

"My...spirit...what...do...you...try?...   This...is...so...unbearable... though... I do...love you," Kymil's meek whisper barely reached his ear nestled not far from her.

Shaking, trembling, his hand reached out farther toward the last splash of leaking acid. His body moved with hers in their shared but unwilled passion. Yet his hand stretched until abruptly a splash of liquid intersected with it and pain seared into the flesh of his hand. Fighting reflex to pull his hand back, Lyndyn forced with his will hand to hover there in the air until another burning pain bit into his flesh and sent pain through his nervous system to his brain. The reflex to move his hand was stronger this time, yet with surprisingly strong will, he opposed the reflexive reaction of his brain. Another droplet of acid splattered onto his hand, and again his nerves hastily transmitted signal to his brain to pull back the hand, however, Lyndyn was in command of his brain now.

Now as he regained some conscious control of his own behavior as his brain began itself to fight the psychic compulsion for procreative urgency, Lyndyn rolled off Kymil and toward the acid leak.

While his eyes blurred with vague images and tears of pain, he heard Kymil scream, "No, not...that, my spirit...some other...way... Not that..."

"What...what...happens... This...sex...not...cherp," Whyvvi mumbled in obvious torment.

However, now that he was able to keep control of his own consciousness for several seconds, Lyndyn realized that he had no choice. The compulsion was still nagging at his brain. His loins were very much activated for procreative act. His blood flowed hotly inside his body, urging for copulation. Yet he must retain this refreshing lucidness, this vision of clarity. He must seek out more pain.

"I want...you...so...much," Kymil moaned, shaking on her hands and knees. "Come...back."

He glanced toward her briefly, afraid he would lose his newly recovered self-control and return to their shared intercourse, but the pain on his hand reminded him of his purpose and Lyndyn panted, "I do as...well...but cannot...now... must...save you...save...all...pups..."

Fear of pain overwhelmed his sexual urges. With encouragement from the face of the thin boy haunting his daydream, he persuaded himself to roll his body into the zone. A droplet of acid stung into his belly near his navel. The splatter effect seared a circle around the initial contact spot. Pain, glorious pain, ran through his body to strike at his brain, to battle all consuming drive to mate. His loins remained full of lust, but his self-control was his own again. He let another burning droplet strike his torso, and then as pain seared into his flesh, he rolled out of the way.

"Oh...my...burn...your skin...bad.." Kymil gasped, trying to twist her own body toward him. "Must...let...me...care...for...you...must stop...this need... for...you."

"No...my spirit...let me do...this..." he groaned against the agony in his flesh and desire to go back to her. "Pain...helps...fight...this compulsion."

"So does...my love...and concern...for you," she panted, struggling to stay on her hands and knees without toppling to the red-streaked floor. "I feel...less... controlled...still want you bad...but can...control...a little."

While painfully forcing himself into kneeling position, Lyndyn noticed that the glitter was now floating away from the overhead of the bubble. The back edge of its vastly wide girth remained overhead. The green balls were in their frenzied random pattern darting about in the dew drop storm below the glitter. Their preoccupation with absorption of dew drops had not apparently waned. Was this a natural habit of procreation of green clusters? This did not matter now, he chastised himself. He was wasting his limited freedom of thought. He needed to focus himself away from continuing sexual desires. He needed to begin some defense against the bloodstar.

"Bloodstar... I must...fight...the bloodstar," Lyndyn muttered, yet his mind did not have a definite plan for him, his mind was dazed and confused still as he fought the nagging primal drives within himself. "For you...my Kymil...and our young...pups... I must...fight...this bloodstar."

"Bloodstar? Can we do?" Kymil struggled to say breathlessly as her back and shoulders slumped between her quivering arms and legs. "So...tired...so tired... much longing...compulsion...."

Turning his partially regained attention to the bloodstar, Lyndyn saw the red-streaked, wide round body with its clinging arms wrapped onto the bubble. This time four arms had seized the bubble so far. The maw was about waist high, less than seven feet from where he lay. Two arms were draped toward the top of the bubble. One of these had created an acid leak and seemed to be working at enlarging the crack. Another was clinging to the right of his position, not far from where Domyn copulated with Whyvvi. The fourth was to his left about head height. Scarlet fluid flowed from each of these arms. This red fluid had now spread around the entire bubble. His eyesight saw all this in only a few seconds.

"Do you...try...my spirit...can I...help?" Kymil asked with honest resolve but a very weak and disheartened voice and slumped posture as she lay back to the floor face-down.

"Rest now...my spirit...prepare...to help...our pups...Hope that...this passes soon," Lyndyn said with more decisiveness in his voice and also in his mind as he seized more control away from external force which had compelled him for so long.

This obnoxious bloodstar had been attacking the bubble for quite some time. Obviously he had not noticed the initial attack originally because of his complete immersion in procreative urge. However, he was not the only one to ignore danger. The green clusters had been most likely consumed by their own urge and perhaps procreative drive as well. To his perspective then, he saw that none of their former guardians had yet to free themselves for compulsion. Would they be able to free themselves? Would the green clusters follow the glitter endlessly seeking the dew drops in the storm under the ocean surface? Would these green clusters desert their human specimens? He had no idea of how long their procreative urge lasted. What could he do alone now?

Croaking through a dry throat and mouth, Lyndyn pleaded, "Jamyk...help us... Send your green friends...to help us now... Am I going insane? Are you really...out there?"

This foolish effort tired him and weakened his internal battle to fend off the still potent sexual desire. Yet he found that he could fight fight. In spite of the annoying lust in his loins and physical difficulty of movement due to this engorged lust, he arose shakily to stand up. While his hands rested on his knees a few seconds, he stared at the pink maw sucking at the exterior of the bubble. Would this mouth-like maw break through the bubble? Could he stop this from happening? Could he save his kindred spirit from the ugly maw? This seemed very overwhelming at the moment.

"Lyndyn... I can...help you," Kymil said weakly as her prone body sagged into the reddening floor, and he realized that she could not, yet she called out softly, "I need...help you."

"No, my kindred spirit...free Nyba...under Milyr," Lyndyn suggested, trying to give her something of importance to do, so she would not give up on herself and yet not put herself into more likely harm by coming to him. "Help Nyba... Maybe two can...help to stop Domyn...wake him from...his desires...with pain maybe... He is tough... He can take pain...just break his...sex lust...maybe."

"But help you...beloved... I need...you," Kymil cried desperately.

"No, help...pups...you are Doc," Lyndyn gasped with exhaustion as he gazed into her frightened face. "Green clusters...under compulsion...also... Should free...selves soon... Get back...to protect."

"I am Doc...yes...must focus...am Doc..." she muttered with obvious turmoil within her own mind, no doubt fighting her own battle between mating urgency and her maternal caring instincts, and then she abruptly mumbled, "Yes, Jamyk... must help... Milyr... Domyn...now."

Witnessing her determination and courage, Lyndyn felt himself encouraged to defeat his own internal lusts and distractions. He must find a way to stop this bloodstar. If not at least attract attention of the green clusters for protection. Yet their compulsion to absorb the raining dew drops seemed overwhelming to the green balls. The green shapes were pursuing the glitter still. A sudden fear that they might not care about humans any more seized his awareness. However, he fought this panic as he fought his lust.

On wobbling legs, he stumbled toward the maw. There must be something which he could do to delay destruction of the bubble until the green clusters could return to chase away the bloodstar. Yet how could he do this? Could he rely on the green clusters to break free of their natural instinct? Would they remember their captives after such a naturally traumatic experience with this compulsion? Yet he must not worry about what he could not control. Focus on your immediate challenge, he scolded himself, and suddenly recalled many of the times he had yelled that same refrain to Jamyk over the years. He had nothing to use to fortify inner layer. No tools, but his own hands, no patching but his own body.

From behind him, Lyndyn heard Domyn growl gasping breathlessly, "Not... strong...enough...to stop...this...sorry... Whyvvi...sorry, Doc."

Whyvvi stammered in an almost hushed voice, "Not your...fault...my... man...blood star...in bubble...layer...must try ...to fight..."

What could he do? Lyndyn was getting furious with himself. He watched with terror as the mouth-like lips of the maw picked away at the exterior shell. Small abrasions and splinters were there in the shell now in front of his face. The maw would eventually crack this shell and be able to get at the people inside. This would not be a good experience, Lyndyn told himself. He must find way to fortify the bubble at this point. Focus, you elderly wolf, like you always lectured Jamyk, focus on your task.

Domyn groaned weeping with despair, "Sorry...can't help...can't stop myself...this sex...not good... Lyndyn?...bubble...repair?...boy...makes... splatters...pulls...pinches...reforms...splatters... Can't... help... Lyndyn...can't stop...sex... Sorry, Whyvvi."

Hearing the bewildered rambling of the big man's words, Lyndyn felt intense sympathy for Domyn at that moment, so he said with compassion, "Care for her... friend...as you do ... Green clusters should ...return soon....their compulsion ends...yours will also... Now I must...prevent...bloodstar...from harming bubble...and all our friends."

Domyn's despairing voice replied, "Boy makes splatters...pulls...pinches... makes bulbs...from soft layers...much fun... Jamyk laughs...cherp memory."

As he tried to comprehend what Domyn had just rambled, Lyndyn observed a few cracks begin to appear in the harder exterior layer of the bubble. The maw was breaking through. Moving more quickly, he fell toward the inner curve of the bubble. Reaching forward to catch his fall, his hands scratched and gripped into the pliable layer.

What had Domyn just mumbled? His brain was afire with lust still, but Lyndyn stumbled on. His momentum and weight caused his fingers to pull a portion of the inner layer away from the bubble. Then he abruptly recalled doing the same thing with Domyn not days ago. The layer was beginning to harden but still had flexibility. Could he make something from this pliable layer?

"Awright, yes...thank your metaphy," Lyndyn croaked in tormented glee. "Thank you...my friend... Both ...my friends...big and small... Now I might... stop this monster."

While people behind him groaned and grunted and occasionally swore now with their efforts to disturb the procreative compulsion and help each other, Lyndyn began frantically pulling at the inner layer of the bubble. He was not concerned about damaging it now as he had been during their original investigation of this bubble. The bloodstar was presently doing much worse. A foot, two feet, he pulled away from the bubble and folded this over and against the area in front of the increasingly persistent destruction of the ugly maw.

At least his mind was his now for the most part, he rejoiced. With a hasty glimpse upwards, he confirmed that the glow of the glitter was beyond his sight now. Perhaps the green clusters would be returning soon. If he could just support this area of the bubble against intrusion of the mouth-like maw, then there could be time for the guardian aliens to return.

Had he just called them aliens, he wondered. Was his mind not really restored to himself? Aliens suggested definite intelligence. When had his very scientific brain determined that the green clusters were truly intelligent aliens? However, this was not focusing, he silently yelled at himself. Perhaps he needed Jamyk to look over his shoulder and do scolding at him to make him focus.

A flash of a mischievous young boyish face startled his attention within his own mind. Yes, focus, Lyndyn told himself as he thanked Jamyk. This could work, this pinching and pulling of the soft inner layer. Yet it had started to harden on the floor just minutes ago. Would this hardening interfere with his intention to overlap this refolded material on top of the original lining? No, in fact if the material hardened after he put it into position, then maybe it would reinforce against the damage to the outer shell. Perhaps he could gain time to allow the green clusters to chase away the bloodstar. Just perhaps this goal had been his wavering focus all along.

Behind him he listened to Nyba and Kymil breathlessly trying to push Milyr's heavy slack body off Nyba as she moaned, "Big...heavy...toxx...need him...so much...now...he's...out."

Still suffering with burning lust to go back to a woman, any woman, Lyndyn tried to block out obvious sexual odors and sounds in the bubble now, and to enhance his own confidence in his strength and self-control, he yelled feebly, "Jamyk...thank you...for focus...but don't...desert us yet...get your green friends...to come back here...soon...my friend..."

When he glanced upwards during his cry, he noticed the yellowish ocean overhead through the widening red streams in the bubble wall. Truly even a faint glow of the glitter was now long gone. Had the green clusters chased after the glitter never to return to this bubble? He wished to suddenly see the small green balls reforming into their clusters and dashing back toward this bubble. But he did not see this. His imagination was no doubt wishing for the sight. Perhaps Domyn's universal metaphy could direct the green clusters back to the bubble.

This foolish speculation was not getting his task completed, he whined silently to himself. The maw was cracking the shell faster than he was folding and making new inside material. His attention was not fully released from procreative urge. In fact his manliness prevented him from getting too close to the substance, which he pinched and formed frantically with his twitching hands. Maybe this wasa ood thing, he thought to himself idly. After all Lyndyn did not desire any part of himself sucked into the maw. That would not be his idea of releasing his iota of awareness. Again he scolded himself for letting his recently freed mind from aimlessly wandering. Yet Domyn had given him notion of using this inner layer as reinforcement against the maw. Perhaps thought of iota of awareness was not so aimless after all.

Just then Domyn cried in dismay, "Sorry... Whyvvi...should not...done...to you...this way..."

Breathlessly Whyvvi's voice stammered, "Big man...love you now...do not regret...natural reaction... Not your fault...green balls...their psychic compulsion...too powerful...for us...to fight."

Trying not to let his concentration waver, Lyndyn ignored the rest of the dialogue behind him. He knew that all wolves there were caring of one another. However, his attention must be on creating as much reinforced inner padding as he could before the cracks in the outer layer shattered. If he could only delay and stall the entry of the bloodstar, then he would have done his best. His goal was to delay the bloodstar, not to defeat it. He was not a warrior, not much of an athlete, he was a counselor. The duty of fighting the bloodstar belonged to the green clusters.

A crackling noise sounded from his left. Then a dull popping noise, as if flesh had ruptured, suddenly struck his ears. He heard Kymil scream. As his focus was on the work in front of his body, movement caught his peripheral vision. When he glimpsed over to look, he saw the arm of the bloodstar had poked through the bubble wall. A barbed point about one-foot long extended from the tip of the arm. This pointed barb looked very nasty. Yet he continued to work his hands as quickly as he could to put as much padding between the maw and himself and inside of this bubble.

"Oh my...watch out... Lyndyn," Kymil screamed and her stumbling footsteps patted on the hardening floor of the shriveling bubble. "This thing... sharp point...moves."

Instinctively spinning around in concern for her safety, Lyndyn felt a brief dizziness and saw his beloved stepping toward him, so he hesitated his movement and instead shouted, "No, Kymil, stay away. Stay there with the others. You are their matron. Protect them. Do not get into reach of that vulching arm. I'll be okay here. It's not long enough now."

Pausing she stared at him with her tired but beautiful eyes, pert little nose, and perfect mouth contorted with worry and said, "Be careful, my spirit... I can't lose...you now...after this day..."

Confirming with his eyes that the swaying arm seemed to be able to reach a limited distance inside the bubble interior at this moment, Lyndyn felt relief for her safety and instructed, "No farther, Kymil, I insist, my kindred spirit. That arm is not extendable as were the tendrils. Stay a safe distance away. Guard our young pups. Watch for other arms should they force entry. I've got to make more layers here. You stay there."

"Oh my, I don't want to lose you, Lyndyn," she murmured, gazing at him steadily but keeping her distance now from the groping arm and its nasty barbed tip.

"I don't want to be lost, my kindred spirit," he said, and then just before returning to his work, added with renewed confidence, "I feel myself again. I think sex compulsion is fading. I hope this brings the green clusters back to protect this bubble."

"I feel more normal now myself, my love. Scared and terrified though. Hurry back here," Kymil pleaded and then added with a hoarse cry, "Help us, Jamyk...please!"

"Yeah, help us, little peener rascal. That's an order," Nyba rasped. "Will the green balls come back to help us? Jamyk, send them back please!"

Kymil turned toward the young woman and said, "Watch over Milyr, Nyba. I believe the green clusters could return soon. If they get over their frenzy as we are beginning to now."

"Yes, my young little peener friend," Lyndyn murmured while he fingered more layers from the bubble. "Help them if you can. I will do my part. You do yours. Help them please!"

Cracks sprang suddenly along the outer layer of the bubble. They were much wider now and spread more quickly. Lyndyn rushed his hands in desperation. Where were his reinforcements, the green clusters? Had they deserted their human specimens? They should have broken their natural compulsion by now, unless they followed the glitter so instinctively that they could not remember their new specimens in the bubble. This was not a cherp thought, he mused as his hands pushed at the flexible substance.

Then the maw abruptly broke through the outer shell in about a foot and a half circle. Frantically Lyndyn pulled his most recent inner layer of substance. Applying his body weight against this last layer of inner skin, Lyndyn attempted to seal the breach with his makeshift layered patch. Since the inner substance had hardened somewhat, his construction held against the intrusion of the big maw. But for how long could he hold it? How long before corrosive properties of the maw ate through this patch? Could that gaping maw swallow him whole? His eyes stared in terror at the maw.

"Look out, Lyndyn!" Kymil yelled in a sudden panic.

Abruptly piercing agony stung his left torso just below his rib cage. His body almost went into shock at the agony, so much worse than acid drops of before. Yet his awareness remained to bolster his consciousness. He felt a barb slide through his lower organs and kidney past his backbone. Then his skin ruptured outward on his back.

"Oh my, no," Kymil wailed in despair. "Not you. Not now!"

Peering down Lyndyn saw the red-streaked arm against his body pull back slowly, and he said realizing that he was doomed, "No, Kymil...don't come... closer...protect them...my...love...my spirit...wait...for...yours...a long... time...wait."

"Oh, Prof, no...this can't happen," Nyba shouted.

"Oh...my... Lyndyn," Kymil murmured. "Not like this. Not you, kindred spirit!"

Then he sensed himself hefted up by the arm of the bloodstar away from the patch. His body felt horrible pain. His brain tried to shock his consciousness into blackness, but his will and awareness resisted. While he was tossed around within the bubble on the end of the arm, his eyes saw Kymil approaching.

"Ky...mil...mus...live," he pleaded to his kindred spirit as his blurring vision glimpsed her face.

Through tears of torment and the red-streaked wall of the bubble, he thought he viewed the green cluster outside the bubble. Then the sparkling silver-gray fluid flowed through the yellow ocean at the bloodstar. When the arm attempted to retract from the bubble, his body was slammed face-first against the inside of the opening through which the arm had entered previously.

Stuck against the bubble with a barb pulling at his body, he whispered as loud as his dying voice could manage, "Love you, Kymil...protect them...iota will be there..."

"I love you, Lyndyn," her angelic voice responded.

Incredible tension pulled against his frame, but the barb claw would not slide through his body. How he was conscious still, he did not know, perhaps a parting joke of universal metaphy, he giggled insanely to himself. Yet he did not care, did not feel, at least he realized his destiny.

His eyes saw the other green clusters approaching closer now. His awareness was hopeful that others could be saved. He rejoiced at this hope.

He thought that he whispered, "Jamyk, save them."

Then suddenly his torso snapped backward at his backbone. A trace of awareness sensed still from his unfeeling body as he was pulled through the hole in the bubble. When acid liquid of the yellow ocean struck his skin, there was no pain. His body no longer had physical feeling. His eyelids blinked reflexively.

The last vision which he witnessed was of the green cluster following, but he realized this was a futile attempt, though honorable.

His last thought was a hope that his iota of awareness could join with his Kymil in some future.

In a flash of blue-white light, Lyndyn died.

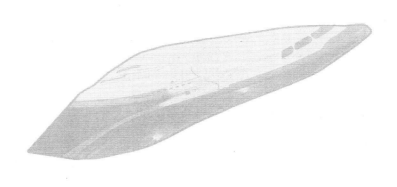

INTERLOG: KYMIL BY LYNDYN

Tears filled her eyes. She could not see clearly through moisture. Yet did she really wish to view the empty space where he had recently occupied? Kymil sobbed and screamed at the same time. He was not there anymore. He was gone now through a ragged hole in the curve of the bubble.

"Vulch, what just happened?" Nyba groaned in despair. "Is Prof really out there? There's no chance he can survive in the acid ocean…"

Kymil ignored the girl. She did not desire to believe this horror yet. Her body shuddered still with passion of his presence. Only minutes ago, they had been in deep intercourse and sharing each other. Now the joy of his being was no longer there for her. Kymil wept with total agony and longing. Her kindred spirit had been stolen by the toxx bloodstar. What was she to do now?

A deep moan from Domyn sounded from vague reality beyond her blurry eyes, and then a worried cry from Whyvvi struck at her ears as the girl squealed, "There is acid…coming into the bubble. From up there where the bloodstar just took Prof, I can see the flow. We must plug this now…"

Acid flowing into their bubble, now was this happening, Kymil gasped silently. Was this alien world trying to kill all of them now? Was she willing to survive without her kindred spirit? However, she did have her young wards still to protect. This was one of last requests of Lyndyn. Could she truly ignore this request, Kymil pondered. No, she realized, she must fulfill this obligation for his sake, as well as her young wolves still alive for the moment.

"Vulching hole up there is leaking in here," Nyba wailed not far away. "I'm too tired to do anything about it… This big toxx Milyr is out in sleepy land now.

He's no help. We're all too tired to care now… Vulching acid is spreading to where he's sprawled like a limp oaf. What can we do now?"

There is acid on the bubble floor now, is this really happening, Kymil wondered in her teary and foggy fugue. Where are the green balls to protect them now? Was there something which she could do now? Lyndyn had tried to be heroic and do something to save the young wolves in this endangered bubble. Could she follow his attempt and try to stop the alien ocean from killing all those still alive in the bubble? Could she awaken her spirit and her strength now after witnessing such a horrible death for her Lyndyn?

"Roll…us…if…you…can," growled Domyn in more exhaustion and lethargy that Kymil had ever heard from big Neer. "We guys…are just no longer…any use now… Just too burned out…from uncontrolled sex… We need strength of…you girls now….to save everyone…"

"Well, big man…we can try… But you are not easy to move," Whyvvi sighed from somewhere beyond the blurred haze still affecting Kymil's sight.

The face and spirit of Lyndyn teased her consciousness again with his challenge for her to safeguard these young wolves, so Kymil shook her weary body with determination and pushed her torso up from the hardening floor of the bubble. She must act now. She must help the wolves go on. She must find a way to force her brain to function again with some creativity and some desire of survival. She must not allow his death to become meaningless now. He wanted them to survive. She must make this happen now.

With energy summoned from her deep awareness, Kymil wobbled to her feet and commanded with authority, which her age and experience sanctioned, "Oh, yes, my young wolves… You must go on now… You must move these weary boys to safer section in this bubble… We must do what we can to channel acid flow to other parts of floor…"

"Now this will be almost impossible," Nyba retorted. "These oafs are just too heavy."

"Well, then we should make the acid go around their lazy bodies," Whyvvi proclaimed with some renewed spirit. "Prof was making the inner layer of this bubble into folds to block the mouth of the toxx nasty bloodstar. And look, see how well his patching is now holding with the bloodstar gone now. We should be able to make drains or at least channels in soft parts of the floor to steer the acid flow away from our bodies."

"Oh my, yes, you have a cherp notion, young lady," agreed Kymil while she stepped cautiously over the prone figure of Milyr toward the splatter of leaking acid beneath the partial hole from where Lyndyn had vanished. "Yes, make indentations with your feet and hands quickly now. Let's create some channels for the liquid acid to travel. Hopefully our guardian green balls get back soon to fix this habitat."

"Vulching green balls should not have left us," Nyba complained while she flopped the limp body of Milyr closer to the side of Domyn and then continued with a breathless grunt, "Vulch, this boy is toxx heavy when he's asleep. Can we really save this bubble, Doc? Can we prevent acid from rising above our little channels and drains? How long can we protect ourselves without any help?"

"Well, you are right about the toxx green balls, Nyba," Whyvvi grumbled as she scuffed a divot into the floor of the bubble and then lengthened this channel with more pressure from her foot. "The toxx balls should not have left us defenseless. The toxx balls should have stayed here, so Prof did not need to die. I hate those useless toxx green balls now."

Yes, Kymil thought silently, the green balls had been protectors of the human occupants of this bubble since beginning of this strange imprisonment. Had they deserted the wolves? Or had Lyndyn's speculations during recent moments of sexual compulsion been correct? Had the green balls been just as helpless and subject to compulsion as human captives? Did this idea suggest that the green balls were a life-form with some form of sexual procreative urge? Was this one of many thoughts and questions which had roamed about in mind of her kindred spirit during his last moments of life? Oh, how she desired his presence already, Kymil moaned.

"Is this one of those vulcher green balls now?" Nyba shouted from her position beside the two boys. "Are those damn things coming back again? I hope so. I don't like those vulching things, yet now I hope those things can help us."

Glancing upwards toward the direction in which Nyba pointed with a finger, Kymil observed a vague green motion moving just outside the bubble in the yellow ocean. The red streaks from the bloodstar were in the bubble shell still and blocked some of the clarity of her vision. Yet she was certain that she could see the oddly-shaped cluster of one of the green balls. This alien thing floated to a spot of leakage. Then a cluster of the balls settled from outside into the hole left by the departing bloodstar. Almost immediately leakage of the acid liquid stopped. The green cluster seemed to shape itself exactly into the ragged hole.

"Well, this is certainly a cherp happening now," Whyvvi said with mild enthusiasm. "At least one of the things has returned to aid us for the moment. I should not criticize those things so much now."

"I still say those vulchers are the things that cost our Prof his life," Nyba spat and then settled herself against the long sprawled body of Milyr. "If those toxx balls hadn't left us, then Prof would be alive now. And these boys would not be lying here like exhausted lumps of male flesh."

With misery and sadness in her heart, Kymil sighed, "Oh my, young woman, I do believe that our men would be just as lifeless now after their exertions during the period of uncontrolled sexual activity. We were all thrust into this recent event without any choice. It was not the green balls that killed Lyndyn. He was stolen from us by the bloodstar. I can already say this with reason, although my heart is torn and saddened by his loss. I cannot blame the green balls."

"Awe...those...tiny....things...did give...me...you... Whyvvi," mumbled a deep voice, "I'm happy...for this...joining...at least."

"Well, you lazy big man, you should be grateful for my recent proximity to you. I do not believe that we would have had any choice of partners then," Whyvvi said with her usual analytical straight forwardness, and then abruptly complained with a groan, "I could have been near Milyr at the wrong moment then. Argh, I could have copulated with him..."

"Now he wasn't so uncherp as you pretend," Nyba muttered, patting Milyr on his naked back.

While she observed the alien green cluster continue to snuggle into the hole in the bubble, Kymil sighed with her own memory of recent sexual compulsion and then admitted to the younger wolves, "Yes, fate or destiny did seem to have us matched perfectly during this event. My kindred spirit was as gentle and loving to me as he could be under such a horrid compulsion. My future memories of his final loving moments should be very pleasant, I hope. If you are as fortunate, then you will each find joy in our recent ordeal rather than focus on the terrible result."

"Doc, you are so much stronger than any of us," Whyvvi proclaimed.

"Yes, I don't believe that I could be so...so...understanding...with destiny," Nyba admitted.

"Fate...universal...destiny...may have...a plan..." murmured Domyn from his prone position beside Milyr's sleeping figure. "Or, perhaps...not... We may... make our own..."

Walking to Domyn, Whyvvi said with some emotion, "Well now, my big man, whichever eventually occurs, I am so cherping pleased that you were my mate this time. We should make a cherping couple in our future."

"Vulch, I'm not sure just how long of a future we will have," Nyba protested while she rubbed the shoulders of Milyr. "We're not really in very cherp conditions here now."

"Oh my, we're alive now. Our habitat is at least sound again for awhile. Perhaps the green clusters will heal this bubble. Perhaps they will tend to our health again. Perhaps they do have our Jamyk somewhere in their alien ocean. Perhaps we will yet meet him again. My Lyndyn may have been a rambling wordy elderly gent, but he always seemed to find a bright side in any situation. I must continue to hope and expect his notion to succeed. I just can't live any other way," Kymil exclaimed with a much more optimistic feeling than she truly believed at that moment.

"Ho, ho, this is cherp philosophy, Doc," Nyba agreed with a gentle slap to the toxx of Milyr. "Even I who am extremely pessimistic now can appreciate your notion. Although I'm not sure I'd wish for a reunion with our rascal Jamyk so hastily..."

"Now, Nyba, you do not really mean this, do you?" Whyvvi asked with a smirk.

"Awe...knows...she does...not," Domyn murmured with a deep weary voice.

"Oh my, we must pray that he is still alive and safe here on this moon. We have lost Swyllo and now my kindred spirit Lyndyn. We must not lose any more of our Wolf Streak Beta pack," Kymil said, and her thoughts churned with memories of faces and past antics of spritely Swyllo and Jamyk and yes, she admitted to herself, her own Lyndyn, as childish as he could be at times.

"Now you're right, Doc. I should not wish for any uncherp thing to happen to Jamyk now," Nyba admitted sheepishly, and then after a few seconds of quiet, she continued, "I'm not sure that this is the way MisCom had planned for our mission to proceed once we reached the Sexto System. This is so uncherp. We could not have known just how ridiculous our mission would turn in this Sexto System."

"Awe...yes... Nyba...the mission plan...was nothing like...the reality," Domyn sighed.

"Well, you are truly correct about this, my big man," Whyvvi agreed with a tired sigh. "We should not complain too much though. Our partner craft Fox Flash Alpha may have had an even more uncherp experience when they reached this system. That is if they reached the Sexto System."

"Yes, you are right about this," Kymil murmured as her mind still toyed with faces of those wolves who were gone or lost now, and she added her memories of faces of eight foxes who were now somewhere out of communication and possibly in jeopardy. "We never did discover why we could not get any signal from their Buffalardi beacon, which they should have deployed once they entered this solar system. I hope that they are having better luck than we are."

"Awe...knows... Khebol...would...know the...sci-tech...to help them," Domyn whispered.

"Well, yes, Khebol should be able to deal with any crisis," Whyvvi declared with a tired voice. "And he should know how to correct any rash action taken by Cap Bhiros."

Yes, foxes were just as youthful as wolves, Kymil reminded herself. Blue Jayer crews of this mission had been challenging for her and Lyndyn, just as they had been for Doc Thebon and Prof Hethep on Fox Flash Alpha. Yet the young people of this mission were worth the challenge, she thought. However, she would miss the support of her kindred spirit now. This would be so difficult to continue on this mission, wherever it led, without Lyndyn. Oh, she prayed, hopefully his iota of awareness is somewhere safe and protected now.

With a peek toward Domyn's large naked form, Kymil mused of his philosophy of iotas of awareness. She must hope that the young man had been correct in his speculations. She must pray that Jamyk was out there still somewhere in this vast acid ocean hopefully with the protection of the strange green balls. And most of all, she prayed that her beloved Lyndyn was still somewhere at least in his form of iota of awareness. Yes, she could go on into the future if she believed that she might have some miniscule chance to reconnect with his spirit again.

Oh my, kindred spirit, where are you now, Kymil wondered.

Thus ends

Wolf Streak Beta: Awareness

1st Tome in Saga

Perspectives of Blue Jay

to be continued in

2nd Tome

Wolf Streak Beta: Alienation